Praise for *The High Tide Club*

"Andrews creates a story that is at turns suspenseful, sad, and hopeful, with plenty of surprising twists. Her dialogue is natural and funny, and even her minor characters are fully drawn with unique voices.... Another satisfying summer read from the queen of the beach." —*Kirkus Reviews*

"A compelling novel about the people and places that shape a life and the secrets that create ripples for generations. With a unique setting, mysterious flashbacks, romance, and a surprising twist, this book will not disappoint readers looking for a juicy escape." —*Booklist*

"Andrews has crafted a smart and wonderful beach read with a lot of rich Southern and historical details." —*RT Book Reviews*

"Andrews skillfully contrasts deception, betrayal, and murder with the scenic beauty of her Southern setting. Readers will enjoy the many twists and turns the novel takes as it moves toward its surprising and heartwarming conclusion. Ultimately a tale about redemption and enduring friendship, *The High Tide Club* links mysteries from the past and present to create a compelling story." —*Mystery Scene*

"*The High Tide Club* is a remarkable novel in which Mary Kay Andrews cleverly intertwines vignettes from the past with a modern-day narrative to give us a cohesive story that compels us to turn the pages to solve one mystery after another. No matter how good you are at guessing what's coming next, this book will surely hold shocking surprises and unexpected smiles throughout." —Bookreporter.com

ALSO BY MARY KAY ANDREWS

The Beach House Cookbook

The Weekenders

Beach Town

Save the Date

Christmas Bliss

Ladies' Night

Spring Fever

Summer Rental

The Fixer Upper

Deep Dish

Savannah Breeze

Blue Christmas

Hissy Fit

Little Bitty Lies

Savannah Blues

The
High Tide Club

Mary Kay
Andrews

St. Martin's Griffin
New York

THE HIGH TIDE CLUB. Copyright © 2018 by Whodunnit, Inc. All rights reserved.
Printed in the United States of America. For information, address
St. Martin's Press, 175 Fifth Avenue, New York, N.Y. 10010.

www.stmartins.com

Title page icon made by Freepik
from www.flaticon.com

The Library of Congress has cataloged the hardcover edition as follows:

Names: Andrews, Mary Kay, 1954– author.
Title: The high tide club / Mary Kay Andrews.
Description: First edition. | New York : St. Martin's Press, 2018.
Identifiers: LCCN 2017060760 | ISBN 9781250126061 (hardcover) | ISBN 9781250199621 (international,
    sold outside the U.S., subject to rights availability) | ISBN 9781250198037 (signed edition) |
    ISBN 9781250126092 (ebook)
Subjects: LCSH: Female friendship—Fiction. | GSAFD: Love stories.
Classification: LCC PS3570.R587 H54 2018 | DDC 813/.54—dc23
LC record available at https://lccn.loc.gov/2017060760

ISBN 978-1-250-12608-5 (trade paperback)

Our books may be purchased in bulk for promotional, educational, or business use. Please contact
your local bookseller or the Macmillan Corporate and Premium Sales Department at 1-800-221-7945,
extension 5442, or by email at MacmillanSpecialMarkets@macmillan.com.

First St. Martin's Griffin Edition: April 2019

10 9 8 7 6 5 4 3 2 1

This one's dedicated with love to Andrew Rivers Trocheck,

whose love of Georgia's wild places inspire me.

Acknowledgments

....

The setting for this novel is entirely fictional. Inspired by the beautiful and fragile Georgia coast, I created a barrier island called Talisa, a county called Carter, and its county seat, St. Ann's, and inserted them into the real geography of the Georgia coast, just north of Cumberland Island, but South of Sapelo Island. I can't offer enough thanks to Blaine and Jenna Tyler for sharing their love of that island.

It's always foolhardy to create a character whose work you know nothing about, but it's a very good idea to have experts who are willing to share their knowledge. Many thanks go to Robert Waller, Sharon Stokes, Beth Fleishman, Mary Balent Long, and Kathryn Zickert for their legal expertise. Any misstatements of fact are due to my own ignorance and not the excellence of their advice.

Savannah friends who contributed their knowledge of local history include Polly Powers Stramm and especially Jacky Blatner Yglesias.

As always, my community of author friends lent their ears and advice during the process of brainstorming and writing *The High Tide Club*. The members of The Weymouth Seven: Diane Chamberlain, Margaret Maron, Katy Munger, Sarah Shaber, Alex Sokoloff, and Bren Witchger, were as always, essential to my process. Special thanks to my favorite low country ladies, Patti Callahan Henry and Mary Alice Monroe for their brilliant suggestions.

I couldn't do what I do without my dream publishing team: the best agent in the whole damn world, Stuart Krichevsky, and the gang at SKLA, marketing genius Meg Walker at Tandem Literary, and of course, my publishing house, St. Martin's Press. There aren't enough words to express my gratitude for editor extraordinaire Jen Enderlin, capo di tutti capi Sally Richardson, and the team who make it all happen: Brant Janeway, Erica Martirano, Jessica Lawrence, and Tracey Guest. Thanks again, Mike Storrings, for yet another gorgeous cover.

I may wander far and wide in search of the next story, but at the end of every quest I'm blessed enough to have the love and support of my family, who know enough about me to leave me alone when necessary, and reel me back home to reality at just the right time. All my love goes to Katie and Mark Abel, Andy Trocheck, my darling grands Molly and Griffin, and most of all, best of all, my starter husband of forty-one years—and counting, Tom.

The
High Tide Club

Prologue

....

October 1941

The three young women stared down at the hole they'd just dug. Their gauzy pastel dresses were rumpled and slightly damp, and the heels of their dainty sandals made them teeter precariously on the rounded oyster shell mound. Their faces were flushed and shiny with perspiration. The fourth in the circle was a girl of only fourteen, dressed in a hand-me-down set of boy's overalls and a pair of worn leather shoes, her eyes wide with terror in a smooth, toffee-colored face. The first shafts of sunlight shone softly through the thick intertwined branches of moss-hung live oaks.

"Give me the shovel," the tallest one said, and the girl handed it over.

The blade of the shovel sliced into the crushed shells and sand, and she dumped the material onto the form at the bottom of the hole, then wordlessly handed the tool to the redhead standing beside her. The redhead shrugged, then did the same, being careful to distribute the shells and sand over the dead man's face. She turned to her friend, a pretty blonde who now had both hands clamped over her mouth.

"I'm gonna be sick," the young woman managed, just before she leaned over and retched violently.

Her friend offered a handkerchief, and the blonde dabbed her lips with it. "Sorry," she whispered. "I've never seen a dead man before."

"You think we have?" the tall one snapped. "Come on, let's get it done. We have to get back to the big house before we're missed."

"What about him?" The redhead nodded toward the body. "When he doesn't come to breakfast, won't people start asking questions?"

"We'll say he talked about going fishing. He went out yesterday too, remember? Before dawn. Millie can say she heard him leave his room. His gun is right here, so that makes sense. Anything could have happened to him. He could have gotten lost in the dark and wandered into one of the creeks."

"There's gators in the creeks," said the young girl in the overalls. "Big ones."

"And there are snakes too," the tall one volunteered. "Rattlesnakes, cottonmouths, coral snakes. And wild hogs. They run in packs, and if they get you . . ."

"Good heavens," the redhead said. "If I'd known that, I never would have snuck out in the dark last night. Snakes and gators?" She shuddered. "And wild hogs? Terrifying."

"We don't know anything," the tall one said emphatically. She searched the others' faces carefully. "Agreed?"

A tiny sob escaped from the blonde's lips. "Oh my God. What if somebody finds out?"

"Nobody's going to find out," the redhead said. "We swore, didn't we?"

"They won't. Nobody ever comes here. They don't even know it exists. Right, Varina?"

The fourteen-year-old looked down at her dusty shoes. "I guess."

"They don't," the tall one said. "Gardiner and I found it by accident, when we were little kids. It's supposedly an Indian mound."

The blond girl's brown eyes widened. "You mean a burial mound? We're standing on dead people?"

"Who knows?" A single drop of water splashed onto the tall one's face, and she glanced up, through the treetops, where the clouds had suddenly darkened. "And now it's starting to rain. Come on, we've got to finish this and get back to the house before we all get soaked and ruin our shoes and have to answer a lot of questions about where we've been and what we've been doing."

Tears welled up in the blond girl's eyes, and she unconsciously rubbed her bruised, bare arms. She was weeping softly. "We're all going to hell. We never should have gone swimming last night. What if somebody finds out what's happened? They'll think it was us. They'll think it was me!"

The redhead, whose name was Ruth, was thoughtful. "It doesn't matter who killed him. Any one of us could have done this. He was a terrible man. He's the one going to hell for what he did. You never should have agreed to marry him, Millie."

"She did, though. And what's done is done," said their leader. "There will be a lot of questions, girls, when he turns up missing. There's bound to be a search, and I'm sure my papa will call the sheriff. But we don't know anything, do we?"

The blonde looked at the redhead, who looked at the tall one, who looked expectantly at the young girl, who nodded dutifully. "We don't know nuthin'."

1

Brooke Trappnell rarely bothered to answer her office phone, especially when the caller ID registered "unknown number" because said caller was usually selling something she either didn't need or couldn't afford. But it was a slow day, and the office number actually was the one listed on her business cards, so just this once, she made an exception.

"Trappnell and Associates," she said crisply.

"I'd like to speak to Miss Trappnell, please." She was an older woman, with a high, quavery voice, and only a hint of the thick Southern accents that prevailed on this part of the Georgia coast.

"This is she." Brooke grabbed a pen and a yellow legal pad, just in case she had a potential real, live client on the other end.

"Oh." The woman seemed disappointed. Or maybe disoriented. "I see. Well, this is Josephine Warrick."

The name sounded vaguely familiar, but Brooke didn't know why. She quickly typed it into the search engine on her computer.

"Josephine Warrick on Talisa Island," the woman said impatiently, as though that should mean something to Brooke.

"I see. What can I do for you today, Mrs. Warrick?" Brooke glanced at the computer screen and clicked on a four-year-old *Southern Living* magazine story with a headline that said "Josephine Bettendorf Warrick and Her Battle to Save Talisa Island." She stared at the color photograph of a woman with a mane of wild white hair, standing defiantly in front of what looked like a pink wedding cake of a mansion. The woman wore a full-length fur coat and high-top sneakers and had a double-barreled shotgun tucked in the crook of her right arm.

"I'd like you to come over here and see me," Mrs. Warrick said. "I can have my boat pick you up at the municipal marina at 11:00 A.M. tomorrow. All right?"

"Well, um, can you tell me what you'd like to talk to me about? Is this a legal matter?"

"Of course it's a legal matter. You are a lawyer, are you not? Licensed to practice in the state of Georgia?"

"Yes, but—"

"It's too complicated to go into on the phone. Be at the marina right at eleven, you hear? C. D. will pick you up. Don't worry about lunch. We'll find something for you to eat."

"But—"

Her caller didn't hear her objections because she'd already disconnected. And now Brooke had another call coming in.

She winced when she glanced at the caller ID. Dr. Himali Patel. Was the pediatric orthopedist already calling to dun her for Henry's ruinous medical bills?

"Hello?"

"Hello, Brooke. It's Dr. Patel. Just following up to see how Henry's physical therapy is coming."

"He's fine, thanks. His last appointment was this week."

"I'm so glad," Dr. Patel said. Dr. Himali Patel was the soft-spoken Indian American doctor who'd treated Henry's broken arm. Brooke shuddered when she thought about the thousands she still owed for the surgery. She'd rolled the dice on an "affordable," high-deductible health insurance policy and came up snake eyes when Henry fell from the jungle gym at the park and landed awkwardly on his arm, leading to a trip to the emergency room, surgery, and weeks' worth of physical therapy.

"If he has any pain or his range of motion starts to seem limited, bring him back into the office. Other than that, he's good to go."

"Thanks, Doctor." Good to go. Easy for her to say. Brooke still needed to call the hospital's billing department to set up a payment plan.

The *Southern Living* magazine article was timed to coincide with Josephine Warrick's ninety-fifth birthday. Which would make her ninety-nine now. Brooke reached for the glass of iced tea and the peanut butter and jelly sandwich she'd brought from home and read the article, and half a dozen others she'd found online, catching up with the colorful life and times of Josephine Bettendorf Warrick.

She already knew a little about Talisa, dating back to a brief, ill-fated Girl Scout camping expedition nearly twenty-five years earlier. Her memory of the place was hazy, because she'd gotten seasick on the boat ride across the river on the way to the island and then managed to get stung by a jellyfish *and* hike through a patch of poison ivy. The assistant troop leader had to arrange for a boat to take her back to the mainland a day early to await pickup by her parents, who were two hours away in Savannah. It had been Brooke's first and last camping trip. The name *Talisa* called up memories of calamine lotion, burned marshmallows, and her sight line, from the backseat of the Cadillac, of her father's neck, pink with barely suppressed anger at having to miss his Saturday golf game.

Brooke jotted notes as she read and chewed her sandwich. Talisa, she learned, was a twelve-thousand–acre barrier island a thirty-minute ferry ride from where she now lived in St. Ann's, Georgia. It had been purchased as a winter retreat in 1912 by Samuel G. Bettendorf and two cousins, all of whom were in the shipping business together in Boston. In 1919, Samuel Bettendorf and his wife, Elsie, had built themselves a fifteen-room Mediterranean revival mansion, which they named Shellhaven.

In 1978, the cousins had sold their interest in Talisa to the State of Georgia for a wildlife refuge, which explained how Brooke's Girl Scout troop had been allowed to camp there. Samuel Bettendorf had retained his property, which was on the southeast side of the island, facing the ocean.

And Samuel's daughter and only living heir, Josephine Bettendorf Warrick, had been engaged in a lengthy court battle with the state, which had been trying, in vain, to buy up the remainder of the island for the past twenty years.

Was this why Mrs. Warrick wanted to see her? Brooke frowned. She'd spent the first three years of her career working at a white-shoe Savannah law firm, doing mostly corporate and civil work. But since fleeing to the coast as a runaway bride, she'd hung out a shingle as a solo practitioner. The *and Associates* part of Trappnell and Associates was pure fiction. There were no associates and only a very-part-time receptionist working in the one-story, wood-shingled office she rented downtown on Front Street. It was just thirty-four-year-old Brooke Marie Trappnell. In life, and in law, come to think of it. She did some divorce work, DUI, personal injury, and the occasional petty civil or criminal work. But she knew next to nothing about the highly specialized area of eminent domain law.

Which was what she'd tell Josephine Bettendorf Warrick. Tomorrow. And why not? She had a 9:00 A.M. appointment to see a client who'd been locked up for assault and battery in the Carter County Jail for a week, following a run-in with a clerk at the local KwikMart who'd tried to charge her ninety-nine cents for a cup of crushed ice. But the rest of her calendar was open. Not an unusual occurrence these days.

There were, by her count, nearly three dozen other attorneys practicing law in St. Ann's, all of them long-term, well-established good ol' boys, who gobbled up whatever lucrative legal work was to be done in this town of seventeen thousand souls. Brooke counted herself lucky to pick up whatever crumbs the big boys didn't want.

If the weather app on her phone was to be trusted, tomorrow would be another sunny, breezy spring day. Why not take a boat ride to reacquaint herself with Talisa on her own terms and meet the legendary Josephine Warrick?

2

....

She heard the music blaring from within the office as soon as she parked the Volvo out front on Friday morning. Twangy guitar, heavy drumbeats, some kind of party-hearty country music. Brooke dug a can of Mace from her purse and quietly moved toward the door, which was slightly ajar.

She eased the door open with her foot and cautiously poked her head inside.

The intruder was so intent on her task, she never even looked up. She was seated with her bare feet propped up on the receptionist's deck, her head bobbing, singing along with the radio. "Play it again, play it again, play it again," she repeated, drumming the desktop for emphasis.

Brooke reached down and tapped the wireless speaker sitting atop the file cabinet.

The girl, startled, jerked upright.

"Jesus, Brooke!" she exclaimed, reaching for the bottle of nail polish she'd been applying to her toenails. "You scared the shit out of me!"

"And you almost gave me a heart attack when I drove up and heard that music and saw the door standing open," Brooke said. She held up the can of Mace. "You're lucky I didn't spray first and ask questions later."

"What are you doing here, anyway? I thought you were supposed to go see

Brittni in the jailhouse this morning," Farrah said, glancing at the clock that hung over the office's sole bank of file cabinets.

"And I thought you were supposed to be in second-period English."

Farrah Miles was a high school senior who also doubled as Henry's babysitter. Brooke and Farrah had met in September after Brooke had given a career-day talk about law at the local high school. Most of the teenagers had napped or stared at their phones during her talk. But the next day, Farrah, a petite blonde with a tiny gold nostril stud, blue-green streaks in her hair, and a penchant for cowboy boots and supershort cutoff jeans, showed up at her office and proclaimed herself interested in the law and a job.

The girl was smart and efficient—when she wanted to be—so they'd struck a deal that Farrah would work five days a week after school and pinch-hit as a babysitter for three-year-old Henry, as needed.

Farrah sat down and resumed her pedicure, dabbing a bit of purple polish on her big toenail. "Mr. Barnhart's a prick. We've only got two more weeks of class before graduation, and I've already got a solid A, but he still won't exempt me from taking the final exam like my other teachers."

"So you're cutting class? Farrah, he could still flunk you. I thought we talked about this. You've got to keep your grades up if you want to get into Georgia."

The girl scowled. "They wait-listed me, Brooke. I'm not gonna get in. I'll just go to Community College like everybody else. It's no biggie."

Brooke rolled her desk chair over to Farrah's desk and sat inches away from her. The girl lowered her head, pretending to concentrate on her toes. Brooke reached out and tilted Farrah's chin, lifting it until they were eye to eye.

"Listen to me, Farrah Michele Miles. You still have a really good chance. You aced your SATs and your ACTs. You've got a solid 3.9 grade point average in mostly advanced placement classes, and plenty of extracurricular activities. You wrote amazing essays, and your teachers wrote you great recommendation letters. Do not screw this up. Please?"

"I'm not screwing anything up." Farrah changed the subject. "So what happened this morning with Brittni?"

"I went over to the jail. Her stepfather still won't post bail, and her court date's not 'til next week, so there's not much I could say except hang tight and try not to get in any more fights."

Farrah shook her head. "I know she's my cousin, but she is such a dumb bitch. She shoulda just paid the ninety-nine cents for the damn cup of ice. It's not like she was broke!"

"I told her the same thing," Brooke said, "but she says the KwikMart cashier was some kind of high school frenemy who thinks Brittni stole her boyfriend."

"Right. That's Kelsy Cotterell, and she hates Britt because she totes did steal Kelsy's boyfriend. And also because Brittni had his name tattooed right across her chest, which is not even hot, despite that boob job of hers," Farrah said. "She thinks because she used to be a cheerleader the whole world owes her something. Mama says she gets that and her lard butt from Aunt Charla."

Brooke pressed her lips together to keep from laughing at Farrah's dead-on assessment of her client and her client's mother. "Okay. Enough about Brittni. As long as you're here, you might as well get some work done. I need you to go online and do some research. See what you can find out about *State of Georgia v. Josephine Warrick*. Print out what you get and start a file."

"Josephine Warrick? Is that the old lady who owns Talisa? What's up with her?"

"She called me yesterday, wouldn't say what it's about. Just that she wants to see me about an unspecified legal matter. I'm headed over there in a few minutes."

"Awesome. A new client. So that's why you're all dressed up today. You look nice, by the way."

"Thanks," Brooke said. "I kinda like that nail polish of yours too. What's it called?"

"Violet Femmes," Farrah said. She held up the bottle. "Want a hit?"

"No, thanks. I'll stay with my Bubble Bath. Gotta look conservative in my line of business."

Shunning her usual casual office attire, Brooke had reached to the back of her closet and brought out an expensive tailored navy pantsuit, which she wore with a white silk shell, pearl earrings, and a pair of black lizard-skin Tod's loafers, throwbacks from her Savannah wardrobe, which rarely saw the light of day in St. Ann's.

"That old lady's, like, filthy rich, you know," Farrah said.

"I doubt that she'll end up hiring me. I don't practice the kind of law it sounds like she needs."

"You're a lawyer, right? Why wouldn't she hire you?"

"I'm a general practitioner, remember? From the little research I've done, it sounds like she needs somebody who does eminent domain law. But she seems like quite a character, so I'm gonna go see her anyway."

"Text me some pictures of the house, okay? I've never actually been inside. Jaxson and I used to ride over to the island on his brother's boat last summer to party at the top of that old lighthouse, but I hear she's got an armed security guy roaming around now."

"Talisa is private property. You and your friends had best stay away from there," Brooke said, trying to look severe. "Unless you want to share a jail cell with your cousin."

"Whatevs." Farrah set the bottle of nail polish aside and turned the music on again.

Brooke promptly turned down the volume. "Who is that, anyway?"

The girl's eyes widened. "You're kidding, right? Seriously? You never heard Luke Bryan before?"

"These days my playlist mostly consists of Kidz Bop and the Wiggles," Brooke replied.

"Girrrrrl, you need to get in the now," Farrah said condescendingly, reeling off her current favorite country music acts before stopping abruptly. "Hey, I almost forgot to tell you the good news."

"What's that?"

"I might have gotten us a new client. Jaxson's mom left his dad again this week, and she swears this time it's for good. So I gave her your card. If she hires you for the divorce, do I get, like, a finder's fee or something?"

Brooke laughed. "We've got to find a way to get you into UGA, kid. Someday, you're gonna make somebody a hell of a lawyer."

The municipal marina was quiet at midday. The tide was dead low, and most of the serious fishermen had set out earlier in the morning. Seagulls screeched and swooped for fiddler crabs scuttling across the exposed gray pluff mud of the riverbank. A couple of derelict-looking shrimp boats creaked at their moorings at the end of the wharf, along with a handful of the open, shallow-hulled center-console boats favored by local crabbers. There were seven or eight shiny new cabin cruisers and three sailboats scattered along the wharf too, but most of the larger, more expensive boats were to be found up the coast, on St. Simon's Island, which was where really wealthy boaters congregated.

Brooke gazed along the length of the long wharf, wondering which of the boats belonged to Josephine Warrick.

She heard a sharp whistle and swung around to see who it was meant for.

Finally, she spotted a modest, faded-yellow craft bobbing at its mooring at the end of the dock. A lone man stood on the bow, waving at her. He cupped his hands around his mouth and called to her.

"Are you Brooke?"

She nodded and hurried toward the boat.

He was skinny, with thinning hair bound into a scraggly gray braid that hung down his neck, bow-legged and sun-bronzed, wearing an ancient green army fatigue shirt with the sleeves hacked off and unbuttoned to his bare bony chest, and cutoff jeans that had seen better days. Clipped to the belt of his shorts was a holster with a large pistol. Brooke wasn't good with guns, but she was pretty sure it was a 9 mm.

His face was shaded by a sweat-stained ball cap, and his eyes were hidden behind cheap aviator sunglasses, but she felt the intensity of his stare.

"Are you C. D.? From Talisa?"

"That's me," he said, offering her a hand. "C. D. Anthony, in the flesh. Come aboard."

He motioned for her to sit atop a cushioned bench at the stern and busied himself untying the boat.

"All set?" he asked, and without waiting for her reply, he gunned the motor and expertly backed the boat away from the wharf.

The man turned to look at her as the boat putted quietly through the marina's no-wake zone.

"Nice day for a boat ride," he said abruptly. "You ever been over to the island before?"

"A long time ago," Brooke said.

"I don't reckon it's changed much, no matter how long ago it was," he said. "You a friend of Miss Josephine's?"

"Not really," Brooke said.

"She don't get a lot of visitors. So I reckon maybe you've got business over there?"

Brooke found herself squirming a little under his stare. "Something like that."

He was sizing her up. "You a lawyer? You look like a lawyer to me."

"Good guess," Brooke said, keeping it light. "How about you? I assume you work for Mrs. Warrick? In what capacity?"

"Whatever needs doin', I do," C. D. said. "Run the boat, work on the vehicles a little. Fetch groceries and supplies from the mainland. Like that."

"How nice."

"She ain't in real good health. Took her to the doctors over in Jacksonville last month. She don't say a lot, but I reckon they gave her bad news. Louette, she's kinda the housekeeper, she says Josephine don't eat much. Makes sense. She was pretty stout when I met her, but lately, she's gotten real skinny. Eat up with cancer probably."

Brooke wondered how Josephine Warrick would feel about one of her employees gossiping about her health with a total stranger.

"If that's true, I'm sorry to hear it," Brooke said politely.

She pivoted sideways, signaling their discussion was over, gazing back toward the mainland. She knew it was a five-mile crossing to Talisa, and she didn't care to spend the trip chatting with this unnerving cornpone Popeye.

He took the hint and gunned the boat's motor the minute they passed the last piling marking the no-wake zone. She gripped the seat with both hands and within minutes found herself being drenched with sea spray every time the small vessel crested one wave and bounced back into the water.

Eventually, Brooke saw a green swath appear on the horizon, and ten minutes after that, C. D. slowed the boat down and they glided into a narrow tidal creek. At the creek's widening, she spotted a long dock jutting into the water. A sturdy black man stood at the end of the dock, his arms crossed over his chest. A child of about eight or nine sat at the edge of the dock, holding a cane fishing pole. Long, bead-wrapped dreadlocks reached to his shoulders.

"Hey, Lionel," C.D. called. "Catching anything?"

The kid looked up and waved. "Ain't no fish biting today. You take me for a boat ride?"

"Sorry, pal, maybe another time."

As they approached the dock, C. D. put the boat in neutral, and the black man tossed them a thick line, which the captain knotted to a cleat on the bow.

"Hey," the man said quietly, nodding politely at Brooke.

"This here's Shug," C. D. said. "He'll drive you up to the house." He busied himself fiddling with something on the boat's console.

Shug bent down and gripped Brooke's arm at the elbow, helping her make the two-foot leap from the boat's deck to the dock.

"You okay?" Shug asked solicitously. "Got everything?"

"Oh," Brooke said, pointing toward the bench on the stern. "Oh no. I left my briefcase."

C. D. grunted, picked up the briefcase, and slung it in the general direction of the dock. Shug reached out and snagged it, midair, before it could hit the water.

"You have a nice visit now, you hear?" C. D. said. "I'll be around when you're ready to go back."

. . .

An ancient, rusted seafoam-green Ford pickup truck was parked at the end of the dock among a motley-looking assortment of junker cars.

Brooke patted the rounded front hood. "Wow. How old is this thing?"

"Mmm, I think it's from around the late fifties," Shug said, opening the passenger-side door. "I do know that Mr. Preiss Warrick bought it new way back when. He's been gone a long time, but Miss Josephine, she don't like to part with nothin' that was his. Likes to keep everything just like it was before he passed."

He turned the key in the ignition and pumped the gas pedal. The truck's motor whined, then stalled. He shook his head, repeated the same motion twice before the engine finally caught. Moments later, they were bumping along the narrow crushed-shell roadway. Brooke poked her head halfway out the open window, marveling at the scenery.

Gnarled, moss-draped live oaks on both sides of the road met in the middle to form a dense, nearly impenetrable canopy of green overhead. Thick stands of palmetto, swamp myrtle, pines, and cedars were festooned with blossoming jasmine, whose heavy scent perfumed the air. As they rounded a bend in the road, she spotted a pair of blue herons intent on fishing for their lunch in a shallow ditch. Another turn revealed an expanse of marsh where patches of sun-bleached driftwood and cypress knees were host to dozens of large, brown nesting birds.

"Wood storks," Shug said, pointing. He gave her a smile. He was a thickly built man, in his fifties, she guessed, with heavily muscled arms. He wore neatly pressed blue jeans and a short-sleeved blue work shirt. "We got lots of birds over here. Famous for it, I guess. Is this your first trip to Talisa?"

"Sort of," Brooke said. "I was here for a Girl Scout campout years ago. It didn't end well."

"You must have been on the other end of the island," Shug said. "Whole different world over here."

"It's beautiful," Brooke said. "So . . . wild. And peaceful. Do you live on the island full-time?"

"We do now. Louette, that's my wife, she was born and raised here. We moved to Brunswick a long time ago for work, but then our kids got grown and moved away, and I got laid off my job at the port. Right around that time, Louette's sister, who still lives here, said Miss Josephine was looking for some help. We come over and talked to her, and we been here ever since. Eleven or twelve years now, I guess."

"I didn't realize anybody but the Bettendorfs or Warricks lived here," Brooke said.

"Oh yeah. There's a bunch of black folks been living at Oyster Bluff, since right after the Civil War. The whole island was part of a plantation that got burned down by the Yankees, because they thought the owners were blockade-runners. Later on, the government gave all these former slaves a little piece of land up at Oyster Bluff. Nobody else wanted it, because it was swampy and they were afraid of yellow fever. Those folks, they stayed and scratched out a living, farming and fishing and hunting. They're what are called Geechee. Louette's people, they're all Geechee."

"And do they still own their own land?" Brooke asked, fascinated by this chapter of Georgia history she knew so little about.

"Nope," Shug said. "People moved off and sold their land to the Bettendorfs, or they had so many kids, and none of them wanted to stay here, so they just abandoned the houses. There's not but ten or twelve families still living at Oyster Bluff now, and Miss Josephine owns all that land. She's nice and all, don't charge hardly anything for rent, but it's still not the same thing as owning your own place, you know?"

"I know all too well," she said wistfully, thinking of the modest two-bedroom concrete block cottage she rented at St. Ann's, as opposed to the restored Italianate three-story town house in Savannah's historic district that she'd walked away from when she broke her engagement to Harris Strayhorn.

The truck rounded another curve, and suddenly, a blanket of bright green lawn spread out before them. The grass was patchy and spotted with clumps of dandelions, wild garlic, and silver-dollar weed. Overgrown formal beds of bedraggled-looking azaleas and camellias were planted in tiers on the gently sloping lawn, and a line of palm trees announced that they were approaching the Bettendorf family compound.

"We're here," Shug said, slowing the truck to a stop so she could get out and take a look.

3

....

Situated at the top of the gentle slope was an astonishing pale pink wedding cake of a mansion, consisting of a two-story central block bristling with vaguely Moorish-looking arches, a pair of peak-roofed turrets, and a crenelated balcony projecting over a porte cochere. This was flanked on either side by wings of only a slightly more modest design. Each was marked by a towering sentinel palm tree. The roof consisted of pale-green fired-clay barrel tiles that reminded Brooke of the frosting on a gingerbread house. The place bristled with leaded glass windows, wrought iron Juliet balconies, heavy plaster bas-relief flourishes, and curlicued ornaments. A thick green curtain of ivy crept across the façade of the house, and crimson bougainvillea traced the outline of the porte cochere.

"Wow."

"Mmm-hmm," Shug agreed. He started the truck again, and as they drew closer, she could see that the curving concrete driveway leading up to the mansion was buckled and potholed, the pink stucco on the house was cracked and faded, and the roof sported great gaps of broken or missing tiles.

Shellhaven was slowly, inexorably crumbling as surely as a century-old layer cake.

"It don't look like it ought to," Shug said, his voice sorrowful. "I keep after it the best I can, but it's only me now. Time was, half a dozen hands worked on the grounds here. One man, his whole job was taking care of the roses. There was a tractor kept the grass cut and a grove with the prettiest oranges and lemons and grapefruit you ever seen. Peach trees and pecan trees, of course. A greenhouse too, just to grow flowers and orchids for the house. All gone now. A pine fell on the greenhouse, and some kind of blight killed all the fruit trees. Just as well, 'cause these days, you can't find nobody wants to live way over here and do an honest day's work. Plus, Miss Josephine, she's pretty tight with a dollar."

If Josephine Warrick was as rich as local legend had it, Brooke wondered why she'd allowed her home to deteriorate to this extent.

"I'm sure you do the best you can, and she's probably very grateful to have you," Brooke said tactfully.

He pulled the truck beneath the porte cochere and pointed to the heavily carved arched double doors. "Go ahead on inside. Louette's waiting to take you to see her."

She pushed the door open and stepped inside timidly, momentarily blinded while her eyes adjusted from the harsh sunlight to the near darkness of the entry hall.

The naked bulb of a tarnished brass wall sconce dimly revealed a high-ceilinged room with black-and-white checkerboard tile floors, cracked plaster walls, and age-darkened wooden beams overhead. The crystal chandelier hanging from an ornate plaster medallion was caked with dust and cobwebs. The air was oppressively hot and damp.

"Hello?" Her voice echoed in the empty room.

"I'll be right there," a woman's voice called from the darkness. A moment later, a woman she guessed was Louette bustled into the room. She looked younger than her husband, with close-cropped graying hair and a freckle-flecked, caramel-colored complexion two shades lighter than his. She had the comfortable thickness and heavy bosom of solid middle age and was dressed in a white synthetic-blend uniform.

"Miss Brooke? I'm Louette. You got here okay? That C. D. didn't ride you too hard coming across the river today?" Her pleasant accent had a distinct sing-song lilt.

"It was bumpy, but I'm here in one piece," Brooke said.

"Well, we don't get a lot of company these days, and Miss Josephine's got herself all worked up waiting to see you, so I guess I'd best take you back there."

She gestured for Brooke to follow her down a wide hallway. They passed arched entryways into what looked like twin parlors, furnished with over-stuffed sofas and chairs and heavily carved tables and chests.

Louette paused outside a closed door at the end of the hall. "This used to be the library, but she can't make the stairs no more, so me and Shug fixed her up a bedroom in here. She don't hear so good, so you got to speak up when you talk, and she's been pretty sick lately, so you need to make sure she don't tire herself out. But don't go thinking because she's nearly a hundred years old she's weak-minded or something. No, ma'am! Not Miss Josephine. She don't miss a trick."

She rapped loudly on the door, waited a moment, then poked her head inside. "Miss Josephine? You ready to see your company?"

"Is that the lawyer I sent for? Bring her in, Louette."

The library at Shellhaven had been a grand room once. But now the dark mahogany paneling was dull, the draperies at the windows faded and tattered. Three walls of the room were lined with bookshelves, crammed with books and rows and rows of the distinctive bright yellow spines of *National Geographic* magazines. Every flat surface was littered with items; birds' nests, sun-bleached seashells, chunks of coral, even a huge set of yellowed shark jaws. A stuffed bobcat sat on a pedestal near the window, muzzle open in mid-snarl, his molting yellow fur drifting onto the dark pine floor. A five-foot-long intact skeleton of an alligator stretched across the top of one of the built-in bookcases, and tall apothecary bottles were filled with sharks' teeth, sea glass, and what appeared to be tiny bird skulls.

A hospital bed had been set up in the far corner of the room, partially hidden by an ornate three-panel chinoiserie screen.

A box fan whirred in one of the two open windows, doing little to dispel the heat or the scent of antiseptic soap.

The lady of the house was ensconced in a brown vinyl recliner. Brooke had been expecting a slightly diminished version of the defiant mink-wrapped, shotgun-toting heiress she'd seen in *Southern Living*, but the passing of years had been as cruel to Josephine Warrick as it had been to her home.

The flowing white mane was gone, replaced by a navy-blue baseball cap that did little to conceal the nearly bald head beneath it. Pale skin blotched with vivid brown liver spots stretched over skeletal cheekbones and a pointed chin. Her lips were thin and bloodless. But a pair of bushy white eyebrows arched over large, dark eyes behind oversized yellow-tinted glasses that carefully studied Brooke as though she were another museum specimen.

In the quick research she'd done, Brooke had seen dozens of photos of Josephine Warrick. She'd been a striking—if not beautiful—woman, a slender, serious-faced debutante with the short, wavy hair of the period, then a dewy-faced bride in the fifties, turned into a rangy, imposing force to be reckoned with in later years. The society pages of the newspapers in Savannah, Atlanta, and Palm Beach showed her dressed in golf togs, tennis wear, and expensive designer gowns, as well as hunting gear, standing with one foot atop a massive buck.

The woman sitting in the cracked vinyl recliner weighed less than ninety pounds and was wrapped in layers of knitted afghans and throws. An oxygen tank stood beside the chair, and a pair of thin plastic cannulas snaked toward the transparent breathing apparatus on her face.

"Hello, Mrs. Warrick," Brooke said, after the momentary shock of the old lady's appearance had worn off. "I'm Brooke Trappnell." She took a step toward the chair, then stopped abruptly.

"Grrrrrr."

She hadn't noticed the dogs, they were so small, and nearly the same beige as the afghan.

"Grrrr."

A pair of miniature Chihuahuas sprang into defense mode; the fur on their necks bristling, teeth bared.

"Hush, Teeny. Hush, Tiny." The old woman stroked their backs, patted their heads. "Don't mind the girls," she told Brooke. "They won't bite. Unless I tell them to. Sit down over here," she said, pointing to a faded chintz wing chair. "And you needn't call me Mrs. Warrick. Josephine will do just fine, and I'll call you Brooke, if I may. The doctors keep saying I'm going deaf, but I'm not really. It's just that people these days mumble and fail to enunciate properly." She gave Brooke a sharp look. "You're not one of those types, are you? I can't abide a mumbler."

Brooke sat down in the chair and balanced her briefcase across her lap. "No, ma'am," she said loudly. "I've got a lot of faults, but that's not one of them."

"You didn't tell anybody why you were coming over here today, did you?"

"No, because you never actually explained why you wanted to see me."

The old lady chuckled. "But you were curious about me and this island, so you decided to come anyway. Is that correct?"

"Something like that."

"Then we'd better get to it, hadn't we? As you can tell by my wretched appearance, I don't have a lot of time these days for social niceties."

"Your housekeeper mentioned you'd been ill. I'm sorry to hear that."

"Louette likes to fuss. I smoked too much and for too long, and I've had COPD for several years, but it's lung cancer now, and that's a different matter. I did the radiation, but I draw the line at chemo. So that's that. Let's talk about something else, shall we?"

"Of course."

"Do you know anything about this island, Brooke?"

"I did some reading after your call, and I was here briefly as a child, on a campout."

"On the other end of the island, which my wretched cousins' heirs sold to the State of Georgia in 1978 for pennies on the dollar," Josephine said. She shook her head. "If they'd offered me the same deal, I would have bought it myself."

"Why didn't they?"

"Bad blood. We'd had boundary disputes over the years, silly feuds over water rights, that type of thing." She shrugged. "Also, from what I heard, they needed the money. As you may know, my father, Samuel Bettendorf, along with two cousins, bought Talisa in 1912."

She nodded toward the bookshelves. "Somewhere I have a copy of the original bill of sale. They each chipped in $10,000, which doesn't sound like a lot of money now, but back then, it was the equivalent of $2.4 million apiece. My mother hated the cold Boston winters, so Father bought the island and eventually built this house. His cousins' wives had no interest in spending time in a place as wild and remote as this, so they eventually partitioned the land, with my father retaining this end of the island. His cousins had more acreage, which was all they were interested in, but Father bought most of their holdings and kept what really mattered—this tract, which has ocean frontage, high ground, and the only freshwater source on the island."

"Clever man," Brooke said.

"He was brilliant, really," Josephine said. "He made his money in the family shipping business, but Father was interested in everything—natural science, the law, literature, the arts. He was the one who insisted I go to college, which was not the norm for girls at that time."

She sighed. "He loved it here. He loved the climate, the wildlife, the peacefulness. That's why I have to preserve his legacy here." She gestured around the room. "Saving Talisa, studying it, understanding its beauty was his life's work. And then after I married Preiss, it was our work."

Josephine's voice grew raspy. "Which is why I've fought so hard all these years to keep the state from taking my land."

Brooke opened her briefcase and took out a yellow legal pad and pen. "I didn't have time to do much research, but I do know from what I've read that your Atlanta lawyers have been fending off the state's offers."

"The state built the campsite you stayed at, they paved roads, and then they cut down some of the oldest trees on the island to build another campground, cabins, and a ten-thousand–square-foot 'conference center.' Can you tell me why Talisa needs a conference center?"

"Maybe as meeting space?" Brooke guessed.

"That ferry of theirs runs four times a day," Josephine rasped. "Hundreds of people tromping around, leaving their fast-food wrappers and beer cans and dirty diapers. It's deplorable. They're deplorable!"

"How do things stand with the state currently?" Brooke asked.

"Their last offer, made five years ago, was for the same amount they paid my cousins nearly forty years ago," Josephine said bitterly. "It's an insult. When I refused, the state filed notice that they'll take my land by condemnation. For the public good." Her lips twisted in disgust. "The public hasn't got any right to traipse across this land. I won't let them."

"What is it you think I can do to prevent that?" Brooke asked. "You already have the best law firm in Atlanta representing you."

"I want you," Josephine said.

"But why? You don't even know me."

"I've been following your career in the newspapers. You've got spunk. And I need somebody with spunk. Besides, you sued the National Park Service, didn't you?"

"And lost," Brooke said calmly.

"But you fought them tooth and nail for three years. You wore the bastards down."

"Not really. You of all people know what that's like. The Park Service decided that Loblolly, my family's house on Cumberland Island, was 'nonconforming,' so they knocked it down. And we're not allowed to build anything to replace it."

"Which is precisely why I need you to fight my last battle," Josephine said. "I won't be around that much longer. I've seen their secret preliminary master plan. The first thing the state will do is to tear this house down. And I can't have that. I can't die knowing they'll ruin everything. All our years of work."

"Tear down Shellhaven? Why would the state do that?"

"You've seen the condition it's in. It would take millions to preserve it. Much cheaper for them to knock it down and build more cabins and conference centers. They'd build a big marina where my dock is—we've got the only deep-water boat access on this end of the island."

Brooke looked down at the few lines of notes she'd taken. "Josephine, I just don't think I can help you. It's true I'm a lawyer, but this is not my area of expertise at all."

"Word is out that I'm sick," Josephine said, ignoring her. "They've already come over here, sniffing around. C. D. ran off a boatload of 'em a couple of weeks ago. Survey crew, they said they were. They'd tied up at our dock, just as C. D. was coming back from the mainland with a load of groceries. He fired a couple of warning shots across the bow of their boat, and they took off like a pack of scalded dogs, but they'll be back."

Brooke shook her head in alarm. "I'm not sure that's such a good idea."

"They were trespassing. As long as I'm alive, this is still private property. They've got no business sniffing around over here. I want this thing settled before I get too sick to fight anymore."

"And how do you propose to do that?" Brooke asked.

"I want my land and this house protected, put in a trust or something, so that nobody, and I mean *nobody*, can develop this end of the island or tear down this house."

"Who'd be the beneficiary of such a trust?" Brooke asked. "Do you have family?"

The old lady put her head back and closed her eyes. "Not really. My brother, Gardiner, was killed in World War Two. Preiss and I never had children." She smiled, briefly. "Never wanted any, either. I didn't marry until I was in my thirties. He was six years younger than me. Bet you didn't know that. No, there's somebody else. My friends. My oldest, dearest friends. The High Tide Club girls."

4

....

Josephine

April 1932

I t was Ruth's idea to "borrow" my papa's Packard to go exploring on the island. At thirteen, she was the oldest, and the bossiest. I was still twelve, and
Millie, whose birthday wasn't until the last week of August, was the baby of
the group. That was the night the High Tide Club was born.

We were on spring break from boarding school, having taken the train down
from Boston a good five days before the rest of the family would join us.

With the run of the house mostly to ourselves and largely unsupervised,
we'd spent the week listening to the radio, playing endless hands of canasta,
and taking turns reading aloud from the naughty parts of *Lady Chatterley's
Lover*, which we'd found hidden in my mother's lingerie drawer.

It was the night before my parents and Gardiner were to arrive.

"I'm bored. Let's go for a drive." Ruth jumped up and ran down the stairs
with Millie and me trailing along behind. We followed her out to the barn,
which had once held racehorses but now housed Papa's "island cars"—a
disreputable-looking collection of automobiles that had outlived their useful
lives back at home in Boston but were still well suited for life on Talisa.

Ruth jumped into the front seat of the Packard. Once, when it had been Mama's favorite car for shopping jaunts, it had been shiny and black with gleaming chrome trim and soft leather upholstery. But now the windshield was missing, along with the bumpers. The leather was cracked, and the chrome was pitted from exposure to the salt air.

"What do you think you're doing?" I stood in front of the Packard's blazing headlamps, my hands on my hips. Somehow, Ruth had managed to start the motor. And now, she blasted the car's horn so loudly Millie and I both jumped, and a chicken, who'd been roosting up in the rafters of the barn, squawked and flapped down onto the sawdust-covered floor.

"Let's go!" Ruth said, tapping on the horn again.

"But . . . but . . . ," Millie sputtered. "You can't drive. You're not old enough."

"I'm plenty old enough," Ruth retorted. "I've been driving for ages and ages. My sister, Rose, taught me how."

That was good enough for me. I opened the door and swung onto the front seat.

Millie stared at the two of us, trying to make us be sensible. "What if somebody finds out? We could get in a lot of trouble."

Ruth was rummaging around in the glove box, but she looked up, annoyed. "*Pfffft*. Who's going to tell on us? We have the whole island all to ourselves."

"That's not true," Millie said stubbornly. "Mrs. Dorris is here, and the rest of the servants, and the colored people who run the commissary, and the man who brought us over on the boat . . ."

"Mrs. Dorris goes to bed at seven o'clock, and the rest of the servants had better mind their own business or I'll tell Papa to fire them," I said, which I never would have done, and Papa wouldn't have fired anybody on my say-so anyway, but Millie didn't know that.

"Lookie here!" Ruth cried. She was holding up a clear pint bottle with a brownish liquid. "Hooch!"

"Ruth Mattingly, don't you dare," Millie said.

So of course, Ruth uncapped the bottle, sniffed, and took a chug. She coughed and gagged, then wiped her mouth with the back of her hand, and handed the bottle to me. I pretended to drink, then tucked it under the seat for safekeeping.

"Are you coming or not?" Ruth asked. "Scaredy-cat!"

Millie barely had one foot in the Packard before Ruth jammed the car into reverse, stomped on the gas, and shot us backward out of the barn.

"Slow down!" Millie pleaded as the Packard lurched forward over the narrow asphalt road the islanders called Dixie Highway. But Ruth just laughed and sped up, and soon the wind was whipping our hair, and the headlamps shone yellow white in the inky darkness.

"Where shall we go?" Ruth turned to me for directions. It was only her second time on Talisa, but I'd been coming to the island my whole life.

That's when I had the brilliant idea. I pointed ahead, toward a huge three-trunked live oak tree that marked a split in the road. "Take a left, just up there. We'll go down to Mermaid Beach."

Without slowing down, Ruth veered so sharply left we almost left the road, and as it was, a low-hanging limb from the tree scraped the Packard's roof and right side, in the process depositing a long, lacy strand of spanish moss in Millie's lap.

"Hey!" I protested. "You almost put us in a ditch."

But Ruth just cackled with that demonic laugh of hers.

Millie planted both hands on the dashboard to brace herself. "Look! There's something up ahead, in the road."

Ruth slammed on the brakes, and the three of us watched as a five-foot-long alligator, its eyes glowing yellow orange, ran across the road.

Millie's screech echoed in the thick night air, but Ruth soon resumed driving.

The asphalt gave out without warning, and then we were in the wildest part of our wild island. The road was a narrow, haphazard trail of crushed shells, and wax myrtles, palmettos, and oak trees crowded against the side of the Packard, the palm fronds slashing at the sides of the car.

"Where are we?" Millie asked. She clutched my hand, and I clutched hers back, trying to act braver than I felt, partly because I had never been to Mermaid Beach at night but mostly because my thirteen-year-old best friend was driving my papa's Packard, at night, in the dark.

"It's not far now," I said, pointing toward the place a hundred yards ahead where the road seemed to disappear in a green curtain of underbrush.

"Stop here," I told Ruth. "We'll have to walk the rest of the way."

But she didn't stop until the Packard was ensnared in a tangle of wisteria and morning glory vines.

Leaves and twigs rained down on our heads as we gingerly stepped out of the car.

"I don't like this," Millie said, gripping the door handle. "I'm staying right here."

"Okay. Fine by me." Ruth set out ahead of us, stabbing at the underbrush with a thick branch she'd picked up. "Go away, snakes!"

"Come on," I urged Millie, grabbing her hand. "It's not that much farther."

The thick, humid air closed in on us, and as we pushed through the vines, we stirred up clouds of stinging, swarming mosquitoes.

"Aaagggghhh!" Millie cried.

The skeeters were in our hair, our mouths, our noses.

"Let's run," I urged. So we did, lunging through the green curtain toward a clearing I prayed was right where it had been during my last trip here, in the daytime, with my brother, Gardiner.

Ruth stopped short at the point where the tunnel opened up to a shimmering platinum world.

She flung her arms wide as though to embrace the spectacle and make it her own.

"Wow," she breathed.

Millie and I stood beside her, breathless from the run.

The wide sandy beach ran down to the Atlantic Ocean, and a huge full moon shone down from a black velvet sky. It was high tide, and the silver-streaked rollers broke just inches from our feet.

"What is this magic place?" Ruth asked, slipping out of her shoes and digging her toes into the cool white sand.

"We call it Mermaid Beach," I said, plopping down on the sand to untie my shoelaces.

"It's wonderful," Millie said. She tilted her head back and gazed up at the sky. "Have you ever seen a moon so big and beautiful?"

"It's called the king moon," I told my friends, feeling important at possessing such knowledge. "I think it only happens once or twice a year."

I glanced at Ruth, expecting her to ridicule or contradict me, but to my astonishment, she was busily unbuttoning her cotton blouse. She dropped it onto the sand and unfastened the gingham skirt she'd dressed in that morning, and soon it joined the blouse.

"What are you doing?" I asked.

"I'm going swimming," she said, leaning forward to unfasten the brassiere she'd just begun wearing earlier that spring.

"But you don't have a swimsuit," Millie said.

"I don't need a swimsuit. I've got my birthday suit." Ruth dropped the brassiere, and next came her panties. She danced toward the waves, wiggling her bare bottom the way we'd seen the sideshow hootchy-kootchy girls do when the carnival came to town. She glanced back at us, over her shoulder. "Come on, you prissy-pants!"

I was hot and sweaty, and I could feel itchy mosquito-bite welts on my face and arms. I pulled my dress over my head and kicked off my cotton panties and the icky cotton undershirt Mama insisted on making me wear. A moment later I was as naked as a jaybird, the breeze ruffling my hair. I glanced over at Millie, who'd averted her eyes out of modesty.

"Come on, Millie," I begged. "It feels great."

"I can't," she whispered.

Ruth was leaping and diving into the waves. She pulled the pins from her long red hair and let it cascade, dripping down her knobby breasts. "Look, Josie. Look, Millie. I'm a mermaid!" She dove backward into the water, kicking her feet at the last minute.

"I'm coming in," I announced, and I made a running leap into the surf. I'd never felt so daring or so free. The ocean was as warm as bathwater. I floated on my back, staring up at the velvet sky, pricked with millions of stars and that low-hanging king moon. The tide carried me back toward the shore, and when my bare bottom scraped the sand, I flipped over and looked toward the beach. Millie was crouched on the sand, her knees pulled up tightly against her chest, looking thoroughly miserable.

"If you don't get in here right now, I'm never speaking to you again," I called.

"And I'll tell you-know-who that you have a crush on him." Ruth ran forward and began splashing Millie.

"Ruth, stop!"

I joined in, and within minutes, Millie was soaked and laughing despite her protests.

"Oh, all right," she said finally. Gritting her teeth, she pulled off her dress and ran shrieking into the waves, dressed only in underclothes similar to mine.

"No fair," Ruth said, splashing Millie again. "It's not skinny-dipping unless you're naked."

"That's right," I agreed. "You can't be in the club unless you are tee-totally stitch-stark naked."

Millie sank down into the water until only her head and shoulders were exposed. "This is stupid," she grumbled. A moment later, she stood and tossed her remaining clothes onto the beach.

"See? Doesn't it feel wonderful?" Ruth asked.

Millie ducked down under the water and popped back up again, spouting a stream of water from pursed lips, like the fountain in the garden back at school. She shook her head, raining droplets on both of us. "Yes! All right. Yes, it feels marvelous!"

After that, we laughed and splashed and floated and swam until our arms and legs were so tired we could barely drag ourselves onto the beach. Finally, we lay flat on our backs in the sand, our fingertips barely touching, while we gazed up at the moon.

"You said there's a club," Millie said, sitting up and looking around for her clothes. "And now you have to let me be in it, because I skinny-dipped too. What's it called?"

"Hmm." Ruth found Millie's wadded-up dress and tossed it at her.

"It's the High Tide Club," I announced.

"Yes!" Ruth proclaimed. She found her skirt and pulled a packet from the pocket, tapping out a cigarette and a book of matches.

"Ruth Mattingly! I didn't know you smoked," Millie said, wide-eyed.

"Oh, sure," Ruth said carelessly. She held out the package. "Want one?"

"No, thanks," Millie said.

I shook my head. Ruth shrugged, lit the cigarette, inhaled, then tilted her head back and blew a series of perfect smoke rings.

"What should we have for rules?" Millie asked as she began to dress.

"Well, skinny-dipping, for starters," Ruth said. She flicked ashes onto the sand, took another puff on the cigarette, and handed it over to me. I hesitated and took a tiny puff. My lungs burned, and I coughed and passed the cigarette back.

"But only when there's a full moon," Millie said. "It's so much more glamorous."

"And a high tide," I added between coughs.

"Next meeting, this summer," Ruth said. "You're all invited to my house at Newport." She waved her cigarette in our faces. "And don't forget your birthday suits."

5

....

Josephine closed her eyes. Her chin sagged, and a moment later, she was softly snoring, the Chihuahuas each nesting with their snouts in the opposing crooks of her elbows. Brooke waited tactfully. Should she leave?

Remembering Louette's warning about overtiring Josephine, Brooke quietly stashed her notes in her briefcase and began to tiptoe toward the door.

Josephine's eyes opened. "Where do you think you're going?"

The Chihuahuas scrambled to alert, yawning, their huge eyes staring expectantly at the intruder.

"Um, I thought maybe you needed some rest," Brooke said.

"I'll let you know when I need some rest. Now, where was I?"

Brooke sat down again. "Well, I asked you who would be the beneficiary of your trust, and you said something about the girls of the high tide? Was that sort of a youth organization? Like Pioneer Girls maybe?"

"I've never heard of that organization, so why would I leave my island to them?"

"Sorry," Brooke said. "Maybe I misunderstood. The High Tide Club?"

"For heaven's sake. Keep up, will you? I just told you, these were my oldest, dearest friends in the world."

"Oh."

"It was all so long ago," Josephine said drowsily. "Sometimes, I almost wonder if I dreamed them. Dreamed the times we had together."

Brooke shifted uncomfortably in her chair. "Um, just how long ago did you have these friends?"

Josephine waved her hand dismissively. "We were just girls. Millie and I were in kindergarten together. Ruth, oh, I don't know. I suppose I met Ruth my first year at boarding school. We were both so terribly homesick. We hated our roommates. So we tricked them into ditching us so that we could room together. Oh, that Ruth. She was the most delicious fun! Sweet Millie, well, she had such a soft heart, the other girls would take advantage of her. So we had to take her under our wing, didn't we? We were peas in a pod. We made our debut together . . ."

Josephine's eyelids fluttered, and Brooke feared she was falling asleep again. Should she leave?

"I want you to find them for me," Josephine said suddenly, fully awake again. "I . . . it was a long, long time ago, but it's begun to eat at me. I'm not sleeping. I want to make amends. Before I go."

"Make amends with these women? Your old friends?"

Josephine gave her a withering look. "Are you always this slow? Have you heard anything I've said so far?"

Brooke wondered what she was missing here. Josephine Bettendorf Warrick was inching up on the century mark. What was the likelihood that these girlhood friends would also still be alive?

"It's just that, well, if these friends were your age, I was wondering . . ."

"If they're dead?"

"I was trying to be tactful," Brooke said.

"We don't have time for tact, dear. Just say what you mean. I find that's the best policy."

"All right. When was the last time you were in touch with these friends?"

Josephine looked down at the dogs in her lap. She stroked their ears, scratched their noses. "Too long," she said softly. "Much too long. Maybe it's too late. Probably it is, but I have to know. I have to try."

"Well," Brooke said. "With computer databases, it's usually not that difficult to track people down these days."

"Computers?" she sniffed. "Never had any use for one. And unfortunately, I have no idea where to start looking." She turned to a small mahogany end table that stood beside the recliner. Sliding the drawer open, she reached in and took out a yellowing envelope.

Brooke leaned in, trying to get a better look at it. Three names were scrawled on the envelope in fading blue ink.

The old lady's hands shook violently, but she managed to unseal the flap. "Put out your hand," she said.

Brooke obeyed, and the old lady shook a small item into Brooke's palm, quickly returning the envelope to the drawer it had come from.

It was no more than half an inch high, a tiny gold-and-enamel brooch depicting the slender silhouette of a girl in a jackknife dive. The girl was nude, and a diamond chip twinkled in the position where her nipple would have been.

"What's this?" Brooke asked.

"We called ourselves the High Tide Club." Josephine's lips curved into a smile. "You see, we had a ritual. Whenever we were together, the four of us, and there was a high tide and a full moon, we'd go skinny-dipping. At Newport, at Ruth's family's home there, or Nantucket, at my grandmother's house, and at Palm Beach, back when Millie's family had a winter home there, before her father lost everything in the crash. Of course, Varina was only with us when we skinny-dipped here, on Talisa. You're shocked, I imagine."

"Not at all. My friends and I used to skinny-dip off the dock at my cousin's house, on the bluff, at Isle of Hope in Savannah." Brooke held the pin up to the light to admire it. "It's lovely."

"Millie had them made for us. As bridesmaids' gifts. For the wedding that never was."

"When was the last time you spoke to your friends?"

Josephine shrugged. "Sometime right after the war, I suppose. Maybe Ruth's wedding? But I don't think Millie was there. It's such a long time ago, I really can't recall."

"You said there were four members of the club? You, Ruth, and Millie? Who was the fourth?"

"Varina." Josephine held out her hand for the pin, which Brooke surrendered.

"And why didn't Varina join you at those other places, Newport and Palm Beach?"

The old lady stared at her as though she were daft. "Varina? Don't be absurd."

"Did your friends come to your wedding?"

"No," Josephine said. "We were . . . estranged." She looked out the window, which was nearly covered by a thick green vine whose tendrils had crept through the window screen. "They're probably all long dead by now. All but Varina. She was younger than the rest of us. She comes to see me, still, although it's harder, because she's getting on in years now. Like me."

"This really isn't the kind of work I usually do," Brooke said. "Have you considered hiring a private detective to find your friends?"

Josephine looked her over carefully. "If I didn't know any better, I'd think you didn't need money."

Brooke felt her face flushing. "What do you know about my finances?"

"I've asked around," Josephine said. "You left a top law firm in Savannah after you broke off your engagement a few years ago, isn't that right?"

"Yes."

"You're a bit of an ambulance chaser these days, aren't you? And representing drunk drivers and shoplifters, between divorces and debt collection?"

Brooke said nothing. Because it was true. She'd take just about any legal, ethical work thrown her way these days. There were bills to be paid. Hospital bills. She couldn't afford pride. Any more than she could afford cable television, dinners out, or a set of new tires for her eight-year-old Volvo. Her car needed work. She needed work.

"And I believe you're an unwed mother? Oh, wait. I beg your pardon. Nowadays women like you are called *single mothers*, isn't that right?"

Brooke felt her jaw clench and unclench. "I have a son, yes, and I'm not married."

Josephine yawned widely. "What do your people think about your having a child? Out of wedlock?"

She considered ignoring the question. But why? Henry's existence was no secret. Except to his father.

"My father and stepmother are scandalized. Dad definitely does not approve. He and Patricia have only seen their grandson once or twice. My mother, at first, was worried, but once she held Henry in her arms, she fell madly in love. She comes down from Savannah to see him as often as she can."

"Your mother is a lovely person. I'm sorry I can't say the same about that unfortunate woman your father left her for. How is your dear mother, by the way?"

"She's, uh, fine."

"I imagine that divorce knocked the wind out of her sails."

"She was devastated," Brooke said truthfully. "She never saw it coming. Nobody did. But I think she's finally come to terms with her new life. So you know my parents?"

Josephine waved the question away. "Savannah's not that big a town, my dear. Everybody knows everybody else. Except for the nobodies that nobody cares about anyway."

"Exactly how do you know my family?" Brooke persisted.

"If you must know, your grandmother was a dear, dear friend of mine."

"You were friends with Georgette?" Brooke asked, confused.

"Good heavens, no! Not your father's mother. I'm sorry to say this, but Georgette Trappnell was truly a horrible woman."

Brooke wouldn't argue that point. Georgette Trappnell had been a dragon. A selfish, self-centered terror whose acid tongue could peel the paint off a wall. Not unlike Josephine Warrick.

"I meant your mother's late mother," Josephine said sadly. "Dear, darling Mildred."

"Wait. Your friend Millie was my granny? The friend you went skinny-dipping with?"

"Yes," Josephine said. She changed the subject abruptly again. "What about your son's father? Do you know who he is?"

Brooke shot to her feet, nearly knocking the chair backward. "I think I'd better be going. I don't need money badly enough to be insulted this way." She reached for her briefcase and her pocketbook. "I suggest you find somebody else for this particular assignment."

Teeny and Tiny, sensing her hostility, went on the offensive, jumping down to the floor, bracing themselves on either side of their mistress's chair, yapping loudly.

"Don't be foolish," Josephine snapped. "I didn't mean to wound your pride. I just wanted to learn more about you."

Brooke's face was hot. "I don't appreciate your insinuation that I'm some sort of harlot." She would have said more, but she hadn't been raised to disrespect her elders. Even elders who were as loathsome as Josephine Bettendorf Warrick.

"That's not what I meant to insinuate at all," Josephine said. She scooped the dogs back up into her lap, stroking their heads soothingly. "I just wondered if your son's father is part of your life—that is, does he provide financial support? Does he see the boy?"

"He doesn't need to be part of our lives," Brooke said. "Henry and I do just fine without him."

"Is this man even aware that he has a child?"

The smaller of the two dogs arched her neck and began licking Josephine's chin.

"No." Brooke still had no idea why she was submitting to this deeply personal line of questioning. Maybe it was because she'd become immune to the intrusive questions asked by strangers who all seemed to feel entitled to ask questions about Henry's absent father.

"Do you think that's fair? To your little boy? Doesn't he wonder where his papa is?"

Brooke sighed. How often had both her parents asked that same question? "Henry's only three. I'm all he knows. Anyway, times have changed, Mrs. Warrick. There's no longer any real stigma to being a single parent. Now that we've established that I'm broke and unmarried, is there anything else, before I catch the boat back to St. Ann's?"

"I really must insist you call me Josephine," the old lady said. "And I've already told you what I want. Two things. I want you to keep the state from taking my island away from me. From ruining all of it. Whatever it takes, that's what I want from you. And I want you to help me make things right by those women I told you about."

She coughed again, then reached for a thick, leather-bound book on the table beside the chair. Opening it, she took out an envelope and extended it toward Brooke.

"That's your retainer. It's a certified check. I'm assuming $25,000 is sufficient for you to get started?"

"I'm sorry," Brooke said. "As I've tried to explain, based on the little you've told me, I really don't think I can help you."

The old lady's eyes were closed again.

"And remember," Josephine said. "Strictly confidential. Not a word to anybody about what we discussed today."

Josephine nodded off once more, leaving Brooke wondering again if she should go or stay. She still smarted from the intrusive questions about Henry's paternity and whether his father knew of the boy's existence.

Henry had straight dark hair, a high forehead, and a short nose like her own. His moods changed moment to moment. One minute he was climbing into Brooke's lap and smothering her face with kisses while she was trying to work at the kitchen table, and the next thing she knew he was scowling and howling, "Bad Mommy!" Strangers stopped her at the grocery store to comment that he was a carbon copy of his mama. But sometimes, when the tantrum clouds passed, and he gave her that full-faced impish smile, all she could see was Pete. He had Pete Haynes's smile, Pete's square jaw, long, Bambi-like lashes, stormy blue eyes, and smooth olive skin. Even the faint sprinkle of freckles across Henry's nose and cheeks were Pete's.

He was his father's son, a son Pete knew nothing about.

6

Josephine

October 1941

S uch a lovely party." Everybody kept saying it, and it was true. Papa and I wanted everything perfect for Millie's engagement party.

The ballroom floor had been waxed and polished until it shone like a mirror. The orchestra, brought all the way down from Atlanta—ten pieces—played all the most popular songs from that year. Caterers had been brought in too. A steamship round of roast beef, silver trays piled high with cracked lobster tails, steamed shrimp and oysters mounded on beds of crushed ice, poached quails' eggs, and the cleverest little pink cakes. Flowers everywhere. Orchids from the greenhouse, huge vases of peonies and roses and lilies, their perfume scenting the gentle breeze blowing in from the open doors to the veranda.

Thank goodness for that breeze! October could still be oppressively warm on Talisa, but even the weather cooperated that evening, with a full moon shining down on the loveliest party that I'd ever seen.

My gown was pale blue silk, with elegant beading and a plunging neckline. Millie was fairy-tale pretty in pink organza, the gown a surprisingly generous gift from her miserly grandmother, and Ruth, in seafoam-green satin to complement her copper hair. "You girls look like a rainbow," Papa had said, nodding in approval.

A hundred people filled the ballroom at Shellhaven that night. Or was it two hundred? Such a pretty, perfect night.

Until Russell strolled back into the ballroom from the veranda. He'd been drinking steadily all night, supplementing the champagne punch from the silver flask stuck carelessly in the breast pocket of his dinner jacket. Poor Millie had been on edge all night, fluttering around, too nervous to do more than nibble at the edges of the plate of food Ruth had tried to coerce her into eating.

"He hasn't danced with her once tonight," Ruth had hissed in my ear, glaring in Russell's direction.

"Too busy drinking and talking sports and smoking cigars with his fraternity brothers," I'd agreed, following her gaze.

Russell Strickland stood by the french doors, holding the stub of a still-lit cigar in his hand, coolly surveying the room. The dance floor was a crush of color and movement because right at that moment the orchestra was playing Glenn Miller.

Ruth slipped her arm around my waist, and we both hummed along and swayed to the rhythm. "Moonlight Serenade." A perfect song for a perfect night.

"What's he staring at?" I muttered.

Russell's eyes were narrowed, his jaw tight with anger.

"Oh Lord," Ruth said. "It's Millie. She's dancing with another man."

"Where?" I craned my neck to see through the crowd.

"Over there, near the punch bowl."

Finally, I spotted Millie's gauzy pink dress. She was in the arms of a lanky man with a white dinner jacket and a deep tan. "Oh, for heaven's sake. It's only Gardiner. He's just being nice. Papa probably made him ask Millie."

"Maybe your brother is just doing the gentlemanly thing, asking his little sister's best friend to dance, but I doubt Russell sees it like that," Ruth said. "He is holding her awfully close."

"Because every single living person in the room is on that dance floor," I said, laughing. "You and I are the only ones who aren't dancing."

"Russell isn't dancing. And he doesn't look at all happy at the way his fian-cée is looking right now."

Ruth was right.

"Should we do something?" I asked. "Maybe try to distract him?"

"And how would we do that?" Ruth's dark green eyes crinkled in amuse-ment. "Strip naked? Faint at his feet? Offer him some cake?"

"Or another flask of whiskey. I've got a better idea, though. You could ask him to dance."

"You ask him. You're the hostess."

"Should I?" My stomach did a little flip. Russell Strickland had always been perfectly polite to me, but there was something intimidating about him. And not just his football-player size. Everything about him was outsized and intense.

"Never mind now. The song's almost over. I think you and I should warn Millie . . ."

But it was too late. The music had ended, and Russell was steaming across the room, shouldering his way through the throng of partygoers until he'd reached the spot where Millie was standing.

She'd been talking to Gardiner, her cheeks pink with excitement. A moment later, Russell clamped his hand around her bare upper arm. She turned, and her eyes widened in surprise. Russell said something to Gardiner, who took a step backward, shaking his head in disgust.

The next moment, Russell was towing Millie toward the ballroom door, not really holding her hand but nearly dragging her. Luckily, most of our other guests didn't notice. The music started again, and Ruth and I stood rooted to the spot where we'd been standing.

"Should we do something?" I asked. "Should we tell my father?"

Ruth thought about it, then shrugged. "Maybe not. It would just make Rus-sell madder. And he'd probably take it out on poor Millie and spoil your won-derful engagement party."

"Poor Millie," I whispered.

.   .   .

"Are you going to help me or not?"

"I want to help you," Brooke said. "But I'm still not clear on what you think I can accomplish. Besides, you never finished telling me about these friends of yours. Or how you plan to make amends with them."

"I certainly did," Josephine snapped. "I told you about Millie. And Ruth. And Varina."

"You told me that Varina is still living and that your friend Millie was my grandmother," Brooke said. "But what about Ruth? And why do you need to make amends with these women?"

"Oh." Josephine looked down at the Chihuahuas, who were dozing on her lap. "Sometimes I do get a little forgetful. And sleepy."

Brooke laughed. "Sometimes I dream of sleeping 'til noon. My son creeps into my room two or three times a night. I don't think I've gotten more than four uninterrupted hours of sleep since he was born."

"Why don't you just lock him in his room? Or lock your own door, for that matter?"

Brooke tried not to show her shock. "You're joking, right? Lock a three-year-old in his room? What if there was a fire? Or he really needed me in the middle of the night?"

"Oh, well, I didn't think of that," Josephine said with a shrug. "That's why Preiss and I never had children of our own. I don't think I would have made a good mother."

Brooke silently agreed with that assessment. "Anyway, it's time for Henry to transition to a big-boy bed. Maybe then he'll let me sleep in peace."

"Is Henry a family name?"

"Yes. He's named for my grandfather. Millie's husband. I suppose you knew him too?"

"I regret now that I never met him. But Ruth said he was a good man, and I heard he was good to Millie."

"Mama was only sixteen when he died, and she was devastated. I think he was much older than Granny," Brooke said.

"I believe that's what I heard." Josephine nodded. "Thank goodness he left Millie well fixed. You know, Millie's father—he'd be your great-grandfather—lost everything in the crash of '29. If it hadn't been for her grandparents, they would have been penniless."

Brooke gazed at the pin fastened to Josephine's chest. "I'm a little confused. Earlier, you said my grandmother had those pins made for her bridesmaids. But you just told me you never met my grandfather."

Josephine ran a bony finger over the pin. "Millie was engaged to someone else. His name was Russell . . . something." She looked up at Brooke. "Can you believe I've forgotten his last name? That's the wedding I was to have been in. But it never came off. Later, Millie married your Henry. Ruth said he was very distinguished. Some type of educator, I believe?"

"He was an English professor at Kenyon College, in Ohio," Brooke said. "His first wife died in one of the influenza epidemics, and Mama said he'd been a widower for years before he met Granny at a party in Boston. They got married a month later. Can you imagine doing that now?"

"Quite the whirlwind courtship," Josephine said, her tone acerbic. "But dear Ruth said the wedding was a lovely, intimate affair."

"You were going to tell me more about Ruth," Brooke prompted.

"She had the loveliest red curls," Josephine said. "And a temper to go along with them. A spitfire, we called her. But she had a tender heart. And she was such an animal lover. She'd find an abandoned kitten behind the dining hall at school and rescue it. Sneak it into our room, feed it milk with a medicine dropper. She hated any kind of injustice, hated cruelty. Ruth was a crusader."

"Whatever happened to her?"

Josephine shrugged. "We . . . had a disagreement. I suppose it came to a head with the '72 election. Ruth despised Nixon. She was what Preiss called a limousine liberal. Came by it honestly. Her mother was a suffragette."

Brooke shrugged. "Was that so awful? She sounds pretty amazing to me."

"You wouldn't understand," Josephine said. "It was a different time. Ruth was so . . . preachy. So damn certain about everything. Now? I see that our quarrel was silly. She and Millie were wonderful friends. We were like sisters. Closer than sisters."

"I know what you mean about missing your oldest friends," Brooke said wistfully. "My best friend, back in Savannah? Holly? She was Harris's sister."

"The man you jilted," Josephine said.

"She was supposed to be my maid of honor. But I ran away the night of the bachelorette party," Brooke confessed. "I was scared and confused. Afterward, I was too ashamed of the way I'd acted to reach out and apologize. It's been nearly four years, and we still haven't spoken."

"Foolish pride," Josephine said, shaking her head. "Foolish, foolish pride."

7

....

o, Ruth and Millie. They were your best friends from boarding school? What about Varina, the woman you mentioned yesterday?" Brooke asked.

"Ah, Varina. Of course she didn't go to school with us. She was black! And much younger than we were. Only fourteen. Her father was Geechee, and her family worked for my father here on the island. Do you know about the Geechees?"

"They're the descendants of slaves, right? From the Gullah tribe in West Africa? Who stayed here on the coast of Georgia after the Civil War and emancipation?"

"That's right. Harley—he was Varina's father—was a Shaddix. The little church graveyard at Oyster Bluff is full of Shaddix headstones. Harley's people were slaves who worked at the plantation that once stood right where Shellhaven now stands. Harley and his wife, Sally, came to work for my papa before he'd even finished building this house. Poor Sally, she was from the mainland, and I don't think she ever got used to living over here. Sally died, leaving Harley to raise their four children. Varina was still a baby, and the only girl."

Josephine fiddled with the trim on the afghan draped loosely around her shoulders. "I'm afraid the Shaddix boys took after their daddy. They were hard workers, and capable enough, but I don't think any of them ever went to school beyond sixth grade."

"But Varina was different?"

"Oh yes. She was the prettiest little thing, and bright as a new penny. After Sally died, Harley's sister, Margie, came to work here, and she'd bring Varina up here to Shellhaven with her most days. She was reading before first grade and had such a thirst for learning. She knew every inch of this island and loved to show us all her secret places."

The old lady's face shone as she spoke of Varina's accomplishments. "At first, Papa didn't think it was right—her spending so much time here. He was a free thinker for that day and time, but even he worried that people would wonder about a little colored girl getting big ideas."

Brooke winced at the term *colored girl*. She'd lived in the South her whole life but had never gotten used to the lingering vestiges of racism.

"But Varina became a friend?" Brooke asked.

"We all doted on her. We gave her clothes and shoes, treated her to gifts— candy, new books, things like that. Harley had diabetes, and the doctor had to amputate his right foot, and then he really couldn't work anymore, so he took up preaching, and the boys all quit school to help out. The Shaddixes never had enough to go around. Varina was like our little sister."

"If your little sister happened to be a colored girl," Brooke said.

The old lady's eyes flared. "You're very rude, you know that? I never called Varina a colored girl. That was Papa. And he didn't mean it in a derogatory way. He never, ever used the N-word, which most people did back then. It was a different time."

"You said Varina is still alive?" Brooke asked, interrupting. "And you've kept in touch all these years?"

"Of course. After the war, Varina worked in Jacksonville. For the railroad. But she missed Talisa and her family. Her brothers were all married, with a dozen children between them, and eventually she moved back here."

"Here? To Shellhaven?"

"Part of the time. She worked here for me after Preiss's death. It was lonely, you know? I never imagined he would die first. He was six years younger than I was. I still can't get over it. I'll never get over his death."

"I'm sorry for your loss," Brooke said. She'd noticed that Josephine's breathing was growing labored, her narrow shoulders hunched, and her voice raspy.

She leaned forward and touched the old lady's hand gently. "Are you feeling all right? Is there anything I can get you? Some water?"

Josephine's cough rattled, and she abruptly yanked her hand back, as though she'd been burned. "I've taken my pills, and there's nothing more to be done."

"I can leave and come back later, maybe when you're feeling better?" Brooke offered.

"I'm not going to feel better," Josephine snapped. "My time is short, so I'd really prefer it if we could get down to business."

"All right. Tell me more about Varina. Does she still live on the island?"

"No. One of her great-nieces—Felicia, I believe is the girl's name—took it upon herself to move Varina to Jacksonville, supposedly to take care of her. Felicia is Homer's granddaughter, or maybe great-granddaughter. He died back in February. Varina has been living with Felicia three or four years now. They tell me the girl is some kind of professor at a college down there, but I don't know where or what she teaches."

"And you've had no contact with Varina since then?"

"I didn't say that," Josephine retorted. "Varina came back here for Homer's funeral, and that girl brought her here to see me then."

"Why is a great-niece caring for her?" Brooke asked. "What about her own children?"

"Varina never married," Josephine said. "Bad luck and bad decisions have haunted that family. There were three brothers, and all of them had their problems. Drinking, gambling, bad women, and of course, the damn diabetes. It killed Omar and Otis before they turned fifty. Varina helped raise her brothers' children and then their grandchildren. Oh yes, they all love their auntie Vee, as they call her."

"And you're on good terms with her?"

Josephine coughed violently, startling the sleeping dogs, who jumped down from her lap.

Brooke waited.

"That pushy Felicia has put all kinds of wild ideas in Varina's head," Josephine said, dabbing at her lips with a sodden handkerchief. "When she came to see me, back in February, I assumed it was strictly a social call. But I was sadly mistaken. Shocked, really."

"What did Varina want?"

"Varina never would have thought of it on her own," Josephine said. "That girl—Felicia—she's just like all the rest of this generation. Think they're owed something. Always looking for a handout."

Brooke waited.

"Can you imagine? She wanted me to deed over Oyster Bluff to the families living there. Just give it to them! Land I bought and paid for. And paid a fair price, I might add, when I could just have easily waited and bought it for next to nothing on the courthouse steps for back taxes."

Josephine's indignation sparked another alarming spasm of coughing. Brooke glanced toward the door. Should she call Louette?

A minute or two later, after the coughing subsided, Josephine's face remained pink with remembered outrage.

"What was your answer?" Brooke asked, her face deadpan.

"I refused! And I let Varina know I was disappointed that she would ask such a thing of me, considering all I've done for that family over the years."

"I thought the land at Oyster Bluff originally belonged to those Geechee families after the Civil War. Wasn't the land given to the freedmen by the government?"

"It was, but as I said, the Shaddixes and the others chose to sell their land. In fact, they came right to this house and begged me to buy, because they needed the money. Nobody made them sell it, and I paid a very fair price."

I'll just bet, Brooke thought. "How much land are we talking about?"

"A little over twenty acres. When Papa was alive, it was a nice little community, with a schoolhouse, a commissary, and a church, but then, over the years, all the young folks moved off, and the families that stayed are either too shiftless or sorry to keep up with their property."

"Don't Shug and Louette live at Oyster Bluff?" Brooke asked. "Do they rent from you?"

"I wasn't referring to them," Josephine said. "What I mean is the others."

"How did Varina take it, when you refused to deed the property to the residents of Oyster Bluff? Did you quarrel?"

"What could she say? She was embarrassed. I tell you, that pushy niece put her up to it. Varina never would have been bold enough to ask such a thing, in the light of our friendship over the years, which is what I told Felicia, right to her face, when she tried to pick a fight with me that day."

"Did you fight?"

Josephine drew herself up as best she could in the sagging recliner. "We had words. She called me some very unpleasant names and accused me of taking advantage of Varina and their family. Can you imagine? Finally, I'd had enough. I told her to leave. And I haven't seen or heard from Varina since that day. It makes me very sad, but what could I do?"

"It seems to me you could have done as Varina asked, if you cared as much about her as you say. It's only twenty acres—and you have what? Twelve thousand? It's not like you need that land. Or what little income you derive from the rent," Brooke said earnestly. "Think of it, Josephine. Varina's people were slaves. Abducted from their homes in Africa, then shipped here where they were bought and sold and worked and treated with less regard than mules or chickens. The government meant for them and their heirs to have that land as restitution. Why not give it back to them?"

"*My* family never owned slaves," Josephine shot back. "Anyway, it's the principle of the thing that I object to. Felicia has no right to make demands of me. That girl has no sense of gratitude, no idea of propriety. I'm afraid she's poisoned Varina against me." The old lady's hands shook in her lap.

"You told me earlier you want to keep the state from taking your land and to make amends with your friends, including Varina, isn't that right? So why not go ahead and deed Oyster Bluff over to the heirs of the original Geechee families, including the Shaddixes? Wouldn't that go a long way toward repairing your relationship with your old friend?"

Josephine brooded over the suggestion, shaking her head. "I resent being backed into a corner like this. It makes me furious."

"Don't think of it like that, then," Brooke suggested. "For one thing, if you deed the land over to those families, you'll reduce your own tax burden. Right?"

"I suppose."

"And you'd be doing a really good thing. You're fond of Louette and Shug, aren't you? Think of what it would mean to them—to own their own home again."

Brooke paused, then reached out again and touched Josephine's hand. This time the old woman sighed loudly but did not shake her off.

"Look, Josephine. You called me over here because you said you want to make things right, because you're not sleeping. You said yourself, you don't have much time left. If that's true, why not start by returning Oyster Bluff to those families who still live there?"

"It'll be a big mess," Josephine grumbled. "Lots of paperwork."

"That's why you have me," Brooke said. "I can get started on it right away, if you'll get me a list of your tenants. My assistant can look everything up in the county tax office."

"Fine," Josephine said, throwing up her hands in surrender.

"Do you have contact information for Varina's niece in Jacksonville?" Brooke asked.

Josephine motioned to the corner of the room, in the general direction of a huge antique mahogany Chinese Chippendale secretary. "There's an address book in the top drawer of the desk. It has a blue leather cover. I might still have the last birthday card Varina sent me tucked in there somewhere."

"What about a phone number for Felicia?"

"I don't know. Just look in the address book."

"While we're on the subject, if I'm going to try to track down your friend Ruth's family, I'm going to need whatever information you have. Old correspondence, anything like that with her last known address."

Josephine's eyelids drooped, first one, then the other, and she leaned her head against the back of the recliner. "Dear Ruth. She always had the cleverest Christmas cards. She was a wonderful writer, Ruth was. That was one of the things I missed, after our quarrel. Those damn Christmas cards."

"Josephine?"

Brooke leaned forward. Her client was perfectly motionless. She gingerly touched her bony wrist. Her skin was cool, the skin dry as paper and brown-splotched. Brooke wrapped her fingers around the old lady's wrist, watching her face for any reaction. There was a surprisingly strong pulse.

Josephine snored softly. Not dead. Just napping.

Brooke stood and walked over to the secretary. She might as well start trying to find contact information for Ruth's heirs and for Varina. She yawned involuntarily. What she wouldn't give for a few stolen hours of sleep. Her son had climbed into bed with her sometime after midnight, nestling against her back, his sweet, warm breath close against her neck. And sometime after that, he'd wet the bed, and they'd both ended up sleeping on the lumpy sofa in the living room.

She heard a hesitant knock at the door, and Louette entered, carrying a silver tray with a plate of sandwiches, a bowl of potato chips, and a silver pitcher beaded with condensation. She cleared some magazines from a tabletop and set the tray down, glancing over at her employer.

"I was hoping she'd eat something," Louette said, shaking her head. "The doctor says she needs to gain weight, but I can't hardly get her to eat anything. I made her favorite—egg salad on toast, and there's a pitcher of iced coffee too. Does that sound okay? I could fix something else if you want."

"Actually, that sounds perfect. My son was a little fussy this morning, so I didn't have time to grab breakfast and I'm starving."

"You need anything else before I run down to the dock to meet Shug? He's bringing our groceries, and I don't want my milk to sour in this heat."

"No, thanks. I'm going to eat this lunch, then go through Josephine's address book for some folks she wants me to contact."

Louette nodded and started to leave the room, but then she turned and came back. "I'm not trying to pry into Miss Josephine's business," she said, her voice low. "But I do know she's not sleeping well or eating, and she's all upset about those state folks coming around, trying to make her sell the island to them. Is that why she wanted to see you?"

Brooke hesitated. "I'm sorry. My business with Josephine is confidential. She specifically asked me not to tell anybody about our discussion."

"Okay," Louette said. "I figured you couldn't say anything. It's just, Shug and me and the rest of us, we're worried about what will happen. You know . . . after." Her dark eyes rested on Josephine, asleep in her chair. She smoothed her hands over her hips. "If the state takes the rest of Talisa, what'll happen to Oyster Bluff? Where'll we go? Shug wasn't crazy about moving over here, at first, but now, he's turned into a real Geechee. He hates the idea of going back to the city. And so do I."

"I don't blame you," Brooke said. "This island. There's something special about it that I can't describe. It's like the last wild place."

"It is that," Louette said. "You know, when I was coming up, I couldn't wait to get off this island. The day I got done with high school, I told my mama I was getting me a job in town and finding me a man from away, and then I wasn't ever coming back here again."

"I felt the same way about Savannah, where I grew up," Brooke agreed. "I didn't even want to go to college in Georgia. And then I ended up moving right back home after law school. So what did your mother say when you told her you never planned on coming back here?"

"She just laughed and told me to go on and get all that running around out of my system," Louette said. "But she always said she knew someday I'd end up right back here on Talisa. And she was right. My mama was nobody's fool."

8

....

The secretary was enormous, with seeded glass doors behind elaborate fretwork, and a drop-front desk with a dozen small cubbies and drawers. Each slot was crammed with yellowing stationery, envelopes, pencil stubs, and notebooks. Behind the glass doors, leather-bound books with stamped gold lettering were shoved up against Chinese export blue-and-white porcelain vases and bowls. The top shelf of the bookcase held a turtle shell, an old mayonnaise jar full of beach glass, and a stuffed squirrel with lifeless brown glass eyes and a tail that seemed to have lost most of its fur.

Brooke tried to open the top drawer. Stuck.

Finally, after prolonged jiggling, one side of the drawer loosened, and as she inched it open, she could see stacks of papers and notebooks inside. She worked on the other side, and after five minutes of tugging and cussing, the whole drawer pulled free of the cabinet, landing on the rug with a dull thud.

"Damn," she whispered.

The drawer was about eighteen inches deep and was as crammed with papers as the bookcase above it. There were stacks of rubber band–bound canceled checks and bills, spiral-bound notebooks and black-and-white composition books, and bundles of letters and cards tied together with faded blue ribbons.

Brooke dug around in the drawer until her fingers closed on something that felt like leather. As she lifted the address book from the drawer, shards of the palest pink rose petals showered down on the faded rug, releasing their faint, musky scent.

She sat cross-legged on the floor and lifted out a rubber band–wrapped bundle of likely looking correspondence, each with the same handwriting on the envelope. Opening one, she saw that it was an anniversary card.

"To My One True Love" was written in thick gold script on the outside of the card, beneath an image of red roses. The inside right side of the card had a treacly Hallmark verse, beneath which the sender had written in a strong, slanting script: "My darling Jo, with love from Preiss." On the opposite side, the sender had copied a poem called "Always Marry an April Girl."

> *Praise the spells and bless the charms,*
> *I found April in my arms.*
> *April golden, April cloudy,*
> *Gracious, cruel, tender, rowdy;*
> *April soft in flowered languor,*
> *April cold with sudden anger.*
> *Ever changing, ever true—*
> *I love April, I love you.*
> —Ogden Nash

"Ohhh." Brooke let out a long, involuntary sigh and looked again at her would-be employer, her crepe-like eyelids closed, nearly bald head slumped sideways, a tiny bead of saliva trickling from narrow, colorless lips. Of course, Josephine Warrick had been young once, with slender limbs and a laughing smile. She had won the love of a much-younger man, this Preiss Warrick, who called her his April Girl.

9

....

An hour later, she'd finished her sandwich and chips and made what she thought was a decent start on completing the old woman's assignment.

"Well?" Josephine was awake again. Her dark eyes glared accusingly. "What did you find?"

Brooke looked down at the notes she'd scrawled on her yellow legal pad. She'd drawn circles around the names *Varina Shaddix* and *Ruth Quinlan*.

"Josephine, if I find Ruth's relatives and Varina, what do you want me to tell them?"

"*When* you find them, I want them to come to Talisa," Josephine said. "I want to see them. Your mother too, of course. She was Millie's only child, wasn't she?"

"Yes," Brooke said cautiously. "And what will you tell them—if they agree to come here to see you?"

"I want to leave this island to them—in a trust," Josephine said promptly. "And I want you to set up the trust and administer it."

"But that's impossible," Brooke said quickly. "If my mother is to be included in the trust, that would present a clear conflict of interest." She shook her head sadly. "I wish you'd told me that from the beginning. I can't represent you, Josephine. It's a matter of ethics."

"Ridiculous," the old lady snapped. "I can hire whomever I want to help me dispose of my property."

"You can, but that person cannot legally benefit in any way from such a relationship," Brooke said. She was already thinking of the $25,000 check. She was going to have to give it back.

So, goodbye to paying down her Amex bill. Goodbye to replacing the bald tires on the Volvo, and goodbye to making a dent in Henry's hospital bills.

"If you really don't trust your Atlanta lawyers, I can help you find an attorney to set up the trust, and contact the others in the High Tide Club," Brooke offered. "It would probably be better anyway, since I have absolutely no experience with estate law."

"You're not listening," Josephine said. "I want you. Only you. Millie's granddaughter."

"That's a lovely sentiment, but I can't ethically do the job," Brooke said. "It's not just a whim of mine. It's the law."

"There must be a way around that kind of thing. A work-around, Preiss would have called it. There's always a work-around."

"Not this time," Brooke said. "I'm sorry, Josephine. I really am. I'm willing to track down Ruth's relatives and Varina, and I'll let my mother know you'd like to meet with her, but that's the extent of the services I'm legally able to offer you. Of course, I'll be returning your retainer."

"I don't want my money back," Josephine fumed. "And I don't need any more damn lawyers complicating what's left of my life." She shoved the sandwich plate aside. "Go on, then. Take your so-called ethics and get out."

Brooke had been standing under the shade of the porte cochere for at least ten minutes, staring down at her cell phone, which still had no service. So she was thrilled and relieved when Shug pulled up in the pickup truck.

Louette leaned out the passenger-side window, a look of alarm on her face. "What's wrong? Where's Josephine?"

"Nothing's wrong," Brooke said quickly. "She just woke up, and she's in a foul mood."

"Sounds about right," Shug said.

"You're leaving already?" Louette asked, climbing down and grabbing two canvas totes of supplies.

"I've got to get back to my son," Brooke said. "Anyway, I've told Josephine I can't represent her in the matter she raised. So there's not much more I can do here." She looked over at Shug. "I hate to ask, but can you or C. D. take me back across to the mainland?"

"No bother," Shug said. "It'll have to be me, 'cause C. D.'s off this afternoon. No telling where he's got to."

She sat in the bow of the boat as they crossed the river. It was hot and sunny, and the water was dead calm. A pair of dolphins skimmed along in the boat's wake, and Brooke felt grateful for the slight breeze.

"So . . . you won't be coming back over to the island after this?" Shug asked, his face impassive behind his sunglasses.

"Probably not," Brooke said.

"Too bad. Louette said Miss Josephine was all excited about whatever it was she wanted you to do for her. She's been kinda low since the last time she went to the doctor. Seems like she perked right up since she got the idea to call you. Even started eating a little bit again."

"I'll help her as much as I can," Brooke said, already feeling guilty. "But there are . . . technicalities that prevent me from providing the services she needs."

"I got ya," Shug said.

He steered the boat toward the first available slip in the marina, and once they were tied up, he jumped onto the dock and helped her off. "You need a ride?" he asked, looking around the crowded complex of boat slips, launch ramps, and bait shop. "We keep a truck over here. It ain't got no air-conditioning, but it runs all right, and I can take you wherever you need to go."

"I'm parked right over there under that oak tree," she said, extending a hand to shake his. "And thanks again."

He smiled and gripped her hand with both of his. "My pleasure. You take care now."

"You too," she said.

He turned to go back to the boat, and she felt a sudden stab of guilt.

"Wait a minute, Shug," she called.

He stopped and walked back to her.

Brooke dug in her purse and handed him her business card. She'd ordered a box of a thousand after setting up practice three years earlier and had barely made a dent in her supply.

"Take this," she said impulsively. "It's illegal as hell for me to discuss this with you, but, well, Louette mentioned that y'all are worried about what will happen at Oyster Bluff once Josephine is gone. Maybe there's something I can do to help."

He looked down at the card and then up at her and frowned. "We got no expectations. And Louette, she shouldn't have said anything to you about that. We can take care of ourselves. Always have."

"I'm sure you can," Brooke said quickly. Had she insulted his pride?

10

....

Brooke eyed the stack of bills on her desk. She'd gone over her budget one more time looking for something else to cut, and turning the pages of her legal pad, she found the notes she'd jotted during her visit with Josephine Warrick.

That seemed like a lifetime ago. She tapped her pencil on the check Josephine had given her. On the boat ride back from Talisa, she'd made up her mind to return the check.

Was there any way, ethically, she could keep Josephine's money? She chewed the end of her pencil for a moment, then opened her laptop and her favorite search engine.

It took less than five minutes to discover the whereabouts of Josephine's oldest friend, Ruth.

The obituary ran in *The Boston Globe* on October 16, 2008.

> Ruth Mattingly Quinlan, formerly of Boston, died October 12 at Hospice Care of Palm Beach, Florida, after a short illness. She was 89.

Born in 1919 to Frederick Eustis Mattingly and the former Prudence Patterson, Mrs. Quinlan attended the Grosvernor School and Smith College, from which she graduated in 1942. In 1946, she married Robert Hudson Quinlan of Highland Park, Illinois. Mr. Quinlan, a former pharmacist, was a successful businessman who owned a chain of midwestern drugstores, which he later sold to Walgreens in the 1970s.

Mr. and Mrs. Quinlan made their home in Winnetka, where Mrs. Quinlan became active in civic and charitable circles in between raising the couple's two children: Robert Hudson Quinlan Jr., born in 1949, and Diana, born in 1951.

A devoted mother and advocate for liberal causes, Mrs. Quinlan became involved in the civil rights movement in the early 1960s, joining the Rev. Martin Luther King's Washington peace march in 1963. She was a delegate to the 1972 Democratic National Convention and was also a key organizer for Walter Mondale's 1984 presidential bid.

Following the death of her husband in 1996, Mrs. Quinlan became a full-time resident of Palm Beach, Florida, where she resumed fundraising for favorite charities and causes. In August, she served as the oldest Florida delegate to the Democratic National Convention, where she cast her state's ballot nominating Barack Obama for president.

Ruth Mattingly Quinlan was predeceased by her daughter, Diana Quinlan, who died in 1968. Survivors include her son, Robert H. Quinlan Jr., of Orlando, Florida, and one granddaughter, Ruth Elizabeth Quinlan, of Los Angeles, California.

No services are planned. At Mrs. Quinlan's request, memorials may be made to the American Civil Liberties Union or Planned Parenthood.

Brooke chuckled at the last line of the obituary. Ruth Quinlan sounded like the lefty liberal Josephine had described. And like someone Brooke would have loved to have met. According to the newspaper, Ruth was survived by a son and a granddaughter. She typed the name *Robert Hudson Quinlan Jr.* into the search engine.

The first hit she got was for an article in the *Orlando Sentinel*. A Robert Quinlan had been arrested in 2009 for breaking and entering, assault on a peace officer, and public intoxication.

She found two more published police reports concerning minor legal skirmishes for the man she assumed was the same Robert Quinlan, another in 2011, and a third in 2012. She found a white pages listing for R. H. Quinlan, in Oviedo, Florida, and called the number, but got a recorded message saying the number had been disconnected. Maybe Quinlan was currently residing in a local jail or prison?

Next she typed the name *Ruth Elizabeth Quinlan* into the search engine and was thrilled to see a list of more than a dozen hits. Clicking on each citation, Brooke learned that R. Elizabeth Quinlan was a somewhat prolific, if not wildly successful freelance journalist.

She wrote for obscure trade journals like *American Hardware Retailer* and *The Journal of Lawn Care Professionals*. She'd penned a handful of travel stories for regional airline magazines, and her most prestigious byline, as far as Brooke could tell, was for a series of stories about midlife dating for the online version of *Glamour* magazine.

Brooke bookmarked the articles to read later. Right now, what she really needed was to locate Ruth Elizabeth Quinlan. She couldn't find a telephone listing for the woman, but after clicking around, she did find a website for R. Elizabeth Quinlan, freelance journalist. Which led her to R. Elizabeth's private Facebook page.

Brooke clicked on the private message button and typed in a missive to Ruth Elizabeth Quinlan, one she hoped would be intriguing enough to elicit a reply.

Hi. I'm an attorney in Georgia, and my client was a lifelong friend of Ruth Mattingly Quinlan, whom I believe was your grandmother. If that is the case, my client would very much like to contact you. Please call or reply to this message at your earliest convenience.

Almost immediately after she'd sent the message, she received a reply.

This is Lizzie Quinlan. My grandmother has been dead nearly ten years. I don't know anybody in Georgia. What does your client want? If this is some kind of a scam and you're looking for money, you're out of luck, because I don't have any.

That made Brooke laugh out loud, and she quickly typed a reply.

Welcome to my world. I'm broke too. I can assure you that this is not a scam. My client was an old classmate of your grandmother's. She is a widow and never had children. She lives alone on a barrier island off the coast of Georgia, and I'm sorry to say that she is terminally ill. She lost contact with your grandmother some years ago, and now she would like to meet and make amends to Mrs. Quinlan's heirs.

Lizzie Quinlan's reply took less than a minute.

Yeah, sure. And I'm the crown princess of Istanbul. Who is this really?

Brooke sighed. It was late, and she was exhausted and in no mood to play games.

My name is Brooke Trappnell. I'm a member in good standing of the Georgia bar. Feel free to check me out. In the meantime, I'm going to bed. If you want to talk further, contact me tomorrow, after 8:00 Eastern time.

Brooke closed her laptop and looked at her phone again. Too late now to call her mother and ask for a loan. Maybe tomorrow she'd call. Maybe tomorrow things would look better.

11

....

October 1941

Millie's head spun. She'd had three glasses of champagne, which was two too many. She was dizzy but strangely happy. She knew Gardiner Bettendorf had asked her to dance out of pity—he felt sorry for her because her oafish fiancé had been ignoring her all evening. But she didn't care.

She let her chin rest on his shoulder and relaxed as Gardiner guided her around the polished dance floor, his hand resting lightly at the waist of her new gown.

In the next instant, Russell was there, wrenching her away from Gardiner. His fingers dug into the flesh of her bare upper arm, and his breath stank of cigars and whiskey as he confronted her dance partner.

"What the hell do you think you're doing with my girl, Bettendorf?"

"Hey, fella," Gardiner said, taking a step backward. "Take it easy. We were just dancing."

"Fuck off," Russell said. "I'll deal with you later."

Without another word, he dragged Millie through the crowded room and out the french doors and onto the veranda.

"Russell," Millie said breathlessly. "Russell, stop. Let go. You're hurting me."

He released his hold on her arm. "But it's okay when that clown Bettendorf grabs you, right?"

"Gardiner didn't grab me," Millie said, trying to keep her tone light. It was always best to keep things light when Russell was drinking. "He didn't even really want to dance. He only asked me because Josephine asked him to."

"And why would she ask her brother to dance with you? What business is it of hers?"

"She's our hostess," Millie said. "You weren't around, and I guess she felt sorry for me because I was sort of a wallflower. She was just being polite."

Russell edged her into the shade of a huge magnolia tree that towered over the slate-floored veranda. The full moon spilled light onto the other end, where a group of young men laughed and joked, passing a silver flask among themselves. Fireflies flitted in the treetops, and Millie could see the glowing tips of the men's lit cigars.

It was like a scene from a movie, Millie thought. Or a book. The creamy magnolia blossoms were the size of dinner plates, and they contrasted brilliantly against the glossy dark leaves. Their perfume filled the night air.

Russell's dinner jacket was white too, although his tie was slightly askew, and his face had a fine sheen of perspiration.

"You weren't a wallflower. You're the prettiest girl here. I was just out here having a smoke with some of the fellas." He looped his arm around her shoulders and pulled her closer. His mustache tickled her ear, and he flicked his tongue just behind her earlobe. "Don't tell me you missed me." His words were only slightly slurred.

Millie shivered, despite the warmth of the evening. "Just a little," she said. "You haven't danced with me all night. And it's our engagement party."

"Too many people around," Russell groused. "You know how I hate crowds and big parties. Too much small talk. Small drinks, small food, small people." He nuzzled her neck and slid his hands around beneath her breasts, pushing them upward until they spilled from the neckline of her dress.

"Russell, please behave," Millie whispered, blushing in the dark. "Somebody will see us."

"Aw, who cares? We're engaged, aren't we?" He pulled her closer.

"I care," Millie said indignantly. "My mother is here. And my grandmother. What if they stepped out here and saw us like this?"

"Your mother is inside, flirting with old man Bettendorf. And your grandmother is blind as a bat. She just asked a hat rack in the foyer if he'd get her a cup of punch. Anyway, if she did see us, that could be good. Maybe your grandmother would have a heart attack and leave all her money to us."

Millie giggled despite herself. She really should not have had that third glass of champagne. Unlike Josephine and Ruth, she wasn't much of a drinker. "That's a terrible thing to say. You're terrible."

"I'll show you just how terrible I am."

Russell's teeth shone white in the darkness. "Come on. Let's get out of here. They've got me staying in the guesthouse, out by the pool. It's way more private there." He tugged her by the hand, but Millie stood her ground.

"But these are our friends. Josephine and her family have been so wonderfully generous to throw us this party, Russell. It would be rude to leave now."

"Who cares? They won't even notice."

"You know I can't go to your room alone. What if somebody saw me? What would they say?"

"I said, let's go," Russell said hoarsely. He grabbed her arm and started towing her toward the walkway that led around the edge of the house, through the gardens to the pool. The walk was narrow and closed in on either side by tall boxwood hedges.

"Russell, no," Millie said, her voice rising. She stumbled along behind him, catching her heel on one of the cobblestones and nearly tripping before he roughly pulled her upright.

"What is wrong with you tonight?" he snarled. He shoved her up against the trunk of another magnolia tree and pressed himself into her until she felt the rough bark scraping against the flesh of her bare shoulders. He forced a knee between her legs and pushed her dress up until it was nearly at her waist. "That's better," he breathed in her ear. "No more games."

She flailed helplessly against his hands, but they were everywhere, tearing at the neckline of her gown, fumbling with the snaps of her garter belt. He thrust his tongue into her mouth, and a moment later, he was unbuckling his belt and unzipping the fly of his pants.

"Stop it!" Millie cried. She pushed against his chest with both hands, but he was stronger, a head taller, and she was pinned there, half-naked, exposed to the world. She felt panicky. She was no virgin—Russell had seen to that—but this . . .

"Just relax, baby," Russell said, chuckling. "Let me just—"

"No! Stop it!"

"Millie?" A man's voice.

She heard the rapid clatter of hard-soled shoes on the cobblestones.

He stopped, a few feet away. It was Gardiner Bettendorf. "Millie? Are you all right?"

Russell kept her pinned, right where she was. "Get lost," he said calmly, not even bothering to turn around. "The lady and I were just admiring the moonlight."

"That's not what it sounded like to me," Gardiner said. "Millie, would you like to go back to the house?" He stepped closer, peering at them.

She squirmed under the weight of Russell's body, mortified at her appearance, desperately trying to cover herself. She took a deep breath, willing herself to sound normal.

"Um, yes. We were just about to come back to the party. But you go on ahead and we'll catch up."

"I think I'll just walk back with you, if you don't mind," Gardiner said. His tone was light, affable.

"I said get lost!" Russell yelled. He whirled around and without warning threw a punch at Gardiner's nose, just barely grazing it. He swung again and connected solidly this time.

"Stop it!" Millie screamed.

Russell was bigger, but Gardiner was faster, and now he swung hard, landing a solid blow to Russell's jaw and then to his gut.

The big man staggered two steps backward, a look of astonishment on his face. "I'll kill you."

A thin stream of blood trickled from Gardiner's nose and onto the spotless starched collar of his white dress shirt. "Enough, all right?" He nodded at Millie. "Why don't you go on back to the party now?"

12

....

B rooke's cell phone rang at precisely 8:01 A.M. She grabbed the phone, hoping the loud ring wouldn't awaken her son.

"Hello? Is this Brooke Trappnell? This is Lizzie Quinlan."

"Oh, hi."

Brooke glanced over at the crib mattress on the floor by her bed, momentarily reassured that Henry was still asleep, his favorite blue-and-white quilt wrapped around him, burrito-style. She took the phone and walked into the kitchen.

"Who's your client?" Lizzie asked.

"Excuse me?"

"His name. You said your client was a dear friend of my late grandmother's. So I'd like to know his name, since you know mine."

Brooke hesitated. Josephine hadn't told her not to reveal her identity, and she couldn't really think of a legitimate reason not to disclose it.

"*Her* name is Josephine Bettendorf Warrick. Does that name ring a bell at all?"

"Never heard of her," Lizzie said. "Spell it for me, okay? So I can Google it?"

Brooke spelled out her client's name. "While you're at it, you might want to do a search for Talisa; that's the island Josephine owns, and it's off the Georgia coast."

"Got it," Lizzie said. "My Wi-Fi is slow as hell, so if you would, fill me in on the details while I wait. Like, what's the deal with this Josephine? And what does she want with me?"

"It's complicated." Brooke took a deep breath.

"You'd be surprised at the depth of my ability to handle complicated issues, Mrs. Trappnell."

"It's Ms. Trappnell, but call me Brooke."

"Okay, Brooke. I'm listening."

"I know there are gaping holes in this story, but what you have to realize is that Josephine is ninety-nine and critically ill. I met her just a few days ago, so she's been feeding me the details in tiny little spoonfuls," Brooke said. "Your grandmother Ruth and Josephine were lifelong friends. They were roommates in boarding school and made their debuts together."

"I never knew Granny was a debutante," Lizzie said, chuckling. "That's just crazy! She was a card-carrying liberal."

"Which Josephine decidedly is not," Brooke volunteered. "Anyway, Josephine and Ruth were also best friends with Mildred Updegraff, who, by the way, was my grandmother. They had another friend, who was much younger, named Varina. The four girls had a little club, sort of a secret society, which they called the High Tide Club."

"Cute, but what's the point?" Lizzie said.

"Sometime after the war—World War II, that is—Josephine had a falling-out with my grandmother Millie and later, your grandmother Ruth. Over the years, she lost contact with everyone except for Varina. Josephine is hazy on the details, but that's it in a nutshell. Now she's got terminal cancer. She wants to reconnect with her old friends' heirs and 'make amends' as she says. I should add that Josephine has been a widow for many years and never had children."

Brooke heard the tapping of keys from the other end of the line.

"Holy shit," Lizzie said. "I'm just reading an article about Josephine Warrick. This says that Talisa is twelve thousand acres. Is that true?"

"Yes. A small portion of the island was owned by distant cousins, who sold it to the State of Georgia for a park in 1978, but Josephine retains ownership of the rest of Talisa, and she's determined not to let the state take her land. That's how I got involved."

"I'm looking at a photo of some gorgeous pink mansion. It looks like a frickin' castle!" Lizzie exclaimed.

"That's Shellhaven. It was built in the twenties by Josephine's father, who was a shipping magnate. It's in pretty bad shape these days, but Josephine is also adamant that the house should be preserved. She wants her land and house transferred intact to her beneficiaries," Brooke said.

"Are you telling me a woman I never met, never even heard of until today, wants me to inherit a twelve thousand–acre island in Georgia?"

"Not exactly," Brooke said. "I mean, maybe. It's not really clear. And yes, I understand how insane this all sounds to you, because it sounds insane to me too, and unlike you, I've met her, and I've been to Talisa."

"This is totally, totally nuts," Lizzie said.

"Agreed. So here's the thing. Josephine wants to meet you. You and your brother. I've been trying to find a way to contact him too, but I'm sort of at a dead end."

There was a long pause on the other end of the line.

"Bobby's dead," Lizzie said.

"Oh. I'm sorry to hear that," Brooke said.

"Don't be. My brother had what we journalists like me call 'a checkered criminal career.' We hadn't talked in years. I only found out Bobby was dead when his landlord called me up to ask for his last three months of back rent. Turns out he'd listed me as next of kin on his apartment application."

Brooke was at a loss for words.

"So you were saying?" Lizzie prompted.

"Josephine would like to meet you. In person. On Talisa. To be honest, I don't know what happens after that. She's old and ornery, and she's dying."

"Is she rich?" Lizzie asked bluntly. "Because if she's not, I have no interest in flying out to Georgia to meet some eccentric old crackpot. I'm on deadline for a crappy magazine story right now, and I can't really afford to take time away from that, not to mention the cost of a plane ticket. So you tell her that. Tell her I'll come if she'll pay my way. All expenses, including airfare, meals, and hotel."

"I'll tell her, but there's no hotel on Talisa. There's hardly even cell phone service," Brooke warned.

"Sounds dreamy," Lizzie said.

Henry pounded on the plastic tray of the high chair with his sippy cup. "Milk! Milk! Milk!"

"Milk, *please*," Brooke said.

"Milk, please, milk, please, milk, please," he chanted.

She refilled the cup and called her mother.

Marie answered on the second ring. "Hi, sweetie. Is everything okay?"

"Of course. Why wouldn't it be?" Brooke asked.

"Don't be so sensitive," Marie said. "You usually don't call on weekdays while you're working."

"Actually, I am calling you about work. I need to ask you something about my new client."

"Is it somebody I know?"

"Well, she seems to think she knows *you*. It's Josephine Bettendorf Warrick."

"You're kidding."

"I'm not. Do you know her?"

"In a roundabout way. She was your granny's oldest friend. Does she still live down there in that creepy old mansion on that island?"

"Yep."

"Good heavens. I had no idea she was even still alive. Let's see. She must be in her nineties, right?"

"She turned ninety-nine in April," Brooke said.

"How did you get mixed up with her?"

"She called me. Out of the blue. She'd seen those old newspaper stories about me trying to sue the Park Service, and she wants me to keep the state from condemning Talisa and taking it for a park. And that's not all. She wants me to find the heirs of her oldest friends. I've already contacted one grand-daughter, who lives in California. I'm trying to track down another woman and her niece. And that just leaves you."

"Me? What's she want with me? Or those other women?"

"She wants to meet with you. And then, if she likes what she sees, I think she intends for the three of you to inherit the island. And the mansion."

"Really? Josephine Warrick hardly knows me. Why would she do some-thing like that?"

"She says she wants to make it up to her oldest, dearest friends. But she hasn't really told me what she's trying to apologize for. It's all pretty sketchy, to tell you the truth. I tried to talk her out of hiring me, but she's absolutely ada-mant that she wants me and nobody else."

Marie mulled that over for a moment. "You say she's ninety-nine? Are you sure she's not suffering from dementia?"

"Josephine is sharp as a tack. Most of the time. But she's been diagnosed with lung cancer, so she tires easily. I gather she was a pretty heavy smoker for most of her life."

"Funny you should mention that," Marie said, "because that's what I re-member about her. Your father and I were at a party, years and years ago, at the Oglethorpe Club, and she was there too, and what I remember about her was that she had this long, jeweled cigarette holder, like something out of *Breakfast at Tiffany's*, you know? I thought she was quite exotic."

"Did she speak to you?"

"Only briefly. I was in the ladies' lounge, fixing my hair, and she came up and introduced herself and said how sorry she was about Granny. She went on and on about what a dear friend Millie was. Which I thought was very odd, since she didn't go to Granny's funeral or send a sympathy card or any-thing."

"That sounds like Josephine," Brooke said. "And you'd never met her before that?"

"Not that I can recall," Marie said.

"Do you remember Granny ever talking about the High Tide Club?"

"Say that again?" Marie asked.

"The High Tide Club. Did Granny ever mention it to you?"

"Granny wasn't much of a club woman. I think she did Junior League because her mother and grandmother did it . . ."

"This was a different kind of club," Brooke said. "According to Josephine, it was just her, another friend named Ruth, Granny, and a young black girl, Varina, who worked for the Bettendorfs and grew up on the island."

Marie gave that some thought. "I remember Granny talking about Ruth and Jo and the scrapes they got into in boarding school. And the name *Varina* sounds vaguely familiar, but what you have to remember is this was all a long time ago. Granny's been gone almost thirty years now."

"Twenty-eight," Brooke said promptly. "She died when I was six."

"Has it really been that long?" Marie said, her voice wistful. "I do miss her, Brooke. And I wish she'd lived long enough to enjoy you and, of course, our sweet Henry."

Brooke glanced over at sweet Henry, who at that precise moment was in the process of trying to climb out of his high chair. He had one chubby leg over the tray, and the chair was starting to tilt.

"Henry, no!" Brooke yelled. "Sorry, Mom. Gotta go."

13

....

Farrah was on the phone when Brooke arrived at the office, talking in what the young assistant liked to refer to as her "takin'-names-and-kickin'-ass voice."

"Hi, Mr. Mabry," she said, the model of crisp efficiency. "This is Ms. Miles, the office manager at Trappnell and Associates."

Farrah frowned and looked up at Brooke in amazement. "He hung up on me! The douchebag hung up as soon as I said your name."

"Was that Steve Mabry, the long-haul trucker who owes me $5,000 for handling his DUI case back in January?" Brooke asked with a sigh. "Forget it. He's a bona fide deadbeat. I'll have to file against him in small claims court, and it's probably not worth my time."

"No way," Farrah said. "He's gonna pay, and I'm gonna make it happen." She picked up her phone and redialed.

"Hi. Steve Mabry? Dude, don't hang up. I mean it. Look. You owe our firm $5,000 for representation on that DUI charge from way back last winter."

Farrah listened, tapping long violet fingertips on the desktop and shaking her head. "Yeah, I am aware that the judge revoked your driver's license. I'm also aware that it was your third DUI in the past five years, and if it hadn't been for my boss, or 'that bitch Brooke Trappnell,' as you just referred to her, your sorry tail would be sitting in the county jail right now."

Farrah's eyes narrowed as she listened to the diatribe on the other end of the line. "Let me get this straight," she interrupted. "You're telling me you have no intention of paying your legal fee, 'cause you don't have a job, 'cause you're not allowed to drive? Then how come you delivered a pizza to my boyfriend's house last night? Yeah, that's right. I was there, and I also took a picture of you behind the wheel of your pickup. Which I'm fixin' to email over to Judge Waller's office unless you deliver the money you owe this firm, in person. Like, today."

Brooke gasped in horror, but Farrah smiled smugly. "That's great. And hey, don't bother bringing a check. We're gonna need either cash or a money order. And if I were you, dude, I'd ask your mama to give you a ride."

She disconnected and gave her boss an angelic smile. "He says he'll be right over."

"Did you really get a photo of him driving last night?"

"Nope. It was way too dark."

Brooke tried to look stern. "Blackmail is against the law, you know."

Farrah shrugged. "So if that douchebag gets me arrested, I'll hire a good lawyer. Know any? I gotta go to class now. Don't forget to give him a receipt when he shows up."

There was a light tapping at her office door. A moment later, it swung open, and a black woman in her midthirties stepped inside. "Come on in, Auntie," she said, grasping the arm of a tiny white-haired woman with a walker.

"Hi," Brooke said, standing. "I'm Brooke Trappnell. Can I help you?"

"This is a nice office," the elderly woman said, looking around. "You reckon this is the right place?" She gave Brooke a warm smile. "We're looking for a lady lawyer."

"I'm a lady lawyer," Brooke said.

"See, Auntie Vee? It is her."

"Wait," Brooke said, startled. "Auntie Vee. Is your aunt Varina Shaddix?"

"That's right. And I'm her great-niece Felicia Shaddix. My aunt's cousin Louette called this week and said you might be in contact. We were coming up from Jacksonville today anyway, to see about a headstone for my great-uncle, and I just decided to drop in and see what you wanted with my aunt."

"This is great," Brooke said, still surprised. She pulled two chairs up to her desk. "Won't you sit down? I'm glad Louette called, although I wasn't aware Josephine had let her know I was looking for your aunt."

Felicia Shaddix got her aunt seated and then sat down in the other chair. She was tall and willowy, with short-cropped hair that had been peroxided nearly white. Her skin was a shade darker than her aunt's. Half a dozen gold-and-ivory bangle bracelets jangled from her left wrist. Her dark, almond-shaped eyes were outlined with kohl, and she wore a form-fitting black tank top, white jeans, and cork-soled gold sandals.

"What's that old bird want from my aunt now?" Felicia said, crossing her legs.

Brooke found herself momentarily at a loss for words. Had she told Louette she wanted to contact Varina—and her niece? Had Josephine Warrick asked Louette to reach out to the two women?

"Um," she said, stalling. "I didn't know Louette was related to your great-aunt."

Felicia gave a wave of her jangling wrist. "Everybody who ever lived at Oyster Bluff is somehow related to everybody else. Except Shug, of course, and he married into the family."

"Right." Brooke took a deep breath. "I'm sorry. You really did take me by surprise. I spoke to Josephine last week about trying to track you and your aunt down. In fact, that was my plan for today. And now you've showed up."

"Josephine wasn't very nice to us last time, was she?" Varina said, looking from Felicia to Brooke. Her skin was surprisingly smooth for a woman in her nineties, Brooke thought. Varina Shaddix seemed swallowed up in the wooden office chair. She wore a neatly pressed pink floral cotton dress, loosely belted at the waist, of a style Brooke hadn't seen since her own grandmother was alive, with pin tucks on the button-front bodice. Varina had undoubtedly made the dress herself. A large white patent-leather pocketbook dangled from her bony wrist. Her rubber-soled, white lace-up shoes were spotless, and her snowy white hair was parted down the middle, braided in a series of cornrows, and fastened with pink plastic barrettes. A tiny silver cross nested in the hollow of her throat, and a pearl brooch was pinned to the collar of her dress.

"Josephine was Josephine," Felicia said, shrugging. "She's only nice when she wants something from you, Auntie Vee." Now she turned again to Brooke. "So what is it she wants this time, and why now?"

"She's been diagnosed with terminal lung cancer," Brooke said. "And she wants to make amends with her oldest friends and their heirs. She's hired me to try to make that happen."

"Make things right how?"

Brooke sighed. "Nothing is in writing yet, but as you know, Josephine has no living heirs. She wants to leave Talisa, and Shellhaven, to her friends and their heirs. And that includes your great-aunt."

"What's that?" Varina leaned in.

"Josephine is dying," Felicia said loudly. She sat back in her chair and crossed her arms defiantly over her chest. "Serves her right, for all the things she and her family did to all of us. Now she wants to make things right by you, Auntie Vee."

Varina blinked rapidly. "Is that right?" she asked, her voice quavering, eyes welling up with tears. "Josephine is dying?"

14

....

October 1941

J ust as fast as Varina finished washing a load of plates and glasses in the big kitchen at Shellhaven, one of the waiters who'd been brought in special for the party from Atlanta toted in a tray with another load of dirty dishes. She had been standing at the big cast-iron sink for three hours with her arms plunged up to her elbows in soapy water, and still it seemed the dishes kept coming.

The back door was propped open with a big electric fan, but it barely made a dent in the heat of the kitchen. It might be October in the rest of the world, but summer lingered on in this part of the Georgia coast. Sweat dripped down her face and her back. Her calves ached.

Whenever the swinging door from the butler's pantry opened, she could hear the strains of music coming from the ballroom. At one point in the evening, she'd been allowed to put on a frilly white apron and take a tray of sandwiches and drinks out to the men in the orchestra while they took a break from playing, but other than that, she'd been cooped up right here in this kitchen.

The ballroom was so crowded she hadn't even seen her friends, but that was just as well, considering how ugly she looked.

She had a brand-new dress store-bought, special for the party, that Josephine had given her. It was her first grown-up dress, a light pinky-orange color with beautiful embroidery and no baby-looking puffy sleeves or silly bows or sashes like her mama used to make her wear. She had almost-new shoes too, which Ruth had brought her, all the way from Boston.

They were pink. Pink shoes! With sassy ankle straps that fastened with rhinestone buckles. Rhinestones! And a little heel, and they were as far from her scuffed-up hand-me-down brown leather brogans as a pair of shoes could be. They looked just like the shoes in the fashion magazines Millie brought her every time she came to the island, and they were almost too perfect to wear.

The biggest mirror they had at home at Oyster Bluff was the one on the bureau in Daddy's room. She'd snuck in there, before leaving for the party, and tilted the mirror just the right way so she could admire how the shoes looked.

Everybody said she was small for her age. She had light skin and good hair, which her auntie said came from her mama's people, who were from away and part Indian. Her brothers called her Skinnystick, and her daddy was always saying she needed "some meat on her bones," because she was not built like the rest of the Shaddixes. Just this year, her bosoms had started to come in, and Auntie gave her a brassiere, which she'd bought from the Sears Roebuck store in Jacksonville, and which was Varina's most treasured possession, if you didn't count her white leatherette Bible.

Looking in the mirror at herself, Varina thought she looked real fine. She had no stockings, but she'd used some lotion Ruth had given her on her legs, and they looked smooth and silky, like the models in the fashion magazines.

She wrapped up the new shoes in a flour sack and carried them on the walk to Shellhaven. After she got to the house, she used the flour sack to wipe her feet off, then put the shoes on and reported to work.

Mrs. Dorris, the white boss lady, took one look at Varina and pitched a fit.

"Girl, what do you think you are doing sashaying in here in that fancy dress and silly shoes? You ain't getting paid to look pretty, and you sure can't work like that."

Varina's face fell. "I can wear an apron so it won't get all messed up."

"No, ma'am," Mrs. Dorris said. She rummaged around in the broom closet until she found one of her own faded cotton housedresses hanging from a nail and tossed it to Varina. "Go put this on, and be quick about it." A moment later, she managed a rare smile. "But first, go find Miss Josephine and her friends so they can see how nice you look. And then you get your tail back in here and start washing those dishes."

Varina had run up the back stairway and managed to catch Josephine just as she and Ruth were walking out of Josephine's bedroom heading toward the guest bedroom where Millie was staying for the week of the engagement party.

"Look here, Jo," Ruth had said, when she caught sight of Varina. "It's a fairy princess!"

"Oh, Varina!" Josephine had exclaimed. "Turn around. Let me see!"

The soles of the shoes were slippery, so Varina did a slow pirouette, her arms poked stiffly out from her sides.

"You look so pretty," Ruth said, touching the sleeve of the silk dress. "Jo, this color is perfect for her. And what a cute figure you have too." She caught Varina's hand in hers. "Come on, let's show Millie how beautiful you look for her party."

Varina glanced at the grandfather clock in the hallway. "I have to get back downstairs. Mrs. Dorris needs me."

"If Dorris fusses, you just tell her I needed you upstairs for a few minutes," Josephine said.

Josephine rapped lightly on Millie's door. "Come on out, bride-to-be," she called gaily. "We have a surprise for you."

Millie opened the door and stepped into the hallway. Her blond hair was tied up in soft rag curlers, and she still wore a bathrobe. There were dark circles under her eyes, but when she caught sight of Varina, her face lit up with a smile.

"Who is this gorgeous creature?" Millie asked.

"It's me," Varina said, suddenly shy.

"And I'm furious at her, because she is much prettier than all three of us put together," Josephine teased. "No boy at this party will want to dance with us after they see Varina."

Varina blushed furiously. "Y'all know I can't really come to the party. Mrs. Dorris only let me come upstairs to see y'all for a minute. She says I got to get back and change out of this dress and shoes so I can work."

"Well, I think I'm just going to sneak you downstairs and into the ballroom for a few minutes so that Papa and Gardiner can see how nice you look," Josephine said.

"Oh no," Varina said quickly.

"Varina's right, Jo," Ruth said. "We don't want to get her in trouble."

Millie gave the girl a quick hug. "Go on back downstairs, then, Cinderella. Before your coach turns into a pumpkin."

"Huh?" Varina gave her a puzzled look.

"Don't tell me you never read the fairy tale about Cinderella and her wicked stepsisters," Ruth said. "With the pumpkin that turned into a coach?"

"And the rats that turned into coachmen, or were they footmen?" Millie asked.

Varina looked from one of the girls to the other. "Are y'all my wicked stepsisters?"

The girls all laughed.

"No, silly girl," Josephine said. "We're more like your fairy godmothers."

"Okay," Varina said. "I'd better go back now, before Mrs. Dorris comes looking for me."

"Wait just a minute, Varina," Millie said. She darted into the bedroom and came back a moment later.

"Josephine gave you this dress, and Ruth gave you the shoes. Now I want you to have something from me. Mama gave me this pearl pin for my sixteenth birthday. You're almost sixteen, aren't you?"

"Not for another year and a half," Varina said. "But I can't take this, Miss Millie. This must've cost a lot of money."

"It really didn't," Millie said, fastening the pin to the collar of Varina's dress.

"Anyway, it's a gift. And it's bad manners not to accept a gift from a friend, isn't it, girls?"

"It certainly is," Ruth said solemnly.

It was ten o'clock before she'd worked her way through the mountains of dirty glasses and plates. Finally, Mrs. Dorris took the dishtowel from Varina's hand.

"Go on home now, girl. Those fancy waiters can finish up in here once the party's over." She fished in the pocket of her apron and handed Varina two crisp dollar bills. "Miss Josephine said this was to be your pay for tonight. I told her that's way too much, but she insisted."

Varina stared down at the dollars. "You sure?"

"I'm sure," Mrs. Dorris said. She peered out the back door. "It's mighty dark out there. Is one of your brothers coming over to walk you home?"

"No, ma'am," Varina said, untying her apron. "It's not that dark. There's a full moon tonight, and anyway, I could walk to Oyster Bluff with my eyes closed." She headed for the broom closet, where she changed out of the ugly housedress and back into her own beautiful dress.

"Girl!" Mrs. Dorris was laughing at her. "You are bound and determined to wear that dress tonight, aren't you?"

"It's the prettiest thing I ever owned," Varina said.

"Well, I can't say I blame you. If I were as young and skinny as you, I guess I'd do the same thing. Just be careful and don't get nothin' on it. That's real silk, you know."

Varina knew she should have gone right home, but she just wanted to get one more peek at the party before it was all over. She cut around the side of the house and positioned herself at the edge of the veranda behind a tall camellia bush. The french doors were open, and when she poked her head around the camellia, she caught glimpses of ladies in their beautiful party dresses and the men in their stylish white dinner jackets. She closed her eyes and hummed a little of the song the orchestra was playing. Josephine brought a record of the song when she came down from Boston, and she said it was called "Moonlight Serenade." She and the girls played it all the time in the days before the party, and they'd even shown Varina how to do a dance called the foxtrot.

At one point, she thought she saw Josephine dance past the doors with a short, stout man with a shock of gray hair, who looked like Mr. Bettendorf. She saw Ruth too, beautiful in a seafoam-green dress with white flowers tucked into her shining red hair.

Suddenly, a huge man in a white dinner jacket burst through the french doors. He had a woman by the arm, dragging her along like a puppy on a short rope.

It was Millie! She recognized the dress, and then a moment later, Millie's voice.

"Russell, stop. Let go. You're hurting me."

Russell. That was the man Millie was fixing to marry. Josephine said he was richer than King Midas. It looked to Varina like they were fighting.

They stopped for a moment, just a few feet away. Varina shrank back behind the bush and held her breath, certain they would see her there.

They were talking now, but their voices were lower, and she couldn't make out what they were saying. She heard Millie's soft laugh and relaxed a little.

Now the man was on the move again, and he was dragging Millie after him. They went a little ways down the walkway, out of sight and earshot. Curious, Varina slipped out from the bush and tiptoed down the walkway, being sure to stay in the shadows.

The moon was so bright that night, she was afraid she'd be seen, but she darted across the cobblestone walk and crept closer.

Millie was crying! Varina tensed. She ducked behind a huge ball-shaped bush and craned her neck to try to see.

The crying was coming from beneath the deep shade of the big old magnolia tree that towered over that part of the garden. Varina could see the white of Russell's dinner jacket, but not much more.

"No! Stop it!" Millie cried. It sounded like he was hurting her. Varina took a deep breath. She had to do something to stop that man. She took a step sideways but then heard footsteps coming from the direction of the veranda, and she slunk back to her hiding place.

Gardiner Bettendorf, Josephine's big brother, hurried past. Mr. Gardiner had just about quit coming to Talisa, ever since Mrs. Bettendorf died. Josephine said her brother hated to come here because it reminded him of his dead mama, and anyway, he'd been in college and started law school, but now, Josephine said, he had dropped out of that and was getting ready to go to Canada to sign up to be a pilot and bomb the hell out of the Germans.

"Millie?" Gardiner called.

Russell said something that Varina couldn't quite make out, and the next thing she knew, he was right there, standing under the magnolia tree, and things were starting to get ugly.

Then Millie screamed, and Varina heard bone meeting flesh. Millie screamed again.

And then it was over. Millie rushed past Varina's hiding place. Her dress was torn at the bodice, and she was crying so hard she never even saw Varina standing there, wondering what to do.

Varina knew she should go too, but she just had to see what would happen next. She darted across the walkway and into the shadows on the other side of the walk. As she crept closer, she could hear the familiar sounds of two men fighting, which she knew well, having older brothers who regularly "tussled," as her daddy called it, sometimes in fun, but mostly out of anger.

"Uuunhhh," would be followed by a low groan, then another blow.

Their voices echoed in the night air, cursing—she knew those words too from her brothers, who mostly did it only when their preacher daddy was not within earshot.

Finally, Gardiner staggered onto the walkway. In the moonlight, she could see one of his eyes was swollen, his lip and nose bloodied, his white dinner jacket spotted with more blood.

"Enough!" he shouted. "We're through here. In the morning, if you're not on the first boat off this island, my father and I will contact the sheriff, and I'll tell him exactly what you did to Millie."

Russell stepped into the moonlight too. A gash above his eye leaked blood, as did one on his jaw. "Charges? What kind of charges? Millie is my fiancée, and what I do to her or with her is none of your goddamn business."

"She's not your property yet," Gardiner said, his voice low. "Now, get out of my sight. And I warn you, if you lay hands on her or try to force yourself on her again that way, I'll leave the law out of it and take care of you the way people down here handle things."

"You don't have the balls," Russell taunted.

Gardiner turned and walked away. Varina shrank back into the shrubbery and watched as he skirted the house and the veranda. She glanced up at the sky. Clouds rolled past and obscured the moon. The temperature had dropped, and the wind had picked up. Rain was coming. She needed to hurry home or her dress and shoes would be ruined. She would have to leave the way Gardiner had gone. But quietly.

She took a step in that direction, and her shoe landed squarely on a dried twig that snapped loudly.

"Who's there?" Russell called.

Varina scurried back into the boxwood hedge and stepped on another twig.

The big man was at her side in an instant, reaching through the tangle of underbrush, grabbing her by the arm. Thorns snagged on her silk dress, scratching the bare skin on her arms and legs. Varina clung helplessly to a branch of the shrub, but it broke off in her hand, and a moment later, he'd hauled her onto the walkway.

"Who are you? Were you spying on us just now?"

She was so terrified she was unable to speak. He slapped her face so hard she felt her ears ringing.

"Damn it, girl, who are you?"

"N-n-nobody," she stammered. "I didn't see anything. I was just walking home."

"What are you doing up here?" he demanded.

"I was working at the party," Varina whispered. "In the kitchen. Mrs. Dorris, she said I could go home, so that's what I was doing."

His eyes narrowed as he looked her over, up and down, the way you'd look at a horse or a mule you were sizing up to buy.

"Where'd a servant girl get an expensive dress like this?" He ran his hand down her shoulder and over her chest, right over her breast. He flicked the pearl pin with one finger.

"I know this pin. It belongs to my fiancée. Did you sneak upstairs in the house and steal this pin? And that dress? What else did you steal, girl?"

At first, Varina was too terrified to speak.

"Nothin'," she finally managed. "I didn't steal nothin', I swear. Miss Josephine gave me this dress as a present. And Miss Millie gave me the pin."

"Liar," he spat. He pinched her nipple so hard she screamed, and he clamped his hand over her mouth.

"Millie never gave jewelry to a colored girl. You stole these things. I know you did. That's why you were hiding out here. Like a thief."

Varina couldn't breathe. She couldn't speak. Finally, he moved his hand. She exhaled and began sobbing.

"I'm not a thief. You can ask Miss Josephine. I'm not. I was just going home. I got to get home now. My daddy will be looking for me."

"Your daddy will just have to wait," Russell said. He jerked her arm so hard she thought it would pull from its socket. "You're coming with me. I think the two of us will have our own private party."

15

....

Felicia Shaddix leaned in close to Varina. "Now, Auntie, you knew that old lady had cancer. Louette told you. I told you."

Varina nodded and dabbed at her eyes with a crochet-edged handkerchief. "Cancer, yes. But nobody said nothin' about dying." She looked over at Brooke. "You sure you got that right?"

"Josephine told me herself."

"I should go see her. Take her some of my soup. She always loved my beef consommé. Mrs. Dorris showed me how to make it so that it was clear as could be. You could see the bottom of the bowl," Varina said. She turned to Felicia. "I used to make that consommé for all you children when you were sick. Remember?"

"We were your family," Felicia said coldly. "You took care of all of us, Auntie. And now I'm taking care of you. But Josephine Warrick is not your family. What did she ever give you besides some old clothes she didn't want anymore?"

"Josephine is my friend," Varina said. "She's got her ways, that's true. But she is my friend. I told you she would do right by us, didn't I? And that's what this lady lawyer is going to see about." She gave Brooke a warm smile. "Isn't that right?"

"Yes," Brooke said.

"We'll see." Felicia looked around the office at the stained, fraying carpet, secondhand furniture, and single bank of file cabinets. She stared at Brooke's framed college degrees.

"Emory Law, huh?"

"That's right," Brooke said.

"Felicia went to Emory University too," Varina said proudly. "They gave her a full scholarship. And she graduated first in her class."

"Undergrad," Felicia said. She turned back to Brooke, crossed and recrossed her slender legs. "You know, my aunt asked Josephine, only a few months ago, if she would consider deeding over the land at Oyster Bluff to our family. And Josephine refused. Threw us out. It was really ugly."

"So I heard," Brooke said. "If it's any consolation, I think she now regrets the way that meeting ended. And that's why I wanted to talk to your aunt. Josephine has authorized me to start the process of returning the property at Oyster Bluff to the people who live there."

"See there?" Varina said. "I knew she'd make things right. Didn't I tell you?"

"I'll believe it when I see it," Felicia said. "Louette told me the state wants to make Josephine sell them all the rest of Talisa, for the state park. How's she going to give twenty acres to our people with the state breathing down her neck? How would that work?"

"I'm not sure yet," Brooke admitted. "I was just hired last week, and I haven't had time to start my research. I can tell you that Josephine intends to fight the state to prevent them from taking her land. And in the meantime, she'd like to immediately begin the process of deeding over Oyster Bluff to the families who still live there."

"About time," Felicia said. "You know what she paid for my folks' house over there? Did she tell you? If not, I will. She paid my widowed mother $1,500. For the house and more than an acre of land. I think Louette's daddy got even less than that when he sold to her."

"Now, Felicia, honey," Varina said gently. "You know as well as I do those houses was in bad shape. Josephine fixed your mama's house up real nice for her after your daddy passed. And Louette's daddy, well, he was my cousin, and

I don't like to speak ill of the dead, but Gerald was bad to drink and didn't care nothin' about patching a leaky roof or painting a porch. That house of his wasn't fit for chickens by the time he died."

Felicia rolled her eyes but didn't argue with her great-aunt.

Brooke sighed. "I can't speak to the fairness of the real estate transactions. It's my job, now, to get a list of the surviving Oyster Bluff families who sold their land to Josephine. My assistant can do some of that research in the court-house, but it would be great if you and your aunt could give me names and addresses."

"We can do that," Felicia said. "Right, Auntie?"

"She's really gonna give back Oyster Bluff?" Varina said. "All of it? The church too? The graveyard where my mama and daddy and brothers are buried?"

"Yes," Brooke said. "All of it."

"Praise Jesus," Varina said. She dabbed at her eyes again and sniffed. "I guess we can go on home now, Felicia."

Felicia stood up and helped the old woman from her chair. She looked around the room again. "Auntie, would you like to visit the bathroom before we get on the road back to Jacksonville?"

"That would be real nice."

After she'd helped her aunt into the bathroom and closed the door, Felicia turned back to Brooke with a stern expression.

"I didn't want to say anything more in front of my aunt, Ms. Trappnell, because she doesn't like to 'fuss,' as she calls it, but I think it's best you know who you're dealing with here. My aunt is an amazing woman. First in her family to finish high school, and then to leave the island to take business classes and work for the railroad. You have no idea what an accomplishment that was in the forties, and in the Jim Crow South. She is the matriarch of this family, and she has been doing for others her whole life. But she still very much suffers from a plantation mentality. She's grateful for whatever stale crumbs Josephine Warrick throws her way."

Felicia crossed her arms over her chest. "But that's not me. In case you're interested, after I finished Emory, I got a master's in American history and a

PhD in African American studies at Northwestern, but I'm currently my aunt's caregiver."

"That's very admirable of you, giving up a career for your great-aunt," Brooke said.

"Please don't patronize me," Felicia said. "Auntie Vee is the one who did without to buy me a secondhand car to take to college. A month didn't go by that I didn't get a card with a little check in it from her. I didn't give up my career. I'm teaching online classes through the University of North Florida and working on a book proposal. All of this is just to let you know—I don't intend to let Josephine continue exploiting my aunt or the rest of my family."

Brooke was startled by Felicia's intensity. "I know it's late in the day, but I honestly do believe Josephine wants to make things right by your aunt and by the others living at Oyster Bluff."

"Do you know anything at all about my people? About the Geechee and how long we've lived on these coastal islands?" Felicia asked.

"Only a little," Brooke admitted. "I know there was a plantation where Shell-haven now stands and that your ancestors were slaves who worked there."

"Typical," Felicia snapped.

They heard the toilet flush through the thin Sheetrock walls, and a moment later, Varina slowly emerged from the bathroom.

"All set?" she asked, smiling at her niece.

"Yes, ma'am," Felicia said, taking her arm. She looked over at Brooke. "Do you have a business card or something? I'll make some phone calls after I get her home, and then I'll email you the names and addresses of the Oyster Bluff folks."

"Any idea how many people we're talking about? Like, maybe a ballpark figure?"

"My guess? Nine or ten families," Felicia said.

Brooke fetched a card from her desk and offered it to her visitor, and at the same time, Varina Shaddix reached up and planted a kiss on Brooke's cheek. "You tell Josephine I'm coming to see her real soon," she whispered in Brooke's ear. "You tell her I'll be praying that demon cancer lets loose of her. Will you do that?"

"Yes, ma'am," Brooke said. "I'll let her know."

16

Felicia Shaddix had hit on a matter that had been worrying Brooke ever since she'd changed her mind and decided to work for Josephine Warrick. The State of Georgia was, as her client said, circling like buzzards, trying to force Josephine to sell Shellhaven and the land surrounding it to add to the existing park on the other end of the island.

Brooke knew little to nothing about statutes pertaining to condemnation law. The good news was that she knew somebody who would be able to school her on the issues. The bad news was that he was a senior partner in her old Savannah law firm. And she hadn't spoken to Gabe Wynant since the day she'd turned in her resignation letter four years ago.

He had actually been the one who'd hired her, been a mentor and a friend to her, and Brooke could still see the look of disappointment on his face the day she'd shown up, unannounced and dripping wet in his office doorway, to tell him she was quitting and leaving town.

The morning she'd quit, Brooke had to make three circles of the block around Calhoun Square, where the Farrell, Wynant offices were located, before finding a curbside parking space a block away. And of course, she'd left her

umbrella at home. By the time she stepped into the office's marble-floored reception area, she looked like a drowned rat.

"Gabe?"

He was sitting at his desk, his suit jacket draped over the back of his chair,
his face still ruddy from having just showered and shaved in the bathroom ad-
joining his office.

"Brooke! My God, what happened to you?"

She gestured toward the bow window that looked out on the live oaks of the
square. "Poor planning," she said. Rain streamed down her face and her legs,
leaving a puddle on the jewel-toned Oriental rug.

He stood, went into his bathroom, and came back with a thick, white monogrammed bath towel. "Here, see if this will help."

She toweled off her hair, made a half-hearted attempt to mop up the worst
of the water, then draped the towel over her shoulders.

"Sit," he said, gesturing toward one of the leather wingback chairs facing
his desk. "Unless you want to go home and change first. I'm sure whatever it is
can wait."

"No," she'd said quietly. "I'm afraid if I leave now, I'll lose my nerve."

"You? Never," Gabe said. "But I don't like the look on your face right now.
As a matter of fact, aren't you supposed to be on your honeymoon?"

Gabe Wynant was then in his late fifties, but he claimed his hair had turned
white overnight after a particularly grueling lawsuit he'd filed against the City
of Savannah. He was lean and tan, with a beaky oversized nose and dark eyes
behind trendy tortoiseshell Warby Parker glasses.

Brooke took a deep breath. "I'm resigning."

"What? Why? Aren't you happy here?"

"I have been. I was." She felt her upper lip quivering and swallowed. "I thought
you would have heard by now. Harris and I . . . anyway, the wedding's off."

"I just got back from vacation, so no, I hadn't heard," Gabe said. "I'm sorry,
Brooke. We all really liked Harris. He's a nice guy."

"The best guy in the world," Brooke agreed. "And I'm the biggest idiot in
the world. But I just can't . . ."

She was crying now, big, huge, crybaby tears. He sat and waited. Finally, he handed her a box of tissues.

"I'm not ready to be married," she said finally. "I thought I loved Harris enough to get past that, but I guess maybe I don't. Love him enough, I mean. In fact, I'm terrified of being married. And I was terrified to tell anybody, which is why I ran away."

"Okay," Gabe said slowly. "But just because you broke off your engagement, that doesn't mean you have to quit your job. Does it?"

"I can't stay here any longer," Brooke said. "I've lived in Savannah my whole life, except for when I was in school. I know this sounds like a horrible cliché, but sometimes clichés are true. For me anyway. I feel like I'm suffocating. I've made a huge mess of my life. I've let my family and friends down, hurt Harris and his family terribly. I'm a disaster. You don't want me working here, Gabe."

"You're the furthest thing from a disaster. You've got a fine legal mind. Your work here has been excellent, and all your clients adore you. The fact that you were savvy enough to walk away before getting entangled in a marriage you had doubts about means you've got a good head on your shoulders."

"I didn't walk away. I ran. All the way to Cumberland Island. I was a coward. I'm still a coward. I snuck into town last night. My parents don't even know I'm here. Harris is still at his parents' house in South Carolina. I've packed up the rest of my stuff, and as soon as you and I are done talking, I'm headed back down there. I can't face anybody, Gabe. It was all I could do to make myself come in here this morning, to hand in my resignation in person. I thought it was the least I owed you."

Gabe nodded. "I appreciate that, Brooke. And you're not a coward, so please stop saying that. A coward would have gone through with the wedding, despite the misgivings. The way I did, twenty-five years ago."

It was an open secret around the office that Gabe Wynant's marriage was over. He and his wife, Sunny, still lived under the same roof, but Sunny was an alcoholic who'd been in and out of rehab three times just in the time Brooke had worked at Farrell, Wynant.

Brooke didn't know what to say to that. "I've gotta go," she said, standing. She stuck out her hand, and Gabe took it and clamped it in both of his.

"Good luck, then," he said.

She'd walked all the way back to her car before she realized she still had the firm's bath towel wrapped around her shoulders.

Brooke still had that towel. And she still had Gabe Wynant's direct number in her cell phone.

"Brooke? Is that really you?"

"Hi, Gabe," she said. "Yes, it's really me."

"My gosh, it's good to hear from you. How the hell are you? Are you still living down, where was it, Brunswick?"

"I'm fine, thanks. I'm living in St. Ann's. I even hung out my shingle here."

"Did you go with an established firm?"

"No, I'm solo," Brooke said. "My practice isn't anything like it was in Savannah. I do a little of this, a little of that, whatever the other guys in town don't want to take on."

"That's great. I'm so glad to hear you didn't quit law. You're not, by any chance, calling to tell me you want to come back to us at Farrell, Wynant, are you? Because my offer still stands. The firm would welcome you back with open arms."

Brooke's face flushed with pleasure. It was nice to be wanted.

"That's so kind of you, Gabe. I can't tell you what it means to have you say that. But no, I'm not calling about a job. What I could use is your advice. I've actually got a new client, and although I've tried to persuade her I don't have any expertise at what she needs, she's insistent that I'm the only lawyer she wants."

"Happy to help out if I can," Gabe said.

"Do you have a few minutes to chat? It's kind of a long story."

"I've got a meeting in ten minutes. Can you give me the condensed version?"

"I'll try," Brooke said. "Have you ever heard of Josephine Bettendorf Warrick?"

"Of course," Gabe said promptly. "The queen of Talisa. My dad was a friend of her late husband, Preiss. I met her a couple of times, years ago, when she and Preiss came up here for parties and such. Is she your new client?"

"Yes."

He whistled softly. "Did she dump her Atlanta law firm? Schaefer-Moody?"

"I wouldn't say she dumped them. But if you know Josephine, you know she's, um, fairly headstrong. And eccentric."

"What's she want from you?" Gabe asked.

"She wants me to keep the State of Georgia from condemning her house and the rest of the island. They want to annex her land into the existing state park on the other end of the island. They've made her an offer, and they're pressing hard."

"How much?"

"Six million."

"For the house and how much land?"

"Twelve thousand acres, give or take."

"I've never set foot on that island and I can tell you right now that's a bullshit offer," Gabe said.

"I agree. She's got the only deepwater dock on that end of the island, all the beachfront, and the only freshwater supply on the island. And get this—the state paid her cousins three million for their little bit of the island back in the seventies. That's where the existing state park is located now."

"So, obviously, you need to fight the condemnation," Gabe said. "Look, Brooke. I need to get to my appointment. Here's an idea. I'll be down at my place on Sea Island over the weekend. You're not that far from there, right? Why don't you come up and have dinner with me, and then you can give me more details and we can throw around some ideas."

"This weekend?"

"Yeah. I've got something Friday night, but I could do Saturday, or even Sunday night if I don't head home until Monday morning. What do you say?"

Brooke sighed. "I don't know, Gabe. That's so generous of you, but the thing is, it's tough getting a babysitter on weekends."

"You've got a kid?" He sounded shocked.

"Henry. He's almost three. That's another long story. Look. My mom is coming down to stay with us, and I guess maybe I could get away for a couple of hours. Is there any way I can let you know over the weekend?"

"Why not? I'm going to be on Sea Island anyway. You've got my number, so just call or text me. I won't make dinner reservations at the club until I hear from you."

Brooke grinned. "Thanks so much, Gabe. Really."

17

....

W here's my little fella? Where's my sweet Henry?"

Marie Trappnell arrived at Brooke's house shortly after 6:00 P.M. on Thursday night with a rolling suitcase and a gigantic tote bag overflowing with groceries and wrapped gifts. She swept past her bemused daughter and into the house.

Hearing her voice, Henry sped across the living room and flung himself at her knees, repeating his name for his grandmother over and over again. "Ree! Ree!"

Marie plopped herself down on the floor and gently pulled him onto her lap.

"Oh, my sweet boy! My poor angel." Marie kissed his face and the top of his head. She looked over at Brooke. "He's breaking my heart. I'm not hurting him, am I?"

"He's not made of glass, Mom," Brooke said. "It's been six weeks and he's fine. Just don't fling him around the room."

Henry held his arm up awkwardly for his grandmother's inspection. "Look, Ree. I got boo-boo."

"I see," Marie said. She kissed his arm. "Better?"

He beamed. "Better." But the colorfully wrapped gifts had already drawn his attention. He pointed. "What's that, Ree?"

Marie pulled the tote toward them and spilled the contents onto the floor. "Well, let's see."

Henry picked up a stuffed dog. "Puppy!" He waved it at Brooke. "I got puppy!"

After they'd eaten dinner and put Henry to bed on the mattress in Brooke's room, Marie took a good look around her daughter's living room.

"This is really nice," she said, taking another sip of her wine. "You've done a lot since the last time I was down."

"It's not Ardsley Park," Brooke said wryly.

She actually had taken pains to fix up her modest cottage. Marie had donated the furniture from her garage apartment in Savannah after the departure of her last tenant. The sofa and matching ottoman were comfortable but with ugly, eighties brown-plaid upholstery, which Brooke had covered with sets of washed and bleached canvas drop cloths.

She'd splurged on an indoor-outdoor rug from a big-box store at the mall in Brunswick and had assembled a gallery wall of inexpensive thrift store paintings along with Henry's framed crayon drawings.

Marie yawned and stretched her legs. Brooke thought she looked distinctly out of place in this room of castoffs. Her mother had an innate elegance and sense of style that Brooke had always envied.

After the divorce, Marie had stopped coloring her dark hair, and her now silver hair was cut in a sleek bob, just below her chin. Unlike Brooke, she never left the house without eyeliner, blush, and lipstick. Her clothes weren't showy, just classics, like the well-fitting jeans and oversized Eileen Fisher white linen blouse she wore tonight. Her hands were long and slender, with nails painted a neutral color. She wore no rings.

"I'm so glad Henry is okay," Marie said. "I was terrified when I heard about the surgery."

"If it makes you feel any better, even though Henry is fine and the arm has totally healed, I'm still a little freaked out about the whole thing."

"You don't show it," Marie said. "You never have. I think you're like your father that way."

Brooke held up her hand, traffic cop–style. "Don't. Please don't compare me to Dad."

"I didn't mean it as a dig, honey. Just a mother's observation."

Brooke took a gulp of wine. "I may look calm to you, but I'm really like those ducks at the Daffin Park pond back home. Gliding over the water on the surface, but underneath it all, I'm paddling like hell trying to keep afloat."

Marie cocked her head and studied her daughter. Brooke's dark hair was pinned up in a messy bun on the top of her head. She wore a loose-fitting T-shirt and denim shorts. She was barefoot and needed a pedicure. And there were dark circles under her eyes.

"I wish you'd called me sooner," Marie said. "I wish you'd let me pitch in and help. Not just with money, but with Henry. I know you prize your independence, but sometimes I feel like you're deliberately shutting me out. And it makes me sad. You and Henry are my world, Brooke."

"I know," Brooke said with a sigh. "I don't mean to shut you out. It's just . . . I guess I feel like I have something to prove. You know, that I can do this. Work. Raise a child. Just be a competent human being. But it's so damn frustrating. If I'm home with Henry, I'm anxious that I should be at work, doing lawyer stuff. And when I'm at work, with a client—not that I have that many—I feel guilty that I'm not home with my child. And, Mom, I suck. At everything. I suck at life. I really do!"

Marie got up and sat down beside her daughter on the sofa. She wrapped both arms around her and laughed. "You don't suck."

"No," Brooke insisted, "I do. What kind of mom lets her kid break an arm at the park? What kind of lawyer can't even make enough money to pay for decent health insurance for her family?"

"Don't you think you're being a little hard on yourself?" Marie asked. "Do yourself a favor and stop trying to be a superwoman."

"I'm not. I just want to be half as good a mom as you were when I was growing up."

"Is that what this is about?" Marie asked, raising an eyebrow. "You're comparing yourself to me? But that's crazy! You're a single working mom, raising a child in a town where you have no support system. I had the luxury of being able to quit my job when I had you, because your father was more than able to support us."

"And you did everything, and you did it perfectly," Brooke said. "Beautiful, spotless house, gourmet cook, on every committee in town . . . and I know Dad wasn't any help with any of that."

"It was a different time. None of the women in our social circle worked outside the home. Even the women who had MDs and PhDs and JDs after their names quit their jobs to stay home with their babies."

"You sound wistful about that," Brooke said. "Did you ever wish you hadn't quit?"

"Sometimes," Marie admitted. "Not at first. I mean, I waited until I was over forty to have you. So I'd had a great career, and when I finally did get pregnant, it was such a shock, I thought, well, I should just stay home and raise this miracle child of mine. And that ought to be enough."

"And then?" Brooke prompted.

"I couldn't get you to sleep or nurse. I was a miserable failure. And I wasn't used to failing at anything. I'd always been good at everything when I was working."

"So what did you do?"

Marie reached over and stroked Brooke's hair, tucking an errant strand behind her ear. "I did what you should have done. I finally called my mother and told her I needed help."

"That's when she moved down to Savannah to live with us?"

"Yes. She literally saved my life. Yours too."

"God. It must be an inherited trait. Remember? I had to quit nursing Henry after two months because he wasn't latching on. And he didn't sleep the whole night until he was almost two," Brooke said, shuddering at the memory.

"You should have told me," Marie scolded. "Why wouldn't you call me up and tell me what you were going through?"

"I don't know," Brooke said. "I guess I thought it would be like surrendering. Admitting that I couldn't take care of my own child."

"You can't do it all alone, honey," Marie said softly. "Nobody can. Not even you."

"I see that now," Brooke said. She stretched out on the sofa and put her head in her mother's lap. "I don't know if it's the wine or just having you here, but all of a sudden, I sort of feel okay. I think maybe it's gonna be okay."

"I'm glad," Marie said. "You've changed, you know, since you moved down here."

"Is that a good thing or a bad thing?"

"I haven't made up my mind yet. One thing that I think is good is that you're not as driven as you used to be when you were working in Savannah. You used to scare me, you were so focused. Work, running, work. I used to wish you'd slow down and have some fun."

"And the bad?" Brooke was almost afraid to ask.

"Oh, Brooke." Marie sighed. "Your self-esteem is so low. What happened to my golden girl? The triumphant soccer player, the kid who went to summer camp by herself at the age of six and never looked back or acted homesick? It hurts me to see you being so hard on yourself."

Brooke felt a tear slide down her cheek. She swallowed hard and tried to find the words.

"I screwed up. Royally. Let you guys down. Left poor Harris standing at the altar. Left Dad holding the bag for that hideously expensive wedding. Quit my job, ran away from home, and if that's not enough, I got myself knocked up. Had a kid out of wedlock. I'm like some big, stupid sitcom. Only nobody's laughing."

Marie pushed Brooke off her lap and prodded her back into a sitting position. "Look at me, Brooke Marie. Tell me the truth. Do you regret not marrying Harris?"

"No," Brooke said quickly. "Just the way I handled everything."

"Do you regret having Henry?"

"Never! He's the best thing that's ever happened to me."

"That's what I thought," Marie said. "So you made some mistakes. Doesn't everybody?"

"Maybe," Brooke said, still unconvinced. "But you can't pretend you were thrilled that I got pregnant the way I did."

"The baby was definitely a surprise," Marie admitted. "I wasn't even aware you were seeing somebody. And you still haven't told me anything about Henry's father. All I know is that you say he's not in your life anymore. That's the part that's really hard for me. I know you, Brooke. I know you don't have casual relationships. So this man . . . this mystery man. He's still Henry's father. Our boy has his DNA. And I'm only human. I can't help but wonder about him. Why aren't you together? Did he hurt you that badly? Are you still in love with him? Is he a good man?"

Brooke looked into her mother's dark blue eyes and saw only love and acceptance. She felt herself exhale slowly. Holding the secret of Pete, she realized, was exhausting. And senseless. And selfish.

"His name is Pete. Pete Haynes," she began. "Henry has his smile. And his big feet. And yes, he's a very good man. I think you'd like him. And I know he'd love you."

The words came tumbling out, like a dammed-up torrent of story and emotion.

She told her mother how she'd met Pete during her summer job in DC. Her harmless secret summer fling. How she'd run into him at the barbecue restaurant in Savannah, at a lunch meeting with her wedding florist, for God's sake!

"Seeing Pete, after all that time," Brooke said. "I can't even describe how I felt. It was terrifying. I was already having these nagging midnight doubts about me and Harris. If we were really right for each other. And then to run into Pete—two weeks before my wedding! It was like seeing a ghost, Mom. I hadn't thought about this guy in years. At the end of that summer, I came home and moved in with Harris and started law school. Mentally, I put Pete Haynes in a shoe box, taped it up, and shoved it in the back of my closet. But that day, at freaking Johnny Harris Barbecue, the tape came off. And I couldn't stop it. I couldn't stop thinking about Pete."

"I wish you'd told me," Marie said quietly.

"I couldn't tell you, because I couldn't admit it to myself. I was having anxiety nightmares. Panic attacks. I got some Xanax from a girlfriend at work, but the Xanax just made me feel stoned. It didn't get Pete out of my head."

"So when you ran away, the night of your bachelorette party?" Marie asked.

"I got in the car and started driving. That day at Johnny Harris, Pete told me he was staying on Cumberland, working on some project for the National Park Service. I didn't have a plan. Not really. I told myself I was going to Loblolly just to hang out and give myself time to think. But that was a lie. I wasn't running away from Harris. I was running to Pete."

Brooke found her half-empty glass of wine and drained it.

"Of course, when I threw myself at him on Cumberland, he turned me down flat. Told me he didn't want to be my rebound boy."

At some point, Brooke got her phone and showed Marie the last photo she'd taken of Pete before he'd left for Alaska. It had been taken while they were kayaking on the river. He was bearded and bare-chested, laughing, the late-day sun making a halo around his shaggy, unkempt hair.

Marie peered down at the phone, enlarged the image, then tapped the photo with her index finger. "The freckles. That's where they came from. I've always wondered."

"It's uncanny," Brooke said. "Henry has the exact same number of freckles sprinkled over his nose and cheeks as his father. I know, because I counted them. While Pete was asleep. The morning after . . ." She blushed. "The morning after Henry was conceived."

Marie didn't seem shocked. "When did things change between you? I mean, you just told me he rejected you when you showed up on Cumberland Island after you called off the wedding."

"We mutually agreed that we should take things slowly. The old 'let's just be friends' kind of deal. I realized I wasn't in any kind of shape to start a new relationship, I was trying to get my law practice up and running, and Pete's a naturally cautious person. We were seeing each other casually, at least at first."

"And then?"

Brooke twisted a strand of hair around her finger, avoiding her mother's probing eyes.

"Pete had applied for this research grant to study elk migration patterns in the tundra. It meant living in this remote base camp in Alaska. That's where he is, by the way. Alaska. It's a three-year project. Out of nowhere, he told me he loved me and wanted to be with me. I guess that's when it hit me that things had changed between us. We'd gotten serious when neither of us expected to. So . . . . one thing led to another. Spontaneous combustion, you might say. And by spontaneous, I mean, I wasn't on birth control."

"Oh, Brooke." Marie sighed.

"The next morning, Pete asked me to go with him."

"And you said?"

Brooke shrugged. "I wasn't very diplomatic. I mean, what was I going to do in the middle of the Alaskan tundra? Sue a moose? I drove him to the airport, and we talked about my flying out to see him at Christmas. Six weeks later, I figured out I was pregnant."

"And you never told him? Never let him know he was going to be a father?"

"I wanted to. We were Skyping every other day, and he was so excited about being in Alaska. Everything was new and fascinating, and his work was really intense. He'd be out in the field, four or five days at a time, camping and tracking these radio-collared elk. I thought, if I tell Pete I'm pregnant, he'll think he has to come back here to take care of me and the baby. It would mean giving up his grant."

"Shouldn't that have been his choice to make?"

"Maybe. But I was having doubts of my own. I loved Pete, but I didn't want to be trapped into having a relationship just because of a baby. What if he did come back? And it turned out we weren't actually good together?"

"That's just a risk you have to take in a relationship," Marie said. "In life. Nothing ventured, nothing gained."

"I'm not sure I agree with you," Brooke said, suppressing a yawn. "Henry and I, we're doing okay. It's not easy. In fact, most of the time, being a single mom is terrifying. But I don't regret it." She met her mother's steady gaze. "What about you, Mom? Any regrets?"

Marie stood slowly, then pulled Brooke to a standing position. "No. I don't regret giving up my career to have time to raise my brilliant, gorgeous daughter. I don't even regret marrying your dad. We had lots of good years, you know. I'd never give Patricia the power to take that away from me. The way I see it now, I got the better part of the deal. The man I married was young and fun, the adventurous and romantic Gordon. Look at him now. Yes, now he has more time and lots more money to spare, but Patricia's got the cranky, high blood pressure, potbellied Gordon. I saw them across the room at a wedding at the Oglethorpe Club a couple of weeks ago, and he looked miserable. Patricia couldn't even get him to go out on the dance floor."

"The two of you used to dance all the time, especially at weddings and Christmas parties," Brooke said. "When I was a teenager I thought it was sooooo gross. Parents dancing together!" She covered her eyes in mock horror.

Marie went into Henry's nursery, fetched a stack of bed linens, and proceeded to make up a bed on the sofa.

"See you in the morning," Brooke said, yawning and giving her mother a peck on the cheek. "I almost forgot. Were you planning on staying over Sunday night?"

"Yes. Why?"

"If you really don't mind staying and watching Henry, I'm supposed to go up to Sea Island Sunday afternoon to meet with Gabe Wynant."

"Really?" Marie arched an eyebrow.

"It's about Josephine Warrick. I'm going to take her case on, after all. But I don't know the first thing about condemnation law. So I called Gabe, and he's agreed to meet with me and try to walk me through it."

"That's awfully nice of him," Marie said. "It's just a shame about poor Sunny. You'd think it might be a kind of relief, after all he went through with her, but I hear he's really quite bereft."

"Bereft? Did something happen to Sunny Wynant?"

"You didn't know? She died."

"No! I had no idea. What happened?"

"Liver cancer. She drank herself to death. I guess it's been over a year ago now. Maybe two? I used to know her from altar guild, before she started drinking. She used to be so much fun. She had a really wicked sense of humor." Marie shook her head. "Such a waste."

"That's terrible," Brooke said. "But I'm glad you told me before I see him."

"You say you decided to work for Josephine, after all?" Marie asked. "What changed your mind?"

"Josephine did. She just wouldn't take no for an answer. And maybe, just maybe, I'm ready for a challenge."

Brooke remembered the last conversation she'd had with the old lady.

"Mom? Did you know Granny was engaged to somebody else? Before Grandpop?"

"Hmm? Who told you that?"

"Josephine did. Her family threw an engagement party at Shellhaven for Granny and this man, but something awful happened, and the wedding got canceled."

"Really? This is the first I've heard of such a thing. It's hard for me to picture my mother with another man. She was so devoted to Pops. Did Josephine give you any more details than that?"

"No. She said the man, whoever he was, wasn't a good person."

"I'd definitely be interested in hearing more about this mystery man," Marie said.

"You can ask Josephine all about it when you and the other two women meet with her over on Talisa."

"You think she's really serious? About leaving the island to the three of us?"

"She's dead serious," Brooke assured her.

18

....

October 1941

Josephine tapped loudly on the guest room door. "Millie? Are you all right?" The muffled reply came a minute later. "I'm all right." In another moment, the door opened slightly to reveal Millie, looking pale and exhausted, still wrapped in a bathrobe.

"It's nearly noon!" Josephine exclaimed. "Your mother and grandmother just left on the boat for St. Ann's." She peered at Millie's face. "You look terrible. Are you sick?"

"Maybe a little hungover. I don't think champagne agrees with me."

"Come down to lunch," Josephine said. "Mrs. Dorris will fix you something nice and light. Some soup or something."

"Ugh. Food. I'll come down, but I think I'll just stick to coffee. What about the others? Has everybody gone already?"

"A lot of people needed to get to Jacksonville to catch the train at two," Josephine said. "Ruth's still here, of course, and I think some of the men were planning an early-morning fishing trip."

"Have you seen Russell this morning?" Millie whispered.

"Not yet, but if I do see him, I might have to slap his face for the rude way he acted at the party last night. What a scene he made!"

"I'm so sorry," Millie said, tears pooling in her eyes.

"Don't you apologize for him," Josephine scolded. "You didn't do anything wrong."

"I shouldn't have danced with Gardiner," Millie said. "It didn't look right."

"Why shouldn't you dance with my brother? He was your host. And it wasn't as if your fiancé was dancing with you. Honestly, Millie, I don't understand why you have to marry him . . ."

"Don't!" Millie shook her head. "I'll be down in a few minutes."

She slipped into the dining room and chose the chair beside Ruth's.

"Good morning," Samuel Bettendorf boomed. "How's our bride today?"

"I'm fine, thank you," Millie said. "Please forgive me for oversleeping. I guess I'm not used to late hours and champagne. But it truly was a lovely party, Mr. B. Russell and I are so grateful for your hospitality."

Mrs. Dorris came into the room and offered a platter heaped high with golden fried chicken.

"No, thanks," Millie said quickly. "Is there any coffee?"

"Where is Russell?" Samuel asked.

Josephine rolled her eyes, and Ruth choked back a giggle.

"He talked about going fishing this morning," Millie said. "Or maybe hunting?"

"I know some of the fellows went out fishing on the big boat with Captain Morris because I saw them off," Samuel said. "Russell wasn't with them. If he did go out later, in the skiff, I hope he got Omar or one of the other boys to go out with him. These tidal creeks have so many twists and turns, it's easy to get lost if you're not familiar with the topography." He sipped his coffee and turned to his daughter. "And what are you young ladies up to this beautiful day?"

Josephine consulted her best friends. "Maybe some bridge, if we can scare up a fourth?"

"Good idea," Ruth said. "Maybe Gardiner can play."

Samuel set his coffee cup down with a clatter, got up, and abruptly left the room.

Josephine watched his departure with a sigh. "Gardiner's gone," she announced. "He took the early boat."

"Gone where?" Millie's blue eyes widened with surprise.

"Canada. He's joining the Royal Canadian Air Force. He says he's not going to sit around and twiddle his thumbs while Hitler invades the rest of Europe. Papa's furious. He and Gardiner have been arguing about this for months. Papa says what happens in Czechoslovakia and Poland is none of our business, but Gardiner is dead set on doing this. You know he's had his pilot's license since he was eighteen."

"Gardiner's a gun jumper? Aren't you proud of him?" Ruth asked.

"He's really gone?" Millie repeated. "To Canada? You're sure?"

"I took him to the dock myself," Josephine said. "He was trying to leave without saying goodbye to anybody, but I caught him sneaking down the back stairs with his valise this morning, and I made him tell me what he was up to. He was afraid Papa would try to stop him from going."

"He never said a word," Millie mumbled.

"Gardiner's like Papa that way. He plays his cards close to his vest. I'm mad at him too, of course. To think he thought he could just disappear like that, without telling anybody. He said he planned to send a telegram once the train stopped in Atlanta, but honestly, that's so like a man."

"I think it's terribly exciting," Ruth said. "Think about it. He'll be going to Europe, fighting those awful Nazis. My father says Hitler won't stop at Czechoslovakia and Poland. He won't stop until he's goose-stepped all the way across the continent."

"Don't let my papa hear you say that," Josephine warned. "He doesn't want our country dragged into another war. You know he fought in the last one."

"My father did too," Millie said. "Mother says he was never the same after he came home from France."

"Let's not talk about war anymore now," Ruth proclaimed. "It's too sad."

Josephine jumped up from her seat. "Agreed. Come on, girls. We'll take a ride in the roadster and stir up some kind of fun. And you know, there's a full moon tonight. I say it's time for the High Tide Club to meet. What do you say?"

Ruth clapped her hands. "Brilliant!"

"I'll get Mrs. Dorris to pack us a picnic dinner, and we'll send for Varina to come too." She looked over at Millie, who was gazing out the dining room's french doors at the garden outside.

"Did you hear, Millie? Tonight's the night!"

"I heard," Millie said.

Josephine drove the roadster to Oyster Bluff, and the others waited while she knocked on the door of the simple wood-frame house where the Shaddixes lived.

It was nearly dusk, and guinea hens roosted in the lower branches of the chinaberry tree that shaded the yard, which was swept sand neatly bordered with sun-bleached giant whelk shells.

"I can't come with y'all tonight," Varina said.

"Of course you can," Josephine said. "It's Saturday night, isn't it?" She lowered her voice. "We're going to Mermaid Beach. For the High Tide Club."

The girl shook her head. "No, I can't. My daddy won't let me."

A man's voice came from within the house. "Varina? Who's that you're talking to out there?"

"It's me, Josephine," the older girl called. "How are you tonight, Harley?"

Harley Shaddix's crutch thumped against the wooden floor with each step. He appeared in the doorway behind his daughter. "I'm fine, Miss Josephine. Hope you are too. I saw Mr. Gardiner over on the mainland this morning. He told me where he's going. Mighty proud of him."

"I'm proud too, but so sad to see him go. Harley, would it be all right if Varina took a ride with us in the car? We're going to take a picnic down to the beach."

Harley looked down at his daughter. Varina was dressed in a pair of her brother's outgrown, cast-off denim overalls and a long-sleeved blouse that had been her mother's. The pant legs and shirtsleeves were rolled up to size. She looked so tiny against her father's powerful mass. "You done your chores? Washed up in the kitchen? Memorized your scripture verses for tomorrow?"

"Yes, sir."

He smiled and patted her shoulder. "You been mopin' around this house all day. Time to get out and have a little fun. Go ahead on with Miss Josephine, then. And you mind your manners, you hear?"

He looked past Josephine at the car parked at the edge of the yard. "Just the ladies tonight? You know there's all kinds of critters skulking around this island at night. What happened to all the menfolk?"

"Most of them left this morning," Josephine said. "But don't worry about us." She patted the pocket of her skirt. "I've got Papa's .45, and I know how to use it."

"Maybe I oughta stay home," Varina said. "I got a headache."

Josephine took the girl's hand. "Come on, Varina. It'll be fun."

"Get out on the beach and get you a lungful of that good salt air, you'll be right as rain," Harley said firmly.

Josephine parked the roadster under a cluster of trees at the end of the crushed-shell path that ended at the point they'd dubbed Mermaid Beach.

A wide sand beach flattened out before them, and the full moon's reflection shone on the surface of the water. Waves lapped gently at the shore.

"Isn't it beautiful, girls?" Josephine asked, turning to her friends, who were seated in the car's rumble seat. "Have you ever seen so many stars in your life?"

"The best," Ruth declared. "And the ocean's so much warmer down here! I swear, my lips were blue for a week after we skinny-dipped last year at Nantucket."

"Brrrr." Josephine laughed. She hopped out of the car, went around to the rear luggage rack, and unstrapped the wicker hamper.

"I'll bring the towels," Ruth said. She looked over her shoulder at Millie and Varina, who hadn't moved from the backseat. "Come on, you two."

Millie climbed out of the car, followed by the younger girl, and they trailed after Josephine to the spot on the beach where she unfolded a large woolen blanket.

Josephine sat down on the blanket, promptly removed her shoes, and dug her toes into the soft sand. "Ahhh."

The other girls followed suit, except for Varina, who was uncharacteristically quiet.

"Look here," Josephine announced, opening the picnic basket. "Champagne!" She produced the bottle and popped the cork, sending a plume of champagne into the warm night air.

"Not for me," Millie said. "I had more than enough last night."

"I've got whiskey too," Josephine said, displaying a pint bottle of Jim Beam. "Gardiner gave it to me this morning, as a goodbye gift."

"No, thanks," Millie repeated, shuddering.

"Don't be such a party pooper, Millie," Ruth said. She found a tin cup in the basket and held it out to Josephine. "Guess I'll just have to drink her share."

Josephine tipped the bottle and filled her friend's cup, then gestured toward the youngest member of the group.

"Varina? Have you ever had champagne?"

The girl shook her head vigorously. "No, ma'am. You know my daddy is a Church of God preacher. He doesn't hold with drinking spirits."

"But your brothers drink," Josephine said, taking a sip from the bottle. "Papa always gives them beer after they've been working at Shellhaven."

"It's different for girls," Varina replied. "Everything's different when you're a girl."

"Just take a sip," Josephine insisted. She poured some into a cup and held it out.

"Leave her be, Jo," Millie said sharply.

"Spoilsport," Josephine said. She crossed her eyes and stuck out her tongue at her best friend, then emptied the cup of champagne in one long swallow, with Ruth following suit.

"What else have you got in that basket?" Ruth asked. "Lunch was hours and hours ago, and I'm famished."

"Let's see what old Dorris gave us," Josephine said, inspecting items as she lifted them from the basket. "Fried chicken. Ham biscuits. Some kind of little sandwiches left over from the party. Oooh. Chocolate cake!"

"Yum." Ruth found tin plates in the basket and helped herself to a ham biscuit and a slice of cake.

"Come on, you two," Josephine said, handing plates to Millie and Varina. "This is a party, not a funeral."

When they'd eaten their fill, Josephine sprawled out on the blanket and stared up at the sky. "Just think," she said. "Pretty soon, Gardiner will be up there, maybe flying across the Atlantic, to drop a big bomb on those dirty Nazis."

Millie set aside the plate with her half-eaten sandwich. "Aren't you afraid for your brother? What if something happens to him?"

"Nothing's going to happen to Gardiner," Josephine declared. "He's too good a pilot for that. You wait, he'll be one of those flying aces in no time." She downed another cup of champagne. "Okay. Let's go swimming!"

She stood up and slipped out of her dress, kicking it aside, and stripped down to her satin-and-lace-embellished panties and bra. Ruth followed suit, leaving Millie and Varina huddled together on the blanket, still fully clothed.

"Well?" Josephine said impatiently.

"Somebody might see us," Varina said, turning and surveying the deserted beach. "If my daddy found out I was swimming naked, he'd skin me alive."

"Nobody's going to see us," Ruth retorted. "And your daddy doesn't have to find out. We'll never tell."

"You two go ahead," Millie said. "I'll stay here with Varina."

Josephine shrugged, then stripped off her undergarments. She stretched her arms overhead. She unpinned her long hair and shook it out so that it fell down her back and across her bare chest. A moment later, she ran toward the ocean and plunged into the waves.

"Wait for me," Ruth called. She gulped the rest of her champagne and peeled out of her panties and bra, then raced toward the waves, screaming at the top of her lungs.

For the next ten minutes the two women laughed and splashed, wading out of the water, then running back and diving into the waves, letting the current pull them out before paddling back toward the beach.

Finally, Josephine and Ruth headed back to their friends, who sat watching from the blanket.

"You've got to come in the water," Josephine insisted. "It's wonderful!" She shook her head like a dog, spraying salt water over Millie and Varina.

"I'll take your word for it," Millie said, drying her face with one of the towels. "I'm fine right where I am, thank you very much."

"Oh no you don't," Josephine said. She pulled Millie to her feet. "Why are you suddenly being so bashful? You didn't mind skinny-dipping at Nantucket, or Palm Beach, or here last year."

"That's right, Millie," Ruth chimed in. She tugged at the cuff of her friend's gauzy long-sleeved jacket. "Come on. You've got to be suffocating in this thing."

Josephine caught the end of the silk scarf wound around Millie's neck and began to unwind it, and in the meantime, Ruth had managed to strip away Millie's jacket and was pulling at the waistband of her skirt.

"Don't!" Millie said, swatting at her friends' hands, which made them more determined to help her disrobe. "I don't feel like swimming. Why can't you just leave me alone?"

"You know the rules. One swims, we all swim. Naked as the day we were born," Josephine said, giggling. "You too, Varina. It's your initiation into the High Tide Club."

The fourteen-year-old hugged her skinny legs tightly to her chest, her arms wound around them. "No, ma'am," she said firmly. "I changed my mind. I don't wanna be in your club."

Josephine managed to pull the scarf free but froze when the moonlight revealed the ring of ugly blue-black bruises encircling Millie's neck, and the corresponding bands of bruises on Millie's now-exposed upper arms and wrists.

"Oh my God," she whispered.

Millie's lightweight skirt fell away from her waist just at that moment. Ruth gasped and pointed. "Jo, look."

Fingerprints, in the form of bruises, marred the creamy skin of their friend's upper thighs.

Weeping softly, Millie sank down onto the blanket, clutching her clothes to her body.

"Russell! He did this, didn't he?" Josephine wrapped her arms around her friend. "Oh, Millie. Why didn't you tell us?"

Instead of answering, Millie reached for the whiskey bottle. She uncapped it and gulped down three fingers of the amber liquid, then handed it to Varina. The girl considered the bottle, shrugged, and took a swig.

"I'll kill the bastard," Ruth whispered. "I will. I swear it."

19

Brooke felt guilty. It was Sunday afternoon. She was making the forty-five-minute drive north to Sea Island, and she was almost delirious with the sense of freedom. She had the Volvo's radio cranked to the max, and she was singing along to Journey. Or maybe it was the Eagles. She didn't know and didn't care.

The weather had cooled a little overnight, but the sun was high, and the sky was a brilliant blue. She rolled the car window down and inhaled the scent of marsh mud and diesel fuel from passing trucks as she drove north on U.S. Route 17.

She couldn't really say why she felt so happy this morning.

Maybe Marie's extended visit was the source of her contentment. Her mother had visited before, but this was the first time she'd stayed more than twenty-four hours. And it was definitely the first time Brooke had revealed the truth about her son's father to anybody. It was a huge relief to finally share all her bottled-up emotions. Talking openly about Pete had dredged up emotions she hadn't allowed herself to feel since Henry's birth.

But for now, Brooke needed to figure out Josephine Warrick's dilemma. How could she hope to fight the state on this condemnation issue when much more experienced Atlanta lawyers who specialized in this issue hadn't been able to fend off the taking of Josephine's island?

Josephine didn't have much time left, and the state's lawyers were obviously aware of that. They could easily keep stonewalling until the old woman was dead. Brooke tapped her fingers on the steering wheel of the car, her mind ticking off all the nuances of this case. Josephine Warrick wasn't the least bit loveable, but you had to admire her determination and her dogged, if late-breaking, sense of loyalty to her oldest friends.

The issue of the High Tide Club girls whom Josephine wanted to leave the island to was another matter. If Marie was going to be a beneficiary of Josephine's estate, there was no way Brooke could have anything to do with it. Maybe Gabe Wynant would be willing to take on that piece of work.

Crossing the Torras Causeway to St. Simon's Island, Brooke glanced over at the cell phone on the passenger seat. Marie hadn't called. There were no emergencies. Life was okay.

Brooke easily navigated the road to Sea Island. She'd been coming here since childhood with her parents on mini-vacations to the Cloister, which was the island's five-star resort, and with friends whose families owned homes here.

Brooke knew rich. Her parents were wealthy, in a modest, understated kind of way. But they weren't Sea Island rich. Sea Island rich meant yachts and private jets. She'd been a little surprised that Gabe Wynant owned a home here.

She pulled the Volvo up to the guard shack and gave the uniformed officer her name. He smiled, handed her a large visitor's pass with the date and time, and gave her directions to Gabe's house, which was on Cottage Lane.

Sea Island was lush and green this time of year. The impeccably landscaped roadway was carpeted with thick fringes of ferns and colorful beds of blooming pink, white, and lavender impatiens. No weed would have dared poke its head here.

Four turns later, Brooke pulled into the driveway of the address Gabe had given her. The house was modest—by Sea Island standards—a U-shaped whitewashed stucco cottage with vaguely Mediterranean aspirations. A pair of wrought-iron gates led into a terra-cotta–tiled courtyard garden. A fountain in the center trickled water from an oversized cobalt pottery urn. The heavy-planked arched door was open, and Gabe Wynant was waving hello.

"Brooke!" His craggy face broke into a grin, and he gave her a bear hug. This was a Gabe Wynant she'd never seen before. He was barefoot, dressed in loud pink-and-turquoise madras Bermuda shorts and a pink collared golf shirt. She'd always seen her mentor and law partner dressed in either sweaty running gear or in a custom-tailored suit and tie.

"Hey, Gabe," she said, feeling suddenly shy. "Thanks for letting me impose on your Sunday off."

"Nonsense," he said, waving her inside. "I was happy as hell to hear from you."

She followed him into the living room. The whole back of the room was a wall of french doors that looked out over an overgrown yard shaded by live oak trees. With a whitewashed brick fireplace and shelves filled with thick coffee table books and pottery, the room looked comfortable and lived in. A life-size portrait hung over the mantel. The subject was a young girl of maybe seventeen or eighteen, dressed in a gauzy embroidered peasant-style blouse and faded jeans. The girl was posed in profile, with her shining mane of long blond hair falling nearly to her waist, like a sixties folk singer or maybe just an affluent hippie girl. Brooke didn't know a lot about art, but this painting, she knew, was the work of an accomplished, confident artist.

"Your home is lovely," Brooke said.

"Like it? It can be yours. I'm getting it ready to put on the market," Gabe said.

"What a shame," she said. "This place, it feels so homey. So charming."

"This was really Sunny's house more than mine. I'd come down occasionally to play golf or tennis or to entertain clients, but it was her getaway."

Brooke touched his arm lightly. "My mom just told me about Sunny. I'm so sorry, Gabe. That must have been very hard, losing her."

He closed his hand over hers briefly and then released it. "Truthfully? I didn't suddenly lose her eighteen months ago. It was more like an incremental loss over the years. She climbed into a bottle of Johnnie Walker Black, and over time, the Sunny I knew just . . . dissolved."

Brooke nodded at the painting. "I'm sorry we never met. Is that her?"

"Yeah," he said, gazing up at it. "That was the girl I married. Or so I thought."

"She was so beautiful. It's a wonderful painting."

"It's a self-portrait," Gabe said. "She was a really talented artist. That's one of the only portraits she ever did. She painted it as an anniversary gift for her parents. This was their house. After we inherited it, she wanted to take it down, but I wouldn't let her. I guess I hoped it would remind her of who and what she used to be, before things changed." He shook his head. "Anyway. That's enough of that. Come on in the kitchen. I hope you haven't eaten lunch yet because I'm starved."

"You cooked me lunch? I'm impressed."

"Don't be. I ordered barbecue from a joint on the island. You didn't turn vegan after you moved down here, did you?"

"Not a chance," Brooke said, following him into the kitchen. A grease-spattered brown paper bag and two jumbo Styrofoam cups sat on the kitchen table.

"Sit yourself down and eat," Gabe said. He opened the paper sacks and dished out the food; big sloppy sandwiches of pulled pork with tangy orange barbecue sauce on oversized buns, vinegary coleslaw, and baked beans.

Brooke heaped some coleslaw on her sandwich and added a couple of pickle slices. She took a greedy bite and rolled her eyes in ecstasy. "Best 'cue on the coast," she declared, washing it down with a sip of sweet tea.

Gabe followed suit. "Tell me about this case of yours," he said between bites.

Brooke quickly recapped Josephine Warrick's standoff with the State of Georgia.

"I had one of our law clerks pull all the recent filings," Gabe told her, retrieving a file folder from the kitchen countertop.

"What do you think?" she asked eagerly.

He took a sip of iced tea. "You've got an uphill battle ahead of you. There are only two legal ways to challenge the state's right to condemn land. One way is to challenge the procedures by which the condemnation is initiated. The state has to make good-faith efforts to negotiate a fair price prior to the actual condemnation."

"Anyway," Brooke said, "the main issue is, she doesn't want to sell her land. Not at any price."

"Why not? She's what? Nearly a hundred years old? No heirs. Why not take the money, give it to her favorite charity, and get a life estate? She gets to live out her life there, and after that, it'll be a nice state park. Maybe they'd even name it after her."

"You don't know Josephine. She claims to have seen some secret long-range development plan that would have the state razing Shellhaven and putting in a big marina to allow for larger boats to ferry campers and visitors over from the mainland."

"Would that be such a bad thing? Just playing devil's advocate here."

"Her father, Samuel Bettendorf, whom she worshiped, hired Addison Mizner to design and build that mansion for her mother. So it's basically a shrine to her parents. Virtually nothing in the house has changed in decades. Bettendorf was an amateur naturalist, and Josephine and her late husband also made it their life's work, studying and preserving the land and the wildlife. As far as Josephine is concerned, Talisa and Shellhaven are her legacy, and she wants them preserved. And I can't say that I blame her."

"Very noble," Gabe said, nodding. "Talking about the wildlife over there. That could be another argument against developing Talisa. Say, if there were some kind of rare or endangered animal indigenous only to that specific island. The navy's development of the big sub base down at Kings Bay in that neck of the woods was delayed for years because of some obscure species of gopher turtles that nested down there. You might ask Josephine about that."

"I will," Brooke promised. "You said there are two ways to challenge the condemnation? What's the second?"

He chewed on some ice. "Well, theoretically, you *could* argue that the condemnation is not intended to serve the public trust. But realistically, how do you claim that a big new state park with acres and acres of pristine beaches and a new marina is a bad thing for citizens?"

Brooke's shoulders sagged, but she struggled valiantly to mount a defense against Gabe's reasoning.

"This state has dozens of parks already—which it doesn't have the funding to staff or maintain. Who's going to pay for not just the acquisition but the development of Talisa?"

"Nice try," Gabe allowed, doodling on a yellow legal pad. "But feasibility is not really something you can litigate." He grinned. "There is one place where that argument might work. The court of public opinion."

"You've lost me," Brooke said.

"I'm talking about politics," Gabe said. "Do an end run. Who are your state representatives down here? Call 'em up. Ask 'em to lunch and make your case to them. Or better yet, have Josephine Warrick call and raise hell with 'em."

"I can definitely call those guys," Brooke said, nodding. "And you're right about a phone call from Josephine. I just don't know if she's up to it. Health-wise."

"She's that sick?"

"End-stage lung cancer," Brooke said. "But she's still razor sharp and full of piss and vinegar. She might really enjoy unloading on some hapless state senator."

"Sounds like that could be your game plan," Gabe said.

He wadded up the empty paper sacks and put them in the trash, then took the lunch dishes and stacked them in the sink before returning to the table. He handed the file folder to Brooke. "This has got all my research and the relevant legal citations you'll need."

"Gabe. I can't thank you enough," Brooke said.

"This is going to be a fun one. I envy you, Brooke."

"That's your idea of a good time? Going up against the majesty of the state?"

"Sure. That's exactly what makes it fun. The law doesn't necessarily have to be dry and dusty. This is your chance to get creative. Think outside the box."

"If you say so." She opened the file and thumbed through the contents. "Hey, there's something else I wanted to talk to you about. Josephine says she wants to create a trust—with three beneficiaries."

"I know you didn't do a lot of estate work when you worked at our firm, but that should be pretty cut and dried," Gabe said.

"It might be, except for the fact that one of the beneficiaries is mom," Brooke said.

"You and Marie? Really?"

"Yeah. It's another long story. Josephine never had children, and she doesn't have any living family members, so she's decided she wants to leave Talisa to the heirs of her oldest, dearest friends, including a woman who worked for her family for many years. Coincidentally, my maternal grandmother, Mildred, who died years and years ago, was Josephine's best friend since kindergarten."

"So you've got a big conflict," Gabe said.

"Afraid so. She wanted me to track down the other friend's heir, which I've done. I contacted her last week to let her know Josephine wants to meet with her. Would you have any interest in handling the estate work?"

"Me?"

"Why not? If you're worried about the money, I don't think that should be a concern. She's apparently loaded."

"Money's not the issue," he said quietly. He looked around the room. "I'm fifty-nine, Brooke. I've been thinking maybe I should slow down my work schedule. Not retire, not yet, but maybe not take on any new clients."

"I guess that's understandable," Brooke said, trying not to show her disappointment. "Okay. I'm sure I can find somebody else locally."

"Oh, what the hell," Gabe said. "Who am I kidding? I'm selling this place because I never come down here. Work is what I do. Tell you what. Talk to your client, and if she agrees, I'll come down and talk to her and get the ball rolling on the trust."

"Really?" Brooke threw her arms around her old boss in an impulsive hug. "That would be awesome! We'll be working together again. It'll be just like old times."

"We'll see," Gabe said, patting her back awkwardly. "We'll see."

20

....

Josephine was standing in the front door at Shellhaven, leaning heavily on a cane. She was dressed in baggy khaki slacks cinched with a worn leather belt and a tucked-in long-sleeved pale pink blouse. A baseball cap with the Audubon Society logo shaded most of her face. With a shock, Brooke realized it was the first time she'd seen her client standing upright and outside the confines of the library-turned-bedroom. It was Monday afternoon.

Shug pulled the pickup truck in front of the door, and Brooke got out. She'd called the house on Sunday, during her drive back from Sea Island, to let Josephine know she wanted to come see her, and Louette had promised to give her the message.

Even before the old lady opened her mouth, Brooke sensed she was in a rare mood.

Shug leaned out the driver's-side window. "Hey, Miss Josephine," he said, also obviously startled by the boss lady's miraculous transformation. "Ain't you lookin' perky today."

"Hello, Shug," Josephine said. She nodded at Brooke. "So you changed your mind. Needed the money, is that it?"

"No. Well, sort of. My son had surgery recently, and my insurance is crappy."

"Surgery? What's wrong with the boy?"

"He fell off a jungle gym and broke his arm in two places."

It didn't miss Brooke's attention that the old lady hadn't offered any empathy or condolences for her son's injury. Not that she'd expected any.

"You must be feeling better," Brooke observed. "I'm glad."

Louette peeked out from the spot where she'd been standing at Josephine's elbow.

"She's got some new medicine making her feel way better."

"Steroids." Josephine grimaced. "They don't cure anything, but I'll admit my breathing is much improved. Although they make me feel like I'm about to jump out of my skin."

"She's eating way better," Louette confided. "Sleeps better too."

"Shug," Josephine called to her handyman. "Just leave the truck right there. I want to take Brooke around and show her the island while I have the energy."

His amiable face showed his alarm. "For real? You don't need to bother about that, Miss Josephine. I can take her anyplace you want her to see."

"Not necessary," Josephine said firmly. She turned to Brooke. "I assume you can drive a stick shift? I know how, of course. But it might be better if I navigate and you drive."

"I know how to drive a stick," Brooke said.

"All right, then," Shug said reluctantly. He slid out from behind the steering wheel and held the door open, then ran around and helped Josephine onto the passenger seat.

"Ready?"

Josephine's face was pink with exertion, and she was breathing heavily as she adjusted the portable oxygen canister hanging from a strap on her shoulder.

She pointed toward the end of the driveway. "Down there, then take a sharp left where the road forks."

The old woman directed her driver on a road that took them toward the state park and nature center. The blacktop was crumbling in places and pitted with potholes. Wooden directional signs pointed toward a bathhouse, wilderness camping area, wildlife interpretive center, and conference center.

They drove under a thick canopy of live oaks, sweet gums, and pines. Clumps of palmettos crowded up against the shoulder of the road, and Brooke caught glimpses of some primitive-looking log cabin structures where the vegetation thinned out.

"Interpretive center," Josephine said, sniffing. "These fools don't know the first thing about the wildlife on this island." She pointed at a low concrete-block building with smoked-glass windows. "That's their conference center. Don't ask me what they confer about, though."

They rode in silence through the half-empty campground. Here and there, Brooke spotted tents and picnic pavilions, and occasionally they passed a family hiking or biking along the road. It looked innocuous—idyllic, even—but Brooke could feel the anger radiating from Josephine as she glared at what she saw as the state's intrusion on the environment.

"This is what they intend to do with my land if they succeed in taking it," Josephine said, scowling at two teenagers who sped by on all-terrain vehicles.

"That's what I wanted to talk to you about today," Brooke said, sensing an opening. "I conferred with a former colleague of mine, and he had some suggestions about how it might be possible to deal with the state's efforts to buy your land."

"Steal it, you mean. What sort of suggestions does this colleague of yours have?"

"First of all, we need to get an independent appraisal of your property. Do you know if your Atlanta lawyers have an updated appraisal?"

"Maybe," Josephine said. "I can't keep track of all the correspondence they've sent over the years."

"I can ask them to share their files, but you'll need to contact the law firm, by registered letter, to notify them that you've hired me to work on the matter. I drafted a letter, and if you approve, you can sign it, and I'll send it out today."

"All right."

"We can certainly continue challenging the state's offer as being unfair and inadequate," Brooke said. "But that doesn't halt the condemnation; it only slows it down."

"I want it stopped," Josephine said. Her bony fists clenched and unclenched. "That's what this is all about. I won't rest until I know the state will never be able to take my land."

"I understand," Brooke said soothingly. "But our options are fairly limited. One way we might approach it is through political means."

"How's that? I don't trust politicians. Never have."

"Do you have any connections in the state legislature?" Brooke asked. "Do you know your local state senators and representatives?"

Josephine wrinkled her nose. "I used to know Jimmy Carter's mama. She was nice, even if she was a Democrat. And Preiss played golf with Talbott Hicks, who was our U.S. senator from this district, but he's long dead. Back in my churchgoing days, I knew Maralai Graham, who was in the general assembly, but she's dead too. And Mike Stovall, he was our state senator, but I believe he got indicted for racketeering last year."

"How about anybody who's alive?" Brooke asked, stifling a laugh. "Or not currently incarcerated?"

"Jenks Cooper is still alive, and I don't believe he's gone to prison yet. He's the state representative from our district."

"Great. Do you know him?"

"I know his grandmother and his mother and his wife," Josephine said. "Lovely women. Jenks is a scalawag, but aren't they all? I believe he's some sort of vice president at my bank."

"Anybody else?"

"There's the governor," Josephine said.

"Ooh, good. You know Governor Traymore?"

"Of course. I've known Tubby since he was a child. I contributed to his election campaign, as a favor to his mother. Personally, I don't think Tubby is all that bright."

"Are you friendly with anybody in local politics? Like somebody on the county commission? Judges, anybody like that?"

"Certainly," Josephine said. "They all come here with their hats in their hands to ask for money. I never give them as much as they expect, but I don't send them away empty-handed."

"Do you feel up to making some phone calls and writing some letters?"

"I don't see why not. Do you really think it will do any good?"

"It might," Brooke said. "The state always seems to be strapped for money. They can't even maintain the parks we have. So how can the state justify spending millions and millions of dollars to acquire land for another park? Especially one you can't even get to by car?"

Josephine gave her an appraising look. "I believe I might have underestimated you."

"Let's not get ahead of ourselves," Brooke said. "When we get back to the house, if you're not too tired, I'll help you write letters to everybody you can think of at the state level, protesting the state's attempted land grab, pointing out what a giant misuse of taxpayers' money it would be, and so on. On the county level, we need to figure out what you pay in property taxes every year and remind the commissioners how much revenue will be lost if your land gets turned into a state park."

"All right," Josephine said. Behind the thick-lensed glasses, her eyes glittered with excitement. "Maybe I'll even call Virginia Traymore. After all, I did make a hundred-dollar contribution to her son's campaign."

Brooke rolled her eyes. Georgia's governor, Tubby Traymore, was a multimillionaire developer. He hardly needed Josephine Warrick's hundred dollars.

"My colleague has also offered to handle your estate work. As I said before, it's a conflict of interest for me to have anything to do with that, since my mother is a beneficiary."

"I'll want to meet him first," Josephine said. "When can he come see me?"

"As soon as you'd like," Brooke said.

They'd reached the exit sign for the state park, where the road veered sharply off to the left.

"Where now?" she asked.

"Take the beach road," Josephine said.

"Sure thing," Brooke said. "That's a part of the island I haven't seen yet."

. . .

After a quarter of a mile, the pavement transitioned to a bumpy crushed-shell road. Palmettos and cabbage palms closed in on either side, their fronds slapping against the side of the truck. Brooke slowed, downshifted into third gear, and steered the truck around the worst of the potholes, but some were unavoidable.

At one point she started to apologize for the rough ride, but a glance revealed Josephine with her head slumped against the passenger door, snoring softly. The interior of the truck was silent except for the soft shunting noise of the old woman's oxygen tank.

She drove for fifteen minutes, unsure about her exact location, but eventually, the terrain changed. Palmetto thickets gave way to dense stands of gnarled and stunted live oaks, whose dark gray trunks acted as a windbreak for the seashore just beyond the tree line.

Here and there on the other side of a towering hedgerow of sea grapes, Brooke glimpsed a stretch of beach and heard the waves crashing. The wind whipped her hair around her face, and she was thankful for the break in the oppressive heat in the truck's cab. Meanwhile, Josephine slept on.

Finally, she saw a pull-off point on her right, a hard-packed section of shell that gave way to a path down to the beach. Brooke pulled in and shut off the ignition. The beach stretched temptingly in front of her, totally empty of any sign of human activity. Blue-green waves lapped at the shore, and seabirds skittered along the sand. A mosquito buzzed against the windshield.

"Josephine?"

"Hmm?" The old woman blinked slowly, seemingly confused.

"Is this the spot you wanted me to drive to?" Brooke asked.

"Hmm?"

"The beach road," Brooke said. "You asked me to take you to the beach road. Is this the spot you had in mind?"

Josephine nodded. She sat up straight, bracing her hands against the cracked vinyl dashboard, staring out at the seascape unrolled before her.

"It's beautiful," she said. "Just as I remembered it. Untouched. Unspoiled."

Brooke propped an elbow on the windowsill, and the two women sat, without speaking, for half an hour. It was mesmerizing, Brooke thought. She felt her pulse slow, heard her breaths begin to match the inexorable rhythm of the waves rolling into the shore. She watched the long-legged shorebirds and smiled at their graceful antics, rushing in and out of the foam, pausing to dip and sieve for food. A pod of dolphins cruised by, rolling in and out of the waves. It made her think of Henry, whose favorite beach pastime was looking for dolphins.

She glanced at her cell phone on the seat beside her, guiltily wondering how her mother was faring with her son, who'd woken up cranky and uncooperative that morning. She couldn't tell whether her mother had called, though, because again, she had no cell service.

"Was there something here you wanted me to see?" she asked her client.

Josephine waved her arm toward the horizon outside the truck's windshield. "This. It's the place I told you about. Mermaid Beach."

"Where the High Tide Club went skinny-dipping?"

Josephine nodded. "I haven't been up here since I got sick. Today, when I woke up, I thought, just for a minute, maybe I'm better."

"You certainly look better."

"Looks are deceiving," Josephine said. "I'm dying. The doctors did scans, and there are new tumors everywhere." She stared out at the water. "And please don't tell me you're sorry. I'm sick of hearing that."

"What should I say instead?" Brooke asked. Since Josephine felt so little empathy for others, it shouldn't have come as a surprise that she expected none for herself. Still, her client's matter-of-fact acceptance of her terminal diagnosis was unsettling.

Josephine turned dark, unblinking eyes toward the younger woman. "Tell me the real reason you decided to work for me. I know a little bit about people. You're broke, but you're not desperate, not by a long shot."

"Maybe it's the challenge. My colleague who's worked on these kinds of cases says that fighting a state on condemnation issues is mostly a lost cause. I like the puzzle-solving part of being a lawyer, and lately, there hasn't been a lot of that in my life."

Josephine's thin lips stretched into a ghostly smile. "You think I'm a lost cause?"

"You said it yourself."

"So you're a fighter, after all." Josephine coughed violently, holding a hand to her chest as though trying to soften the racking spasms.

"I found the women you wanted me to look for," Brooke said abruptly.

"Tell me."

"Your friend Ruth has a granddaughter who lives out in California. Her name is Lizzie. She's a freelance magazine writer."

"Lizzie. She must have been named after Ruth's daughter, who died when she was a teenager. Did you speak to this Lizzie person? When can she come?"

"I did speak to her, and she said she'll only come if you pay her way."

"Hmmph."

Brooke let it drop, knowing that if she pushed the matter her skinflint client would probably push back and refuse to underwrite Lizzie's travel expenses.

"Also, Varina and her great-niece Felicia came to see me."

"They came to you? How extraordinary."

"Not really. Louette told them how ill you are and mentioned that you'd hired me to help with fending off the state."

The old woman scowled. "Louette had no business saying anything to that girl about my private business."

"Felicia brought her great-aunt to town to pick out a headstone for her great-uncle. Louette's a cousin. Saved me the trouble of tracking her down. If it means anything, Varina wants to come see you."

"Because of the money. That Felicia is all about the money."

"You're the one who wants to see her old friend. Who, by the way, is in her nineties and suffering from diabetes herself, but whose first concern is praying for your health."

"Preacher's kid," Josephine said dismissively.

Brooke threw up both hands in mock surrender. "I give up. Do you like anybody? Trust anybody? You asked me to find these women. I found them, and now you're looking for reasons to turn them away."

"Just being realistic," Josephine said. "Did you talk to your mother? Tell her I'm dying?"

"Yes. She's actually at my house right now, helping with Henry."

"And what did she say? When you told her about my intentions?"

"She doesn't understand why you feel so strongly about leaving the island to her and the others." Brooke paused. "You didn't even go to my grandmother's funeral. You didn't so much as send a card."

Josephine looked away. "Things changed. I've changed. Did she say she'd come?"

"She'll come."

21

....

Josephine dozed off on the way back to Shellhaven. Her face was pale again, and her breathing sounded a little labored, or maybe Brooke was just feeling particularly anxious about her client. After several fits and starts, now that she'd taken on this oddball case, she realized that she really wanted to see it through to its conclusion.

Brooke touched the old woman's shoulder lightly after she'd pulled the truck around to the front of the house. "Josephine?"

No reaction. Brooke touched the side of her face and was relieved to feel that it was warm and her client was still breathing.

"Josephine, we're home."

The old woman's eyes opened slowly. She sat up and looked around. "So we are."

"Do you feel okay?"

"Tired," Josephine said. "What time is it?"

"It's after three. I need to get home to my little boy. Shall I get Shug to carry you into the house?"

"No!" she said sharply. "I can walk. Just give me your arm and I'll be fine."

The front door opened, and Louette came out and opened the passenger-side door. She must have been watching and waiting for the truck's return.

Brooke took one arm and Louette took the other, and they easily lifted Josephine out of the seat and into the house. The two Chihuahuas met them at the door, eagerly barking and jumping at their mistress's leg.

"Silly girls," Josephine said, but she reached into the pocket of her slacks and tossed each of them a biscuit.

After they'd gotten the dogs calmed down and the old lady settled back in her recliner, Brooke sat down and rested her briefcase across her knees. "Do you feel like signing this letter to your Atlanta lawyers?"

"I'm fine," Josephine said. "Stop fussing over me."

Brooke produced the papers, which Josephine signed.

"What else?"

"We talked about your making phone calls and writing letters to the governor and any other politicians you think might help stop the condemnation effort."

"Not today," Josephine said. "What day is it anyway?"

"Monday."

"Come back Wednesday. We'll do it then. Bring your lawyer colleague too. I've wasted enough time on this already. I want to get this done. And I want to see those women."

"Lizzie Quinlan won't come unless you pay for her expenses," Brooke reminded her. "And she lives all the way out in California. So this could take some time."

"Time is what I don't have. So yes, I'll pay her way."

"Shall I make the arrangements?"

"I certainly can't, so yes, you'll have to do it."

"And how will I pay for it?"

"Don't you have a credit card?"

"Don't you?"

"It's in my pocketbook, which is somewhere around here," Josephine said vaguely. She waved in the general direction of the room. "I'm not paying for first class," she warned. "You tell her that. I never took a first-class plane ride in my life, and she won't be taking one on my dime."

C. D. rode up to the dock on a small black motorbike just as Shug was dropping Brooke off. He leaned the bike against a tree, then motioned Brooke to follow him to the boat. He jumped easily onto the boat and started the motor before extending a hand to help her aboard.

"Thanks," she said, sinking down onto the fiberglass seat.

"You ready?" the boatman asked, and without waiting for her reply, he cast off the stern line and backed away from the Talisa dock.

Brooke clasped her briefcase to her chest and tried to steel herself for another jaw-rattling ride across the river to the mainland.

Instead, C. D. was content to putter across at a leisurely pace.

Brooke tilted her head back to look at the sky. She was running through the list of chores she needed to complete before her return to the island.

"How's your client doing today, Miss Lawyer?" C. D. blurted. "I saw y'all riding around the island in the truck earlier. That's good, right? I mean, last time I took her over to the mainland to see the docs down at Jacksonville, she looked like one good breeze might knock her down. She don't hardly go out of the house at all since she got sick."

"What?" Brooke was startled by his sudden concern for his employer. "Um, yes, she did seem better today. I think the new medicine is helping."

He nodded, chewing the plastic filter of his unlit cigarillo.

C. D. was an odd-looking creature, Brooke mused, with his sun-seared skin, bowlegs, and ever-present cigarillo, plus the braided gray ponytail that hung down almost to his waist.

"Hear tell she's fixing to give Oyster Bluff back to Shug and Louette and the rest of them Geechees living up there," he said. His aviators shaded his eyes, so she couldn't tell from his expression whether or not he approved of Josephine's largesse.

"Where did you hear that?" Brooke asked, careful to neither confirm nor deny.

"Around," C. D. said. "Next thing you know, she'll be giving us all raises and insurance."

"Maybe so," Brooke said. She stared off into the distance.

"Wait 'til she hears I run off another set of assholes from the state." He chuckled. "She'll for sure give me a raise for doin' that."

"You saw some people from the state? On Talisa? When was that?"

"Early this morning, right after sunup. Caught a couple of 'em tied up at the dock with a mess of what looked like surveying instruments. One of 'em tried to show me some piece of paper claiming they had a right to be there. Something about an appraisal they needed to do on account of the state making the old lady sell up. I told 'em unless they had the sheriff with 'em, they needed to stay the hell off this island."

"I certainly hope you didn't threaten them," Brooke said.

He patted the holstered revolver on his bony hip and chuckled again. "Hell, I didn't even draw down on 'em. They saw I was carrying, and that was the end of that conversation."

"You took a risk, running those surveyors off. It might not have been the wisest thing to do, but I'm sure Josephine would appreciate your loyalty."

He shrugged. "Her island, her rules. Can I ask you something?"

"You can ask, but I can't guarantee I'll have an answer."

"What happens to all of us, when she dies? Can the state come in and run us all off?"

"When she dies," Brooke said carefully, "it's my understanding that the state will still have to negotiate to buy Josephine's land from her estate. They can't take the land without fair compensation. That's the law."

"And that's where you come in," C. D. said. "She wants you to make the state go away. So she can keep the island."

"Something like that."

"You say no matter what, the state has to buy the island from her estate. But who's that? She ain't got no family I ever heard of."

"I'm not at liberty to discuss that," Brooke said firmly.

"Oh."

"Are you worried about losing your home on the island, C. D.?"

"I got a little place," he said. "Comes with the job."

"So did you grow up on Talisa?"

"Here and there," he said, suddenly cagey. "Mostly Savannah."

"I thought I detected a Savannah accent. I'm from Savannah too."

"Oh yeah?"

"Born and raised. How about you? What high school did you go to?"

"I bet I know what high school you went to," he said. "Probably St. Vincent's. Or maybe Country Day School. That's where all the rich kids went when I was coming up."

She ignored the taunt about being rich. "Did you go to high school in Savannah?"

"Never finished. Dropped out, bummed around, got drafted, went over to Vietnam, and managed to come back alive. School of hard knocks, as they say."

Brooke didn't try to hide her surprise. "You're a Vietnam vet? Mind if I ask how old you are?"

He shrugged again. "Born in '42."

"I can't believe you're that old. Wow."

"I take care of myself," he said, preening a little, flexing a sinewy, tattooed bicep featuring an eagle atop a globe pierced with an anchor.

"You were a marine?"

"Semper fi, baby," he said. "How'd you know?"

"I used to know a marine," she said.

It was her turn to be cagey. Pete Haynes had gone to college on an ROTC scholarship, fulfilled his obligation with one tour in Iraq, gotten out of the service, and immediately enrolled in grad school on the GI bill. He'd been sheepish about his own tattoo, claiming he'd gotten it on an impulse, which he'd immediately regretted. Brooke had found it sexy, although she'd never told him so.

The tattoo was only one of a long list of things she'd never talked about with Pete, she realized. And now it was probably too late.

22

Farrah waltzed into the office an hour late on Tuesday. She wore an oversized off-the-shoulder black T-shirt and skin-tight white jeans so shredded Brooke could see more skin than jeans.

"You're late," Brooke said, looking up in annoyance.

"And you're not very nice," Farrah said, sticking out her tongue at her boss. "Especially since I got out of school an hour early just to get to the courthouse to work on this." With a flourish she produced a piece of lined loose-leaf notebook paper covered with her girlish handwriting.

"What is it?"

"Just that list of former landowners at Oyster Bluff on Talisa you assigned me."

"Good job." Brooke did a seated half bow. She scanned the list, which covered both sides of the paper. "Geez. This looks like a lot more names than Josephine told me there would be."

"For reals," Farrah said. "I counted twenty-three names. It wasn't easy. People owned a house, then left it to four or five kids, and then the kids sold off pieces of the land to somebody else . . . it's a mess. And so many people had the same last name. Like, there are Shaddixes and Hobarts and Langs and Franklins and Johnsons . . . it's hard to know who owns what if you look at the county's old deed books."

"Well, it's an island, and Louette says a lot of people intermarried," Brooke said.

"I researched as many names as I could online, and at least six of these people have died," Farrah said. She removed her backpack and dropped it on the receptionist's desk. She unzipped a pocket on the bag and produced another sheet of notebook paper.

"I managed to find six addresses that I think are current," Farrah said, handing her the list.

"Okay. Maybe Louette or Varina or her niece can help with some of the missing addresses," Brooke said. "At least it's a start."

The office phone rang, and Farrah grabbed for it. "Law offices of Brooke Trappnell and Associates," she said. "This is Farrah. How may I help you?"

Brooke picked up her own desk phone to start checking off items on her to-do list. She'd already called Gabe Wynant first thing that morning and arranged the meeting with Josephine.

Next up was Lizzie Quinlan.

"Hi, Lizzie. It's Brooke Trappnell in Georgia."

"Who? Oh yeah. The lawyer, right? What's the word?"

Brooke took a deep breath. "Mrs. Warrick would very much like for you to fly out here this week. The sooner the better."

"Not happening," Lizzie said. "I've got to finish a piece I'm working on, and then I've got a bunch of interviews to do for another piece. I could maybe get out there late next week."

"Couldn't you do the phone interviews from here?"

"Maybe, but what's the big rush?"

"Mrs. Warrick's most recent scans show several new tumors," Brooke said. "You might have all the time in the world, but I assure you, she does not."

"Okay, I'll come. But she pays all my travel, right? Room and board, everything."

"That's correct. I'll book your flights today. Could you be here by Thursday?"

"This is already Tuesday. Are you crazy? I'll have to find a cat sitter, finish my magazine article . . ."

"Friday, then," Brooke relented. "I'm afraid there aren't a ton of hotel options here in town. Just chains."

"I'll leave it up to you. Just something clean and near a liquor store," Lizzie said. "And I need to be home no later than Monday. Understood?"

"Perfectly," Brooke said. "I'll text you the flight details. See you then."

Felicia Shaddix wasn't as easily persuaded.

"Friday? I teach a class on Friday. And even if I didn't, my aunt has a standing hair appointment on Friday. I promise you, she won't go anywhere without that hair fixed just right. Not even if it was lunch with Barack Obama himself."

"Isn't your class an online one? Could it be taped? I've got one of the other beneficiaries flying in from LA on Friday morning, and it's going to be tricky to reschedule her."

"I don't know," Felicia grumbled. "The dean likes the classes to be live, with student interaction. She's pretty strict about that."

"Look," Brooke said, lowering her voice. "I don't want to upset your aunt, but Josephine really doesn't have a lot of time left. I was with her yesterday, and she said the latest scans showed that the cancer has metastasized. I'm sure you know the implications of that. I really need to get all of you together with her so we can move forward with the arrangements."

"Fine. I'll tell the dean it's an emergency, and I'll tell my aunt's hairdresser it's an emergency too, see if she'll fit her in on Thursday afternoon instead."

"Thanks so much," Brooke said.

Her own mother was the last piece of the puzzle, and a surprisingly hard sell.

"Friday? Oh no. That's out of the question," Marie said. "I have a committee meeting on Friday morning. I was going to tell you tonight. I'll have to head home to Savannah on Thursday."

"Mom, I really, really need you to meet with Josephine and those other women Friday on the island. I've been through hell getting everybody's schedules lined up. I didn't expect it would be a problem with you."

"Sweetie, I'm sorry, but this is my Fresh Air Home board meeting. We're going through the applications for the children for summer camp. I really can't miss it."

"Mommmm." Brooke knew she sounded like a petulant teenager, but she couldn't help herself. "You're the chairman of the committee, so can't you just make an executive decision and reschedule? Those women don't have jobs or day care to figure out."

"Are you saying my friends and I are just idle, rich ladies who lunch?" Marie asked.

Damn it, Brooke thought. She'd bungled that one badly.

"No, not at all. I know how much good work you and your friends do and how hard you work at it," Brooke said hastily. "But couldn't you let your co-chair run the meeting? Please, Mom? For me?"

"Well, if it really means that much, I'll do it for you, but not for her. This seems like a lot of fuss," Marie complained. "I don't mean to second-guess you, Brooke, but how do you even know Josephine really and truly means to leave the island to a bunch of strangers? It's just so unbelievably odd. Are you sure this isn't some ploy, just to get attention or sympathy?"

"It had better not be," Brooke said.

23

....

Gabe Wynant was dressed for his Wednesday morning meeting with Josephine Warrick in what was apparently his idea of island casual— white button-down oxford cloth shirt (sans necktie), pressed khakis, and navy-blue blazer, accessorized by Topsiders (sans socks) and a briefcase. Brooke didn't have the heart to tell him that Shellhaven didn't have air-conditioning.

"Who's this?" C. D. asked Brooke as the two boarded the boat.

"Gabe Wynant," the visitor said, extending a hand in greeting.

C. D. reluctantly shook hands. "C. D. Anthony. You got a business card?"

Being the Southern gentleman he was, Gabe produced a thick velum card and handed it to the boatman.

"Another lawyer?" He raised one bushy eyebrow.

"How are you today, C. D.?" Brooke asked.

"Same as ever. Bursitis, arthritis, and gastritis. Them VA doctors are all a bunch of quacks, if you ask me."

Gabe started to offer his condolences, but Brooke gave him a warning shake of her head to telegraph *Do not engage.*

. . .

"I haven't been over to Talisa probably since the eighties, when it was included on one of the Georgia Trust for Historic Preservation's rambles," Gabe said as they puttered slowly through the marina's no-wake zone. "At the time, the house wasn't open for tours. I've always been fascinated with the place."

"It's pretty much a living time capsule," Brooke said. "Josephine has tried to keep everything the same as it was at the time of her husband's death."

"When did he die?"

"Sometime in the sixties, I think." She glanced at C. D., whose back was turned to them. "The house and grounds are in pretty sad shape. Unfortunately, she doesn't have the manpower to keep up with all the needed maintenance. Even in its current condition, you can tell it was once pretty magnificent."

"I'm looking forward to seeing it. And, of course, to working with the lady of the house," Gabe said.

"You might change your mind about that once you actually meet her," C. D. said. He'd turned around and was facing them now, ready to insert himself into their conversation.

Brooke frowned and shot her colleague the *Do not engage* look again, which Gabe cheerfully ignored.

"Why's that?"

"Just sayin'. She's a tough old bird. Stingy as hell."

"Why do you stay?" Gabe asked. "I mean, if she's as bad as you say."

"I'm seventy-six years old. I got a bad leg and some might say a bad attitude. I ask you, who else is gonna hire me and give me a place to live, sorry as it is?"

"Exactly," Brooke said. She pointedly turned toward the bow of the boat, leaving her back to the boat's captain and effectively ending the conversation.

When C. D. pulled the boat alongside the dock at Shellhaven, the same little boy was stationed at the end of the dock, waiting. "Hey, C. D.," the boy called.

"Gimme a hand with the bowline, will ya, Lionel?" C. D. tossed him the bowline, and the kid knotted it around a cleat.

"You take me for a motorcycle ride?" Lionel asked eagerly.

"Maybe later," C. D. said, nodding at his departing passengers.

It was Louette, and not her husband, who was waiting for them at the dock this time. She was driving a vehicle Brooke hadn't seen before, a gleaming aqua-and-white four-door Chrysler with the exaggerated tailfins of a fifties muscle car.

Brooke gamely climbed into the backseat of the car and introduced Gabe Wynant. "Where's Shug today?" she asked.

"He's up on the roof, trying to patch another hole," Louette said. "Silly me, I never did learn how to drive a stick shift, which is why I had to come fetch you in Nellybelle." She gave the turquoise vinyl dashboard a fond pat.

"My dad had a Chrysler like this, only his was brown and cream," Gabe said. "I can't believe this thing still runs."

"Shug likes to tinker with Miss Josephine's cars when he has the time," Louette explained. "This is one of his favorites."

"There are others?" Gabe asked.

"Oh, sure. The barn is full of 'em. She don't like to get rid of anything, especially if it had something to do with Mr. Preiss. Let's see, there's the Cadillac he bought her after they first got married. I guess it's from the fifties, like this. And there's her daddy's old Packard. I don't know how old that thing is. Shug can't find parts for it no more. The oldest car, the roadster, is one that belonged to her brother, Gardiner, the one who was killed in the war."

Gabe gestured at the cars parked nearby. "Is this some kind of junkyard?"

"Looks like it, don't it? No, this is where island folks leave their cars when they're going across to the mainland. We just leave the keys in 'em, in case somebody needs a ride somewhere," Louette said.

"And nobody worries about car theft?" Gabe asked.

"Who'd steal any of this mess?" Louette scoffed. "Anyway, it's an island. How far is somebody gonna get in a stolen car?"

"How's Josephine feeling today?" Brooke asked.

"She *says* she feels fine, but I know she didn't sleep much last night. I heard her get up two or three times in the night."

"You're sleeping in the house now?" Brooke was taken aback.

"Uh-huh. Miss Josephine fell and hurt herself Monday night. Said she tripped over one of the dogs. Somehow she managed to get up and get back in the bed. It's a miracle she didn't break a hip or crack her skull wide open. She fought me on it, but last night I fixed me a bed on the sofa in the living room, and that's where I'm gonna be staying until . . ." Louette's voice trailed off.

"Do you think Josephine needs round-the-clock nursing care?" Brooke asked.

"Maybe. But I know her, and she ain't gonna do that. No, ma'am. She ain't gonna want to spend the money on a nurse. It's funny. She's been telling me the doctor says this cancer will kill her, but she really ain't ready to admit yet just how sick she is."

Gabe turned around to Brooke. "Maybe that's something I could discuss with her, if we're redoing her will. She probably already has an advanced health care directive."

"It's worth a try," Brooke said.

"Y'all go on inside, please, while I park Nellybelle out back," Louette said when they'd reached the house. "She's in the living room. Got herself all fixed up today, on account of having herself a 'gentleman caller.'"

Gabe got out of the car and took a few steps backward to take in the house. The grass had been freshly cut, the formerly overgrown shrubbery nearest the house had been trimmed, and the flower beds weeded. He let out a low whistle under his breath. "So this is Shellhaven. Even with the decay, the photos don't do it justice. It's magnificent."

"Just wait," Brooke warned. "If you're into shabby gentility, this is the place for you."

She led the attorney through the foyer and down the hallway to the living room, where they found the lady of the house sitting in a high-backed chair angled in front of the fireplace, facing the sofa.

True to Louette's word, Josephine seemed to have transformed herself into an old-style grande dame for today's meeting. She was wearing a floor-length flowered silk caftan with a stunning double-strand pearl necklace and matching earrings, and a fluffy silver bouffant wig that sat slightly askew on her head. She wore bright pink lipstick and a thick application of face powder that failed to hide a bruise on the right side of her face, but she still managed to look formidably regal. A box fan had been propped in front of one of the windows, its blades barely managing to stir the blanketlike heat in the room.

"Josephine," Brooke said, "I want you to meet my former boss, Gabe Wynant."

"Forgive me for not standing to greet you," Josephine said, offering her hand to Gabe. "I took a tumble the other night and I haven't quite regained my equilibrium."

Gabe gently shook the old lady's hand. "It's a pleasure, Mrs. Warrick. Both to meet you and to see your beautiful home."

"Not as beautiful as it once was, but we do our best," their hostess said. She gestured toward the sofa, which had been liberated from its dust cover. "Please sit."

They exchanged pleasantries for a few minutes, the way Southerners do at a first meeting, while Gabe discreetly unbuttoned the top button of his dress shirt and slipped out of his blazer in deference to the heat.

"I believe I knew your father," Josephine said. "He was a lawyer too, isn't that right?"

"That's right. He was one of the founding partners of our law firm," Gabe said.

"And your mother's people?" she asked.

"Mama was a Poole. She grew up in Macon," Gabe said.

"Macon? I don't believe I know anybody from Macon." It was clear that to Josephine Bettendorf Warrick, Macon might as well have been Mars.

"Gabe's the senior partner at my old firm," Brooke said, hoping to move the conversation along to business. "I've filled him in a little on your legal situation."

"But I'd appreciate it if you'd tell me exactly what your wishes are in regard to this proposed trust and, of course, your estate planning," Gabe said, sliding a yellow legal pad from his briefcase and balancing it on his knees.

"We'll get to that," Josephine said airily. "Where did you grow up and go to school, Gabe, if you don't mind my asking."

"Don't mind at all," Gabe said. "I grew up in Ardsley Park, went to prep school at Benedictine, like most of the guys in my neighborhood. Went to University of Georgia, undergrad. Came home from school, messed around in Savannah for a year or so, and then my dad pointed out that it was pretty inevitable that I would go to law school. So I did."

"And what law school did you attend?" Josephine said. "UGA?"

"No, ma'am. That's where my dad went, but I was just ornery enough to want to go a different route, get a little farther away from home. I'm a proud Duke Blue Devil."

Josephine looked impressed. "You know, I believe Richard Nixon went to law school at Duke University."

"So I've heard," Gabe said, grinning. "It was a little before my time."

"Well, yes, you're obviously much, much younger," Josephine said. "More attractive too, I might add."

"You're too kind," Gabe said.

Brooke felt her jaw drop slightly. The old lady was actually flirting with Gabe Wynant. Ninety-nine years old and batting her eyelashes like a Chi O at a KA mixer.

"I suppose you've been married a long time?" Josephine asked.

Brooke held her breath for a second.

"I was, yes. Unfortunately, my wife passed away nearly two years ago," Gabe said.

"Oh, dear. I had no idea. I'm so sorry." Josephine looked flustered.

"You couldn't have known, so please don't apologize," Gabe said. "She, uh, had liver cancer, so I will say that it was mercifully quick."

"I have cancer myself," Josephine said. "The doctors tell me it's terminal. I just hope my illness will be as mercifully short as your late wife's."

"I hope so too, ma'am," Gabe said. He coughed politely. "Which is why, if you don't mind, we ought to get down to talking about the disposition of your estate."

"Yes, time is fleeting," Josephine agreed. She looked out the open living room window at the expanse of green lawn flowing down toward the ocean, and she touched the pearls at her neck. "As fleeting as summer."

"Josephine says she wants to leave the island and Shellhaven to three women," Brooke put in quickly, hoping to get the old lady to focus on the task at hand with Gabe.

"I've been thinking about that. Since Varina is in her nineties and Marie is in her midseventies now, I think I'll include Felicia and you, Brooke. Let's make it five beneficiaries."

Gabe's eyebrows rose slightly, and Brooke took a deep breath. "That's very generous of you, Josephine, but that makes it doubly important that I excuse myself so the two of you can talk."

"What do you mean?" Josephine demanded. "I want you here too."

"It's like I explained to you the first day we met," Brooke said patiently. "My participation in planning for your estate is a conflict of interest."

"Be that way, then," Josephine huffed. "I wanted to meet with Gabe privately anyway. Go on to the kitchen with you."

Brooke exchanged a look with Gabe. He would use his considerable tact to settle her down. "I think I'll go see what Louette is up to."

24

....

B rooke pushed the kitchen door open and found Louette stirring a boiling pot on the stovetop with a long wooden spoon. The housekeeper wore a faded blue bandanna over her hair and a white butcher's apron fastened around her waist.

"Can I get you something?" Louette asked, mopping her face with a dishtowel. Another box fan was propped in a large double window over the old-fashioned cast-iron sink, but it did little to cool the oven-like room.

"Sorry to intrude," Brooke said, stationing herself in front of the fan. "Josephine had to talk to Gabe in private. What are you cooking?"

"Chicken soup," Louette said. "Miss Josephine's gotten real finicky, but I can usually get her to eat some if I fix it special. White meat only. A tiny bit of onion and celery and carrots."

"Soup," Brooke grimaced. "How can you even stand to turn on the stove in this heat?"

"My mama used to say air-conditioning wasn't good for you. Gives folks head colds. She told us that to keep us from complaining, I know, but I guess I'm just used to it now. Wouldn't know how to act if I did have it."

Louette went to the refrigerator, a rust-spotted relic of a fifties-era Frigidaire, and brought out a heavy cut-glass pitcher of iced tea. She opened the icebox and brought out an aluminum tray. With one deft motion, she cracked the handle and dumped half the ice cubes into a tall glass. "Drink some iced tea, and that'll cool you down."

Brooke gratefully accepted the tea, resting the cold glass against a sweat-dampened temple. She placed her briefcase on the scarred red Formica counter-top and produced the piece of notebook paper Farrah had prepared from her courthouse research.

"Hey, Louette. This is the list my assistant made of all the people who at one time owned property at Oyster Bluff. I'm wondering if you could take a look at the list and tell me who's still living and where I can contact them."

The housekeeper reached into the pocket of her apron, brought out a pair of reading glasses, and ran a finger down the list.

"Yeah, that's Angela. She's still living in the old home place. And that's Jerome. He moved off a few years ago after his wife died, but I know his son works at the Family Dollar store on the mainland. I can get Jerome's address from him."

She tapped the list. "This here's my sister Loreen, and she lives with my other sister Latrelle. They're both widows."

She kept reading names as Brooke made notes on each entry. "Did that help?" she asked when she'd reached the end. "How long do you think it'll take, 'til she gives us our houses back?"

"For people like you, who still live on the island, it's a fairly straightforward process," Brooke said. "I'll get the paperwork drawn up, and if Josephine signs off as she promised, it shouldn't take long at all. Tracking down the other families is a different matter."

"You don't think she'll change her mind?" Louette asked, putting her glasses back in her pocket. "About us getting our property back? Especially the church and the graveyard?"

"You know Josephine better than I do," Brooke said, wanting to be honest. "But she seems sincere in her desire to make things right."

"All I can do is pray," Louette said with a heavy sigh. "The rest is up to Jesus."

Brooke finished her iced tea and set it in the sink before bringing up another matter. "Something I've been meaning to ask you about. What's the story with C. D.?"

Louette laughed. "He's an odd one, isn't he?"

"How did he come to work for Josephine?"

"He just showed up one day, probably about a year ago. Knocked on the front door and asked if we had any work we needed doing. He claimed he knew about boats, so Miss Josephine hired him on."

"Where does he live?"

"He's got himself a little place fixed up in the old chauffeur's cottage by the barn. There's no real kitchen out there, just a hot plate, so he comes around and eats here sometimes."

"I hate to make more work for you, Louette, but Josephine is going to have company arriving on Friday."

"Friday? Miss Josephine didn't say nothing about company coming."

"I just firmed up the arrangements yesterday. It'll be four women."

"But that's the day after tomorrow," Louette said. "That means I got to get guest rooms ready and beds made up. Get some groceries in here . . . that's more company than we've had since, well, I don't rightly know when."

"They're not staying at Shellhaven. In fact, they're not even staying on the island. Except maybe Varina and Felicia, who I guess will stay with one of the nieces and nephews. The other woman, Lizzie, I'll get her a room on the mainland, and of course, my mother will be staying with me."

"Am I allowed to know why these folks are coming over here?" Louette asked, returning to the stove. "Something to do with Miss Josephine's will?"

"Something like that," Brooke said. "I'm sure Josephine will tell you what she wants as far as food."

"Lord Jesus," Louette muttered. "Now I got to get that dining room straightened out. Got to get me a grocery list together, probably need to bake some rolls and pies . . ."

The kitchen door swung open just then, and Gabe Wynant stuck his head inside. "Her Majesty has retreated to her bedchamber for a nap," he announced with a grin. "And we're dismissed."

. . .

When they got back to St. Ann's, Gabe followed Brooke to the restaurant where she'd promised him lunch, parking beside her in the nearly full lot outside Screen Door Seafood.

"Really?" Gabe nodded toward the restaurant behind him. "This is your idea of an awesome place to dine?"

In its past life, the building had been a wholesale seafood processing plant, and a pair of shrimp boats were still tied up to a wharf that ran along the riverfront. The low-slung rusting corrugated steel building was perched on wooden pilings, with large rollup doors on the side facing the street. These had once provided access to refrigerated tractor-trailer rigs. Now the doors were rolled up, with metal-cased windows revealing tables crowded with happy diners.

"Trust me," Brooke said. "You're gonna love it."

"Miss Brooke!" The young black man's face lit up with a wide smile, revealing a row of gleaming gold-capped front teeth. He flung muscular arms around her shoulders and hugged her tightly.

"Table for one like usual?" he asked, but before she could answer, he spotted Gabe and released her.

"Hey there! I bet you're Miss Brooke's daddy." He grabbed Gabe's hand and pumped it enthusiastically. "How you doin'? I'm Myles. I wanna tell you, this daughter of yours is a great lawyer. Really. She helped my mama so much. Took care of business. She's a great lawyer, sir, and I know you're real proud of her."

Gabe's face turned crimson.

"Uh, Myles, this is actually my friend and associate, Gabe. He's a lawyer too."

"Oh. Me and my big mouth." Myles slapped his forehead, then shook Gabe's hand again. "Wow, man, I'm sorry. I just . . . well, I know Miss Brooke don't have no husband, so I figured, you know, white-haired dude . . . hey, man, no offense."

"None taken," Gabe said quickly. "Although, for the record, her *actual* father is at least twenty years older than I am. And not nearly as good looking."

"Heh-heh." Myles grabbed two menus and flagged down a passing waitress. "Hey, Addie, take Miss Brooke to that two-top by the window and treat 'em real special, you hear?"

"That was awkward," Brooke said after they were seated at a prime table overlooking the river.

"Brutal," Gabe agreed.

Their waitress reappeared at their table with a frosty pitcher of frozen margaritas, two oversized goblets, and a complementary basket of hush puppies. "From Myles," she said. "On the house."

Brooke glanced at the host stand, and Myles waved and flashed her a thumbs-up, which she returned.

"Your buddy Myles is certainly a big fan," Gabe said. "How'd you meet him?"

She took a gulp of the margarita, then fanned her face. "Sorry. Brain freeze. Gimme a minute."

He waited.

"Myles's mom, Lillian, works in the county clerk's office, which is where I spend a lot of time. Anyway, Lillian hired some crooked contractor to put a new roof on her house. The guy ripped the old roof off, then demanded payment in full before he'd finish the job. She paid, and of course, he cashed the check and never came back. Even left his ladder, the dumbass. Lillian hired me, and I went after him in small claims court. She got her roof and even some damages. So now I'm a superhero in the eyes of the extended King family."

"Did you get paid?" Gabe asked.

"A little. Enough." She gestured at the pitcher of margaritas. "This happens every time I'm in here. You wait. We'll be getting dessert too, whether we want it or not. Also, Myles and his brother show up faithfully, every week, to take care of my yard. But best of all, there's Lillian. She knows all the judges and where all the bodies are buried in this county. She takes care of my filings. You can't buy that kind of loyalty. Right?"

. . .

They placed their orders—fried seafood platter for Gabe and for Brooke, broiled, stuffed flounder. And a craft brew for Gabe, who confessed he wasn't much of a margarita drinker.

"So," Gabe said after the waitress had gone, "you have a child. I had no idea. At all."

"Henry. He'll be three in July. Want to see?"

"Of course."

She took out her iPhone and scrolled through the photo library, holding it out for Gabe to see. "This is his preschool photo. Here he is at the park, with my mom. That's us, eating ice cream in the backyard . . ."

"Good-looking little guy," Gabe said, picking up a hush puppy from the basket the waitress had left on their table. He chewed and processed the images and the information. "He really is a miniature version of you."

"I think he looks more like his father, especially when he's mad at me."

"And the father?" Gabe said, taking the opening. "If you don't mind my asking."

She downed a third of her margarita, then dabbed her lips with a napkin. "I don't mind your asking," Brooke said calmly. "But I would prefer that you keep this just between us. I know how people gossip in Savannah."

"You think I don't know gossip?" Gabe said bitterly. "All those years with Sunny? Arriving late or not at all to dinners with friends? Making excuses for when she was passed out cold in the middle of the day. I knew what people were saying."

"I'm sorry," Brooke said. "If it matters, I think you were a good and loyal husband all those years."

"Thanks." Gabe smiled. "It matters."

"His name is Pete." She blurted it out.

"Huh?"

"Henry's father. My baby daddy. His name is Pete. We first met the summer before I started law school. We had sort of a thing, I guess you'd call it."

"This guy Pete? He's why you left Harris?"

"No. I ran off because I wasn't ready to be married, to anybody. I'd been having doubts, but once that wedding freight train got rolling, I didn't have the balls to derail it."

"Probably for the best, then," Gabe said.

"Tell that to my dad," Brooke said.

"You mean your *actual* dad?"

They laughed in unison, and with perfect timing, their food arrived.

When he'd worked his way down to everything but the lemon-and-parsley garnish and the shrimp tails, Gabe groaned and pushed back from the table. "You were right about this place," he told Brooke. "Don't know when I've had seafood this fresh."

"Glad you liked it," Brooke said. She'd finished most of her salad and the flounder.

"You were telling me about Henry's father. Pete? When did he come back into the picture?"

"Pete's a wildlife biologist. He was working down here on the coast, over at Cumberland Island, doing some research. And when I left Savannah, I came down here, because I didn't have anyplace else to go."

"And that's when you got together with this Pete?"

"Not at first," Brooke said, blushing. "We were just friends."

"Until you weren't."

"Something like that. I suppose it was probably inevitable. One night, he announced he'd gotten a grant to do research on elk migration patterns. In Alaska. And he wanted me to go with him."

Gabe cocked one eyebrow. "To Alaska?"

"Yeah. Big shock. At which point, things got, um, real serious real fast. I did give it some thought, but in the cold light of morning, the whole idea seemed impossible. So I took him to the airport and kissed him goodbye, and six weeks later, I realized I was pregnant."

"And what? He dumped you?"

"He doesn't know," Brooke said.

Gabe set his beer down carefully on the tabletop and gave her a quizzical look.

"I had my reasons for not telling him," Brooke said. "But according to my mom, he has a right to know that he has a son."

"And what do you think?"

"I'm . . . conflicted," she admitted. "Things are complicated between Pete and me. And the more time that goes by, the harder it is for me to reach out and tell him. I don't want anything from him. I don't expect anything."

"But maybe you're afraid Pete will want to have some part in raising your son? Maybe even attempt to take him from you?" Gabe asked.

"There's that. Henry's all I have."

"I think it suits you. Motherhood, I mean. Are you happy down here, Brooke?"

"Happy?" With her fingertip, she drew circles in the tabletop water rings.

"I guess that's relative. St. Ann's is a small town, and the lawyers here are a pretty clannish bunch. They didn't actually throw me a welcoming parade. So I take whatever cases I can get. As for the rest of it, I've been lucky. I've got good childcare, including Farrah, who helps out in the office and babysits when I need her. And my mom comes down as often as she can. She's here right now, watching Henry, and she'll stay until after this weird meet and greet with Josephine on Friday."

Now it was Brooke studying her old law partner and mentor. "Speaking of Josephine, are you going to tell me what that 'confidential meeting' was about?"

"Nope. Sorry, but she was insistent."

"I really can't figure her out. I mean, why hire me? I told her I have no experience with the legal work she needs done, but she's adamant that I'm the only girl for the job."

"She has her reasons," Gabe said. He looked down at his watch and then around the room. "I'd better get going if I'm going to make it back to Savannah."

As if on cue, Addie, their waitress, was back, with two towering slices of what looked like key lime pie. "From Myles," she said.

They turned to look, and Myles waved again.

25

························

Brooke and Marie Trappnell stood outside the baggage claim door at the Jacksonville airport. It had rained earlier, and now steam rose from the still-damp sidewalk and road. Brooke's cell phone dinged.

The automatic doors slid open, and a handful of passengers emerged: a young family with a baby in a stroller, a pair of suited businessmen, two college-aged girls dressed in tight white shorts and matching sorority jerseys, and the last, a tall, striking-looking woman with short, spiky, blue-streaked hair who had an animal crate tucked under one arm and was dragging a rolling suitcase.

"That's gotta be Lizzie," Brooke told her mother.

"And she brought a friend," Marie added.

Brooke stepped forward. "Lizzie?"

"That's me," the woman said. "You must be Brooke. Here," she said, thrusting the carrier at her. She gestured toward the Volvo parked at the curb. "I hope that's yours. We've got to get Dweezil into some air-conditioning. She's not used to this crazy humidity."

As if on cue, the animal inside the crate yowled loudly, reached a paw through the crate's metal bars, and raked Brooke's arm with her claws.

"Dweezil! That wasn't very nice," Lizzie said, taking the crate back. She looked up at Brooke. "Let's go. We've been up since midnight. I need a drink, and she needs a litter box."

Brooke looked down at the bleeding claw marks on her forearm. "Uh, sure."

Marie turned around from the front seat and extended her hand toward their passenger. "Hi. I'm Marie. Brooke's mom."

"I figured," Lizzie said, taking her hand and shaking it briefly. "Same nose and all."

She opened the carrier, and an enormous fluffy gray cat exploded onto her lap, yowling indignantly. "And this is Dweezil."

"My goodness," Marie said. "I've never seen a cat that large. She's beautiful. And so unusual looking. What kind of cat is she?"

"Maine coon cat," Lizzie said, burying her nose in the cat's fur. The cat purred happily and licked Lizzie's face. "Three-time, All-West best-in-breed." She looked out the window at the passing traffic. "About that drink?"

Brooke followed the airport signs toward the interstate. "We're about an hour or so away from St. Ann's. Can you wait until we get to your hotel? I think there's a bar in the lobby."

"They don't have liquor stores in Florida?" Lizzie said pointedly.

"Riiiight," Brooke said. She flipped her turn signal and maneuvered the Volvo into the far-right lane. "I think there might be one at this next exit."

They waited in the car while Lizzie went into the liquor store. Dweezil was perched on the backseat, her face turned expectantly toward the window. A moment later, her owner was back, clutching a large brown sack under one arm and holding a smaller package with a straw poking out the top. Lizzie opened the back door and set the large sack on the floor, then clipped a leash to the cat's collar and tucked her under her arm.

"This could take a while," she warned. "Dweez doesn't like to poop in new territory."

"You walk your cat?" Brooke asked.

"Unless you want her to poop in your backseat, I do," Lizzie said. She slammed the door and walked around to the side of the liquor store, where she gently set the cat down on the concrete.

"Interesting woman," Marie said, raising one eyebrow.

Lizzie settled herself into the backseat with her cat on her lap. She reached into the paper sack and brought out a six-pack with one can missing. "Anybody want a mojito?" she asked. She took a sip from her own can. "No clue what's in this, but it's not half-bad."

"I'm good," Brooke said.

"No, thank you," Marie added hastily.

"So," Lizzie said, after they were back on the road. "Tell me about this island we're about to inherit. Got any idea what it's worth?"

"Um, well, the State of Georgia previously offered her $6 million," Brooke said. "But Josephine doesn't want to sell her portion of Talisa. Not under any condition. She's going to fight the condemnation."

"But we could sell it after she's dead, right?" Lizzie asked. "That is, I could sell my portion, right? I mean, no offense to you girls, but I live in California. What do I need with an island in Georgia?"

"Actually, Josephine is adamant that the island shouldn't ever be sold," Brooke said. "That's why she hired me. She wants to establish a trust to ensure that it's left just as it is."

"In perpetuity," Marie added.

Lizzie took a long pull on her canned mojito. "Shit. But you're a lawyer, right?"

"Yes."

"If the state does force her to sell the island, who gets that money? When she's gone? I mean, you told me she's pushing the century mark and she doesn't have any family. That just leaves us, right?"

"Let's not get ahead of ourselves," Brooke cautioned. "At this point, Josephine wants to meet with you, Marie, and Varina. After that, I can't predict what will happen. She's, um, eccentric, to say the least."

"Are you trying to say that if she doesn't like me, she might write me out of her will?" Lizzie asked. She scratched the cat's ears. "That won't happen, will it, Dweez? Everybody loves your mommy. Right?"

Brooke and Marie exchanged amused glances.

"You'd asked about Talisa," Brooke said. "It's an amazing place. Mostly wild. There's a state park on the north end of the island, but otherwise, Shell-haven, the home Josephine's father built, and a small community called Oyster Bluff are the only houses on the island. The scenery is spectacular—and the beach, well, when you see it, I think you'll begin to understand Josephine's determination to keep things untouched. You really have to see the island before you can begin to appreciate its beauty."

"Doubtful," Lizzie said. "I'm a city girl. Dweezil and I don't really *do* nature. Do we, Dweez?"

The cat yowled loudly as if in agreement.

"According to my research, there used to be a plantation on the island. Is anything left of it?" Lizzie asked.

"No. Union troops burned it during the Civil War," Brooke said. "I think there are some tabby ruins, but they're on a part of the midsection of the island that's largely gone wild."

"And the only way to get to the island is by boat? Is there, like, a ferry?"

"There's a small state-operated ferry that goes to the park on the north end, but Josephine keeps a boat at the dock on her end of the island, and that's how we'll get over there today," Brooke said. "It's only about a half-hour ride."

Lizzie glanced down at the cat stretched across her lap and frowned. "Dweez doesn't really like water. Or boats."

"Maybe you can leave her in your room at the hotel," Marie suggested.

"No way," Lizzie said flatly. "She goes where I go. But it's not that big a problem. I brought some chill pills. She can have some of mine."

Marie smiled weakly. "Lizzie, tell me about your grandmother Ruth. I think it's so interesting that she and Josephine and my mother were best friends."

Lizzie yawned. "Grandma was definitely a pistol. She dyed her hair flame red right up until her hairdresser died, and then I did it for her. She had great legs, and she loved to show them off every chance she got. And she was a real original thinker. My dad always said I was more like Grandma than him or my mom, which was true. Grandma was the one who turned me on to books and writing. My dad said Grandma was living her life through me. She never worked after she married my granddad, because, let's face it, he was rich as sin, and women in her circle didn't really have careers back then. If she'd been born in my mother's generation, she probably would have been in Congress or maybe even president. Instead, she marched and protested and raised funds and raised hell for the liberal causes she cared about."

"Brooke tells me Ruth was your paternal grandmother?" Marie asked.

Lizzie shrugged. "She pretty much raised me, off and on. My mom split when I was just a kid, and my dad, well, he wasn't really what you'd call *dad material*. They weren't even technically married, it turns out. Grandma said my dad was super smart in school, but then he got drafted and went to Vietnam, and he was pretty messed up when he got back. He drifts around, always has some crazy scheme he's working on. Grandma left him some money in her will, so I guess that's what he lives on."

Brooke glanced at her guest in the rearview mirror. "It's none of my business, but when I contacted you, the first thing you told me was that you're broke. I guess I'm wondering why your grandmother didn't leave you any money."

"The broke part was just in case you were a scammer. Anyway, I didn't say she didn't leave me any money," Lizzie said, her smile tight. "Grandma didn't want me to end up like my dad—you know, just a stoner. Most of Grandpa's fortune she left to the American Civil Liberties Union, Planned Parenthood, and Greenpeace, which she told me she intended to do, so no surprise there."

Marie turned around in her seat to face Lizzie. "Didn't you resent that?"

"Not really. It was something she talked about a lot. She paid for me to go to a good college, said she was investing in me having a career so that I could make my own way without having to depend on some man to support me. She left me enough to buy a house—which, if you know anything about California real estate prices, was a pretty good chunk of change. I started out working at newspapers, but that's no longer sustainable. So I freelance, and I do okay."

"Why wasn't newspaper reporting 'sustainable'?" Marie asked.

"It was for a few years, right up until they fired me," Lizzie said. "I might've survived the downsizing, but they wouldn't accept Dweezil as my emotional support animal."

"You mean you took your cat to work with you?" Brooke asked. She was beginning to wonder if maybe Lizzie had inherited some of her father's instability.

"Of course," Lizzie said. "But one day she ate my editor's desk plant and coughed it up on the linoleum floor of the break room. The publisher stepped on it, slid to the floor, and broke a hip. So they banished Dweez from the newsroom, which was entirely their loss, I assure you. Without her, my anxiety level soared. So when cuts were made, I was one of the first to go."

Brooke wasn't sure she wanted to hear how Lizzie's anxieties manifested themselves, so she decided to change the subject. "Your grandma sounds like somebody I would have loved to have known," Brooke said. "I guess it makes sense that she and Josephine were such good friends."

Now it was Lizzie's turn to ask the questions. "What was Millie like, Marie?"

"Mama was pure sweetness. Quietly religious, in her own way. She played the piano beautifully, and she was devoted to her home and her family. I know she and Josephine were in nursery school together, and later they met Ruth in boarding school, and they all went to the same college together, but I think she dropped out after her sophomore year. Her family had financial issues, the war had started, and she got married not long after that."

"I wish Granny had lived long enough for me to have really known her," Brooke said. "I just have these tiny fragments of memories—like, I remember her perfume. It smelled sort of like lilies. And I remember her hands. She had long, slender fingers, and I'd sit on her lap and she'd let me play with her rings."

"By the time you came along, she'd already started to show signs of early dementia," Marie said sadly. "She'd get frustrated and was so easily agitated. Holding you seemed to calm her down."

"It's funny to think about Granny and Ruth and Josephine being best friends," Brooke mused. "From what I can tell, listening to you two, they all had such different personalities."

"I have a couple of old pictures of the three of them together that I found in one of my grandmother's photo albums," Lizzie said.

Marie's face lit up. "You do? Oh, I'd love to see those."

"Me too," Brooke said.

"They're in my suitcase," Lizzie said. "I made copies for you."

"That's so thoughtful," Marie said. "I don't have many family photos at all. Mama was never much of a saver," she said wistfully. "I think she didn't see the point of it."

"Grandma was the opposite," Lizzie said. "She saved everything. Newspapers, old letters, play programs, diaries. And scrapbooks! I have an entire trunkful of her scrapbooks. I've always thought someday I'd get a book out of that stuff. Maybe even more than one."

"What kind of a book?" Brooke asked, intrigued.

"Well, there's that unsolved murder on the island, of course," Lizzie said.

Brooke stared at her passenger in the rearview mirror. "You don't mean Talisa."

"Of course I do," Lizzie said. "Hasn't Josephine mentioned Russell Strickland to you?"

"Noooo," Brooke said. She looked over at her mother. "Does that name mean anything to you?"

"Never heard it before," Marie said.

Lizzie sucked loudly on her mojito. "It was a huge mystery at the time. Let's see . . . 1941? Think that's right. I say it's a murder, but actually, nobody really knows what happened to the guy. One minute he was there, at a big fancy party at Shellhaven, and the next morning, he was gone. Poof! Never seen or heard from again."

"For real?" Brooke asked.

"Absolutely. It was in all the newspapers back in the day. There was even a piece in *The Saturday Evening Post*. I found all the clippings in Grandma's scrapbooks."

"Who was this Russell Strickland?" Brooke asked. "Why was he on Talisa? How did he know Josephine?"

Lizzie took the last sip of her mojito. "He was from a wealthy family in Boston. According to the newspapers, he came down to Talisa because Josephine's family was throwing an engagement party for him and his fiancée."

"Who was his fiancée?" Marie asked.

Lizzie stared at her intently. "Her name was Mildred Everhart."

26

....

October 1941

Ruth gingerly touched one of the angry bruises on Millie's exposed upper thigh. "Did he . . . ?"

Millie reached again for the whiskey bottle and gulped. "Not this time. He was about to, but Gardiner followed us out into the garden. He saw what was happening and made Russell stop." She blinked back more tears. "Gardiner said he'd kill Russell if he didn't get off the island. And then he took me back to the house."

"You said he didn't do it *this time*," Josephine broke in. "Does that mean he'd . . ." She lowered her voice. "Has he forced himself on you before?"

Even in the moonlight, they could see Millie blush deeply. She looked away. "He only does it when he's drunk."

"When isn't he drunk?" Ruth demanded, her fists balled up as though she were about to launch a counterattack on her friend's fiancé. "You can't marry him, Millie. We won't let you, will we, girls?"

She looked to Josephine and Varina for an answer.

"No!" Josephine said.

Varina shook her head mutely, her eyes wide. She snuck another sip from the bottle of Jim Beam and this time immediately began coughing and wheezing.

"It burns!" she sputtered.

"Here, Varina," Millie said, handing the younger girl the cup of champagne. "This tastes much nicer."

Varina hesitated, then took the cup.

"Just a sip at first," Ruth suggested.

Varina took a cautious drink. "It tickles," she reported, giggling.

"Exactly," Ruth said. "That's the whole point of champagne. It's tickly and bubbly, and it makes you feel giddy."

"Even when you shouldn't," Millie added.

Varina smiled and took another sip, and then a few more. "Oooh," she said, looking up at the sky. "I'm dizzy!" She flopped backward onto the blanket. "Why you gotta marry that man?" she asked, poking Millie in the arm. "He hurt you bad, didn't he?"

Millie sighed. "You wouldn't understand, Varina. You have a father and three brothers to help take care of you. My father is dead, and Mother and I don't have any money. We have to depend on my grandmother to support us, and she's so mean about it."

Varina looked at Josephine and Ruth. "Your friends have money. Maybe they can share so you don't have to get married."

"She's right," Ruth said. "I bet if I told my father how awful Russell is, he'd help you."

"My papa would give you money too. Russell Strickland is not the only man in the world," Josephine declared.

"He's the only man in my world," Millie replied. She held out her left hand and waggled the finger upon which perched a perfect five-carat diamond solitaire. "My family is broke, girls, and that's no joke." She giggled at her rhyme.

"My mother says your granny is richer than God," Ruth scoffed.

"Ain't nobody richer than God," Varina said solemnly.

"We really are broke," Millie insisted. "Grandmama has been living on the interest of the money Granddad left her, but now that's gone, and she's dipping into capital to keep the house going. You girls know Mama sold our house last year and moved in with Grandmama. I just can't ask her to support me too."

"You could get a job," Josephine pointed out. "You're a smart girl, Millie. You always made the best grades in school."

"Doing what?" Millie scoffed. "I've never had a job in my life. I don't know how to type. I don't even have a college degree. Russell says there's no need for me to finish school, since we're getting married. And he'd never let me take a job, even if I could find one."

"You're not going to marry him," Ruth said fiercely. "We won't let you."

"Ruth is right. I don't care what we have to do, you are not going to marry Russell Strickland," Josephine said.

Millie picked up the champagne bottle and took another drink before handing the bottle to Ruth. "Let's not talk about it anymore. It's too depressing." She paused, then unfastened her bra and stepped out of her panties.

In the moonlight, the women could see the bruises on her thighs, hips, upper arms, and collarbone.

"Come on, girls. Eat, drink, and be merry, for next month I'll be married. This could be the last meeting of the High Tide Club!" She whooped loudly, then raced for the shore. Josephine shrugged and gestured at Varina.

"Come on, Varina. We can't let her swim all by herself."

Varina giggled and stood unsteadily. "Ooh. My daddy will tan my hide if he finds out I went swimming naked." She hesitated, then took off her shoes and unfastened the strap of her overalls.

"Come on in, girls," Millie called, splashing in the waves. "And bring the champagne!"

Two hours later, dressed again, the four young women lolled on the blanket, gazing up at the stars.

Varina held up the empty champagne bottle and sighed heavily. "Too bad. I sure do like the taste of that stuff."

Ruth propped herself up on an elbow and yawned. "Wonder what time it is?"

"I don't know, but I'm hungry." Varina sat up and began rummaging through the picnic hamper. She held up a sandwich and greedily wolfed it down.

"Do you think we should be getting back?" Millie asked. "It has to be after midnight."

"I don't feel like going back yet," Josephine declared. "It's our last night together before everybody leaves the island. Let's make it special."

"Yes!" Ruth agreed. "Why should we go back to the house? Let's stay out all night."

"Whoopee!" Varina chortled. "I ain't ever had a spend-the-night before."

Josephine glanced over at her young friend. "Girls, I believe Varina is officially tiddled."

"Tiddled?" Varina frowned.

"Yep," Ruth nodded. "Sloshed. Rip-roaring."

"What's that?" Varina asked, grabbing another sandwich.

"Sweetie," Millie said, "I think you're . . ."

Before she could finish the sentence, Varina grimaced. "Uh-oh." She stood and dashed toward the nearest dune, before bending over and being violently sick.

"Drunk," Josephine agreed.

Varina made it back to the blanket, where she collapsed, holding her head between both her hands. "I don't feel so good. My head is spinning."

Millie found a napkin in the basket and dabbed Varina's face with it. "Sit up," she said gently. "You'll feel better."

"It's all my fault," Millie said after Varina made two more trips to the sand dune. "I never should have given her that champagne. She's too young to drink. I feel awful that she feels so awful."

Suddenly, they saw a flash of lightning on the water, followed by the low rumble of thunder in the distance. A moment later, fat, warm raindrops splashed onto the blanket.

They all looked up at the sky, where black-tinged clouds drifted across the full moon.

Josephine swatted at a mosquito feasting on her arm. "Storm coming, girls.

I think we'd better go. And these darned skeeters are eating me alive." She pointed at Varina, who was sitting with her head buried in her hands. "But we can't take her home like this. Her father would never forgive me. He's a teetotaling Church of God preacher." She stood up and brushed the sand from her clothes.

"Should we take her back to Shellhaven?" Millie asked.

Josephine had a gleam in her eye. "I've got a better idea."

"I hope it's better than combining bourbon and champagne," Ruth said.

"We'll go to the old lighthouse. To the lighthouse keeper's cottage."

"What about the lighthouse keeper?" Millie asked. "Won't he object?"

"He's long gone. The government decommissioned the lighthouse a couple of years ago, and now the cottage is abandoned. Locked up tight."

"So how do we get in?"

Josephine grinned impishly. "I'm not supposed to know, but Gardiner keeps a key under the floor mat of the roadster. I think he used the cottage for his secret assignations."

"Assignations?" Ruth said with a hoot. "If it's such a secret, how do you happen to know about it?"

"That's easy. Like the good little girl detective I am, I followed him one night and peeped in the window."

"You didn't!" Millie said, shocked. But a moment later, she asked. "Who was he with?"

"Some silly little blond floozie that he met at a dance at the Cloister," Josephine said dismissively. "You should have heard her carrying on when Gardiner took off his shirt."

"Jo!" Millie said, shocked to her core. "You didn't actually watch!"

"Of course not," Josephine said. "There's no electricity, and Gardiner blew out the candle before things got really good." She rolled her eyes for comic effect. "But I sure could hear those old bedsprings squeaking."

"You're awful," Millie said, tossing the napkin at her best friend.

"Awfully resourceful, you mean." Josephine began gathering up the picnic hamper. Raindrops began to pelt them, and the wind picked up. "Ruth, Millie, I'll get the blanket, and you girls had better help Varina to the car."

"We're going for a car ride?" Varina asked, rousing herself. "Whoopee!"

. . .

"Hold the flashlight, Millie, so I can see." Josephine handed the flashlight to her friend while she fumbled with the old-fashioned skeleton key.

"Hurry up," Ruth whispered, trying to crowd closer to the door. "We're getting soaked!"

"Ta-da!" Josephine turned the rusted knob, and the heavy wooden door swung slowly inward. She stepped inside, gestured for the others to follow, and they all heard something scurry across the wooden floor.

"Rats!" Millie squealed. "I'm not staying here."

"Probably just a possum or a raccoon," Josephine said, putting on a brave face.

Varina made a show of holding her nose. "It stinks in here."

"Don't be so prissy." Josephine took the flashlight and swept it around the room.

The beam revealed a single large room. A makeshift kitchen with a sink, a propane stove, and an ancient icebox stood against the front wall. The room was sparsely furnished with a wooden table and two chairs, a davenport with cotton stuffing erupting from its cushions, and a large brass bed haphazardly covered with a faded cotton quilt. The wooden floor had a thick coating of cobwebs, leaves, and long-dead insects.

A small brick fireplace stood opposite the bed, and its hearth was littered with twigs, leaves, and bits of sofa stuffing, indicating that an animal had made a nest in the chimney.

Josephine hurried over to the window above the sink and, with effort, managed to raise the sash. She did the same with three other windows, and a tattered curtain remnant at the kitchen window fluttered faintly in the breeze coming off the ocean.

"See? Much better."

"Can you turn on the lights?" Millie asked, creeping closer.

"I could, but it won't do any good. There isn't any electricity anymore," Josephine said.

"How about plumbing?" Ruth asked. "I really need to pee."

"Me too," Millie echoed.

Josephine turned on the kitchen faucet and after a moment, a thin stream of rusty water trickled into the sink. She pointed to an open doorway in the far corner of the room. "It should be okay. At least we have water. I think the bathroom's over there."

Ruth hurried over and gave the toilet a test flush. "Hooray!" she called. "Good thing I can't see what this commode looks like."

"I'm next," Millie said.

Varina sank down onto the bed and wrapped thin arms around her abdomen. "I don't like this place," she whispered. "It's spooky."

"You don't have to whisper," Josephine pointed out. "It's just us. And anyway, my papa owns this cottage, so it's not like we're really trespassing." She sat down beside the younger girl and put a protective arm around her shoulder.

They heard the toilet flush again, and the rusty water pipes groaned when the faucet was turned on. Millie emerged from the bathroom carrying a damp cloth, which she placed on the back of Varina's neck.

"Better?" she asked. She sat down beside Josephine and Varina, and the three of them laughed out loud when the bedsprings loudly protested.

"But where will we all sleep?" Ruth asked. "Is there another bed?"

"Nope. Just this one, although if you want the sofa, be my guest."

Ruth glanced at the ripped stuffing and shuddered. "No, thanks."

At Millie's insistence, they stripped the sagging mattress from the bed and turned it over. Then they all took turns sponging the salt spray off themselves in the bathroom's claw-foot bathtub.

When Josephine returned from her makeshift bath, she found that Millie had managed to find a broom, sweep the floor, and remake the bed using the coverlet as a bottom sheet and their blanket as a bedspread.

"Well, Millie, you really are going to make somebody a wonderful wife someday," Josephine said.

"Just not that bastard Russell Strickland," Ruth added.

The four of them crowded onto the bed, and Josephine switched off the flashlight.

"This isn't so bad," Millie said after a long yawn. "Remember, we used to do this all the time when we were at boarding school and I was so afraid of the thunderstorms."

"What I remember is that Jo snores worse than my grandpa," Ruth said drowsily.

"And you had terrible gas," Josephine retorted. "And Millie likes to talk in her sleep."

Varina giggled in the darkness.

"This'll probably be the last time we get to do something like this," Millie said, sounding wistful. "Once I'm married . . ."

"You are not marrying him," Jo said. "And we would never forget about you."

"I ain't ever getting married," Varina said.

"Sure you will," Millie answered. "Not right away, of course. But someday you'll find some nice boy and get married and have the sweetest babies ever."

"No, ma'am," Varina said forcefully. "I ain't ever gonna let some bad man beat up on me or drink too much or tell me what to do. Someday, I'm gonna get off this island, and I'm gonna get me a job and have me a house of my very own."

She expected an argument from the others, but after a moment, all she heard was a low rumbling snore emanating from Josephine on the far side of the bed. Varina closed her eyes tightly and turned on her side, toward the wall. She felt Millie's slight body, spooning into her back, heard her mutter something incoherent.

She heard the rain pelting the tin roof and saw flashes of lightning through the windows. The wind picked up and the curtains danced. She pulled the edge of the quilt over her eyes and burrowed deeper into the lumpy mattress.

The last thing Varina heard before drifting off to sleep herself was a faint *phhhhhht* coming from Ruth, who was stretched out between Josephine and Millie. She giggled softly.

27

....

Marie whipped her head around to stare at Lizzie. "What do you mean? Are you saying my mother was engaged to marry this man who just vanished?"

"According to the old newspaper accounts my grandmother saved, yes," Lizzie said calmly.

"That's impossible." Marie shook her head. "I've never even heard of this Russell . . . what did you say his name was?"

"Strickland. I can't believe this is news to you. It was a really big story back in the day."

Brooke reached over and touched her mother's hand. "That must be the man Josephine told me about. She said his name was Russell. Granny never said anything at all? About being engaged to somebody before she married Pops?"

"Never," Marie said. "In fact, after Pops died, I teased her once, saying she should find another husband. She was so young to be a widow, only in her forties, and so pretty too. She got really angry at me for even suggesting such a thing. I can still remember what she said. 'I had one true love—and he's gone. That's enough for one woman.'"

"So . . . is it possible she was talking about Russell Strickland and not Pops?" Brooke asked.

Marie didn't hesitate. "No. Mama was devoted to Pops. As he was to her."

"Maybe your mother just felt uncomfortable talking about this guy," Lizzie suggested. "That generation—your mother's and my grandmother's—could be pretty stoic. Or in denial. Or both. Take my dad. It was clear to anybody who met him that he had issues. I mean, he once set fire to my grandma's Cadillac when she wouldn't give him the keys—this after he showed up at her house, at nine in the morning, stoned out of his gourd. But she never once admitted that he might be an addict."

"Well, this certainly puts a whole intriguing new light on our trip to Talisa," Marie said.

The desk clerk at the Seafarer Motel looked at Lizzie Quinlan and then pointedly at the cat carrier she'd placed on the counter at the reception desk.

"Sorry, Miss, uh, Quinlan. But we don't allow cats."

Lizzie's eyes narrowed. "Dweezil is not just a cat. She's a certified emotional therapy support pet." She slapped an envelope on the counter. "Here's her registration from the California secretary of state's office."

The clerk ignored the envelope. "Ma'am? This is Georgia. And it's management policy. No cats, no dogs, no ferrets. No pets of any kind."

"Policy?" Lizzie shrieked. "Is your policy posted on your website? Is it posted on the property? I don't see any signs."

Brooke stepped up to the counter to intercede. "Can you recommend any of the other local hotels that do accept pets? It's just two nights."

He shook his head and pointed out the lobby's plate glass window, where knots of gaudily costumed adults dressed up in pirate garb strolled past on the sidewalk. "I guess you could try the Happy Wanderer. Myrtice, the owner, is a crazy cat lady. But you know, it's Buccaneer Ball weekend, and every hotel in town has been booked for months. We're all pretty slammed."

Dweezil yowled her annoyance.

"What the hell is a Buccaneer Ball?" Lizzie asked.

Brooke slapped her forehead. "I'd totally forgotten that was this weekend. It's a local festival. A big tourism draw. Grown men and women dress up as pirates and wenches and take turns invading each other. There's even a big parade."

Lizzie gave Brooke a winning smile. "Maybe I could stay with you. As you say, it's only two nights."

"I'm so sorry," Brooke said. "I have a tiny two-bedroom cottage, and I share it with my three-year-old son."

"A kid? Never mind. I don't do kids," Lizzie said quickly.

"And Mom is already sleeping on my sofa," Brooke added.

Lizzie's shoulders sagged as she gathered up the cat carrier and her rolling suitcase. "I guess it's Shellhaven and Talisa, then," she said, heading for the door.

"I'll call Louette and let her know to expect an overnight guest," Brooke said.

C. D. took Lizzie's suitcase and stowed it in the bow locker. "Y'all having some kind of a convention over on the island? This is the third boatload I've had today."

"Third?" Brooke asked. "I know Felicia and Varina were going over this morning, but who else have you taken to Talisa today?"

"That other lawyer fella," C. D. said, casting off the lines and easing the boat away from the pier. "Louette called me first thing this morning to tell me to pick him up. Wasn't even daylight."

"Lawyer? You mean Gabe Wynant?"

"Yup," C. D. said. He gestured toward Lizzie, who was clutching the pet carrier with both hands. Inside, despite having shared a tranquilizer with her owner, Dweezil yowled loudly and pitched herself against the carrier's sides. "A cat, huh?"

"Good guess," Lizzie said coldly.

C. D. stretched his neck to see inside the carrier. "Wow. That's one pretty kitty. Never seen one like that before."

"She's a Maine coon cat," Lizzie said, preening just a little. "She was actually cover kitten of the July 2015 issue of *Cat Fancier*."

"Have to check that out," C. D. said as the boat puttered away from the city dock.

Lizzie looked over at Brooke. "Wynant. Is he the lawyer who's making Josephine's new will?"

"That's right," Brooke said. "He was my boss at the law firm I worked at in Savannah."

"Why don't you just draw up the will yourself?" Lizzie asked.

"I thought the same thing, but Brooke can't do it because of me being involved in the trust," Marie explained. "It's a conflict of interest."

"Who are the other two women he took over earlier?" Lizzie asked.

"Varina Shaddix is the only other surviving member of the High Tide Club, and Felicia is her great-niece," Brooke said. "Varina's Geechee, and as a young girl, she worked for the Bettendorf family."

"What's a Geechee?" Lizzie wanted to know.

"They're called that, for the Ogeechee River, which is one of the big tidal rivers in South Georgia," Marie said. "In South Carolina, they're called Gullah."

"The Geechees are the descendants of the slaves who were brought to Talisa from West Africa," Brooke added. "Varina's family, the Shaddixes, have lived at Oyster Bluff, in that settlement, for generations."

"So this Varina, she was black, and yet she was friends with Josephine and Millie and Ruth? Wasn't that kind of unusual? This being the South and all?" Lizzie asked.

Brooke shrugged. "Josephine's an unusual woman. Very conservative, politically, but on the other hand, she's deeply concerned about the environment and keeping Talisa from being developed. She said she and her friends regarded Varina as a sort of little sister, because she was five years younger."

"Even so, that puts her in her midnineties," Lizzie observed. "Does she still work for Josephine?"

"Not anymore. After she retired from her job in Jacksonville, she got homesick and moved back to Talisa and worked for Josephine in some capacity, but she currently lives with her great-niece Felicia, who's become her caregiver."

"What's Felicia like?" Marie asked, gazing back toward the rapidly disappearing waterfront.

"Very smart and polished. She's a PhD, teaches African American studies. A little prickly, maybe. She's convinced Josephine has taken advantage of her Auntie Vee her entire life."

"And has she?" Lizzie asked.

"Not for me to say," Brooke said with a shrug. "I can tell you Josephine feels genuine affection for Varina. But there's something else, something she obviously feels guilty about in her relationship with all these women."

"Any idea what it is?" Marie asked.

"Wait until you meet her," Brooke said. "Josephine Warrick is not somebody who easily relinquishes her secrets."

Twenty minutes later, they were within sight of the island when the boat's motor sputtered, coughed, and quit.

"Sheeeuttt," C. D. muttered under his breath. The cigarillo fell from his lips onto the floor, but he didn't seem to notice.

"What's wrong?" Lizzie said. "Why'd we stop?"

"Mechanical difficulties," C. D. said. He switched the key in the ignition, and the engine turned over for a moment, then died again. His second and third attempts to start the motor achieved the same result.

"Damn it." He stood and yanked the cover from the outboard, fiddling and cursing for a full five minutes as the boat fell and rose gently with the tide.

"Don't tell me we're stuck out here," Lizzie said, sounding panicky. She wrapped her arms protectively around the cat carrier.

"Naw, it's probably just a fouled spark plug," C. D. said. He opened the door to the stern locker, reached in, and rummaged around but came up empty.

"Damn it." He stood with his hands on his narrow hips as the boat rocked up and down. The sun beat down on the three women who stared expectantly at their captain. The drug-addled cat mewed loudly, thrashing against the sides of the carrier.

"Now what?" Even Brooke felt a tiny prickle of anxiety. They could see the faint green outline of the island, just tantalizingly out of reach.

The old man sighed heavily and went back to the locker, finally extracting a long wooden oar.

"Now we paddle." He nodded at Lizzie, still seated on the bow. "You might wanna move, ma'am."

For the next thirty minutes, C. D., standing on the bow like a Viking boatman, poled the craft in the direction of the island. The tide and the current aided somewhat, but sweat drenched his shirt, and he finally took it off, using it to mop his gleaming face. His bare chest was sun-blackened, the skin as saggy and leathery as a saddlebag, with patches of kinky white chest hair. His damp pants hung limply on his hips, and he panted with exertion as the boat inched toward his target. Brooke worried that he might keel over at any minute, and from the worried look on her mother's face, she knew Marie was thinking the same thing.

A hundred yards from the dock, the wind died, and their progress slowed dramatically. "Tide's changed," C. D. said grimly. "Can't fight this current."

Without another word, he set the oar down, removed a timeworn billfold and a box of cigarillos from his hip pocket, and tucked it into the glove box.

Then he jumped into the water. Dogpaddling, he called to Brooke, "Throw me that bow line, would ya?"

"What are you doing?" Lizzie cried. "There are sharks in this river. I read all about it. Get back here immediately!"

"Gonna walk it in," C. D. said calmly, standing on the shallow river bottom. "Unless you know a better way."

"Call somebody," Lizzie ordered.

"Like who?"

"I don't know. The police. The Coast Guard. Get them to send a helicopter."

He chuckled. "My phone's dead. Anyway, we ain't out in the open ocean, and this don't count as no life-threatening emergency. Ain't nobody gonna send a helicopter over here when we're just a hundred yards from the island. You ladies just sit tight."

As they watched, he tied the bow rope around his narrow waist and proceeded to do as he'd promised, walking the boat, at an agonizingly slow pace, toward the island. When they finally reached the dock, he tossed the line to Brooke. "See if you can tie us up to that piling," he instructed. "Then tip the outboard back into the water so I can climb up on the prop."

Five minutes later, the old man hauled himself up into the boat. He lay panting on the fiberglass floor, as dark and wet as an oversized otter.

Then, with effort, he heaved himself to his feet. "Goddamn, I need a drink."

"Me too," Marie said weakly.

Louette stood next to the red pickup truck, squinting into the sun. When she saw the boat arrive at the dock, she ran out to the end. "What happened?" she called. "I've been waiting here for an hour. I could see you out there, but there was nothing I could do."

"Engine conked out on me," C. D. replied. "Where's Shug?"

"He took the ferry into town to pick up Miss Josephine's medicine after I tried to call you but didn't get an answer."

"Phone's dead," C. D. said.

"Is Josephine okay?" Brooke asked, climbing out of the boat.

"Last night wasn't a good one," Louette said. "The doctor called in something stronger for the pain."

"Oh, my," Marie said quietly. "Will she feel well enough to see us?"

"Louette, this is my mom, Marie," Brooke said before climbing into the bed of the pickup. "And this is Lizzie. Her grandmother Ruth was one of Josephine's best friends."

"Nice to meet you ladies," Louette said. "Just slide up here on the front seat with me, if you don't mind being a little close for a few minutes. As for Miss Josephine, she's got herself set on seeing you no matter what. It's all she's talked about for days now."

She started the truck's engine, waved goodbye to C. D., who was tinkering with the outboard motor, and started off down the road toward Shellhaven.

28

....

L ouette pulled the truck up to the front door at Shellhaven, and Marie, and then Lizzie, cat carrier in hand, hopped out.

"What a dump!" Lizzie exclaimed, looking up at the crumbling pink mansion. "The pictures made it look a lot nicer."

"I think it's beautiful," Marie said, looking over her shoulder at Brooke, who'd climbed out of the truck bed. "Didn't you say a famous architect designed it?"

"Addison Mizner," Brooke said. "Very famous, especially for the homes he designed in Palm Beach and Miami."

Louette stood motionless by the side of the truck, her usually cheerful, round face lined with worry.

Brooke walked over to her. "What's wrong, Louette?"

The older woman shook her head mutely.

"Where are the others?" Lizzie asked, pausing between taking photos of the house with her cell phone.

"Varina wanted to show Felicia her old house at Oyster Bluff, so Mr. Wynant drove them over there in my truck," Louette said. "They ought to be back pretty soon."

"I want to see that old slave settlement and the site of the plantation," Lizzie said. "But first, Dweezil needs to stretch her legs." She set the carrier down on the ground, and the cat bolted out, streaking across the lawn.

"Dweez!" Lizzie cried, taking off after her. Marie followed right behind.

Brooke pulled Louette aside. "Louette? What's wrong?"

"It's Josephine. She fired me and Shug."

"What? That can't be true."

"Yes, ma'am." Louette nodded for emphasis.

"But why? How? She can't mean it. She wouldn't fire you."

"But she did. I told you, she hasn't been sleeping; the pain's been so bad. So last night, I called up her doctor and told him he needed to give her something stronger. Which he agreed was the thing to do. What I didn't know was, somehow, Miss Josephine managed to get herself up out of bed and come looking for me in the kitchen. She heard me talking on the phone."

"Uh-oh," Brooke said.

"I've never seen her so mad. She said I had no cause to go messing in her private business and calling her doctor behind her back. She yelled at me and carried on so bad, she had me crying. Called me names nobody ever called me. Then, Shug came in, and he heard the ruckus, and when he tried to stand up for me, she took after him too!" Louette bit her lip and blinked back tears. "Finally, Shug told her if she felt that way about us, we would just quit, and she could get somebody else to work for her."

"Oh no," Brooke moaned.

"That's when Josephine said we couldn't quit, because we were fired. And then she said, 'Oh yeah, I changed my mind too, and I'm not gonna give y'all back Oyster Bluff, after all.'" Louette burst into tears.

Brooke hesitated, then folded her arms around Louette's bulky shoulders. The older woman heaved with every sob. After a moment or two, she pulled away, obviously embarrassed by her outburst.

"I'm sorry," she said, taking a neatly pressed handkerchief from the pocket of her white uniform. "I didn't mean to be such a crybaby. I know Josephine's only acting this way 'cause she's old and sick and hurtin', but I just don't understand how she could be so ugly to me."

"I don't understand it either," Brooke said.

"I'm still sleeping in that room next to hers, and I hear her at night, she can't hardly breathe right, and she's not sleeping, and that's why I called the doctor. He told me there's no reason she needs to be in pain, so close to . . . you know. Her time."

"You absolutely did the right thing," Brooke said. "And I don't care how sick Josephine is. There is no excuse for this kind of behavior. You and Shug would certainly be justified in quitting, if that's what you want."

"Shug wants us to go. We've got money saved. We could go someplace like Brunswick and buy us a little house for our own. He can work anywhere, and he wants me to retire. But I don't know what I'd do if I wasn't working." Louette sniffed. "And then what happens to her?" She jerked her head in the direction of the house. "She can't take care of herself. She don't know how to cook, and she's weak as a kitten. Who'll stay here and look after her if we leave?"

"We caught her!" Lizzie emerged from a thicket of overgrown azaleas on the north side of the house, clutching the errant cat. "Jesus, I need a drink!"

Marie was close behind. She frowned when she saw Louette's distress. "Everything okay here?"

Brooke took a deep breath and tried to swallow the anger bubbling up from her gut. "It will be," she said. "Louette, I know Josephine thinks she fired you, but could you please take Lizzie and my mom to the kitchen and give them something cold to drink? It was pretty hot out there on the water today."

"Of course. I should have offered that as soon as we got here," Louette said. She opened the front door. "Y'all come in and get out of this heat."

"And I'll go speak to Josephine and get this firing thing straightened out," Brooke said.

She found Josephine dozing in her recliner. Her face was paler than it had been, her lips cracked and bloodless. There were deep purplish circles under her eyes. Her mouth was ajar, and she snored softly, as did the two Chihuahuas who were cradled in her lap. As soon as Brooke approached, both dogs scrambled to their feet, instantly alert and on the defensive.

"Hi, girls," Brooke whispered. She reached out and touched each dog's head. Then she pulled a wooden chair closer to the recliner, sat down, and stared at her client.

Josephine's red-rimmed eyes opened slowly. She coughed violently, and when she could finally catch her breath, she spoke with difficulty.

"Teeny and Tiny must be used to you now," she said, wheezing. "They didn't even whimper when you came into the room."

Brooke was so angry she didn't trust herself to speak at first. "Why are you so hateful?" she blurted.

"Me?"

"You. Hateful, cruel, spiteful, ungrateful. How could you treat Shug and Louette the way you did?"

Josephine coughed again. "She had no right—"

"She had every right," Brooke interjected. "Unlike you, Louette is a good, kindhearted person. She has empathy for others, which is a quality you were seemingly born without. Louette saw that you were suffering, and she tried to do something about it. And for that you fired her and threatened to take away her home? I can't even deal with you, Josephine."

Josephine struggled to catch her breath between words. "Louette knows I didn't mean it."

"No, she doesn't. And here's the irony. It's not herself she's concerned about. She's worried about who'll take care of you when she and Shug are gone."

"No . . . no," Josephine protested. "I didn't mean it. I was upset. The doctor wants me to take more pain pills. I don't want them. They make everything fuzzy. Make me so groggy I can't think straight. And I need to be able to think."

She closed her eyes, and Brooke thought she'd drowsed off again.

But Josephine was only gathering strength. "Where is everybody? Did you bring them? I need to see them. Tell them to come here. Right now."

"No."

Josephine blinked. "What's that?"

"I said no. Something you're not used to hearing. I'm not going to enable your cruelty and bullying. Either you apologize to Louette and take back everything you said to her, including the part about you not giving back the land and homes at Oyster Bluff, or I quit."

Josephine coughed so violently the dogs jumped from her lap and began barking at Brooke, their mistress's tormentor.

"That's blackmail," she wheezed.

"Sue me," Brooke said, folding her arms across her chest.

"Louette," the old woman croaked. She raised her voice. "Louette, damn it! I need you."

Gabe Wynant sat at the table in the kitchen, squeezing lemon into a tall glass of iced tea, surrounded by the women who'd been called to gather on the island. They were all drinking tea and laughing and munching on pale iced cookies from a platter in the center of the table.

Lizzie's and Marie's faces were pink with sunburn, and Brooke realized she too had gotten burned during their breakdown on the trip to the island.

"What's so funny?" Brooke felt like a party crasher. "What'd I miss?"

"Varina was telling us about the first time she tried to bake these cookies," Gabe said, biting into one, ignoring the crumbs scattering across his shirtfront.

"In a wood-burning stove in their family's cabin—which didn't even have electricity until after the war," Lizzie added. "How is that even possible in the twentieth century?"

"Wouldn't have made a difference," Varina said with a chuckle. "This tea cake recipe—my mama had it written down on a piece of paper in her Bible, but I couldn't read her handwriting too good. Where it said to put in a quarter teaspoon of salt, I did four teaspoons! My daddy said those tea cakes weren't hardly fit to feed to the hogs."

Marie broke off a portion of one of the cookies and nibbled at the edge. "These are delicious. I wouldn't mind having this recipe myself."

"Louette got all the cooking talent in this family," Varina said. "I never did learn how."

"But I thought all Southern women were great cooks," Lizzie said.

"Not me," Varina said. "I wanted to be a career girl. My daddy used to fuss that I'd never catch a husband if I couldn't cook, but I didn't care."

"She's doing good to open a can of soup," Felicia said fondly.

Gabe cocked his head in the direction of the library. "Louette seems pretty upset. What's going on?"

"Josephine threw a conniption fit last night because Louette called her doctor without her permission. She threatened to fire both Louette and Shug. From what Louette told me, I wouldn't blame them if they both left her high and dry," Brooke said.

"Oh no," Varina said quickly. "Louette wouldn't do that to Josephine. Her being so sick. She would never."

"Oh noooo," Felicia said, her tone mocking. "Couldn't leave missy in the big house to take care of herself."

"Hush now," Varina said fiercely.

Lizzie looked around the homey kitchen with interest, taking in the outdated appliances, the worn linoleum, and the water-stained plaster ceiling. "As rich as Josephine is, I can't believe how shabby this place is." She pointed at the open kitchen window. "No air-conditioning? It's barbaric. How do people stand it?"

"That air-conditioning isn't healthy," Varina said. "Poisons your lungs. Good fresh air is what people need."

"Not me," Lizzie declared. "The air here is as thick as a swamp. Give me air-conditioning any day. That and a shot of tequila. Which reminds me. Wonder where the old lady keeps her liquor?"

Louette bustled back into the kitchen with a wan smile, dabbing at her eyes. "What kind of liquor do you want?" She opened a pantry door and sorted through cans and bottles with faded labels that looked like something out of a museum. "We got gin and vodka." She held up a bottle with a brown label. "Wild Turkey. Will this do?"

Lizzie took the bottle from her hand and studied the contents. "It's not tequila, but it'll do. You do have ice cubes, right?"

Brooke glanced at the kitchen clock. It was already after three. "As soon as everybody's finished their ice tea, I think we need to meet with Josephine. It's late, and I promised my babysitter I'd be back by six."

Louette looked startled. "Josephine said y'all are spending the night. I got all the guest rooms cleaned and ready."

"Can't," Brooke insisted. "I've got a three-year-old at home."

"I haven't heard from C. D. about the boat motor being fixed yet," Louette said.

"Can you call him?"

Louette turned to a black rotary phone mounted on the wall beside the pantry and started to dial. "I'll try calling him, but if I know C. D., it won't do no good."

"My God, it's like being in medieval times around here," Lizzie muttered.

"Right?" Felicia agreed. "Time-warp city."

"Went right to voice mail," Louette said, hanging up the receiver. She took a set of keys from a hook by the back door. "I'll be right back."

"What happens if the boat's not fixed?" Marie asked. "Can somebody else on the island give us a ride back to the mainland?"

"There's the ferry," Louette said. "Last trip of the night is six thirty."

29

Brooke felt odd being the one to usher the others through Shellhaven. Lizzie and Felicia gaped at the disused rooms as they made their way to the library.

"It's like Miss Havisham's dining room in *Great Expectations*," Lizzie murmured.

"All it lacks is a moldy wedding cake," Felicia agreed.

Marie cast an appraising eye at the furnishings, tsk-tsking at the state of decay. "What a shame." She sighed, running a hand over the dining room table whose mahogany top was cloudy and freckled with grayish mildew. "This was once a gorgeous antique piece. It would probably sell for over ten thousand in an antique shop in Savannah. But the finish is ruined."

Brooke looked up and saw that the plaster ceiling around the chandelier had sustained water damage, leaving crumbling plaster and exposed lathe.

"Mmm-hmm." Varina clucked her tongue in agreement. "Louette does her best, but this house is too big for one woman. Time she gets one room cleaned, the next one is about to fall in."

"Louette?" Josephine called from the library. "Where is everybody?"

. . .

The old woman's dark eyes gleamed with barely suppressed excitement as Brooke ushered them into the library. In just the few minutes since she'd last seen Josephine, a transformation had taken place. She'd removed the knit cap and was wearing the bouffant wig again. Bright lipstick made a vivid slash across her pale face, and she'd changed into a rumpled periwinkle-blue dress that had probably last seen the light of day during the Johnson administration.

"Hello," Josephine said as the women filed into the room with Gabe trailing behind. She pointed at the semicircle of straight-back chairs, which had been dragged in from the dining room. "Please, sit. Did Louette give you something to drink?"

"Sure did," Varina said, taking the chair next to her oldest friend. "Fixed us cookies too." She grasped Josephine's hands in hers. "I been praying for you," she said softly.

Josephine started to say something, but Brooke caught her eye and subtly shook her head. "Thank you," she said simply.

Brooke made the introductions, and Josephine silently studied the newcomers' faces.

"Thank you all for coming," she rasped.

"What do you want?" Felicia asked abruptly.

Varina gave her great-niece a disapproving look.

"What's that?" Josephine was clearly taken aback.

Felicia leaned in and raised her voice. "I said, what do you want from us?" She gestured at Varina, Lizzie, and Marie. "Why are we here?"

"Want? I don't want anything. I want to give you all the most precious thing I own. This house. This island."

"But why us?" Lizzie crossed and uncrossed her legs. "You never spoke to my grandmother again after the '72 election. You don't know anything about me or the rest of my family. Why give me anything?"

Josephine didn't seem put off by the younger woman's brashness. "You're Ruth, made over. Aren't you? Not in looks, of course. She was much prettier.

All that glorious red hair. But personality-wise, you've definitely got her DNA. Her spunk. You're a fighter. I like that."

"And what about me?" Marie asked. "Brooke tells me you seem to think there's something you need to make amends for with us." She gestured at the women sitting in the semicircle, with Josephine at the center.

Josephine was studying Marie. "You're very like her, you know. Your mother had a quiet beauty. She radiated sweetness. I don't mean to say she was a pushover. But there was a gentleness that drew people to her. Ruth and I . . . I don't know how she put up with the two of us. We were bossy, brassy. Opinionated."

"Ha!" Varina chuckled. "Opinionated. You two sure were. But Millie? My goodness. She was an angel to me." Varina glanced over at Felicia. "You know, Millie gave me my first pair of high-heel shoes. Pink satin with rhinestone buckles and ankle straps. I was only fourteen, but I thought I was real grown up. They were the prettiest pair of shoes I ever owned. And Millie gave them to *me*." She tapped her chest with pride.

"High heels with rhinestone buckles? On this island?" Felicia looked dubious. "You, Auntie Vee?"

Her great-aunt looked down at her feet, shod today in sensible beige crepe-soled walking shoes. "I didn't always wear ugly old-lady shoes, you know. I used to spend *all* my folding money on stylish shoes. Back when I was working for the railroad, if it was payday, I was going straight to the shoe store."

"Whatever happened to those shoes, Auntie? Do you still have them?"

Varina's face clouded. "No, child. I . . . lost 'em. Wore them that one time and never saw them again."

While Varina spoke, Josephine struggled to pull herself to an upright position in the recliner, ignoring the dogs on her lap, her eyes riveted on Varina, her face tense. Her breathing was raspy and irregular, and Brooke panicked for a moment. Should she call the doctor?

Teeny, or was it Tiny? Whichever one it was whined softly and delicately licked Josephine's chin, which seemed to relax her.

Brooke relaxed a little too, and sitting back, she spotted Gabe out of the corner of her eye. He'd seated himself in a distant corner of the room, and he was doing the same thing, his eyes darting back and forth between his client and Varina.

What did he know that she didn't? Had he drawn up the new will Josephine requested? Surely, that's why he was here. But she hadn't had time since they'd arrived on the island to pull him aside and inquire.

"You still haven't told us what you want from us," Marie reminded her hostess.

Josephine was still staring at Varina. "Forgiveness."

"What did you do that was so unforgiveable?" Lizzie asked.

Josephine folded her hands in her lap. "It was a long time ago. I've spent nearly seventy years trying to put it out of my mind. And now I'm dying, and it seems the chickens have come home to roost."

"Does it have anything to do with that man? The one who disappeared at the party here on Talisa—back in 1941?" Lizzie asked.

What little blood remained in Josephine's face seemed to drain away in the blink of an eye. "How do you know about that?"

She turned to Varina. "We all swore. We took an oath. Did Ruth say something?"

"Relax," Lizzie said. "Granny never mentioned it. But she kept a scrapbook. She clipped all the newspaper articles about the disappearance of . . . what was his name again?"

"Russell Strickland." As Josephine whispered the name, she reached over and briefly clutched Varina's hand.

"Right." Lizzie snapped her fingers. "Russell Strickland. Big mystery back in the day. There was even a story in *The Saturday Evening Post*. Granny pasted that in the scrapbook too. Along with some photos of three girls dressed up in fancy evening gowns. I'm guessing it was Granny, Millie, and you."

Josephine pressed her lips together and said nothing.

"Was this man actually engaged to my mother?" Marie asked. "Is it really true?"

Josephine's chest heaved and fell. She coughed, covered her mouth with her hand, and finally grabbed an inhaler from the table beside her chair and took two puffs.

"It was a mistake," she said when she'd regained her breath. "He was all wrong for Millie. A dreadful man. We tried to get her to break it off."

Brooke was intrigued. "What was so awful about him? And if all of you hated him, why would she agree to marry the guy?"

"She had no choice," Josephine said. "Millie's father . . ." She nodded at Marie. "Your maternal grandfather lost everything in the stock market crash in '29. He took his own life not long after that."

Marie looked shocked. "I didn't know."

"It was hushed up. I doubt Millie ever knew the truth. My papa told me, strictly in confidence. But Millie's mother was destitute. They had no money and were dependent on her grandmother."

Josephine continued with her story, meeting Marie's gaze as she spoke. "Your maternal grandmother's people, the Prestons, still had money and a certain position in Boston society." She smiled ruefully. "We all did. Our families— mine, Ruth's, Millie's—were what people called *robber barons*. We weren't Rockefeller or Vanderbilt wealthy, nothing as showy as that . . ."

"Oh, I don't know," Lizzie drawled. "I'd say owning your own private island is pretty damn showy."

"Touché," Josephine said. "Anyway, after her father died, Millie's mother and grandmother were determined that she would make a brilliant marriage. Russell Strickland's people—his grandfather, that is—owned banks, railroads, a seat on the New York Stock Exchange."

"In other words, he was mega-rich," Felicia said.

"I suppose." Josephine tugged the afghan on her lap, drawing it up to her shoulders. The room was suffocating, with only the box fan droning away in an open window, and everybody except the hostess dabbed at the perspiration on their faces.

"She met Russell at Ruth's coming-out party in Newport." Josephine's lips twisted into a bitter smile. "He cut quite the figure in white tie and tails. He was tall and rangy. Broad shoulders, dark hair, and the most arresting deep blue eyes. What we used to call *matinee idol looks*. He had buckets of money, and he threw it around like it was water. Anyway, he swept Millie off her feet— or rather, he swept Millie's mother and grandmother off *their* feet."

Marie's brow puckered. "He doesn't sound like Mama's type at all."

"No. Forgive me, dear Marie, but he was rich, which meant that he was your grandmother's type. By then, Millie had dropped out of college. Her mother didn't see the point of spending money on educating a girl, and anyway, Russell was in hot pursuit."

Felicia fanned herself with her hands and yawned. "Can we cut to the chase, please? Like, how did this Russell Strickland just up and disappear?"

Josephine fixed Varina's great-niece with an icy glare. "I was getting to that."

"Russell proposed, and Millie accepted," Josephine said. "At first, Ruth and I were happy for her. But then, the more we saw of him, the less we liked. He was loud and could be very intimidating. He was so possessive of Millie. Jealous, especially of her friendship with us, and he drank too much. And when he drank, he was mean. *Abusive*, we'd call it now.

"The wedding was set for November. Of 1941. Ruth and I were to be bridesmaids. Papa was so fond of Millie. He thought we should give an engagement party for her. Here on the island."

"Not back in Boston?" Lizzie asked.

"No. My mother had passed away the previous year, and Papa was devastated. He loved Talisa and spent as much time here as possible, especially after Mama was gone. So we planned the party. We brought in an orchestra from Jacksonville and the best caterer in Atlanta. It was the social event of the season. White orchids and gardenias flown in from Miami. The ballroom looked like a fairy tale."

"There's a ballroom?" Felicia asked incredulously. "Here?"

Josephine seemed not to have heard her. "Millie looked so beautiful that night. She had a couture gown, flowers in her hair. We all had new dresses." She looked over at Varina and smiled. "Even Varina."

"Oh yes," Varina said dreamily. "Josephine gave me a dress, pink, the nicest thing I'd ever owned. And Millie gave me those pretty shoes to match."

"You were invited to the party?" Felicia looked dubious. "In the Jim Crow South? In 1941?"

"Not exactly," Varina said.

"We wanted her to come, but my father thought it wasn't the right thing," Josephine said. "Remember, she was only fourteen at the time."

"And black," Felicia said.

"I was getting paid to work in the kitchen that night," Varina said. "But the girls, they knew what a special night it was for all of us, and they wanted me to be all dressed up, to be a part of it."

"Before Cinderella's coach turned into a pumpkin," Felicia said caustically.

Brooke glanced down at her watch. It was getting late, and Josephine's narrative about the party was close to being derailed. She needed to nudge things along.

"What happened at the party?" she asked.

"Russell had been drinking all night with his fraternity brothers who'd come down for the party. And not just champagne. They were out on the veranda, passing a flask around. Poor Millie, he never even danced with her. She was a wallflower at her own engagement party. So Papa asked Gardiner, my brother, to dance with her. It was totally harmless. Gardiner had known Millie for years. She was like a kid sister to him. Unfortunately, Russell came into the ballroom, saw them dancing together, and there was an incident."

"You mean, like a fight?" Lizzie was clearly intrigued.

"Not there in the ballroom. Even Russell Strickland wasn't that gauche. He said something to Gardiner—I couldn't hear what—then he grabbed Millie by the arm and dragged her out of the ballroom."

"Poor Mama," Marie said. "She must have been terrified."

30

....

There was a soft knock at the library door, then Louette poked her head inside. "Miss Josephine, sorry to interrupt, but I need to let these ladies know that I finally tracked down C. D. He says the water pump on the boat motor is broke."

"What does that mean?" Brooke asked. From the expression on Louette's face, Brooke had a feeling that this was not good news.

"Too late to do anything about it today. He'll have to go on up to Brunswick tomorrow to try to get a new one," Louette said.

Brooke glanced again at her watch. It was nearly five o'clock. "If he can't take us back to the mainland, can we take the ferry?"

"Afraid not. I called the office, and they said the whole boat is booked with some folks who've been up at the conference center for a two-day corporate retreat. Not even a single seat is available."

"Is there another boat on the island—one we could charter to take us back?" Gabe asked, half standing.

"Not one you'd want to get on," Louette said. "A few folks at Oyster Bluff have boats, but they're just little bitty wooden bateaux for fishing in the creek. I'm sorry, but it looks like you'll have to stay over tonight."

Gabe sank back down onto the chair and pulled out his phone. "I'm supposed to take a deposition in the morning. I need to call the office."

Brooke took her phone from her pocketbook and glanced down at the screen. As she'd feared, it read, NO SERVICE.

"Don't bother," she told Gabe. "Cell phone reception is almost nonexistent over here."

"So what do we do?" he asked, annoyed. "I really have a busy day tomorrow. Not to mention a dog at home who needs to be let out and fed."

"And I've got to call my babysitter and let her know I'm stuck over here," Brooke added. "I just pray she'll agree to spend the night with Henry."

"Come on out to the kitchen. You can use the landline there," the housekeeper offered.

As they followed Louette down the hall, Gabe checked his phone one more time. "You'd better believe I'm billing Josephine if I have to spend the night."

Which made Brooke laugh despite her worry over childcare arrangements. "Good idea. I'll bill her for the cost of my babysitter, assuming Farrah will stay."

"Is everything okay?" Marie asked when Brooke and Gabe returned to the library.

"As good as can be expected," Brooke said, sitting down again. "Thank God, Farrah broke up with her loser boyfriend, Jaxson, today. She's usually not available to sit on Friday nights. She volunteered to take Henry out for pizza, and then they have a date with some LEGOs."

"I got a neighbor to feed and walk my dog," Gabe reported. "And I arranged for my paralegal to handle the deposition."

"Did Louette tell you she has rooms ready for you?" Josephine asked. "I thought I'd made it clear that I expected everybody to stay over."

Brooke bit back her retort. Josephine Warrick at ninety-nine was still very much used to getting her way.

Instead, Brooke shrugged off her irritation. "Louette gave me a tour of the upstairs and showed me our rooms and asked us to let you know dinner will be ready at seven, if that's all right."

"That'll be fine," Josephine said regally.

Brooke held out a white paper bag. "And in the meantime, Shug got back from the mainland with your new medicine. You're supposed to take it at dinnertime."

"Pills. Always more pills," Josephine fretted.

"She also suggested you probably need to rest before then, since you didn't sleep at all last night," Brooke said. "And I have to agree." She looked at the others. "Since we're apparently all staying for dinner, I guess the rest of this story can wait until then."

"And people say *I'm* bossy," Josephine said, making a face. She waved her hand. "All right. For once, she's right. I suppose I could close my eyes for a few minutes."

Brooke led the group up the broad staircase to the second floor. The silk damask wallpaper in the stair hall was peeling off in sheets, the Persian stair runner was faded and threadbare, and the curved mahogany handrail wobbled beneath their hands.

"I can't even imagine what it cost to build this place over a hundred years ago," Marie said, pointing up at the once glittering, multitiered chandelier above them. "If I'm not mistaken, that's Waterford crystal."

"I can't imagine what it would cost to make it livable again," Lizzie said. She glanced back at Gabe, who was bringing up the rear of the caravan, behind Felicia, who was slowly guiding her great-aunt up the stairs. "Is she leaving money for the upkeep of this white elephant?"

He smiled and said nothing.

At the top of the landing, Brooke pointed to the right. "Lizzie, your bedroom is the second doorway from the end. There's a bathroom right next door, although it's not attached. Mom, you and I are doubling up in what used to be the master bedroom, which is at the very end." She pointed to the left. "That's Gabe's bedroom down there. Louette said it was Gardiner's before the war, and it does have a bathroom, although there's a tub and no shower." She pointed to a double doorway halfway down the left wing. "Felicia, this room is yours and Varina's. There are two double beds, but the best thing is there's an attached bathroom."

"I need that bathroom right now," Varina said, a note of urgency in her voice. She took her walker from Gabe, who'd carried it upstairs, and scuttled in the direction of the bedroom.

"God," Lizzie said, wiping her glistening face with the back of her hand. "Tell me there's air-conditioning in my room."

"It's only a window unit, but Louette turned it on and she swears the room will cool down nicely," Brooke said.

Dweezil yowled and batted against the side of the cat carrier, echoing Lizzie's annoyance.

Brooke sat gingerly on one side of the narrow bed and patted the lumpy mattress, which was covered with a quilted satin throw. "Isn't it funny to think of married couples sleeping on something this small?"

The master bed had a towering carved mahogany headboard that reached halfway to the ceiling and a footboard so high that being in the bed felt like being in a boat.

Marie sat down on the other side of the bed, the one nearest the window, and bounced up and down. "Your father and I slept on double beds for years when we first got married. We didn't think anything of it at the time. Now I get claustrophobic sleeping alone in a queen."

"Sorry about having to share a bed with me," Brooke said.

"It'll be fine," Marie said lightly. "Taking family closeness to a whole new level. Although I do wish I had a toothbrush and nightie with me."

"Louette put new toothbrushes in the bathroom for both of us," Brooke said, "and she said we should just help ourselves to whatever we find in the closet for clothes."

Marie flopped backward onto the bed. "Later," she said wearily. "Right now, I feel like I'm the nonagenarian. There has been a *lot* of drama already today."

She turned onto her side and yawned. "Wake me up ten minutes before dinner so I can at least wash my face. Okay?"

Brooke curled up beside her mother and stared at the wall. The wallpaper was a scenic toile featuring flowers and trees and birds and animals that she guessed were native to Talisa, all done in shades of pea green. She managed to pick out a sea turtle, a running deer, some kind of long-necked seabird, pine trees, oaks, palms . . . and the next thing she knew, her mother was gently poking her in the side.

"Come on, Brooke," Marie said, laughing. "It's dinnertime. And did you know you snore?"

"Do not," Brooke yawned, sitting up.

"Do too," Marie said. "Let's go. I'm starved."

The others were already seated in the dining room, which had also undergone a transformation. A snowy white damask tablecloth covered the table, which was set with gold-rimmed porcelain dishes, heavy sterling flatware, and crystal stemware. A pair of tall silver candelabras adorned the center of the table with lit tapers.

Josephine sat at the head of the table, sipping from a glass of wine. She was dressed in the silk caftan again, and diamonds twinkled from her earrings, necklace, and a solitaire cocktail ring on her right hand. When Louette bustled into the room, delicious scents wafted from the direction of the kitchen.

"What are we having tonight?" Josephine asked.

"Paper-bag baked redfish," Louette said. "C. D. was fishing off the dock when he oughta have been fixing that boat motor, but at least we got dinner out of it. There's red rice to go with the fish, salad from the garden, and some lady peas out of the freezer. I didn't have time to bake yeast rolls, but I managed to throw some biscuits together."

Gabe moaned out loud. "Redfish. My favorite. And lady peas. My mother used to fix them with fatback."

"Mmm-hmm, that's how I do 'em too," Louette said, setting the dishes on the sideboard. She held up a bottle of white wine that had been sitting in a silver cooler. "Can I pour anybody some more wine? The man at the wine store says this is real nice with fish."

Josephine held up her nearly empty glass. "You can top me off."

Louette shook her head vigorously. "Noooo. You know your pain pills have it written right on the bottle—*Do not consume with alcohol.*" She moved around the table, filling the other extended glasses.

"Louette, I said you can top me off." Josephine's voice held a warning note. "What does it matter if I drink with my medicine? I'm not operating heavy machinery. And I already have stage-four lung cancer, so what's the worst that can happen?"

The housekeeper muttered something under her breath but did as she'd been ordered.

Dinner proceeded, with the guests around the table complimenting the fish, which was the best Brooke had ever tasted, and the wine, which was also a surprisingly good quality. Their hostess, Brooke noticed, barely picked at her plate, merely moving food from one side of her plate to the other and occasionally tossing morsels to Teeny and Tiny, who sat on the floor by her chair.

At last, Marie folded her napkin and placed it beside her plate. "Josephine, that was absolutely a divine dinner." She toyed with her dinner fork. "Do you want to know something funny? I think I have this same silver pattern. Francis First, right?"

Josephine sipped her wine. "Yes, I believe that's the name of this pattern." She waved her hand at the table with its elegant trappings. "I don't really care for this kind of thing, but Louette insisted. This was my mother's wedding silver."

"Mine was my grandmother's," Marie said. "The war was going on when Mama got married, so she said she didn't really get a lot of wedding gifts."

Lizzie picked up her fork and looked at it. "Granny had boxes and boxes of this kind of family stuff. I think it's all still in storage. At some point, I guess I'll get it all out and deal with it, but what do I need with pickle tongs and monogrammed pillowcases? I live alone and mostly eat carryout Chinese."

Brooke tried not to think about all the wedding gifts she'd had to return after she'd canceled her own wedding to Harris Strayhorn.

She turned to their hostess. "Josephine, you didn't go to Millie's wedding, did you? Or Ruth's either, for that matter. Isn't that what you told me?"

Color flooded the old woman's parchment-like skin. "As Marie pointed out, it was during the war. Gas was rationed, and travel was difficult. And, well, as I've admitted, we were estranged."

"Did you have a fight?" Felicia asked eagerly. "What did you fight about?"

"No fight," Josephine said. "We just . . . drifted apart."

"Because of the thing with Russell Strickland?" Lizzie asked. "Don't forget, you promised to tell us the rest of the story."

Josephine's fingers toyed with something on the collar of her dress. Brooke leaned closer and saw that it was the brooch she'd shown her previously. The High Tide Club pin.

"Yes. What happened after that man dragged my mother out of the ball-room?" Marie asked.

The door to the kitchen swung open, and as Louette walked in, Brooke glimpsed C. D. sitting at the kitchen table, mopping up sauce with half of a huge biscuit.

"I made coffee," Louette announced, brandishing a pot. Josephine glared at Louette. "But you're not having any, and I don't care how much you fuss at me. It's too late for you to be drinking coffee."

"Fine. Open a bottle of port and bring me that," Josephine said. She looked around the table. "At one time, Papa had the finest wine cellar on the coast. We might as well have some of his port, don't you think?"

When the coffee had been drunk and the port poured, Josephine resumed her story.

"Russell was absolutely livid after he saw Millie dancing with Gardiner," Josephine said. "I wasn't out in the garden where he attacked her, so I only know what we managed to coax out of her the next night."

"I seen it all," Varina said quietly.

Every head in the room swiveled to look at her. She was such a tiny figure, almost child-sized, against the bulk of the enormous chair she sat in.

"You did?" Josephine seemed taken aback. "You never said so, all those years ago."

"Nobody asked," Varina said, shrugging. "Anyway, I was just a girl. I was so shocked at first, I couldn't believe what I was seeing and hearing."

"Auntie, how did you happen to see it?" Felicia asked. She reached over and gently removed a crumb of biscuit from her great-aunt's blouse, which was when Brooke noticed, for the first time, that Varina was also wearing a High Tide Club pin.

"I'd finished up working in the kitchen, and Mrs. Dorris—she was the housekeeper back then—she told me to go ahead on home. I was supposed to wait for my brother to come fetch me and walk me home, but I knew he wasn't coming for another hour, and anyway, I wanted to peek at all the fancy dresses in the ballroom. So I changed back into my pink party dress and heels, and I sorta snuck around to the back of the house so I could look in the doors from the veranda. About the time I got there, I saw that man hauling Millie out of there." Varina looked over at Marie. "I'm sorry you have to hear this."

"It's all right," Marie said. "It was a long time ago."

"Millie was crying, telling him he was hurting her, but he didn't care, and he didn't slow down," Varina said. "He drug her into the garden, way back where the camellia bushes were head-high. And that's right near where I'd jumped into the bushes to hide."

Varina closed her eyes as though she were reliving the scene from memory. "It was a full moon that night, so I could see things I wished I hadn't. That man, he shoved her up against a tree, and he had his hands all up and down in her dress."

She glanced over at Gabe, blushed, and looked away. "Millie was begging him to stop. She was afraid somebody would see them, like her mama or her grandmama, but he said he could do what he wanted because they were getting married. I saw him push her dress up, and then he unfastened his trousers . . ."

"Oh my God." Lizzie breathed. "He raped her. The bastard raped her."

Marie was clutching her napkin in both hands, twisting it into a rope, her face ashen. Brooke reached over and touched her shoulder, but her mother didn't seem to notice.

"He didn't get the chance," Varina said. "Right about that time, Mr. Gardiner came busting in on them. I think he must have followed her out of the ballroom, because just before that, I saw him standing on the veranda, like he was looking for somebody. I guess he caught sight of Millie's dress, because he ran right over to them. He yelled at that man to stop it, and the bad man told him to mind his own business because he could do what he wanted, and the next thing I knew, Mr. Gardiner yanked him clean away from Millie. They had a fight, and even though the other man was way bigger, Mr. Gardiner punched him in the face and the gut and knocked him clean off his feet."

"Good for him," Lizzie said. "What happened after that?"

"Mr. Gardiner had already told Millie to go on back to the house. So then he told that bad man he'd better leave this island. He told him if he was still there in the morning, he'd kill him. And then he left."

"Gardiner really was a hero," Josephine said, sighing. "Not just a war hero, although he was that too. He was all our heroes. The best brother a girl could ask for."

Her face sagged, and her speech was slightly slurred. The pain meds, Brooke thought, must be kicking in.

"Did he . . . make it through the war?" Lizzie asked.

"No. He didn't," Josephine said. "His plane was shot down at Midway. Gardiner was a gun jumper, you know."

"What's that?" Felicia asked.

"He got tired of waiting for the United States to get into the war. He'd gotten his pilot's license just about the same time he got his driver's license. Gardiner hated what was happening in Europe. After Hitler marched into Poland and then Holland and Belgium, his mind was made up. He and Papa had terrible fights about it because my father was still an isolationist at that point. Anyway, Gardiner decided to join the Royal Canadian Air Force. The morning after the engagement party, he took the early ferry to the mainland, and from there he took the train to Canada."

"You must have been so proud of him," Marie said.

"At the time, I thought it was terribly romantic," Josephine said. "And heroic. Of course, that was October, and in early December, Pearl Harbor happened, and the United States did get into the war."

"Did you ever see Gardiner again?" Marie asked.

"Just once, and only for a few hours. He came home briefly, after training and before he was shipped out. By then, Papa had closed up this house. Most of the men on the island, including all the Shaddix boys, went off to fight the war, plus German U-boats were prowling the coast, and he didn't think it was safe for us to stay."

Gabe looked up from his glass of port. "I never heard that before."

"Oh yes. In 1941, at least five Allied merchant ships were torpedoed by the Germans between here and Savannah, and I believe four or five U-boats were sunk, right off the coast here." Josephine drained most of her port and, setting the glass down, tipped the rest onto the tablecloth, watching idly while the deep purple stain pooled on the white damask.

"I should really be getting to bed," she said. Her eyelids drooped, and she slumped back in her chair.

"Oh no," Lizzie objected. "You still haven't told us how Russell Strickland disappeared."

31

....

Louette hovered in the doorway, anxiously observing her employer's body language. "Y'all need to let her go to bed now," she warned as she mopped up the spilled port. "She's flat wore out."

Josephine's eyelids fluttered, and she seemed to struggle to stay awake. "No," she protested, raising a bony hand. "No, it's all right." She coughed, then recovered. "I owe them this much. Go back out in the kitchen, Louette, and leave me be."

"You were saying?" Lizzie prompted.

"We all slept late the morning after the party, but at breakfast, Millie seemed different. She was edgy and agitated. Of course, at the time, we had no way of knowing what had gone on the night before. As Varina said, it was a full moon. We had this silly custom—a ritual, I suppose you'd call it—of skinny-dipping on a full moon at high tide if we were near a beach. We called ourselves the High Tide Club."

Josephine's fingers found the brooch on her collar, and with trembling fingers, she managed to unfasten it and hold it out in the flat of her palm for the others to see. "Millie had these made for Ruth and me, as bridesmaid's gifts."

"She gave me one too," Varina said proudly, pointing to the pin fastened to her chest.

"Mom? Did Granny have a pin like this too?"

"May I see it?"

Josephine handed the pin to Marie.

"No, at least I never saw her wear one like this, but then she never wore much jewelry. Just her wedding band and engagement ring. Is that a diamond . . . on her nipple?" she asked, raising an eyebrow. "I never knew Mama had a naughty side to her."

"Yes," Josephine said. "She could be as silly as the rest of us. We were just girls. Anyway, we'd skinny-dipped at Millie's grandmother's beach house and at Ruth's family house at Palm Beach and at Cape Cod, all during the full moon, and that weekend seemed like the perfect time. The moon was full and high tide was around nine that night. Millie claimed she had a headache and didn't want to go, but Ruth and I pestered her until she finally gave in and agreed to come with us."

Felicia gave her great-aunt a sideways look. "Auntie Vee—did you skinny-dip too? I'm shocked!"

Varina ducked her head and then looked away.

"It was peer pressure," Josephine said. "We took Gardiner's roadster, picked Varina up at Oyster Bluff, and sweet-talked her daddy into letting her go with us. We said we were having a beach picnic, which was true, but we left out the part about skinny-dipping."

"My daddy was a Church of God preacher," Varina told the others. "He never would have let me go if he'd known what those fool girls were up to."

"There's a place on the island—not far from the lighthouse, a little secluded spot that we named Mermaid Beach. That's where we were headed," Josephine said. "I'd gotten the cook to fix us a picnic basket, and I snuck in a bottle of champagne and a bottle of Gardiner's bourbon. We had a fine supper, but when it came time to go swimming, Millie flat refused."

"Mama was always so modest," Marie said. "I don't think I ever saw her undressed the whole time I was growing up."

"It wasn't just that," Josephine said sadly. "Ruth and I had both been drinking, and we were sort of teasing Millie, telling her she had to swim, and I guess I pulled at the jacket she was wearing—long-sleeved, even in the heat—and that's when we saw the bruises."

Brooke felt herself recoil at the thought of Millie, just a girl of nineteen, and a victim of sexual abuse.

"She had bruises up and down her arms and on her shoulders and thighs," Josephine said. Her eyes filled with tears. "Our dear, sweet Millie. That's when she broke down and told us what that bastard Russell had done to her. She as much as told us Russell violated her whenever he was drinking—and he drank a lot. He was a violent, abusive drunk."

"Dear God," Marie said. She was clutching the edge of the table like a life preserver.

"Ruth told her she couldn't marry Russell. So did I. We both tried to talk her into breaking the engagement, but she said it was too late. She said it was the only way out of her mother's money problems."

"I'd never heard of rich people with money problems before," Varina said. "I thought rich folks didn't have problems like the rest of us."

"Millie insisted there was no way out of her predicament. She drank some more, and then we all went skinny-dipping and finished off the champagne and the whiskey," Josephine said. She looked over at her old friend, sitting at the opposite end of the table.

"You too, Auntie?" Felicia said, her eyes widening in disbelief.

"I'd never had a drop of alcohol before," Varina said. "That whiskey tasted nasty and burned my throat, but the champagne, that was a different story."

"It was very good champagne," Josephine added. "Moët & Chandon."

"I did like that champagne," Varina admitted. "It had bubbles like a Coca-Cola, only it tasted different. I didn't have but maybe a whole cupful."

"But you were so small, it didn't take much to get you drunk," Josephine said.

"My first and last time drinking alcohol," Varina said. "I guess I was cutting up pretty bad."

"It had gotten late, after midnight. And we didn't dare take her home drunk," Josephine said. "And anyway, none of us wanted to go home. We had this crazy idea about staying out all night—under the stars. Millie wanted to do it. She thought it would be her last night with all of us before she got married."

"But the bugs . . . oooh, the bugs were bad back then," Varina said.

"And it started to rain. Then I remembered the old lighthouse keeper's cottage. The government had decommissioned it several years earlier, but I knew Gardiner had a key to the cottage hidden under the roadster's doormat. So I drove us over there, the key worked, and we all piled onto the only bed in the place."

"Four girls in one bed?" Lizzie wrinkled her nose at the idea.

"Four very drunk girls," Josephine said. "I was the tallest, and Ruth wasn't exactly tiny, but Millie and Varina were so petite, they didn't take up any room at all." She yawned, not bothering to cover her mouth. "Oh my. Maybe I over-did it tonight. Or maybe it's just these damn pills." The old woman shook herself slightly as though she were shaking off her weariness. "I can't remem-ber who woke up first, but I know it was early, because that bed was facing east, so the sun was shining right in our eyes."

"Y'all didn't hear me creeping out of that bed, getting sick in the middle of the night, I guess," Varina said. She held her head between her hands at the memory of it. "Ooh, I had a headache, and I'd never been so sick in my life."

Felicia laughed. "I'm sorry, Auntie. I just can't picture you hungover."

"Girls do lots of crazy things when they're young," Varina said. "I seem to remember your mama and daddy putting up with all kinds of foolishness from you."

"That's true," Felicia agreed. "I was a real handful."

"We were all a little worried, because it was Sunday morning, and we didn't want Varina to get in trouble for missing church, so we got dressed and hurried back to Oyster Bluff. We hadn't gotten very far when I spotted something up ahead, in the middle of the road. As I got closer, I could see it was buzzards. Three of the biggest, boldest buzzards I'd ever seen. There was another, peck-ing at something off in the tall grass. And they didn't fly off, even when the car was almost on top of them. At first I assumed it was a dead animal, like a deer or a feral hog or something. But as we got closer, I realized it was . . . a person."

"I'll bet it was Russell Strickland," Lizzie said.

"Was he . . . ?" Marie's hand reached for her wineglass, but it was empty.

"Yes. He was dead." Josephine looked back at the sideboard, where another bottle of port rested on a silver trivet. She pointed at Gabe. "Be a dear and fetch that, will you? We're all going to need another drink."

When everyone but Varina had a refilled glass, Josephine went on talking.

"He must have weighed nearly 250 pounds, and of course, all of it was dead-weight. I still don't know how we managed to lift him. I suppose it was adrenaline or something. Somehow, we got him into the rumble seat, and then, of course, we had to figure out what to do with the body."

"Wait! Hold the phone," Felicia said, her voice rising. "How did he die? Who killed him? Are you saying you just hid the body?"

"Mmm-hmm." Varina nodded calmly. "That's right."

"But how did he die?" Lizzie persisted. "It was Russell Strickland, right? So who killed him?"

"Yes, it was him. He'd been shot. He didn't tell us who did it, and we didn't ask," Josephine said.

Gabe had been silent throughout most of the dinner, but now he was shaking his head. "You didn't notify law enforcement?"

"We did not," Josephine said.

"Why not? He'd been murdered. A crime had been committed."

"Russell Strickland was a monster," Josephine said, her voice cold, detached even. "We've already established that. Varina saw him assault Millie. He was twice her size! He would have kept on assaulting her, and nobody could have stopped him. Whoever killed him did the world a favor."

"So you got rid of the body. Just like that?" Gabe reached for the port bottle. "You didn't wonder who the murderer was?"

"It didn't matter. The four of us—Millie, Ruth, Varina, and me—we all agreed not to ask any questions. And never to tell what had happened. And we didn't."

"Until tonight," Brooke said.

"Do I dare ask what you did with the body?" Gabe asked.

Josephine regarded him with cool dispassion. "Why do you want to know? Are you going to report me to the authorities?"

"I am an officer of the court," Gabe said. He nodded toward Brooke. "And so is she. Did you kill him?"

"If I had, I wouldn't tell you," Josephine said.

"Do you know who killed him, Auntie?" Felicia peered at her great-aunt.

"Maybe I do, maybe I don't. We swore that night, and I won't go back on my word," Varina said.

"It couldn't have been you," Felicia said forcefully. "You're the most God-fearing woman I've ever known. You wouldn't hurt a fly."

Varina gave her an indulgent smile. "Child, we are all sinners in this world. I have tried to live the Lord's word the best way I know how, but the Bible tells us we are all born sinners, craving the Lord's forgiveness."

"It couldn't have been Granny, no matter what he did to her," Brooke said. "I bet she didn't even know how to fire a gun."

"We *all* knew how to shoot," Josephine corrected her. "We learned to shoot sporting clays at summer camp. And of course, Gardiner taught me how to hunt." She pointed at a pair of impressive deer mounts on the wall above the sideboard. "That eight-point buck is one I shot when I was twelve. That one"— she pointed to the mount on the right—"Gardiner shot just a week before the party."

She nodded at Varina. "You know how to shoot, don't you?"

"Oh yes," Varina said. "On an island like this—with rattlesnakes and gators and wild hogs, every family has a gun and every child learns how to shoot it, even little bitty girls like me. My daddy had a big ol' pistol, and he made me learn how to use it."

"This is just unbelievable," Lizzie said, slapping the tabletop for emphasis. "But it doesn't really solve the big mysteries of the night. What happened to Russell Strickland's body? Was it ever discovered? Granny's scrapbooks just covered the year he disappeared. And it was a huge story at the time."

"To my knowledge, the body was never found," Josephine said.

32

....

October 1941

Harley Shaddix's shoulders sagged as he parked the rusted pickup in front of Shellhaven. Samuel Bettendorf had been waiting for him, nervously pacing back and forth in front of the house, wearing a path in the lush green grass.

Dusk was approaching. Most of their houseguests had departed on the four o'clock ferry, including Millie Everhart's mother and grandmother, but it had been hours since anyone had seen or heard from Russell Strickland. The knot of worry burned in his gut.

The hound tethered to a cleat in the bed of the pickup truck hung his head over the side, panting heavily.

"Anything?" Bettendorf asked.

"No, sir," Harley said. He pointed at his dog. "Butch, he picked up a scent out in that dove field and followed it right close to the deer stand. Then, coming back down the road, he acted like he picked it up again, but I couldn't find no sign of Mr. Strickland."

"His kit and all his clothes and suitcases are still in his room," Bettendorf said. "I can't tell what's missing, other than his shotgun. Poor Millie is so upset, I hate to ask her to look through his things. Josephine and Ruth are with her now, trying to keep her calm."

"I talked to my boys," Harley said. "Homer said he showed Mr. Russell the spot where we seen that big ol' buck Mr. Gardiner's been tracking. And Friday, he talked about he was gonna bag him a trophy while he was on the island." Harley winced as he tried to take the weight off his bad leg. "I got Omar and Otis out in the bateau, looking in the creek in case he decided to go fishing."

"Good idea," Bettendorf said. "I wish to God Gardiner were here right now. He'd know where to look."

"Varina tells me your boy's gone off to fight in the war," Harley said.

Bettendorf's posture stiffened. "He's a goddamn fool. What happens in Europe is not this country's concern. But I couldn't talk him out of it. Couldn't stop him from going."

"He's a grown man," Harley said. "My boys, they say they're gonna sign up first chance they get." He sighed. "I can't talk no sense into them neither."

The two men, one black, one white, leaned against the bed of the truck, gazing up at the sky, where the last orange streaks of sunlight were visible through the tree line.

"Getting dark," Harley said, scratching at the stubble of beard on his chin. "City boy like that, how's he gonna do alone at night in a place like this?"

Ruth peered out the window at the scene below. "Your father's back with the truck," she told Varina, who crouched uneasily on the chair at the dressing table. "He's got a huge dog with him. I've never seen a dog like that."

Varina craned her neck to see. "That's Butch. My brothers take him coon hunting. He can scent anything. Daddy must have been out looking for that bad man." She wouldn't say his name out loud. She would never say his name.

Millie sat on the bed, her knees drawn up tightly against her chest. "What if they find where we put Russell? What if the dog finds that place and they dig him up?"

Josephine stood by the window now, looking down at the two men. "They won't go near that oyster mound. It's a special Indian place for the Geechees. Right, Varina?"

"Mmm-hmm." Varina nodded agreement. "Supposed to be evil haints there."

"But you're Geechee, aren't you?" Ruth asked. "And you were right there with us."

"Dead Indians don't scare me," Varina said. "And I don't believe in haints. Anyway, I'm not gonna be afraid anymore."

"I'm not going to be afraid either," Millie said, lifting her chin. "I'm going to be like you girls."

"The High Tide Club," Josephine said. "We're like the Three Musketeers, plus one."

"All for one, and one for all," Ruth said.

Millie clapped a hand to her mouth and jumped up from the bed. She scrabbled in her suitcase, spilling slips and stockings and dresses onto the carpet. "Oh my gosh! I almost forgot."

She brought out a small package. "Here!" She opened the wrapping and brought out three small black velvet boxes, which she passed around to each of the girls. "These were to have been your bridesmaids' gifts," she said.

Josephine was the first to open the box. She held up the tiny brooch, squinting at it and then laughing delightedly. "Millie, you scamp! She's naked!"

Ruth clapped her hands. "Mildred Everhart, this is the most perfect gift anybody has ever given me. And I will treasure it always."

Varina stared down at the pin nested in its white satin wrapping. "But I'm not a bridesmaid."

"Neither are we. Now," Ruth drawled.

"You're better than a bridesmaid," Millie said, hugging the younger girl. "You went skinny-dipping with us last night, didn't you?"

"And helped us bury you-know-who this morning," Josephine pointed out. "I'd say you've paid your initiation fees in full."

Varina lifted the pin from the box and held it up to the light. "That ain't a real diamond, is it?"

"They're just chips, but they're real. Granny gave me a pair of her earrings, and I had the jeweler use them for the pins."

From outside, they heard an engine starting, then backfiring. Ruth parted the curtains again. "Your father is leaving, Varina. And, Josephine, your father is in the truck with him."

"Maybe they're going for the sheriff," Millie fretted. "Maybe they'll bring more dogs and men who aren't afraid of dead Indians and haints. And they'll figure it out and we'll all be arrested."

"It won't matter. They won't find Russell. As long as we stick together, nobody will ever know what happened to him," Josephine said.

33

No, the body was never found," Josephine said.

"And the family never did anything about that?" Lizzie persisted. "They didn't, I don't know, hire a private detective or try to call in the FBI?"

"Russell Strickland's parents were both killed in a car wreck when he was a boy. He was raised by his grandparents, who were old and ill at the time. They did send somebody down to conduct an investigation, but you have to understand, the sheriff in this county at that time was part of a political dynasty who'd run things here for generations. He didn't appreciate having a Boston lawyer question his methods and practices."

"And I'd venture a guess that your father, being the wealthiest taxpayer in these parts, probably had some political sway with the sheriff and his cronies," Gabe said.

"Papa believed in being generous to this community. Among other things, he paid for two new squad cars, and he built the high school football field. The sheriff was . . . grateful," Josephine said.

"So the investigation never went anywhere," Felicia said.

"The war started, and people had bigger things to worry about," Josephine said. She pushed her chair back and stood with great effort. "And now, if you'll excuse me, I think I really must go to bed." She snapped her fingers at the dogs, asleep on the carpet. "Come along, girls."

The old woman took one faltering, wobbly step.

Gabe jumped up and offered her his arm. "May I assist you?"

She shrugged. "If you must."

34

....

"Miss Brooke, Miss Brooke." Someone was knocking on the bedroom door. She sat up in bed, awakened from a deep, dreamless sleep. She looked around the room, disoriented. Her mother was in bed beside her. Where was she? And then the knock again. She saw the wallpaper, the blurry green tangled vines and creatures, and it came to her. She was in a bedroom at Shellhaven. She reached for her phone on the nightstand and glanced at the digital time readout. 7:15 A.M.

She jumped out of bed and opened the door. Louette stood in the hallway, barefoot and wild-eyed, with a cotton bathrobe cinched loosely around her waist. Brooke stepped into the hallway and gently closed the door to keep from waking her mother.

"What's wrong, Louette?"

"It's Josephine. I think she's dead. I need you to come downstairs and see about her."

Brooke felt as though she'd just touched a live wire. "What happened?" She was already moving down the hallway toward the stairs with Louette in tow.

"I don't know. I found her on the bathroom floor. She must have fallen. There's blood. And she's not moving, and she's not breathing."

They'd reached the door to the library-turned-bedroom, which was closed, but Brooke could already hear the dogs inside, whining and scratching at the door.

"That's what woke me up," Louette said as they slipped into the library, quickly closing the door behind them. "Since I been sleeping in the house, I usually get up at six, because she's up by then, needing her medicine and such, but today when she wasn't up, I thought that was a good sign. Maybe she was sleeping late. I went back to sleep, but then I heard Teeny and Tiny barking and carrying on, so I went to check, and that's when I found her."

The dogs were in a state of frenzy, barking, jumping at their heels. Brooke saw puddles of urine on the carpet. "Better grab them, Louette, before they wake up the whole house. I'll see about Josephine."

Louette nodded, scooping up a dog with each hand.

Brooke walked toward the bathroom door, but as she got nearer, she saw a ghostly white foot, turned at an odd angle, and then the pale, blue-veined leg belonging to the foot and then the other foot, and then, finally, Josephine Bettendorf Warrick.

There could be no doubt she was dead. The body was sprawled on the tiled floor. She was dressed in a moth-eaten gray sweater over a pale yellow cotton nightgown, her body awkwardly twisted, faceup on the tile floor, in a pool of blood.

Brooke swallowed hard, once, twice, and clenched her jaws, fighting the wave of nausea that swept over her. She knelt beside the old woman and tentatively touched the side of her neck. It was cool to the touch, and there was no sign of a pulse.

She heard the library door open and looked over her shoulder. Louette stood motionless in the doorway, a dog tucked under each arm. "I was right. She's dead, isn't she?"

"I'm afraid so," Brooke said, standing and backing out of the bathroom.

"That poor old thing," Louette said. "It's all my fault. I never should have given her that wine last night. Not when she was taking that medicine. She hadn't had no wine since she got sick, so she wasn't used to it. Mixing it with those pills, that's what killed her."

Louette began to cry, and to her surprise, Brooke felt tears streaming down her own face. Louette set the Chihuahuas gently onto the floor, reached out, folded Brooke into her arms, and they stood like that, quietly crying. Teeny and Tiny sat on their haunches, their ears pricked up, small bodies trembling, attuned to the emotions unfolding before them.

Brooke finally pulled away and wiped her eyes with the sleeve of the man's cotton pajama top she'd found neatly folded in the master bedroom upstairs.

"What should we do?" Louette asked, wringing her hands. "Should I go get Shug?"

"Let me think," Brooke said, taking a deep breath. But her mind was a whirl of emotions. Panic, dread, grief, confusion. Josephine was dead. What happens next?

"Look here," Louette said, pointing down at the top of one of the dog's heads. "Is that blood?"

Brooke scooped up the dog and examined her head. Sure enough, there were several droplets of dried blood on the dog's face and muzzle, but as she searched the dog's body, she could find no obvious wounds.

"I bet I know what happened," Louette said. "Josephine probably got up in the middle of the night to go to the bathroom, and it woke up these dogs. They followed her wherever she went. She wasn't right last night, doped up on those pills and all that wine. Probably she tripped over Teeny, or maybe Tiny. And that's how she fell and hit her head."

"You're probably right," Brooke said. "I guess you'd better go get Shug. In the meantime, I'll use the house phone to call the sheriff."

"Sheriff?" Louette stiffened at the word.

"I think that's the correct procedure," Brooke said. "But before you fetch Shug, I think we're going to need a big pot of coffee ready before I wake the others."

35

Carter County Sheriff's Office. Is this a life-threatening emergency?" The dispatcher's voice was calm and detached, the exact opposite of how Brooke was feeling at that moment.

"Er, no—that is, the person is already dead," Brooke replied.

She could hear the tapping of computer keys on the other end of the line.

"Ma'am, can you tell me the manner of death?"

"She's, uh, ninety-nine years old, and I believe she fell and hit her head."

"Accidental, then. I see you're calling from over there on Talisa Island?"

"That's right."

"Name of deceased?" More tapping.

"Josephine Bettendorf Warrick," Brooke said.

"Ohhhhh," the dispatcher said. "That's so sad, and I'm very sorry to hear it. Miss Josephine did a lot of good things for this community."

"Yes, it is a shame."

"All right, hon. I'm gonna call Sheriff Goolsby, because he was a personal friend of Miss Josephine's, and I'll ask him to call you right back. Is this a good number?"

"It's the only number," Brooke said. "My cell doesn't have good reception here."

"Okay, well, you sit tight while I get ahold of the sheriff. What's your name, hon?"

Brooke told her.

"I know you!" The dispatcher's voice warmed. "My niece Farrah works for you. This is her aunt Jodee. Now, you being a lawyer and all, you probably already know this, but y'all just leave Miss Josephine right where she's at. Don't try moving her or nothing like that."

"I promise you, nobody is going to move her body."

After she'd hung up, Brooke took a few more sips of coffee and waited. She really wanted to call Farrah and check on Henry, but she also didn't want to miss the sheriff's call.

She paced around the kitchen, looking out the window for the return of Louette and Shug, trying not to think of Josephine's lifeless body stretched out on the bathroom floor. Ten minutes later the phone rang, and she grabbed it.

"Sheriff Goolsby here. Is this Brooke Trappnell?"

"This is she."

"Jodee tells me Miss Josephine has taken a fall and died?"

"Yes. We think she got up in the middle of the night to go to the bathroom and perhaps tripped over one of her dogs and hit her head when she fell. There's quite a bit of blood."

"Don't touch a thing," the sheriff said sternly. "At all. Are you able to close off that bathroom?"

"Yes."

"Do that. I'll call the funeral home and try to raise the coroner, and we'll be over there ASAP. Don't touch anything. Understand?"

Brooke rolled her eyes. "Yes, I've got the message. If you'll call this number when you're close to the Shellhaven dock, somebody will come down and bring you up to the house."

She glanced over at the kitchen clock. Just past eight. Henry would have been up for at least two hours by now. She dialed her babysitter's number, crossing her fingers that all would be well. One crisis per morning was all she was equipped to handle.

"Farrah? How's it going?"

"Oh, Brooke, hey. Everything's cool. Henry's being a really good boy. Aren't you, Henry?"

She could hear the tinny theme song of her son's favorite cartoon show. Then her son's voice. "Yes! I'm good boy."

"He really has been pretty good," Farrah said. "I got him to sleep almost the whole night in his new bed. He's had breakfast, and now we're just chilling with some *Caillou*."

Brooke smiled despite herself. "Ugh. I hate that show."

"For real. Whatever happened to Barney the purple dinosaur like I used to watch?"

"Dunno. Listen, Farrah. Would it be possible for you to stay 'til later in the day?"

"I guess. I mean, it's not like I've got anything else to do since me and Jaxson are broken up. How late are we talking about?"

"Not sure yet."

"Is everything okay? You sound kind of stressed."

"Yeah, well, stressed is putting it mildly. The thing is, Josephine is dead."

"What! For real? What happened?"

Brooke described the scene she'd found in the bathroom.

"Oh, man. That really sucks. What happens now, with the island and everything?"

"It's way too soon to tell. I've called the sheriff's office, and he'll be over pretty soon. In the meantime, I've got to deal with things here, which could get complicated. Which is why I'd really, really appreciate it if you could keep watching Henry. I'll pay extra, of course."

"No problem. It'll be fun. Maybe we'll head over to the park in a little while."

"Good idea," Brooke said. "I can't thank you enough, Farrah. Can you put Henry on the phone?"

"Sure thing," she said. "Henry!" the babysitter called. "Hey, Henry, come here. Your mama's on the phone. She wants to talk to you."

"No!"

"Come on, buddy," Farrah coaxed. "Don't you want to tell Mama about the awesome thing you did last night?"

"No!"

"Never mind," Brooke said, sighing. "I'll get home as soon as I can. Give him a kiss for me, okay?"

"All day long," Farrah promised.

"Just out of curiosity, what did he do last night?"

"Oh. Big news. Huge news. He pooped in the potty."

"Major breakthrough," Brooke said, laughing. "I'll call you later."

Gabe Wynant was just emerging from his bedroom, dressed, with his briefcase tucked under his arm. "Oh, good," he said, seeing Brooke approach. "You're up. I was going to see if somebody could give us a ride to the ferry . . ." He left the sentence unfinished, noticing her pained expression. "What's wrong?" He clutched her arm.

"Josephine's dead," she said.

"Oh no." He shook his head. "Heart attack?"

"Maybe, but maybe not. Louette found her lying on the bathroom floor. It looks like she fell and hit her head on the tile."

He glanced up and down the corridor at the closed doors. "Have you told the others?"

"No, I just got off the phone with the sheriff's office. He'll be over with the coroner as soon as he can. I was just about to start the process of letting the others know. My mom's still sleeping. But I'm glad you're the first. I guess we need to talk about what comes next, right?"

"Yeah," he said with a long sigh. "But first, coffee. And maybe some aspirin."

When they'd reached the first floor, Gabe turned away from the kitchen and toward the library. Brooke intercepted him before he opened the door.

"Gabe, the sheriff said not to let anybody near the body, or to touch anything."

He pulled his cell phone from his pocket and nodded. "I promise not to touch anything, but as her attorney, I think I need to see her body."

Brooke used the hem of her shirt to turn the doorknob. Inside, the room was already hot, despite the early hour and the fan whirring in the open window. "She's in there," she said, pointing to the open bathroom door. Unwilling to see her client's body again, she posted herself beside Josephine's recliner. The knitted afghan was carefully folded across the back of the chair, but the covers of the nearby bed were rumpled. Josephine's favorite sneakers, with the laces removed, were neatly lined up at the foot of the bed, and the wig was on the nightstand.

She looked up when she heard Gabe's cell phone shutter clicking off multiple frames. When he emerged from the bathroom, his face was pale under his ruddy tan. "Coffee," he said.

Gabe helped himself to a mug of coffee, then poured more for his associate. "This has been a hell of a twenty-four hours," he said, draining half the cup.

"What comes next?" Brooke asked.

"Assuming the authorities don't think foul play is involved, I suppose the body will be removed to the funeral home at St. Ann's."

"Will there be an autopsy?" Brooke cringed as soon as she'd said the word.

"Up to the sheriff and the coroner. I mean, she was old and terminally ill. And as far as we know, nobody would have a motive to want her dead, right?"

"Not that I know of," Brooke said.

"If that's the case, they'll start the work to issue a death certificate. After that is when the fun begins."

"What's that mean?" Brooke asked. "You drew up a new will and executed it yesterday before I got here. Right?"

He set the coffee mug on the table and massaged his temples with both hands. "Not quite. I did draw up the will. Josephine read and approved it, but we needed two witnesses. Louette was supposed to fetch a couple of folks from Oyster Bluff, but then there was the trouble with the boat, and Josephine was excited about seeing your mother and Lizzie, and the will got pushed onto the back burner."

"Oh no," Brooke moaned. "I thought everything was signed and sealed."

"Christ!" He stared down at the table. "This is going to be a hell of a mess, and it's totally my fault. I knew I should have pressed her to get those witnesses over here yesterday, but Josephine was adamant about greeting her guests first."

"Not blaming you at all, but couldn't you have gotten Louette and maybe C. D. as witnesses?"

"No. She'd left them small bequests, so they had the same conflict as you."

"Which means that Josephine died intestate."

"As far as I know, yes."

Brooke gestured upward with her chin. "So this means we tell everybody—Varina and Felicia, Lizzie, Mom, and of course, Louette and Shug—that they don't inherit?" She stood and began rifling cupboards, banging the warped wooden doors as she searched.

"What are you looking for?" Gabe asked.

"Aspirin. Let's hope there's an industrial-sized bottle somewhere in here."

36

....

"Good morning, ladies," Louette murmured, head down, eyes averted. She set a tray of fruit, coffee, and tea down on the sideboard. "Breakfast will be just a few minutes."

Brooke looked around the table, wondering how she would break the news to the women that their hostess was dead. As a delaying tactic, she got up and began filling coffee cups.

"I'll get your tea, Auntie Vee," Felicia volunteered.

"I reckon Josephine is sleeping late this morning," Varina said, chuckling. "We sure did have a late night." She reached over and patted Lizzie's hand. "How did you sleep last night, honey, after that long plane ride all the way from California?"

Lizzie yawned. "Not that great. The sun was shining right in my eyes. Plus, that mattress in my room felt like it was stuffed with corncobs or something."

"Sorry about that," Brooke said. She cleared her throat nervously, looking down the table at Gabe, who'd just joined the group in the dining room.

"Is something wrong?" Marie asked, studying her daughter's face.

Brooke hesitated. Marie knew her all too well. She'd never been able to hide anything from her mother's all-seeing gaze.

"I'm afraid so."

Every pair of eyes in the room turned toward her, coffee cups suspended in midair.

"There's no easy way to tell you this, so I'm just going to say it. Josephine is gone."

"You mean she's dead?" Felicia looked from Brooke to Gabe and then back at Brooke again.

"Yes."

"Lord Jesus!" Varina exclaimed.

"How?" Lizzie frowned. "I know she was old and sick, but she seemed fine last night."

"The Lord took her," Varina said, tears streaming down her face. She clasped her hands over her chest.

"Exactly how did Josephine die? And when?" Felicia asked.

"That's what I'd like to know," Lizzie echoed.

Marie said nothing, watching her daughter over the rim of her bone china coffee cup. The swinging door from the kitchen opened again, and Louette placed their breakfast on the table, a platter of scrambled eggs, bacon and sausages, a bowl of steaming grits, and a basket of biscuits, covered with a checked napkin. Through the open door, Brooke spied C. D. hunched over a plate of food at the kitchen table. He gave her a solemn nod, then kept eating.

But all eyes in the dining room were riveted on Brooke.

"We can't be sure, but from the looks of it, Josephine got up sometime in the night to go to the bathroom, and she tripped, maybe over one of the dogs, and fell and hit her head," Brooke said. "Louette found her there this morning, and that's when she came and woke me up."

"I thought she was just tired from being up so late last night," Louette said, wiping the palms of her hands on the skirt of her polyester uniform. "But then I heard the dogs scratching at the door wanting to get out. So I went in to take them outside, and that's when I found her . . . ." She bit her lip and looked away, tears welling up in her eyes.

"Oh, Louette," Marie said. "That must have been so upsetting for you."

"Yes, ma'am," Louette said. "I ain't gonna forget that sight. Not ever." She turned and quickly left the room.

Lizzie shrugged and reached for the food, sliding bacon and eggs onto her plate. She looked askance at the steaming bowl of grits with a melting pat of butter in the middle. "What's this? Mashed potatoes? For breakfast?"

"It's grits," Felicia said, rolling her eyes. "Your first time in the South?" She took a biscuit from the basket, sliced it, paused, then reached for the butter dish. "So that's it? Josephine is gone?" She glanced at her great-aunt. "I'm sorry, Auntie Vee."

"She was my oldest friend in the world," Varina said, dabbing at her eyes with a tissue plucked from the sleeve of her blouse. She looked out the open dining room window, past the thick green screen of overgrown azalea branches. "Josephine, she was the last of the line. All the Bettendorfs, all of them, Miss Elsie, Mr. Samuel, Mr. Gardiner, and now, Josephine. All gone. I can't believe it. And what's going to happen to this house now? To Talisa?"

"That's what I'd like to know," Lizzie said, gesturing with her fork at Gabe. "Mr. Wynant? Can you enlighten us?"

"Surely that can wait," Marie demurred. "This is hardly the time."

"Why not?" Felicia said. "Josephine invited all of us here to discuss leaving her estate to us. She told us last night, told all of us, that she wanted to make amends. And it's my understanding she intended for us to be her beneficiaries. Isn't that right, Brooke?"

"That was her intent," Brooke admitted.

"Then let's get down to brass tacks," Lizzie said. "No disrespect or anything, but I just met the old girl for the first time last night. So it would be totally insincere of me to pretend I'm grief-stricken. She was ninety-nine years old, and she was dying. But the rest of us are alive, and I think I can speak for all of us when I say, what's next? When do we inherit?"

"Leave it to a Yankee," Felicia muttered, shaking her head.

"I'm not a Yankee. I'm a Californian, although technically, Ruth, Josephine, and Millie were all Yankees." Lizzie grabbed a biscuit from the basket and dipped it into the bowl of grits. She took a bite, chewed, and nodded. "Hmm.

Not bad." She added, "Are you saying you don't care what happens to Josephine's estate, Felicia?"

"Nooo," Felicia said cautiously. "I mean, yes, I do care, but for God's sake, have some tact. The woman's body is barely even cold."

Varina sniffed loudly.

"What about funeral plans, Brooke?" Marie asked. "Do we know anything about arrangements yet?"

"No. I've notified the sheriff's office, and he and the coroner should be on the way over by now," Brooke began.

"Coroner!" Lizzie and Felicia said in unison.

"It's strictly procedural," Gabe said. "Especially in a case like this, when the, uh, deceased has met with an accident."

"So after that?" Lizzie crossed her arms over her chest.

"Assuming everything is, uh, as it should be, Mrs. Warrick will be taken to the funeral home in St. Ann's, and a death certificate will be issued."

"And then we start probate, or however you do things in Georgia, correct?" Lizzie asked. She jerked her head in Felicia's direction. "I only ask because at some point, Dweezil and I need to get back to California. I've got stories to write and deadlines to meet. It would be good if we could get all the paperwork wrapped up ASAP."

Gabe frowned and nodded meaningfully at Brooke.

"We have a problem," Brooke said.

"What kind of problem?" Felicia demanded.

"It's about the will," Brooke said slowly.

"Oh, shit. Here we go," Felicia said. "What? She changed her mind?"

"This is all my fault, so I think I'd better be the one to tell you," Gabe said. "Mrs. Warrick had every intention of leaving her estate to be put into a trust and divided among you five women—Brooke, Marie, Lizzie, Varina, and Felicia. I drafted the will as she dictated it last week, and as you know, I brought it back here yesterday for her to review and approve. Which she did."

"Thank God for that," Felicia said.

"Unfortunately . . ."

"Oh, shit," Lizzie said.

"Unfortunately, for the will to be legally binding, it had to be signed by Mrs. Warrick in the presence of two witnesses. And that, I regret to tell you, did not happen. I had every intention of sending for two witnesses first thing this morning, but as you now know, it would have been too late."

"Run that by me again?" Lizzie said. "Are you saying we don't inherit? Like, anything?"

"Yes," Gabe said, looking defeated. "That is correct. For all intents and purposes, Mrs. Warrick died intestate."

Felicia pounded the tabletop with the flat of her hand, sending coffee cups and plates bouncing and clattering. "I knew it! I knew this was just some bullshit white guilt trip."

"All because of a frigging piece of paper you didn't get signed?" Lizzie demanded. "We can fix that. Send for the witnesses now. Get Louette and that weird guy who drives the boat. Have them sign the will, backdate it, then slip them a couple of hundred bucks to keep their mouths shut, and it's all good. The will is in effect, and everybody's happy."

Gabe shook his head. "It's not that simple. For one thing, Mrs. Warrick left both Louette and C. D. bequests, which means they are ineligible to be witnesses. But more importantly, even if they hadn't been named as beneficiaries, such an action would constitute fraud, and as an officer of the court, I cannot and will not be a party to that."

"The sheriff just called. He and the coroner should be docking in a few minutes," Louette announced, returning to the dining room. "I said I'd send Shug to fetch them." She circled the table with the coffeepot, hovering quietly in the background as the unhappy news sank in.

It was Lizzie who asked the question that had already occurred to everybody.

"If none of us inherits everything, who does? Josephine didn't have any family, right?"

"Actually, she did," Brooke said. "There are a couple of distant relatives. Second or third cousins, I believe?" She looked to Varina for verification.

"Those Underwood girls." Varina frowned. "Josephine never did take to them."

"She couldn't stand those women," Louette agreed. "She always blamed them for ruining that end of the island by selling their land to the state to make a park out of it."

"Did either of you ever meet these cousins?" Gabe asked.

"Just the one time," Varina said. "Those two . . . I forget their first names . . ."

"Dorcas and Delphine," Louette put in. "But I don't know their married names."

"Ooh, yes," Varina said. "Long time ago. Josephine wouldn't even let 'em in the house. She stood right in that front doorway out there and told them they could get off her property and never come back. Then one of them started to say something about burying the hatchet and acting like family again, considering they were all cousins, and that's when she told them they'd better not hold their breath waiting on her to leave them anything, because she'd leave it all to her dogs before she gave them a single red cent," Varina said.

"But guess who'll be having the last laugh now?" Lizzie said gloomily.

"Is that right, Mr. Wynant?" Varina asked, turning to Gabe. "Will everything really go to those Double D girls? Isn't there anything you can do to stop that from happening?"

"That's for a judge to decide, but yes, barring any other claims on the estate, and if these cousins truly are her only other living relatives, that's a possibility."

"Excuse me, Mr. Wynant, but what happens in the meantime?" Louette asked. "To the house and the island and to me and Shug and C. D.? And all the folks living at Oyster Bluff? She was going to give that land back to all of us, wasn't she, Brooke?"

"Yes, that was her intent. I had all the paperwork drawn up, but again, it was never signed and witnessed."

"So we're all out of a job, and now we're fixing to get kicked out of our houses and off this island," Louette said sadly. She turned and hurried back to the kitchen.

"Isn't there anything we can do?" Brooke appealed to Gabe. "I know the law's the law, but you and I also know how Josephine wanted her estate disposed of. This all seems so heartless."

"I can petition the county to be named administrator of the estate," Gabe conceded. "If approved, I would be able to keep the staff on here, to maintain the house and grounds. That might buy us some time."

"Time to do what?" Lizzie asked, draining her coffee cup.

"I don't know," Brooke admitted. "Do some research. See if Josephine left an earlier will, anything that would keep her cousins—or ultimately the state—from taking over the island. It's a long shot, but I can tell you this—Josephine Bettendorf Warrick had been living in this house full-time since the war was over. That's nearly seventy years. And judging just from the papers she had me look through in the library, when I was trying to track you and Varina down, she was a world-class pack rat."

"Can we do that? Legally?" Felicia asked.

"Maybe." But Gabe sounded dubious.

37

....

S heriff's here," Louette said, gesturing to the man and the woman who stood
in the front hallway at Shellhaven.

The man stepped forward and held out a hand to Gabe and then to Brooke.
He was trim, probably midforties, with steel-framed glasses and dressed in a
khaki uniform. When he removed his cap, his closely shaved head gleamed in
the dim light.

"Good morning," he said. "Howard Goolsby, Carter County. And this here,"
he said, referring to his companion, a sturdily built middle-aged brunette dressed
in civilian clothes, "is Kendra Younts, our county coroner."

After the introductions were made, Goolsby wasted no time.

"Who found the body?"

"I did," Louette said.

"And you are?"

"Louette Aycock. That was my husband, Shug, who just picked you up at
the dock. We both work for Miss Josephine."

"Can you show us?"

"Yes, sir," Louette said. "Right down this hallway."

"Will you need us?" Brooke asked, not anxious to revisit the death scene.

"Stick around, if you would. I'll need to talk to you after this," Goolsby said.

Brooke and Gabe sat on the stiff upholstered furniture in the living room.

"I feel like I'm living in the middle of an Agatha Christie novel," Brooke said, clasping and unclasping her hands.

"If Agatha Christie had ever written a book set on the Georgia coast," Gabe said.

"You don't think they'll think something . . . bad happened, right?"

"I don't see why they would," Gabe said. "This is all strictly procedural."

"This is all just so . . . bizarre," Brooke said. "I'm sorry I dragged you into this mess."

"Don't be. I'm glad I got to meet Josephine Warrick and see all of this," he said, indicating the house. "The whole story she told us last night was unbelievably fascinating. And of course, I'm glad to be working with you again, Brooke. I just wish we'd gotten that damn will executed."

She heard herself say her father's favorite phrase. One she'd always hated. "It is what it is." Brooke nodded in the direction of the closed library door. "Yeah. About that. Should we mention Russell Strickland to the sheriff?"

"God, no," Gabe said quickly. "It's just a story, right? No need to muddy the water, especially since we have no firsthand knowledge of what happened back then."

"That's what I hoped you'd say," Brooke said. "I also don't want to drag Varina into any kind of trouble since, as far as we know, she's the only living witness to . . . that night."

The library door opened, and Louette emerged. "They want to talk to y'all," she said.

Brooke was relieved to see that a blanket had been placed over Josephine's body. Kendra Younts was busily dumping Josephine's medications into a plastic bag, and Sheriff Goolsby was sitting on the chintz wing chair, scribbling in a small notebook.

"Y'all can come in," he said without looking up from his notes. "Just finishing up here."

"Okay, Howard," Kendra said. "I'm gonna bring in the stretcher if you're all set here."

"All set," the sheriff said.

He looked up at Brooke and seemed puzzled. "You look awful familiar. Have we met before?"

"Probably. I'm a lawyer, and I think our paths have crossed at the courthouse."

He snapped his fingers. "Now I got it. You're Brittni Miles's lawyer, right?"

"Afraid so," Brooke said, laughing. "But please don't judge me by my clients."

"I'll try not to," Goolsby said. "That is one crazy little gal, though. You know she went on a hunger strike because my deputies wouldn't bring her a Diet Dr. Pepper?"

"She's still in your jail? I thought her stepfather was going to bail her out."

"Not yet. If he doesn't come get her pretty soon, though, we're fixing to take up a collection and bail her out ourselves." He closed his notebook and rested it on one knee. "What's your connection to Mrs. Warrick?"

"She hired me a couple of weeks ago, in a legal capacity, to help her find the heirs of her oldest friends. And she also wanted me to draw up a new will."

"And did you do that?"

"We ran into some complications. It turns out that one of the people she wanted to leave a bequest to, the daughter of her late best friend, is my mother, Marie Trappnell. Which is why she hired me in the first place. Once I realized we had a conflict, I suggested she hire Gabe, who I used to work for in Savannah."

Goolsby nodded at Gabe Wynant. "Savannah, huh? You know Wayne duBose?"

"I know Sheriff duBose quite well," Gabe said. "We're in Rotary Club together."

"Wayne's a good man," Goolsby said. "Comes down here fishing with me when he can get away from the big city." He tapped his notebook with a pen. "I think we're about set here. I'd heard Mrs. Warrick was terminally ill, and the housekeeper confirmed that. She was on some pretty strong new pain meds, is that right?"

"Yes."

"And she consumed some alcohol at dinner last night, even though the housekeeper warned her against mixing the pills with alcohol?"

"That's correct," Gabe said. "We finished dinner around ten o'clock, and I helped her from the dining room because she was somewhat unsteady on her feet."

"Did she seem okay, otherwise?"

"She was groggy," Brooke said.

"And there were some dogs in here? The housekeeper mentioned she might have tripped over them?"

"Two Chihuahuas," Brooke said. "Teeny and Tiny. You rarely saw Josephine without those dogs at her feet. I guess Louette must have put them in another room now. But they were here this morning when I came down."

"Okay, then," Goolsby said. "Kendra and I agree, this is a textbook accidental death, likely alcohol-and-drug-related. Hell of a way for the old lady to go, though. She was pretty much a legend around here. Her family did a lot of good in this county."

"She told me her father was always very community-minded, even though he wasn't originally from here," Brooke said.

"That was way before my time, of course, but my granddaddy used to talk about what a fine person Mr. Bettendorf was. What happens to all of this now?" Goolsby asked. "She never had any kids, did she?"

"No children, no close surviving family," Gabe said. "And unfortunately, as far as we can tell, she died intestate."

Goolsby blinked. "I thought you said you did her will."

"I did, but she died before it could be witnessed."

The door opened, and Kendra Younts wheeled in a gleaming chrome collapsible stretcher.

"Son of a bitch," the sheriff said.

Gabe pointed at the stretcher. "That might not be necessary. Mrs. Warrick specified that she wanted to be buried in the family plot here on the island. According to Louette, she even has a handmade casket out in the barn. So why transport the body over to the mainland when it's just going to end up back here?"

"That's a pretty unusual request," Kendra said.

Brooke imagined the coroner mentally calculating the amount of money her family's funeral home would not be billing to Josephine's estate. No transport. No embalming or cremation. No bronze coffin, no visitation in the Younts Mortuary's Palmetto Parlor, no hearse . . .

"Josephine Warrick was a pretty unusual woman," the sheriff said. He nodded at Kendra. "We're agreed it's an accidental death, but I think we might want to touch base with her doctors to confirm their diagnosis of her illness and all. So we'll go ahead and take her over to the morgue at the hospital just in case. Afterward, we can release the body to be brought back over here."

"That sounds reasonable," Brooke agreed.

"First thing Monday, I'll petition with the court to be named administrator of the estate," Gabe said. He stood and handed business cards to the sheriff and the coroner. "Please let me know if you have any questions, and of course, I'd appreciate it if you could notify me when the death certificate is ready."

Brooke quickly left the room before they began transferring Josephine to the stretcher. The dining room was empty and had been cleared of all traces of breakfast. When she went looking for more coffee, she found Louette and Shug standing in the kitchen. Shug had his arm around his wife's waist, and Louette's head rested on his shoulder. Their backs were to her, but she could hear Louette's racking sobs from where she stood.

She backed out of the room to leave them alone with their grief.

She was walking back toward the living room when she heard scratching and whining from behind another door.

Brooke opened the door slightly, and Teeny and Tiny came scrambling out, barking indignantly and flinging themselves at her ankles.

On an impulse, she scooped them both up and cradled one under each arm. "Hey, girls," she crooned. "Poor little girls. I guess we sort of forgot about you in all this excitement."

One of the dogs raised her head up and began licking Brooke's neck. She read the tag on the collar. "So you're Tiny." She held the dog at arm's length.

"How am I gonna tell you apart from your sister? Oh, okay. Your ears are way longer than Teeny's. And no offense, but you've kind of got an overbite. How did I miss that?"

The back door opened, and C. D. poked his head inside the hallway and cleared his throat.

"Hey, uh, Brooke. Can I talk to you for a minute?"

"Of course. Did you already take the sheriff back to the dock?"

"Yeah. Them and Josephine."

"I probably need to let the girls outside for a potty break," Brooke said. "Can we talk outside?"

"Yeah. That'd be okay."

It took her eyes a moment to adjust to the dazzling sunlight after the dim half-light of the house. The moment she set the dogs down, they ran straight for a clump of oleander bushes at the edge of the veranda.

Brooke pointed at a rusting wrought iron table and two chairs. It was the only furniture left on what must have once been a beautiful spot overlooking the ocean. The slate tiles were crumbling, with weeds poking up through the cracks. Still, a fine breeze ruffled the palms at the edge of the low wall, bringing the scent of gardenias blooming in what was left of the garden just beyond.

She studied C. D., who sat stiffly, staring out at the ocean. He still wore his ever-present oversized aviator sunglasses, but today he was dressed in a loose-fitting short-sleeved shirt, tucked neatly into a pair of baggy jeans whose hems just brushed the top of his bare brown feet. This, she realized, was as dressed up as she'd ever seen him.

"What's on your mind?" she asked finally.

He looked at her now. "This morning, I was out in the kitchen, and I heard y'all talking about Josephine and how she didn't have no close kin or nuthin'."

"That's right," Brooke said. "If you're worried about your job, though—"

"The thing is, she does have kin."

"Yes, we know about the cousins, and they'll be notified—"

"I'm not talking about the cousins. I'm talking about me." He thumped his bony chest and raised his glasses to look her straight in the eye. "Me. I'm Josephine's son. I reckon that's about as close a kin as you can get."

38

May 1942

Y ou're the doctor? Thank God!" The woman who'd met him at the door was wrapped in a thin cotton bathrobe and didn't wait for his answer. "She's having an awful time. Please hurry."

Thomas Carlyle was getting accustomed to receiving urgent phone calls in the middle of the night. All the younger physicians in Savannah, even the middle-aged ones, had enlisted in the war effort in the immediate aftermath of Pearl Harbor. But he was in his seventies, and his fondness for gin was well known among a certain clientele in the city.

Still, he was surprised to be summoned to this particular address. It was a handsome, pale pink double town house on one of the most fashionable blocks of West Jones Street, so he'd dressed for the occasion; his only black suit, too large for him now and full of moth holes, and a heavily starched white dress shirt, although no necktie. He was poised to ring the bell when the door opened.

He heard the moans and shrieks as soon as he began to climb the narrow stairs, which did nothing to quicken his steps. He'd heard it all hundreds of times before, and in his experience, babies took their own time.

He found the patient stretched out on a bed with an elaborate mahogany carved headboard. She'd thrown off most of the bedcovers and was thrashing around on the mattress, wild-eyed and clearly terrified. Her face, neck, and narrow arms were slick with sweat. Blood pooled on the white sheets.

"How long has this been going on?" Carlyle asked. He removed his suit coat, tossed it onto a chair, rolled up his shirtsleeves, and opened the satchel he kept packed by his front door.

"The labor pains started around two this afternoon," the woman said, leaning down to stroke the younger woman's hair. She crooned something inaudible, which seemed to calm the patient a little.

"And how far along is she?"

"Maybe seven months? It's too early, I know. The bleeding won't stop. I didn't know there would be so much blood."

"She should have been taken to a hospital hours ago," Carlyle said, frowning down at the patient.

"I told you, that's not possible."

"No!" the patient cried. "No hospitals. My mother died in the hospital." Her eyes widened again, and she cried out as another wave of contractions racked her body.

He sighed and reached into the satchel, bringing out a small clear vial and a hypodermic needle, which he set on the table beside the bed. He rummaged around again and brought out a brown paper packet of cotton balls. "Damn it," he muttered. He reached for his jacket and extracted a half-empty pint of gin from the inside pocket.

Carlyle uncapped the gin and dribbled some on the cotton ball. He stuck the hypodermic in the vial of liquid, drew back the plunger and flicked the tube once, twice with a forefinger, to dispel any air bubbles.

He nodded at the woman. "I'll need you to hold her down for a moment."

"I'll try," she whispered, standing to lean across the bed.

"Noooo!" the patient cried.

"Just a small prick," he said pleasantly. "Then you'll have a nice sleep, and when you wake up, this will all be over."

Her body tensed as another contraction began, and she writhed in pain.

"Hold her down!" he barked, and he jabbed the needle into her arm.

When he emerged from the bedroom, he carried a tiny, squalling infant wrapped in a pillowcase.

"It's a boy," Dr. Carlyle said, thrusting the baby into the woman's arms.

"Healthy?" She looked down at the beet-red infant. "He's so tiny."

"Because he's too early," Carlyle said. His shirt was sweat-soaked and clung to his chest, his forearms were flecked with blood, and his white hair was plastered to his skull.

"Where's the bathroom? I need to wash up."

"Just there." She pointed to the next door. "And how is she?" The woman gazed anxiously through the open doorway where the patient lay unconscious atop a mound of blood-soaked sheets and towels.

"She'll live. But there won't be any more surprise pregnancies, I'll tell you that."

"Just as well," she murmured.

She heard water running. She looked down at the baby, no bigger than an undersized roasting hen. She didn't particularly like babies, but she felt a strange pang of sympathy for this one. She touched a tentative finger to his fist, and he stopped crying, grabbed hold, and clung on with a surprising ferocity.

Carlyle was wiping his hands on a clean towel. "You'll want to wash her properly when she wakes up, keep the incision clean, watch that she doesn't run a fever, which is a sign of infection. If she does seem feverish, call me immediately before she becomes septic."

"And what about the baby?"

"What about it?"

The woman looked down at the now sleeping infant and then pointed with her chin toward the bedroom. "She's not married, you know. If anybody found out..."

He yawned, impatient to get home to his bed. "What are you trying to say?"

She bit her lip. "It would be better if she thought... well, if she thought the baby died."

Carlyle bristled and feigned shock, though in his line of work this was a very old story.

"What if we could find somebody to take care of it?" the woman went on.

"What are you suggesting?"

"Surely there are orphanages?"

"This baby is not an orphan," he said. "In any case, orphanages require paperwork. Questions would be asked."

"Oh."

He looked at her, waiting, expectant.

She sighed and went for her pocketbook. He took the money without comment.

The woman slumped with exhaustion. He considered her, considered his surroundings. He knew the owner of this house, had even socialized with him, in long-ago, happier times. Money would not be an issue for this family. If he could provide the answers to nosy questions, perhaps everybody's problems would be solved.

"I know a couple," he said slowly.

When he left, he took the sleeping infant with him, bundled in a wicker shopping basket. She went into the bedroom and began gathering up the soiled linens. Carlyle's gin bottle stood on the nightstand, empty now.

39

··

abe Wynant was getting accustomed to the unexpected that day at Shellhaven. But nothing could have readied him for the story he was about to
hear in the library-turned-bedroom so recently vacated by Josephine Bettendorf Warrick.

Brooke caught him as he took the last stair. He was dressed and ready to
leave, his briefcase again tucked under his arm.

"What now?" he said, noting the grim expression on her face.

She glanced upward, toward the second floor. "Where are the others?"

"I heard lots of cursing coming from Lizzie's bedroom. And the cat was
yowling, so it's a good guess they're getting ready to leave. I think Felicia and
Varina went out somewhere with Louette."

"I think you'd better come with me," she said.

C. D. had seated himself in the recliner and was idly leafing through a leather-
bound book he'd picked at random from one of the bookcases.

"You remember C. D.," she told Gabe.

"Yes?" Gabe said, leaning against the doorjamb.

"C. D., could you please tell my colleague what you just told me?"

"You mean the part where I tell him I'm Josephine's son?" C. D. seemed pleased to have a story worth telling and retelling.

Gabe blinked and looked at Brooke for her reaction. She nodded. "Yes. And start from the beginning, please."

"Which beginning? You mean how she dropped me off at the orphanage in Savannah when I was just a baby? Not even a month old? And bribed them nuns to keep me and not tell anybody she'd had a bastard? Or do you want me to begin when I got too old to stay with the little kiddies, so they packed me off to Good Shepherd Home for Boys?"

"Whoa. Whoa!" Gabe exclaimed. "She? You are referring to Josephine Warrick?"

"Who else?" C. D. asked.

"You're telling me you are Josephine Warrick's son?"

"And only living heir," C. D. said. He picked up a pen and extended it toward the lawyer. "Write it all down if you want, 'cause it's all true and I can prove it."

40

....

C. D. folded his sunglasses and placed them in his breast pocket. His pale blue eyes flickered around the library, taking inventory, finally resting on the side-by-side oil portraits of Josephine and Preiss Warrick.

Preiss was posed casually in a tweed jacket, sitting on a tree stump, with a shotgun propped in the crook of his elbow. His left hand rested on the head of a black-and-white English setter who had a dead bird clenched between its jaws. Preiss had been a handsome man, with a narrow, bony face, deep-set eyes, and full lips. The painting's backdrop was a romanticized version of Talisa with moss-draped oaks, blue sky, and puffy cotton-candy clouds.

Josephine appeared to have been costumed for a fancy dress party in her portrait, in a floor-length emerald-green satin dress, triple strands of pearls, and a full-length mink tossed artfully around her shoulders. The backdrop matched the portrait of her husband, right down to the tree stump and the trailing Spanish moss. But in Josephine's portrait the setter was curled up, asleep at her feet.

C. D. drummed his fingertips on the leather-bound book cover.

"We're waiting," Gabe said, tiring of the dramatics.

"You were raised at Good Shepherd? In Savannah?" Brooke asked. Like most in Savannah, she knew that the former children's home, founded in pre–Revolutionary War times, was considered the oldest child-caring institution in the country.

"Back in my day, it was called Good Shepherd Home for Boys," C. D. said. "They changed the name along the way. But I didn't get sent over to Good Shepherd until the nuns closed up the orphanage I'd been in. St. Joseph's Foundling Home, it was called."

"Never heard of it," Gabe said flatly. "And I'm Catholic, and I was raised in Savannah."

C. D. shrugged. "You probably never heard of it, 'cause like I said, the nuns closed it up a long time ago. It was on Habersham Street, right where there's a grocery store today. They shut St. Joe's down sometime in the fifties, but they kept on running the girls' orphanage. I reckon they decided boys were too much trouble."

"How does Josephine Warrick figure into all of this?" Gabe asked.

"How do you think? She got herself knocked up. And she wasn't married, either, so she did what rich girls did back then. She paid somebody to take the kid—that's me—off her hands. The nuns took me in, then when I was five, they shipped me out to Good Shepherd."

C. D.'s mouth smiled, but his eyes were wary. "And that's where I stayed, working on that damn cattle farm of theirs, until I got into trouble, and then I ran away before they could bounce me out."

"How old were you when you left Good Shepherd?" Brooke asked.

"Sixteen."

"And where did you finish high school?"

That smile again. "Who says I did? I was on my own, had to get a job, which I did. After a while, I was sick of Savannah, so I hitchhiked clear out to California and then back east. I ran into a recruiter in Baton Rouge, after an all-night bender, who promised me that I'd see the world if I signed up for the marines. Next thing I know, I'm at Parris Island, then right after that, I started seeing the world with the Third Marine Division in Vietnam."

C. D. rolled up his shirtsleeve to display the tattoo on his bicep. "Semper fi, motherfucker." He nodded at Gabe Wynant. "How 'bout you? Did you ever serve?"

"Nope. I turned eighteen in '72, but I had a student deferment," Gabe said.

"College boy," C. D. said. "Figures."

"I suppose you have some proof that Josephine Warrick was your birth mother?" Gabe asked. "Adoption records, birth certificate, something like that?"

C. D.'s smile dimmed a bit. "That ain't how it worked back then. Everything was hush-hush."

"Okay, what proof do you have?" Brooke asked. She couldn't decide whether she was intrigued or horrified by C. D.'s unfolding story. A little of both, probably. "It's not up to us, but a judge is going to want proof of the validity of your claim."

C. D. leaned forward and brought out a worn leather billfold that was attached by a chain to his belt. He slid a packet of papers from the billfold and smoothed them out across his knees.

He held out a photocopy of a black-and-white newspaper photo of a small child of no more than two or three, dressed in cotton print pajamas and holding a toy truck, balanced on the knee of a woman who was looking away from the camera. "That's me," he said, tapping the image of the child. "And that's Josephine."

"Can I see that?"

C. D. passed the clipping to Gabe Wynant, who examined it closely and then handed it to Brooke.

The newspaper photo was date-stamped SAVANNAH MORNING NEWS, June 18, 1945. The woman in the photo was dressed in a dark dress, with a frivolous feathered hat perched on her dark hair. She held the child stiffly at arm's length from her chest.

LOCAL BENEFACTRESS VISITS CHILDREN'S HOME, the caption read. Underneath, the copy said:

> Miss Josephine Bettendorf distributed smiles and Christmas gifts to orphaned boys this week at the St. Joseph's Foundling Home. Three-year-old Charles Anthony delighted in receiving a new toy truck.

Brooke studied C. D.'s face.

"Charles Anthony is me," he said. "And I still got that truck."

"That's an amazing coincidence," Gabe said. "But Josephine was probably just doing what wealthy socialites did back then. It was a charity visit, not a mother-son reunion."

"No way," C. D. said. "She came to that home every year while I was there, at Christmas. She handed out candy and toothbrushes and pajamas to them other kids. But I was the only one who got a real toy." He leaned forward, showing off a narrow white scar that ran through his left eyebrow. "Some other kid tried to take my truck the last year I was at the orphanage. I slugged him, and he hit me with the truck, which is how I got this scar and how he lost his two front teeth."

"Sorry, but that's not really proof that you were her child," Gabe said. "Maybe she just thought you were cute, or she felt sorry for you."

"I figured you'd say something like that," C. D. said. He leafed through the packet of papers on his lap and held up another document. It was a photocopy of a typed page.

"Now this here is what's called the intake report from St. Joseph's. The sister in charge filled it out when they took in a kid. This is a copy of my intake page. Take a look at that, why don't you?"

Brooke scooted her chair next to Gabe's, peering over his shoulder. There were spaces on the page for the date, name, and address of parent or parents, child's name and date of birth, weight, height, eye and hair color, and race. At the bottom, a space was reserved for comments.

According to the report, on May 5, 1942, a male child named Charles D. Anthony arrived at the orphanage. Weight was eleven pounds, six ounces. The child's hair color was listed as brown. Eye color: blue. Race: W. In the spaces for the child's mother and father, someone had typed *Unknown*. Also unknown were the child's exact date of birth, although someone had typed *Approx. six months of age.*

The comments block had been filled out in Spenserian black script.

Father Ryan brought male child to home last Sunday, stated he was found asleep, under pew, in church today, after 8:00 A.M. mass. No parishioners have any knowledge of child. Father stated hopes parent will return to claim child, but fears child has been abandoned. The boy is docile, in good health. Father Ryan believes that boy was born out of wedlock. Mother Superior advises we will accept child pending further investigation.

"Somebody left a child? A six-month-old baby in a church?" Brooke said, aghast.

"Yeah. That was me," C. D. said. "Turns out since they didn't know my real name, they named me after that priest. Charles David. For a last name, they gave me the name of one of the nun's favorite saints, which was St. Anthony." He chuckled. "Can you imagine that? Me named after a saint?"

Brooke found herself speechless, pondering the reality of C. D.'s childhood. She'd always known who she was, who her people were, and who *their* people were. Family and a sense of family identity were ingrained in every Southerner she knew, especially Savannahians, who were obsessed with family connections. What would it be like to wonder your entire life who you really were?

"How did you find out about all of this?" Brooke asked. "Or did you always know about the orphanage?"

C. D. rubbed the gray stubble on his chin. "I always remembered bits and pieces from the time I was in the orphanage. Like how us little kids all slept in one big room, with rows and rows of these iron cribs that had high sides so you couldn't climb out. Even when we got older and were big enough to sleep in a real bed, they kept us in those cribs, almost like a cage, you know?"

Brooke thought guiltily about the crib her own Henry had been sleeping in until recently. Would he too remember, someday, and wonder if he had been kept a prisoner there?

"How were you able to track down these records?" Gabe asked.

"That's kind of a funny coincidence," C. D. said. "After I came home from Vietnam, I'd been living in Savannah off and on for about twenty years. Retired there, after working as a longshoreman out at the Port Authority, and I knew a couple of guys, like me, who were Good Shepherd alumni. One of 'em told me about a reunion they were having a couple of years ago. It was the home's

275th anniversary. So I went along out there, 'cause I was curious to see how the place had changed."

"I imagine there's been quite a bit of change since you lived there," Gabe offered.

"Yeah, the 'cottage' I lived in, it's some kind of classroom now," C. D. said. "The whole place is a boys' prep school now, 'cause you really don't have a lot of honest-to-God orphans these days."

"My mom has a friend whose father and two brothers grew up at Good Shepherd, back in the Depression years," Brooke said. "Their father had died, and their mother had to work and couldn't care for three boys. So she kept his sisters and the boys were raised at the Children's home."

"That happened a lot," C. D. said. "Anyway, at the reunion party, I ran into a guy who lived in my cottage. He was a couple of years older than me, but like me, he'd been at St. Joseph's before Good Shepherd. And he was telling me that he'd been able to look up his records. In the church office. I forget what they call it."

"The archdiocesan office," Gabe said. "All the diocesan records were moved there after the girls' orphanage was closed and remodeled."

C. D. snapped his fingers. "Yeah, that's what it's called. Anyway, they won't let you look at the records unless you can prove you were what they call a for-mer 'resident.' I told the woman there, 'Hell, I wasn't a resident, I was an or-phan.'" He rattled the papers on his lap. "That's where I found all this stuff." He smoothed the newspaper clipping. "They let me look in my file. How about that? I found this clipping. And when I saw the picture of *her* holding me on her lap, something clicked. And I remembered her. How she come to see me, every year, at Christmas, and on my birthday, or what they told me was my birthday. I remembered she smelled like some kind of flowery perfume. And she had a pearl necklace, and I tried to play with it, but she'd slap my hand away."

C. D. paused in his story. "Now you tell me, why would she come see some little kid in an orphanage, bring him presents and all like that, unless she had a connection to him?"

"Good question," Gabe conceded.

"When you came to work here, did you tell Josephine you thought she was your mother?" Brooke asked.

He shook his head emphatically. "No. Because I wasn't sure yet. I kinda wanted to get the lay of the land, check things out. I came over on the ferry, talked to Shug and asked about a job, and he's the one brought me up to the house and told Josephine maybe I could run the boat and help with some other stuff around here."

"And she never recognized you? Didn't recognize your name?" Gabe sounded skeptical. "Come on, C. D. This is an entertaining story, but none of it proves that you are her son or her heir."

"How about this?" C. D. asked. He handed over a faded color snapshot of a brick cottage surrounded by towering oaks similar to the ones on Talisa. Brooke squinted to read a plaque.

"That's the Samuel Bettendorf Cottage at Good Shepherd," C. D. said. "I looked it up in the records. Josephine donated the money for it to be built in 1946—the year I got put over there once they closed the orphanage."

"And what do you think that signifies?" Gabe asked.

"It means she felt guilty about walking away and giving me up," C. D. said, throwing up his hands in exasperation. "Hell, I can't explain why she did the stuff she did. I just know I am her son, and after all these years, it's about damn time she did right by me."

He looked from Brooke to Gabe, then back at Brooke again, and then donned his sunglasses. "Kinda upsets your apple cart, don't it? You and your mom and those women upstairs? Looks like none of y'all are gonna be heiresses after all."

Brooke shrugged. She didn't know what to say or how to feel. Just the night before, the mistress of Shellhaven had shocked them all by telling them about a murder that had happened nearly eighty years ago, right here on this island. This morning, Josephine was dead, her estate left in limbo. Horror, grief, shock, disbelief. And now this. She was numb.

She stood up and held out a hand to C. D. "Good luck to you, C. D. I hope you're able to prove your claim. And I truly mean that. If Josephine really did walk away and leave you in an orphanage all those years ago, you deserve to inherit. But in the meantime, I need to get back to the mainland. To my own son."

41

....

They found Marie and Lizzie in the kitchen, having lunch. Louette looked up from the sandwich she was eating.

"Did C. D. tell y'all that crazy story of his? 'Bout how he's Josephine's son?"

"What's that?" Marie asked, startled. "You mean C. D., the man who pilots the boat? He's Josephine's son?"

"That's what *he* thinks." Louette's voice dripped scorn. She stood up and motioned for Brooke to take her chair. "Sit here. You want some lunch? I got chicken salad and crab salad."

Gabe dragged a chair up to the table. "I'd love a crab salad sandwich."

"I'm not really hungry," Brooke said. "But if it's all right, I'd like to call the ferry to book a ride back to the mainland."

"Oh, I already took care of that," Louette said. "You're on the two o'clock, if that's all right."

Brooke gestured to Lizzie. "Will that give us enough time to get you to the airport for your flight back to California?"

Lizzie reached for a potato chip from the bowl in the center of the table. "I'm not going home. Not just yet. I canceled my flight."

"But . . . I thought you were in such a rush to get back. For your deadline and everything," Brooke said.

"I was, until last night, when Josephine started spinning that amazing story of hers, and then, after what happened this morning, it dawned on me, there's a story right here. Like, a once-in-a-lifetime story. And I'm a part of it. So instead of packing this morning, I pounded out a query letter and emailed it to a couple of magazine editors I know in New York, and I heard back from one right away, and she loves the idea. So I'm staying."

"Here?" Gabe asked. "At Shellhaven?"

"Why not? Louette doesn't have a problem with that, do you, Louette?"

"Be nice to have company, especially with Josephine gone," Louette said.

"Do you have a problem with me staying here?" Lizzie asked Gabe pointedly.

"No. I mean, as I said, I'll petition the court to be named administrator of the estate, but in the meantime, I guess there's no reason you couldn't stay on."

"Then it's settled," Lizzie said. "Now what's all this about C. D.? He really claims he's Josephine's long-lost son?"

While Gabe polished off two crab salad sandwiches, a homemade pickle, and a couple of tea cakes, Brooke recited what the lawyers had just heard from C. D.

"This story just keeps getting better and better," Lizzie said, rubbing her hands together gleefully. "Josephine, an unwed mother! Now it's not just a magazine article or a book. We're talking potential movie deal."

"I wouldn't go that far," Gabe said, brushing cookie crumbs from the front of his golf shirt. "I hated to burst the guy's bubble, but an old newspaper clipping of her holding a little orphaned tyke at Christmas probably isn't going to hold water in court."

"That man is crazy," Louette said, shaking her head. "I never heard a story so crazy. Even if it were true, don't you think Josephine would have recognized her own flesh and blood?"

"It does strain the imagination," Marie said. "Abandoning a baby in a church? And then going to the orphanage every year at Christmas to visit him? How could anybody be that cruel? Even Josephine?"

. . .

Varina pushed her walker slowly into the kitchen, with Felicia following behind. "Is Josephine . . . gone? Did the funeral home man come?"

"Yes, but actually, the coroner is a woman. Her family owns the funeral home too. They took her body back over to the mainland, just until the funeral arrangements can be made," Gabe said, scrambling to his feet to offer his chair to the old woman.

"But they'll bring her back, won't they?" Varina asked anxiously.

"Yes, I understand those were her wishes," Gabe said.

"Auntie Vee, you need to eat some lunch before we get on the ferry so your blood sugar doesn't get too low," Felicia said.

"I got her a nice sandwich right here," Louette said, sliding a plate of food in front of Varina.

"She's all the time fussing over me," Varina told Marie. "Does Brooke fuss at you like that?"

"Usually not," Marie said. "More likely I'm fussing at her."

"What time does that ferry leave?" Varina asked, nibbling on her sandwich.

"Not 'til two, so you've got plenty of time to eat," Louette said.

"Then maybe Shug will take us by the old place at Oyster Bluff first." Varina looked across the table at Brooke. "Have you been over to Oyster Bluff yet?"

"No, ma'am," Brooke said. "I've heard a lot about it, though."

"I'd love to see it," Lizzie said. "Research for my magazine article. What is this Oyster Bluff place?"

"It's my home. Where my people have always lived," Varina said, her voice quivering slightly. "Where I'm going to stay, 'til the good Lord decides to take me."

"Maybe someday," Felicia said with a vague smile.

"Not someday. This day," Varina said, her face serene. "I was reading my Bible just now, and the scripture spoke to me, clear as a bell. Isaiah. This island here is my home, where I am fixing to stay until such time as my Father takes me to his home."

"Now, Auntie, we have talked about this," Felicia said. "You're living with me now, because the doctors say you've got to have somebody to make sure you eat and take your medicine."

Varina nodded and ignored her great-niece. "Louette, could you please ask Shug to ride us over to Oyster Bluff in that fancy new truck of his before these ladies need to take the ferry back?"

Louette reached for the phone. "I'll call him right now."

Shug turned off the paved main road onto a wide shell road. Varina was propped up next to him, and Brooke sat by the window. Lizzie, Marie, and a grumbling Felicia sat in the second row of cab seats.

Varina pointed to a wide, weedy pasture area surrounded by cypress and oak trees. A pair of rusted-out trucks were parked at the edge of the field along with a tractor that leaned crazily on rotted tires. "That there is part of the old plantation, where they grew cotton and sugarcane. It was way before my time, of course, but my grandmama used to talk about working in that field."

"What was the plantation called?" Lizzie asked from the backseat. "Did the Bettendorfs own it?"

"Oh no. Mr. Samuel didn't buy the island until long after plantation times." Varina turned to her great-niece. "What did they call that place, honey?"

"Friendship," Felicia said. "Great name for a business that bought and sold slaves, don't you think?"

Shug turned the truck in a wide arc around the pasture, and in half a mile the small community came into view. A hand-painted sign tacked to a tree proclaimed, "Historic Oyster Bluff. Pop. 45."

"More like twenty. Or twenty-five on a good day," he observed. He slowed the truck over the rutted dirt road as two chickens raced across it. Varina pointed to a long, low, wood-frame building with a rusted tin roof. Six or seven junked cars were parked haphazardly in the crushed-shell parking lot, their hoods up, weeds growing out from broken windshields.

"What's up with all the abandoned cars?" Lizzie asked.

"Costs fifty dollars to barge a vehicle back over to the mainland," Shug said. "If it can't be fixed, that car dies right here."

"That's the old commissary," Varina said, pointing to the building. "Back when I was a child, Mr. Samuel paid all his people in script we called 'Bettendorf Bucks.' You could use it like money to buy whatever you needed. We didn't need much back then. Everybody had a garden, and we fished in the creek, raked oysters. My daddy knew how to knit a cast net, so we had as much shrimp as we wanted. There's wild cows on the island, and every year, my daddy and brothers would catch one, fatten him up, and then butcher it. They hunted too; deer and hogs and turkey and dove. But it was a big treat when I used to take my little bit of money to the commissary and buy candy and Coca-Colas."

"One of Louette's cousins runs it now, we just call it the Store," Shug said. "It ain't open except Thursday through Sunday, and that's only if he's sober and out of jail."

He turned down another lane and pointed proudly to a snug cottage with a wide front porch that looked out onto the marsh. Baskets of ferns and geraniums hung from the ceiling beams, and a carport housed another car and a golf cart.

"That's our place. I built that front porch so we can sit out there and watch the sunset. Got me a deck on the back where I do my grilling. Louette wants me to put in a new kitchen, but we were waiting to see if Miss Josephine was gonna let us buy the place back before we put any more money in it." His shoulders sagged, and he passed a hand over his jaw. "Don't know what will happen now."

The truck rolled slowly down the road, passing half a dozen small homes in various states of disrepair, while Varina provided a running commentary of residents past and present. "That's the Johnsons, but I think they all moved off. That there was where the preacher used to live. This house right here is where my best little friend Marjean lived. Her mama was real sweet to me, because I didn't have a mama of my own. Miss Stokes had the best garden on this whole island. Grew the sweetest corn and the prettiest flowers you ever saw."

"How'd she keep the deer and hogs from eating everything up?" Shug asked.

"Ooh, she had her a stout wooden fence all around that garden plot, and she had a big mean dog, Mitzi, would scare anything away that came near," Varina said, laughing.

Shug pulled the truck in front of a small wooden tin-roofed cottage. Faded green paint peeked from behind thickly festooned vines that threatened to swallow the house whole. The front porch columns were whitewashed tree trunks, and the windows on either side of the front door were boarded up with plywood.

"This is my house," Varina said, her eyes glowing with pride. "My daddy built it with his own two hands. He cut the trees down and milled the planks right here on this island. Mr. Samuel counted on my daddy. He sold him the land for our house, and I been keeping up with the taxes all this time."

"It must be a really special place for you," Marie said from the backseat.

"It's adorable," Lizzie said, peering out the window at the cottage. "It's like one of those tiny houses they show on HGTV. I wish I could move in here myself."

Felicia glared at Lizzie and silently mouthed the word, "*Nooooo.*"

"Yes, ma'am," Varina said. "And now I'm fixing to move right back home."

"Here?" Felicia's voice was panicky. "I know it's special, but look at this place, Auntie. It's falling down."

"Then I'll fix it back up." Varina patted Shug's arm. "This man here can do anything. You'll help me, won't you, baby?"

"Why not?" He opened the door and planted one boot onto the weedy yard and appraised the house with a thoughtful eye. "This house has been standing all this time, so it must be sound. Gonna need a new roof, though."

"You can't stay here," Felicia insisted. "Does it even have plumbing? Or electricity? Tell her, Shug."

"It actually does have plumbing. And electricity, although we probably need to update the panel. Homer was living here until he got too sick and moved over to hospice. It hasn't been empty but a couple of years."

"Okay, but it's gonna need a lot of work before it's even remotely habitable. It'll probably take months and months. And where will you stay in the meantime? You can't get up and down the stairs at Josephine's house."

"Plenty of room at our place," Shug said. "The kids and grandkids hardly come over at all anymore 'cause they've got sports and all that. Louette's gonna be getting lonesome without having Josephine to look after and cook for."

"Oh no, we couldn't put you out," Felicia started.

"We got two guest rooms. Plenty of room for both of y'all," Shug said.

"Thank you, baby," Varina said, beaming at her benefactor.

"Auntie, that's just not possible," Felicia said. "It's sweet of Shug to offer, but I'm your caregiver, and I have to work."

Varina's jaw set stubbornly. "Didn't you tell me you do all your teaching on a computer now? And don't they have computers and all that here on Talisa?"

"Yes, ma'am, we got Wi-Fi here," Shug said. "Me and Louette FaceTime the grandkids all the time on our computer."

"See that?" Varina nodded enthusiastically. "So it's all set, then. We can go on back to Jacksonville today and pack up our stuff and then be back for the morning ferry. Isn't that a blessing?"

Lizzie grinned and poked Felicia in the ribs. "Sounds like a blessing to me."

42

....

The ferry was waiting at the dock, along with a crowd of three dozen passengers—campers, day-trippers, and a group of middle-aged bird-watchers bristling with cameras, binoculars, and backpacks. Brooke was surprised to see just how large the ferry was, a gleaming white affair with two observation decks, with the name painted in large letters across the stern: *The Miss Elsie Bettendorf*.

"I wonder if that was Josephine's mother," Marie said as the group approached the boarding dock.

"That's right. Miss Elsie was Josephine's mama," Varina said, coming slowly up beside them. "Those state people thought they were buttering Josephine up, naming the ferry after Miss Elsie, but that made her madder than a mule with a mouthful of bumblebees. She wrote all kind of letters trying to make them change the name, but it was too late. She wouldn't even get near this new ferry, no matter what."

"I guess it's a good thing Josephine's not still alive to know that her final trip across the river was on *The Miss Elsie*," Felicia said.

"Ooh, child," Varina said, chuckling despite herself. "She'd come back and haunt us all."

. . .

They found an empty row of shaded wooden seats on the first deck.

"Remind me why you're going back across to the mainland, since you're staying on at Shellhaven?" Felicia asked Lizzie.

"Supplies," Lizzie said, ticking off her list. "Cat food for Dweezil, a few more clothes, including a bathing suit, since I only packed enough stuff for the weekend, white wine, tequila, Xanax . . . just the basics."

Felicia cocked her head and regarded Lizzie with real interest. "So you're going to write a magazine article about Josephine and Talisa? Seriously? Who'd want to read about some backwater island in the middle of nowhere?"

"Who wouldn't? This story has more turns and twists than a daytime soap opera, but the best part is, it's all true. Just look at the latest development: this C. D. character coming to Brooke and Gabe this morning to say that he's Josephine's long-lost son and only living heir. How surreal is that?"

"Oh, please," Felicia said with a snort. "If he's kin to Josephine, I'm Diana Ross."

"What did you just say?" Varina leaned forward from her seat next to Felicia to face Lizzie. "Who's kin to who?"

Lizzie raised her voice and enunciated slowly. "I said C. D. is now claiming to be Josephine's son."

Varina's eyes behind her thick-lensed glasses widened. "Oh no. That can't be right. That boy is crazy. What's he saying that for?"

"Easy. For the money," Felicia said, frowning. "He wants to inherit the house, the island, Josephine's money, all of it." She glared in Gabe's direction. "Just because *somebody* didn't get her will signed and witnessed before she died."

Gabe flushed slightly but said nothing.

"Brooke, Mr. Gabe, did that man really say Josephine was his mama?" Varina asked.

"That's his story," Brooke said. "It's kind of complicated, but in a nutshell, C. D. says he believes that Josephine abandoned him as an infant—left him in a church in Savannah. The church turned him over to a Catholic orphanage there, and they, in turn, placed him in Good Shepherd Home for Boys, where he lived until he ran away at sixteen."

"No, no, no," Varina insisted. She clenched the wooden bench slats with both hands. "That's not true. It can't be true. I would have known." She continued, shaking her head, "How old is that man?"

"He told me this weekend that he's seventy-six. Born in '42, I think he said."

Varina's forehead puckered in distress. "See, that's a lie. No, ma'am. Josephine never had no baby, never. I would have known if she'd had a child. She didn't even meet Mr. Preiss until the war was over."

"His story is pretty far-fetched," Marie said gently, "but isn't it just possible that since Josephine was unmarried, she would have kept her pregnancy a secret because of the scandal? She could have told you and everybody else that she was going away to 'visit family.' That's what young girls did back then. At one time, there was even a home for unwed mothers, The Florence Crittenton home, just a few blocks from my house in Ardsley Park, where girls went to have their babies. Afterward, the babies were adopted and the girls went back home and nobody was any wiser."

"I don't care. It's a lie. That man is telling a lie," Varina said angrily.

Lizzie leaned back and stretched and yawned. "I think I'll see about renting a car. That way I can shoot up to Savannah this week to try to verify C. D.'s story."

Gabe reached into his pocket and brought out a plastic bag containing two smaller plastic bags.

"You can double-check his story if you like. I think it's a good idea. But in the meantime, I took the liberty of getting Louette to collect some of Josephine's hair from her hairbrush. And I paid a visit to C. D., who, after some persuading, donated a bit of that ponytail of his."

"Hair?" Varina wrinkled her nose. "What are you gonna do with that?"

"It's for DNA testing, Auntie," Felicia said.

"I'll send it off to a testing laboratory, and they should be able to tell us whether or not C. D. is related to Josephine," Gabe explained.

"I don't need a bag of hair to tell you that," Varina said. "Because that man is definitely no kin to Josephine Warrick." Her hands shook slightly as she gesticulated.

Felicia placed a hand on her aunt's arm. "Auntie, I think we need to test your blood sugar and see if it's time for your meds. Let's go to the ladies' room. Okay?"

The old woman was still muttering under her breath as her great-niece helped her to her feet and they began making their laborious way to the ferry's restroom.

After the ferry landed and their group had disembarked, Brooke motioned for Lizzie to follow them to her car. "I don't think you'll be able to rent a car in St. Ann's. We might need to take you to Brunswick to the airport for that."

"I'm headed back to St. Simon's, so Brunswick is on my way, and I'm happy to give you a ride," Gabe said.

"Fine with me," Lizzie said. She turned and watched as Felicia tried to juggle two overnight bags and Varina. "Let me go see if I can give those two a hand."

"You're not going back to Savannah?" Brooke asked Gabe.

"No, I want to get to the courthouse here first thing tomorrow to petition the court to become administrator of Josephine's estate."

"I need to figure out what my next move is too. Josephine paid me a retainer, and I need to make a good-faith effort to follow through and stop the state from taking her land."

"Your client is dead," Gabe said. "Your obligation to her has expired. I suppose you can raise the matter with her heirs, when and if we track them down, or learn the truth about C. D.'s claim." He leaned in closer to her, his voice low in her ear. "Have dinner with me tonight, Brooke. Please?"

"Tonight? I can't, Gabe. I haven't seen Henry in two days. I'm already feeling guilty about leaving him with Farrah for this long. Maybe we can catch up tomorrow, after you make your filing? We can compare notes."

He sighed. "Okay, if lunch is all you can do. But, Brooke, I didn't mean for this to be a business meeting." He searched her face for a reaction.

Her face grew hot, and she could feel herself blushing.

"Never mind," he said quickly. "Call me tomorrow if you want, and we can meet. Strictly professional if that's how you want it."

He turned and walked hurriedly toward his car.

43

....

M arie waited until they were in the car. "What was that all about?"

"What?" Brooke felt heat creeping up from her collarbone.

"That whispered conference back there with Gabe."

"Oh, you know, just legal stuff. He's going to stay over at Sea Island tonight so he can be at the courthouse here first thing in the morning to petition to become administrator of Josephine's estate."

"This is your mother, Brooke. I know something else was going on back there."

Brooke sighed. "I think maybe Gabe just asked me out on a date."

"Maybe? You're not sure?"

"Okay, so yes, he asked me to dinner. But I totally blew it and embarrassed both of us."

"What did you say?"

"The first thing that occurred to me. Which was that I'd been away from Henry for two days, and I couldn't possibly go out to dinner. Then he asked me to have lunch with him, and at that point he made it very clear that he wasn't talking about a business meeting when he asked me out for dinner."

"Ohhhh. So how do you feel about that? About seeing Gabe socially?"

"I don't know," Brooke wailed. "God, I suck at this boy-girl stuff. I never was good at it. Maybe that's why after I started dating Harris in college, I decided he was the one. It was such a relief, you know, to not have to go through this whole bizarre dating ritual."

Marie laughed. "How did I raise such an odd duck as you? Brooke, honey, this is not all that tricky. Take it slow. Break it down to the basics. A nice man asked you out to dinner. He's single; you're single. Now. How do you feel about Gabe? On a personal basis?"

"Don't you think he's way too old for me? I mean, the last time we went out to dinner, somebody mistook him for my dad! It was super embarrassing."

"Gabe Wynant is much younger than Gordon and, just between us girls, much better looking. Anyway, why do you care what I think or what some stupid waiter thinks? What do you think? That's the only thing that matters."

Brooke took a deep breath. "He's a nice guy. When we worked together, he never talked down to me, never hit on me like some of the other, older partners in the law firm. We used to run together, you know? He really listened to me and respected my opinions."

"What else?"

Brooke shrugged. "I guess I like how he treats women. He never said anything negative about his wife, ever, even though she must have put him through hell. He's old-school like that, but not an old fogey, like Dad."

"And?"

"Okay, I guess he is kind of hot, in a silver-haired-fox kind of way. He's fit, but not obsessed with himself. Does that make sense?"

"Yes. And I'd agree with everything you said."

"Then maybe *you* should go out to dinner with him."

"He didn't ask me," Marie said. "Or I would. Now, what are the negatives?"

"Like I said, he's way too old for me. What do we even have in common?"

"Hmm. You both like to run. You're both interested in the law. I don't know. That's the reason you go to dinner with somebody. To figure that stuff out. It's part of that whole 'bizarre dating ritual thing' that you seem to think you suck at."

"I do suck at it," Brooke insisted. "Anyway, the big thing is, it's creepy. It's like that whole Woody Allen obsession with younger chicks thing."

"It's nothing like that," Marie said sharply. "You're not an impressionable teenager. If you're not interested, just say, 'No, thanks.' Gabe's no dummy. He won't pursue it if you decline."

"But I don't want to hurt his feelings! I like him. I like him a lot!"

"Then go to dinner. Or lunch. Or meet him for a drink. Or coffee. But if you think you have even a little interest, say yes. That's the one thing I've learned, getting older, going through a divorce, reinventing myself. Say yes to the possibility."

Brooke pulled the Volvo into the driveway of her house. "You sound like you have some personal experience in this whole game. Are you saying you've been dating?"

Marie's smile was sphinxlike.

"Mom! You have been dating. Why didn't you say so?"

The front door to the cottage opened, and seconds later, Farrah stood in the doorway, waving at them as Henry hurtled through the yard and into his mother's arms.

44

....

Hey," Farrah said as soon as Brooke walked into the office on Monday afternoon. "We need to get over to the jail. There's a situation with Brittni."

"We?" Brooke asked. "Did you graduate from law school and pass the bar exam over the weekend?"

"No, but Brittni's mom called me a little while ago. Britt got locked up again yesterday and she's in deep shit."

"Her stepfather still owes me for Brittni's last scrape with the law," Brooke pointed out.

"I told Aunt Charla that, and she's gonna meet us at the jail with the money she owes you, plus another check for $5,000 as a retainer. Happy?"

"What exactly did Brittni do?" Brooke asked as they were getting into the Volvo.

"Aunt Charla was kinda hysterical when she called, but she kept using words like *kidnapping* and *aggravated assault*. Also *criminal trespass*," Farrah said.

. . .

Brittni Miles had bleached-blond hair, two black eyes, and an orange jumpsuit. She glared at her visitors from the other side of a plexiglass divider in the visiting room at the Carter County Jail.

"I told Mama not to call y'all," Brittni said sullenly.

"Too bad," Farrah said. "Since your mama is the one who's payin', she gets to do the sayin'."

Brooke looked down at the copy of the arrest report she'd been given, but the police officer's handwritten narrative was nearly unreadable. "Brittni, if I'm going to represent you, I need you to tell me what happened. This says the victim's name is Kelsy Cotterell. Is she the cashier from the SwiftyMart? The one you threw the ice at?"

"She doesn't work there anymore," Brittni said smugly. "Got fired for gettin' arrested for what she done to me."

"Which was what?" Farrah asked.

"Put a big ol' bag of flaming dog poop on my mama's doorstep Friday night," Brittni said. "Only she didn't know Mama put one of those motion-activated video cameras on our front porch. The dumb ho looked right at the camera while she was doing it. The bag caught the whole porch on fire, and Mama called Aunt Jodee, and the cops looked at the video and arrested her, right there at the SwiftyMart."

"Oh-kayyyy," Brooke said slowly. "But that doesn't explain the criminal trespass, kidnapping, and aggravated assault charges against you. Do you want to walk us through that?"

"Kelsy posted bail the same night she was arrested!" Brittni exclaimed. "Then she called my cell and left a message saying next time she'd burn down our whole house. So I decided to, like, keep an eye on her. Saturday night, I followed her Camaro, and you know where she went? Right to Wayne's place! That ho."

Farrah glanced over at Brooke. "Wayne is Brittni's boyfriend."

"Ex-boyfriend."

"Whatever," Farrah said. "Does Wayne still live in those apartments by the school?"

"Uh-uh. He bought an RV, which he parks at his sister's place. Wayne told me he had to work a late shift Saturday night, but his truck was parked right there in his sister's driveway. The lying sack of crap. I watched her go in, and five minutes later, I saw the lights in the RV go out, and the next thing you know, that thing was rockin' back and forth to beat the band."

"Uh-oh," Farrah said.

"Right then, I think I might have had, like, an outer body experience," Brittni said. "I, like, lost control. Next thing you know, I was running over to the cab of the RV. I was just gonna bang on the side to scare them, but the keys were in the ignition, so I fired it up and floored it. Who knew a twelve-year-old Winnebago could do sixty on a dirt road? I could hear Wayne and Kelsy bouncing around back there and hollering at me to stop, but it was like the devil took hold of me. You know how that is, right?"

"Uh, no," Brooke said.

"Wayne came up front, buck naked, and he was trying to yank the wheel away from me, and then Kelsy was right on top of me too, pulling my hair and screaming at me to stop, and while I was trying to fight her off and defend myself, the RV went off the road and slammed into a pecan tree. The airbags deployed, and I was knocked unconscious. And when I came to, all I saw was blue lights and gold badges."

"Okay," Brooke said. "Do you still have Kelsy's message on your phone?"

"Yeah."

"Good. Forward that to me. That's called making terroristic threats. Serious stuff. If she came onto your property without permission, that's trespassing. How much damage did the flaming dog poop do?"

"A lot!" Brittni said. "The fire spread from the porch to the carport, and the whole thing collapsed on top of my stepdad's 1968 El Camino, which he's been restoring."

"All good stuff," Brooke said. "I've got to get back to the office now, but I'm going to call the district attorney and offer to show him the video of Kelsy trying to burn down your house, and I'll let him know about the threats too, and hopefully he'll see that this was just a love triangle gone wrong. In the meantime, if they do drop the charges, I'd urge you to stay away from Kelsy."

"She'd better stay the hell away from me too," Brittni said, glowering.

. . .

Charla Miles was waiting outside when Farrah and Brooke emerged from the jail.

"How'd it go?" she asked, handing an envelope to Farrah.

"As well as can be expected," Brooke reported. "I'll speak to the district attorney and see if we can't work out something that doesn't involve jail time. Best-case scenario, Brittni pays for the damage to the RV, does some community service hours, and takes some anger management classes."

Charla threw her arms around Farrah and hugged her tight. "Thank God!"

"No, Aunt Charla," Farrah said, "thank Brooke. And don't forget, if she gets Brittni off without doing any more jail time, you agreed to let her represent you on your next divorce." She handed the envelope of money to Brooke.

"I won't forget," Charla said. "Martin's so mad about Brittni getting his El Camino burned up, I could be callin' y'all any day now."

When they returned to the office, Brooke spotted an envelope lying on the middle of her desktop. The envelope had the official seal of the University of Georgia.

"What's this?" she asked, turning to Farrah.

"Oh my God, I almost forgot with all of Brittni's drama!" Farrah exclaimed. "I did it, Brooke. I got in! I got into UGA!"

She grabbed both of Brooke's hands and the two of them hopped up and down in an impromptu happy dance. "We did it!" Farrah shouted.

"You did it," Brooke corrected. "Yaaaay!"

They were both out of breath and laughing and crying at the end of the dance.

"I told you so. I knew you'd get in, but I thought you said you weren't going to apply," Brooke said with a mock-accusing tone.

"I just told everybody that, so that way, when I got rejected, nobody but me would know," Farrah said. "I didn't even tell my mom. Or Jaxson, which I felt kind of guilty about."

"Jaxson's not an issue anymore, right?"

"Maybe. I'm not sure. He wants us to get back together. He's been texting me, and I've seen him drive by the house a bunch of times at night. I think he's checking up on me."

Brooke knew better than to give unsolicited advice, but she couldn't help herself. "Farrah, please listen to me. You've got such an incredible, bright future ahead of you. I hate to see you tether yourself to your hometown honey."

"I didn't say I was getting back with him."

"But you're thinking about it. And if he's texting you, he's going to come around begging you to take him back. And he'll make you feel guilty about going off to school in Athens and leaving him behind. And the next thing you know, you'll think about what *he* wants, instead of what *you* need."

Farrah's phone dinged. She took it out of the pocket of her jeans, read the text, typed something rapidly, and pushed Send.

"Okay, I'm ready to get to work," she announced, sitting at her desk and powering up her computer.

"Was that Jaxson?"

Farrah nodded but didn't look up from the document she'd just opened.

"Did you tell him you didn't want to get back together with him?" Brooke asked.

The girl still didn't look up. "Brooke?"

"Yes?"

"Not another word."

Brooke's own cell phone rang. She checked the caller ID screen. It was Gabe Wynant.

She glanced at Farrah, picked up the phone, and headed for the powder room, which was, for her, the equivalent of a conference room. She closed the bathroom door, took a deep breath, and answered. "Hi, Gabe!"

"I know it's last minute, but is there any way you could sit for Henry tonight?" she asked Farrah, trying desperately to sound casual.

"Sure. I could use the extra money. UGA ain't cheap, ya know." She flashed a big grin.

"Great. Why don't you come over around 6:30? I'll fix something for dinner for you and Henry, and you can give him a bath and get him ready for bed before I leave around 7:00."

"That's fine. But you're going out on a weeknight?"

"Yes."

"Business meeting?"

"Not exactly. More like an, uh, date."

"Oh. My. God!" Farrah spun around on her chair so that she was facing Brooke. "Finally. Who's the guy?"

"Just a lawyer I used to work with in Savannah. An old friend, that's all."

"Suuuuure."

"Farrah?"

"Yeah?"

"Not another word."

45

....

Farrah peeked out the small window in the front door. "I think he's here."

"Get away from that window," Brooke said. "Aren't you supposed to be putting my son to bed?"

"Oh my God. He's totally driving a Porsche 911. Who is this guy?"

"Farrah!"

"Just let me get a good look at him. You know, to make sure he's not an ax murderer or something. I wish I could see his license plate."

"Farrah!"

"Okay, he's getting out of the car. Wait. He's got white hair. Seriously, how old is this dude?" She whipped her cell phone out, held it against the window, and clicked off three frames in rapid succession.

"Farrah!" Brooke's teeth were clenched. She wiped her sweaty palms on the side of her white jeans. Her stomach was doing flip-flops, and she could already feel the familiar heat creeping up from her collarbone. She'd felt like this for the past hour. It was as though she were reliving junior high again. Why in God's name had she agreed to go out with Gabe Wynant?

"Okay, he's standing by the car, but he's not moving. He's looking at his watch. He actually dresses kind of cool for an old guy. He's not even wearing dad jeans." She snapped off a few more photos.

"What do you think you're doing?"

"I'm taking his picture, so if you don't come back tonight, I'll have something to take to the cops."

"Farrah!"

"I'm going."

The doorbell rang. Brooke took a last gulp of her white wine and pasted a smile on her face.

"Hey, you," she said.

"Hey, you too," Gabe said. He was dressed casually, in dark wash—but not dad-style—jeans and a crisp, pale yellow dress shirt with rolled cuffs. He wore Gucci loafers, but no socks. "Ready to go?"

"Come on in for a minute. I just need to look in on Henry and kiss him good—"

"Noooooooo!" The three-year-old ran into the living room, dressed in his pajama top, but naked from the waist down. He threw himself against Brooke's legs, wrapping his arms around her knees. "Nooooo. I don't want you to gooooo!"

Farrah darted into the room after him. "Sorry," she said breathlessly. "I turned to grab his pull-ups and he made a run for the door."

"Come on, Henry," she said, gently trying to coax the boy away from his mother. "It's story time. *Good Night, Good Night, Construction Site*. Your favorite."

Henry tried to slap away the babysitter's hands. "No. I go with Mama."

Brooke leaned down and hoisted the boy into her arms. "Hey, little man. It's time for bed. You go with Farrah and help her read, and I'll be home before you know it."

He shook his head, then stared at Gabe. "Who that?"

Gabe smiled nervously. "Hi, Henry. I'm Gabe."

"This is Mama's friend," Brooke added. "Can you say, 'Hi, Gabe'?"

"Gimme five!" Gabe said, holding his hand out, palm up.

Henry buried his face in Brooke's shoulder. "Noooo!" he wailed.

Farrah reached out and managed to peel the boy off his mother. "Let's go, Henry McBenry," she said, heading back to the bedroom. "Have a good time, Brooke," she called over her shoulder. "Nice to meet you, Gabe."

He'd chosen a new restaurant she'd been meaning to check out. It was Italian, located in a restored craftsman cottage a block away from the waterfront. There were flowers and candles on the table, which actually had a white table-cloth.

Gabe smiled at her as the waiter brought their wine. "Are you as nervous as I am?"

She sipped her wine. "That depends. Is your pulse racing? Do you feel like you might vomit at any moment?"

"Check and check. Plus I had to change my shirt twice before I left the house tonight, because of all the flop sweat."

She laughed. "Okay, I didn't require a wardrobe change, which makes me feel marginally better, so thanks for that."

"It's just dinner. That's what I've been telling myself all night. Right? Dinner with an old friend and colleague."

"Absolutely." She nodded and sipped her wine.

He took a gulp of his own wine. "I'm sixty-three, by the way."

"Okay . . ."

"I just thought I'd get that out of the way. In case you were wondering and trying to figure out if I really am too old for you, which I hope I'm not."

"I've got a confession to make," Brooke said, emboldened by the wine. "I already knew that. I checked on Martindale-Hubbell."

"I Googled and checked you on LinkedIn," he countered. "Very impressive. I'd forgotten you graduated near the top of your class."

"So we're two smarty-pants lawyers. We should be able to get through a simple no-risk dinner together, right?"

"Not a problem," he said. "And since you mentioned the lawyer thing, I've got good news. The court appointed me administrator of Josephine's estate today."

"Wow. That was fast."

"One of the circuit judges was a law school classmate of mine," Gabe said.

"Ah yes, the good-old-boy network," Brooke said, hoping she didn't sound bitter.

"In this case, it was helpful. We can speed things up and start wrapping up Josephine's estate."

"It's hard for me to believe she's gone," Brooke said wistfully. "Even though I only knew her for a short time, and of course, her illness diminished her on an hourly basis, she was such a strong life force with such an amazing story to tell."

"I agree. It's sad."

"I'm really pissed she died without telling us who killed Russell Strickland or where the body is buried," Brooke admitted. "My one hope is that Lizzie really will be able to unravel all of Josephine's secrets while she's staying at Shellhaven."

Gabe frowned. "I'm not sure it's such a good idea for Lizzie to be living there. I mean, I personally don't really have a problem with it, but as administrator, once I track down those cousins of hers—the heirs apparent, as it were—they might not like it at all."

"It's not like she's moving in for the rest of her life," Brooke protested. "And it's a good thing that Shellhaven isn't empty, with Josephine gone now. What's it going to hurt?"

"Maybe you're right," Gabe said hastily. "Anyway, for the short term, I suppose it's okay."

Their appetizers arrived then, and the discussion segued into favorite restaurants, gossip about Savannah, old clients, and mutual friends.

It wasn't until their desserts arrived—chocolate sea salt gelato with biscotti for her, a glass of port for him—that Brooke realized two hours had flown by.

She dug out the last bite of gelato with the tip of a biscotti, tasted, and rolled her eyes. "So good."

"Like this evening," Gabe said, watching her over the rim of his glass. "I love seeing you like this, Brooke."

He reached over with his napkin and dabbed at a bit of gelato on the corner of her mouth. His hand lingered there for only a moment, but she felt herself blushing.

"You mean with food all over my face? That's an everyday occurrence. I'm an even messier eater than my three-year-old."

"He's a pretty cute kid, by the way. No, I meant seeing you relaxed, enjoying yourself, just being yourself."

"Are you saying I've changed? Since we worked together in Savannah?"

"Definitely. You were always so driven and focused when you were working for the firm in Savannah. I don't think I was ever with you when you completely let your hair down, the way you have tonight. It's a nice change. It suits you."

"Well . . . thanks. I've had kind of a rough three years, raising a child by myself in a new town. There were weeks and months I didn't think I'd make it. Henry was not an easy baby, and I didn't get a lot of sleep. But somehow, I guess we weathered the storm. Henry sleeps through the night now, mostly. My practice is finally starting to grow, slowly. I've got good childcare—Farrah, who you met tonight, is a godsend. She's my right-hand girl in the office too. She adores Henry, and the feeling is mutual, and she's smart as a whip. I don't know what I'll do in the fall when she goes off to school in Athens."

Gabe swirled the port in his glass. "And what about your personal life?"

She raised an eyebrow. "Personal life? Who has time for that?"

"Now you sound like the old Brooke," he chided. "Don't you have any desire to see what life is like outside the office? Or Henry's nursery?"

"You mean date?"

"Yeah. That."

She sat back in her chair and took a long look at him. His silver hair glinted in the candlelight, and his eyes were frank and appraising.

"I haven't given it a lot of thought," she said finally. "For one thing, there's not exactly a deep dating pool of eligible men in these parts. I mean, sure, I get hit on by your garden-variety rednecks and the occasional horny, inappropriate married guy. And I've had some very tempting offers to provide oral gratification to some of the inmates at the county lockup . . ."

Gabe laughed.

"But otherwise, I haven't met anybody down here that I'd want to date. And I haven't felt the need to go looking, despite Farrah's pleas to set me up with a Tinder account. Now. Turnabout is fair play, Gabe Wynant. What about you? Are you a Match.com guy, or are you more of an eHarmony type? Or maybe Christian Mingle?"

"None of the above. I swear. You know how it is in Savannah, though. For a while after Sunny died, I was fresh meat in the dating supermarket. Her old friends—hell, *my* old friends—all wanted to set me up, either with themselves or somebody they knew. And I'll admit, it was lonely. I went out a few times, saw a couple of women for third or fourth dates, but there was never any real connection, so I just kind of gave up."

"It's much less stressful to stay home in my yoga pants, read a book, have a glass of wine, and enjoy my own company," Brooke said.

"Bingo," Gabe said. "The easy way out. But that gets old too, you know?"

She smiled noncommittally.

The waiter brought the check, Gabe presented his credit card, and he and Brooke drifted out of the restaurant. A breeze was blowing off the river, and as they walked to his car, which he'd had to park a block away, Gabe caught his hand in hers in an easy, natural movement.

"Nice night out," he said. "Not even that humid."

"For Georgia. In May," she agreed.

"Want to take a walk?"

She hesitated, trying to estimate the time.

"Aw, come on. It's not that late," he said, reading her thoughts. "It's not even ten."

"Okay. But just down to the docks and then back. It's a school night for me, and Henry's up at six every morning."

They swung their hands companionably as they walked along the waterfront. The air smelled of marsh mud and salt water and faintly of fish. The sky was pricked with stars. She thought if she squinted she could see the lights of shrimp boats headed out to sea.

"You look beautiful tonight, by the way," Gabe said as they reached the municipal docks.

"Um, thanks," she said. She'd deliberately dressed down for the occasion; white jeans, a simple V-necked navy cotton sweater, and a necklace she'd splurged on at a local boutique, white coral beads with an oyster-shell medallion in the middle.

"Nice to see you not swathed in your typical lady lawyer battle armor of a business suit and heels," Gabe said.

"Not much call for business suits and heels down here," Brooke said. "I'll wear one if I'm in court, in front of a judge, but this is as dressy as it gets for me these days."

"If you did feel the urge to dress up, I'd love to take you to dinner up at the Cloister," Gabe said. "They've got a great new chef, and there's an orchestra and dancing on Saturday nights."

"Oh my gosh. They still have those? My parents used to take me to those when I was a teenager. Mom would make Dad dance with me, and it was total agony."

"Oh." He looked disappointed. "You don't like to dance?"

"I love to dance. And so did he, but it was so damn embarrassing, dancing with your father, who was trying to be all hip and happening. I'll never forget the night he tried to do the Macarena. The memory is permanently seared onto my brainpan."

Gabe winced. "If I promise not to try to break out any new dance moves, would you consider coming to dinner with me Saturday night?"

"At the Cloister? But that's like an hour away."

"You could stay over," Gabe said. "Not at my place. I mean, you could stay at my place. There's room, and I swear I wouldn't hit on you. But what I meant was I'd book you a room at the hotel. And I'd bring you home first thing in the morning."

"I don't know," she said slowly. "I'd have to see if Farrah is available to stay over. It's a lot. And you saw how clingy Henry can be. Don't get me wrong, it sounds like fun, but . . ."

"Just think about it, okay?"

"I will. Now I'd better get home, or Farrah will have the state patrol out looking for me."

The ride home took only five minutes. When Gabe pulled into the driveway, they saw a quick flick of the front window curtains.

"Told ya," Brooke said. "She's very protective of me."

"Hmm," Gabe said.

"But she totally approved of this car. Whatever happened to the Mercedes?"

"I still have it. The Porsche was a complete surprise. Turns out, Sunny bought it without ever saying a word to me. I found it covered by a tarp in the garage at the house at Sea Island the first time I came down after she died."

"A Porsche 911? She just bought it on a whim?"

He shrugged. "More like on a toot. I'll sell it eventually, when I sell the house, but for tonight, I thought maybe I'd impress a girl with it."

"You totally did," Brooke said.

And before she could say anything else, he leaned over and kissed her softly on the lips. "Don't tell the babysitter," he whispered.

46

....

B rooke?" There was more than a note of panic in Louette's voice.

It was Wednesday morning. She'd just walked into her office and hadn't even had time to fire up the coffee maker or laptop before her cell phone rang.

"What's wrong?" Brooke asked.

"Those cousins of Josephine's, Dorcas and Delphine, they're here! They just come riding up here in a Jeep with some man from the state park. I let 'em in, 'cause I didn't know what else to do, but now they're walking around, talking like they own the place. I think you'd better come quick."

"How the hell did they even find out Josephine is dead?"

"They said there was a big piece in the newspapers yesterday. They already called a lawyer, and he told them they're fixin' to inherit this whole island, including the house."

"What newspaper?" Brooke walked around the office, looking for her copy of the local paper, a weekly that was published on Wednesdays.

"I don't know. Maybe the Savannah paper? Or Atlanta? We don't get a paper over here. Shug reads the sports page online."

"I'll head over there right now. Can you have C. D. pick me up at the city dock?"

"We ain't seen C. D. in a couple of days. I'll send Shug over. He's off work today."

"Okay, see you soon. And try not to worry, Louette."

Brooke flipped her laptop open and did a quick Google search on Josephine's name. The first citation was an article from the previous day's edition of *The Atlanta Journal-Constitution.*

Talisa Island, GA. Josephine Bettendorf Warrick, the legendary heiress owner of this wildest of Georgia's untamed barrier islands, died last week at the age of 99. Her death signals what is almost certainly the last chapter of private ownership of the 12,000-acre Talisa.

Mrs. Warrick's father, Samuel G. Bettendorf, was a Boston shipping magnate who purchased the Carter County island more than a century ago with two cousins. He commissioned famed Gilded-Age architect Addison Mizner to design and build a pink stucco Beaux-Arts-inspired twenty-room mansion he dubbed Shellhaven.

Carter County sheriff Howard Goolsby confirmed Mrs. Warrick's death, saying that the nonagenarian, who'd recently been diagnosed with terminal lung cancer, died of a head injury last Saturday after a fall. There are no known survivors.

Bettendorf's only son, Samuel Gardiner Bettendorf Jr., who was known as Gardiner, enlisted in the Royal Canadian Air Force at the age of 23 and was killed when the Spitfire he piloted was shot down over Nazi-occupied France in early 1942. The senior Bettendorf died one year later, leaving his daughter as sole owner of much of the island, with the exception of a smaller tract of land on the northern tip of Talisa, which was retained by distant relatives who sold their land to the state for a park in 1978.

In 1949, Josephine Bettendorf married Preiss H. Warrick, a naval captain she met at a bridge party on Sea Island, Georgia. The couple,

both amateur naturalists, made the protection of Talisa and its wildlife
their life's work. Preiss Warrick died in 1966 of renal disease.

The couple never had children, and Mrs. Warrick spent the remainder of her life as a fierce guardian of the island, mounting a thirty-year
fight to fend off the state's efforts to buy it.

Brooke closed the laptop and called Gabe Wynant. The phone rang three
times, and she got his voice mail.

"Hi, Gabe. Sorry to bother you, but Louette just called to say that Josephine's
long-lost cousins turned up at Shellhaven this morning and are already acting
pretty possessive. I'm going over there right now, and I just wanted to give you
a heads-up. Talk soon."

Shug eased the boat away from the slip at the municipal dock. The water was
calm, and seagulls wheeled and soared overhead as they crossed the river.

"How are Varina and Felicia doing?" Brooke asked, as they rode through the
no-wake zone.

"Varina's happy as a clam, but that Felicia, I don't think she really takes to
island life," Shug said with a chuckle. "She spends most of her time on that
computer, teaching her online classes and reading. And she doesn't leave the
house unless she sprays all over with bug spray. Still, she's got a good heart,
taking care of her auntie the way she does."

"Have you started working on Varina's house?"

"Oh yeah. We got all the vines and brush tore off outside, and cleared out
a whole nest of raccoons that had been living in the chimney. The roofing
shingles and insulation and windows and such I ordered should be here by
Friday. And you ought to see that little old lady Varina, leaning on her walker
and sweeping and mopping the inside of that house."

"You're a saint to house them and help them out this way, Shug."

"Just doin' what's right," he said. "Family's family."

"And what about Louette? How's she holding up with all this stress?"

"Not so good," he admitted. "Her blood pressure's up, and she's worried somebody's gonna make us move off the island. I told her, 'Honey, we got money, and we got a place to go,' but we both know she's true Geechee. Only place she's ever gonna be happy is right there in that little house at Oyster Bluff."

Louette met her at the front door at Shellhaven. She pointed down the hall toward the library. "They're back there, and I'm afraid Lizzie is about to snatch 'em bald."

"I'll see if I can referee," Brooke promised.

She heard raised voices as she approached the library's open door.

"You can't just ransack our family's belongings this way," a woman was saying.

"Hi!" Brooke said, stepping inside.

Two women whirled around to confront the newcomer.

The cousins looked enough alike that they could have been twins. They were skinny, probably in their mid- to late seventies, with dyed strawberry-blond hair so thinned that large patches of pink scalp showed beneath their matching golf visors. They wore T-shirts tucked into their elastic-waisted khaki slacks and sturdy, blindingly white tennis shoes, and they were both glaring at Lizzie, who'd constructed a makeshift office on a card table in the middle of the room.

"Hi, Brooke!" Lizzie looked profoundly grateful for her arrival. She gestured at the women. "These are Josephine's long-lost cousins, Dorcas and Delphine. Or is it Delphine and Dorcas?"

"I'm Dorcas Fentress, and this is my cousin Delphine McElwain," said the taller of the two, whose T-shirt was hot pink with a design of sequined kittens. "And you're the lawyer our cousin supposedly hired to handle her affairs, despite the fact that she had a perfectly capable law firm in Atlanta?"

"That's me," Brooke said, extending her hand. "Brooke Trappnell. My grandmother Millie was one of Josephine's best friends growing up."

"And my grandmother Ruth Mattingly Quinlan was one of her other best friends," Lizzie said. "They all went to boarding school together."

"I never heard Josephine mention either of those names," Delphine said. Her blue T-shirt had a motif of dancing dolphins, and her wire-rimmed glasses had blue-tinted lenses.

"When was the last time you ladies saw Josephine?" Brooke asked.

The two women exchanged glances. "It's been some years now," Dorcas admitted. "Josephine had become such a shut-in late in life, you know, but Delphine and I made several attempts to contact her."

"It was my understanding that she refused to see you," Brooke said. "She was still furious at you for selling your land to the state."

"That's all water under the bridge now," Dorcas said, pressing her narrow lips together. "I must say, it was very upsetting for both Delphine and me to learn about Josephine's death through a newspaper article."

"Horrifying," Delphine said. "We had no idea Josie had even been sick. It breaks my heart to think of our cousin spending her last months so ill and then dying here, all alone, with none of her family around. If only somebody had had the decency to notify us . . ."

"Oh, she wasn't alone that night," Lizzie said cheerfully. "I was here, Brooke and her mother, Marie, were here, Varina and Felicia were here, and of course, Louette, the housekeeper, was here too. And her other lawyer. We had dinner together."

Dorcas favored Lizzie with a withering stare. "I find it hard to believe that a dying woman would have hosted a dinner party."

"More like a house party," Lizzie said. "We all spent the night."

"And why would she have invited a bunch of strangers to a house party?" Dorcas asked.

Lizzie gestured around the library. "She was going to leave—"

"She was feeling nostalgic," Brooke said, deliberately cutting Lizzie off. At this point, there was no need to let the cousins know of Josephine's intent to create a trust to protect Talisa. She would let Gabe Wynant deal with all that. Maybe there was still hope that he would find some loophole to prevent the dreaded Ds from inheriting.

"We should have been notified that she was sick," Dorcas said. "We would have come immediately. We were her only living family, you know."

Brooke shrugged. "No offense, but I think Josephine would have contacted you herself if she'd wanted to see you. She was by no means a shut-in. She was making regular visits to her doctors in Jacksonville, and she knew the cancer diagnosis was terminal. That's why she reached out and asked me to gather these women together. She wanted to meet them and make amends."

"So you say," Delphine said.

"Amends for what?" Dorcas asked. She glanced down at Lizzie's work space, with the scattered file folders, yellowing newspaper clippings, and stacks of old correspondence. Brooke realized that Lizzie, the journalist, had begun digging into Josephine's past, delving into the secrets she'd been so reluctant to share.

"Old slights. Fractured friendships. It was Josephine's story to tell, not mine," Brooke said.

"Very touching," Dorcas said. "But none of that explains what this woman"—she pointed at Lizzie—"is doing here, trespassing in our family's home, meddling with our cousin's private papers."

"Just some genealogy work," Lizzie said with an impish grin. "I'm harmless, really."

"By whose authority?" Delphine asked.

"Mine, actually," a man's voice said.

Gabe was standing in the doorway, with Louette and Felicia right behind him.

Gabe was dressed in a somber gray business suit. "Gabe Wynant," he said, extending a business card to each of the cousins. "I'm the court-appointed administrator of Josephine Warrick's estate. Mrs. Warrick had mentioned that she had some distant cousins, but we had no names or addresses, since it seems you were estranged. I asked Lizzie here to search Mrs. Warrick's papers for your contact information."

"We certainly were not estranged," Dorcas said, bristling.

"Never mind," Delphine said, reading the business card. "Mr. Wynant, is it?"

"That's right," Gabe said.

"My cousin and I have hired a lawyer to see that our rights as Josephine's closest heirs are protected. He'll be in contact with you."

"I look forward to speaking to him," Gabe said. "Anything else I can do for you ladies today? No? Shug is outside with his truck, and he'll be happy to take you back to the ferry if you'd like."

Lizzie waited until the women were out of earshot before offering Gabe a high five.

"Well done, sir." She laughed. "Here's your hat, what's your hurry? And not even offering to have Shug take them back to the mainland instead of waiting on the ferry? I call that cold!"

"Shug has other work to attend to," Gabe said. "I've asked him to stay on here and take over the outside maintenance again."

"Thank you, Jesus," Louette said fervently. "That grass was getting so high I was afraid what might be hiding in it."

Gabe reached into the inner pocket of his jacket and brought out an envelope. "I've brought both your paychecks too," he said. "And I hope the past few days haven't been too stressful for you."

Louette tucked the envelope in the pocket of her slacks. For the first time, Brooke realized that with the death of her former employer, Louette had stopped wearing the white uniform and switched to more casual clothing.

"Thanks for coming over so quickly," Brooke said to Gabe. "Things were getting pretty sticky with those two."

"Yeah, they look like they're gonna be major pains in the ass," Lizzie said. "I think they thought I was going to put a match to Josephine's papers."

Gabe frowned. "I hate to say it, Lizzie, and I didn't want to mention it in front of the cousins, but it is somewhat problematic for you to be riffling through Josephine's personal effects."

"Why?" Lizzie asked. "I'm just doing research for my magazine article, that's all. And I'm actually doing you a favor, organizing and indexing everything I find." She gestured at the cardboard file boxes surrounding the card table. "Besides, maybe I'll find a clue to who actually killed Russell Strickland and where he's buried."

"If they do get a lawyer involved, he may raise an objection with the court," Gabe said.

"You're now the administrator of the estate, right? You could counter that by pointing out that Lizzie's research is necessary to make sure Josephine's papers are in order," Brooke said. She pointed to the secretary. "Josephine was a total pack rat. That thing is full to overflowing with old letters, cards, correspondence, and who knows what? Josephine had me going through it on one of my first visits here, to try to track down Ruth's and Varina's families, and I barely scratched the surface of what's in there. Maybe there actually are other living heirs that need to be notified of her death. Maybe she'll find something that will either prove or disprove C. D.'s claim that he's Josephine's son."

"Doubtful," Gabe said, shaking his head. "I'm sorry, but this is just not a good idea."

Lizzie rolled her eyes but said nothing.

"Look, Gabe. Just let her finish cataloging the contents of the secretary and whatever else is in the room. Okay? If some judge asks questions, you can say you hired her to provide archival services."

"Except that Lizzie, as astute a journalist as she is, is not a forensic archivist," Gabe said.

"Give me a week. One week, that's all I ask," Lizzie chimed in. "I'll put everything in order and notify you of anything and everything I find."

"Please, Gabe?" Brooke asked.

He glanced at his watch. "All right. I've got court up in Glynn County this afternoon. You've got a week, Lizzie, then I really have to insist that you decamp. Let me know what you find."

47

W ho died and left him boss?" Lizzie asked.

    "Josephine did, remember?" Felicia said. She picked up an envelope from the card table. "Find anything interesting yet in all this mess?"

"Lots. Josephine really led a fascinating life. She was a prodigious letter writer." Lizzie picked up a file folder. "She was mad as hell at her 'dear cousins' for selling their land to the state. There are carbon copies here of all the letters she sent—to them, to her state representative, the governor. She even wrote letters to Jimmy Carter. Turns out she contributed a hundred bucks to his campaign when he ran for governor of Georgia, so naturally she thought he should intervene on her behalf."

"Did he write back?"

"Nope. And when she didn't hear from him, she fired off a scathing follow-up letter telling him she was glad she'd voted for Ronald Reagan against him," Lizzie said.

Brooke sighed. "Well, you heard the man. You've only got a week before Gabe kicks you out of here and cuts off your access to these papers."

"What exactly are you looking for?" Felicia asked, sitting in Josephine's recliner, a seat Brooke had consciously.

"Answers. Why did Josephine cut off contact with Millie and Ruth—and Varina, to some extent? I mean, she went to all that trouble having Brooke invite us over here, but she never really gave us any answers. And of course, I'm hoping to figure out this thing with the unsolved disappearance of Russell Strickland," said Lizzie.

"Wasting your time," Felicia said. "Why don't you find some way to prove that C. D. wasn't Josephine's son?"

"I've been trying, but like Brooke said, there are a ton of papers just in that secretary. I did find these, though." She picked up a shoe box and held it out.

Felicia and Brooke peered into the box, which held a jumble of small, thin leather-bound books. Brooke picked one up at random. The cover was stamped in gold with *1965*.

"Datebooks?"

"Yup. They start in 1938 and run all the way through the mideighties. And before you ask, I've looked at the relevant years. No mention of killing anybody or birthing any illegitimate babies."

Brooke riffled the pages of the book in her hand and read aloud from the first entry. "'Dentist appointment, Brunswick, January 12.' And then there's this, in February: 'Lunch with Emma.'"

Lizzie nodded. "From what I can tell from skimming her calendars, she had a lot of lunch dates, played bridge with some ladies at the Cloister every other week, went to fund-raisers for various good causes, and she was diligent about getting her teeth cleaned and her cars and boat serviced. She also noted the tide charts, how many deer and feral hogs were shot on the island, and how many sea turtle nests she observed on the beach every summer."

"Do we know what year C. D. was born?" Felicia asked.

"He claims he was born in '42," Brooke said.

Lizzie sifted through the shoe box contents. "Here's the datebook from 1942. Help yourself, but I'm telling you there's nothing about having a baby."

Felicia pulled a pair of glasses from her pocket and began skimming, turning pages, occasionally reading aloud. "Josephine was living in Savannah then, right?"

"Yes," Brooke said. "Once the war started, her father closed up Shellhaven.

I believe he went back to Boston, but Josephine lived in a town house in Savannah that her family owned."

Felicia ran her finger down the calendar pages. "War bond drives. Bridge parties. Luncheons. Dinners. Josephine was quite the social butterfly. Wait. Here's a notation about a doctor's appointment. In February," Felicia said.

Brooke looked over Felicia's shoulder. "But it doesn't say the doctor's name."

"No." Felicia turned over a few more pages. "Another one in April. Still no doctor's name."

Brooke looked down at the penciled notation. "That doesn't necessarily mean anything. I mean, maybe she had heartburn. Or migraines. Or bunions."

"Or God forbid, a bun in the oven," Felicia said dryly.

"Hey!" Lizzie said, lightly punching Felicia's arm. "That was funny! You actually *do* have a sense of humor."

Felicia looked from Lizzie to Brooke. "Did you think otherwise?"

"You seem pretty serious most of the time," Brooke said.

"I think that's Southern for 'You go around acting like you have a stick up your butt,'" Lizzie said. "Maybe you could lighten up just a little?"

Felicia blinked, then pushed her glasses farther up the bridge of her nose. "You sound like some of my students. I mean, I teach African American studies. It's serious stuff. And as an African American woman, I've spent my whole career trying to take my work seriously."

"We're not your students," Lizzie pointed out. "We're your friends. Or we're trying to be."

"Okay. Point taken. Lighten up. Loosen up. Anything else?"

"Yeah. Turn the page on that datebook. Any other interesting entries?" Lizzie asked.

"Hmm. Red Cross committee meeting. Junior League committee meeting." Felicia flipped pages. "Bond drive." She looked up, startled. "March 20. Maternity clothes."

Lizzie reached for the datebook. "Let me see that."

Felicia stabbed the notation with her index finger. "Right here. See?"

"It actually says, 'Mtnty clothes,' but yeah, you're right. Shit. Maybe C. D. is for real," Lizzie said. "Why else would she be shopping for maternity clothes?"

"Okay, I think we shouldn't start jumping to conclusions," Brooke said, trying to be the voice of caution. "Lizzie, maybe you and Felicia can team up to finish going through all Josephine's papers."

"Or maybe—" Lizzie started.

"We go to Savannah and start doing some primary research," Felicia finished. "Talk to that Catholic whatever-it-is. Visit the orphanage where C. D. says he was raised."

"Brilliant!" Lizzie beamed at her newfound colleague. "Let's do it." She turned to Brooke. "I say we head up to Savannah first thing in the morning. And since you're a native daughter, you can be our Savannah tour guide."

"I can't just drop everything. I've got a job, you know. And a child," Brooke said.

"Have your calls forwarded to your cell phone and get the babysitter to take care of the kid," Lizzie said. "Come on, Brooke. You know people in Savannah, and we don't. This is important. To all of us."

"It's just one day," Felicia said.

Brooke sighed. "Okay. This is crazy, but I'll do it."

"High fives!" Lizzie declared, and the three slapped palms and bumped fists. "Now group hugs!" she added.

"Let's not get carried away," Felicia drawled.

48

Brooke was standing beside the Volvo, waiting, as Felicia and Lizzie walked toward the marina parking lot.

"Shotgun," Felicia said, climbing into the front seat.

Lizzie rolled her eyes and opened the rear door. "Um, Brooke?"

Henry was belted into his car seat, quietly munching on a toaster waffle. His face and hair and hands were smeared with peanut butter.

"Ladies, this is my son, Henry. Henry, that's Lizzie. And this is Felicia, up front with me."

"Hi, Henry," Felicia said, turning around to wave.

"Heyya, Henry," Lizzie added.

"He was running a little temperature this morning, which meant I couldn't take him to day care, and Farrah, my babysitter, has graduation practice today and she couldn't keep him," Brooke explained. "So we're going to drop him off at my mom's house in Savannah before we go do our thing. And Henry's going to be a really good boy today. Aren't you, Henry?"

"No," Henry said, throwing his sippy cup onto the floor.

"He'll fall asleep any minute now, I promise," Brooke said.

"He'd better," Lizzie muttered. "So what's our game plan?"

"I thought we'd start where C. D. says he got his initial information, at the archdiocesan office in Savannah. It's just a few blocks from my mom's house in Ardsley Park. Depending on what we find out, we'll hopefully also make it out to Good Shepherd too."

"Remind me exactly what that place is?" Felicia said.

"It *was* the oldest continuously operating home for boys in the country. But their mission has changed over the years, and now it's morphed into a privately operated all-boys prep school," Brooke said. "C. D. says he lived there from the time this Catholic orphanage placed him there at six until he ran away at sixteen."

"Louette says she almost hopes we can prove C. D. is Josephine's son," Felicia said. "He's definitely a strange one, but she says he's way better than those awful cousins."

"I think we have to try to go into this with an open mind," Lizzie said. "Ask the right questions and just follow the bread crumbs until we reach the truth."

"Agreed," Brooke said. "But realistically, I don't have high hopes that the archdiocese will share much information with us, especially where it relates to those old adoption records. I'm sure they'll cite privacy concerns."

Lizzie leaned forward in her seat. "Listen, I dig up dirt for a living. It's my job to outrun or outsmart every version of the answer *no*. When we get there, how about I ask the questions?"

"Works for me," Felicia said.

"So whatever kind of pretext I come up with, you guys just go with it. Okay?"

Brooke felt uneasy. "You're not going to tell any outright lies or try to make me do anything unethical, right?"

"We'll see," Lizzie said.

Marie met them at the front door of the Ardsley Park home where Brooke had grown up. She transferred the limp, dozing toddler to her mother's outstretched arms.

"He feels a little warm," Marie whispered, touching the child's pink cheek.

"There's some children's Tylenol in here," Brooke said, handing her mother the diaper bag. "Give him that with some juice."

"We'll be fine," Marie said. "Call me and let me know how it's going."

"I will. Thanks again for pinch-hitting, Mom. Love you."

Brooke made the turn from Victory Drive onto the impressive-looking grounds of the Catholic diocese campus. "This used to be a children's home too," she told her passengers. "When I was growing up, it was St. Elizabeth's. But the grounds were so overgrown with trees and moss, it looked really spooky."

They parked and started walking toward the entry. "Rule number one for seeking information you probably don't have any right to is always make friends with clerks and secretaries," Lizzie said as they mounted the marble steps.

"You mean suck up to the man?" Felicia asked.

"No. Not the man. The man's secretary or assistant or clerk, who is almost always a woman. The gatekeeper, if you will. Now watch and learn," Lizzie said.

She swung open the door and approached a middle-aged woman at a reception desk.

"Hi," she said brightly. "I'm Lizzie Quinlan."

"Hello." The woman looked quizzical. "How can I help you ladies?"

"I'd like to see some records from a now-defunct Catholic children's home here in town, and I understand you have those on microfilm? The years I'm interested in are roughly 1942 through 1948 or '49. And I'd be happy to pay whatever photocopying costs are incurred."

"I'm sorry. We have strict privacy rules. Those records are only open to the actual children who were placed in the home and their biological mothers."

"Oh." Lizzie's shoulders slumped dramatically. She stared down at the clerk's nameplate, which said *Debbie Winters.*

"Well, I guess I did see something about that on the archdiocesan website, but I just thought maybe, because of the special circumstances, you all might make an exception, just this one time. And we've come such a long way too."

"That's a shame," Debbie said. "Where are you ladies from?"

"I'm actually from California, and she's from Florida," Lizzie said, pointing to Felicia. "You see, Debbie," she continued, "our dad is very, very ill. He's in his seventies and we really don't know how much longer we'll have him with us."

"Is it . . . ?"

"Cancer? Yes. Very advanced. And very, very aggressive."

"My sympathy to you girls," Debbie said.

"He only recently shared with us the story of how his mother left him—abandoned him, actually—in a church here in Savannah. It was the first time he's completely opened up to any of us about this. Naturally, my sisters and I wanted to follow up and get to the truth."

"Naturally." Debbie nodded.

"He told us that the priest in one of the churches in town found him under a pew when he was an infant after mass one Sunday morning."

Debbie's face registered her disbelief. "But that's horrifying."

"Shocking," Felicia put in. "We had no idea."

Debbie looked from Felicia to Lizzie, obviously puzzled. "Who is this?"

"Oh, uh, that's my sister, Felicia. From Florida."

"Half sister," Felicia corrected. "Same dad. Different mamas."

"Same for me," Brooke said.

"Three daughters by three different women? How unusual," Debbie said.

"Anyway, the three of us, we're at that time in our lives, we really need some answers. For our peace of mind, and of course, to find out about our family medical history," Lizzie went on. "You can empathize with that, can't you?"

"Yes, but—"

"Before Dad dies," Lizzie said.

"Ticking clock," Felicia added.

"Dad told us the parish priest who found him took him to a Catholic orphanage here."

"From the sound of it, that would be St. Joseph's. It closed in the mid-1950s, and the children were moved over here to St. Elizabeth's," Debbie said.

"You still have all the records though, right?" Felicia said eagerly.

"As I said, those records are sealed to the general public."

"But we're not the general public," Lizzie said.

"If you bring your father in here, with some proof of identity, we'd be happy to share the records with him," Debbie offered.

"Not possible," Felicia said.

"Or his authorized representative. If you could bring in a notarized letter, signed by your father, I could speak to my supervisor and I think we could possibly work something out," Debbie said.

"But we want it to be a surprise," Lizzie said.

Brooke had an idea. "Daddy said he'd heard that the priest's name was Father Ryan? Maybe Charles Ryan? He's the one who turned him over to the nuns at St. Joseph's. We know it's a slim chance, but maybe if Father Ryan were still alive..."

"What year did you say this was?" Debbie asked.

"Nineteen forty-two. We think," Felicia said.

"I'm sure Father Ryan is long gone," Debbie said.

Lizzie sighed heavily. "Is there, like, a roster or something in your computer that you could check?"

Debbie's fingers danced over the keyboard of her desktop computer. "Well, just as I suspected. Father Ryan, God rest his soul, passed away in 1982. According to our records, he was pastor at Church of the Apostles until his retirement in 1976. Unfortunately, that church was closed in 1987, and its parish was absorbed into another church."

The three women looked at each other, waiting for an idea to occur to their self-appointed leader.

"I just wish, for Dad's sake," Lizzie said dramatically. "I wish there were some way to find out if the story is true, about him being found under a pew. I mean, it's so bizarre, you'd think somebody who was around back then would remember."

"It was a very long time ago," Debbie said.

Lizzie snapped her fingers. "All right. Let's try this from another angle. After a good bit of prodding from us, Dad said he's always believed his biological mother was a woman named Josephine Bettendorf Warrick. Would it be possible to see if she was a parishioner?"

"I can check, but not all the parishes in the diocese kept good records. And in some cases, when churches closed, their records were simply destroyed, which I think is a shame, don't you?" Debbie began typing. "Spell that name, please?"

Lizzie spelled it out, then repeated it.

"No. Not in our database."

"Dad has an old newspaper clipping from that time," Brooke said. "He showed it to us. It shows Mrs. Warrick at the orphanage at Christmastime with a child identified as Charlie Anthony on her lap. Dad says he remembers she came every year to donate toys and gifts, and every year, he got special gifts the other children didn't."

"That's right," Lizzie said. "Why would Josephine do that, if she didn't have a connection to our dad or to the orphanage or to the church where Dad was left?"

"Right." Debbie's brow was wrinkled as she considered the question. She chewed on the end of a pencil. "Maybe . . . ," she said slowly. "I think you should go speak to Sister Theresa. She's the oldest nun still living in Savannah from that time. She's ninety-nine and almost blind, but she's still sharp as a tack. If anybody would remember this story, it would be Sister Theresa."

"Perfect," Felicia said eagerly. "How do we find her?"

"She lives at the Rose of Sharon Apartments, in midtown." Debbie spun the wheel of a Rolodex and plucked a yellowing card. "One of the younger nuns from her order does all Sister's shopping and acts as a sort of de facto caregiver. Let me call Joan and see if she thinks Sister is up for visitors today."

A moment later, Debbie scrawled an address on a scrap of paper. "Joan says Sister loves company, and you're welcome to go see her right away, if that's convenient."

"Oh!" Lizzie exclaimed. "God bless you, Debbie! We'll all keep you in our prayers."

"My pleasure," Debbie said, blushing.

"Laying it on a little thick back there, weren't you?" Felicia asked as they climbed back into the Volvo.

"The Lord moved me," Lizzie said with a broad wink.

49

S ister Theresa Monahan's grip was firm as she greeted each of her visitors. "I'm so pleased to meet you," she said in a quavery voice that still bore traces of a Boston accent, despite having lived in the South for more than seventy years. "Now, Joanie says you girls have some questions for me?"

She was a short, plump woman, and she wore a navy-blue St. Vincent's Academy sweatshirt and navy sweatpants. Her bright blue eyes were clouded, but her round face was miraculously unlined. She sat in an overstuffed armchair in a neat but sparsely furnished studio apartment. The television was turned to a Braves baseball game but she pointed the remote at the set and turned down the volume.

"Now. I'm all set. Ask away."

Lizzie repeated the pertinent parts of their pretext story.

Sister Theresa nodded sympathetically. "I'll put your father in my devotionals," she said. "Charles Anthony, you said his name is?"

"He goes by C. D. now," Lizzie said. "He has some memory of the nuns at St. Joseph's telling him he was named after the priest who found him, Charles Ryan."

"Of course. I knew Father Ryan."

"The sisters gave him the last name of Anthony, after their favorite saint," Brooke added.

"Goodness. I haven't thought of this in years and years!" Sister exclaimed. "Now, I don't remember the baby's name, I'm afraid, but at the time, back in the war years, I went to St. Joseph's once or twice a week to teach music to the little ones, and I do remember the story about Father Ryan finding an infant in that church. He was a scrawny little thing."

"Yes?" Lizzie said anxiously.

Sister hesitated and picked up a string of well-worn rosary beads. "Now, I would never want to speak ill of the dead or call dear Father Ryan a liar, but I will say that we always wondered if that story was completely truthful."

"Why is that?"

Sister Theresa smiled. "Of course, we take vows of poverty when we accept our vocations, you know. I think Father Ryan came from a very, very impoverished part of Ireland. But when he came to the States, and Savannah, he discovered he had a taste for the nicer things in life. Things that don't come easily when you're the pastor of one of the poorest inner-city churches in Savannah."

"He had a black parish?" Felicia asked.

"Yes. That's right. Many of his parishioners worked for some of the wealthiest families in Savannah as maids or gardeners or handymen. Wonderful people, but of modest means. So it did raise some eyebrows when Father started driving a shiny new Packard. Coincidentally, right around the time the sisters took in that poor little baby you mentioned."

"Did Father Ryan say how he was able to buy such a nice car?" Felicia asked.

"A generous gift from an anonymous benefactor," Sister said with a mischievous glint in her sightless eyes.

Wow! Felicia mouthed.

"And you and the rest of the sisters, you didn't really believe that story?" Lizzie said.

"We might have been nuns, dear, but we weren't dummies," Sister said tartly. "We did wonder what Father Ryan did to deserve such a splendid gift."

"What do you think he did?" Brooke asked.

"It was just speculation, you know. We all assumed one of his parishioners, who worked for one of those very wealthy families, was asked to be the go-between between the baby's mother and Father Ryan—and that Father Ryan was handsomely rewarded in return for his discretion," Sister said.

It was Brooke's turn now. "Wow," she whispered.

"Sister? Did you ever know a woman named Josephine Bettendorf Warrick?" Lizzie asked.

The nun smiled. "I never did have the pleasure of meeting that great lady, but of course, we were all very gratified when she donated the money for the new nursery wing at the children's home. Such a lovely gesture, especially considering she wasn't even of our faith."

"She paid for a wing at the children's home, yet she didn't have children and she wasn't Catholic?" Lizzie asked.

"Oh no. I believe her family attended St. John's Episcopal. As for the children part, I don't believe she was married at that point. The new wing was named the Bettendorf Nursery."

Brooke spoke up, choosing her words carefully. "Was there, well . . . was there any speculation, at the time, about the baby Father Ryan claimed he 'found' in his church? Were there any rumors that the baby could have been Josephine Bettendorf's own baby? Maybe a child she had out of wedlock? Could Josephine have been the anonymous donor of the Packard? And could that be the reason she donated the money for the nursery at the home?"

"You think baby Charlie was Josephine Bettendorf's?" The idea seemed to intrigue the elderly nun.

"We've heard a story to that effect, but we don't have any real proof," Lizzie said. "That's why we came to you."

"I don't think any of us, at the time, thought anything like that," Sister Theresa said. "We all just assumed Josephine was a wealthy young lady from a good family who'd been raised to perform good works. Although, now that I think about it, I remember one of the sisters was always puzzled about why Miss Bettendorf made such a point of visiting the home and spending time

with the children, especially at Christmas, when she was so very clearly uncomfortable around little ones."

"Good question," Felicia said.

Sister nodded. "Is there anything else I can help you with? I've really enjoyed our visit, but I'll confess, I'm anxious to get back to my ball game. I try
never to miss a Braves game. Can one of you tell me the score?"

Brooke stepped closer to the television. "Looks like it's the top of the ninth,
and it's all tied up, and the Braves are at bat."

Sister clapped her hands gleefully. "Who's on deck?"

"Um, I can't pronounce that name," Brooke said. "Lots of consonants."

"Never mind. That must be Vlad. He's my favorite." She put down the rosary beads and picked up the remote, turning the volume on high.

"Goodbye, Sister Theresa," Lizzie said, leaning down to give the old woman
a peck on the cheek. "We've enjoyed talking to you, and really appreciate the
information."

"Entirely my pleasure, I assure you. Come again, anytime. I always enjoy
talking about the old days."

"We'll do that," Brooke said, heading for the door.

"One more thing, girls!" Sister called out. "Something I just thought of. You
said the nuns named Charlie after St. Anthony because he was their favorite
saint. I'm afraid that's wrong. I'm quite sure he was named that because Anthony of Padua is the patron saint of the lost. And that poor baby was definitely lost."

"Excuse me?" Felicia said.

"Obviously you're not Catholic." Sister chuckled. "My late mother, God rest
her soul, whenever she misplaced her pocketbook or house key, she would
always make us children get down on our knees and pray to St. Anthony for
assistance. I can still remember the prayer. 'Tony, Tony, turn around. Something's lost and must be found.' Probably highly sacrilegious, but I still pray to
St. Anthony when I can't find my doggone remote."

50

The women sat in the parked Volvo in the parking lot at the rebranded Good Shepherd Academy.

Felicia gestured toward the manicured grounds dotted with moss-hung towering oaks, head-high azaleas, and redbrick buildings. "This place doesn't look at all like a children's home. I've been on college campuses that don't look this impressive. Hell, I've worked at campuses that weren't this nice."

The bronze plaque over the door told them they were looking at the administration building and visitor's center.

"Remind me what we're doing here?" Felicia asked.

"We're trying to dig up the truth about C. D.'s origin story," Brooke said. "That orphanage he was taken to as an infant is long gone, and this was his next stop. He says he lived here from the time he was six until he was sixteen. To tell you the truth, I'm not really sure what we're looking for."

"After what Sister Theresa said, I think we might be on the right track," Felicia said. "That sweet old lady wouldn't lie, would she?"

"I believed her. And now I'm thinking maybe there really is something to C. D.'s story. It's just weird enough to be true," Lizzie agreed.

"I don't know," Brooke said. "Josephine was so intent on making amends with her oldest friends, and by extension, us. Right up until the night she died. But if she wanted to make things right, why wouldn't she mention the fact that she'd given a child up for adoption? Why wouldn't she try to find him?"

"Not just given him up. Abandoned him," Felicia said. "And bought off a priest in the process to keep her secret."

"Of course, we don't have any proof of that," Lizzie reminded them. "Just an elderly blind nun's suspicions."

"You know what I've been wondering?" Felicia said. "What's C. D. been using to prove his identity all these years? Does he have a birth certificate? Social security card? How'd he get those things if he was supposedly the equivalent of a Catholic Cabbage Patch Kid?"

"Good question," Lizzie said. "Maybe I can look it up online."

"Except you can't," Brooke said. "Privacy issues again. Only the holder of the birth certificate, or a first-degree relative, or a duly authorized representative of the party in question, like a guardian or attorney, has access to those records in Georgia."

"So what's our approach when we get in there?" Felicia asked. "Is Lizzie still our liar in chief?"

"Same general pretext," Lizzie said. "I'm probably just going to wing it. So nod and agree with whatever I say. I think the aim is to see if we can get a gander at C. D.'s records."

Brooke had been staring at the administration building, trying to recall some obscure detail that had been nagging at her since she'd driven through the Good Shepherd entrance arch. Something C. D. had said.

She got out of the car and walked toward a nearby building, a brick one-story affair. A brass plaque proclaimed it the Halberg Cottage. She turned and got back in the car.

"What was that all about?" Lizzie asked.

"Just remembering something C. D. said. It was the morning Josephine died when he came to tell us he was Josephine's son. He said he'd come to a re-union here at Good Shepherd and bumped into a man he'd known all those years ago. Somebody who'd been at St. Joseph's and then transferred here to Good

Shepherd, the same way C. D. had, when he turned six. He was the one who told C. D. he could look up the old records at the archdiocesan offices."

"Did he mention a name?" Felicia asked.

"I don't think so," Brooke said. "If he did, I don't remember it. Maybe this man could corroborate C. D.'s story." She pulled out her cell phone and found Louette's number in her contact list.

Louette answered on the third ring. "Hey, Brooke. How you doing? Finding out anything up there in Savannah?"

"We've made some progress, but I'd like to ask C. D. a couple of questions. Do you have his phone number, Louette?"

"I got a number for him, but he don't ever use a phone," Louette said. "Half the time it's turned off or he's left it behind somewhere."

"Can you tell me the number anyway? It's worth a shot. And if you see C. D., will you ask him to call me?"

"I will, but I don't know where that man's got to. Haven't hardly seen him at all this week."

After she disconnected from Louette, Brooke tried C. D.'s number. Her call went directly to voice mail. She left a message. "C. D., it's Brooke. I'm in Savannah, trying to track down any records that might prove you're related to Josephine. Call me, please, as soon as you get this."

A small sign in the lobby of the administration building directed visitors to the upstairs offices. It was late afternoon, nearly four, and the open space with office cubicles lining the outside walls was mostly deserted.

"Hello?" A trim, middle-aged man with a salt-and-pepper goatee walked out of his office with a smile. The placard on the wall said DON SMALLS, DIRECTOR OF DEVELOPMENT.

"Anything I can do for you ladies?"

"Hi," Lizzie said smoothly. She went into her pretext again, this time adding more drama and substance.

"Dad is at the end of his life," she said sadly. "And this place has meant so much to him. He's sort of searching for his identity, I guess, so that he can pass it along to his daughters."

Smalls adjusted his wire-rimmed glasses. "Are all three of you sisters?"

"Half sisters," Felicia said, picking up her cue. "We had three different mothers. They're all gone now, and Dad's all we have left."

"I totally understand," Smalls said. "Was your father looking to make some sort of bequest to Good Shepherd? As a memoriam?"

"Not at this time, although that could change," Lizzie said. "His birthday is coming up and we thought we'd put together a memory book as a surprise. He suffers from dementia now, you know. The problem is, we don't have anything substantive to put in there from his childhood."

"We were hoping maybe the home had some old photos or documents in their archives that we could make copies of," Felicia said.

"We'd be happy to pay any copying charges," Brooke added.

"Well . . ." Smalls crossed his arms over his chest. "I don't know what documents you're looking for. Most of that stuff would be considered confidential."

"Really?" Felicia wrinkled her nose in disbelief. "After all these years? I mean, he's nearly eighty. Why all the secrecy?"

"You have to remember, at the time this institution was a children's home, there was somewhat of a social stigma attached to having been placed here. After all, living here meant either that you had no parents or that your parents were too poor or unfit to raise you themselves. Most of our alumni are quite proud of what they achieved, coming from such humble beginnings, but others would just as soon hide their connection with Good Shepherd."

"So there's nothing?" Lizzie asked, shoulders drooping dramatically to signal her disappointment.

"You're welcome to look through the exhibits in the museum and the scrapbooks," Smalls said. "They're all downstairs in our museum, and they're organized by year. Maybe you'll find some photos or clippings from his time here. And although it's not usually done, I don't see any harm in letting you make photocopies here in the development office."

"Awesome!" Lizzie said.

"We do ask for a minimal donation for entry to the museum," Smalls said, reaching for his key ring. "Seven dollars."

After the women had paid, he walked them downstairs and unlocked the doors. "I'll be upstairs finishing a report. Look around all you want, and if you do see something you want to copy, feel free. And, ladies? We close at five. I have a board meeting tonight, so I really won't be able to keep the museum open any longer than that."

They spent ten minutes or so browsing the exhibits and then made their way to a small anteroom where they found metal shelves loaded with rows of black leather-bound scrapbooks.

Brooke ran her fingers over the spines of the books, searching for the right years.

"C. D. would have come here in 1948, by my reckoning," she said, pulling a book with the appropriate year stamped in gold on the spine.

The three women crowded around a table as Brooke opened the scrapbook. The pages were of brittle black construction paper with newspaper clippings, black-and-white snapshots, and the miscellanea of a bygone era glued to the paper.

"Look at this," Brooke said, tapping a faded mimeographed sheet of paper. "It's a play program. *Oliver Twist.* Appropriate, huh? Orphans putting on a play about an orphan boy." She ran her finger down the names of the cast and was surprised to see a name she recognized.

"Oh my gosh. Here's George Trautwein. He used to own the biggest Cadillac dealership in Savannah. I went to Savannah Country Day with his granddaughter Ginger."

"Fascinating," Felicia said. "Let's keep going. We don't have much time."

"Right," Lizzie agreed. "Eyes on the prize."

She flipped more pages, and some of the old paper seemed to crumble under her fingertips. "What's with all the pictures of cows?" Lizzie asked.

"They've always had a cattle operation here, and a working farm," Brooke said. "I think it was part of the whole vocational, self-sustaining model."

A few pages later, they found a typed report of the minutes of the Good Shepherd Alumni Association annual meeting.

Lizzie read aloud. "Okay. Discussion about raising funds for a new roof for the hay barn. Announcements about new cottage parents. Announcements about fellow alumni, births, deaths, marriages . . . oh, hello!" She tapped a line item with her fingertip. "'Construction has begun on a new cottage, to be named in memory of local benefactor Samuel G. Bettendorf.'"

"Looking better and better for our buddy C. D.," Felicia muttered. "First Josephine bought a new wing at St. Joseph's, and then a new cottage here. Some guilt trip, huh?"

"Keep flipping those pages," Lizzie said.

Two-thirds of the way through the book, they found a section devoted to black-and-white group photos of boys, organized by cottages.

"Here!" Felicia stabbed a slightly out-of-focus photo of eight young boys posed in front of a small brick house. "These kids look to be the right age."

The boys stared into the camera, squinting in the sunlight. They were dressed in dungarees mostly, with two of the smallest ones wearing knickers and high socks. Their clothes were rumpled, and some wore baseball caps. A small balding man who wore pince-nez glasses stood behind the children, his hand on the shoulder of a dour-looking woman in a dark print dress.

The handwritten caption on the page read: "Cole Cottage, 6–8 yrs."

"Do any of these kids look like C. D. to you?" Lizzie asked, peering down at the photo.

"I've only laid eyes on him a couple of times, so I can't imagine what he looked like over seventy years ago," Felicia said. "One thing catches my eye. They're all white kids, right? What happened to black children who had nobody to look after them?"

"There used to be a home for black children in Savannah, according to my mom, but I don't know too much about it. As for recognizing C. D., I've seen him and talked to him several times, but I've got no clue either," Brooke admitted. "But look. You can see some writing on the back." With a fingernail, she worked at the glued-down corners at the bottom of the photo. A moment later, she carefully turned the photo over to find a handwritten list of the children.

"Dicky Abbott, Buck Anthony, Frank Armour, Sid Babcock, Bobby Bass, Mickey Beaman, Chick Garber, Timmy Potts."

"Buck Anthony," she repeated. "That's gotta be our guy. Bingo."

"Which one?" Lizzie asked, leaning down to get a closer look.

Brooke shook her head. "I don't know. It looks like they listed the kids' names alphabetically, but there's no telling if they're lined up that way."

Lizzie reached for her cell phone and snapped a photo of the list, then flipped the photo over and shot one of the picture itself.

They leafed rapidly through the rest of the scrapbook but found nothing else that showed a boy who could be C. D. "Buck" Anthony.

"Now what?" Brooke asked, looking at her watch. "We've only got ten more minutes before closing. That's not really enough time to go through any more scrapbooks."

"We've got a list of the boys who lived with him in that cottage," Lizzie said.

"And we know at least one of them is still living, or he was as of a few months ago, when C. D. ran into him at that reunion," Brooke said. "But which one? And how do we contact him?"

"Through the alumni association," Felicia said. "That's how my alma mater always reaches out to put the squeeze to me for donations."

They heard the door open, and Don Smalls popped his head inside. "All set, ladies? I need to set the alarm and lock the place up now."

"But it's not five yet," Lizzie protested.

"Sorry. I can't be late for that board meeting," Smalls said.

"Can you do us a huge favor?" Lizzie asked, walking rapidly toward him. "We found a picture of my dad, along with the rest of the boys who lived in his cottage in 1948, the year he came here. And we found a list of the names of the boys on the back. I took a photo with my phone. Maybe you could take a look and see if you recognize any names? Dad said he ran into one of his pals at the last reunion, but he couldn't remember the name because of the dementia. But it's likely this man belongs to the alumni association if he came to a reunion, right?"

"Maybe," Smalls said.

Lizzie scrolled through her camera roll until she found the photo, and then she enlarged it.

Smalls read the list aloud. "Hmm. No, never heard of Dicky Abbott or Sid Babcock. Dowling, Garber, Potts, I've seen their names in old alumni newsletters, but I believe they're all deceased. But Mickey Beaman, yeah. Mickey's still active in the association. His son drives him to all the meetings and functions."

Brooke's heart leaped. "Do you by chance have contact information for Mickey Beaman?"

"No, but this time of day you can usually catch him at his son's business. He likes to hang out there and chat with any old-timers who wander in. Mickey's pretty loquacious. He'll talk your ear off if you give him half a chance."

"What's the business?" Lizzie asked eagerly.

"Mr. B's Quality Beverages," Smalls said. He jangled his key chain to signal that their time was up.

51

....

Mr. B's was a liquor store on West Broad Street, on the fringes of the Savannah College of Art and Design campus.

"We used to try to use fake IDs to buy booze here when I was in high school," Brooke remarked after she'd parked.

An electronic doorbell rang as they entered the store, which was dark and cramped with narrow aisles built of liquor cartons, the walls lined with shelves of cut-rate wine. A glass partition separated the cashier stand from the rest of the shop, and behind it, an Asian woman with white-streaked dark hair was counting back change to a college kid with a case of beer tucked under his arm.

"I don't think this place has been cleaned since the last time I was in here," Brooke muttered to Lizzie. "And that's definitely the same lady who called the cops on us."

She waited until the store's sole customer had departed and stepped up to the counter and gave a friendly smile to the cashier, who remained stone-faced.

"Hi. I'm looking for Mr. Beaman?"

"My husband's out," the woman said. "What do you want? Not another charity donation, I hope. You people are bleeding us broke with all these silent auctions and wine dinners."

"I'm actually looking for Mickey Beaman," Brooke said.

"Why?" The cashier looked over Brooke's shoulder, regarding Lizzie and Felicia, who were loitering near the door, with growing suspicion.

"Well, uh . . . ," Brooke stammered, caught off guard by the woman's hostility.

"We're trying to find somebody who lived at Good Shepherd at the same time as a relative," said Lizzie, stepping into the fray. "We just came from there, and a man in the development office suggested we talk to Mr. Beaman."

The woman rolled her eyes and turned toward a partially open door behind her. "Dad!" she hollered. "Dad! Some people wanna talk to you out here."

She waited a moment. "I'm warning you, once you get him talking about that place, he'll never shut up."

The door opened, and an old man shuffled out of the back room. His thinning gray hair was combed across his balding head. He wore a Budweiser-logoed golf shirt stretched tightly over a massive stomach.

"These ladies want to ask you some stuff about one of your Good Shepherd cronies," the woman said.

Mickey Beaman's eyes lit up at the mention of his alma mater. "What do you want to know?" he asked, leaning against the counter.

"Not here," his daughter-in-law said. She pushed a button and they heard a buzz, and then a door opened between the store and the cash stand. "Take them back to the stockroom."

A small card table and four folding chairs were shoved up against an ancient refrigerator in the stockroom, delineating what passed as Mr. B's break room.

"You ladies have a seat," Beaman said with a gallant gesture toward the table.

"Mr. Beaman," Lizzie started.

"It's Mickey. Nobody calls me Mr. Beaman anymore," he insisted. "Now, what can I tell you about Good Shepherd? Have you been out to see the new museum? Did you see the video? That's me at the three-minute mark, talking about the values that were instilled in boys like me."

"That museum is very impressive," Lizzie said. "We only got to spend a few minutes there today, so we missed out on the video. I guess we'll check it out the next time."

"You do that," Mickey urged. "Jimmy Yaz—that's Jimmy Yazbek, he was three years younger than me—lived in the Blatner Cottage. His son is a big-deal cameraman on one of those TV shows, I forget the name of the show, but Jimmy Junior made that video. For free."

"Speaking of your classmates, we're trying to help a relative of ours, C. D. Anthony, put together some information about his early life, both at St. Joseph's and at Good Shepherd," Brooke said.

Mickey's brow furrowed. "Say the name again?"

"C. D. Anthony. The nuns called him Charlie, but when we were at Good Shepherd just now, we saw a photo showing all the boys who lived in your cottage. He was listed as Buck Anthony," Lizzie said. "Does that name ring a bell?"

"Buck? Oh yeah. I knew Buck Anthony. Like you say, we were both at St. Joseph's, and then when we turned six, we were sent to Good Shepherd. I think I was maybe older than him. I'm seventy-nine, you know. Still drive, although Yvonne out there, she's trying to get my son to make me stop. What can I tell you about old Buck? He was a hell-raiser as a kid, that's for sure. He was always small for his age, but you didn't want to cross him. The guy had a temper and a wicked undercut. We used to box, you know. I don't think they teach boxing to boys these days, which is a shame. Boxing is a great life lesson."

"It sure is," Lizzie said, trying to steer Mickey back toward the topic at hand. "Do you remember ever hearing about how Buck came to live at St. Joseph's?"

"Somebody left him in a church was what I always heard," Mickey said promptly. "Not like me. My mom passed when I was two, and my dad was a traveling salesman. My grandma did what she could, but she was too old to raise a kid like me. And then my dad got killed in the war, Iwo Jima, so then I was a real orphan. But my grandma would come see me, when she could, take me out for my birthday, stuff like that. I don't think hardly anybody ever came to see Buck, which maybe explains why he sort of had a chip on his shoulder, excuse the expression."

"By any chance, do you remember a woman named Josephine Bettendorf, who might have visited him while he was living at St. Joseph's?" Brooke asked.

"Bettendorf? The family the cottage is named after? At Good Shepherd?"

"Yes," Brooke said. "C. D.—I mean, Buck—says he remembers her coming every Christmas while he lived at St. Joseph's. He says she brought all the kids gifts, but he got special ones. Like a toy truck."

"You want a drink?" Mickey asked suddenly. He stood and opened the refrigerator door. "We get all kinds of samples, for free. The sales reps are always trying to get us to order whatever's new in their lines." He held up a can. "Red Bull? The SCAD kids all love Red Bull. Or lemme see, how about a Peach Sunset Tea? Or maybe some Chocolate Mint wine? What will you have? It's on the house. Just don't tell Yvonne."

"No, thanks," Brooke said. "We were talking about the Christmas visits? From Josephine Bettendorf?"

"I wouldn't mind trying that wine," Lizzie spoke up. "Strictly for research."

"Great! Take the whole bottle," Mickey handed her the bottle and a plastic wineglass. "Now what were we talking about?"

Lizzie twisted the metal cap from the bottle and poured an inch of milky brown liquid into the glass. She sipped, shuddered, shrugged, then sipped again.

"Christmas visits? At the children's home?" Lizzie reminded him.

"There were several ladies who used to come around the holidays. They'd bring us kids candy canes and oranges. One year a Jewish lady whose husband owned a shoe store downtown brought us each a pair of new shoes. I tell ya, I was so proud of those shoes, I wore 'em 'til those nuns made me turn 'em over to one of the younger kids because they were way too small for me. I can't think of the name of that store. But it's right there on Broughton, near Levy's Jewelers. Or used to be."

"How about Josephine Bettendorf?" Lizzie prompted. "Can you remember her coming to the home? She was tall, with dark hair. Very striking. And C. D. says she gave him a toy truck one year."

"The truck!" Mickey said, roaring with laughter. "I don't remember that dark-haired lady, but I do remember a red truck. A beauty. The other kids were real jealous of Buck and his truck. This one boy—I can see his face, but I can't remember his name . . . a big red-headed kid with freckles—grabbed that truck and bashed Buck in the eye with it. Buck yanked it back and busted the boy in the mouth. Kid bled all over the place. After that, nobody tried to take nothing offa Buck."

"That's what he told me too," Brooke marveled. "Do you have any other memories of Buck? From his time at Good Shepherd? Did the dark-haired woman ever visit him there?"

Mickey popped the top on a can of Budweiser and sipped. "Not saying it didn't happen, just saying I don't recall it. But I remember him staying in trouble. Wouldn't do his chores. Wouldn't listen to the house parents. Fighting, like that. I heard he ran away after he got caught stealing cigarettes from a candy store nearby."

"That sounds about right," Brooke agreed.

"I was surprised he showed up at the reunion, to tell you the truth," Mickey said. "I've never missed one since I left—been president of the alumni association. But that's the only time he ever came to one. I don't judge, but it looked to me like he'd had a hard kind of life."

Brooke glanced at Lizzie to see if she'd thought of any more questions for Mickey Beaman.

Lizzie cleared her throat. "Mickey, there's something I'm curious about. The nuns named him Charles, after the priest who found him, and they called him Charlie. So why did everybody at Good Shepherd call him Buck?"

"It was just a nickname. Everybody had a nickname back then. My name was Mickey, but the guys called me Mouse. You know, for Mickey Mouse? We had a guy called Jughead because he had big ears."

"Where did the name *Buck* come from?" Brooke asked.

Mickey glanced at Felicia, then looked away. "It was different times back then, you know? We weren't what you'd call politically correct. If you really want to know, *Buck* was short for *Buckwheat*. You know? Buckwheat, the little colored kid from the *Our Gang* shows?"

"I remember Buckwheat," Felicia said, her voice icy.

"How did he get the nickname *Buckwheat?*" Lizzie asked.

The stockroom door swung open, and Yvonne stuck her head inside. "Dad, I've gotta go home and get supper started. I need you to come run the register until Michael comes back."

"Sure thing," Mickey said, lumbering to his feet, eager to escape the prying eyes of these three women. "Sorry, ladies, I gotta go to work now."

"The nickname," Lizzie repeated. "How did Buck get that nickname?"

Mickey squirmed and gulped his beer. "I didn't name him that, you understand. It was one of the older guys who started it, and after that, it just stuck. Charlie, or C. D., whatever you wanna call him, he had this wild, kinky hair. You know, like that colored kid from *Our Gang*."

Lizzie thought about that for a moment. She pulled out her cell phone and pulled up the photo she'd copied from the Good Shepherd yearbook.

"This is a photo of the boys from your cottage, isn't it?"

The old man's face softened. "Son of a gun. It sure is. Look at that. We look like the Dead End kids, don't we? There I am, right there in the middle."

"Which of the boys is Buck?" Lizzie asked, handing him the phone.

He stared down at the photo and finally tapped one face. "I can't be sure, but I think maybe this is him. He was for sure the smallest kid in our cottage, and he's wearing a ball cap, like Buck always used to do. Maybe because he was trying to hide the kinky hair."

Felicia's eyes were blazing, but her voice was calm. "Are you saying Charlie looked black? Like he was African American?"

"His skin wasn't all that dark, not as dark as yours," Mickey said. "Like maybe just real tan. You know how kids are. They say stupid stuff. The guy who gave him that nickname, he said he bet Buck was part colored. And that's why his mama left him in a church. Because she didn't want anybody to know she had a colored baby."

"Dad! Are you coming?" Yvonne screeched.

Mickey downed the rest of his beer and scurried out of the stockroom.

52

....

"What planet was that old dude from?" Lizzie asked as they drove away from the liquor store. "'Buckwheat'? 'Colored kid'? What a dinosaur."

"Nothing new to me," Felicia said, turning around from her perch in the front seat of the Volvo. "You've been living in your little bubble out in California all this time. Wake up, girl. This is the Deep South. We got more crackers here than a box of saltines."

"Could it be true?" Brooke asked. "Could C. D. be Josephine's son? And biracial?"

"You think just because I'm black I can spot that one drop of chocolate in the glass of milk?" Felicia demanded.

"That's not how I meant it, and you know it," Brooke said, the blood rushing to her face.

"Relax," Felicia said, laughing. "I was just yanking your chain. 'Cause I've lightened up." She held out her hand to Lizzie. "Let me see that picture again."

Lizzie pulled up the photo and handed over the phone.

With two fingers, Felicia enlarged the image until the blurry face of a runty six-year-old filled the iPhone screen. Shadow cast from the bill of his cap obscured most of the upper half of his face, but the slight smile was visible.

"It's possible," she said, studying the photo. "His lips are sort of full, and maybe his nose is a bit flatter and broader. His skin tone? No darker than some of my Italian friends. Of course, I can't see his hair because of that cap. But yeah, he could be passing."

"I don't think I've ever seen C. D. without a hat. And a cigarillo," Brooke said. "And he's spent a lifetime out in the sun. The question is, what do we do with this gem of information?"

"Let's go see Sister Theresa, show her this photo, and ask if there was ever any discussion that Charlie, or Buck, or whatever you want to call him could have been biracial," Lizzie said.

"Can't. I've gotta pick up Henry from Mom's by five, and I'm already late," Brooke said.

"And I've got to make sure Auntie Vee has eaten and taken her meds," Felicia said. "Louette's been great about letting us stay there, but I'm the one responsible for Vee's health."

"Maybe you could tactfully broach the subject of C. D. with Varina again, given what we learned today," Lizzie said.

Felicia laughed. "She was absolutely adamant that Josephine never had a child. I don't know what her reaction would be if I ask her if Josephine had a child with a black man. Her head might just spin all the way off her head at the very idea."

"If C. D. would ever return my call, I'd ask him about it," Brooke said, glancing at her own phone, which hadn't rung. "I guess I'll let Gabe know what we learned today. After all, he's the administrator of Josephine's estate. Let him sort it all out."

53

By the time she'd fed and bathed Henry and yawned her way through story time and bedtime, it was after nine o'clock, which was an hour past his normal bedtime and what felt like an eternity past her own.

Brooke peeled out of her clothes and crawled into her unmade bed wearing an old T-shirt. Her laptop rested on her nightstand, but she didn't have the energy to even lift the top. She had emails to return, legal issues to research, documents to draft. The corner of her bedroom was piled high with this week's dirty laundry and last week's laundry that she'd never gotten around to folding. She wouldn't get to any of it tonight, and based on what she knew of her upcoming schedule, tomorrow wasn't looking good either.

Which left only Saturday. In her past life, Saturdays were for long runs followed by endless Bloody Mary–soaked brunches, followed by a trip to the nail salon and maybe shopping with a girlfriend, and then date night with Harris.

But that life was ancient history. It would be a miracle if she managed to muck out her house, get to the grocery store, and maybe do some laundry this Saturday.

Saturday! She flopped backward onto the mattress. This Saturday was supposed to be date night with Gabe Wynant. She'd allowed herself to be sweet-talked into going to a dinner dance with him at the Cloister, but she'd forgotten to line up a babysitter.

She reached for her phone, keeping her fingers crossed that Farrah would be available.

There was a missed call on her phone from an unfamiliar number and an area code she'd never seen before. The caller had left a message. She touched the Play button, and as soon as she heard the voice her pulse rocketed.

"Hey, Brooke. It's Pete. Look, I know it's short notice, but I'm back on the East Coast, headed to a conference in Miami. I've got a stopover in Savannah, where one of my former colleagues from the Park Service is picking me up, then we're driving down to the conference together. I'm wondering—no, I'm hoping, you might agree to meet me at the Savannah airport. I bought a cheap plane ticket, which means I'm about to board my first of three legs of the flight, which is supposed to get me in around ten tomorrow morning. Maybe we could do an early lunch and catch up before my colleague picks me up? Okay, anyway, I really hope to see you tomorrow. I've missed you, you know?"

Pete Haynes missed her. He wanted to see her. Have lunch. Catch up. After three plus years. She could already picture the conversation.

Her: How was Alaska? How are the caribou? Is it really cold there?

Him: Alaska's great. The caribou are awesome, and it's cold as shit. How about you? What have you been up to?

Her: Oh, you know, the usual. Practicing law and raising your son. Wanna split dessert?

She ran her fingers through her hair and groaned. This could not be happening. The call had come in while she was bathing Henry. It was too late to call Pete and try to beg off.

Instead, she texted Farrah.

Hey. Can you keep Henry for me tomorrow morning? Gotta run up to Savannah. Also need sitter for Saturday night. Heavy date. I'll pay double your usual rate.

Farrah's reply came back in less than a minute.

So sorry! Can't tomorrow. It's graduation. I'm a maybe for Saturday night. Can I tell you tomorrow?

No! she wanted to shout. *Commit already.* But she couldn't really blame Farrah. This was a big weekend for a graduating senior. Who wanted to be saddled with babysitting? And maybe it was for the best. Maybe this was the universe telling her she needed to stay home and take care of her kid and concentrate on building some kind of a career.

Or maybe it was the universe telling her to call her mother.

Good thing Marie was a bit of a night owl, Brooke thought.

"Hi!" Marie said. "Shouldn't you be in bed by now?"

"I was, and then I had a missed call. From Pete."

"Oooh. Tell."

"He's got a layover at the Savannah airport tomorrow on his way to a conference in Miami, and he wants me to meet him for lunch and to catch up."

"You're going, right?"

"Not sure. He gets in at ten. But Henry gets out of day care at noon tomorrow because of teacher conferences. And Farrah's graduation is tomorrow, so she can't pick him up and keep him. I hate to ask, especially after you had him all day today . . ."

"Bring him to me," Marie said quickly. "How was he tonight? I didn't want to jinx anything, but he was a little crabby. And he hardly ate anything."

"He seemed fine," Brooke assured her. "We were both wiped out after the long drive home. In fact, he fell asleep in the bathtub after dinner."

"How are you feeling about seeing Pete tomorrow? Are you excited? Nervous?"

"I haven't had time to process it yet. A little of both. Oh, shit!" Brooke wailed. "I have to figure out what to wear. I haven't even done laundry since I got home from Talisa."

"I looked in your closet when I was putting away clothes last time I was there," Marie said. "You have half a dozen pairs of white jeans. Put on a cute top that shows some cleavage. Wear those sexy black sandals I gave you for your birthday. Pull your hair back with those tortoise clips, and wear some dangly earrings."

"Mom! Pete gets in at ten. I'll look like a hooker on the stroll for a john if I show up at the airport in cleavage and spike heels at that hour of the morning."

"You wish. And don't forget to wear makeup, for heaven's sake. You do still know how to apply makeup, right?"

"Very funny. I wear makeup all the time."

"Like when?"

"Like if I have a court date or something."

"You're going to tell Pete about Henry tomorrow, aren't you?"

"I haven't decided," Brooke said. "I thought I'd see how it goes."

"No matter how it goes, you have to tell him," Marie insisted. "Henry is his son. He has a right to know, and you have a responsibility to your son to allow him to have a father in his life. Even if you decide that your relationship with Pete is over, you need to do this, Brooke."

"We'll see," Brooke said. "I gotta hang up now. See you in the morning."

"Makeup. Heels. Cleavage. Earrings," Marie said. "And courage."

She rang the doorbell at her mother's Ardsley Park house and then fumbled in her purse for the house key. The door swung open.

Marie stood in the hallway dressed in her bathrobe and slippers, which was unheard of. This was a woman who never left her bedroom unless she was dressed and perfectly groomed.

But there she stood with lank, unwashed hair. Her eyes were red-rimmed with dark circles beneath. She held a tissue to her nose.

"Mom!" Brooke shifted Henry from one hip to the other. "You look like death. What's wrong?"

"Fever. Chills. Started an hour ago. You look nice," her mother said, giving an approving nod to Brooke's deep V-neck top and eyeliner. "I, on the other hand, feel like I've been run over by a dump truck." Marie's voice was a hoarse rasp.

"You should have called before I left home. I would have just canceled," Brooke said. She stepped into the hallway and took Marie by the elbow. "Come on. I'll fix you some tea with lemon and honey, then you need to get back to bed."

"No," Marie croaked. "Go. Just go. I'm going back to bed. But you need to go to the airport and see Pete. Go. Shoo." She made shooing motions with her hands.

"And take Henry? Are you nuts? What'll I say? What will he say?"

"You two will figure it out," Marie said, turning her head aside to cough. "No matter what else happens, he'll fall in love with Henry. Who wouldn't? Promise me you'll go. Promise me you won't back out and run away again."

Run away. Again. Like she had the weekend of her wedding. The words stung. Because they were true.

"All right," Brooke said. "We're going."

Pete had neglected to tell her where he was flying in from, so she had no idea of his flight number or where they should meet. She'd been so keyed up about the meeting that she'd arrived at the airport thirty minutes early and had spent the past ten minutes pacing up and down the airport's carpeted retail concourse. Her back ached from carrying the heavy toddler, so she finally put him down.

"Toy!" Henry cried, pointing to a gift shop where a giant stuffed Snoopy was perched in the front window. He set off at a run for the shop.

"Whoa there," she said, following after, scooping him up just before the boy made it to his quarry. The back of his pants were damp. She held him aloft, sniffed, and gagged.

"Oh, Henry, nooooo. Not now."

"I poop," he said proudly.

"We poop in the potty, remember?"

"No potty," Henry said.

She'd almost left his diaper bag in the car but at the last minute had shoved her purse inside and looped the bag over her shoulder. It was navy blue, quilted cotton with a pattern of elephants and tigers. Not nearly as cute as the black designer clutch she'd planned to carry. She hurried to the ladies' room, breathing through her mouth while she stripped off the boy's shorts on a drop-down changing table. "What we have here is a shituation," she muttered, stuffing his soiled shorts, shirt, even his socks into a plastic sack she kept in the diaper bag for just such emergencies. She used half a bag of baby wipes cleaning him up, then dressed him in a fresh outfit.

Finally, she went to the sink to wash her hands and check her makeup. "Oh God," she moaned, looking at the mirror. Her cute low-cut top had somehow come into contact with Henry's soiled backside. Gagging, she scrubbed at the top with a wet paper towel. The quarter-sized damp spot grew to the size of a half-dollar, directly over her left nipple.

Brooke grabbed Henry's hand and dragged him in the direction of the gift shop. Surely they sold a few items of women's clothing, right?

She was in the process of paying for the only top she could find, a hideous bile-green tank top with SAVANNAH spelled out in sequins when Henry spied his heart's desire. It was a board book featuring his favorite thing in the whole world, the hairless Canadian cartoon character, propped on a display next to the cash register.

"Caillou!" Henry crowed, grabbing for the book at the same moment Brooke was in the process of handing her credit card to the cashier.

Without thinking, Brooke snatched his chubby hand away from the book, which shared shelf space with dozens of tiny cheesy breakable souvenir trinkets. "Henry, no," she said sharply. "You already have that book."

Her son's face crumpled into agony. "I want it!" he cried. "I want Caillou!"

"Anything else?" the cashier asked, her hands poised over the register. "Chips, gum, soft drinks, magazine?"

"Just the shirt, thanks," Brooke said tersely, keeping an eye on the concourse. It was ten after ten, and a sudden wave of passengers had disembarked their flights and were passing by, laughing and talking.

"Please, Mommy," Henry whined. "I want Caillou."

"Can I have your email for your receipt?" the cashier asked.

"No!" Brooke said. "Stop it right this minute."

"Excuse me?" the clerk said.

"Sorry, I was talking to my son. Just print out the receipt and put it in the bag, please," Brooke said through clenched teeth. She released Henry's hand to retrieve her card.

Henry saw an opening and seized it. He grabbed the book with both hands. "Mine!"

Without thinking, she snatched the book back. She knelt down so that she was at eye level with her son. "Absolutely not. You have this exact same book at home, and I am not buying you another one."

She stood up and tried to compose herself. Another wave of passengers was passing. She saw a familiar face in the crowd. It was Pete, striding down the concourse, one arm flung casually across the shoulder of a young blond woman. She was in her midtwenties, slender and petite with a long Nordic-looking braid cascading down her back. She wore form-fitting green hiking shorts and had a backpack over one shoulder. Pete leaned in, laughing and talking with her.

Brooke felt herself shrink away from the gift shop entrance. She wanted to flee, to melt into the woodwork. As soon as Pete and his friend had passed, she tugged gently at her son's hand. "Come on, buddy. Let's go home."

"Noooooo!" Henry wailed, throwing himself onto the floor. He grabbed the book and hugged it to his chest. "I want Caillou! I want it, I want it!" His face was scarlet with rage. She bent over and tried to pry the book away. "*Noooooo!*" he screamed, kicking his tiny feet at her ankles.

Brooke saw Pete pause. He turned, said something to his female companion, and frowned, looking to see where the commotion was coming from. His eyes met hers. People surged around him, but Pete Haynes stopped dead in his tracks.

54

....

He strode toward the gift shop. Stopped, then wrapped Brooke in an awkward embrace. "I'm so glad you showed up," he murmured in her ear. "I wasn't sure you would."

"I wasn't sure either," Brooke said, her voice shaky. "It's been so long. But I'm really glad you called." She saw the woman who'd been walking with Pete, standing discreetly nearby, watching their reunion with undisguised interest.

Sensing he'd lost his audience, Henry abandoned his tantrum, stood and raised his arms. "Mama. I pick you up."

Brooke took a step backward and scooped her son into her arms.

"Who's this?" Pete asked warily.

"Pete, this is my son, Henry. Henry, can you say hello to Pete?"

Henry turned away, burying his face in her shoulder.

"Hi, Henry," Pete said, lightly tapping the boy's back. "How old are you?"

Henry lifted his head and observed the stranger, his expression grave. He held out three chubby fingers. "I'm fwee."

"Obviously, we've got some catching up to do," Pete said.

"Who's your friend?" Brooke asked, gesturing toward the girl who was now slouching against a nearby wall.

"That's Hope, a grad student I've been working with. Hey, Hope," he called. "C'mere. There's somebody I want you to meet."

"Hello," the young woman said, offering a wide smile showing perfectly straight, blindingly white teeth. "You've got to be Brooke. Pete's told me so much about you."

"Great to meet you, Hope," Brooke said. "This is my son, Henry, who was doing his best howler monkey impression a minute ago."

"Oooh, Henry, is that Curious George on your shirt? I used to love him, and the man with the yellow hat."

Henry peeped shyly at the girl, nodded, then turned his head and hid again. Hope's face registered a flicker of recognition as she looked from Henry to Pete.

"Okay, well, uh, Pete, I'm going to hit the ladies' room and then maybe find a magazine for the ride to Miami. I'll let you two have some private time together," Hope said.

"Thanks. How about we meet outside at noon?"

"I'll see you there. Bye, Brooke. Bye, Henry."

They found a corner booth at the bar. When the waitress arrived to take their order, Brooke gave her what she hoped was a winning smile. "Is it okay for me to have my little boy in here?"

The waitress looked around at the lounge, which was half-empty at that hour. "Okay by me, but if one of my other customers complains, you'll have to leave."

Pete ordered a beer, and although Brooke longed for something to quell her bad case of jitters, she ordered coffee for herself and orange juice for Henry.

"You don't want any food?" Pete asked, scanning the menu. "I've gotta eat something. I've been on planes for twenty-four hours, and all I've had was some mini-pretzels and a stale bagel." He ordered crab cakes and french fries, and Brooke ordered a grilled cheese to split with Henry, who was already curled up on the booth with his head in her lap.

They made polite, inane conversation about the weather in Alaska, southern Atlantic hurricanes, blue crabs versus snow crabs, and politics while waiting what seemed like an interminable amount of time for the food.

She tried not to stare at Pete. His hair was longer than she'd ever seen it before, brushing his shoulders and falling across his eyes. He'd grown a thick beard too and had lost weight so that the planes and angles of his face stood in sharp relief. But his biceps bulged beneath the short sleeves of his dark gray T-shirt, and his belly was noticeably flat.

Brooke was vaguely aware that Pete was talking about the GPS devices they'd implanted in the caribou to allow them to track migration patterns, but she was only half listening. Instead, she was mentally mapping the contours of his shoulders, the scar on his lower back where he'd impaled a fishhook in his own flesh as a kid, his chest and the way it had felt to lay her cheek against it that one fateful night more than three years ago.

She longed to reach out, touch a finger to his lips. *Shh,* she wanted to say. *No more talk of caribou or grizzly bears or how they collected blood samples to measure hormone levels in the female caribou. Later. All that can come later. Tell me about you,* she wanted to say. *Tell me it was lonely without me. Tell me you love me.*

He stopped talking once or twice. Sat back, sipped his beer, and seemed to be taking measure of her, puzzling something over in his mind. Had he guessed? Did he know?

After the waitress brought their order, Pete dove into his crab cakes, and Brooke picked at her sandwich, tearing off bites and offering them to her drowsy son like a mama bird feeding her chick. She had no appetite, although she would have loved a glass of wine.

Finally, Pete stopped eating. His face was unreadable. "So. Got any news you want to share with me? Your child is three, and that's about how long it's been since we last talked."

"Pete, I'm sorry," Brooke started.

"He's the real reason you wouldn't come to Alaska that Christmas? The reason you quit Skyping and then just quit answering my phone calls and emails altogether?"

The lump in her throat felt like concrete. She nodded, miserable.

"And his father? Anybody I know?"

Brooke felt herself tense. How could Pete look at Henry and not recognize his own DNA? How could he gaze into the boy's eyes and not see in them a mirror image of his own smoky blue eyes, fringed with lashes so thick and lush they seemed to weigh down his eyelids?

"Are you married?" Pete asked incredulously. "When did that happen? Were you seeing this guy the whole time we were together? Damn it, Brooke, don't just sit there, staring at me like that."

"I'm not married," she managed. "He . . . Henry's father isn't in our lives. He hasn't been in a long time."

Pete frowned. "The guy just left you? Pregnant with his kid? What kind of swine does something like that?"

"It's not his fault. I'm the one who let myself get pregnant. You know how I am. I decided I could do it all by myself. And I have. Mostly. I found a place to rent at St. Ann's, hung up my shingle. I'm practicing law again."

He pushed his plate away. It was dotted with the breading from the crab cakes, and the streaks of ketchup from the french fries reminded her of blood, and the stabbing pains she felt in her chest as she so artlessly avoided telling Pete the truth about his son. Not lying. Just not being entirely honest.

His voice was hoarse. "Any chance you and this guy will get back together? For Henry's sake?"

She saw Hope approaching. She'd applied fresh makeup and her braid was brushed out, with blond hair flowing loose over her shoulders. She wore black jeans and a spotless white T-shirt and looked as fresh and lovely as a wildflower. Brooke was painfully aware of her own appearance, the large damp spot over her left breast, her shirt and lap covered with bits of Henry's sandwich. She was a hot, unwed mother of a mess.

"It's not looking good for me and Henry's dad. Not right now anyway. What about you and her?" She jerked her head in the girl's direction. Pete turned and flashed her a smile as she neared the table, then backed away, aware that she was interrupting something intense.

"She's a colleague," he said firmly. "She's been collecting data on caribou from another location on the tundra, and we've collaborated on this paper we're presenting at the conference in Miami."

"And there's nothing between you?" Brooke raised an eyebrow, hoping she sounded as though she didn't care.

"We're colleagues. And friends. I thought, I mean, I hoped, maybe, there was still some chance of us, you know, you and me, reconnecting. I successfully defended my dissertation three months ago. When I get down to Miami, I'm meeting with the head of a nonprofit foundation that has funding to study the deer population on all the barrier islands—Talisa, Sapelo, Ossabaw, Cumberland. They've got deep pockets, and it's a great opportunity for me."

"Pete! That's wonderful," Brooke impulsively reached out to grasp his hands in hers.

"Hey, Pete," Hope said, edging toward their table. "I hate to break this up, but Ralph just texted me. He's parked in a no-parking zone at the curb, and he says if we don't get our butts out there right now, we can find our own way to the conference."

"Coming." He stood and threw money on the table. "This should cover the check."

Brooke made a move to stand, but she was trapped in the booth with Henry, sound asleep with his head in her lap.

"Don't wake him up," Pete said. He leaned over and touched the top of Henry's messy curls. "Cute kid." Then he straightened. "This was probably a bad idea, huh?"

"Not at all," Brooke said. "It was great to see you. I just wish we'd had more time to talk. My mom was going to take Henry, but this morning she woke up with some kind of bug." Her mouth was dry, and she didn't know what to say.

He hesitated. "I'm flying out of here next week. This time, the ball's in your court, Brooke. If you call me, we'll meet. If not, I'll know it wasn't meant to be." He brushed his lips against her cheek, turned, and hurried out of the lounge, with Hope following.

"You didn't tell him, did you?" Marie's tone was more resigned than accusatory. They sat at the kitchen table. It was a dark Irish Georgian oak with carved ball and claw feet, and the chairs were of the same wood, but in a Chinese Chippendale style.

Her mother squeezed lemon into a glass of iced tea and handed the glass to Brooke.

"How are you feeling? You look a little better than you did this morning. Have you taken your temperature?" Brooke asked.

"I'm okay. Now, did you or did you not tell Pete that he has a son?"

"I wanted to," Brooke said, sipping her drink. "But when he didn't even notice how much Henry looks like him, I don't know. Something inside me just shut down."

"Your backbone?"

"How could he not recognize his own child?" Brooke cried. "Even that alleged colleague who was with him, the enchantingly lovely Hope, I know she saw the resemblance the minute she laid eyes on Henry."

Marie sipped her own tea. "Oh, Brooke, you know how clueless men are about stuff like that. When you were born, your father stood outside the nursery window at Candler Hospital proudly telling everybody within listening distance that a total stranger's newborn was his beautiful new daughter. And get this—the child was a boy, and he weighed twelve pounds, eight ounces, which was exactly twice what you weighed."

"I've never heard that story before," Brooke said. "Are you sure you didn't just make it up?"

Her mother slid her phone across the table. "Call and ask him if you don't believe me." She glanced fondly at her grandson, who at that moment was happily coloring at a child-sized table Marie had brought down from the attic for him. "Did Pete even get a really good look at him?"

Brooke shrugged. "You know how shy Henry gets around strangers. He sort of buried his head against my shirt when Pete was talking to him. But he did tell Pete he was three, which, if the man had any brains in his head, should have told him that Henry was the fruit of his loom. He even had the nerve to ask me if I'd been seeing Henry's father while we were together!"

"What did you tell him?"

"I told him the father hadn't been in our lives in a long time, which was the truth."

"I just don't understand why you didn't simply tell him the truth: that you got pregnant the last night you were together and then couldn't quite get up the nerve to tell him about his child."

Brooke jiggled the ice cubes in her glass. "I wanted to. Truly, I did. But the food took so long to get there, and it was so weird and awkward between us, and then after the food did arrive and we finally got around to talking about us, that damn girl showed up to say that their ride was there and they needed to leave. I swear, she did it on purpose."

"Didn't he tell you they were just colleagues? Nothing romantic?"

"I guess. Maybe I'm just paranoid. Pete did tell me he's coming back through town to fly back to Alaska after the conference ends next week. He said I should call him if I want to see him—and that this time the ball's in my court."

"Fair enough," Marie declared. "Next week, you call him. You get a sitter for Henry, and you arrange to meet Pete somewhere other than the airport, at a nice restaurant, and without his little friend Hope. And you sit down and put all your cards on the table."

"He'll hate me," Brooke said. "Or worse. What if he decides he doesn't want to be with me but he wants me to share custody of Henry? What if he tries to take him away from me?"

Marie rolled her eyes. "He has a right to be angry, but he's not going to try to take your son. You're being ridiculous, and you know it. Stop being so paranoid. I know you, Brooke. If you cared enough about this man to sleep with him, you know his character. Right?"

"Maybe. But it's been three years. Maybe he's changed. He grew a big, awful Grizzly Adams beard that hides his beautiful face. And he's been pumping iron too. He's, like, beefcake now. Who knows what else is going on with him?"

"You're giving me a headache," Marie said wearily. "I can't talk any sense into you. Are you going to see Pete again or not?"

"Truthfully, I don't know. My life is complicated enough right now. And part of that's your fault."

"Mine? What did I do?"

"You're the one who told me it was okay to date Gabe Wynant. So I'm doing it. He's taking me to the dinner dance at the Cloister tomorrow night, and he wants me to spend the night at his place after."

"Oh, he does, does he?"

"He swears he'll be a gentleman," Brooke said.

"They always do," Marie said primly. "Are you on any kind of birth control?"

"That's none of your business," Brooke said. But she wasn't. There hadn't been any need in a long time. As far as she was concerned, the combination of a rambunctious three-year-old and an exhausted single mother was the most effective birth control on the market.

Marie cocked her head and studied her daughter.

"What? What's that look?" Brooke demanded.

"Nothing. Just thinking."

"I hate it when you do that. It's like you're psychoanalyzing me."

"Has it occurred to you that you're at a fork in the road? The father of your child apparently wants to be in your life again. And in the meanwhile, Gabe Wynant has come a-courting. I know I encouraged you to see Gabe, but that was before all this business with Pete."

"Yes, Mom, it has occurred to me. Trust me, I know what I'm doing."

"I certainly hope so. Anyway, you never told me what you and the girls found out on your fact-finding mission yesterday. Do you really think there's a chance C. D. is Josephine's son?" Marie asked.

Brooke shared the results of the previous day's investigation, and Marie listened carefully. "Have you spoken to C. D. yet? If it's true that his father might have been black, that's going to come as a huge shock to someone of his generation."

"I've left him messages, but nobody's seen or talked to him. I'm starting to get a little worried about him, to tell you the truth," Brooke said. "Lizzie was going to try to track him down today. I'll call her on my way home to see what she knows."

"Keep me posted," Marie said. "And be careful driving home. Call me Sunday and fill me in on all the gory details of your night with Gabe."

"A lady never kisses and tells," Brooke said, grinning impishly.

"Except to her mother," Marie said.

55

....

When Shug dropped her off at the dock at Talisa, Felicia and Lizzie were waiting, with Lizzie behind the wheel of the pickup truck. Shug waved goodbye as he backed the boat away from the dock, headed back to the mainland to run errands for Louette.

"I was kind of surprised to hear from you this morning," Lizzie said as the two other women scooted in close to her in the front seat of the truck.

"After you told me yesterday that C. D. seems to be missing in action, it made me a little nervous. I mean, right now, he's Josephine's heir apparent," Brooke said.

"Or at least, he's *our* preferred heir apparent," Felicia said. "Not that we have any say in the matter."

"Did you talk to Varina? Ask her about the possibility that a black man could have fathered Josephine's child?"

Felicia shook her head. "I can't. She's still pretty frail. And she's so protective of Josephine's reputation. Her main concern right now is when Josephine will be buried. She hates the idea of her body locked up in a freezer drawer at the morgue. Have you heard anything?"

"We're waiting on the sheriff to release the body," Brooke said. "I'll ask Gabe when I see him tonight. Maybe, now that he's been named administrator, he can speed things up."

"You're seeing Gabe tonight?" Lizzie asked, nudging Felicia.

"You two are so juvenile," Brooke said.

"I told you so," Felicia said, addressing Lizzie. "I definitely sensed some kind of a spark between those two."

Lizzie wrinkled her nose. "It's none of my business, but . . ."

"It really isn't, so let's change the subject," Brooke said good-naturedly. "Talk to me about C. D. When was the last time anybody actually saw him?"

"Shug rode him over to the mainland last Monday," Felicia said.

"Did C. D. say where he was going? And how does he get around when he's over there? Does he have a car in St. Ann's?"

"According to Shug, C. D. has an old Vega. A real rust bucket he keeps parked at the city marina," Felicia said. "And Louette thinks he might have a girlfriend there too."

"How does he get around on the island? Does he always use Josephine's truck?"

"I've seen him a couple of times on a motor scooter," Lizzie said. "Don't know if it's actually his or if it belonged to Josephine."

"I find it hard to picture Josephine on a motor scooter," Brooke said. "Does anybody know where C. D. was headed when he went to the mainland?"

"He told Shug he was going shopping for a new boat so he'd be ready to buy it when his inheritance from Josephine comes through," Felicia said. "Which gave everybody a good laugh."

The trunk bounced down the long drive to Shellhaven.

"Looks like Shug's been busy," Brooke said. The huge expanse of grass had been mowed. All the fallen palm fronds and tree branches had been picked up, and the flower beds had been weeded.

"Finally getting a paycheck was a real morale booster," Lizzie said. "But Shug can't keep these grounds up all by himself. He's got to have help, from C. D. or somebody."

"Louette says C. D. wasn't that much help with the lawn maintenance anyway," Felicia said. "He mainly wanted to take care of the boat and run errands on the mainland. She says he's forever wandering off and disappearing for a day or two."

"Does she have any guess where he goes?"

"Maybe shacked up with the girlfriend?"

They walked over to the barn, a creaky wooden structure that seemed to lean at a near forty-five-degree angle. It was painted a weathered white, and sunlight shone through cracks in the old boards.

"Shug says the barn roof is in worse shape than the house," Lizzie remarked. "He'd finally talked Josephine into shelling out the money to hire roofers to do it, but then, after she got so sick, the roof sort of got put on the back burner."

"She wanted her husband's cars preserved, Louette says," Felicia added. "I walked over here and looked at them this week. If you're into cars, it's a pretty amazing collection."

Lizzie grasped one of the barn doors, and the rusted hinges squealed a protest. Inside, it was dim and relatively cool and smelled of mildew and mouse droppings. Four shadowy hulks were shrouded in dusty tarps.

She walked over to the car on the end and yanked off the cover to reveal a gleaming vintage roadster.

"This was the last car Gardiner owned, and we know Josephine worshiped him. And this car," Brooke said, running a hand over the hood of the roadster.

Felicia walked slowly around the roadster and peered in the back. "Is this the same car she told us they dumped Russell Strickland's body in when they went to bury him?"

"It must be," Brooke said.

Felicia jumped away from the car, eliciting a belly laugh from Lizzie.

"What's the matter, Felicia? You getting spooked by an old car?"

"Must be 'cause I'm spending all my time with these Geechees," Felicia admitted. "I had no idea how superstitious my people are. Even Auntie Vee. You can't leave a broom in a corner because she says that means somebody's fixing to die. And don't you let her catch you leaving a pocketbook on a bed, either. I've started writing it all down. It's really pretty fascinating."

Brooke carefully returned the dustcover to the roadster. "How far is C. D.'s place from here?"

"Just a little ways away," Lizzie said. "It used to be the chauffeur's house."

The house stood in the shadow of an enormous oak tree. It was a step up from the humble slave cottages they'd seen at Oyster Bluff—wood frame, with a small front porch ornamented with simple Victorian-inspired gingerbread trim. Once, the house had been white, but only traces of the paint remained now. A front door with a small window was flanked on either side with tall windows.

Lizzie stepped onto the porch and boldly jiggled the doorknob.

"Lizzie!" Felicia scolded.

"He could be in there, hurt and unable to call out to anybody," Lizzie said. She stepped to the right and pressed her face against the wavy window glass, which was smeared with ancient layers of grime and cobwebs. "Can't see a thing through all this dirt," she complained.

Brooke peered through the other window but saw only a shadowy interior.

"Let's look around back," Lizzie said, leading them around the east side of the house. A lean-to roof jutted off the back of the house. The wooden floor-boards groaned under her footsteps. A weathered broom, rag mop, and dust-pan hung from nails, and a fishing pole and plastic bait bucket stood beside the door.

Lizzie rattled the door handle. "Locked." She took a step backward and lifted the edge of the doormat. Grinning, she extracted a large brass skeleton key, which she fit into the lock.

"Stop. You can't just break into the man's house," Brooke said.

"Technically, it's not his house. Louette says he doesn't even pay rent. Josephine just let him stay here as part of the job. So technically, it belongs to the estate. Also, he could actually be in here, hurt or passed out or something, so really, this is a welfare check." Undeterred, Lizzie opened the door and stepped inside.

"Nobody home." She popped her head outside the door. "Come on in. Don't be so prissy. If he comes back and catches us, you can say I was the evildoer."

Felicia looked at Brooke and shrugged. "Might as well."

They were standing in a compact galley kitchen. There were exactly four wooden cabinets, their doors warped from humidity. An opened plastic Sunbeam bread bag on the Formica countertop held a moldy heel of bread, swarming with black ants, and a jar of store-brand mustard was open, with a butter knife stuck into it. A greasy plastic ziplocked container held only the red stringy rinds of a half pound of bologna. The small stainless steel sink held a used coffee mug, a teaspoon, and a plate. An ashtray on the counter was full of cigarillo butts.

Lizzie sniffed the air. "Yeah, this is C. D.'s place, all right."

"It looks like wherever he was going, he decided to pack a picnic," Felicia said.

They followed her into the small front room, which looked like it had been furnished with cast-offs from the big house. The sofa, a 1940s relic, had worn maroon tufted upholstery and another overflowing ashtray was perched on the arm. The glass-topped coffee table was part of an old wrought iron patio set. It was littered with file folders and photocopied news clippings.

Lizzie ducked into the adjacent room. "Here's his bedroom. No sign of C. D., though."

"We should get out of here," Brooke said uneasily. "This doesn't feel right."

Felicia perched on the edge of the sofa and began sifting through the papers. "Hey. Looks like he's been reading up on Josephine and the Bettendorfs. Look at all this stuff."

"Let me see." Lizzie sat beside her. She picked up a paper. "He's been spending time in the library, going through the old microfiche issues of the Savannah and Atlanta newspapers, dating all the way back to the mid-1930s. I'm kind of surprised he knew to do that."

"Yeah, he doesn't strike me as the researching type," Felicia agreed. She looked up at Brooke. "He's gotten copies of the old property tax records from the Carter County courthouse too."

"It's a matter of public record," Brooke said. Against her better judgment, she stepped into the bedroom. Like the rest of the house, it was tiny, with worn wooden floorboards. The cracked plaster walls were bare except for a calendar from a marine supply store, the page turned to the current month. The old brass bed was unmade, covered with a cheap white cotton bedspread and a pair of lumpy feather pillows. A nightstand held an ugly, oversized lamp, an empty beer can, and the usual ashtray full of cigarillo butts. A pair of worn jeans hung from the doorknob of a narrow closet.

The drawers of a cheap wooden dresser facing the bed were pulled out.

"I feel like a Peeping Tom," Brooke muttered.

But she looked inside the top drawer, which held balled-up crew socks and a folded stack of worn-looking white cotton briefs that had been pushed aside. An empty leather binocular case lay atop the briefs, and beside them was a half-empty cardboard box of bullets.

She felt queasy. "Hey, y'all," she called.

Lizzie and Felicia approached and stared down at the cardboard box. "Nine-millimeter bullets," Lizzie said. "I guess they're for that holstered pistol he carries."

"So wherever C. D. went, he left in a hurry, and he took binoculars and extra ammo," Felicia said. "And a picnic."

"And he probably lied when he told Shug he was going boat shopping," Lizzie added. "But why? And where was he really going?"

"I think we should leave," Brooke said, slamming the dresser drawer closed. "As soon as I get back to St. Ann's, I'm calling Gabe. Something weird is going on here."

56

Henry reached across the kitchen table and touched Brooke's sparkly diamond-and-pearl-drop earrings. "Pretty!" His face and hands were smeared with spaghetti sauce, but at that moment something in his expression so closely resembled Pete Haynes it took her breath away. She caught her son's chubby hand in hers, kissed it, then pretended to munch on his fingers.

He giggled, then presented his other hand for similar treatment, but the doorbell rang.

"Farrah's here," she told him.

Her heels clicked across the wooden floor, and she caught a glimpse of herself reflected in the living room window. She couldn't even remember the last time she'd gotten really dressed up for a date. But fortunately, the strapless black cocktail dress she'd bought to wear to a long-forgotten party in Savannah still fit, and the earrings her parents had gifted her as a law school graduation gift were timeless.

Brooke opened the door and frowned. Not at Farrah but at her companion, Jaxson, who stood beside her on the doorstep.

"Wow!" Farrah said, following her into the house. "You look amazing." She nudged Jaxson. "Doesn't she look great?"

"Uh, yeah, awesome," Jaxson said. He'd changed since the last time Brooke had seen him. The greasy blond mullet and scraggly Fu Manchu mustache were gone. His head was newly buzzed, and he was clean-shaven. He carried a large cardboard pizza box in both hands and was setting it down on the coffee table.

"New haircut?" she asked as he settled himself on the sofa.

"Yeah," he said, opening the box and shoving a gooey slice of pizza into his mouth.

"Jaxson's going into the army!" Farrah announced. "He leaves Monday for basic training."

"Congratulations, Jaxson. Farrah, why don't you come into the kitchen and say hi to Henry. He's just finishing his supper."

"Fawwah!" Henry called, reaching out his arms to his favorite babysitter.

The teenager lifted him out of his booster chair and swung him up in the air. "Henry McBenry!" She sat him on the kitchen counter, wet a paper towel, and began cleaning him up. "I already know what you're going to say about Jaxson," she said, her voice low. "So save it. We are not getting back together. He's just a good friend, okay?"

"That's fine, but it would have been nice if you'd asked me if he could come with you tonight," Brooke said. "I'm not really comfortable leaving you and Jaxson here alone with Henry while I'm away overnight."

"For God's sake, we're not going to have sex on your sofa or anything," Farrah retorted. "We'll eat some pizza, watch some television, and then he'll go home. Okay? Don't be such a buzzkill. Like my mom."

Brooke glanced at the kitchen clock. "I don't have time to argue with you about this now. I should have left fifteen minutes ago. Jaxson can stay, but I want him out of here by no later than eleven o'clock. Understood?"

"Whatever." Farrah set Henry on the floor and began cleaning up the kitchen table.

"There's breakfast stuff in the fridge," Brooke said. "I think there are some Cokes somewhere around here too. Don't forget to lock the front and back doors before you go to bed, okay? I put clean sheets by the sofa bed. And let's see. Remember to—"

"Quit stalling." Farrah handed Brooke the overnight bag she'd packed earlier in the evening. "Henry and I will be fine. I'll see you tomorrow."

"Call me if anything comes up. Okay? No matter what time. In fact, I want you to check in with me at eleven. The pediatrician's number is on the fridge. I'll text you Gabe's cell number too. And you've got my mom's phone number, right? Just in case?"

"Yes, yes, and yes. And remember," Farrah said, giving her an exaggerated wink, "don't do anything I wouldn't do."

She called Gabe on the drive to Sea Island to tell him she was running late.

"Damn. Well, I guess that means we won't have cocktails at the house before we head over to the Cloister," he said, sounding annoyed. "Dinner starts at seven."

"Sorry. Babysitter complications. I'll fill you in when I get there."

"I've left you a guest pass at the gate. Park at the Cloister and meet me inside."

As soon as she'd driven through the gatehouse at Sea Island, Brooke felt herself slipping into her privileged past. Everything about the grounds and buildings at the resort and second-home community whispered power and money and taste. There was even a row of moss-draped oaks, each of which had been planted by successive presidents, starting with Calvin Coolidge right up to the most recent occupant of the White House. She pulled up to the entrance to the Cloister, and a uniformed doorman stepped out to whisk her car away.

The lobby was crowded with people dressed in elegant evening wear, and when she saw Gabe beaming as he walked rapidly toward her, a martini in one hand and a glass of champagne in the other, she realized that her date might be the most attractive man in the room.

Black tie suited Gabe Wynant. His jacket was custom-tailored to his slender frame, and his silver hair was just long enough to be hip, but short enough to be considered not trying too hard. Her pulse blipped at the sight of him, and she couldn't have said if she was nervous or giddy at the prospect of the evening ahead.

He handed her the champagne and kissed her lightly on the cheek. "You look beautiful," he said before tucking her arm in his. "And I am the luckiest man on this island tonight. Maybe in this state."

They were seated at a round table with three other couples, all of whom were Gabe's old friends or business associates. Despite her misgivings that she'd be seated with a bunch of strangers, theirs was a congenial group: the Johnsons, who'd recently retired and moved from Minneapolis to Sea Island, Dave and Susie (he was a business consultant, she did something in marketing), and Jack and Sharon, both closer in age to Brooke, and from the looks of it, still celebrating their recent marriage, because they held hands every moment they weren't eating or drinking.

The new chef Gabe had touted lived up to his reputation, producing a French-accented five-course dinner that had them all oohing and aahing—and groaning at the thought of the calorie count.

Even the orchestra was a nice surprise—a versatile sextet that played everything from Big Band standards to sixties soul to eighties rock.

"Hope you're not too bored," Gabe said as he led her out to the dance floor. The band was playing a respectable version of "Unchained Melody," and it felt good to be in a man's arms again. He held her closely, his hand resting lightly on the small of her back, and he was easy to follow.

"You smell nice," he said, his lips close to her ear. "I know this perfume. You've worn it for years, right? Even when you were at the law firm?"

"Since high school," Brooke said. "It's Joy. Mom gives me a bottle every year for Christmas. I can't believe you remembered my perfume from when we worked together."

"I notice a lot people don't give me credit for," Gabe said. "What does Marie have to say about your seeing me?"

"She was all for it," Brooke said. "She says age shouldn't matter."

"Smart lady. And your dad?"

"He'd probably call you a dirty old man. He doesn't approve of much that I do anymore, but then, I can't say I approve of all his choices either."

Gabe chuckled and let his hand slide farther down her back. "If I'm gonna get called a dirty old man, I might as well act like one."

"I like your friends," Brooke said. "I was afraid I'd get stuck listening to a bunch of grumpy old men talking about tax reform and prostate surgery tonight."

"Not a chance. They like you too. Especially Byron. Which is good, because he just sold his share of a startup tech company, and he wants to start doing some estate planning. It'll be a nice piece of business. He's got two sets of kids: one set from his first wife, all of whom are in their early thirties, and his kids with Micki, who are eight and six."

"Really?" Brooke looked over his shoulder at the Johnsons, who were dancing together at the far side of the ballroom. "He's got grade-school kids? How old is he?"

"Only a couple of years older than I am. Do you think that's too old to have young kids?"

"I guess I'm just surprised he'd want to start over raising a family."

Gabe looked down at her. "Personally, I wouldn't rule it out. Why not? I'm healthy, I can afford it, and I've always wanted kids."

"But Sunny didn't?"

"No," he said succinctly. He tilted his head. "How about you? Has being a single mom turned you off to having more kids?"

"Not necessarily," Brooke said. "I was an only child of an only child. It can be lonely, you know?"

"I was never an only child. I have two brothers. But I do know about loneliness. People treat you differently when you're not half of a couple. They might bring casseroles and potted plants when you're first widowed, but after that, it's a whole lot of single-serve microwave dinners and Netflix binge-watching."

"You should try being single in a town like St. Ann's," Brooke said.

"Maybe you should move back to Savannah and find a nice guy to settle down with," Gabe said, nuzzling her neck. "Somebody who'd bring you coffee in bed in the morning and rub your feet at night."

"Mmm," she said, sighing and sinking into him. "That does sound tempting. Where do I sign up?"

"Right here," Gabe said.

She looked up at him. He'd had two or three martinis before dinner, and they'd both had a little wine with dinner, but what she'd thought had been casual flirting had suddenly taken an unexpected turn.

He was still holding her hand when they returned to their table. Coffee and after-dinner drinks were being served, and jokes were being told. Gabe scooted his chair next to hers, so close her bare shoulder brushed his dinner jacket. Brooke glanced surreptitiously at his gold wristwatch. It was nearly eleven. She excused herself and headed for the ladies' lounge.

Checking her phone, she saw that she had no missed calls and no text messages. She combed her hair, reapplied lipstick, then sat in one of the lounge chairs and stared at her phone, waiting for the babysitter's call. At five after eleven, she called Farrah's cell. No answer.

"Damn it, Farrah," she muttered.

She went back to the table and waved away Gabe's offer of more champagne. "I was about to send out a search party for you," he said, his voice low. "Everything okay?"

She shook her head. "Farrah promised to check in with me at eleven. I waited a few minutes and then I called, but there's no answer."

"She's eighteen, right? Just graduated from high school?"

"That's right."

"And she's usually very responsible? I mean, she works in your office too, right?"

"Yes, but this is different. When she showed up tonight, she had her boyfriend with her. Or ex-boyfriend. I'm not sure which. I let her know I wasn't happy about the situation, but what could I do? That's why I was late leaving the house."

"She probably forgot and fell asleep," Gabe said.

The band was breaking into another slow song, "When a Man Loves a

Woman." It was one her parents had danced to back during the rosy-hued years when they'd dragged her along to parties at the Cloister. She could remember being deeply embarrassed at the way they'd clung to each other on the dance floor.

"Come on," Gabe said, taking her hand. "The band will be packing it in pretty soon. Let's dance, and then you can try calling the babysitter later."

He held her even closer than before as they danced. "I was dead serious about that offer I made you earlier," Gabe said, taking her hand and kissing the back, and then the palm. "I can tell you're struggling with the solo practice, single parenting, finances, all of it. I've thought a lot about this, Brooke. Come back to Savannah. You can practice law with me again, or not. Let me take care of you and Henry."

She was so taken aback by the proposal, she stumbled briefly, but he helped her regain her footing. "I . . . don't know what to say," she said, feeling herself blush.

Gabe smiled. "I'm rushing you, right? Damn it! My timing is usually better than this. Look, we can talk about this later. Just chalk it up to the music and the wine." He nuzzled her neck again. "And that perfume of yours, which is driving me out of my mind."

The party was breaking up. Goodbyes were said, hugs and contact information exchanged. The moon was three-quarters full as they stood outside, with a salt-scented breeze gently ruffling the palm fronds near the entrance, waiting for the valet to bring their cars around.

"Gorgeous night tonight," Gabe said, his arm around her shoulders. "What do you say we take a walk on the beach when we get back to my place?"

"That sounds nice," Brooke said, trying not to sound distracted. It was after midnight, and she still hadn't heard from Farrah.

The Porsche sped around the corner from the parking deck and stopped abruptly inches from where they stood. The booming thump of head-banging rock music assaulted them when the valet driver hopped out of the car.

Gabe snatched the parking stub from the driver's hand. "Where the hell do you think you are, you dumb fuck? This isn't the Indie 500. That's a $175,000 car you just mishandled."

"Sorry, sir," the driver said. "I'm not used to all that horsepower."

Gabe whipped his cell phone from the inner pocket of his dinner jacket and quickly snapped a photo of the driver, who wore a brass nameplate pinned to his uniform shirt.

"Lopez, right?" Gabe said. "I'll email this to your supervisor in the morning."

Before the kid could reply, another valet pulled up, at a more sedate speed, in Brooke's Volvo.

Gabe held the door while she slid behind the driver's seat, his rage seemingly forgotten. "You remember the way to my house, right? Turn left at the first roundabout, then a quick right and two more lefts."

She waited until she was out of sight of the clubhouse before calling Farrah again. She called two more times, each time waiting until the girl's voice recording played.

Hey, this is Farrah. Leave me a message, and I'll hit you back later.

Brooke pounded the steering wheel in frustration. This wasn't like Farrah. Something had to be wrong. Instead of taking a left at the first roundabout, she made a right. When she'd reached the causeway that would take her back south to St. Ann's, she winced and tapped Gabe's number on her cell phone. He'd be pissed, she knew, but if he was sincere in his concern for her as a mother, he'd have to understand. Henry came first.

He answered on the first ring. "Are you lost? I knew I should have had you follow me home."

"Actually, I'm not coming to your place. I'm so sorry, Gabe, but Farrah hasn't answered any of my calls, and I'm already sick with worry. I'm heading back to St. Ann's. I'm hoping you'll give me a rain check."

There was a deafening silence from the other end of the call. "You're kidding, right?"

"Not at all. This isn't like Farrah. I'm terrified something could have happened. You understand, don't you?"

"Not really." His voice was cold. "You said yourself the girl is very responsible. It seems to me that this is you looking for an excuse to pull another disappearing act."

His words felt like a slap in the face.

"I see. Well, thanks for a lovely evening." She disconnected the phone, her cheeks burning with anger and indignation.

57

....

Brooke kept the Volvo's speedometer at seventy-nine miles per hour on the drive back to St. Ann's. Any faster than that, the car's whole chassis would have vibrated, plus she would have been ticket bait for the cops, who ran a notorious speed trap on that section of highway. She was grateful she'd limited her alcohol intake to two drinks over the course of the long evening. And she didn't really slow down until she reached the turnoff for St. Ann's.

Jaxson's black Ford F-150 truck was still parked at the curb in front of her house. She could see the lights in the kitchen window, but the front of the house was dark. She'd been rehearsing the lecture she'd give Farrah when she got home—assuming she still had a home when she got there—but seeing the boy's vehicle further fueled her anger.

She opened the front door, which she noted was unlocked, and stepped inside. The television was on, and two bodies were slumped sideways on the sofa. Brooke gasped. And then she saw the coffee table. The pizza box was still there, along with an empty liter bottle of Coke and a mostly empty liquor bottle.

Brooke stomped over to the sofa and picked up the bottle. Captain Morgan rum. An inch of brown liquid sloshed in the bottom, and from the looks of it, the rest had been consumed by Farrah and Jaxson. His head lolled against the back of the sofa cushions, mouth open, snoring. Farrah's head rested on his chest, and a thin trickle of drool dampened his T-shirt. She slammed the bottle back down onto the table, but neither of them stirred. They were both alive, but dead drunk.

Henry was asleep in his bed, tucked between his green stuffed Ninja Turtle and a large Clifford the Big Red Dog stuffed animal. She bent down and kissed his cheek, then went to her own room, where she quickly stripped out of her party dress and diamond-and-pearl earrings and into a pair of lightweight summer pajamas.

She took a cotton bedspread from the closet and draped it loosely over the sleeping couple. It was nearly two o'clock. In the morning, she promised herself, she would raise hell with those two. But for now, she needed to sleep more than she needed to vent.

Bleeeeechhhhh. Bleeechhhhh. Brooke sat up in bed, momentarily confused. Where was she? It was still dark outside—6:15 A.M. according to the digital clock on her nightstand. The horrific noise was coming from the hall bathroom. She got out of bed to investigate.

Farrah was hunched over the commode, her head nearly invisible.

"Hey." Brooke sat down on the edge of the bathtub.

The girl raised her head and gazed at Brooke from bloodshot eyes. She looked like hell.

"Hey," she said weakly.

"You look like hell," Brooke said. "I'd say Captain Morgan is no friend of yours."

Farrah retched for another five minutes. Brooke found an elastic band and fastened the girl's hair. She ran cold water over a washcloth and placed it on the back of her neck.

Brooke tiptoed out to the living room in time to see the black pickup zoom away from the curb. Picking up the pizza crusts, Solo cups, and rum bottle, she noted with grim satisfaction that Jaxson had been in such a rush to depart that he'd left behind a pair of nearly new, expensive-looking basketball shoes. She picked them up and deposited everything in the trash.

Back in the bathroom, she found Farrah sprawled, facedown, on the tile floor. "Your super-classy boyfriend had to leave," she said.

"Uuuuggghhhh. He is *so* not my boyfriend." Farrah managed to pull herself up to a sitting position. "And I want to die."

"Okay," Brooke said pleasantly. She turned on the shower. "But we need to clean up your corpse before we bury you. A hot shower is your first step to salvation."

By the time Farrah stumbled into the kitchen, Henry had finished his frozen waffle and was happily knocking back a sippy cup of milk. She sank down onto a chair and gratefully accepted the mug of coffee Brooke offered.

"Fawwah!" Henry yelled. He held out his cup. "You want some milk?"

The girl's face turned a new shade of green. "You drink it, Henry."

"How're you feeling?" Brooke asked. "Any better?"

"Not really. I mean, I stopped barfing, so I guess that's something." The girl looked balefully at her employer. "I'm really, really, really sorry I let you down, Brooke."

"Yeah. Me too. I expected better of you."

Farrah hung her head. "I know. I was so stupid. I should never have let Jaxson come over here with me last night. You were right. He's nothing but bad news."

"Whose idea was the rum?"

"His. But I went along with it, you know? He didn't pour it down my throat or anything."

Brooke took a sip of her own coffee. "Was Henry awake when you started drinking?"

"No! He was asleep. I swear. But I wouldn't blame you if you wanted to fire me."

"I don't *want* to fire you. My son adores you. I adore you, or I did until I drove back here like a maniac last night after you didn't call, only to find you and Jaxson passed out on my sofa."

"I really fucked up your big night, didn't I?" Farrah pressed her fingers to her temples. "I bet Gabe is really mad."

Brooke mentally replayed Gabe's cutting remark about her pulling "another disappearing act." It hurt as much now as it had when he'd said it last night.

"He wasn't thrilled. He had big plans for the rest of the evening, and then I pulled the plug. I think it's safe to say our fine little romance is kaput."

"Oh God. I'm such a screwup."

"Just as well it happened now. Gabe never had kids, so he doesn't understand where my priorities are. And if he can't understand that, there's really no future for the two of us."

Brooke went to the pantry and got a packet of crackers. She placed them on the table in front of Farrah. "Eat those."

"Food? No. Gross."

"They'll help settle your stomach. I'll get you some ginger ale too. Then, if you keep that down, you can take some aspirin for that headache I'm sure you have."

Farrah took fifteen minutes to nibble half of one cracker, washed down with four sips of ginger ale. Brooke handed her two aspirin, which she swallowed. She held her head in both hands, a pathetic, miserable sight.

"Are you going to tell my mom?" Farrah asked.

"What would she do if I did tell her?"

"Probably ground me for the rest of the summer. Maybe take away my car. For sure she wouldn't let me see Jaxson again."

"If she grounds you and takes away your car, that hurts me as much as it hurts you. If I hadn't been so tired last night, I would have throttled you both with my bare hands."

"I deserve it. And so does he."

"True. But I need an assistant at the office, and Henry needs a babysitter who loves him so very much, so I'm going to give you a second chance, and I'm not going to tell your mom. This time."

Farrah let out a long sigh of relief. "Thanks. I'll make it up to you. I swear. And hey, no charge for last night."

"Oh, don't worry," Brooke said. "I wasn't going to pay you anyway. Go on home and get some sleep now, okay? And if Jaxson calls, you can tell him I threw his shoes in the trash."

Brooke puttered around the house most of the morning, doing multiple loads of laundry, cleaning and disinfecting the bathroom, dumping the clothes Farrah had left on the floor into a grocery bag, and helping Henry put together one of his puzzles. He'd begged to go to the park, but by mid-morning it was broiling out, the temperature already hovering around ninety with sauna-level humidity, so she'd compromised by letting him watch an hour of cartoons on her laptop. Did that make her a terrible mother? Maybe, but she didn't care.

At eleven, she put her son down for a nap and decided to color her hair. Like Marie's, Brooke's hair had begun going gray when she was in her midtwenties. In the past, Genevieve, the stylist at her trendy Savannah salon, had colored her hair, but these days, rather than spend $175 a pop every six weeks, she colored her own hair with the stuff that came in a box from the drugstore.

It took thirty minutes to apply the grape gravy–colored goop to her wet hair. She was still barefoot in a ratty terry cloth bathrobe when the doorbell rang. *Probably Farrah returning to reclaim her clothes,* she thought as she went to open the door.

Gabe Wynant stood on the doorstep with a huge bouquet of pink peonies in one hand and a large Harris Teeter paper sack in the other. "Hi," he said, eyeing her uneasily. "Um, maybe I should have called first?"

Brooke's hands flew to her hair. "Oh, shit." She must have looked like something from a bad seventies sitcom.

"I just wanted to apologize for last night," he said, thrusting the flowers at her. "I was a jerk and an unforgiveable ass."

"You really were," Brooke agreed, sniffing the flowers.

He held the paper sack in both hands now, looking like a penitent first grader. "I brought you a peace offering. Coffee, fresh-squeezed orange juice, croissants..."

"Come on in, then," Brooke said, opening the door wider. She gestured toward the small, shabby living room, grateful that she'd picked up all the toys and preschooler detritus that usually littered the room. "Sit there and pour yourself some coffee. I have to deal with this." She pointed toward her head.

Thirty minutes later, she emerged from her bedroom dressed in shorts and a T-shirt, her hair freshly blown dry and styled. She'd even applied a little lipstick.

"Hi," Gabe said, standing when she walked into the living room. He'd found a vase for the peonies and arranged a buffet on the coffee table; a bowl of rasp-berries, blueberries, and strawberries, a carafe of orange juice, a plate of crois-sants, plates, napkins, silverware, even a miniature jar of marmalade, and two steaming mugs of coffee.

Brooke nodded and sat down on the sofa. "I'm sort of amazed you didn't head for the hills just now, after you saw me in my natural habitat."

"It takes a lot more than that to scare me off," Gabe said, smiling. "And I'm the one who's amazed—that you didn't tell me to take a hike when I showed up here uninvited."

She fixed herself a plate of fruit and buttered a croissant. "The least I can do is listen to your apology. Anyway, I didn't have any breakfast this morning."

Gabe looked around the room. "I see the house is still standing. So, I guess everything was okay when you got home last night?"

"Farrah and her boyfriend were drunk, passed out on the sofa," Brooke said, biting into the croissant.

"Christ! Where was your kid? Was he all right?"

"Henry was sound asleep in his bed," Brooke said, taking another bite of the croissant, ignoring the shards of pastry showering onto her shirt. "Crisis averted, narrowly."

"I hope you fired the girl," he said.

"Nope. Farrah's a good kid. She made a really dumb decision. I'm giving her a second chance."

He gave her a winning smile. "So . . . how about me? Do I get a second chance? I don't know what came over me last night. I could blame the martinis. I should have stopped after two."

"You really should have," Brooke said. "Nobody likes a mean drunk. And that's what you were last night, Gabe. You were mean. First when you went off on that poor valet kid, threatening to get him fired, and then to me. You were mean and rude."

"I know." He shook his head. "So no excuses. I want you to know I went back over to the Cloister this morning. I left the kid a note of apology and a big tip."

She sipped her coffee and waited for what would come next. Did she even want to hear it?

He ran his fingers through his hair, which was uncharacteristically messy. Come to think of it, Gabe was uncharacteristically messy this morning. Gray stubble, dark bags under his eyes, and he wore beltless khaki slacks that needed ironing, a faded gray T-shirt, and scuffed up Topsiders.

"Look," he said, his dark eyes pleading. "I'm not a kid anymore. I haven't courted a woman in . . . well, a long time, and I'm not sure I was good at it back in my twenties. I'm in foreign waters here, you know?"

He took Brooke's hand and pressed it between his. "I wish you could forget the ugly turn the evening took last night. Because I want to. I'll never forget how it felt, holding you in my arms, watching every other man in the room watching you and envying me, because I was the lucky guy you were with."

He brushed a tendril of hair behind her ear. "I had so many plans for us last night. A walk on the beach, a kiss in the moonlight. And when you called to say you were leaving, I guess I lost it. I lashed out, and the moment those words were out of my mouth, I hated myself." Gabe leaned forward and kissed her lightly. "Can you forgive me?"

"Honestly? I don't think this is about forgiveness," Brooke said, drawing away. "It's about understanding. What you said last night—about me pulling a disappearing act? It showed you don't really know me, even after all this time. I left Harris Strayhorn because, ultimately, I wasn't ready to be married. I've admitted that was wrong. I don't regret canceling the wedding, but I do regret the careless way I did that and how deeply I hurt both our families. But I've changed. I have a child now, and he has to be my first priority. If you can't understand that, there's no future for us."

Gabe nodded solemnly. "I get it. Really, I do. That's part of what attracts me to you. Your fierceness. And your intelligence. Can we start over? Can I have that second chance?"

"Mama? Where Fawwah go?"

They both turned. Henry stood in the doorway, naked from the waist down, clutching his stuffed Ninja Turtle. "I pooped," he said solemnly.

"This is my life now, Gabe," Brooke said. "Are you really sure this is what you want?"

58

Brooke walked Gabe out to his car, blinking in the white-hot sunlight. "Any news on probating Josephine's estate?"

"I've filed all the paperwork, and I'm still tracking down all the assets," he said. "It's still amazing to me that she allowed the house to deteriorate to the extent it has, even though she had millions in cash and stocks."

"I think she wanted time to stand still after Preiss died. She only allowed Shug to do the barest minimum maintenance."

"Crazy old bat," he said, shaking his head. He turned the key in the ignition. "So . . . are we good? Can I call you again? I need to head back to Savannah this afternoon, but maybe I could take you to dinner when I'm down here next time on estate business?"

"Let's take it a day at a time," Brooke said. "Lizzie and Felicia and I are worried about C. D. Nobody's seen or heard from him in several days."

"He called me just this morning, demanding to know when he can get his inheritance," Gabe said.

"Did he say where he was calling from? I meant to tell you, we checked his cottage at Shellhaven, and it looks like he hasn't been there in a while. It looked like he'd left in a hurry."

"You broke into the guy's house? Bad idea. C. D. is certifiable. He's paranoid, and he's got a gun. There's no telling what he'd do if he caught you prowling around his house."

"We didn't actually break in. Lizzie found the key. And we weren't prowling. We were conducting a welfare check. Anything could have happened to him."

"And did you find anything interesting?"

"No. Just copies of some old newspaper clippings and things of that nature."

Gabe frowned. "C. D. has a record, Brooke. Mostly petty stuff—public drunkenness, disorderly conduct, and a misdemeanor assault. My point is, until we have the results of that DNA test back, I'm not assuming he actually is Josephine's heir."

"But what about the stuff we found out in Savannah? The photos of Josephine with him at the orphanage? The truck she gave him? He still has it, you know. And if he wasn't her child, why was she so benevolent toward the orphanage and the boy's home?"

"The Bettendorfs believed in philanthropy. Josephine's father built hospital wings, paid for local ball fields and libraries. He endowed university chairs, underwrote all kinds of things. Going through her tax records, I can see that up until her husband died, she gave away hundreds of thousands of dollars every year. That truck could be meaningless in the larger scheme of things."

"Or it could be proof that Josephine felt deeply guilty about abandoning her child," Brooke said stubbornly.

"We'll see," Gabe said. "So Lizzie is still living at Shellhaven?"

"Is there a problem with that?"

"Those cousins don't like the idea of anybody who isn't family living there," Gabe said. "They've called me twice to complain that she's trespassing. I thought Lizzie understood that. Magazine article or no, she has no business digging through Josephine's effects. I hate to be the bad guy here, but she really can't stay there any longer."

"But that's so silly," Brooke protested. "She's not hurting anything."

"Lizzie has no standing in this estate," he said firmly. "Please let her know she needs to go. Or I will."

59

On Monday, Brooke attended a child custody hearing, took a deposition on behalf of a client who'd shattered an ankle after slipping on a newly waxed floor at a fast-food joint near the interstate, and on Tuesday, after a day's worth of negotiating, managed to get all the charges against Brittni Miles dropped. Her feeling of triumph was short-lived.

Farrah called shortly after nine. Brooke could tell from her voice that there was an issue.

"What's up?" she asked.

"Don't hate me, but I need to miss work tomorrow," Farrah said. "My granny's back in the hospital in Jacksonville, and Mom says I need to go with her to visit."

"I'm sorry." Farrah's grandmother's declining health was a source of continued concern for the tight-knit Miles family. "You'll be back to work on Thursday, right?"

"Absolutely."

"Good, because I need to take a run over to Talisa, and I'm going to need you for Henry in the afternoon."

"I'll be there."

. . .

Henry squealed with happiness as soon as she pulled into the parking lot at the library. He loved Wednesday morning story hour.

"Hey, stranger!" Janice, the head librarian, a chunky brunette with a fondness for gaudy jewelry and big hair, approached and gave Brooke a hug. "We haven't seen you in a while. Where's Farrah this morning?"

"Family issues," Brooke said. She watched as Henry ran off toward the cozy book-lined children's room, eagerly taking his place among the chattering semicircle of preschoolers seated around Miss Myra, their beloved octogenarian storyteller.

"Life treating you all right?" Janice asked as Brooke plucked the Atlanta newspaper from the periodical rack.

"I'm good," Brooke said. Seeing the newspaper reminded her of something that had been bothering her. "Janice, have you had an older guy in here a lot lately?"

"Tons," Janice said. "The retirees come in to research their stock picks and read their hometown newspapers online, the unemployed want help writing résumés, and the homeless ones like the air-conditioning and use our bathrooms. Which old guy are you looking for?"

"He's short and wiry, has a gray ponytail, always wears a baseball cap?"

"And smokes those stinky cigarillos? Don't tell me he's a friend of yours."

"No. He's an, um, acquaintance."

"He's a pain in the butt is what he is. He's been researching back issues of the Savannah and Atlanta newspapers, doing all kinds of online searches. He seems to think I'm his personal computer instructor."

"Any idea what he's looking for?" Brooke asked.

"He's very interested in local history. Especially the Bettendorf family. Do you know about them? They owned Talisa Island, and the last remaining member of the family died recently."

"I know them," Brooke said.

"I showed him how to search the local genealogical society databases here and in the next county over. And then we had to order him some books through interlibrary loan. One was an old out-of-print book about Josephine Bettendorf Warrick that she apparently commissioned back in the 1970s. He was incensed that we charged him three dollars for ordering those materials and having them shipped here. Gave me the whole line about being a Vietnam vet and how his tax dollars paid our salaries."

"What kind of books?"

Janice lowered her voice. "I don't mind telling you, because you're a long-time patron, but that man, Mr. Anthony, was obsessed with privacy. To the point of being paranoid. He wanted to make sure we weren't keeping any records of what he was looking at."

"Which was?"

"Hmm. Well, he looked at the county property tax records. I know, because I helped him with that. He printed out some records concerning Talisa. And then he also researched legal records from Glynn and Chatham counties."

"Did he say why he was interested in those counties?"

"I tried not to get too close to him, to tell you the truth," Janice said. "His personal hygiene isn't the best, if you know what I mean. But I think I printed out some tax records for him. And he was looking at civil and criminal dockets for those counties too. I remember because he raised holy you-know-what because we charge ten cents apiece for printouts!"

"Weird," Brooke said.

Janice looked around to make sure she couldn't be overheard. "Pretty sure he was also trying to look for online pornography sites too. We have blocks to keep people from doing that, but a couple of times, when he left before signing off the computer, I saw the record of his Google searches. Yeesh!"

"Anything else you can think of?"

"He was very interested in wills and trusts and that sort of thing. Funny, because he didn't strike me as the kind of person who would stand to inherit anything from anybody."

"Fascinating," Brooke said. "Has he been in here lately? Like in the past week or so?"

"I didn't see him myself, because I was at lunch, but Myra mentioned that he was here last week. She finally had to ask him to quit standing outside the doors smoking those cigars of his, because the other patrons were complaining. Excuse me," Janice said, hurrying off to quiet a table of giggling teenage girls.

60

....

"Brooke?" Lizzie's voice was crackling with excitement when she called early Thursday morning. "I found something. You need to get over here right away and take a look."

"I was planning on coming this morning. Are you at Shellhaven now?"

"Yeah, I'm here."

"Can you ask Shug to come pick me up? I can be at the marina by nine o'clock."

"He just pulled up with Louette," Lizzie said. "I'll ask him now."

Lizzie met Brooke at the Shellhaven dock, and it struck Brooke that although she'd been on the island only a short time, the change since she'd arrived from California was remarkable. She wore shorts, a white tank top, beat-up sneakers with no shoelaces, and a baseball cap. She held Dweezil in the crook of her elbow.

"My chariot awaits," she announced grandly, pointing at a battered blue VW station wagon.

"Where'd you get the car?" Brooke asked, jumping into the front seat.

Lizzie handed over the cat. "Shug knew a guy who knew a guy. So for the price of a battery and new tires, I am now the proud new owner. I had it barged over Monday."

Brooke looked down at Dweezil, who was butting her hand with her head.

"She would like you to scratch her ears," Lizzie said. "And neck and chin. In that order."

Brooke did as instructed, and the cat purred her approval. As she scratched the cat, she brooded once again about how to tell Lizzie that she was about to be evicted.

"Oh, hey, that's Lionel." Lizzie slowed the car as they approached a young Geechee child. He was barefoot, with a fishing pole propped against one shoulder, lugging a bucketful of fish.

"Lionel, what's happenin'?" Lizzie called, pulling up alongside him.

"Hey, Miss Lizzie. You give me ride?"

"Sure thing. Hop in the back."

He wrenched the back door open and slid the bucket across the seat. The smell of fish filled the car. In an instant, Dweezil leaped onto the backseat and began pawing at the bucket.

Lizzie turned to look at the boy. "Did you catch all those fish?"

"I cotched some, but Dobie, he give me some he had extra."

Lizzie frowned. "Those fish look pretty small, Lionel. They're not really keepers."

"Oh yeah, they keepers. My mama gonna keep 'em and fry 'em for supper tonight."

"Next time, Lionel, they need to be fourteen inches long. Otherwise, you need to throw them back while they're still alive, so they get big enough to make some more fish babies. If the ranger man comes around and finds you with those little fish, you could get into trouble."

Lionel shook his head vigorously, sending his dreadlocks flying. "The ranger man already come 'round today. Dobie, he see him coming, so he give me these fish and tell me go home."

Lizzie rolled her eyes. "Dobie knows better than to keep undersized fish, Lionel," she said. "It's probably better if you don't take any more fish from him."

"But he's my friend," Lionel protested. "He give me money to go to the store to get his smokes and let me keep the change and get me some candy and Cokes."

Lizzie pulled the car to a stop in front of the Oyster Bluff sign. "Okay, pal, this is as far as we go today."

She watched the child trudge away. "Dobie is sort of the town drunk of Oyster Bluff. He ignores all the local game and fish regulations. According to Shug, the Department of Natural Resources ranger regularly issues him tickets, but he tears 'em up and ignores the fines."

"Seems like you've settled in and gotten to know the locals," Brooke said.

"They have a covered-dish supper Sunday nights at the Oyster Bluff community house. Louette invited me." She patted her belly with a rueful grin. "The food is unbelievable. Baked redfish, shrimp pilau, deviled crab. The island's not such a bad place once you get used to the humidity and the gawd-awful bugs," Lizzie said. She slapped at an invisible bug on her forearm and grimaced. "I'll never get used to the damn no-see-um gnats." She glanced over at Brooke, noting her glum expression. "What's wrong? You're not looking too cheery today. How did your date with sugar daddy Gabe go?"

"It started out great, but then I had to cut the night short because of a crisis at home," Brooke said. "The thing is, Gabe wants you out of Shellhaven. Like, right away."

"What's the big hurry?"

"I'm sorry," Brooke said. "I hate to be the bearer of bad news, but the odious Dorcas and Delphine have apparently been kicking up a fuss. They say you're trespassing, and Gabe agrees that you really don't have a right to be going through Josephine's papers."

Lizzie's answering smile was enigmatic. "Just wait until you see what I uncovered in those papers. You can tell Dorcas and Delphine to take a flying leap."

. . .

"Step into my office," Lizzie said as they entered the library.

Brooke set Dweezil on the floor, and the cat immediately leaped onto the windowsill.

Lizzie pointed at a battered green footlocker. "I found this shoved way at the back of the closet in here. The lid was covered in an inch-thick layer of dust and spider eggs. Louette said she's never seen it before, and I'm pretty sure it hadn't been opened in decades."

S. G. Bettendorf—RCAF was stenciled on the side of the trunk, and the lid was unlocked.

Lizzie plopped down on the floor, and Brooke sat down beside her. "This was Gardiner's air force footlocker. I found a letter from the RCAF inside, indicating that it was shipped back here to Shellhaven after he was killed in 1942."

Brooke peered inside the trunk, not knowing what to expect, but it was empty except for a lingering, dank odor.

"I had to throw most of the stuff away," Lizzie said apologetically. "The clothes were moldy and full of silverfish." She turned and retrieved a thin packet of papers.

"Fortunately, these were wrapped in some kind of oilcloth, so they were pretty well preserved." She handed over a gray cardboard folder.

Inside was a hand-colored studio photograph of a young woman. Her blond shoulder-length hair was parted on the side and swept back from her face. She wore a blue sweater and a sweet smile.

Brooke stared down at the photo, transfixed. "It's Millie, right?" She turned the photo over.

In girlish looping script, the sender had written, *To Gardiner: All my love, Millie.*

"She looks so young," Brooke murmured. "But I don't understand what Gardiner was doing with this."

Lizzie handed over the packet of papers, and a yellowed newspaper page fluttered to the floor. It was from the front page of *The Florida Times-Union*, dated October 10, 1941. BOSTON INDUSTRIALIST STILL MISSING; FOUL PLAY FEARED.

"Read the letters and you'll understand." Lizzie said.

Oct. 29, 1941
Hingham, Mass.

Dear Gardiner:

Thank you for your kind letter of condolence concerning Russell. I'm so torn and confused right now, your letter was a great comfort. Perhaps you're right, and he and I were never meant to be. His poor grandparents are distraught, of course, but your dear father has been wonderful dealing with everything, and I will be forever grateful to him.

Please tell me all about your training. Is it exciting? Fascinating? Terrifying? Things are very quiet here at home with Mother and Grandmama. We never speak of what happened on Talisa, but I believe they feel I'm somehow to blame for Russell, and I fear I will never be able to move past this awful doubt. Maybe I will become an old maid and crochet doilies and shout at small children who ride their bicycles past our house. We read the newspapers every day and listen to the radio for war news, and I can't help but be frightened for you. Please let me hear from you soon.

Your good old friend,
M

Nov. 10, 1941
Hingham, Mass.

Dear Gardiner:

I believe our last letters must have crossed in the mail. I think of you often too and pray constantly for your well-being and safe return home. Of course I would love to see you when you are back in the States on leave at the end of the month, but are you certain you wouldn't rather spend your precious time with your family? I know Jo would be so disappointed not to see you. We had lunch together last week, and she spoke of you constantly. We had a fine time gossiping. Did you know she is doing volunteer work with the Red Cross? And Ruth has a new beau. He is from Chicago and very dashing. Not nearly as dashing as you, though, in your splendid RCAF uniform, so I do thank you for the photo, which I have hidden in my Bible,

because Mother has become such a terrible snoop. She quizzes me con-
stantly about who I am seeing and speaking to on the telephone. She has no
idea of our friendship, because I am the one who brings in the mail every
day, and I keep an eagle eye out for letters from my favorite airman.
Speaking of the mail, must stop now before the postman arrives.

Fondly,

M

Brooke sighed. "Wouldn't you just love to read the letters Gardiner wrote to Millie?"

"I would. And I looked for his letters but didn't find any," Lizzie reported. "They weren't in the trunk, which makes sense."

WESTERN UNION: DEAREST G: CONFIRM I WILL BE ON TRAIN FROM BOSTON, ARRIVING GRAND CENTRAL STATION AT 12:10 P.M. NOV. 27. UNTIL THEN, M.

Nov. 30, 1941
Hingham, Mass.

Darling Gardiner:

I know it's terribly selfish of me, but I was so very glad to have had
you all to myself last weekend in New York. I never dared to dream in all
the years we have known each other, since I was a funny-looking little kid
pestering you for a ride in your car, that you would feel the same way
about me as I do about you. My darling, I cannot believe that we wasted
so much time pretending otherwise. But now that we are older and wiser,
I don't intend to let a moment go by without telling you that I love you,
have always, will always. The trip home was fine, but the train was
awfully crowded and overheated. You asked me what I told my mother
about my trip, and I am ashamed to report that I told her I was meeting
Ruth in the city for some shopping. I did take Ruth into my confidence
about our feelings for one another. First, because I simply had to share
my happiness with someone, and second, in case Mother checks up, Ruth
will cover for me. Unfortunately, I don't think it's wise to let Josephine

know just yet about our relationship. I love Jo so, but you of all people know how prickly she can be and how jealous and protective she is of her beloved big brother. Gardiner. There are so many things I regret in my life—Russell and so on—but the hours I spent in your arms last weekend are something I will never forget or regret.

Your most loving M

Dec. 11, 1941
Hingham, Mass.

Darling G:

Well, it's war. We all listened to President Roosevelt on the radio this week, and afterward, I hid in my bedroom with a pillow over my head while I had a good long cry. I try not to worry about you, but since your training has ended and you'll be flying missions soon, that is impossible. So whenever I feel a black mood coming on, I pick up my knitting needles. Yes, your girl is knitting, and the results are ghastly. Which you will see for yourself—as soon as Grandmama manages to teach me how to cast off. The war is all we talk about and think about now. Ruth's beau has signed up and shipped off to Camp Pendleton in California. Maybe now that the United States has joined the fight, we will be that much closer to beating the Germans and the Japs. All I know is that I live for the day when we will be together next. Is there any chance for New York again? Maybe at Christmas? You did mention that you might get leave again before you receive your orders, so I live in hope and am already making up a fine whopper of a tale to tell Mother. In the meantime, I am enclosing something to keep you warm in my stead.

Your loving, lousy knitter,
M

Brooke looked up, and Lizzie thrust a bulky woolen bundle at her. "Here.

It was a gray woolen scarf, knobby, full of dropped stitches, knots, and holes, but Brooke held it to her nose and inhaled. The scarf had retained the scents of cigarette smoke and camphor.

"Millie knitted this," Brooke said wonderingly, stroking the coarse woolen fabric. "Over seventy years ago." She sighed and looked down at the diminishing stack of letters in her lap. "This is so amazing and unexpected. But I feel like such a voyeur, reading my grandmother's love letters."

"I know," Lizzie said, nodding sympathetically. "Keep going anyway."

Jan. 8, 1942
Hingham, Mass.

Darling G:

Christmas came and went without you, and I was in a terrible, foul black mood. Please forgive my selfishness. You warned me that it was unlikely you could get away again, so this is all my fault. Can you forgive me for not writing sooner and sending you buckets of love and cheer? I did receive your sweet gifts. We all loved the maple syrup, which was such a treat with all the sugar rationing now. And the cashmere sweater was much too extravagant, and a totally improper gift from a gentleman to a spinster such as myself, which made me love it—and you—that much more. We actually spent Christmas Day with Jo and your papa at the house in Boston. There was a ham sent up from Talisa and oysters and as much jollity as we could muster under the circumstances. I believe Mr. Samuel has finally come around to agree with your views on the war, and at any rate, he and Jo are so terribly proud of their royal airman. I know you can't tell me much about your orders or where you're being sent, but I pray every moment that God will keep and protect you until we are together again.

Your loving, bratty M

Brooke's eyes filled with tears as she tucked the letter back into its envelope. "I want my mom to read these letters. This is a side of Millie I don't think either of us ever saw. I know I didn't. Even despite the war, she seems so young and alive and joyful and frank and funny in these." She found a tissue and dabbed at her eyes. "This is so unbelievably poignant, knowing Gardiner actually didn't make it back to Millie." She sniffed.

"From the documents I found with the footlocker, Gardiner's Spitfire was shot down by the Luftwaffe while he was on a bombing raid in northern France at the end of January '42," Lizzie said. "He'd just strafed a railway station in Boulogne and was headed back to base when his plane was hit."

Lizzie passed a hand over her own glittering eyes. "I researched it, you know? Online? These kind of RAF missions were called 'Rhubarb Raids.' They were basically just a nuisance to distract the Germans and keep them from concentrating on fighting on the western border. I think Gardiner and the men in his squadron were considered collateral damage."

"Fuckers," Brooke whispered.

"There's one more letter from Millie," Lizzie said hesitantly, holding it in her outstretched hand. "And it's what Grandma Ruth would have called a doozy."

61

....

Darling Gardiner:

It's nearly midnight here at home. We've had so much snow this month, the drifts have nearly covered the dining room windows. Grandmama has had the flu, and now Mother has a fever too, but the weather has been so terrible the doctor can't get here to check on them. Right now, I am tucked into bed under my quilt. I have all your beautiful letters saved in the now empty chocolate box you gave me in New York. Nights like this, when I am lonely and afraid, I read and reread them, and your sweet words of love give me strength. I'm praying that I'll receive one of your letters any day now. It's been a month, and I miss you so terribly, my darling. I follow the war news and believe your squadron must be in England by now, though I know the censors won't allow you to say more. The thing is, darling, I have some news of my own that I'm afraid can't wait. I'm pregnant! By my calculations, the baby is due in August. I finally saw a doctor in the city this week, and he confirmed my suspicions.

I am so terribly sorry to bring you this news now, but I really don't know what else to do. We talked about marriage in New York, and I know I was the one who was afraid of creating a scandal by marrying so soon after Russell, but now I realize just how foolish I was. Oh, if only we had married in November, and I could call you my husband and announce this news to the world and hold my head high.

Of course, I dare not tell Mother. Do you know, she still seems to be mourning Russell? So far, I think my secret is safe. I've barely gained any weight, and aside from a little bit of morning queasiness, I feel fine. I did confide again in Ruth, and she has been my rock. She suggests that if you can somehow get emergency leave to come home, we could have a quick wedding. Eyebrows might be raised, and tongues would be wagged, and months would be counted, but that is the least of my concerns right now. But we both agree Jo cannot hear about the baby until after we are married and you have made a "respectable woman" of me. You know your sister can be terribly old-fashioned.

Write to me soon, darling Gardiner, and tell me what to do. I love and miss you with all my heart, but the thought that I will soon hold our own sweet baby in my arms has me giddy with excitement. And terror. Do you know, I've never held a newborn or changed a diaper?

Your expectant M

Brooke read the letter a second time and again a third time. She heard the loud ticking of the grandfather clock in the corner and the whir of the box fan in the window, and she felt the slow slide of sweat trickling down her back. Finally, she looked up at Lizzie, who was watching her with open curiosity.

"My God," Brooke said finally. "Millie was pregnant with my mother. And Gardiner was my mom's father. Not Pops. Gardiner."

"That's what it looks like to me," Lizzie said. "Gardiner Bettendorf was your grandfather. Which means that Josephine was your great-aunt."

Brooke's hand trembled as she handed the letter back to Lizzie. "I've got to talk to my mother."

"Agreed," Lizzie said. "And then you'd better call Gabe too."

"Gabe?"

"Uh, duh. If Gardiner was Marie's father and your grandfather, unless I'm sadly mistaken, that makes the two of you Josephine's closest family. Her heirs."

Brooke let that sink in for a moment, especially in light of what they'd learned during their visit to the children's home in Savannah.

"Don't count out C. D. yet," Brooke cautioned. "If he really is Josephine's long-lost son, he'll be calling all the shots around here."

"And he'd be your mom's cousin."

"Eeeewww," they said in unison.

Brooke flopped backward onto the carpet and stared up at the ceiling, whose plaster was water-stained and flaking. "This whole thing is too weird to be true."

"I know. It's gonna make a great story. And just think! You'll have every right to tell Dorcas and Delphine to kiss your grits."

"Kiss my grits?" Brooke said. "Now I know you really have gone native."

62

....

Brooke and her mother sat in the small room her parents had added to the back of the 1920s-era Ardsley Park home. Marie had transformed the former den into a cozy sunroom, painting the dark pine paneling, ripping down the drapes, and installing a pair of flowered chintz love seats, wicker armchairs, and huge baskets of ferns and pots of pink geraniums.

"I fixed us an early supper," Marie said. There was a large club salad with wedges of juicy red tomatoes, hard-boiled eggs, sliced, poached chicken breasts, and bacon bits. She served Brooke a plate and handed her a linen napkin rolled around the flatware.

Marie had never flagged in keeping up the standards Millie had instilled in her. Bone china, linen napkins, and always the good silver. The only time Brooke could ever remember eating off paper plates was when the family went on beach picnics.

"Okay," Marie said. "You've got me on pins and needles. What's so important that you had to drop everything and drive up here today? Is it something about Josephine? Have the DNA results come back on C. D.?"

Brooke sipped her iced tea. "Yes, it's definitely about Josephine. But this isn't about C. D., Mom. It's about you. And Millie. And Gardiner."

"Oh yes," Marie said. "The pilot. He was killed in the war, right?"

"That's right." Brooke handed her mother the packet of letters. She'd had Farrah make photocopies of everything before leaving the office, but she wanted Marie to read the originals.

"Before I forget, your dad wants you to call him."

"Why? What does he want?"

"He'd like to speak to you. Could you just do me a favor and call him, please?"

"No." Brooke abruptly set her glass down on the table. "I'm not calling him. He can call me if it's that important."

Marie handed the letters back. "I'm not looking at these until you call your father."

"Mom! This is really important. It's why I drove all the way up here today."

Her mother folded her arms across her chest. "What your dad has to say to you is important too. So I'd say we're at a stalemate."

"Okay, fine. You read the letters while I call Dad."

"Good idea." Marie picked up the first letter and adjusted her reading glasses.

Brooke was too jittery to sit and watch her mother read Millie's letters to Gardiner Bettendorf anyway. She walked slowly up the stairs and without really thinking about it pushed open the door to her old bedroom.

It was a small room, with a low, sloping ceiling and pink-and-green-striped wallpaper, last decorated when Brooke turned fourteen. Marie hadn't gotten around to redecorating it yet, for which Brooke was thankful.

She sat on the white-painted canopy bed and scrolled through her contacts until she found Gordon Trappnell's cell number. She checked the time. Not yet five. With luck, he'd still be at his office and out of earshot of Patricia, his second wife.

Gordon and Patricia had been married for five years now, but Brooke still refused to refer to her as her stepmother. Once, Patricia and her first husband had been close friends with Gordon and Marie. They'd been members of a neighborhood supper club, and Patricia had been part of Marie's book club.

But the divorces had shattered both those groups, not to mention Brooke's own fondest notions about her parents' "perfect marriage."

She tapped his number, silently hoping he wouldn't pick up. But he did, on the first ring.

"Brooke? Is that you?"

"It's me, Dad. Mom said you wanted to talk to me. What's up?"

"Oh. Well . . ." Her father seemed to be at a momentary loss for words. "How are you? How's that boy of yours?"

Fifteen seconds. She was only fifteen seconds into a call with her father and already doing a slow burn.

"His name is Henry, Dad. H-E-N-R-Y. And he's fine."

"I know his name, Brooke. Your mom keeps me up to date on everything. Is his arm healing? Maybe next time you come up, we could get together. I'd really like to see him."

An acid, sarcastic response was on the tip of her tongue, but she chose to let the moment pass. "That would be nice. His arm is totally healed. I'll see what I can do about a get-together. In the meantime, what's so important that you needed to talk to me about?"

"Marie tells me you've started seeing Gabe Wynant. Actually dating?"

"Don't start on me about the age difference, Dad," Brooke warned. "We've seen each other socially a couple of times. It's no big deal, and besides, we've known each other for years."

"Actually, you don't really know him at all," Gordon said. "This isn't about that, although it's ridiculous for a man his age—"

"Whoa! I'm thirty-four years old, you know. A little past the age when I want dating advice from my daddy."

"Listen to me, damn it! Patricia says Gabe is a charlatan—"

"Okay, just stop right there. I'm not going to listen to your new wife's character assassination of a man I've known and admired for the past decade."

"If you'd just let me finish," Gordon said.

"Nope. Not interested. Nice try. Bye, Dad."

Brooke disconnected, still fuming. She stared at the assortment of framed photos on her old white-painted dresser, Brooke laughing into the camera with her best friend, Holly, on the beach at Tybee Island. There was Brooke in her cap and gown after her graduation from Savannah Country Day. She picked up the oldest photo, a three-generation snapshot of her grandmother Millie seated on the sofa next to an impossibly young-looking Marie, who held an eighteen-month-old Brooke in a frilly white Easter dress.

Millie was gazing adoringly at the baby, and Marie was beaming proudly.

Brooke's memories of Millie, her granny, were hazy now. She remembered a crystal lidded dish, always placed on the coffee table and filled with pink jelly beans for her visiting granddaughter. She remembered stacks of library books and record albums, mostly classical music, that Granny played on a bulky turntable in what she called her "hi-fi cabinet."

She took the photograph, left the bedroom, and walked slowly downstairs, where her mother was still seated in the sunroom.

"Mom?"

Her mother's beautifully composed face was in ruins. She stared numbly at the letters. "Where did you find these?"

"Lizzie found them. In Gardiner's footlocker, which was shoved way in the back of a closet in the library at Shellhaven. The military shipped it there to Josephine after he was killed."

Marie scowled. "That horrible, horrible woman."

"Who? Josephine?"

"Yes." Marie tossed the stack onto the table. "She read these letters, then hid them. She knew Mama was in love with Gardiner, was having—I mean, had—his child. Mama was her oldest, dearest friend. And Josephine just cut her out of her life. No wonder she wanted to make amends with us."

"I've been thinking about that," Brooke said. "Maybe that's why Josephine quit talking to Ruth too—because she knew Granny had confided in Ruth but not in her. Of course Josephine read all the letters. She must have been furious at her best friends."

"Why? Why, after Pops died, didn't she reach out to Mama? The secret wouldn't have mattered so much then, not between the two of them, anyway."

"I don't know," Brooke admitted. "There's so much I didn't understand about Josephine. After Preiss died, she was essentially alone for the next forty years or so. All those years, she had no family, and she isolated herself from her oldest, closest friends. But she did have family—she had us, and we were what? An hour and a half away, in Savannah? A phone call, that's all it would have taken. Instead, she waited until she knew she was dying."

"Mama never said a word," Marie said, twisting and untwisting the napkin she held in her hands.

Brooke sat down in the chair opposite her mother's and gripped her hands in hers.

"Do you think Pops knew?" It was a question that had haunted Brooke since she'd read Millie's last letter to Gardiner.

"He must have, but he certainly never let on to me," Marie said, attempting a smile. She dabbed at her eyes with the napkin. "Pops was my father," she said finally. "He was! He was the most patient, most loving and gentle man in the world."

"I can't believe Granny kept this a secret, all these years. And none of us had any idea."

"I can," Marie said. "Looking back now, I can understand why she was so private, and self-contained. I always thought it was just that famous New England reserve."

"It must have been awful for Millie, keeping that secret. Pregnant and un-married, knowing it would cause a scandal, wondering if Gardiner would come home from war to marry her. And then having to grieve him all alone," Brooke said.

"I'm glad Josephine didn't reach out to us," Marie said. "I couldn't have for-given her for the way she treated my mother. She didn't deserve to call us her family."

Marie jumped to her feet and went into the kitchen. When she came back, she had an open bottle of wine and two glasses. She poured a glass and offered it to Brooke.

"No, thanks. I've got to drive home, remember?"

"Right." Marie took a long drink of the wine.

"These letters change everything, you know. You're Josephine's niece, her closest relative and her heir, unless we find out that C. D. actually was her son."

"I don't need Josephine Warrick's money." Marie's voice dripped scorn. "I had a career and saved my money, your father was generous with the divorce settlement, and I've done well with my investments. I thought it was a nice gesture when she reached out to us. I thought I'd be indulging her by going over to Talisa to meet her. And yes, I wanted you to have whatever bequest she wanted to give you. But knowing what we know now?" She drained the wineglass. "I'd be willing to *give* that damn island and the house to the state just to spite Josephine."

"Who are you kidding?" Brooke said. "You're the least spiteful woman I know. Anyway, are you telling me you're not even just a little bit curious about Josephine's estate? Don't you want to know what it's worth? Call me a mercenary little money-grubber, but I am. I've been wondering ever since I first set foot in Shellhaven."

"I feel like I'm suddenly living in some weird parallel universe. All of a sudden, I'm not who I thought I was. I can't even begin to process this. Anyway, what if this is all some kind of a mistake? And we're jumping to conclusions?" Marie asked.

Brooke pointed to the letters. "Do you think they're fake? Does that look like Granny's handwriting?"

With a fingertip, Marie traced the elegant slanting script on a brittle envelope.

"It's Mama's handwriting," she said slowly. "And the voice in these letters, it's hers. I can hear her so clearly as I read them. She used to write me letters like these when I was away at college. I still have them, you know. Packed away somewhere in the attic. I even have a few letters Pops sent me when I was away at summer camp. He knew I was homesick, so he'd draw these funny little cartoons of my cat, Mrs. Whiskers, with the silliest balloon captions."

She sniffed and dabbed at her eyes again. "I wish you'd known Pops, Brooke. I wish he'd known you. And Henry, of course."

"I wish it too." Brooke stood up. "I'd better hit the road."

Reluctantly, Marie handed her the letters. "You'll need to give these to Gabe, right?"

"Yes. I had Farrah make copies of everything for you, but he'll want the originals," Brooke said. "And I wouldn't be surprised if the cousins, once they hear this news, don't insist on getting your DNA compared to Josephine's."

Marie shuddered. "Does that mean needles? You know how I feel about blood. And needles."

"I think it's just a matter of something simple. Like a cheek swab," Brooke said.

They walked toward the front door.

"Did you talk to your dad?" Marie asked.

Brooke tensed. "Briefly."

"Gordon wouldn't tell me what he wanted to discuss. From the look on your face, I'm guessing it didn't go well."

"You could say that. He doesn't like the idea of me dating Gabe. I wish you hadn't told him I was."

"I didn't think it was classified information. Did Dad have a specific objection, or was it just the age thing?"

"Patricia has some malicious gossip about Gabe that she's just dying to spread, but I shut him down before he could get started."

"Maybe you should have listened," Marie said. "Gordon is many things, but a gossip isn't one of them."

"I've known Gabe for years. I think I know him a lot better than Patricia does," Brooke said.

Marie kissed her daughter on the cheek. "Sometimes the people we think we know the best are the ones with secrets we can't even fathom. Drive carefully, okay?"

63

On Friday morning, Brooke's cell phone buzzed to signal an incoming text. It was from a number she didn't immediately recognize. It was a screenshot of a court document. She squinted as she read the tiny print. It was a copy of a Chatham County property tax lien against Gabe W. Wynant, in the amount of $90,000, on behalf of KPW Roofing Inc.

Beneath the screenshot was the text message:

> Heard you've been looking for me. Your boyfriend Gabe is a phony. If you want to know what I know, come over to island and we'll talk.

Now she knew the number. It belonged to C. D. She was relieved that he was apparently alive and well but annoyed at his reference to Gabe as her boyfriend. And what was this about a lien?

> Okay, when and where?

> My friend Ramona has a boat tied up at the municipal pier. It's called *Foxxy Lady*. She's waiting. I'll pick you up at the Talisa dock. Come now, okay?

She hesitated, wondering why she felt uneasy about responding to a text from the old man. He was harmless, wasn't he? But where had he been hiding, and why was he reaching out to her now? Her thumbs flew over the phone's keyboard.

Waiting on my assistant to arrive at office. Can't leave 'til then.

She glanced at the clock on the office wall. Farrah was thirty minutes overdue. So this was what the old man had been furtively researching in the library databases. The real estate lien must have been the result of a clerical error. Gabe's town house in Savannah was on West Jones Street, one of the most beautiful streets in the downtown historic district. It was easily a $2 million property. She frowned. What was C. D. up to?

The office door opened, and Farrah breezed in, her cell phone wedged between her shoulder and left ear as she sipped from a huge Styrofoam Slurpee cup. Brooke fixed her with a disapproving stare. "Gotta go," Farrah told her caller. "My boss is giving me the death stare."

The girl set her backpack and Slurpee on her desk. "Sorry about that. What's up?"

"You're late," Brooke said. She picked up her phone and texted C. D., and she reached for her pocketbook.

Leaving now.

His return text was almost immediate.

Come alone and don't tell nobody.

"I've got to go," she told Farrah. But the idea of a secret meeting with this paranoid old man was making *her* feel paranoid.

"Go where?" Farrah asked, sifting through the stack of papers piled atop her desk.

"I'm meeting C. D. over on Talisa." Brooke quickly filled her assistant in on her mission. "It's probably bogus, but he claims to have some damaging information about Gabe. Do me a favor, will you? Just in case, take a look at the online tax records for Chatham County. See what you can find in the way of tax liens." Another thought occurred to her. "While you're at it, check the plaintiff and defendant indexes and see if Gabe has been party to any recent civil actions."

Farrah nodded as she scrawled notes to herself. "How far back should I look?"

"Maybe the past three years? And while you're at it, check the Glynn County records too. I can't remember the exact address, but his house on Sea Island is on Blue Heron Street. It might be listed under Sunny Wynant."

"Who's she?"

"His wife. She died two years ago."

"For real? I mean, he drives a Porsche."

"It's called due diligence," Brooke said. She fixed her assistant with what Farrah called her death stare again. "This is all highly confidential stuff. A man's reputation is at stake. If anybody asks, just tell them I had an appointment this afternoon. Not a word about my going over to the island or who I'm meeting with. Right? I'm not sure how long I'll be over there, so can you pick Henry up from day care if I'm not back by 2:30?"

"Sure thing."

"And Farrah? If you're late picking Henry up? That's a firing offense."

C. D.'s friend Ramona had jet-black hair that fell nearly to her waist. She wore flowered board shorts and a neon-orange bikini top that displayed a pair of saggy sixtysomething-year-old breasts. "All set?" she asked after she'd helped Brooke onto the eighteen-foot *Foxxy Lady*.

Brooke nodded, and Ramona backed the boat away from the slip.

"You're a friend of C. D.'s?" Brooke asked. "Have you known him a long time?"

Ramona's smile was enigmatic. "Been knowing him off and on for a while. More off than on, but since last week, I guess you'd say we're on again."

"Has he told you what all the secrecy is about?" Brooke asked.

"He *says* he's fixin' to come into an inheritance—which, knowing C. D., is a lot of crap. He also says I should keep my mouth shut about what I know, so that's what I been doing." Ramona turned her back to Brooke, and a moment later the boat was flattening out, skimming across the calm waters of the river with Talisa straight ahead.

C. D. was seated on a black motorbike at the edge of the Shellhaven dock. He raised a hand in greeting to Ramona, who returned the salute. Lionel, the little Geechee boy who'd been sitting on the dock, waved too.

As Brooke walked toward C. D., she heard the boat's engine start and turned to see the *Foxxy Lady* pull away from the dock.

"Get on," C. D. said in lieu of a greeting.

"No helmet?" Brooke asked nervously, straddling the bike and gingerly wrapping her arms around the old man's midsection. She noted the leather holster clipped to the waist of his shorts.

"We ain't goin' that far," he said. "You didn't tell nobody you were comin', right?"

"Right," she lied.

He steered away from Shellhaven, turning in the opposite direction. The small bike's engine labored beneath the weight of two riders. Bits of rock and crushed oyster shell sprayed her ankles and calves as they rode along, and she kept her lips clamped together and eyes squeezed shut against the stirred-up sand and grit.

The bike finally slowed after they'd been riding for ten minutes. She looked up when she heard the waves pounding ashore and saw the old lighthouse looming in front of them.

"We're here," C. D. said.

She was grateful to hop off the bike and have both feet on the ground again. He pushed the bike off the roadway, leaning it against the abbreviated porch of a small wooden edifice that Brooke realized must be the lighthouse keeper's cottage, the same one Josephine, Millie, Ruth, and Varina had stayed in the night before discovering Russell Strickland's body.

Was this where C. D. had been hiding out?

Instead of entering the cottage, C. D. turned and walked toward the lighthouse itself.

"In here," he said, pushing against the heavy wooden door, which opened inward on long-disused hinges. An open padlock hung from a rusty hasp screwed into the rotting wooden doorframe.

"Here? In the lighthouse?" Brooke peered uneasily inside. The landing in front of her was narrow, maybe six feet wide, and green-painted wooden stairs spiraled up the exposed brick column. Dust motes swirled in the shaft of sunlight pouring down from the top.

"You got a better place?" He started up the stairs, and she was surprised at how nimble he was. She stood, rooted in the doorway, already regretting having come this far. She saw now that C. D. Anthony wasn't just a harmless, aging eccentric. He was paranoid, and he was armed.

C. D. read her expression. "Come on, now. You think I'm gonna hurt you? I swear, that ain't what this is about."

"What is this about? Why can't we just talk down here?" Brooke hoped her voice sounded steadier than she felt.

"I like it up top." He jerked his chin upward. "You got a 360-degree view up there. I can see anybody coming or going. See the whole island. That's why I chose it. Anyway, I got my dossier up there. That's what I want you to see."

He started up the stairs again, calling over his shoulder. His high, reedy voice echoed off the curving walls. "Your friend Gabe? He ain't what you think he is, and I can prove it. I know you don't believe me, but ain't you curious?"

She was, damn it. Almost against her will, she began to climb, higher and higher. Once, halfway up, she stopped to catch her breath. She made the mistake of looking down and was seized by a sudden wave of terror. The stairs spun crazily beneath her feet, and she felt herself about to pitch backward. Panic-stricken, Brooke clawed at the brick wall, trying to gain a handhold. Bile rose in her throat, and she felt a crushing weight on her chest. She knelt and gripped the wooden stair risers at waist level.

"You coming?" C. D.'s disembodied voice floated from above.

"I can't do this!" Brooke cried when she could catch her breath. "I'm dizzy. I'm afraid of falling!"

"Happens all the time. Don't look down. Just keep coming."

Hot tears streamed down her cheeks. She managed to stand upright. She took a step. Paused, took a breath then took another step, and then another.

C. D. leaned casually against the glass-enclosed turret. "Took you long enough," he said when Brooke finally crawled onto the wooden landing. Her hands and knees were blackened from the gritty stairs, and she was sick and scared and bathed in her own sweat.

"Dizzy," she gasped.

He reached into a Styrofoam cooler and handed her a bottle of water. "Don't be such a crybaby."

After she'd regained her hard-won composure, she looked around at what must have been the lens room when the lighthouse was still operational. Queasy as she was, even she would admit that the view was, as advertised, spectacular. She understood why Farrah and her friends trespassed here. From 120 feet up, she could see the roof of Shellhaven and its outbuildings, the dock, and the river, and in the far distance, the mainland. The sweep of untouched beach and endless ocean felt calming. When she turned toward the north end of the island, she could see the state's ferry boat churning away from the island.

But the sudden head movement brought on another spasm of anxiety and nausea. She slumped down onto the floor.

"You done sightseeing?"

C. D. had made himself a rat's nest of dirty clothes and a sleeping bag. A backpack was stashed beside a wooden soft drink crate, atop which sat a file folder and a heavy, lethal-looking flashlight.

"Here's what I wanted to show you," he said with a smug smile. "My dossier."

Brooke opened the folder and made a show of leafing through the documents, but trying to read the already blurry printouts made her even queasier.

"What exactly do you want from me, C. D.?" she asked.

"I need your help. Your lawyer buddy Gabe tried to kill me."

Humor him, Brooke thought. *Isn't that what you do with delusional people?*

"I don't understand," she said slowly. "Why would Gabe try to kill you?"

"Because I know stuff about him. Stuff he doesn't want anybody else to know. He tried to kill me once, and he'll try it again unless you help me."

Oh God. C. D.'s paranoia was in full flower. She eyed the holster on his hip. If challenged, would he become violent or unhinged?

"You're saying Gabe actually tried to kill you? When was this?"

"Last week. I don't know the day. I been running and hiding, and I lost track of time."

"Tell me what happened."

"I been calling him a lot to, you know, try to get him to speed up this inheritance thing. Or just float me a loan, you know, until the court or whoever decides that I'm Josephine's son and I'm her heir. I guess it pissed him off, because last week when I called, he said I was full of shit, just some damn drifter who was trying to cash in on a sick old lady. He said he'd done some research and found out some bad stuff about me."

"Like what?" Brooke asked.

"I ain't a damn saint. Never said I was. Maybe I wrote some bad checks when I was between jobs, and maybe I got in some bar fights and got locked up for public drunkenness for pissin' on somebody's tires."

"Okay," Brooke said soothingly. "Those kinds of things happen. Totally understandable."

"Ticked me off, you know? Some damn lawyer digging up dirt on me. So I decided I'd see what kind of dirt I could dig up on him."

"Is that when you went to the library in St. Ann's?"

"You know about that?" C. D. asked. "They keep records of who all looks up that stuff? Them librarians said they didn't do that."

"I have a confession to make," Brooke said, coloring slightly. "We—that is, Lizzie and Felicia and I—were worried when you just disappeared. So we went over to your cottage, and we found the key where you'd hidden it, and we went in. I'm sorry, C. D., but really, we were worried that you might be sick or something."

"Snooping. Spying on me," C. D. said accusingly. "Big Brother always watching."

"We found some of those papers you printed out from the library, the old newspaper photos and clippings. I was in the library yesterday, taking my son to story hour. I asked the librarians if they knew you, and they told me you'd been doing a lot of your own research and that they'd helped you figure out how to use the computers and access databases."

"You know they charge you for stuff?" C. D. said, indignant. "I mean, that library is paid for with my tax dollars. And hell, I'm a senior citizen and a Vietnam vet. But yeah, that's where I was doing my research. After that crook Gabe dug up his dirt, I figured two could play that game. So I got them library ladies to show me how to look at the clerk's records in Savannah and up there at Sea Island, where he's got that fancy house of his."

Brooke pulled out her phone and pointed at the text message he'd sent her. "Is that where you found this?"

"And there's a bunch more like that too," C. D. said smugly. "He's plastered bad paper all over Savannah. And that place of his up at Sea Island, it's got all kinds of liens on it." He tapped the file folder. "I'm not just talking about tax liens, either. Roofers, electricians, landscapers. Hell, the guy that cleans his swimming pool has a lien on that house."

"Are you sure you've got the right address and the right Gabe Wynant?" Brooke asked. "I've known Gabe for years. We worked in the same law firm. He's a wealthy man with a thriving legal practice. I've been to his house downtown on West Jones Street several times. It's probably worth $2 or $3 million. The same for the Sea Island house. Gabe is one of the most respected attorneys in Savannah."

"He's a damn crook is what he is. Look at all them small businesses he stiffed."

Brooke said. "Look, C. D., Savannah's still a small, gossipy Southern town. If Gabe were in some kind of financial trouble, there would be rumors, and I'd have heard something."

"How long you been living down here?" C. D. asked.

"Three years," she admitted. "I guess I have kind of cut myself off from the rumor mills."

"You know the guy in the $2,000 suit and Rolex watch that drives a Mercedes and a Porsche," C. D. said. He took off his cap and bent his head down. "Look here."

There was a knot the size of a hen's egg on the back of C. D.'s skull with an angry, jagged red scar running through it. "This is the guy I know."

"Oh my God. Gabe did this to you? When? How?"

"Last week. I called him up and told him I wanted to talk to him about getting an advance on my money, and he just laughed. Said I wasn't getting a dime. So I texted him the same photo I sent you, of those bad check charges, and all of a sudden, his calendar got freed up in a hurry. He said he couldn't get down here until early evening. I was supposed to meet him at seven, but it was closer to eight. He said he'd got tied up in traffic, which I think now was just a lie.

"Anyway, I sat in the boat, had some beers, waiting. Hell, I been waiting my whole life, what's a couple of more hours? He showed up, and it was dark, but I wasn't too worried, because the boat's got running lights, and anyway, I could cross that river blindfolded if I had to.

"He come on the boat, acting kind of nervous, and I offered him one of my beers. We talked a little bit about me getting my money, and he was acting like he actually had the money on him, but he wanted to talk more once we got to the island. I was just about out of the no-wake zone, had my back to him, when out of nowhere, he took that full beer bottle and bashed me on the back of my head. Before I knew it, he'd flung me off the side of my boat."

"You could have been killed," Brooke said.

"He thought he had killed me," C. D. said. "I don't know how, but I never even blacked out. I swam under water until I thought my lungs would explode. He took off and headed back toward the city dock. Me, I managed to make it over to the creek bank. I was bleeding and had a hell of a headache, I'll tell you that. Lucky for me, the tide was coming in. I swam to a dock a little ways away. Climbed up, walked back to town, and got ahold of Ramona. She took me to the emergency room, and they stitched me up. I stayed at her place that night, then I got her to bring me back over to the island. Just wanted to sleep in my own bed and figure out what my next move was, you know?"

"But you didn't stay there," Brooke said. "Louette and Shug checked. We checked. It looked like you'd packed up and left in a hurry."

"I got to the cottage that night, and the lights were on. I could see him, through the window, going through my stuff."

"Who?"

"Wynant. He was real careful not to mess stuff up, but I seen him take those papers, the ones that showed all the bad check charges and liens. I watched him, and after he'd gone, I went in, and like you said, I packed up some stuff, got some food, and got the hell out of dodge. Come over here and let myself into the lighthouse, and I been staying here ever since."

"I'm glad you reached out to me, but why now? And why hide out at all? Why not go to the sheriff? That's attempted murder, C. D."

"The sheriff? The same one who locked me up for pissin' on his deputy's tires? You think he's gonna believe me over the lawyer with the suits and the watch and the Porsche?"

"But you could show him those same papers you showed me; it's pretty incriminating evidence, C. D. He seems like a reasonable guy to me."

"That's because you're a cute young lawyer lady, not a crusty old bastard like me," C. D. said. He rooted around in his cooler and brought out a sandwich. "Want one? Well, this is my last one, but I got some chips you can have if you're hungry."

"No," she said weakly, fighting another wave of nausea. "God, no."

Her phone, tucked into the pocket of her jeans, pinged softly, startling her, because her cell phone reception on the island was usually so spotty. She reached for it and saw she had an incoming text from Farrah.

G was here. Told him I don't know where u r, but seemed suspicious. FYI.

"Who's that?" C. D. asked, instantly wary.

"It's from my babysitter. C. D., does your phone have cell service up here?"

"Yeah, best reception on the island usually, 'cause we're up so high, but it ain't got no juice now, and I left the charger at my place."

Her own phone indicated she had only one bar, and her battery was running down, but she tapped Farrah's number, praying the call would go through.

"Who you calling?" he demanded.

"My babysitter. I need to tell her to pick up my son from day care, okay?"

"Hey," Farrah said, her words rushing together. "Brooke, I'm sorry. I was telling Gabe you had an appointment, and just then, Brittni pulled up outside and honked her horn. I went out to talk to her. I swear, I was only gone a minute. But I had all those printouts on top of my desk. I think maybe he saw them."

"Are you sure?"

"No, but he left in a big hurry," Farrah said. "I tried to call you for like, half an hour, but then I remembered you don't have cell service over there, so I tried a text."

C. D. was staring at her intently, his hand resting lightly on the gun on his hip.

"Okay," Brooke said cautiously. "That's fine."

"Huh? You seem kinda weird. Is something wrong? Where exactly are you?"

"Yes," Brooke said pleasantly. "I think that's a great idea. You and Jaxson can pick up Henry. Take him to that place the two of you used to go last summer, with the great view, okay?"

"Huh? Are you talking in code?"

"Come on, wrap it up," C. D. said.

"Yes. Okay, gotta run," Brooke said. "Also, maybe pick me up a bottle of Captain Morgan?"

"What the hell, Brooke?" Farrah said, just as Brooke was disconnecting.

C. D. sighed his annoyance. "Look, I called you because I need help." He looked her square in the face, his voice pleading. "I need you to go to the sheriff with me and tell him I'm telling the truth. Don't let that lawyer get away with what he done to me. Don't let him cheat me out of what I'm due from Josephine."

"All right," Brooke said finally, tucking her phone away. "I'll see what I can do." She stood, but the room seemed to swim beneath her feet again. She swayed slightly, then slumped against the glass.

"Hey, you don't look too good," C. D. said. He took her arm and tried to steady her. They heard a car coming, and he was on instant alert. He picked up the binoculars resting on top of the fruit crate and looked.

"Shit. That's Wynant."

64

....

C. D. whirled around to confront Brooke. "You lied, damn it. You led him right to me!"

The truck was the ancient turquoise one that belonged to Josephine. She'd noticed it earlier, at the dock, parked with the other vehicles under the shade of a twisted cedar tree. She watched as it pulled up to the grassy area at the foot of the lighthouse. Gabe hopped out and looked around. He darted toward the lighthouse keeper's cottage, trying the locked door and peering in the window, before staring up at the lighthouse. C. D. ducked down onto the floor, and Brooke reflexively followed suit.

"I didn't tell him anything. I swear I didn't," Brooke said. She didn't know whether Gabe's arrival was a rescue mission or not.

"How did he know we were here?" C. D. grabbed the front of Brooke's shirt. "Was that him you just called? I should have known you're in cahoots with him. Lemme see that phone." He took her phone, and stared down at the screen.

Brooke wrenched away from the old man. "Think about it, C. D. I had no way of knowing you were here at the lighthouse. And I have no idea what Gabe is doing here."

C. D. duck-walked away from the window, then stood, his fingers resting nervously on the holster on his hip again. "If you're lying to me . . ."

"I'm not."

They heard the door open below.

C. D. cursed softly. "Forgot to lock the damn door." He stood looking down the stairwell. "Wynant, I seen you down there. You need to not come up here. I already told Brooke what you've been up to. You're done, asshole."

"Brooke?" Gabe yelled. "Are you up there with him? Are you okay? Has he hurt you?"

"I ain't ever hurt a woman in my life," C. D. called. "You're the one that bashed me in the head, threw me into the creek, and left me for dead. But the joke's on you. I'm alive, and I'm fixing to tell the sheriff everything I know."

Gabe's footfalls echoed off the brick walls. They heard his labored breathing, and then he stopped.

"Brooke, whatever he's told you is bullshit. He's been trying to blackmail me. It's true, I had some money problems right after Sunny died. I was out of my head with grief, I had no idea about the kind of money she'd been spending. But that's all it was."

Could that explain the source of Gabe's financial distress? Had C. D. overreacted?

"Yeah, right!" C. D. hollered. "How do you explain what happened on the boat the other night? How'd I get that gash on the back of my head?"

More footsteps, and Gabe stopped again. "He's been trying to blackmail me. Calling me repeatedly. I agreed to meet with him, but once we got on the boat, he started threatening me, waving that gun of his around. He'd been drinking. When I refused to give him any money, he shot at me! He missed, and that's when I hit him with the beer bottle and took off for the dock. He could have killed me."

Brooke glanced over at C. D. He'd admitted to taking potshots at park service rangers, so why wouldn't he have shot at a lawyer he suspected of defrauding him?

"Brooke?" Gabe shouted. "Talk to me. Are you okay? C. D., you just let her go. She's not involved in this. Let her go, and you and I will settle our differences."

She felt C. D.'s fingers dig into the flesh of her upper arm. He released her for a moment, pulling his revolver from the holster.

"I'm fine, Gabe!"

"Shut up, damn you." C. D. jerked her backward. "Don't you know he's a liar?" She flinched as his sour breath sounded hot and low in her ear. "Tell him to get out of here. Get out, and then I'll let you go."

"He says if you go away, he'll let me go," Brooke called.

"He's lying!" Gabe yelled back. "If he means what he says, he'll let you walk down these stairs and leave with me."

Gabe's voice echoed in the stairwell. They heard his footsteps, sensed him coming closer.

"Don't you come up here!" C. D. yelled. His rheumy, red-rimmed eyes darted around the room. His hands shook badly as he tried to slot bullets into the pistol's chamber. Brooke had the sense that he was coming unglued before her eyes, the raw nervous energy sizzling through every cell of his body.

Agonizing seconds passed, each one marked with the sound of Gabe's inexorable upward climb.

Brooke's eyes were riveted on the old man. Right now, he was focused on Gabe, but in his hyper-paranoid state, he might turn the gun on her at any moment. She mentally measured the distance to the stairs, tried to calibrate the trajectory of bullet to human bone and blood—hers, Gabe's, C. D.'s. She had to do something to pause this nightmare, but she felt paralyzed. Finally, she inched away from him, pressing her back against the wall, trying to slide out of his sight line.

In the next second, the footsteps accelerated. Gabe was running. He burst onto the stair landing, a black pistol aimed directly at C. D.'s head. Startled, the old man scrabbled backward, firing wildly, his bullets ricocheting off the ceiling. Gabe leveled the gun, his finger on the trigger.

"No!" Brooke screamed, lunging toward Gabe, who fired.

The gunshot roared, echoing and bouncing off the brick walls, louder than anything Brooke had ever before experienced. She screamed and watched in horror as C. D. dropped his gun and fell to the floor, howling in pain. He writhed on the floor, blood pooling from his shoulder.

"Come on. We've got to get out of here." Gabe grabbed her arm and tugged her toward the stairwell.

Brooke pulled away and knelt beside C. D., whose face was already ashen. "We can't leave him like this." She grabbed a T-shirt from the mound of C. D.'s clothing and clamped it against the shoulder wound, which burbled blood.

"Leave him," Gabe barked. "The bastard tried to kill me twice."

"No. He'll bleed to death. He's a crazy, sick old man. I can't leave him like this." Brooke looked up at Gabe. The warm, caring, courtly barrister had vanished, and in his place was this cold-eyed killer, ready to exact vengeance from anyone who crossed him.

"He killed Josephine," Gabe said calmly. "He would have killed you too if it hadn't been for me. Why do you think he lured you up here? You're what's standing between him and Josephine's money."

"No!" C. D. growled, trying in vain to sit up. "I never."

Brooke pressed down on the wound, and C. D. moaned. She shook her head. "I don't believe that. He could have killed me before you got here. He wouldn't hurt me. He's bleeding badly. You've got to go for help, Gabe. I'll stay here with C. D., but you've got to get help."

Gabe's face as he stood over her was twisted with fury. "I tell you, he's dangerous. And I'm not leaving you here with him. Let's go," he said abruptly, waving the gun at her.

"No," Brooke reached for another shirt to stanch the flow of blood.

"Now, goddamn it!" Gabe slapped her hard with the flat of his hand, so hard her ears were ringing, so hard the band of his thick class ring cut a gash in her cheek. Stunned, she felt the warm trickle of blood down her face. He grabbed her arm and began dragging her toward the stairwell. He stepped off the landing and onto the next step, intent on bending her to his will.

Brooke looked down, and suddenly the endless, dizzying nautilus shell staircase spun beneath her feet. "No!" she screamed as the panic seized her and swallowed her whole. "Leave me alone." She fell to the floor and grasped the iron handrail with both hands.

Gabe grasped her by the ankle, and she instinctively kicked out, catching him square in the gut. His face registered a momentary flash of shock before he toppled backward, down and down and down, the sickening thud of his falling body echoing in the brick stairwell.

Time stopped. She was conscious of crawling to C. D.'s side, of wadding up another shirt, pressing it to his shoulder. The old man was deathly quiet, his breathing shallow.

She reached for her cell phone. She had only half a bar. She tapped the number for the house phone at Shellhaven, but before the call could connect, the phone went dead. She had to go for help before C. D. bled to death. She tried to stand, but the floor swam beneath her feet.

"Brooke! Brooke!" Two distinct women's voices floated up from below. "Are you up there? Are you okay?"

"I'm here," she managed. "We need help."

Their footsteps pounded on the wooden steps, pausing only when they'd reached the lawyer's body, corkscrewed across the stairwell, his head resting at an unnatural angle.

"Oh my God!" Lizzie gasped.

Another moment and they were both on the landing, surveying the carnage before them—the blood, the forgotten pistol, and a barely conscious old man and his makeshift nurse, who was softly weeping.

"Get help," Brooke croaked. "He's been shot, and he's lost a lot of blood."

"The sheriff is on the way," Lizzie said.

Felicia gently pried Brooke's hands from C. D.'s shoulder. "Let me do this," she said. She gingerly lifted the shirt, blanching at the sight. "The bleeding seems to have stopped."

"Gabe," Brooke said, her throat dry. "Is he . . ."

"Dead?"

Lizzie and Felicia exchanged a look that confirmed Brooke's worst fears.

"I killed him," Brooke whispered. "I did this. After he shot C. D., Gabe was trying to get me to leave. But I couldn't leave C. D. And then, I looked down, and the stairs." She shuddered. "Dizzy. I nearly blacked out. I couldn't move. The nausea. He hit me. And then he started to drag me down those stairs. I just couldn't. I could feel myself falling. So I kicked him." She was weeping again. "I kicked him, and he fell backward, down the stairs. I didn't mean to, but I killed him."

"Hush." Felicia wrapped her arms around Brooke. "Don't talk."

They heard cars approaching. Lizzie looked out the windows. "Sheriff's here. He's got a deputy and Shug with him. I'd better go down there and tell them we need a stretcher, for C. D."

"And a body bag for Gabe Wynant," Felicia said.

"They'll arrest me for murder. I'm going to prison. And Henry. My Henry . . ." Brooke buried her face in her hands.

"You're not going anywhere," Felicia said. "It was self-defense, right, Lizzie?"

Lizzie paused at the stair landing. "That's right." Her voice was matter of fact. "Gabe shot C. D. in cold blood. And he would have shot you too. He had the gun to your head, you were afraid for your life. You kicked at him, and he fell backwards." She nodded at Felicia. "Right?"

"End of story," Felicia agreed.

There was a flurry of activity then. Sheriff Goolsby and his deputy seemed to fill the tiny landing with their male presence. Brooke shrank back against the wall, her knees drawn tightly to her chest, as an EMT and an ambulance, hastily summoned from the state park, arrived to bandage C. D., hook up IV tubes, and transport him out of the lighthouse and to the sheriff's boat waiting at the dock at Shellhaven. Before they left, Brooke allowed them to clean and bandage the gash on her cheek.

"Might need stitches," the burly EMT muttered.

Lizzie and Felicia hovered protectively beside Brooke as she numbly answered the sheriff's questions, while the deputy quietly went about his business photographing the scene and taking notes and measurements.

"She's told you everything she knows," Felicia said after the sheriff asked for the third time why a rich, successful Savannah attorney like Gabe Wynant had ended up dead on Talisa Island.

"She's in shock," Lizzie agreed. "No more questions. You can call her tomorrow if you think of anything else."

They waited until the others had gone. "Okay, the coast is clear," Lizzie said, watching the parade of trucks motoring away from the lighthouse. "Let's go home now, Brooke."

They pulled her to her feet. Brooke took two steps, then froze. "I can't," she gasped. "The stairs . . . dizzy."

"You've got this," Lizzie said firmly. She wound an arm around Brooke's waist. Felicia took Brooke's left arm and placed it across her own shoulders.

"We're just going to take it nice and slow," Felicia said soothingly. "Close your eyes. Take a step when we tell you."

"I'll fall!" Brooke started to tremble. "I'll fall, and I'll pull you down with me."

"You won't," Lizzie said. "We've got you. We won't let you fall. Not ever."

65

....

The emergency room admitting clerk called her name loudly. "Brooke Trappnell?"

Felicia and Lizzie walked with her to the doors leading to the triage area, where a nurse in purple scrubs stood waiting, a clipboard tucked under her arm. "Sorry. I can't let visitors back there. Family only."

"We're her family," Felicia said.

"Sisters," Lizzie agreed.

The nurse rolled her eyes at the improbability of the statement but showed them back to a curtained-off treatment room. "The doctor will be with you shortly."

Brooke sat on the narrow bed while Felicia leaned against the wall and Lizzie perched on a low rolling stool. Her head was pounding, and the gash on her cheek throbbed. She looked down at herself. Her hands and arms were bruised, her clothes were filthy and blood-spattered. "God, I'm a mess."

"You're alive. That's what counts. You scared the living bejesus out of us, you know," Felicia said.

Lizzie nodded solemnly. "Yeah. We heard the shots just as we were pulling up to the lighthouse. We didn't know if you were dead or alive, or what."

"How did you even know where I was?"

"It was Farrah. You'd better give that girl a raise," Felicia said. "After that wacky call from you, she knew something bad was going down over there. I guess you gave her some clue about being at the lighthouse. Where she and Jaxson partied? She called the sheriff, and then she called the house phone at Shellhaven."

"And I picked up," Lizzie said. "The poor kid was frantic. She was trying to tell me about Gabe and some tax liens and bad checks, and I didn't really know what any of it meant, but she convinced me that you were in some kind of trouble."

The nurse pulled the curtain aside. "You've got more company. I'd say this is probably your real family." She glared at Lizzie and Felicia. "You two will have to leave."

Marie and Gordon stepped into the already cramped space.

Gordon's face paled when he saw his bruised and blood-spattered daughter. "Jesus! What did that animal do to you?"

Marie nodded at Lizzie. "Thanks so much for calling to let me know what happened."

"It looks worse than it really is," Brooke said. "The EMT said they'll probably just give me a few stitches. I'm fine, really."

"You two," the nurse said, pointing to Felicia and Lizzie. "Out."

"Can't they stay? Just for a few minutes?" Brooke pleaded.

"The doctor is finishing up with a patient now. When he's ready for you, they'll have to leave," the nurse relented.

"I spoke briefly with somebody in the sheriff's office while we were driving down here," Gordon said. "They wouldn't tell me much. Just that there'd been an incident over on Talisa and that two people were injured. I hope to God Gabe Wynant is the other injured party."

"Gabe is dead," Brooke said quietly.

"Good. Saves me the trouble of doing it myself."

Brooke's head felt like it was in a vise. "I don't understand. Dad, what are you doing here? What's any of this got to do with you?"

"You're my daughter. You were nearly killed today. Why wouldn't I be here?" Gordon said, bristling.

"Your dad called me this morning. He was insistent that I make you listen to the truth about Gabe," Marie said.

"You always assume the worst about me," Gordon said bitterly. "And Patricia. Who was only trying to warn you about that snake—"

"Gordon?" Marie's voice held a warning note. "Let's not get into the family dynamics. Just tell our daughter what you told me this morning."

"Um, maybe we'd better let you guys have some space," Felicia said.

Lizzie nodded. "We'll go check out the coffee situation in the cafeteria."

The two beat a hasty retreat.

"Gabe Wynant was the executor of Patricia's uncle Robert's estate," Gordon began. "Robert Zehring founded Chatham Community Bank, which got bought out by a bigger bank in Charlotte fifteen years ago. Robert's been dead six or seven years. Patricia's aunt Ellie is in a nursing home, suffering with dementia, so Patricia's been trying to help untangle her finances, but she could never get a straight answer out of Gabe. She started doing some digging and discovered there was some funny business with the trust accounts. We hired a forensic accountant and, long story short, discovered Gabe had been treating Ellie's trust account like it was his personal piggy bank. Hundreds of thousands of dollars had gone missing."

"And that's not the only client he's defrauded, right?" Marie looked at Gordon.

"I've been making quiet inquiries around town," Gordon said. "There are two others that I know of. Gabe was slick, I'll give him that."

Brooke's stomach heaved. She made it into the adjacent bathroom just in time. Marie was by her side in an instant, holding her hair as Brooke hunched miserably over the commode, then helping her back to the examining table.

The curtain parted, and a white-coated doctor appeared. "Brooke Trappnell? I'm Dr. Schaefer."

"We're her parents," Marie said. "Can we stay?"

The nurse came in, bearing a plastic-covered stainless steel tray.

"Better not to," Schaefer said. "Stitches and all. I'll send for you when we're done here."

He turned to Brooke. "How do you feel?" he asked when they were alone, leaning in to look at her face. "This cut is pretty deep. Does your head hurt?"

"It's killing me," Brooke said.

"Nauseous?"

"Very," she admitted.

He held a small penlight and examined her closer. "Does this light hurt your eyes?"

"Yes." She winced, closed her eyes, and turned away.

"And how did you get these injuries?"

She gave him the condensed version, telling him about the dizziness and panic that seized her as she was climbing the lighthouse stairs, and about falling and hitting her head, and then being struck by Gabe.

He nodded. "Vertigo. That could account for the nausea, but I think you've probably also got a concussion. We'll get your wound area numbed, then I'll stitch you up. With a concussion, I want somebody to check on you every few hours. Do you have somebody who can stay with you tonight? Your parents or one of your sisters?"

"I think so," Brooke said. Her head hurt too much to correct him about the status of her real and newly adopted family.

"The man I was with, C. D. Anthony? Do you know how he is?" she asked.

"He'll be all right. It was a through-and-through gunshot wound. He's one tough customer. We'll keep him overnight, mostly because of his age and the amount of blood loss, but barring any surprises, we should be able to cut him loose tomorrow."

"Can I see him?" Brooke asked.

"Tomorrow. There's not much to see. He's been sedated. You should go home and get some rest."

Lizzie and Felicia were in animated conversation with Brooke's parents as the nurse wheeled her out to the waiting room.

"Who gets these?" the nurse asked, holding up Brooke's discharge papers.

"I'll take them," Marie said. She looked down at her daughter. "The girls and your dad and I have been talking. You're going to need some quiet time at home, so I'm hoping you'll let me take Henry back to Savannah to my house, at least for the weekend."

"Lizzie and I can hang with you," Felicia said.

"Is that really necessary?" Brooke asked, pressing her fingers to her throbbing temples.

"Yes," Marie said, ushering her out the door. "No arguments."

Henry and Farrah were working on a puzzle when they got home. "Ree!" the child cried, ignoring his mother and flinging himself at Marie's knees. She swung him into the air and spun him around as he laughed in delight. Gordon stood just inside the door, an awkward, silent outsider.

"Omygod, Brooke!" Farrah cried. "I was so worried about you. Gabe showed up to take you to lunch. I told him you were at an appointment, but I knew he didn't believe me."

Brooke gave her a wan smile. "You kinda saved my life today. If you hadn't figured out where I was . . ."

"I knew something was bad wrong when you said me and Jaxson should pick up Henry, but it took me a minute to figure out you were telling me you were at the lighthouse," Farrah said, giggling.

"Hey, buddy," Brooke said as Henry reached for her.

His dark blue eyes widened when he spotted her bruised and bandaged face. "Boo-boo?" he asked.

"Just a little one," Brooke said, taking him in her arms. "All better now."

Henry kissed his fingertip and touched it to her cheek. He stared and pointed at Gordon. "Who's that?"

Gordon's voice was hoarse. "I'm your grandpop, Henry." He took the child's chubby hand in his and solemnly shook.

"Grandpop is my daddy," Brooke explained. "Just like Ree is my mommy."

"Let me take him," Marie said. "I can tell your head is hurting. I can pack his bag, and then we'll be on our way."

Catching the cue, Lizzie stepped up and took Brooke by the arm. "Come on. Show me to your bedroom."

"Henry, would you like to go stay at Ree's house and sleep in the big bed tonight?" Brooke heard Marie ask just as Lizzie pulled the covers back from her bed and urged her to get some sleep.

66

....

Every four hours, Lizzie and Felicia took turns shaking Brooke awake, asking the questions outlined in the emergency room discharge instructions. Brooke's cheek still throbbed, and her head still hurt. She was disoriented and sleepy, but the women were relentlessly efficient.

When she awoke on her own, she could see the sun through the slats in the window blinds. Felicia was asleep on the other side of the bed, facedown on a pillow.

She found Lizzie in the kitchen, making coffee. "You're alive!" Lizzie said, pouring her a mug.

"Barely." Brooke sat at the table and sipped her coffee. A moment later, they heard water running in the bathroom, and then Felicia joined them.

"How did you sleep?" she asked.

"Badly," Brooke admitted. "All night long I kept dreaming I was falling down the stairs at the lighthouse. Down and down and down. And then one of you would wake me up and ask me what day it was."

"Sorry," Felicia said. "Doctor's orders."

"The past twenty-four hours all seem like a bad dream. I still can't believe any of it happened. I can't believe Gabe is dead. That he did those things my dad says he did. None of this makes any sense." Brooke looked from Felicia to Lizzie. "Does it make sense to you?"

"We sat up talking last night after you were asleep," Lizzie said, "trying to piece it all together, but some of it's just a guess, and some of it, let's face it, we might never know."

"We took a look at all the stuff Farrah dug up on Gabe yesterday," Felicia said. "The man was having serious financial problems. There were tax liens on his house in Savannah and at Sea Island. He'd even had some bad check charges, although it looks like those were dismissed once he made restitution."

"Probably that's why he looted his clients' trust accounts. He figured he'd be able to pay back all the money before he was found out," Lizzie said. "But the question is, why?"

"Sunny," Brooke said.

The two women gave her a questioning look.

"His wife. She'd been in and out of rehab for years. That couldn't have been cheap. Gabe told me she would go on spending sprees when she was drinking. He claimed he didn't even know about that Porsche he's been driving until he found it in the garage of the house at Sea Island shortly after she died of liver cancer two years ago."

"Classic," Felicia said. "Blame it on the dead wife."

"He needed money, and he needed it fast," Lizzie went on.

Brooke shook her head. "And when I called him and asked him to meet with Josephine to handle her estate, it must have looked like the perfect opportunity. My God, I've been so stupid and so naive."

"You couldn't have known he was broke," Lizzie said. "He fooled everybody."

"I was *such* a chump," Brooke said. "He charmed me, romanced me, convinced me that he was a lonely widower looking for a second chance at love. I wish you'd seen him at the Cloister in black tie and tux. He was in his element. He basically proposed to me Saturday night. He wanted me to give up my practice here, move back to Savannah, and let him 'take care of' me and Henry. Oh my God! He even hinted that he'd love to have a child with me!"

"But you didn't say yes," Felicia pointed out. "You didn't sleep with him, right?"

Brooke blushed and looked away. "I was tempted. Gabe made it pretty clear he intended to seduce me that night. But thanks to Farrah and her lowlife boyfriend, I cut the evening short and drove back home."

"And that's the only reason you didn't fall for all his smooth talk?" Lizzie asked.

"No. A couple of times, he let the mask slip. He yelled at the valet parking kid and threatened to have him fired. And then, when I called from my car to tell him I was leaving instead of spending the night at his house, he got in a really nasty dig about me running away. Of course, the next morning he showed up here with flowers and croissants and a lame apology. Still, it was an eye-opener."

"Never trust a man who hollers at the help," Felicia said.

"This whole time, he's been angling to get his hands on Josephine's money," Brooke said. "That first time he met with her at Shellhaven? I think Josephine must have told Gabe her secrets. I think she told him that day that Gardiner was my mom's father, and that's why he was suddenly, passionately in love with me—he figured if he married me, he could eventually get his mitts on that money."

"Don't be so hard on yourself," Lizzie said. "We saw the way he looked at you. Like Dweezil when she sees a can of sardines."

"Is that supposed to make Brooke feel better about herself?" Felicia asked.

"You know what I mean. It wasn't only dollar signs he was seeing when he looked at Brooke. There was some real attraction there."

"I think the attraction was that I was vulnerable. I've been so isolated from family and old friends since I moved down here to St. Ann's." Brooke gave the women a sad smile. "Okay, maybe vulnerable and isolated is a nice way of saying I was horny. It's been more than three years since I had a man in my life."

"Seven years for me, unless you count the drunken one-night stand I had at a wedding two years ago," Lizzie said. She turned to Felicia. "You?"

"Next question?" Felicia said.

Brooke stared down into her coffee. "You know what else I think? I think Gabe killed Josephine."

67

....

Both the women stared at Brooke in disbelief.

"I thought the cops agreed that it was an accident," Lizzie said. "We all saw her that night. Josephine was groggy from mixing the new pain meds with the wine. She tripped over the dogs, fell, and hit her head on the bathroom floor. Right?"

Felicia chimed in. "Josephine was ninety-nine years old, and she had end-stage cancer. I mean, she would have been dead in a matter of days anyways. Why would Gabe risk murdering her?"

"That's what I was asking myself all night long," Brooke said. "And then it came to me. Josephine was ready to sign a will that would have divided her estate between five people—the three of us, plus my mom and Varina. She also planned to leave pretty generous cash bequests to Shug and Louette. And she planned to deed back the property she owned at Oyster Bluff to the original landowners."

"Which would have all gone into effect if Gabe had gotten that will witnessed," Felicia said.

"But he didn't get it witnessed when he easily could have. Which meant that when Josephine died, that will was invalid. She died intestate—so that meant her estate would be left to her closest blood relatives," Brooke said.

"Meaning your mom," Lizzie said. "And if you're right, Gabe Wynant was the only person who knew about that connection. And I'm not disagreeing with you, Brooke, but it's still so hard for me to think of Gabe as a murderer."

"Why?" Felicia demanded. "Just because he was an apparently rich, classy-looking white dude?"

"Well, yeah, now that you mention it," Lizzie said.

"I wouldn't have believed it either, if I hadn't seen him try to shoot C. D. at point-blank range. If you'd seen his face..." Brooke shuddered. "He meant to kill C. D. And I'm not sure he wouldn't have killed me too..."

She left the sentence unfinished, but her friends knew she was still dwelling on the way Brooke's would-be suitor fell to his death. They sat sipping their coffee until Lizzie spoke up.

"I get that Gabe had the perfect motive to kill Josephine, but so did C. D., if you look at it like that."

"Huh?" Felicia said.

"We know C. D. is convinced he's Josephine's son, but the will she dictated didn't include him, so he had just as much motive, maybe even more than Gabe, to kill Josephine. Like revenge. Because as far as he's concerned, she dumped him like a cast-off shoe at an orphanage," Lizzie said.

"Maybe you're right," Felicia conceded. "I mean, what does anybody really know about C. D., besides the fact that he was raised in an orphanage? Don't you think it's an awfully big coincidence that he showed up at Talisa, looking for a job, only six months ago?"

"Stop!" Brooke clutched her head with both hands. "I'm already dazed and disoriented. You two aren't helping matters any."

"You're the one who brought up the topic of murder," Felicia said. "What do you want to do now? Do we just keep our mouths shut about our suspicions?"

Brooke sighed. "Lizzie's right. We don't actually know if Josephine's death was an accident or a homicide. I'm so mixed up right now. Gabe gave me my first job right after law school. He was my mentor and my friend. Something changed in him, and I never saw it. But I keep thinking about what my mom said. 'The people we think we know the best are the ones with secrets we can't even fathom.'"

"Who doesn't have secrets?" Lizzie said. "My grandma Ruth used to say there's a little felon in the best of us."

68

....

October 1941

Millie peered into the steam-clouded bathroom mirror and gingerly touched the bruises on her neck and chest. Blackish-purple handprints bloomed on her breasts. His handprints.

She'd lain awake all night, pondering her situation. Her bruises would fade as they had in the past, but what of her future with a man like Russell Strickland?

Only one solution occurred to her. She found the packet of razor blades in the medicine cabinet, alongside the Pepsodent, the cotton balls, and the Pond's Cold Cream, all so thoughtfully stocked by the Bettendorfs' housekeeper in anticipation of any need a guest might encounter. With a fingernail, she slit the paper wrapper and held the shining blade up to the light. One deft swipe across her wrist would surely do the trick, wouldn't it? But the mess. How inconsiderate. And who would find her? Josephine? Her own mother? Her grandmother? She could only imagine their horror at finding her in a pool of her own blood. She shook her head. No, it was just too ghastly.

Millie's hand closed on the bottle of sleeping pills she'd pilfered from her mother's pocketbook. Almost a whole bottle. These would do the job nicely. She shook them into the palm of her hand. Tiny pink tablets, as sweet and promising as a first kiss. One swallow. Not nearly as messy. She would take the pills, then climb into the bathtub for a long, lovely nap. But what if the pills didn't work? She could barely choke down baby aspirin. What if she vomited them back up? Or worse yet, what if she woke up, still engaged, still doomed to the life with Russell Strickland that had been so neatly planned for her? She could picture the shock and disappointment on her mother's face.

That wouldn't do either. She frowned and dumped the pills into the sink, turning on the tap to wash them down the drain.

Millie looked back in the mirror again. She was no longer the coed who'd met and flirted and become infatuated with Russell Strickland. That girl disappeared the first night he'd forced himself on her, months ago, in the backseat of his car, taken her in the same violent way he took anything he regarded as his property.

The woman who'd emerged from that car was someone who had to stay hidden. But she was there, just beneath the innocent veneer Millie presented to the world. She turned away from the mirror quickly, having glimpsed the resolute, rage-fueled visage who came and went in the blink of a long, fluttery eyelash.

She brushed her teeth and combed her hair and returned to her bedroom, where she dressed quickly in dark slacks because there was a chill in the air this morning.

The house was eerily quiet as she tiptoed past the closed bedroom doors of her oldest, dearest friends, Josephine and Ruth. What would they think if they saw this version of Millie? She crept down the stairs and into the big kitchen. Someone had put a pot of coffee on the stove, and she was tempted to pour herself a cup to soothe the throbbing in her temples, but time was of the essence. She must act before the sleeping household awakened.

She slipped out the back door and made her way in the predawn darkness toward the garage. She would have her pick of the Bettendorfs' vehicles. The Packard, the roadster, the truck. All the keys were kept in their ignitions, because who would steal a car on an island? She'd read about carbon monoxide poisoning. A length of garden hose inserted in a tailpipe and then wound into a nearly closed window. Just the trick. No fuss, no muss.

A male voice cut abruptly through the morning stillness. "Millie? What are you doing out here?"

Her stomach roiled at the sound of his voice. Her first instinct was to run and hide as far from here as she could get. But just how far could she get on an island?

69

Mary Balent was a presence in Carter County. According to her website, she was a fifth-generation native and had gone to undergrad and law school at the University of Georgia, which made her what faithful alum referred to as a "Double Dawg." Her law office stood directly across the square from the county courthouse, and since moving to St. Ann's, Brooke had watched her with envy as she skillfully navigated the local legal landscape.

Now, a week after her harrowing experience at the lighthouse and Gabe Wynant's demise, Brooke and Marie sat in Ms. Balent's office, seeking representation as they attempted to untangle Josephine Bettendorf Warrick's estate.

Mary Balent had already read the wartime letters from Millie to Gardiner Bettendorf, which Brooke had dropped off a week earlier, and Marie had submitted a cheek swab for DNA testing to compare with Josephine's hair sample.

"We still don't know the outcome of a DNA sample Gabe sent off, comparing Josephine's DNA to a local man who believes he could be Josephine's son," Brooke explained.

"Really?" Ms. Balent said, intrigued. "It was my understanding that Mrs. Warrick never had children."

"There is a chance that she could have had a son out of wedlock while she was living in Savannah in 1942 and given him up for adoption," Brooke said. "My friends and I did some sleuthing. We found some anecdotal evidence that shows Josephine was interested in a boy who was raised at two different children's homes there, but we didn't find any concrete proof. As far as I know, Josephine never acknowledged having a child, and of course, we have no idea who the father might have been."

"But this man, C. D. Anthony, is convinced that he is Josephine's son. He's the man Gabe tried to kill last week," Marie said. "Brooke saved his life."

"We'll have to have this man retested," Ms. Balent told her. "But in the meantime, I'd say your next-of-kin status to Mrs. Warrick is entirely provable. I can get the paperwork started to have myself appointed administrator of the estate this afternoon, and given the circumstances of the previous administrator's death, that shouldn't be a problem, but it's probably going to take a while to get this mess straightened out. It could take months."

"We understand that," Marie assured her. "My most immediate concern is going forward with my aunt's burial. It's been a month now. Josephine's oldest living friend is ninety-one years old and is still heartbroken over her death. For her sake, at least, we'd like the closure a funeral could provide."

"Have you been in contact with the cousins you mentioned earlier? Do they have any objections to a burial?"

"I called them," Brooke said. "They were pretty shocked—and disappointed to discover that Gardiner Bettendorf had a daughter and that she was Josephine's closest blood relative—but they indicated they don't oppose a funeral."

"I'll see what I can do to expedite that. We'll have to get the body released. Have you talked to the sheriff?"

"That's my next appointment," Brooke said.

Marie spent the next ten minutes filling out legal documents as Mary Balent explained what each one meant.

"You know," she told Brooke, "I served on a couple of different bar association committees with Gabe Wynant over the years. I wouldn't say we were friends, exactly, but I respected his expertise. I have to say, all these revelations coming out of Savannah are sending shock waves through the legal community, even all the way down here in little-bitty Carter County. I hear his former law firm has really taken a hit from this, which is a shame. You worked there, right?"

"Yes. Gabe hired me right out of law school," Brooke said, glancing at the clock. "Mom, while you finish up here, I'd better get over to the sheriff's office."

Ms. Balent gave her an appraising look. "I know the sheriff pretty well. Is there anything I can help with?"

"He says it's just a few more routine questions so he can close out the death report on Gabe," Brooke said. "But if it's anything more than that, I might take you up on your offer."

The Carter County courthouse was a looming brown brick Spanish revival–style two-story building from the early 1920s, but the courthouse annex where the sheriff's office was located was a squat 1970s-era concrete bunker with leaky smoked plate glass windows.

Howard Goolsby offered Brooke a seat in his cluttered office. "How're you feeling? I heard you had a concussion."

"I'm much better, thanks," she said, making an effort to sound and look composed. "You have some questions for me?"

"Just a few," he said, opening a file folder and leafing through the papers inside. "We took statements from those other two women, Elizabeth and Felicia, who witnessed Mr. Wynant's fall. They both said Mr. Wynant struck you. And you feared for your life?"

"Yes." Brooke crossed and uncrossed her legs. "He'd already shot C. D. Gabe grabbed me and was dragging me toward the stairs, but I couldn't leave C. D. there to bleed to death. When I resisted, grabbing for the handrail, he pointed the gun at me. I thought he would kill me. I kicked him, thinking he might drop the gun, but instead, he fell backward."

"I see," the sheriff said, scribbling in a stenographer's notebook. "Could you tell me again how you came to know Gabe Wynant?"

"Again?"

"Please." The sheriff seemed amiable and relaxed.

"He was my boss when I worked for his law firm in Savannah. As I said in our last interview, Josephine Warrick called me over a month ago and asked me to visit her on Talisa. She first said she wanted me to draft a new will for her, and then said she intended to make me and my mother, as well as three other women, her beneficiaries. I explained that I had no expertise in trusts and wills, plus, I had a conflict, since that will would potentially benefit me and my mother. That's when I reached out to Gabe, because I knew he did a lot of estate planning work."

"So . . . the relationship was strictly professional?"

Brooke felt the flush creeping up her neck. "At first, yes. But recently, Gabe let me know he wanted something more. We had a couple of dates."

"But nothing came of it? Was that your idea or his?"

"Why are you asking me this?" Brooke asked, wishing now that she'd asked Mary Balent to accompany her to this interview.

"Just doing my job. We found your name and number several times in Mr. Wynant's phone log. He'd tried to call you several times the morning he was killed."

"My phone has lousy reception on Talisa."

"Mine too," he said with a conspiratorial smile. "That's when the old two-way radios come in handy, right?"

"I suppose." She looked at the sheriff. "Do you know how he figured out where we were?"

"We think so. We found a fisherman who keeps a boat at the city dock. He said Wynant flagged him down and offered him twenty bucks for a ride over to Talisa. That little Geechee kid Lionel? Hangs around that dock all the time? He said a white-haired fella asked him if he'd seen you and C. D., and Lionel obligingly said he'd seen the two of you riding a motorcycle in the opposite direction of the house.

"Now, back to my questions. Remind me why Mr. Wynant would have tried to kill C. D. Anthony? Not once but twice, according to Mr. Anthony?"

There was a rapping at the glass door.

"Come in," Goolsby barked.

Mary Balent stepped into the office. "Sorry I'm late," she said, nodding at Brooke. "Howard, Ms. Trappnell tells me she's already told you everything she knows about this unfortunate matter. Now, what else do you need from my client?"

Without waiting for an invitation, she dragged a chair from the corner of the room and sat beside Brooke, who found herself momentarily speechless.

"Just tying up some loose ends," Goolsby said. "She's a lawyer, the dead guy's a lawyer, I didn't think we'd need to get any more lawyers involved."

"Just one more," Mary said sweetly.

"I was asking your client why Gabe Wynant seemed so intent on killing Mr. Anthony," the sheriff repeated.

"Did you ask Mr. Anthony that question?" Mary asked.

"I did. This office has had some past dealings with Mr. Anthony, who isn't always the most reliable witness. So now I'm asking her."

"Gabe told me C. D. had been hounding him for money, even trying to blackmail him over some financial irregularities C. D. uncovered. C. D. thought it was just a matter of some bad checks, but I think what he'd unwittingly uncovered was something much more serious—the fact that Gabe was in such bad financial straits he'd started stealing from his clients," Brooke said. "Gabe must have known C. D. would tell me everything and that I'd figure out the rest. That's why Gabe tried to kill C. D. He pretended it was to protect me from C. D., but that was a lie."

"Okay." The sheriff scribbled some more notes. He reached into the top drawer of his desk and held out an envelope in a sealed plastic bag. "We found this in Mr. Wynant's car, which was parked in the lot at the city marina."

"What is it?" Brooke asked.

"Lab results on DNA testing performed on hair samples from C. D. Anthony and Josephine Warrick."

"Which show what?" Brooke asked, not bothering to try to hide her excitement.

"No familial relation," Goolsby said. "No big surprise there. I could have told you that old drunk was no kin to Miss Josephine."

"Could we have a copy of that report, Howard?" Mary asked. "For my client's peace of mind?"

He shrugged. "Don't see why not." He walked to the outer hallway with the envelope. They heard the mechanical whir of a photocopier, and a moment later he was back with the copy of the report, which he handed to Brooke. "Anything else?"

Mary Balent spoke up. "Yes, actually, Howard, we'd appreciate it if you could release Josephine Warrick's body as soon as possible so her family can have a funeral."

Goolsby tapped his pen on the edge of the desk and looked at Brooke. "I understand you've only recently learned that you and your mother are Mrs. Warrick's next of kin?"

"Yes," Brooke said. "It was . . . a shock, to say the least."

He rolled the pen over and over between his fingertips. "You being next of kin, I guess I owe it to you to tell you that we now consider Josephine's death a homicide."

"What did you just say?" Mary Balent asked, leaning forward.

"It was set up to look like an accidental death." Goolsby chuckled. "Hate to say it, but Kendra Younts, that hotshot new coroner we got now, she's the one who made a believer out of me. You know she used to be a homicide detective up in Atlanta, until her granddaddy talked her into coming down here to take over the family funeral parlor business and run for coroner. I was dead-set certain when I saw that poor old soul laid out on that bathroom floor at Shellhaven that it was just an unfortunate accident. But Kendra, she had her suspicions. She took all kinds of photos and measurements of the scene and convinced me not to release the body for burial, even after Gabe Wynant called over here raisin' all kinds of hell about it."

"So it was Gabe who murdered her," Brooke said quietly.

"What makes you think so?" the sheriff asked.

"He had the best motive for wanting her dead. Money. Josephine must have told Gabe that my mom was her immediate next of kin. And as far as we know, he was the last one to see her alive that night when he helped her to bed."

"How did the coroner conclude that Mrs. Warrick's death was a homicide and that Wynant was the murderer?" Mary Balent asked.

"Just a feeling she had. She was looking back over the death scene photos and noticed that when we arrived, Miss Josephine was wearing her eyeglasses."

"I never saw her without her glasses," Brooke said. "She was nearly a hundred."

"But if she'd tripped and fallen, don't you think those glasses would have gone flying off? Probably would have been smashed too. But hers were right there on her face. We fingerprinted those glasses, and found a partial print from Gabe Wynant. Plus, our new coroner determined that she was struck on the side of the head with an unknown object, which caused the fall that killed her. And no, we don't have a murder weapon."

"Not much here that would hold up in court, is there, Howard?" Mary Balent asked.

"I won't argue with you. But it wouldn't have taken much for him to have done it. She weighed all of eighty pounds and was eaten up with cancer, on top of which she had some powerful prescription opioids in her system. And since we can't exactly ask a dead man if he was a murderer, that's the best we're going to get," the sheriff said.

"It's more than enough for me," Brooke said firmly. "I've got a son to raise and a law practice of my own and a funeral to plan. So if you'll excuse me . . ."

70

....

Brooke had barely settled in at her desk the next day when her cell phone rang. The caller ID said *Younts Mortuary*.

"Miss Trappnell?" The woman's voice had a soft, rural Southern accent, which was different from the harder-edged accents of urban Atlanta, Birmingham, or Charlotte. "This is Kendra Younts from the funeral home. I believe we met over on Talisa, the day of your great-aunt's death."

"Yes, I remember." Brooke took a sip of the coffee she'd just poured.

"I spoke to Howard Goolsby last night, and we've gotten the okay to release Miss Josephine to the family."

"That's great. And by the way, the sheriff told me about your theories about Gabe Wynant. Thank you for your diligence."

"I'm sorry for your loss," Kendra said, sounding properly somber. "The other reason I'm calling is because Miss Josephine has a pre-need plan in place with us."

"Pre-need?" Brooke was drawing a blank.

"Yes. She actually set it up with my granddaddy twenty years ago. All the charges have been prepaid, and of course, we have her instructions."

"Which are?"

"Cremation with remains in our Eternal Slumber Bronzesque urn. Now, that model is no longer in production, of course, but the finish on our new Odyssey urn is very similar. Will that be acceptable?"

"Um, sure," Brooke said. "You should probably ask my mom, just as a technicality, but what the hell, I don't think she'll know the difference."

"And Miss Josephine won't care, will she? Oh, sorry, that's a little funeral home humor. Anyway, I'm afraid that's about the extent of your great-aunt's wishes. The notes in the file say that she opted against a hearse or a funeral procession or reception here at the mortuary, and I see that she already has a headstone and a plot in the family cemetery on the island. It's a fairly bare-bones plan."

"More funeral home humor?" Brooke asked, chuckling.

"Sorry! Can't help myself. My three-year-old didn't sleep last night, and I'm a little punchy."

"I totally understand. I have a three-year-old myself," Brooke said. "What happens next?"

"We can have the remains ready for you by the end of the week," Kendra said. "And if the family decides they would like a reception or something a little more formal, we would love to accommodate you. Miss Josephine was a much-beloved figure in this community, you know."

"I'll consult with my mother, but my feeling is that she'll want to honor Josephine's wishes," Brooke said. "So just plan on having the remains ready on Friday, please."

Shug picked her up at the municipal marina. It had rained the night before, which lifted the oppressive June heat a little but left the air as thick and humid as a wet wool blanket.

"How are things on the island?" Brooke asked. "Is Varina feeling all right?"

"Varina still gets a little blue, but Felicia just jokes her out of it, and once she takes her over to see how her house is coming along, she's all smiles," Shug reported. "Your mama called to say she's sending a roofing crew over to Shellhaven next week, and Louette hasn't been that happy in months. She says I'm too old to be getting up on rooftops, and I can't disagree."

"Have you seen much of C. D.?"

"He comes around. That shoulder's still bandaged up, but I see him out walking most days. That man's like a cockroach, you know? Can't nothing kill him." Shug cast her a sideways glance. "How about you? You gave us all a scare that day. I saw that blood all over you, and I could have sworn you'd been shot too."

She touched the bandage on her cheekbone. It seemed to be healing, and the headaches had also subsided. "I guess I'm almost as tough as C. D.," she said.

He nodded his approval. "Good to hear."

Lizzie was waiting at the Shellhaven dock, behind the wheel of the blue VW. "You look almost human," she said as Brooke climbed into the car.

"Thanks. I'm feeling better every day. Everything good over here? How's your research on the magazine article coming?"

"I've got enough material for ten articles, or one book. Josephine and Preiss had an amazing life. Quite the partnership. Their correspondence is so sweet. It makes her seem like a real person. Almost. I've even found old records dating back to the plantation days. So what have you been up to?"

"I'm finally ramping up my campaign to stop the state from condemning Josephine's land. I've been reaching out to the county commission and our state representatives, asking for a meeting so I can make my case. Also, we're going to have Josephine's funeral on Saturday."

"I heard. Louette's been in a frenzy, getting the house spiffed up. And Felicia and Varina are here, getting started on their baking. I get a sugar buzz just walking past the kitchen. Are you really having the service in the African Methodist Episcopal Church at Oyster Bluff?"

"It's what Josephine wanted."

"Is that why you're over here today?"

"Not really. I need to talk to C. D."

"He's keeping kind of a low profile. Has he been pestering you about his inheritance?"

"He's called me once or twice. The thing is, I've got news."

"Do tell," Lizzie said.

"The sheriff found the report on C. D.'s DNA testing in Gabe's car."

Lizzie pulled the VW around to the back of Shellhaven and parked. "And?"

Brooke held out the copy of the report. Lizzie read it carefully.

"As you can see, there's zero evidence of a DNA match with Josephine," Brooke said. "He's going to be devastated."

Lizzie was too busy reading to reply. After a few minutes, she looked up at her friend. "Did you read the whole report?" she asked. "Even the fine print?"

"Not really. Why?"

Lizzie thrust the report at Brooke, stabbing at it with her finger. "Check out this part right there."

Brooke squinted at the print, reading it once, and then again, and finally a third time.

"Holy shit."

"Right? Are you sure you want to give the whole report to him? Maybe you should just tell him there's no match and leave it at that."

"No. He's got a right to know. He's waited his whole life for this. This report might not have the answers he wanted, but he deserves to know something."

"Do you have to go see C. D. right this minute?" Lizzie asked.

"No. He doesn't even know I'm coming."

"Good. I know Varina's going to want to see you."

71

....

Felicia was taking a cake from the oven, a dishtowel tied around her waist for an apron and a scarf wrapped turban-style around her short-cropped hair. Varina sat at the kitchen table, chopping pecans. Both the women's faces were shiny with perspiration.

"Oh, Brooke girl!" Varina cried. "Come here and let me see what that rascal did to you."

Brooke and Lizzie sat at the table on either side of Varina, who gingerly touched the bandage on Brooke's cheek. "I've got some salve I want you to start putting on that thing," she said. "You do that every night, and you won't ever have a scar on that pretty face of yours."

Felicia mopped her own face with her apron. "Auntie has become a conjure woman since moving back to Oyster Bluff. You watch out, or she'll bury some chicken bones at midnight and put a spell on your enemies."

Varina took a playful swipe at her great-niece's hand. "This one here thinks because she has a PhD, she's smarter than her elders."

"Varina," Lizzie said, her voice unexpectedly serious. "You know I've been going through Josephine's old papers, working on a magazine article. I found something I don't understand, and I wanted to ask you some questions, if that would be okay."

Felicia shot her friend an inquisitive look, but Lizzie brushed it off.

"I'll try," Varina said cheerfully. "I might be an old, old lady, but I still remember a lot of things. What can I help you with, baby?"

"I found an old letter from the fall of 1942 to Josephine from a Catholic priest in Savannah. His name was Charles Ryan. The letter is sort of a progress report for a baby boy named Charlie. It says the couple who took the baby can't continue to care for him anymore, so he's decided to take the baby to the nuns at St. Joseph's. That was an orphanage in Savannah. It closed a long time ago."

"Oh?" Varina said with interest. "Well, I know Josephine used to give money to those orphans. She had a good heart, and she did a lot of good things, but she didn't want people to find out because then they'd think she was weak or silly." Varina set her knife on the cutting board. "But now, if this is about that crazy C. D. saying Josephine is his mother, you just need to stop with that foolishness. Josephine never had no baby. And I'd know, because I was living with her and working for her back then."

"I believe you," Lizzie said, her voice soothing. "But I think, maybe, the person who had a baby was you. Can that be true, Varina? Were you the one who had a baby?"

72

Varina

The first year after the war started, Josephine went to my daddy and asked could she take me with her to Savannah so I could go to a real school. Josephine told him I was so smart, I should go to a school in Savannah so I could make something of myself. But the real reason was that I had a big secret I couldn't tell anybody about.

Josephine was the only person in the world who knew. And I only told her because I was scared. And ashamed. So ashamed.

My mama died right after I was born, and I never had any sisters, so there wasn't anybody to explain women's things to me. The first time I had my monthly, when I was thirteen, I thought I was bleeding to death. That's when Josephine sat me down and explained things. She was the one who taught me how to take care of myself when I got my monthly.

Josephine was the only person I'd told about that bad man grabbing me at the party for Millie. And I never would have told her at all, except that night when it happened, afterward, when everybody was asleep or gone, I came creeping up into the house as quiet as I could to try to wash him off me because I couldn't go home and let my daddy and brothers know what that man had done to me. When I came out of the bathroom, Josephine was standing there.

And after I told her, she took me upstairs to her bathroom and let me take a hot bath. My beautiful new pink dress was torn and dirty, so she gave me some clean clothes to put on and she took that dress and burned it in the fireplace. And then she drove me home in her daddy's Packard. And I promised not to tell nobody.

And Josephine was the one I went to, right after Christmas that year, when I figured out that I had missed my monthly three times.

"Sweet Jesus!" she said. We went up to her bedroom and she locked the door and she looked at me and said, "Well, Varina. This is my fault. And I feel awful about it, and I will help you the best way I know how, if you trust me." And then we both cried and cried.

And that's how I came to move off the island.

Josephine said the public high school for colored students in Savannah was too crowded and not very good, so she put me in a school called Most Pure Heart of Mary, which had been started by some Catholic nuns from Baltimore who wanted to give colored children in the South a better education.

Oh, I loved that school so much. I got to wear a pretty uniform with a white shirt and a plaid pleated skirt and new black-and-white saddle shoes. We had nuns for teachers, and they were strict, but sometimes they could be kind too. My favorite teacher was Sister Helen, who taught English and social studies.

The best part about that school was getting to learn. Sister loaned me her own books to read, because at that time, colored children were not allowed in the big pretty public library on Bull Street. Because of Sister, I read *The Count of Monte Cristo* and *Gulliver's Travels* and *Little Women* and *Jane Eyre*, which was very sad.

73

....

Varina's face crumpled, and her dark eyes filled with tears.

"What are you saying?" Felicia asked indignantly, her hands on her great-aunt's shoulders. "Where would you get an idea like that? Tell her, Auntie. Tell her it's not true. In 1942, you were what, fourteen? Just a child."

Varina's hands trembled as they clutched for Felicia's. "Oh, Felicia, honey, I'm sorry. I'm so sorry I never said nothing." She turned and faced her niece. "You think I'm a bad person? Maybe I was. Or maybe you just had to know how it was back then."

Felicia knelt beside her aunt. "Auntie, I'd never think anything bad about you. You're the best, the godliest woman I've ever met. I would never judge you. Never. Do you want to talk about it? You don't have to, you know. It's your secret. Not Lizzie's or mine, and especially not Josephine's."

"Get up off that floor now," Varina chided, sniffling. "I guess maybe it's time to talk about this thing. It's been clawing at my heart all these years. Maybe now's the time to let it out."

She took a deep breath and folded and unfolded her hands. "Lizzie has found out my story. My secret. Josephine told you about Millie's engagement party. And I told you while I was hiding in the bushes, I saw that man, the one

Millie was supposed to marry, attack her and paw her. I told you I saw Gardiner and him fighting. But I didn't tell you that after Millie and then Gardiner went back to the house, I was trying to sneak on home, and he caught me."

"Who?" Felicia demanded. "Russell Strickland? What did he do to you, Auntie?"

Varina picked up the knife and began chopping the pecans again. "He dragged me back to the guesthouse, where he was staying. And he . . ."

"He raped you?" Felicia whispered.

The old woman nodded, continuing to chop the pecans until they were less than dust.

74

Varina

I never was what you'd call a grown-looking girl. "Skinny Minnie" is what the other kids called me. So I kept on going to school at Most Pure Heart of Mary, keeping my secret the whole time. When my belly started to pooch out a little bit in the spring, I moved the buttons on my school uniform, and then moved them again.

The crazy thing is, except for my secret, I was happy as could be. I missed my daddy and brothers and friends on the island, but I loved my new school and getting to learn about the world outside Talisa. In April, at a school assembly, Sister Helen called me up on the stage and gave me a prize for being the best student in her class. It was a little gold statue of Mary, and I got a framed certificate too.

But that afternoon, Sister asked me to stay after school. I thought maybe she had a new book for me to read, but when the other students were gone, Sister closed the classroom door, and when she turned around, she had a real serious look on her face.

I knew she had figured out my secret. I sat at my desk and I folded my hands on the top, just like all the students at Most Pure Heart were taught to do, but my hands were shaking and my mouth was so dry I couldn't swallow, and that secret in my belly was kicking so hard I was sure Sister could see it from where she sat at her own desk. In my head I was saying that Catholic prayer we said every morning, right after we said the Pledge of Allegiance.

Hail Mary, full of grace, the Lord is with thee. Blessed art thou amongst women, and blessed is the fruit of thy womb, Jesus.

"Oh, Varina," she said, and she sighed. Her face was as white as that wimple she wore on her head that covered her hair. "What have you done?"

I didn't say a thing. Just stared at my hands.

Holy Mary, mother of God, pray for us sinners, now and at the hour of our death.

"For several weeks now, I've seen something different about you. I thought maybe you were gaining a little weight, and that was good, because you are such a skinny little thing. But today, on that stage, I realized, you are . . . that is . . ."

I looked up and Sister turned her head, and when she looked back at me, her cheeks were bright pink.

"I had such high hopes for you," Sister said. "And now you are about to throw all of that away because you've been a wicked girl."

What could I do? I couldn't look at her, and I couldn't tell her it wasn't me that was wicked, it was that bad man whose name I would never say.

I felt something wet hit the back of my hand and realized I was crying.

"Does your employer know?" Sister Helen asked, meaning Josephine.

I nodded, but I still couldn't speak. It was like my mouth was full of cotton.

Sister sighed. "Well, I'm afraid you will have to leave this school immediately."

I jerked my head up then. "Leave school?" I whispered. "But graduation isn't until two more months."

"You will not be graduating with your class," Sister said. "And I'm sorry about that, but Mother Superior has rules. We can't let the other girls and boys in this school be exposed to something like this. Most Pure Heart is not a school for fallen girls like you."

"No, Sister," I whispered.

She drummed her fingertips on the top of her desk.

"Is there something you'd like to tell me? Some...special circumstance you'd like to tell me about?"

"No, Sister."

"Was it a boy at this school? This is very serious, Varina, because if the boy is a student here, I will see that he leaves this school too."

"No, Sister."

She drummed her fingertips some more. "Would you like to see Father? I realize you are not Catholic, but perhaps a good confession and an Act of Contrition..."

I shook my head hard. That priest went around with a mad face all the time. I could never tell him what had happened to me. Besides, I was kicked out of school, so there was nothing more to say.

"May I go, Sister?" I said.

"I suppose." She rummaged around in her desk drawer and brought out a black leather change purse. I'd seen her take that change purse out before, on the sly, when some of the boys and girls who came to school looking hungry and raggedy and didn't have enough money to buy milk in the school lunchroom.

She walked over to me and put one hand on my shoulder as I stood for the last time beside my desk, and she pressed a coin into my hand. "For the streetcar fare," she said.

I wanted to throw that money back at her face. I wanted to scream that I hadn't been wicked and that I wanted to stay in school and read all the books and someday, maybe, be a teacher, like her.

Instead, I said, "Thank you, Sister. I still have your book. Would it be all right if I brought it back to you tomorrow?" Sister lived at the brick convent attached to the school.

She wrinkled her brow. "What book do you have?"

"It's *Treasure Island*, Sister." I didn't tell her that Mr. Robert Louis Stevenson's book was my favorite one so far, even better than *Jane Eyre*.

She hesitated, looking down at me, and that's when I saw her eyes get all watery. "You keep it, Varina. Keep reading. Keep learning, no matter what."

"I'll try," I whispered.

"Take care of yourself, Varina. And the baby."

75

....

A nd you never told anybody?" Felicia asked.

"He told me he'd kill me if I told anybody what he'd done. And he took my pretty pearl pin that Millie gave me, because he said I'd stolen it," Varina said. "I couldn't go home the way he left me, so I snuck back here, to try to clean up, and that's when Josephine found me. She guessed, just as soon as she saw me, what had happened, and she made me tell her everything."

"That bastard," Felicia said, the color rising in her cheeks. "Raping a child. I wish you had killed him, Auntie. I wish he were still alive so I could kill him for you."

"No need," Varina said. "He's dead and gone. Everybody, all my family, all my friends, they're all gone. Josephine was the last one, and now she's gone too."

76

Varina

March 1942

After I got kicked out of that school, there wasn't much for me to do. Josephine thought I shouldn't go out, because nice people would see me and figure out I was going to have a baby, so I stayed in her house and I did laundry and some cooking and listened to the war news on the radio.

We didn't really talk much about what would happen next. Just the one time, really.

One night, Josephine came home from a party and she came up to my bedroom on the third floor of that town house her daddy owned. I was reading *Treasure Island* again, thinking about pirates and buried treasure and such.

She knocked on the door and then came in and sat on the little chair. "Varina, we need to talk about what will happen when your baby comes."

"I know that," I said, struggling to sit up in the bed.

"It's going to be very hard on you, trying to raise a baby as young as you are. And there are going to be people saying terrible things about you, because that baby is going to be half-white," Josephine said. "Your family might not want to take you back once they find out."

"I don't want to go back home," I said, because I'd been thinking a lot about that. "I want to finish high school and then get me a job."

"All right," she said. She looked tired. "We still have a couple of months to figure things out. I know lots of people here, and maybe somebody will be looking for a maid or a live-in babysitter."

The first thing I thought of when she said that was *Jane Eyre*.

I couldn't tell Josephine I didn't want to do the kind of work Geechee ladies on the island did, cooking or cleaning or watching other people's children, because that would make me seem ungrateful for all she'd done for me. I really wanted a real job, like in an office. The nuns taught us what they called vocational skills, and I could type fast as anything.

I didn't tell her I dreamed of going to college and someday maybe being a teacher like Sister Helen. It sounds bad to say this, but I was all mixed up inside. Nothing that had happened to me since that night at the party seemed real to me. Not any of it. Not even after the baby started kicking so hard I woke up in the middle of the night. Not even when I had to go to the bathroom every hour and my back hurt every time I went up and down all those stairs at her house.

It didn't start seeming real to me until that very next day. We were in the kitchen, listening to *The Romance of Helen Trent*, our favorite radio program, and all of a sudden I got this awful cramp in my belly—like a lightning bolt or a live wire. It hurt so bad I doubled over. When I looked down, I saw all this warm water running down my legs.

"Josephine!" I screamed.

77

....

Felicia buried her head in her arms and wept. Her sobs echoed in the big kitchen.

Varina patted her back and tried to soothe her. "Now, honey, that was a long, long time ago. You don't need to be crying for me. I cried all the tears a long time ago."

"How can you say that?" Tears ran down Felicia's anguished face. "After everything that happened to you?"

"Hush now," Varina said, handing her a paper towel to wipe her eyes. "You're getting yourself all worked up about something that's in the past. You think I do that? Look back at those bad times? No, ma'am. Every morning when I wake up, I think, *Thank you, Lord, for giving me one more day in this beautiful place you made for me.*"

"You amaze me, Varina," Brooke said.

Felicia got up and poured four glasses of iced tea. She brought them back to the table and handed a glass to each woman.

When she sat down again, Felicia took a deep breath. "What happened to your baby, Auntie Vee?"

Varina's face clouded over. "The baby came too early. I was only seven months along. Josephine got the doctor over to the house as soon as she could, but there wasn't anything he could do. My baby was too little and too weak. Jesus took my baby home. And I never even got to hold him."

Lizzie and Brooke looked away, each hating the burden of the secret that they shared.

"Oh, Auntie, I'm so sorry," Felicia said.

"Don't be. It's like Josephine said—maybe that was just a blessing. You know, I was just a baby myself when all that happened. And I don't know what my daddy or brothers would have said if I'd come home with a baby from a white man. Josephine took real good care of me. I was sick with a fever after I lost the baby, but she got me medicine and looked after me just like I was her own little sister. Then, when I was better, she found me a new school to go to. I finished high school, and I went to business school and learned to take dictation, and then she helped me get a good job in a real office."

"Good old Josephine," Felicia said bitterly.

"You don't realize it now, but that was a real hard thing for a little black girl like me," Varina said proudly. "Back then, not many colored girls in the South worked in offices. I worked at the shipyard in Savannah, and then, after the war, I went down to Jacksonville, where one of my brothers worked, and I got a job at the railroad."

Brooke's throat felt dry. She sipped her iced tea and tried to ignore the laser stare Lizzie was giving her. "Varina," she said finally. "You know Josephine had all these secrets she kept all those years. And that's why she hired me and brought me over here to Talisa. Those secrets were eating away at her. She knew she didn't have long to live, so before she died, she wanted to make things right with the people she'd hurt."

"Josephine always did play things close to the vest," Varina agreed. "When Felicia told me about your mama being Josephine's niece, you could have knocked me over with a feather. I never would have known that sweet Millie had a baby with Mr. Gardiner—and then that baby was your mama!"

"How does Marie feel about Josephine keeping that little tidbit to herself all these years?" Felicia asked.

"She was pretty angry," Brooke said. "But then, Millie kept it a secret too.

All these years, my mom had no clue that her pops wasn't her biological father. She's slowly getting used to the idea, but it's going to take some time."

"Didn't Josephine tell you that Millie and Ruth and Varina were her best friends? All that High Tide Club stuff, that was just a bunch of crap," Felicia said.

"Josephine had one more secret she was keeping," Brooke said, looking at Felicia. "Lizzie found it by accident this week as she was going through Josephine's papers looking for material for her magazine article, but it didn't make much sense until yesterday when the sheriff gave me the report on the DNA comparison between Josephine and C. D."

Lizzie nodded. "After I found that letter from the priest, Father Ryan, telling Josephine about that little boy, Charlie, I started to wonder again why Josephine was so concerned about that particular boy and no other child."

Felicia's eyes widened as she realized what was coming. "Oh my God," she whispered. She grasped her great-aunt's hand. "Josephine lied, Auntie. She told you your baby was dead, but that was a lie. She gave the baby away! To an orphanage." She turned to Brooke and Lizzie. "I'm right, aren't I?" she asked. "C. D. isn't Josephine's son. He's hers!"

"What's that?" Varina asked, confused. "You're saying my son is alive? He didn't die? How can that be?" She shook her head violently. "No! Josephine wouldn't have done me that way. She wouldn't hide my child from me for all these years. Let me think he was dead when he wasn't?"

"I'm so sorry, Varina," Brooke said. "There's no explanation for it, but yes, we think that's exactly what she did. A priest who was the pastor at a black church in Savannah was the go-between. He found a couple, probably in his parish, who took the baby for a few weeks, and then he turned the boy over to a Catholic orphanage, where he stayed until he was six. After that, he went to live at the Good Shepherd Home for Boys."

"And you think my boy, my grown-up son, is C. D.? Living right here on this island, working for Josephine?" Varina asked. "I don't understand."

"That bitch!" Felicia exclaimed. "Playing God with people's lives. How dare she!"

"My baby is alive," Varina said, looking from Lizzie to Felicia. "I can't believe it." She turned pleading eyes to Brooke. "How can you be sure it's him after all these years?"

"The only way we can be really positive is if we tried to DNA match you with C. D. There are so many compelling facts it can't be a coincidence. The DNA report we had done on C. D. showed he had African heritage. C. D. was told he was named after the priest who found him abandoned in his church after Sunday mass. That's the same priest who wrote Josephine to give her an update on the baby. We talked to a nun in Savannah; she's nearly a hundred years old, but she remembers the little boy named Charlie who came to live at St. Joseph's Children's Home. The nuns gave him the last name of Anthony, for St. Anthony, who is the patron saint of the lost. And the priest who brought him there, he was driving a new Cadillac not long after that. The rumor was that the Cadillac was given to him by that baby's family as a reward for keeping his mouth shut. When Charlie was six, he was sent to the Good Shepherd Home for Boys. We talked to a man who lived in the same cottage at the boy's home. He remembers C. D. from that time."

Brooke reached for her phone and scrolled through her camera roll. She found the photo from Good Shepherd of the boys standing in front of their cottage. She enlarged it and handed it to Varina, tapping the photo of the boy the others had nicknamed Buck. "That's him."

"Oh, my. Oh, my," Varina whispered. "He looks like my brother Omar." She thrust the phone at Felicia. "See? Doesn't he look like a Shaddix?"

"I've never seen a blue-eyed Shaddix before," Felicia snapped. But she examined the photo closer, reluctantly nodding. "He was light enough to pass, wasn't he? You know, I've seen that old man dozens of times since we started staying over here, but I never saw it until now."

Varina could not take her eyes off the photo. "When it was my time, the pains were awful. We knew something was wrong. There was so much blood! When the doctor came, he gave me a shot. And when I woke up, there was no baby. Josephine said the baby was born dead, and the doctor took it away with him. She said it was better that way so I wouldn't be so upset."

"I hope she rots in hell," Felicia said. "I'm glad Gabe killed her. Josephine needed killing. I only wish I'd done it myself." She stalked over to the counter, picked up the cooling cake layers, and dumped them into the trash. "I'll be damned if I'll bake a cake and sit in a church and pretend to be sorry that old bitch is gone." She looked over at Varina. "Come on, Auntie. We need to get you home and give you your meds. I don't think I can stand to be under Josephine's roof for one more minute."

"No, ma'am," Varina said. Her voice was loud and clear.

"Now, Auntie Vee," Felicia started.

"You go along home," Varina said. "You're upset. I'll be along in a little while. Lizzie will bring me home, won't you?"

"Happy to," Lizzie said, earning her a glare from Felicia, who stomped out of the kitchen, slamming the screen door as she went.

"Fetch me those cake layers out of that trash, will you, honey?" Varina said. She pointed in the direction of the door. "That girl has had a temper her whole life. There wasn't no reason for her to throw those cakes out. I'll put some icing on 'em and nobody will know the difference."

Lizzie reached into the trash and rescued the cake layers, which had split in half. She brushed away some stray potato peels and placed them on a plate.

"Are you all right?" Brooke asked as the old woman returned to chopping pecans. "I know you've had an awful shock."

"I'm going to pray about this," Varina said, not looking up. "I don't rightly know what to think." She blinked back tears, and a moment later, her shoulders shook as she sobbed quietly on Brooke's shoulder.

Lizzie slipped from the room. A moment later she was back. Varina had regained her composure. Lizzie put two items on the table in front of her. One was a small prayer card with a color rendering of the Virgin Mary, eyes cast heavenward. The other was a string of mother-of-pearl rosary beads.

"These were with one of the letters the nuns sent Josephine, after she'd paid for a new kitchen and hot water heater at St. Joseph's. I thought you might like to have them."

Varina picked up the rosary, letting the smooth beads slide between her fingertips. She clutched the silver crucifix dangling from the end. "Thank you." She looked up. "Could you take me home now?"

"Of course," Lizzie said.

"I'm going over to visit C. D. in a little bit," Brooke said. "I have to tell him that his DNA didn't match Josephine's. Should I tell him about you?"

Varina wound the string of beads around and around her narrow wrist. "What's he gonna say when he finds out? How's he gonna feel about having a mama who's black and a daddy . . ." Her voice trailed off.

78

······································

This really sucks," Lizzie said as they trudged toward the chauffeur's cottage.

"Totally. I don't blame Felicia for being outraged. I feel like burning down the house too. I don't see how Josephine was able to live with all the pain she caused all those years," Brooke said.

"I guess, at the end, she thought her money would absolve her of all her sins," Lizzie said.

As they approached the cottage, they spied C. D. on the porch, sitting on a wooden kitchen chair. His right arm was in a sling, and as they grew closer, they smelled the acrid smoke from his cigarillo.

He was awkwardly pawing through the contents of a rusted red metal tackle box with his left hand. "Hey," he said. "Excuse me for not standing up."

"How are you feeling, C. D.?" Brooke asked.

"Still kicking," he said. "How about you?"

"Better. The headaches from the concussion are gone, and my face seems to be healing."

"Glad to hear it." He touched his shoulder. "I did a tour in Vietnam, came home and worked on the docks, and been thrown out of just about every bar on this coast, and this is the first time I've ever been shot. Some folks would say I was overdue." He studied the two women's serious expressions. "You just come over here to check up on me?"

"I brought you something," Brooke said, holding out the envelope. "The sheriff found this in Gabe's car. After the shooting."

"You mean after you killed the son of a bitch? Best day's work you ever did." He took the envelope, glanced at the return address, then handed it back. "Can't open it with my bum arm. It's the DNA report from the lab, right? I reckon you already know what it says."

"I do," Brooke admitted.

"And?"

"There is no DNA match between you and Josephine. I'm sorry, C. D. She wasn't your mother."

He reached for the cigarillo and took a puff, letting the ash drop unnoticed onto his lap. "Well, shit. And that's 100 percent?"

"They say 99 percent in the report, because it's scientifically impossible for anything to be 100 percent," Brooke said.

He looked past them, out at the barn, and then the green lawn that sloped gently down toward the road to the beach, the landscape dotted with huge moss-draped live oaks.

"I guess you and your mama own all this now. Y'all will be wanting me to move along. Right? I mean, I ain't no good to nobody with my arm like this."

"You can stay put. We've hired a new lawyer—an honest one this time—to handle the estate. You can stay as long as you like."

"Okay." His nod was as close as he'd come to saying thanks. He pulled himself up by his good arm, went into the cottage, and came out holding a bottle of beer. "Open that for me, if you would."

Brooke obliged, and he knocked half the beer back in a single long gulp, setting the bottle on the porch rail and letting out a beery belch.

"Back to being an orphan again. It was nice for a while, you know, letting myself believe I might own a piece of this. I ain't ever really owned anything before, except a truck or a boat, stuff like that."

"I'm truly sorry. I know it's not enough, but my mom wanted you to know she intends to honor all the bequests Josephine made for her employees here on the island."

"How much?"

"Twenty-five thousand. You won't get the money right away, because the estate will be probated, but she'll continue to pay your salary, the same as she will with Louette and Shug."

"Guess that's better than nothing, but why's she paying me to sit on my can on this porch? Docs can't tell me yet how long I'll be laid up."

"Consider it worker's comp," Brooke said. "And before I forget, if you're interested, Josephine's service is Saturday, at 6:30 P.M., at the AME Church."

"I can give you a ride if you want," Lizzie offered.

C. D. finished off the beer and belched again. "I'll let you know how I feel."

"Okay, well, I guess I'll see you around," Brooke said.

They were halfway down the path toward the barn when he suddenly called out. "Why'd she give me that toy truck, then?"

Lizzie raised one eyebrow, then followed Brooke back to the cottage.

"If I wasn't her kid, why'd she give me that truck for Christmas? Why'd she treat me special, over all them other kids? Hold me in her lap and act like I meant something to her?"

Brooke took her time answering the question, walking the tightrope between truth and fiction.

"We think your mother was somebody Josephine cared about. Somebody who was special to her. Which made you special."

"Just not special enough to adopt. Or raise as her own," C. D. said bitterly. "Got it."

79

....

The Episcopal minister imported for Josephine's funeral looked out at the tightly packed pine pews in the small wood-frame African Methodist Episcopal Church on Talisa Island. Her face gleamed with perspiration, and a fly buzzed persistently around the podium.

She was short and young, in her midthirties, with a cherubic face and a tangle of enviable black curls that touched the collar of her vestments. The Reverend Patricia Templeton admitted that she'd met Josephine Bettendorf Warrick only once, six months earlier, when she'd stopped in at her church on the mainland to ask her to preside over her funeral.

"I say *asked*, but really, it was more of an order," Rev. Templeton said.

"I know that's right," mumbled a woman near the back, loud enough to provoke scattered laughter and rib-poking.

"Miss Josephine explained to me that she believed in God and believed that he was calling her home, and she said that although she had sinned mightily in her life, she had come to believe the promise of redemption that we, as Christians, cherish," the minister said.

"Hmmph," muttered the same woman. Just as Brooke turned to see who the commentator was, she was astonished to see C. D. slip into the only open seat remaining at the back of the church. He was nearly unrecognizable in a starched white dress shirt and baggy black trousers. He clutched his ever-present ball cap in his good left hand, and his wiry gray hair was slicked back to reveal his balding forehead. He saw Brooke's stare and nodded a greeting.

Brooke and Marie were wedged into the "family pew" at the front of the church, alongside Lizzie and Louette and Shug. Varina sat on the right end of the pew, but Felicia, her great-niece, had declined to attend the service. The room was uncomfortably hot, so the AME church members fanned themselves with the photocopied funeral programs.

They'd deliberately planned an early evening service, hoping the June temperatures would have cooled off by six, but Brooke was certain it must have been at least ninety degrees. She felt her eyelids sag. The church, with its simple whitewashed plank walls and Gothic arched windows, had only a single, barely functioning air-conditioning unit installed in a window near the altar. Large brass vases brimmed with bunches of white gladioli, asparagus ferns, and palmettos lovingly arranged by members of the church's altar guild, and gardenias, which had been wired onto chicken wire–framed crosses, hung at the end of every pew, their overpowering scent filling the air.

All of this, even the menu for the reception to be held afterward at Shellhaven, had been spelled out in a letter that Josephine had entrusted to Louette right after her cancer diagnosis.

Brooke had stressed the need for brevity to the pastor and was thankful when, fifteen minutes later, Marie roused her from a nap with a subtle tap on the arm in time to hear Rev. Templeton intone the final words from the Book of Common Prayer.

They recessed from the church while a joyous version of "Amazing Grace" was played on the AME Church's organ and then they gathered outside, shaking hands and accepting condolences from two dozen islanders, most of them current or former residents of Oyster Bluff, along with a smattering of old friends from the mainland whom Josephine had specifically included as invitees to the funeral.

Marie had rebelled on only one point of Josephine's instructions and invited the cousins, Dorcas and Delphine, despite Josephine's specific ban.

"They're her family too," Marie had insisted. Still, she'd been relieved when the women begged off, instead sending a huge, hideous arrangement of carnations in the shape of an open Bible.

As they stood in the late-afternoon heat, Brooke was grateful for the light breeze that ruffled the fronds of nearby palmettos. She was even more grateful when, thirty minutes later, Shug pulled Samuel Bettendorf's Packard up to the front of the church.

It had been another of Shug's thoughtful gestures. He'd fine-tuned the old engine, then washed, polished, and buffed the car until it gleamed in the dimming sunshine like a burnished coin. He held the driver's-side door as Marie climbed behind the wheel with Varina in the front passenger seat and Lizzie and Brooke in the back.

The funeral-goers milled around inside the house, helping themselves to the buffet provided by Louette, Varina, and other AME church ladies. Platters of golden fried chicken vied with trays of deviled crab, potato salad, pickled shrimp, baked ham, macaroni and cheese, and sliced tomatoes on the polished dining room table. The sideboard was loaded down with more desserts than Brooke had ever seen in one place. Coconut cake, caramel cake, pound cake, chess pie, lemon meringue pie, pecan pie, brownies, and three different colors and shapes of congealed Jell-O salads. Pitchers of iced tea and lemonade stood on a huntboard alongside an enormous crystal punch bowl that held a vivid red concoction that resembled Hawaiian Punch and lime sherbet.

Lizzie brought a plate of food to Varina, who, as the oldest living member of Oyster Bluff and Josephine's oldest friend, held court in a high-backed chair near the fireplace, then joined Brooke and Marie, who stood near a pair of open windows in a corner, hoping for a bit of cool air.

"I don't know about you, but I could really use a drink," Lizzie told the women. "And I can't wait to get out of this dress. I'm melting!"

"Amen to that," Marie said, fanning herself. "I wanted to have an open bar, but Louette and Varina were appalled at the suggestion. They said Josephine didn't mind drinking, but she wouldn't want to be 'likkerin' up half the island,' as they put it."

"How much longer before everybody clears out?" Brooke asked. She'd smiled and nodded and accepted the sympathy of strangers for what seemed like an eternity. Her feet hurt, and she desperately wanted a cocktail.

"It's nearly eight," Marie said. "But it seems like everybody is just settling in."

Brooke looked out at the sky, which had turned a deep bluish purple. She leaned forward and spotted what she was looking for. "It's a full moon tonight."

Lizzie looked out. "Are you thinking what I'm thinking?"

"There's C. D.," Lizzie said, nodding toward the dining room, where C. D. was clumsily attempting to load a plate with fried chicken.

"I saw him in church," Brooke said. "It's sweet that he made such an effort to dress up for Josephine, especially considering what we know now."

"Uh-oh," Lizzie said as Felicia walked into the dining room. "Look who the cat dragged in." Felicia was dressed up too, in a long, black halter-necked dress. She wore subtle makeup and large gold-hoop earrings. Once again, Brooke was struck by how stunning Felicia was.

She stood for a moment, leaning down to chat with her great-aunt before noticing the other women and walking over to join them.

"My goodness, C. D. really does resemble Varina," Marie muttered. "It's uncanny."

Felicia spotted C. D., who'd found a spot on the sofa and was balancing his plate on his lap. "It looks like he's taking the news in stride. Better than I would." She looked at Brooke. "I'm sorry I lost it and blew my stack at you yesterday."

"It's understandable," Brooke said.

"Here's the thing. Auntie is over it. She was upset when she came home, but this morning, when I got up, she was dressed in her church dress, all ready to go. At 7:30 in the morning! She was sitting in a chair, reading her Bible, clutching a string of rosary beads, of all things. And she proceeded to cite me chapter and verse on forgiveness."

Marie smiled. "I think I've marked some of those same verses in my Bible lately."

"She waited until ten, then she went into Louette's kitchen and fixed a plate of food from all the stuff the church ladies have been cooking, covered it with foil, and then she asked me, sweet as pie, if I would take her to see C. D."

"She what?" Lizzie said.

"She wanted to be the one to tell him. I tried to talk her out of it, but Auntie was not having it. So I took her over to C. D.'s cottage. She told me to wait in the big house, then she went up and knocked on the door, and he peeped out, and she offered him his plate of takeout."

"I would have loved to have heard that conversation," Brooke said.

"Me too. I waited an hour, then I walked back over there, and they were sitting on that teeny little front porch, kind of talking and staring at each other."

"How did C. D. seem?" Marie asked.

"Shell-shocked," Felicia said. "Auntie said he had no idea."

"Did she tell him the whole story? About Russell Strickland and the rape and how they somehow disposed of the body and kept it a secret all these years?" Marie asked.

"Yep," Felicia said. "She spilled it all. Then I took her home, and she had a nap and insisted on going over to her house at Oyster Bluff to check on the progress. And then she fixed two dozen deviled eggs and her famous 7UP Jell-O salad to bring over here. I can't keep up with her, y'all."

"Your aunt is a marvel, Felicia."

"She's my superhero," Felicia agreed. "God, I wish I had a drink."

"Look at that moon tonight," Brooke said. "We need to figure out what time the tide is high."

"I'll go ask C. D.," Lizzie volunteered.

She maneuvered through the crowd, then pulled up a chair and sat down beside the old man. They talked quietly for a moment, then he became visibly agitated, gesturing wildly with his good hand and occasionally pointing at Varina, who was in turn watching him.

"That was a whole lot of conversation just to get a tide report," Brooke said.

"You're not going to believe this," Lizzie said as she rejoined them. "That old goat does not miss a beat. Varina told him about being attacked and raped by Millie's fiancé, but she still won't say his name. That's what he was asking me. I figured the secret's already out, right? So I told him everything I know about Russell Strickland, how he disappeared the day after the party and was never seen again. I told C. D. that Russell's grandparents hired a private detective to come down here from Boston to look for Strickland. C. D. wanted to know all about Strickland's family—where they were from and whether they had money. I told him Josephine said the family was stinking rich and that Russell was an only child. His face lit up like it was the Fourth of July."

Brooke laughed. "He'll be over at the library in St. Ann's before the doors open Monday morning, badgering those poor women to help him track down the Strickland family fortune."

"And why not?" Felicia asked. "If there's any money anywhere, why shouldn't C. D. get it?"

"Did you ever get around to asking C. D. about high tide tonight?" Brooke asked.

"It's at 9:10. We've got forty minutes." She glanced at Marie. "Are you in?"

Marie's smile was impish. "You know, I'm seventy-six years old, and I've never done it in my life."

"No way," Felicia said.

"It's true," Marie insisted. "Let's do it."

"But we can't just leave with all these people here," Brooke said. At least a dozen stragglers seemed to have made themselves at home, lounging on the sofas, leaning in corners, chatting with old friends.

"I'll ask Louette to put away all the food. That'll clear stragglers out," Marie said. "I've got a couple bottles of good white wine in the fridge. I'll pack them up and sneak them out to the car."

"And I'll run upstairs and get some beach towels and a quilt out of the linen closet," Lizzie volunteered. "Felicia, will Varina come with us? Do you think she can manage?"

"I'll help her manage. Going out to Mermaid Beach tonight is just what she needs. I think it's what we all need, after the past few days."

80

....

Marie eased the Packard off the pavement and as far as she dared drive down the sandy beach overlook before stopping and setting the hand brake.

The ocean spread out before them with the full moon a glowing white orb, spilling silver onto the surface of the deep blue sea.

"Look at all those stars," Marie marveled.

Brooke and the others scrambled out of the backseat, and Felicia hurried around to her great-aunt's side, taking her arm and guiding her carefully through the soft sand.

"This looks like a good spot." Brooke pointed toward a flat stretch of beach just above the high tide line. Lizzie spread the quilt onto the hard-packed sand and unfolded the beach chair she'd brought for Varina.

"Perfect," Marie agreed. She set down the basket she'd brought from the house and slipped out of her shoes, easing herself down onto the quilt beside Brooke, Lizzie, and Felicia.

Brooke uncorked the wine, pouring it into plastic cups that she handed around to the others.

"Auntie Vee?" Felicia held out a cup.

"Oh, no, honey," Varina said.

"Just a sip? To toast the full moon?" Felicia teased.

"All right, a sip."

When everyone had been served, Brooke raised her cup. "Let's drink to Josephine."

Felicia frowned and looked away, muttering something unintelligible.

"Felicia Shaddix, don't you go acting ugly," Varina chided.

"Well, I don't mind toasting Josephine," Lizzie said. "She's the one who brought us all together here on this island. She helped me understand a little about my grandmother Ruth and, indirectly, my messed-up, dysfunctional family." She looked at the other women. "Did I tell you I got my ex to go through the boxes of my grandmother's stuff I've had in storage? He's sending me the rest of her letters and scrapbooks so I can look for more of Ruth's correspondence with Josephine and Millie."

"You've got an ex-husband?" Felicia asked.

"Josephine's not the only one with secrets," Lizzie said with a touch of sadness. "We were together for nine years but never actually married, which might have been our problem."

"Sorry," Felicia said. "I know what that's like."

"Not to mention Josephine seems to have reignited my stagnant writing career," Lizzie said, brightening. "I've never been as productive as I've been since I came to Talisa. I've sold my piece about the High Tide Club ladies to *Vanity Fair*, and I've even started fiddling around with a screenplay. So here's to Josephine."

Brooke tapped her cup against Lizzie's. "She made me take a closer look at my family too. I've gained a new appreciation for my amazing mom, and I'm suddenly on speaking terms again with my dad. More importantly, I've reconnected with my own son's father."

"Does that mean you and Pete . . . ?" Marie asked.

"We'll see," Brooke said. "He's coming back into Savannah tomorrow, and he wants to have a serious talk about the future. Whatever that means."

"Josephine almost got you killed," Felicia reminded Brooke, pointing in the direction of the lighthouse.

"That was my own fault. I fell for Gabe's lies. I wanted easy answers, and he was only too willing to give them. Maybe if I'd listened when my dad tried to warn me about him, none of this would have happened."

Varina took a tiny sip of the wine and made a face. "Why do folks like this stuff? Tastes nasty to me. Josephine was my first friend and my oldest friend." She patted Felicia's shoulder. "I know you can't understand it, but that's a fact."

"Auntie! She stole your child, told you he was dead, then gave him to strangers to raise. It's obscene! She treated you just like those plantation owners treated their slaves right here on this island. It kills me to think about it."

Varina was unfazed by her niece's brutal judgment. "Or maybe she did what she did out of love. I was so young. Had no money, no friends or family in Savannah. No education. How could I raise a child? And maybe I wouldn't have been able to love that baby, knowing how he came into the world. I had nightmares for a long time about that bad man. Sometimes I would wake up, crying and sweating, thinking about him, about what he did to me. Maybe I would have seen his face every time I looked at that baby."

"But she had no right," Brooke said. "That should have been your decision, not hers. And what about C. D.? How different would his life have been if he hadn't been dumped in that orphanage and then shuttled off to a children's home?"

Varina shrugged. "I guess that was God's plan. For him and for me." She looked at Brooke, and her eyes seemed to brighten. "I know it was God's plan that brought me back to this beautiful island where I was born, and then, it brought my son here too. After all these years. You see that, don't you?"

"No," Felicia said, shaking her head again. "I don't. I don't see it that way at all."

"Try it this way, then," Varina said. "It's easier to walk around with love in your heart than with hate." She clutched her chest. "I don't want that burden. I let go of all that mess. You need to do that too."

"I'll drink to dear old Aunt Josephine," Marie said. "It's been painful, I'll admit, but finding out that my biological father was Gardiner Bettendorf has been a blessing in disguise. It gives me a new appreciation for Pops, who loved and raised me as his own, and it's deepened my admiration for my mom. I had no idea of the depth of her courage and quiet determination. And her strength. And now . . . all of this." She waved her arm at the landscape around them. "Talisa is such a wonderful opportunity and a challenge, especially for somebody my age. Ever since I found out, I wake up every morning and my head is spinning with plans and ideas for Shellhaven and Talisa." She grinned. "After all those years of being a wife and stay-at-home mother, of being a volunteer and a fund-raiser, I have a project again. And it's big and inspiring and intimidating. I tell you, it's like a youth tonic!"

"What kind of plans do you have?" Felicia asked, sipping her wine.

"I really want to fulfill Josephine's dream of saving the island and keeping it out of the state's hands, but I'm going to need all of you to get on board."

"Us?" Felicia looked skeptical.

"All of you," Marie said. "Josephine had the right idea."

"But the wrong lawyer," Brooke said. "Which was my fault."

"I'm going to honor her intentions as best I can. I'll create the Talisa Trust, with all of you as partners. First priority is to preserve and update Shellhaven."

"Please tell me that means central air," Lizzie said.

"Central heat and air, a new roof, updated electrical. All new bathrooms and a new kitchen. I've got a contractor coming over Monday to start working on an estimate."

"Does that mean you're moving to Shellhaven?" Lizzie asked.

"Full-time? No. I've got a much better idea. I want to turn Shellhaven into a nonprofit retreat house for writers, painters, musicians. We could offer residencies for creative types to come for, say, two weeks or maybe even a month's stay. That's why all the bedrooms will need new en suite baths. Then, I want to convert the barn into studio spaces, maybe with moveable walls so there could be a central performance space for readings or art exhibits or concerts. I'm not going to live here full-time, but I was thinking maybe you"—she pointed at Lizzie—"might agree to that. I wouldn't want you to give up your writing, now that it's going so well again, but maybe you could live on-site and help vet the writers applying for residency."

"Twist my arm," Lizzie said.

"Mom, that's a genius idea!" Brooke exclaimed. "Why didn't you tell me?"

Marie tapped her skull. "A lot of it's still just up here. But you won't mind, will you? Not inheriting some big old white elephant of a house to clatter around in during your old age?"

"No." Brooke laughed. "And I definitely won't mind missing out on the up-keep or the tax burden."

"What about all of Josephine's cars? She loved those old things," Varina said wistfully.

"I'll have a new garage built, and of course, I'll keep the Packard, but those other cars are too rare and valuable to keep here on the island, where the salt air is so destructive and nobody really drives them. I want to sell them and use the money for something that does real good."

"What kind of good?" Felicia asked.

"I'd like to buy a new, larger capacity boat for the children going over to the mainland for school. Right now, they have to rely on the state-run ferry, which stops running at five on weekdays. This way, they could participate in after-school enrichment programs they miss out on because they don't have a reli-able way to get back to the island late in the afternoon."

"I notice you haven't said much about Oyster Bluff in all your grand schemes," Felicia said.

"That's my department," Brooke spoke up. "You all know that Josephine had finally decided to sign over all the deeds for the houses she bought there over the past twenty years or so. I was working on that before she died. It's complicated, but we'll get there."

"Felicia, it sounds like you're still not really on board with any of this," Marie said.

"I don't want to sound ungracious, but it's still hard for me to believe good can come out of all the destructive things that woman did," Felicia said. "I know you mean well, Marie, but do you really believe you can just wave some money around and think that fixes things?"

Marie gave it some thought. "You're right. Money won't fix everything. It will certainly help with things like roofs and plumbing, but I'm under no illu-sion that I can turn Talisa into some kind of utopia. So I'm going to invest in brick and mortar, but I also want to establish an after-school tutoring program and a college scholarship fund for Geechee children on the island. Maybe that's something you could get involved with. You'd sure be a great role model for them."

"Too many children leave the island and never come back here," Varina said sadly. "You know there's only ten school-age children living at Oyster Bluff right now? When I was coming up, we had our own schoolhouse. Every house had five or six children."

"There are no jobs to keep them here," Felicia reminded her. "Talisa can seem so closed off from civilization. I remember I couldn't wait to get off the island to go to school and drive through a McDonald's and shop at a real mall." She leaned back on her elbows and looked up at the sky with its dazzling array of stars twinkling in the blue velvet sky. "It didn't occur to me that one day I'd choose to come back here just to get away from the fast-food restaurants and the malls and the traffic and pollution. And to be able to look up and see all these stars, so far from the city lights."

"You're a Geechee girl," Varina said fondly. "Ain't nothing you can do about it. You got salt water in your veins, and it pulls you back here just as surely as the moon pulls that tide."

Felicia refilled her wineglass. "Maybe. Oh, hell. You know what? You're right, Marie. It's a start. It'll make a difference."

"We'll make a difference," Brooke said, taking the bottle from Felicia. "All of us."

"Okay, I'll toast to that," Felicia said. She raised her cup, then clicked it against Brooke's, who clicked hers against Lizzie's, who clicked against Marie's glass. Varina touched her glass to Felicia's, completing the circle.

"Here's to the High Tide Club," Felicia said. "Here's to us. And here's to the ones who brought us here."

"To Varina," Felicia said, blowing her great-aunt a kiss.

"And Ruth," Lizzie declared.

"And even Josephine, God forgive her," Marie said, raising her glass.

"But mostly to Millie," Brooke said, tears springing to her eyes.

They all drained their glasses.

81

October 1941

Russell had backed the pickup truck out of the barn. He was dressed in what Millie recognized as his hunting clothes—long-sleeved tan shirt, tan trousers with leather chaps meant to deflect the burrs and brambles of the island's thick undergrowth, and stout boots. He was loading a pair of rifles into the back of the truck.

"I, uh, was looking for you. Where are you going?" she asked.

"Where does it look like I'm going?" He slammed the tailgate up and walked around to the front of the truck. "What do you want?"

She swallowed hard and gave him her a demure smile. "About last night. I'm . . . sorry. It's just there were so many people around, and I was afraid Mother might catch us in the act." She giggled innocently.

Russell opened the door of the truck. "Hadn't you better get back in the house?"

"Why don't I go with you?" Millie asked, placing her hand on his arm and giving it a slight squeeze.

"Hunting? Don't be ridiculous. You don't know the first thing about it. You'd probably wet your panties or faint if you heard a gun fired."

She shook her head vigorously. "You're wrong, darling. Papa was a great shot, and he taught me. And we practiced skeet shooting at boarding school."

"Hunting isn't the same as sporting clays," Russell retorted. He looked up at the sky and seemed to consider her request. "It'll be daylight soon. I should be up in a tree stand by now."

"Let me come," she wheedled. "It'll be fun. My first kill."

"All right, you can come along if you like." He gestured at her clothing. "Will you be warm enough? I don't want to hear you whining about the cold, and there's no time to go back to the house to change."

"I'll be fine," Millie assured him. "Anyway, like the song says, I've got my love to keep me warm."

"Get in, then, before I change my mind."

She clapped her hands softly. "I can't wait to show you what a good shot I am."

The old truck bounced and jounced over every rut in the crushed-shell road, jarring Millie so thoroughly she was sure she could hear her bones rattling. The headlights illuminated a narrow tunnel through the lush greenery.

"Where are we headed?" she asked.

"One of the colored boys showed me Gardiner's tree stand just up the road here," Russell said. He had one hand on the steering wheel, and the other arm was slung carelessly across her shoulders. "There's a big buck—the fellows call him Zeus—an eight-pointer. I was out here early Friday morning and saw him, but before I could get a shot, something spooked him."

"I'm sure you'll get him this morning," Millie said. His fingertips massaged her shoulder, and she cringed inwardly.

"Damn right I will. And I can't wait to see the look on Bettendorf's face when I show up with the carcass of his buck strapped across the hood of his truck."

He whistled tunelessly as they rode through the inky darkness. "How can you tell where we're going?" she asked, peering through the windshield. "There are no road signs, and it's so dark, I'm hopelessly lost."

"It's just up here, where the road forks," Russell said. "If you go to the left, that's the road to the dock; to the right is where we're going." A hundred yards later, he turned the steering wheel sharply to the right, and several hundred yards later, he pulled the truck off the road. The headlights illuminated a path cutting through the tree line.

He cut the engine and jumped out of the cab. Millie joined him as he pulled the first rifle from the truck bed.

"Where—"

He clamped a hand hard across her mouth. "Quiet, goddamn it," he whispered. "You'll spook the damn deer."

She nodded her understanding, and he removed his hand. "Now listen, because I'm not going to explain it again." His voice was a harsh whisper. He pointed at a towering live oak across the meadow. "The stand is in that pine tree just up there by the oak. You can come with me, but you don't say a word, don't move, don't breathe until I give you the nod. Okay?"

"Okay," she whispered.

He sat down on the tailgate and pulled a flask from the inside pocket of his jacket and took a swig.

Picking up the rifle, he jammed three cartridges into the magazine before turning it right-side up again. He yanked the lever down and propped it beside him before taking another swig of bourbon. "See how I did that?"

He demonstrated the aiming process and blabbed endlessly about the trigger and firing. Finally, he handed her the rifle. "Got that?"

Millie took the rifle and cocked it. "Like this?"

"Don't point it at me, goddamn it!" He nearly knocked the rifle from her hands. "Didn't that useless father of yours teach you anything? Never point a loaded weapon at somebody unless you mean to fire it."

She took exactly five steps backward, her heart pounding. The words she heard in her head weren't Russell's but instead, her dear, sweet papa's.

"That's the girl, Millie," he'd said. "Plant your feet wide to absorb the shock of the recoil. Sight it. Hold your breath. Pull down steadily on the trigger."

Russell was tipping the flask up to his lips. His eyes widened in disbelief. Millie held her breath and pulled.

The blast echoed across the field and knocked her onto the ground. Slumbering birds rose up, squawking from the treetops, but Millie was momentarily deafened. She stood up, her ears ringing, knees shaking badly, her hands still trembling.

The minutes ticked away slowly. Finally, she forced herself to walk back to the truck. The single shot knocked Russell onto his back in the bed of the truck. The silver flask, her engagement gift to him, was still clutched in his hands. She picked it up and tucked it into the waistband of her slacks. Somehow, she managed to push his body backward far enough to close the tailgate.

Millie slid behind the wheel of the truck and clutched the steering wheel with both hands, trying to still the waves of nausea and panic.

The first few purplish-pink streaks of sunlight broke over the distant treetops. It was nearly dawn. She had to get back to the house. Finally, when her hands quit shaking, she pulled out the flask and drank the last few swallows of bourbon.

She was searching for the cap when out of the corner of her eye, she saw movement. As she watched, wide-eyed, a buck emerged from the tree line. His rack was so magnificent it seemed like he might topple over from the weight of it. He walked slowly into the emerging daylight, swung his head in the direction of the truck and, for just a moment, seemed to be staring directly at her. Two seconds passed. The buck turned his muzzle upward, alerted to something. Finally, with a swish of his white tail, he bounded back into the tree line, back to safety.

"Goodbye, Zeus," Millie whispered.

Swallowing her fears, Millie gripped the steering wheel to head back to the mansion. Just as she was about to pull onto the main road, she heard a car coming and stopped, just short of the intersection. It was the roadster! She dove for the floor, praying she wouldn't be noticed, and by the time she pulled herself back to a seated position, she saw Josephine's dark hair whipping in the breeze, and Gardiner, upright in the passenger seat, beside his sister.

She felt a deep wave of longing and regret—and something else—as the car passed. And then Millie squared her shoulders and drove back toward Shellhaven. She allowed herself to feel nothing. Except relief.

82

....

Brooke stood up and kicked off her shoes. She unzipped the sleeveless black sheath dress she'd worn to the funeral and pulled it off over her head. "Who's up for a swim?" she asked.

Lizzie and Felicia jumped to their feet and immediately began to strip.

"Come on, Marie," Lizzie urged. "There's a first time for everything."

"Yeah, Mom," Brooke said, reaching down to help her mother stand.

"Oh, my goodness." Marie giggled. "I'm too old for this nonsense." But she turned around to allow her daughter to unzip her chic black silk dress, then folded it neatly and placed it on top of the basket with the wine bottles.

"I'll just swim in my bra and panties," she said.

"Nuh-uh. No way," Felicia said. "Skinny-dipping means naked."

"As a jaybird," Brooke agreed, tugging at the back of her mother's bra.

"Y'all going in without me?" Varina struggled to get out of the lawn chair.

"Auntie Vee! Of course we're not going without you." Felicia and Lizzie each took Varina by the arm. She stood, and her fingers fumbled as she tried to work the buttons on her blouse.

"Let me," Felicia said, and a few minutes later, the old lady stood naked and beaming up at the full moon overhead.

By unspoken agreement, the five joined hands and walked slowly toward the waves, pausing as the warm ocean lapped at their ankles, wading farther in until the water was neck-high on the tiny nonagenarian Varina.

"Ooh, this feels so good," Varina squealed. "But don't let go, y'all. You know I can't swim. I'm afraid that tide will pull me clean out to sea, and I'll end up naked in some country where they don't even speak English."

"We've got you," Lizzie promised, clutching Varina by the elbow.

The old woman let the water sweep her off her feet, and for a few minutes she floated, bobbing tranquilly in the gentle waves, until one swept her under and she emerged, sputtering and coughing, then giggling at the sheer absurdity of the situation.

It was nearing midnight as the women, laughing and talking softly, finally made their way back to the Packard.

It took two tries, but finally the engine turned over, and Marie carefully backed the car onto the pavement. They were passing the lighthouse when Lizzie tapped Varina on the arm.

"Varina, do you ever think about that night? The night y'all skinny-dipped and then slept at the lighthouse keeper's cottage?"

"Hmm?" Varina yawned. "Sometimes I do. Other times it seems like everything that happened that night and the next day was all a dream, it was so long ago. I miss my old friends Ruth and Millie. And now Josephine. Can't hardly believe I'm the last one here."

Lizzie gave her a conspiratorial look. "Since everybody else is dead now, it wouldn't hurt, would it, if you told us where Russell Strickland is? I mean, it would make such a powerful ending to my magazine story if we knew."

"Hush!" Felicia said fiercely. "She doesn't want to think about that. Or talk about it."

"It's all right, honey," Varina said. "I don't reckon it matters anymore. Maybe it would give C. D. peace to know it."

"You really don't have to tell us," Marie assured her.

"No. I think it will be like finally owning my own story," Varina said. "Go on down the road here a little ways, Marie, then turn like you're going to the dock. When you come to the two oaks that look like they've grown together, right before the road to the dock, you take a right at that fork, and you keep going until you see the creek running in front of you."

Marie drove slowly, following Varina's directions until the pavement ran out, and they were on a narrow shell road that grew narrower still, and darker, with the thick oak canopy overhead nearly blocking out the moonlight.

Varina peered into the inky night. "I hadn't been back here since that night. We all swore we'd never come near here again."

"It's okay," Marie assured her. "You don't have to do this. I'll back out of here, and we'll go on back to the house."

"No," Varina said stubbornly. "It's right up here. See that break in the trees? Stop there."

Marie cut the engine but left the headlights on. The warm night air folded in on them like a blanket. They heard the insistent thrum of cicadas and the croaks of tree frogs. From somewhere overhead, a pair of owls hooted from the tops of opposing trees.

A swarm of stinging gnats descended upon them, and soon the women were frantically slapping and trying to wave them away.

"This is the place," Varina said solemnly. She opened the car door and stepped out, clinging to the side of the car for balance. The others followed suit, with Felicia taking her great-aunt's arm.

"Just a little ways up here," Varina said. Her steps quickened, and in two minutes they stood in a clearing dominated by an imposing oyster shell mound.

"This is where we put him," Varina said. "Nobody else on the island would come back here. It's an Indian mound, you see."

"Geechees are superstitious about Indian things," Felicia whispered. "When I was a kid, we used to dare each other to come back here, but nobody ever would because it was supposed to be haunted."

Varina stared at the shell mound, then turned her back to it. "No," she said firmly. "Not haunted. Not anymore." She turned to Marie. "I'm ready to go home now, please."

83

....

Kavanaugh Park was a lush, green enclave of oaks, magnolias, and head-high azaleas a short walk from Brooke's childhood home in Ardsley Park. She'd dropped Henry off at Marie's house, then bought a picnic lunch at Back in the Day, a nearby bakery and restaurant. Now she sat on a bench under the shade of an oak tree and checked her phone for the tenth time in as many minutes.

He was late. She'd texted Pete earlier in the week, asking him to meet her in the park where she and the neighborhood kids had romped and played as children. It was the same park Marie liked to walk to, back in the days when Henry agreed to sit placidly in a stroller, something he rarely agreed to these days.

Would Pete show up? His return text had been a terse, three-word reply.

See U there.

Her stomach was in knots, her pulse racing. She'd dressed with care that morning, trying to look casual but pretty, sexy but not desperate. It was hot. Of course it was hot. This was June in Savannah. She could feel her mascara already starting to run, and the concealer she'd painstakingly applied to the still-healing scar on her cheek was melting. What had she been thinking when she'd planned this ridiculous affair? She should have met him in a restaurant, or better yet, a bar, where she could have soothed her nerves with a drink. She found a paper napkin and blotted her face with it, then glanced at her phone again. He was ten minutes late. Maybe he'd had problems calling a cab from the airport. Or maybe he was having second thoughts and had caught an earlier flight back to Alaska. If he was having second thoughts, so was she.

She twisted the platinum-and-diamond ring on her right ring finger. Marie had found it in a box of jewelry in Josephine's room and insisted she take it. "If you and Pete don't get together, you can at least wear it on your left hand and tell people you used to be married."

"Ha-ha, Mom. Good one," Brooke had said. But the ring was stunning, and let's face it, nobody else had offered her a diamond ring lately.

Where the hell was Pete? Why hadn't he called? Her cell phone hadn't rung. Really, it was so thoughtless. Hashtag rude. She clutched the bag and decided she would leave. It would serve him right. Maybe she wouldn't tell him he had a son. Maybe he didn't deserve a child as wonderful as Henry.

She saw a yellow cab pass by on Forty-fifth Street, slow down, then drive past. A few minutes later, the car was back. It rolled slowly past, then stopped again. The back door opened, and Pete climbed out. Brooke jumped up and waved as the cab sped away.

The Grizzly Adams beard was gone, and his straight, square jaw was back. Her pulse did funny things as he drew closer. He'd gotten sunburned in Florida. His smile seemed self-conscious. Well, maybe hers was too.

"Hey!" he said, reaching the bench.

"Hey," she said, leaning in to kiss his cheek. He drew back a moment as though he were startled.

Bad idea, bad idea, bad idea. The kiss made her look anxious or desperate. Or both.

"Let's sit," she said finally. "How was the conference?"

"Great," Pete said. "Our paper was a huge success, and it's been accepted by a pretty prestigious journal."

"And the job interviews? How did they go?" Oh God. She sounded like his mother. Next thing you knew she'd be asking if he'd been eating vegetables and flossing.

He nodded. "They went better than I'd expected. The wildlife foundation position would be a perfect fit for me. I'd be based on the Georgia coast, but they'd want me to travel as far south as Amelia Island, Florida, and as far north as Daufuskie, in South Carolina. Pay's good, and they're establishing a relationship with the University of Georgia Marine Institute, so I'd have access to lab facilities."

"That does sound nice," Brooke said, trying to sound noncommittal.

"I'm not the only applicant, but I'd say there's an 85 percent chance I'll get an offer."

"You said there was another position too?"

"Yeah. It's with the U.S. Fish and Wildlife Service, and that one would be based out west, in the Sierras. I could continue my work on migration patterns, which would be sweet. The guy who interviewed me told me in confidence that I'm pretty much their number-one choice."

"Is there a downside to that one?" Brooke asked.

"I'm worried about the political situation," Pete admitted. "Conservation isn't exactly a big priority with the current administration. If there are layoffs or budget cuts, I'd be the first one to be let go."

Brooke tried to clandestinely wipe her sweaty palms with the crumpled paper napkin she still clutched in her fist. "So," she said cheerfully, "would you want to go back out west?"

Pete's gaze was level and direct. "That would depend on where I stand with you, Brooke. I mean, I've been thinking about this ever since I saw you last week. I still have no idea how you feel about us. I mean, give me a clue here, will you?"

He looked down at her hands and frowned. He gestured toward her hand. "What the hell? Is that an engagement ring? You got engaged since I last saw you?"

"No! I mean, no, it's not an engagement ring. It's a gift from my mom, who just inherited it, which is another long story."

She took a deep breath and reached into her pocket. She handed him a color photo of Henry as an infant, his hair downy, eyelashes thick and lush.

"This is Henry at six months, right after he started sitting up. I named him that after my grandfather, my mom's father, who we called Pops. He died before I was born. You want to know something funny? Last week, I found out that Granny had a secret affair with her best friend's older brother. His name was Gardiner Bettendorf. It was at the very beginning of the war. She'd been in love with him most of her life but never dared let anybody know. They had a one-night stand, and then his plane was shot down over France."

Pete looked puzzled.

"Granny got pregnant that night. But by the time her letter arrived, telling Gardiner he was going to be a father, he was already dead. Being an unwed mother back then, in her social circles, would have been unthinkable. So she married another man, Henry Updegraff, my pops."

He was still looking deeply confused.

"Here," she said, thrusting the bag at him. "I brought us lunch. Have a sandwich. They make these amazing sandwiches at Back in the Day. From their own bread. There are cookies too." She was babbling, and she knew it.

He unwrapped a sandwich and took a bite, chewing slowly. "Why are you telling me all this? I mean, it's interesting, but what's it got to do with us?"

"Take a good look at that picture of Henry, please. Tell me what you see."

"I'm not sure. I mean, I guess he looks like you. He has your lips."

She sighed. "And he has his father's eyes. And nose. And jaw. Henry's yours, Pete. He's your son."

Pete's sandwich dropped onto the bag on his lap. "You said the other day it was some guy who wasn't in your life anymore."

"Which was true. I let you slip out of my life, Pete. You were so far away, and things were so new and raw between us. You were so excited about your work in Alaska, I told myself I couldn't ask you to give that up and come back here. You said it yourself, remember? A once-in-a-lifetime opportunity. I thought you would have resented the baby and resented me."

"No!" Pete said. "Goddamn it! You had my baby and you didn't even tell me?"

Brooke bit her lip. "I know now how wrong I was. You had a right to know. And you have a right to know your son now, if that's what you want."

Pete's eyes narrowed. His voice was hoarse, choky. "You mean you didn't want me to come back when you found out about the baby, isn't that it? I would have come back. I would have been here for you, no question. Don't you know that about me? Do you think so little of me that I would resent you or our child?"

"It's not you that I think so little of, it's me," Brooke said, looking away. "When I figured out I was pregnant, I wouldn't allow myself to believe that you would want me. Who would? I was a mess. And now I am a mess with baggage. A kid."

Pete stared down at the photo of Henry.

"I'm telling you about him now, Pete, because I finally realize what a horrible thing I did. I hope it's not too late. Henry needs a father. He deserves a family, whatever that means."

She reached out and touched the hand holding the photo. "I'm so sorry I screwed this up. Seeing you now, all my careful reasoning doesn't hold up. It never did."

Pete got up and slammed the bag lunch into the trash. He whirled around to face her. "So what am I supposed to do with this information? You spring this on me out of nowhere. 'Hey, guess what? You've got a three-year-old son.' What the hell, Brooke?"

"You do whatever you want with this information," she said, her voice strained. "I can't say I'm sorry enough, I know. But I couldn't keep this secret any longer. It should never have been a secret."

He paced back and forth in front of the bench, staring down at the photo of Henry. "What time is it?"

"Quarter to one," she said.

"I gotta go," he said abruptly. "My flight's gonna leave soon. You think I can catch a cab or an Uber or something from here?"

"I'll drive you," Brooke said. "My car's parked at my mom's house, right around the corner."

. . .

He kept staring down at the photo of Henry on the short walk to Marie's house. "My son," he said, his voice full of wonder. "Who is he? I mean, I saw him at the airport, for what, thirty minutes, and he wouldn't even look at me for most of that time. Maybe you could catch me up on the first three years of his life. What's he like?"

"He's a funny little guy," she said, ignoring the sarcasm. "He walked at exactly nine months. I thought he'd never sleep through the night. He loves to be read to. He has a favorite cartoon, this heinous Canadian kid, Caillou. He adores Caillou. He's crazy smart, Pete. He asks a million questions. He's a climber. He broke his arm climbing on a jungle gym in the spring. He's almost potty trained, but I think he gets a subversive thrill from pooping in his pants at the most inappropriate times. Please talk to me," she pleaded. "Tell me how to fix this. Tell me what to say."

He gave her a long, steady look. "If you don't already know what to say, then it's goodbye." He started to walk away, his long legs eating up concrete. He stopped suddenly and turned to her. "I'd like to keep the picture of our son, if that's okay."

"You're really going back to Alaska without seeing him?" she asked.

He stopped walking.

"Henry's at my mom's house. Right up there." She pointed at the two-story brick house two doors down from where they were standing.

"What if I want to do more than just see him occasionally?" Pete asked, his jaw still set in anger.

Brooke held her breath for a moment, wondering what that meant. "Are you talking about some kind of joint custody thing?"

Pete shrugged. "Maybe. I mean, I just learned I have a son five minutes ago. It's gonna take time to figure this out."

"Whatever you want," Brooke said softly. "Henry needs a dad. He needs you in his life. I know that now. But I guess how that happens is up to you."

They were standing on the front porch at Marie's house. Brooke's hand was on the doorknob. "Are you seriously thinking of taking the job out west?" She was holding her breath, waiting for him to say something, when the door opened.

"Hey," Marie said, looking from her daughter to Pete. "I thought I heard voices out here."

Brooke exhaled slowly. "Mom, this is . . . Henry's dad. Pete, this is my mom, Marie."

Marie smiled and held out her hand. "So good to finally meet you, Henry's dad. FYI, Henry's up from his nap. Do you two want to come inside?"

"Nice to meet you too," Pete said, shaking her hand. "Could we, uh, have a minute or two in private?"

Marie closed the door softly, and Brooke felt herself sag against the frame. She realized with a start that this was the same doorstep where she'd gotten her first goodnight kiss after her first car date, at fifteen.

"Tell me what you want, Brooke," Pete said, looking directly into her eyes. "And don't make it just about Henry. Do you want me to stay?" He traced the scar on her cheek with a fingertip. "What happened here?"

"Another long story," Brooke said. "Resulting from a near-fatal lack of good judgment. Could you please repeat that last question?"

"Do. You. Want. Me. To. Stay?"

This time she was ready with an answer. "Yeah," she said softly. "Yeah, I think it would be good if you could stick around to see what happens next. Do you think maybe you could kiss me now? Like, for old times' sake?"

He put a hand on either side of her face and did as she asked, kissing her with a sweet intensity that left her aching for everything she'd missed.

"Okay," he said finally. "I'll move to the coast. We'll figure us out. And the dad thing."

"I hope you know what you're getting yourself into," Brooke said.

The door opened a crack, and they hastily pulled apart. Henry stepped onto the porch, dressed in his favorite SpongeBob T-shirt and a sagging pair of pull-ups. "I pooped," he announced proudly.

Brooke scooped up her son and handed him over to Pete. "About that dad thing . . ."

Epilogue

....

October 2018

Moonlight dappled the water, and a stiff wind rattled the fronds of palm trees and swirled sand around the ankles of the five women standing at the water's edge.

Felicia tightened the blanket draped around her elderly aunt's shoulders. It had been an unusually chilly October on Talisa, with temperatures dipping into the forties and high winds buffeting the fragile dunes.

"Are you warm enough, Auntie?" she asked.

"There's an extra blanket in the back of the Packard," Lizzie offered.

"Don't y'all be fussin' over me now," Varina said. "I've lived this long, and I haven't frozen or blown away yet."

"Well, I for one am chilled to the bone," Marie said with an exaggerated shiver. "I know we agreed to do this every time we're together on a full moon, but nobody said anything about getting frostbite in the process."

Brooke gestured at the quilt, beach chairs, and picnic basket they'd set up a few yards away. "Don't be such a whiny baby, Mom. We've got hot toddies in the thermoses and plenty of beach towels."

"And what about that fire I built?" Lizzie asked. She'd spent hours digging a pit in the sand and circling it with bricks left over from the latest island restoration project. They'd hauled down a load of wood in the beach cart, and now the flames leaped high into the frigid night air, crackling and sending up showers of sparks.

"I think we should wait until the weather warms up again in the spring," Marie said. "After all, we didn't swim last month when you had court in Brunswick, Brooke, and it seems to me that Felicia was off island in August, visiting her new beau."

"No, ma'am," Varina said firmly. "Y'all know what today's date is?"

"It's October 21," Felicia said.

"Same exact date as the first time, the night after Millie's engagement party," Varina said solemnly. She pointed up at the star-shattered night. "You know what that is? It's a hunter moon, just like that night it all started. We only get one of those a year. Might be the last one I ever see."

"Don't talk like that," Felicia said.

"It's the truth. I'm ninety-one. Nobody in my family ever lived this long. I could go tonight or tomorrow, and I'm at peace with that," Varina said.

"Why is this so important to you, Varina?" Lizzie asked. "I can't believe you don't want to forget this date and everything associated with it. What happened to you—"

"Is in the past. And that's why I cast that ugliness out of my heart. I'm not letting it fester there like a poison-filled boil," Varina said. She grasped Lizzie's hand tightly and gazed out at the moon in wonder. "You know I wouldn't ever say that man's name after that night. I couldn't. But when I woke up to this sunny morning and realized what today is, it struck me from out of nowhere. I can't hate him no more. He is long dead, cold and in the grave, and I am alive and more blessed than I deserve. I got me a son I never even knew about. I got my own little home right here on this island, got family and friends . . ."

Marie nodded and grasped her daughter's hand. Wordlessly, Brooke reached for Felicia's hand.

"His name was Russell Strickland," Varina said. She repeated the name, enunciating and pausing between each syllable. "Russ. Sell. Strick. Land."

Without prompting, the women repeated the name.

"Russell Strickland is powerless over me," Varina said. She shrugged out of the blanket and took one tentative step into the water, and then another, letting out an involuntary yip of shock as the cold water reached her knees and then waist. She turned once, looking over her shoulder at the four women, standing naked on the shore.

"Y'all coming?"

1. How does the prologue set the tone for the rest of the novel? What kind of story were you expecting after the prologue? Did the novel turn out to be the kind of story you thought it would be, or were you surprised?

2. Andrews describes the beautiful island of Talisa and Shellhaven, Josephine's crumbling house, in an extremely evocative, vivid way where you can easily imagine yourself there. Have you ever been anywhere like Talisa? If you had the opportunity, would you want to live on a wild, remote island?

3. What kind of parallels do you see between Brooke and her grandmother Millie, both in their personalities and in the ways their lives have played out? Do you think that Josephine saw those similarities as well?

4. On page 45, when Brooke is talking about how she ran away from her own wedding, Josephine makes a comment about pride, "foolish, foolish pride." Where can you see Josephine's own "foolish pride" throughout the novel? Do you think it hindered her in her relationships with other people? Why or why not?

5. Over the course of the novel, many shocking truths are uncovered. Which revelation surprised you the most? Which did you have an inkling of before you knew for sure?

6. How did the dual timelines—one in Josephine's present and one in her past, as a young High Tide Club girl—affect your reading experience? How do you think that one timeline informed the other?

7. How do you think this novel demonstrates the effects class and race can have on friendships? Where do you see this playing out in Varina's friendship with the rest of the girls? How do you think things might have been different if Varina were wealthy and white, like them?

Discussion
Questions

8. Much of *The High Tide Club* is about the complicated and wonderful relationships between women—daughters, mothers, and friends. Who are the women in your life who you turn to when you need a second opinion or a shoulder to cry on?

9. In the novel, Brooke has a difficult time figuring out what she thinks of Josephine, who had such strong, loving friendships in her past but has become so prickly in her old age. On page 131, Brooke says, "I give up. Do you like anybody? Trust anybody?" What do you think—does Josephine like anybody anymore? If not, what events in life do you think led to her distrust of people?

10. How did the ending of the book leave you feeling? Surprised? Shocked? Did you guess the identity of the murderer, or were you completely surprised? What do you think is going to happen for Brooke and her family in the future?

Turn the page for a sneak peek at
Mary Kay Andrews's next novel

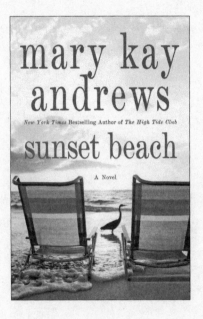

Available May 2019

1

Sunset Beach, April 2018

Drue turned the key in the ignition and the white Bronco's engine gave a dispirited cough, and then nothing.

Come on, OJ," Drue muttered, trying again. This time the engine turned over. She gave it some gas and the motor roared to life.

"Thanks, babe." She gave the cracked vinyl dashboard an encouraging pat, then shifted into reverse and eased her foot onto the accelerator. The motor gave a strangled wheeze and cut off again. Now every single indicator on the control panel began blinking red.

She tried again, but the third time was not the charm. The engine caught briefly, the Bronco's battered chassis shuddered, then fell still.

"Noooooo," she moaned.

She glanced down at her watch. She now had fifteen minutes to get downtown to work. "No way," she muttered.

Back when life was good, when she was living in Fort Lauderdale, she would have taken an Uber or called a friend for a lift when the 1995 Bronco she'd bought off Craigslist was having what Drue thought of as PMS. But she hadn't exactly had time to make friends since moving back to Florida's west coast, and she no longer had a viable credit card for Uber, or even viable credit, for that matter.

Drue had a vague memory of seeing city buses lumbering past on nearby Gulf Boulevard. She pulled her phone from her backpack, found the transit authority website and schedule, and determined that with any luck, she just might catch a bus that might get her to the downtown St. Petersburg offices of Campbell, Coxe and Kramner in the next thirty minutes. Which would make her late for her first day of work.

She started walking. It was barely eight-thirty, and only April, but the temperature already hovered in the mid-eighties, and within two blocks of leaving her house, her cotton tank top was damp with perspiration and her right knee was throbbing.

Shit. She should have gone back to the house and put on the tight elastic brace the surgeon had given her. In fact, she should have been wearing it anyway, even if she hadn't had to walk five blocks. But the damn thing was so hot. The elastic chafed her skin and gave her a rash, so she left it at home more times than she wore it.

Drue gritted her teeth against the pain and kept walking. She was on Gulf Boulevard now, the busy north–south thoroughfare that threaded through all the tiny beach towns before eventually making a sharp right turn at Treasure Island Causeway, heading east toward downtown St. Pete. A clutch of giggling teenage girls, spring breakers, probably, dressed in bikini tops and microscopic neon-bright shorts with the waistbands rolled down to their navels, approached on the sidewalk, headed in the opposite direction, and made an elaborate show of sidestepping her.

She heard a quavery voice behind her.

"Excuse me, darling." She turned her head to see an elderly man, his bony bare chest glistening with sweat, power past, pumping small dumbbells in each hand.

She squinted and saw, just half a block ahead, the shaded bus shelter. Thank God. She wasn't sure if she could walk much farther. Half a block, though.

That, she could do. She picked up the pace, trying to ignore the red-hot stabbing pain in her knee.

Brüiing, brüinnng, a bike's bell and then a booming woman's voice: "On your left!"

She stumbled over her flip-flop and toppled onto the grassy verge just in time to avoid being mowed down by a white-haired octogenarian wearing wraparound sunglasses and a Tampa Bay Rays sun visor furiously pedaling past on an adult tricycle.

"Hey!" Drue yelled after her. "Get on the bike path."

"Up yours," the woman called, turning around briefly to flip her the bird.

As she struggled to her feet, she saw, almost in slow motion, the city bus passing her by. She winced in pain, but also at the ad emblazoned along the side of the bus.

SLIP AND FALL? GIVE BRICE A CALL! The ad was accompanied by a five-foot-tall airbrush-enhanced color portrait of W. Brice Campbell, arms crossed defiantly, his chiseled chin jutting pugnaciously, a stance Drue knew all too well.

The bus slowed momentarily at the bus stop. The air brakes whooshed. "Stay there," Drue muttered. "Stay right there." She broke into her current version of a run, a lopsided, sorry, limping affair.

A young Hispanic woman stepped off the bus, turned, and waved goodbye to the driver.

"Hey," Drue yelled breathlessly, closing the gap, now maybe only three buslengths away. She waved her arms over her head. "Hey!"

The woman turned and gave the stranger a hesitant smile. "Hey."

The bus's brakes whooshed again and it started to move.

"Tell him to stop," Drue cried. "Tell him to wait."

But it was too late. The bus picked up speed. It moved on. The woman stood by the bus shelter. She was dressed in a gray and white uniform smock, her name, Sonia, embroidered above her left breast.

"Sorry," she said softly, as Drue approached, limping badly. "Are you okay?"

Drue grasped the back of the bench as she tried to regain her breath. The bench was painted blue and white, with the Campbell, Coxe and Kramner signature logo superimposed across Brice Campbell's visage. HAVE A WRECK? WE'LL GET YOUR CHECK!

"No," Drue managed, as she collapsed onto the bench. She jumped up immediately, gingerly extracting a half-inch wood splinter protruding from her right butt cheek. "No. Definitely. Not. Okay." She looked down at the screen-printed face of Brice W. Campbell. Her new boss. Her long-lost father, and as always, a major pain in the ass.

A job in his law firm had been the very last thing Drue had wanted from her long-estranged father. But what choice did she have? That five-second midair kiteboard collision three months earlier, and her mother's subsequent death, only reinforced the fact that she no longer had any reason to stay in Fort Lauderdale.

Drue had been adrift, self-medicating with tequila and Advil and wallowing in self-pity on the day of her mother's funeral. As she was leaving the memorial service, with the bronze urn containing Sherri's remains tucked under her arm, she'd been shocked to spot a well-dressed businessman standing uneasily at the back of the church.

At first, she wasn't even absolutely sure it was really him. His hair was longer, touching the collar of his open-neck shirt, and flecked with silver. He was tanned and slim, and in his expensive tailored blazer and sockless Gucci loafers looked distinctly out of place in the former fast-food restaurant turned Fortress for All Faiths Chapel of Prayer.

She approached him warily. "Dad?"

"Hi," he'd said softly, giving her an awkward hug.

She'd endured the embrace with what she thought was admirable forbearance.

"What are you doing here?"

He shifted from one foot to the other. "Why wouldn't I be here?"

"I mean, how did you know? That mom died? I didn't even put an obituary in the paper until today."

"Sherri called me. To tell me she was sick. And I asked the hospice people to let me know . . . when it happened." He glanced around the church, which was nearly empty now. "Look, can we go somewhere else to talk about this?"

"Like where?" Drue wasn't about to let him off that easy. Twenty years ago, he'd shipped his sullen teenage daughter across Florida, from St. Pete back here to Lauderdale, choosing peace with his second wife and her obnoxious sons over loyalty to his only daughter. He'd dutifully sent the birthday cards and child support checks right up until her eighteenth birthday, but she hadn't laid eyes on him since that boiling hot summer afternoon so long ago. She wasn't about to let him waltz in here today and play the grieving dad and ex-spouse.

"I thought maybe we could go to lunch somewhere." His blue-gray eyes took in her frumpy black dress, the only remotely funeral ready dress she owned, and the too-large black pumps, which she'd appropriated from Sherri's closet.

"Why?"

He let out a long, aggravated sigh. "Why? Because your mom is gone and I'm now your only living relative. And because there are some business matters we need to discuss. Okay? Can you just cut me some slack and go to lunch? Or do you really need to keep busting my balls for the rest of my life?"

She shrugged. "I guess I could do lunch. Where do you want to go?"

"I heard there's a bistro on Las Olas that has great mussels."

"Taverna." Why was she not surprised that he'd chosen the most exclusive, expensive restaurant in town?

Outside, in the parking lot, Brice pointed a key fob at a black Mercedes sedan and clicked it. Drue went to the backseat and opened the door.

He stood by the driver's side, looking puzzled. "You're getting in the backseat?"

"No," Drue said, carefully stretching the seat belt across the bronze urn. "Mom is."

When the waitress brought their drinks Drue knocked back half her margarita in one gulp.

Brice sipped his martini and rearranged the silverware on the tabletop.

"Can I ask you something without your getting pissed at me?"

"Maybe."

He pointed at her right leg, with the knee ensconced in the hideous brace.

"What happened there?"

"I had a kiteboarding accident. Right after Mom got diagnosed."

"So you're still into that? Guess it wasn't a phase after all, huh?"

Kiteboarding had been a major source of friction between Drue and Brice and her step-mother. Joan had objected to the cost of her board and kite (although it was money Drue earned from working at a surf shop), her kiteboarding friends (an admittedly motley looking crew), and especially, her obsession with the sport—to the detriment of her already mediocre grades.

Drue chewed the inside of her cheek. "Definitely not a phase. How is Joan, by the way?"

He picked the olive from his drink, chewed, and smiled bitterly. "Let's see. She soaked me for a waterfront house, a new car, and attorney's fees to keep both Kyler and Kayson out of prison. Last I heard she'd moved up the marital food chain and married an orthopedic surgeon. So, I'd say she's doing great."

"So you two split up? Sorry to hear that."

He sipped his martini. "No, you're not."

"That's true. She never liked me, and the feeling was mutual."

He started to say something, stopped, shook his head, and took another sip of his martini.

"You said you had some business to discuss with me?" Drue prompted.

"That's right." He reached into the inside pocket of his blazer and brought out a key ring with a tacky pink plastic flamingo fob. Two keys dangled from the ring. He slid the key ring across the table toward his daughter.

"What's this?"

"It's the key to Coquina Cottage."

"Nonni and Papi's house? The old place on Sunset Beach? I thought Mom sold it after Nonni died."

"She almost did, but in the end, she decided to keep it. I think maybe she thought one day the two of you would move back and live there. Anyway, it's yours now."

Drue picked up the key ring and turned it over and over. "You're serious? For real? Like, I own Papi's cottage?"

"You do," Brice said. "Before you get too excited, though, I should warn you it's in pretty rough shape. The last tenant lived there for six or seven years, and he was kind of a hoarder. He always paid his rent on time and never had any complaints about the place, so I sort of let things slide. It wasn't until last year, after the hurricane damaged the roof and the old guy moved out, that we realized how bad things had gotten."

Drue's eyes filled with unexpected tears. "Mom never said a word. All those years, she drove crappy secondhand cars and we lived in shithole apartments. She could have sold that place—it's right on the Gulf, right? I bet it was worth a lot of money. I can't believe she hung on to Papi's house."

"Your mom was never the sentimental type, as you know, but I think she regarded the cottage as her legacy to you. It was the one thing of value in her life. Well, that and her daughter."

Not trusting herself to speak, Drue could only stare down at the keys.

"What are your plans now?" Brice asked.

"I don't know," she admitted. "Things are kind of up in the air right now."

"Sherri said you've been waitressing at a bar?"

"That's right."

His raised eyebrow spoke volumes.

"And . . . no romantic ties keeping you here in Fort Lauderdale?"

She scowled. Since Trey, her faithless boyfriend, had been a no-show at the funeral, she'd already relegated him to ex-boyfriend status. "Are you deliberately gloating over the fact that I'm thirty-six and have a shitty job and no life?"

He raised his hands in surrender. "I was going to offer you a job, but obviously that's a deeply offensive move on my part."

"A job? Doing what?"

"Working at the law firm. We've affiliated with half a dozen boutique personal injury firms in the Southeast in the past year. Business is crazy good. Another firm in town just poached my most senior intake associate. I'm really short-handed."

"No thanks," Drue said firmly. "I have no interest in moving back to St. Pete and zero interest in the law."

"You mean, zero interest in working for me."

Her eyes met his. "That too. Sorry. I mean, I appreciate the offer. And your coming over for Mom's funeral. And letting me know about the cottage. Thanks. I really mean it." She looked down at her watch. "Can you get the check now? I've got to work tonight."

He let out a long sigh. "You're as goddamn stubborn as she was. More, even."

"I'll take that as a compliment," Drue said.

Bill Miles

Mary Kay Andrews is the *New York Times* bestselling author of *The Beach House Cookbook, The Weekenders, Beach Town, Save the Date, Christmas Bliss, Ladies' Night, Spring Fever, Summer Rental, The Fixer Upper, Deep Dish, Savannah Breeze, Blue Christmas, Hissy Fit, Little Bitty Lies,* and *Savannah Blues.* A former journalist for *The Atlanta Journal-Constitution,* she lives in Atlanta, Georgia.

I've Found My Keys, Now Where's My Car?

Florence Littauer

Author of *Personality Plus*

Thomas Nelson Publishers

NASHVILLE

Published in Nashville, Tennessee, by Thomas Nelson Publishers, and distributed in Canada by Word Communications, Ltd., Richmond, British Columbia, and in the United Kingdom by Word (UK), Ltd., Milton Keynes, England.

Portions of this book were orginally published as *The Pursuit of Happiness* by Florence Littauer (Harvest House Publishers, 1981).

Scripture quotations designated KJV are from the *King James Version*.

Scripture quotations designated NIV are from *The Holy Bible: New International Version,* © 1973, 1978, 1984 by the International Bible Society. Used by permission of Zondervan Bible Publishers.

Scripture quotations designated TLB are from *The Living Bible,* © 1971 by Tyndale House Publishers, Wheaton, Illinois.

Scripture quotations designated NASB are from *The New American Standard Bible,* © The Lockman Foundation 1960, 1962, 1963, 1968, 1971, 1972, 1975, 1977.

Library of Congress Cataloging-in-Publication Data
Littauer, Florence, 1928- .
    [Make the tough times count]
    I've found my keys, now where's my car? / Florence Littauer
        p.   cm.
    Originally published under title: Make the tough times count. San Bernardino, CA: Here's Life Publishers, c1990.
        ISBN 0-7852-8185-1
        1. Littauer, Florence, 1928- . 2. Christian biography—United States. 3. Consolation. 4. Encouragement—Religious aspects—Christianity. 5. Christian life—1960- I. Title.
    [BR1725.L487A3 1994b]
    209'.2—dc20
    [B]   93-37370
                                                        CIP

Printed in the United States of America
98 97 96 95 94 — 7 6 5 4 3

One Mother to Remember

I lovingly dedicate this book to the memory of my mother and acknowledge she deserves far more credit than this account gives her.

While I looked for flashy faces and worldly wonders, my mother stood on the sidelines, patiently waiting for me to abandon my fitful grabs for glory. It was she who encouraged me to play hymns on the piano while she harmonized on the violin. Her sincere, Christian principles, her quiet and gentle spirit, and her devotion to motherhood prove the biblical admonition, "Bring up a child in the way he should go and when he is old, he will not depart from it."

Even thought we grew up during the Depression and had none of the furnishings and appliances that we take for granted today, Mother made the best of bad situations and helped us all to make the tough times count.

Other Books by Florence and Fred Littauer

THOMAS NELSON
Get a Life Without The Strife
Freeing Your Mind from Memories That Bind
The Promise of Healing

WORD BOOKS
Silver Boxes
Dare to Dream
Raising Christians Not Just Children
Your Personality Tree (also in video album)
Hope for Hurting Women
Looking for God in All the Right Places
Wake Up Women
Wake Up Men

FLEMING REVELL, BAKER BOOKS
Personality Plus (also available in French, German, Spanish)
Personality Puzzle (with Marita Littauer)

HARVEST HOUSE PUBLISHERS
Blow Away the Black Clouds
After Every Wedding Comes a Marriage
It Takes So Little to be Above Average
How to Get Along with Difficult People
Out of the Cabbage Patch

HUNTINGTON HOUSE
Personalities in Power

CLASS BOOKS
Christian Leaders and Speakers Seminar (tape, album, and manual)
The Best of Florence Littauer

For information on "Promise of Healing" recovery workshops conducted by Fred and Florence Littauer, please call 1-800-433-6633.

Contents

1

Lost
Keys

1994

Among the funny stories I tell about my life, losing my car in the seven-story parking garage is everyone's favorite. It was in the mid-60's in New Haven, Connecticut, when I went shopping at Macy's. I parked my car in the grim, gray garage which was so austere it made even the cars feel they'd been sentenced to prison. Oblivious to the dullness of my surroundings, I was happy; I was going shopping. A few hours later I emerged from that week's white sales laden with bundles. As I looked across the street to the garage a frightening fact came to mind! <u>You don't know where you left your car!</u> That thought so gripped me, I stopped in my tracks.

Gratefully a kind man happened upon me and asked, "Is there something wrong?"

"I've lost my car in the seven-story parking garage," I replied sadly.

Wanting to help, he queried, "What kind of car is it?"

"I don't know."

He was stunned. "You don't know what kind of car you drive?"

"Worse than that," I answered. "I have two cars and I don't know which one I drove today."

"You do have a problem!"

I told him what the two cars looked like and he suggested I find my keys so we could tell which car I had.

Now, if I lost something as big as a car, did I know where to find my keys? I tried to get into my handbag, but with all those bundles in my arms I could hardly move. My new friend offered to hold the packages. He was now committed. He couldn't abandon me.

My handbag was huge and full of assorted items, some of which had lived there so long they were close friends. To go through the bag piece-by-piece to locate the lost keys was more than I could do standing up, so I knelt down in the driveway and began emptying things out onto the curb. I found possessions I'd been missing for years. As I was lining up bottles and boxes on the curbstone, another man came along and asked the first man, "What's the lady doing in the gutter?"

"She's lost her car and she's looking for the keys."

"What kind of a car is it?"

"She doesn't know what kind of car she drives! Worse than that, she has two and she doesn't know which one she brought today."

"She does need help!"

By this time a group of ladies had joined us and were fascinated, watching me pull things out of my bag like a magician. Finally, under the debris of candy wrappers and crumpled kleenex, I found the keys—but I had both sets so it didn't solve the problem! I was so happy to locate the keys I held them up and proclaimed, "I've found my keys, now where's my car?"

The first man repeated, "She's found her keys, now where's her car?"

Some of the women helped me stuff everything back into my bag and off we went to find my car. We had so much fun parading through the seven-story parking garage and became such good friends that when we found my car on the fourth level in the corner I was ready to start a club and be president!

When I tell this story on the platform, I ask the audience if anyone has a large handbag, like mine. Women hold up huge bags all over the audience, and my husband picks out what he deems to be the gaudiest and the fullest. The audience loves to watch me pull things out and make ad-lib comments on each item. We have found the most unusual treasures anyone could imagine. Aside from the usual gum wrappers, used kleenex, make-up, and candy bars, I've pulled out sandwiches, baby bottles, diapers, aspirin, vitamins, panties, toys, a banana peel stuffed with paper napkins, loose dollar bills, broken sunglasses, a revolver, and even a plastic examining glove in the bag of a woman attending a gynecologists' convention.

At the first break, women come running up to me with their huge handbags and insist I forage through them, "Mine would have been better than the one you chose," they say. Also, they proudly tell me about losing their cars, keys, and even their children, hoping their story will be bad enough to be just as amusing.

One woman, Terry, told me she had a history of losing her car. On one particular day she was elated to find a parking spot right near the mall entrance, <u>easy to remember</u>, she thought. She didn't have to count rows, she only needed to remember to turn right out of the building and there was her car, first in the row. With this position fixed firmly in her mind she happily scurried off. When the day was over, and she was clutching her purchases, she headed for the garage. A banner day for Terry, she had her keys in her jacket pocket and knew where her car was. She wouldn't have to search for either of them!

So, off she went toward the garage. She turned right, opened the car door (she hadn't remembered leaving it unlocked), put her bundles on the backseat, and got in herself. She tried to push the key in, but it didn't seem to go. She jammed it in, but it just wouldn't fit. She had several keys on her chain left over from past cars and she tried each of them in vain. She was getting upset with the keys when she realized this car didn't smell like hers. It didn't even look like hers—in fact it was blue and hers was red!

As she jumped out to take another look the security cart drove by. "Stop, stop!" she cried out. "My car's been stolen and there's another one in its place!"

The guard calmly suggested she retrieve her packages and get in his cart. He told her he had an idea of where her car might be even though she reaffirmed that she had left it in that exact spot. He drove to the other end of the mall to an identical parking structure. They turned right at the entrance and there was her red car, first in the row.

"How did you know?" Terry asked the attendant.

"Because I do this several times a day," he replied. "You're not the first woman who doesn't know the difference between East and West."

When Terry told me this story she was so excited. "Imagine it. Here I was in the wrong car, with the wrong color, and the wrong smell, and I didn't know it until the keys wouldn't fit!" She then philosophized. "You can have your keys and still not have the right car."

Another woman, Sally, could hardly wait to tell me about the day she couldn't find her keys. She gave her usual glance over all the normal places she might have dropped them to no avail. In dramatic despair she went to plead with her husband, Sid, who was always her last resort. Sid never did anything the simple way, and Sally felt he made a big deal out of some of her errors.

True to her fears, Sid gave her a lecture. "I can't believe you've lost your keys again. You'd lose your head if it wasn't attached. The last time I let you take my keys you left them in the ignition while you went shopping. Do you remember that? Do you think there is a ghost of a chance that you could do any better today? Have you learned anything?"

Sally admitted she was a slow learner and promised to do better if he'd only give her his keys. Sid pulled them out of his back pocket. His keys were always in the same spot and he never lost them.

As soon as Sally drove away, she felt better. She'd taken the necessary medicine from Sid and had looked appropriately repentant. Now she could go shopping and have fun. Her last stop was the small local supermarket. The checkers all knew Sally because she was so friendly and made each one feel he was her best friend. Once home, she was unpacking her groceries when the phone rang. It was one of the checkers calling to see if Sally had lost her keys. They had found some shortly after she'd left.

Sally had no idea, so she looked in her huge handbag and was relieved to see her keys right on top. She thanked the man but assured him she had her keys.

At this point Sid came into the kitchen and asked for his keys. Hers were right there, but she panicked as she searched her bag for his and couldn't find them. Suddenly, a horrible thought occurred to her. She had started out with Sid's keys and somewhere along the line had found hers and switched. Then where were his?

As Sid stood watching, Sally emptied out her handbag onto the counter. Sid's keys weren't there. In a flash of brilliance Sally realized the keys at the store must be Sid's! She tried to flee out the door before Sid could lecture her but she did hear the parting words ringing out behind her. "I knew better than to trust you. That's the last time—the last time. You could die first before I ever give my keys to you again!"

Are you a little bit like me, or Terry, or Sally? Or are you more like Fred or Sid? Whether you are the one who loses keys, or finds them, you will laugh with me, or at me, as I lead you through my search for the keys to life, particularly during tough times.

Making the Tough Times Count

As I've looked back over my life, I've observed many tough times. In retrospect, many of these times are humorous; some are even hilarious (like my car keys incident) if you're not going through them yourself. Weighing the events of my life on the scales of time, I can see that the trials, temptations, tragedies, testings, triumphs and tough times did count.

Before my brother Jim, a career chaplain in the Air Force, left for a year's duty in Taiwan without his family, his wife Katie said, "It will be tough here trying to raise the five children alone, but be sure you don't waste your time. Make it count."

As Katie cared for the children, Jim spent his year in creative and charitable work. He organized the Council of Concern which matched Air Force groups with charitable organizations in Taiwan to aid those in need. Through this council the base civil engineers built a two-bedroom home for a Chinese grandmother who had been raising her grandchildren in a mud hut. Along with the normal responsibilities of the chaplaincy and the additional charitable work, Jim managed to write his thesis for a master's degree in political science and organize the building of a new chapel on the base. Though their year apart was a difficult one, neither Jim nor Katie wasted the time.

They made the tough times count.

There's not one of you reading this book who couldn't write a fascinating, unique story of your own life. Even children growing up in the same house don't see the circumstances from the same point of view. As I share my life with you, I want you to ask yourself, "Was my life like hers? Was it better? Was it worse? Have I learned to make the tough times count? Have I found my keys *and* my car?"

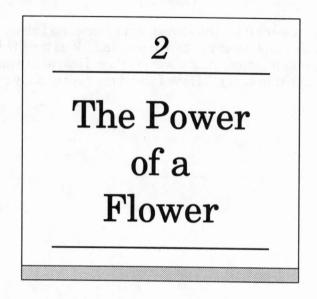

2

The Power
of a
Flower

*Miss Badashaw handed me the little clay pot
with one lonely geranium at the top of a long
stalk. I had a flower of my own.*

"Could we have wallpaper in the kitchen?" I asked
Fred as we discussed our new home. "Could we have
flowers?" I added. "That's what my name means—Florence: 'blooming flower.' "

We were moving from a large house we no longer
needed to what we had already labeled our love nest: the
first place in thirty-five years where we would live alone.
Our last home was built during the energy crunch when
the aim of architects had been to make houses energy
efficient by extending the rooflines into massive over-
hangs and setting the windows where even an aggressive
sunbeam couldn't seek them out. And although we saved
on air conditioning, for ten years we had lived in semi-
darkness. Now, in what was to be our final home—that
last one before "In my father's house are many mansions"—I wanted light. We chose a town house on top of a

hill with tall windows and skylights grabbing each passing ray. We'd never be in the dark again.

Our last house had no wallpaper. It had been monotonously washed in Navajo white. Even though I had hung pictures and posters on every wall, the white stuck out behind them as if to say, "You can't get rid of me." I did paint one room brick red in a rebellious effort to take control away from the Navajos, but the room never fit in. It never got comfortable with itself or compatible with its sisters. It remained a step-child, the prettiest room but always out of step with the rest.

I could have done more with the house, but with my busy schedule it never seemed quite worth the effort. I could have put up some wallpaper, but I never had the time to go through those huge books and make a choice. But now it was different. This was to be my last house. "Whatever you want," Fred answered, "whatever will make you happy. Get it now, because this will be your last chance. We're not going to move ever again."

I'd never moved into a last house before. It was almost like decorating a tomb. There was an eternal tone to it. We'd bought a one-story house so we wouldn't have to worry about stairs when we were too old to climb. We had chosen a tiny yard in anticipation of being too old to weed. We had the eternal white walls, but I could paper those quickly before my eyes got too feeble to see the flowers.

"Could I have flowers?"

"Anything that will make you happy."

Instantly, a roll of wallpaper dropped from heaven. I looked up as eager as a child in a garden and began to pick pink posies off the paper and hold them in bunches in my arms. Suddenly all the flowers were gone from the paper and all that remained was a geranium—one lonely red geranium in a little clay pot. As I reached out for it, Fred asked, "Why are you crying? I said you could have whatever wallpaper you wanted."

"I want geraniums, lots of geraniums."

"Just geraniums? How come?"

For once in my life I didn't have a ready answer. Why did I want geraniums?

I suddenly saw myself as a little child standing on the steps outside our store. In front of the three cement steps was a blacktop sidewalk leading to the gas pump—an orange Gulf monster that spewed gas into the cars that honked for service. Behind the pump was a patch of weeds that belonged to the drugstore next door and next to our building was a strip of dirt.

I'd tried to plant some flowers there, but like the seeds in the Bible, they fell on hard soil and never took root. Some up close to the store forced their way up but died for lack of water. A few hardy seedlings popped up through the cracks in the blacktop sidewalk, but they were quickly trampled down by the feet of those who didn't know I cared. I'd sit on those steps in the evening and wonder, *Will I ever have any flowers?*

Say It With Flowers

Across the street from our store was the local church. It was the only social center we had and we were there every time it opened. Once a year we had Children's Sunday, a special day in June when we got our awards for perfect attendance and were given recognition for any honor we might have received throughout the year. It was a dress-up day when we happily put on the best we had because we knew we would be called up front by name. I remember the excitement as we met in our Sunday school rooms and were given our instructions on how to behave in "big church."

We marched in a quiet, awe-struck army and dutifully took our assigned seats. Helen Badashaw, our perpetual Sunday school superintendent, stood at the appointed time and walked to the platform. I always wondered why her legs puffed out over her shoes. Did it hurt to walk with legs like that? She would read off the winners' names and we'd walk forward with dignity. No one ran or giggled. This was church.

The most exciting part came at the end of the service: the giving out of the geraniums. The platform was ringed with little pots of bright red geraniums and we knew from the start we would each get one. The toddlers went first and I can still see my brother Ron's big eyes as he brought his first geranium up the aisle to his seat. My other brother Jim gave me a proud grin as he passed by and then it was my turn. I always wished I had a prettier dress or curly hair, but at least I was going to get a geranium. Miss Badashaw handed me the little clay pot with one lonely geranium at the top of a long stalk. I had a flower of my own.

I'd take my little pot home and each year I'd vow to make my geranium last forever. One year it fell off the porch railing where I'd put it for decoration. Once it shriveled up and died in the dark kitchen. Another time I planted it outside in the hard dirt and a hurried customer stepped on it. "Sorry," he called back to me as he hastened on, unaware that he had trampled the only flower I'd have for another year. I sat on the steps and wondered, *Will I ever have a geranium that will last?*

I realize now why my favorite hymn was always "In the Garden." The words expressed my childhood dream, that I might trade the blacktop and the gas pump for a garden. I wanted to find an Eden full of geraniums. I wanted to "come to the garden alone while the dew is still on the roses." I wanted to walk with Him and talk with Him and have Him tell me "I am His own."

When I chose this hymn for my baptism back in 1966, I didn't realize that my choice sprouted from that inner childhood longing for a garden full of fresh flowers—or at least one little lonely geranium.

As I thought about my childhood with no flowers and my desire for some touch of beauty, I asked Fred again,

"Could I have a little pot of geraniums?"

"You can have all the geraniums you want," he answered. "You can have geraniums on the wall and on the curtains. You can have pots at the front door and window boxes full of them. You don't need to cry for a geranium ever again."

Reflections

How about you? Have you lived a bleak life without beauty? Did you long for flowers you couldn't find?

Whenever I share this story of my longing for a flower to call my own, women come to me in tears, crying out for some token geraniums. One lady told me how she grew up in West Texas where nothing was alive but the wind and the tumbleweeds. As she told me how she'd tried to plant some flowers and nothing grew, she got emotional and I put my arms around her. I looked toward her husband. He was obviously embarrassed that his wife would burst into tears over a lack of flowers in her childhood. As I gently moved her over to him I suggested, "Why don't you stop on the way home and buy her a geranium."

"She doesn't need any geraniums," he retorted as he pushed her toward the door. "She just needs to grow up."

How sorry I felt for that lady whose husband had missed the point and who was no doubt going to reprimand her for making a scene in front of the speaker. Here was a man more interested in himself than in filling some gaps in his wife's childhood.

Oh, let us be like little children. Let us reach out for the flowers we never had. Let's fill pots and vases and surround ourselves with beauty.

A pastor came to me that same day and told me a story about his first pastorate. He had decided to give every lady in the church a carnation for Mother's Day. After the service he had a box of carnations left, so he and the elders decided to take them to the mothers of the church who had been unable to attend. One suggested a certain old lady who had not been to church in years. "Oh, she won't even let us in," another elder said. "We've tried to visit her and she slams the door in our face. There's no point in going to see her."

The pastor's interest was aroused and his nature challenged. He determined to give it a try. Just as had been predicted the lady snorted out a nasty, "What do you want?" as they stood outside her screen door.

"We're from the church," one replied.

"I haven't been to church and I don't intend to go. Just leave me alone."

She was about to slam the inside door, when the pastor quickly said, "I've brought you a flower."

The lady looked out through the screen and saw the pink carnation. Her harsh voice softened and she replied, "Well, I guess you could come in for a few minutes."

The astounded men entered. The pastor pinned the carnation on her dress, and she burst into tears.

"This is the first flower I've ever had in my whole life."

The next Sunday she was in church.

Let's not ever underestimate the power of a flower.

One Sunday morning I was called to the platform in a church where I had told about the geraniums on the previous day. When I stood by the pastor, he reached under the pulpit and pulled out a little clay pot with a geranium. He had searched through every geranium at the nursery until he had found this spindly specimen: a few green leaves at the bottom with one long stem and a lonely little red flower at the top. It was so ungainly that it was laughable for the audience but I became nostalgic. I remembered that one day I waited for each year when I received my very own geranium.

Is it possible you had a childhood without flowers? Did you long to touch a tulip or reach out for a rose? You don't need to live another day without the smell of a gardenia, the smiling face of a pansy or the bright color of a geranium. Find some fresh flowers at your florist or purchase a potted plant in your supermarket. Hang silk flowers in a basket from your ceiling. Paper the walls with bouquets of lilacs and nosegays of violets.

Make up for what you missed out on as a child. You don't have to be without flowers ever again.

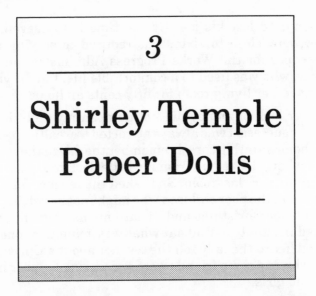

3

Shirley Temple Paper Dolls

Although I was too young to recognize this gathering as a charity affair, I was bright enough to observe that I was on the wrong side of the stage.

If ever a fairy godmother wandered through the state of Massachusetts in search of a child in need of a change, she would have chosen me. I was a perfect candidate for Cinderella—poor, plain and plump. Born during the Depression to a struggling shopkeeper and fragile violinist, I needed all the help I could get.

My parents, Walter and Katie Chapman, married late in life and when I was born in Newton Hospital on April 27, 1928, my mother was thirty and my father fifty. Because I was an eight-pound, first child of a ninety-pound mother, my birth was a trauma for both of us. She was hospitalized for weeks and I emerged with a twisted foot that had to be put in a plaster cast.

When I was born, my father managed an S. K. Ames Butter and Egg store, but as the Depression grew deeper, the stores were sold. After twenty-eight years with the company, he lost his job. By the time I was seven, my father, now close to sixty, was reduced to serving as a timekeeper for the Works Progress Administration. My mother, who was used to a comfortable life, taught violin lessons in her living room for fifty cents an hour.

Our lack of money did not dampen my ambition or drive for success. I was always attracted to wealthy people, large homes and big cars. I remember the day in the second grade when I looked up from my little desk to see a lovely lady enter our classroom. She asked the teacher for a list of names of the poor children who might not be getting any presents for Christmas and I heard my name mentioned. I tuned in closely to find out what was going to happen to me and heard the lady tell the teacher about a Christmas party she and some friends were sponsoring for poor little boys and girls.

When the day came, we were picked up after school by a chauffeur in a big black Packard. I didn't even know what a chauffeur was, and I had never been in such a large car. We arrived at the local Grange hall along with many other children and after some cookies and Kool-Aid we were asked to take our seats. I was on the end chair in the third row and I watched wide-eyed as the "lovely lady" came out on the stage and called us up one by one.

When my name was called, I went up front to receive my gift—three books of Shirley Temple paper dolls. Although I was too young to recognize this gathering as a charity affair and the terms "disadvantaged" and "deprived" had not yet been invented, I was bright enough to observe that I was on the wrong side of the stage. I wished then that I could be that lovely lady in the elegant gown giving out the books and toys. I wanted to be on the stage giving out and not receiving.

That night I began to look at myself in a more critical light. I decided I didn't like the dresses the Works Progress Administration turned out in three pastel colors: pink, blue and yellow. Once they were washed they all turned beige. These little dresses had puffed sleeves, a peter pan collar and a sash tied in the back. They came in three sizes—small, medium and large—none of which seemed to fit.

I was tired of looking like all the poor little girls in class. I wanted a fairy godmother to give me a whole new wardrobe. My mother explained I should be grateful for the clothes I had. "There are some children who have nothing," she said. But because she understood my hurt, she embroidered a big black lion on the pocket of my plain yellow dress. I was hopeful no one would recognize this as a charity contribution.

From that time on I determined that when I grew up I was going to have plenty of clothes and they weren't going to be plain pastel colors—even with a lion on the pocket.

Reflections

Did you grow up in the lap of luxury or were you, like many of my generation, on the list of "poor children"? Did you long for the big car and the fancy home? Did you receive charity? Did you know you were on the wrong side of the stage?

Gratefully, I was able to get on the right side of the stage and today I spend my time giving out to others. But some of us stay on the wrong side of the stage for a lifetime because we were made to feel there was no hope for us. We believed the lie. For those of you who may have been forced into retaining a poverty mentality, you don't need to stay there any longer. Read my book *Get a Life Without the Strife*. Get self-help books from the library. Have your hair styled. Give yourself a lift.

Think about the simple possessions you had as a child. See if you can find some replacements or perhaps the originals in your mother's attic or garage. My friend Patsy Clairmont loves to search through antique shops and for my birthday she gave me two pages of original

Shirley Temple paper dolls from 1935. She also located a Shirley Temple doll and a blue milk pitcher with Shirley's picture on it. When I saw the pitcher I remembered how we had sent in box tops from Wheaties to get the Shirley Temple dishes free. We had a cereal bowl with Shirley's picture on the bottom and we would race to eat all our Wheaties so we could find Shirley's smiling face beaming back at us. When I look at those objects some very happy memories come to mind.

What special objects did you treasure as a child? Bring them out where you can look at them. Have the fun search- ing for replacements. Don't blot out the simple and uplifting souvenirs of childhood.

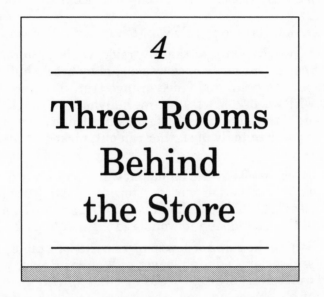

4

Three Rooms Behind the Store

*With an air of optimism, Father showed us the
rest of our new home. Mother continued to sob
and clutched Baby Ron as if he were her security
blanket.*

When I was nine, my father borrowed $2,000 from his
best friend, bought the Riverside Variety Store in Haverhill, Massachusetts, and went ahead to prepare for us.
When everything was ready, Aunt Sadie picked us up from
our tenement in her Model-T Ford. We drove from Newton
Upper Falls to Haverhill with Mother sitting up front
holding baby brother Ron and my five-year-old brother
James sitting in the back with me.

As we approached our new town, Mother said, "So
here we are, starting all over from scratch, and at our
ages."

"I don't have much hope for this whole venture," said
Aunt Sadie, shaking her head.

I left them to their thoughts as I eagerly looked out

the window. I could hardly wait to see our new home.

As we drove up to the Riverside Variety Store, my heart sank. Our new house was a shabby brown building with peeling paint and faded orange trim. The yard was high with weeds and a few sparse hollyhocks struggled up the side of the store. Three cement steps led to the warped front door. Excitedly my father ran out, picked us up and hugged us.

I took James by the hand and walked into our newly acquired combination variety store and living room. I noticed a nickel on top of the *Haverhill Gazette* on the news rack at the front door and wondered if I should pick it up.

Behind the stand of newspapers was a long table piled high with brightly dotted loaves of Wonder Bread, packaged cakes and jelly rolls. I was fascinated with the prospect of a house crammed with cakes, free cakes at my finger tips. James tugged my attention to a big glass case full of candy—trays and trays of all kinds and colors of candies! Gum drops, Fleer's bubble gum and licorice twists.

A perfect heaven for children, I thought.

Soon James and I found the sliding doors behind the case holding the Tootsie Rolls. As we stuffed our pockets with goodies, I heard my mother crying.

"Chappie," she sobbed, "how will we ever fit our furniture into these three rooms behind the store?"

"Katie," said my father optimistically, "it's going to be all right."

I followed their voices past the cash register, the Coca Cola case and the ice cream freezer, through to the kitchen. There I saw my mother staring into a black slate sink edged with warped green linoleum. There was one brass cold water faucet and beyond the sink was an ugly black stove. Gurgling behind it was an upside-down bottle of kerosene. Faded flowered chintz curtains that had long since lost their glaze hung in shreds over the windows.

Sagging squares of painted tin served as the ceiling.

With an air of optimism, Father showed us the rest of our new home. Mother continued to sob and clutched Baby Ron as if he were her security blanket. The back hall was so narrow that Father had to go sideways past the wooden icebox that leaked its way to the back door where we peeked out into the backyard full of garages, mechanics, gas pumps and broken cars.

"Is that where my little boys are going to play?" asked Mother. It was.

Father quickly brought us back in and showed us the tiny den. The wallpaper looked like a jungle, and my father, trying to relieve the tension, said, "When you look at that paper, you almost expect a monkey to jump out at you." We children laughed although Mother didn't think it was funny. The final stop was the bedroom where we all had to sleep on unpainted bunk beds my father had ordered from the Sears catalog.

Mother was near collapse as the full force of her new life hit her. "How can anyone bring up decent children in three rooms behind a store?" she asked.

Yet Mother did. From that day on I remember Mama, serious and sad, trying to bring up decent children, and Father, enthusiastic and joyful, trying to make fun for us and force the frown off Mother's brow.

Visions of Grandeur

As I look back now, I realize how difficult it must have been for Mother to keep going at all. She was so frail the doctor made her drink heavy cream to put "some meat on her bones," and yet she worked night and day. Since there was no hot water, Mother constantly kept a boiling pot on the back of the stove.

She did our laundry in the black slate sink, where her tiny hands, made for the violin, wrung big sheets and heavy corduroy pants. It always embarrassed her to hang our clothes on the clothesline that ran from the back door to one of the garages. The mechanics would laugh, hold up their greasy hands and say, "Do you need any help, honey?"

My brothers loved playing with real cars in the backyard, but Mother constantly worried about the vulgar language they heard. One day little Ron asked one of the mechanics, "How come Jesus could walk on water?" My mother was aghast at the reply: "I guess it was because He had such big feet." How could she bring up decent children in surroundings like this?

While my brothers enjoyed the cars, candy, cake and chewing gum, I picked up my mother's pessimism. I wondered why I had to live in three rooms behind a store where to go from the bedroom to the bathroom I had to pass the cash register. I wondered why the bathroom had no tub and why we all had to take baths in the kitchen sink while Mother held up a big towel to shield us from the customers. I was embarrassed and fearful that some day Mother would drop the towel and the customers would see me sitting naked in a sink.

To escape my unpleasant surroundings, I sat on our one couch and read romantic novels where the heroines all live in magnificent mansions with huge white columns. I imagined myself in a beautiful ball gown, sweeping down the circular staircase into the arms of an awaiting prince. I even wept a little when the hero marched off to the Civil War and the heroine had to spend long lonesome evenings in her wing chair by the bedroom fireplace reading love poetry.

I knew that *if only* I could live in one of those plantation houses with the columns, stairs and fireplace, I could be happy. But, as I closed the book and looked around the three rooms behind my father's store, I realized the only column we had was the rotating barber pole for the shop next door; the only staircase was a ladder that dropped from a trap door to the oil tank room where we pumped kerosene by the gallon for the customers; the only fireplace was a gas grate in the bedroom where all five of us slept in layers.

In order to improve our circumstances, I was constantly creating and cleaning. I made new curtains for the kitchen out of white dish towels scattered with strawberries. I repainted the drop-leaf table and chairs, and I tried desperately to keep the top of our old sideboard cleaned off.

One day after seeing a magazine picture of a mahogany buffet set in an elegant fashion, I swept away all the junk that had collected on top of ours and put tall candles at each end with a large bowl of polished apples in the center. When I came home from school later, I found that my brothers had used the candles for hat stands and had eaten all the apples and left the cores turning brown in the bowl. Where was that pleasant plantation living that I longed for?

I desired to be a heroine, but instead I was a discouraged damsel in distress; I wanted to go to important places and be with beautiful people, but instead I was stuck in three rooms behind a store in Haverhill, Massachusetts.

Family Fun in Spite of It All

Although I felt sorry for myself, we did have family fun sitting around our one table in the store. My father kept us laughing and our dinner table conversation, frequently attended by an audience of customers, was often sharper than today's situation comedies. While Mother jumped up to wait on customers, Father kept us sitting at the table by giving a running commentary on politics and current events. He stimulated our imaginations with provocative questions.

One day during World War II he asked, "Do you think it would be possible to make buildings that would go up and down to save on elevators?"

Immediately we started on the plans and verbally designed a skyscraper on pulleys. We began with the economy and ease of eliminating elevators and having the building move so businessmen could walk out from their own floors. We put light switches on the outside so that when the building sank, each floor would automatically light up. Our design was also a great boon to window washers as they could do a whole skyscraper without ever leaving the ground.

One of the outstanding advantages of our brilliant creation was its versatility during air raids—the building could sink rapidly into the ground! We planned the roof as a pasture with peacefully grazing cows so that when the bombers flew over they would have no idea that under the cows was a business building.

Sometimes customers would join in with additional ideas. One night a man phoned from his home to tell us he had just figured out how to put toggle switches on nearby trees to increase the leverage of the pulleys. With his timely suggestion, we were able to add five more floors to our building!

As we spent night after night on our inventions, Mother would just shake her head and say, "This is ridiculous. How can I bring up decent children when their father keeps their minds on foolish things?"

Not only did Father keep us laughing and thinking, he kept us playing. One of our favorite pastimes was Monopoly. We always had a game in progress on our one table in the store. Some of our steady customers even owned property and we rolled their dice by proxy if they were not around. Father taught us how to buy and sell wisely, how to build hotels on the right side of town, and how to expand our fortunes while avoiding bankruptcy. Our longest game lasted thirty-seven days!

While Father and the three of us focused on the fun of life, Mother's steady hand kept a quiet, even keel on our tipsy boat. She washed and ironed our clothes, cooked on the oil stove and had good meals on the table on time. She helped us each night with our homework and faithfully went to PTA. She kept us in church and made us sing in the junior choir, listened to me recite my elocution pieces and played the violin to keep me practicing the piano. She encouraged James with his piano and singing lessons, and scrimped to buy Ron a trumpet. On Sunday evenings she gathered us around the piano and led us with her violin as I played hymns on the piano, Ron strained at the trumpet, and James and I sang. In every way Mother tried her best to bring culture and dignity to a family forced to live in a variety store surrounded by garages.

Reflections

Where did you grow up? What kind of a house did you live in? Were you ever ashamed of your circumstances and afraid to bring your friends home?

When I share my story of the three rooms behind the store, people laugh and cry as they think of their childhood homes. One lady told me she'd lived in three rooms over a saloon. My friend Emilie Barnes grew up in three rooms behind her mother's dress shop in Los Angeles. And one girl had come from a one-room depot at a railroad crossing in the desert of Needles, California. No matter where you lived, it has had some influence on your adult life and choices. For me the lack of a normal home gave me the driving desire for a large house with a real front door and furniture that matched.

On Christmas Day, 1989, our whole family gathered at our Redlands home to open presents. Marita was unusually excited about the gift she was giving me. When it was time to open it, she went out into the garage and made me shut my eyes while she brought it in. Even without peaking, I could tell the object was large. She and her husband Chuck struggled to get it through the door! The item was placed in front of me, covered with a sheet. I was told to feel it and see if I could guess what it was. I ran my hands down the side and I guessed it was a table. I felt the drop leaf on the side and I cried out, "It's the table from the store!" And it was.

My mother had kept that old table which she had purchased new as a bride. When she moved to California, she had left the table in Aunt Jean's basement where Marita had found it. Chuck had taken it apart, put it in a box and brought it back to California on the plane. They had stripped off the different layers of paint we had put on through the years and had it stained and polished.

When I opened my eyes and looked at the table, I was transported back to those many years in the store. Sitting around that table we would play games, piece puzzles and do homework. Often customers would watch us eat. I could see mother mopping off the oilcloth after supper and picture Daddy and me sitting there reviewing the newspaper and listening to politicians on the radio. That table was our gathering place, the center of our lives in the store.

Though that table doesn't match my other furnishings, I display it proudly as a memorial to a life long ago and far away.

Perhaps there's a piece of furniture, a family picture or a doll that has been ignored in your family. Revive it and revere it. Let it serve as a remembrance of what once was.

5

The
Barber
in the Attic

We couldn't understand how a person who was our friend, who was intelligent and had a sense of humor, could turn into an incoherent, babbling old man within a matter of hours.

It wasn't enough that we had to live behind the store and that a heavy-footed family rented the apartment overhead, but we also had an alcoholic barber who made his simple home in the attic. His name was Bill, and when he was sober he was Ron's best friend. He called Ron "Snookie," and when there were no customers in his store, he would pump Ron up and down in the barber chair. Barber Bill dropped by our store each day and sometimes ate with us as a family.

The stairs leading up to Bill's room went right by our bedroom. On those nights when Bill had been out drinking, he would stumble halfway up the stairs and begin to sing, "It was on the Isle of Capri that I met her." He only seemed to know one song and would intersperse his singing with, "That Snookie's a good little kid. Snookie's all right." He would then condemn himself, sob out loud and fall asleep. We children, of course, were awake during his whole performance and I could hear Mother tell Father what a terrible influence this was on the children.

One Thanksgiving afternoon, after Father had closed the store for two hours so we could eat together, we heard a knock at the back door. It was the lady next door and she wanted to speak to Father. We had set our one table in the den for the holiday and because it filled the whole room, it was difficult for Father to get out. But the lady was insistent. She would only talk to Father. We all got up, moved the table against the piano, let him through, and followed him out. I'll never forget the woman's remark. "I didn't want to upset your family," she said quietly, "but your attic is on fire."

Frantically we raced outside and looked up to see flames shooting out the attic window. While I called the fire department, Father and the boys ran up the stairs where they found Barber Bill drunk and unconscious. In his drunken stupor he had tipped over his little oil stove which caught the room on fire.

They pulled him out and down the stairs before the trucks arrived to put out the fire. As an ambulance took Barber Bill to the hospital, Mother shook her head and muttered, "Even when we close the store, we can't have one peaceful meal."

Reflections

Our early acquaintance with the evils of drink influenced our lives in a dramatic way. We couldn't understand how a person who was our friend, who was intelligent and had a sense of humor, could turn into an incoherent, babbling old man within a matter of hours.

People would come looking for Bill to cut their hair and my father would say, "He's on a little vacation." Sometimes Bill would come into the store sobbing and beg

Daddy to give him money. I can remember the answer, "I won't give you anything to buy more liquor, but when you're ready to eat again I'll give you money for food." And he did.

We children would hide behind the candy case when Bill came in drunk and wonder how long his "vacation" would last this time. Mother would give us little temperance lectures which were very effective with our friend Bill as a living example.

When did you first learn about substance abuse? When were you first aware that a drink could turn a loved one into a different person? Did you grow up in an alcoholic home where you learned very young to cover up the problem? Were you forced to deny the difficulties and spread a blanket of deception?

So many of the couples I counsel have grown up in dysfunctional families and didn't realize the damage their childhood abuse had on their adult relationships. In our CLASS seminars for the training of Christian leaders, an average of 40 percent have experienced alcohol problems in their immediate families. While the statistic is frightening, there is more help available today than ever before. With the formation of Adult Children of Alcoholics and an abundance of material on co-dependency, people can find answers.

If you don't remember parts of your childhood or are not sure whether what you lived through has become a negative influence on you as an adult, read and work through our book *Freeing Your Mind From Memories That Bind*. You can't help where you've been, but you can change where you're going.

Make the tough times count!

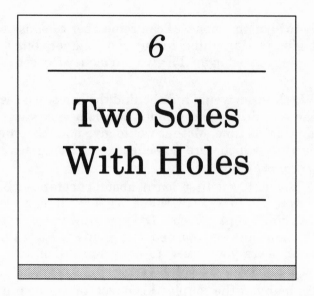

6

Two Soles
With Holes

Once, in desperation, I painted the brown clod-hoppers with white enamel paint only to be depressed when they looked bigger in white.

I was not only embarrassed by my sad little drab dresses and my life in the store, but I was often upset over my shoes. Because of our poverty we could barely afford one pair of shoes a year for each of us. They were always too big at the start—we needed room to grow into them—and too tight for the last few months. There never seemed to be that magic moment when my shoes and feet met in harmony.

Besides the sizing mismatch was the fact that my feet were bigger than I was. I wore size 9 in eighth grade. In those days a child's size 9 had to be custom ordered and they only came in brown tie oxfords. I can clearly remember the shame I felt because I had to wear these ugly shoes. Once, in desperation, I painted the brown clodhoppers with white enamel paint only to be depressed when they looked bigger in white. Eventually they cracked and peeled, showing veins of dull brown through the shiny enamel.

Besides the wrong size and the ugly shape and color was what happened when the soles wore out before it was time for the year's new pair. At the sign of a hole in the sole, my mother cut cardboard to fit the shoe and inserted it for our protection. As the hole widened, the cardboard had to be replaced frequently until mother would sigh and say, "Chappie, you're going to have to fix these shoes."

Fixing was a major procedure. Daddy took a package of rubber soles from the nail on the wall where they hung for the customers' convenience. These soles looked like tire treads, black ugly rubber with waffle marks. They came in two sizes, men's and women's, and Dad had to cut them down to create a children's size. I remember him taking mother's bread board and an ivory handled butcher knife to carve up the piece of rubber to make it fit the shoe. Interested customers would watch and make comments like, "The kid sure has big feet" and "Why don't you buy her new shoes? It would be a lot easier."

Once the new sole was carved to the correct size, give or take a jagged edge here or there, it was time to rough up the bottom of the shoe. Included in the set of soles was a "rough up" tool that looked somewhat like a little cheese grater. My brothers were assigned to scrape this vigorously across the shoe sole until it looked as if a dog had chewed it up. This mock destruction was such fun that they fought for the tool and attacked each shoe as an enemy.

When the shoe was gouged up enough, Dad would squeeze the cement out of the tube included in the set and spread the glue across the sole with a knife as if he were frosting a cake. There was an art to this step because not enough glue would cause the sole to drop off and too much would run over the edge and eat off whatever was left of the original finish. The final trick was to place the rubber treads on to the sticky soles and hold them down tight without gluing yourself to the shoe.

Once the procedure was complete, we were supposed to let the shoe and glue set for twenty-four hours. But usually I became impatient and would put my shoes on prematurely, causing my socks to be cemented into the original hole. I remember once pulling my feet out and leaving the socks in the shoes for several days because they were firmly attached to the sole by the hole.

But this procedure, which could give Bill Cosby a whole show's worth of material, was only a temporary solution. As the months went by the sole would loosen and the tread would flop with each step. How humiliating it was to be teased about the flip-flop of the phony soles as they came unglued. How I longed for a new pair of shoes more than once a year. How I wished for a fairy godmother who would wave her wand and give me glass slippers.

Reflections

Is it any wonder that I have a closet full of shoes today? When I pass by a shoe sale anywhere in the country, I rush in!

A man came up to me one day and said, "Do you know what I like best about your speaking?"

Expecting some meaningful compliment, I answered, "What?"

With a smile he replied, "Your shoes always match your dress."

I realize that purchasing the perfect pair of shoes to accent each outfit has become a hobby with me and looking at the many different styles and colors on my closet shelves says to me, "You'll never have to glue rubber treads on your shoes ever again." What a relief!

As I look back on the embarrassment of wearing tire treads on my shoes, I realize that most of us have had something glued onto us as children that made us ashamed of ourselves. It may not have been a rubber sole but perhaps you were given a derogatory name by an angry parent. Perhaps there was some failure that had been repeatedly pointed out so you couldn't get loose of it, or an abuse that made you feel you were wearing a Scarlet Letter on your chest.

When you think back, what was glued on you that you've never been freed from? Until we uncover the phony sole over the hole, we won't be able to

Make the tough times count!

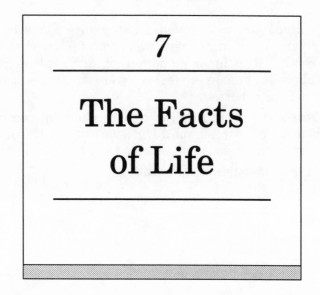

7

The Facts of Life

The closest Mother had ever come to an explanation of sex was when she casually stated that the lady down the street seemed to get pregnant every time her husband hung his pants in the closet.

In spite of the fun we had with Father, I was still embarrassed about living in a store and wanted desperately to change my circumstances. Not only were my surroundings in need of transformation, but I was also far from the heroine I wanted to be. By the time I was thirteen I knew I was hopeless. I had eaten myself chubby on store candy, and the few dull clothes I owned fit poorly. My feet were too big and my hair was too straight.

I had spent my childhood peering out from under the bangs of a Dutch Boy cut, and when I finally convinced my mother to give me a home permanent, it produced an Afro. When I had to get glasses I knew my life was doomed forever. Dorothy Parker had just told the world, "Men never makes passes at girls who wear glasses." What could be done with a poor, shapeless, frizzy-headed teenager with spectacles? Oh, how I needed a fairy godmother! *If only* I could be beautiful, I could be happy.

Not one to let circumstances get in the way, I decided if I couldn't be beautiful I would at least get organized. Before I entered high school I wrote down my unlikely goals for life:

1. get educated
2. get money
3. get clothes
4. get popular
5. get married

The fact that each goal started with "get" didn't, at that point in my life, seem selfish. I reasoned that a person got only what he set out for, and since I was so far behind, I needed to move twice as fast as others. Furthermore, I felt deprived because I didn't have a regular house like normal people and, since my parents hadn't gone to college, I was disappointed at their lack of knowledge. My brothers, on the other hand, enjoyed the frantic pace of life in the store and even thought double-decker beds were fun.

I was alone in my quest for the grand life. I could see that my only hope was to get out of there and find people who would appreciate my lofty aims. But how could I achieve my goals?

My Life as an Actress

While I was neither an athlete nor a beauty queen, I felt I was somewhat of an actress. This inclination toward the stage started at age three when my father taught me the second chapter of Luke and had me recite it by heart for the church Christmas pageant. Father placed a high premium on articulate enunciation and trained each of us from early childhood to speak fluently.

By age three, my brothers and I had each memorized such statements as, "People who live in transparent domiciles should refrain from hurling geological specimens promiscuously." Before each one of us went to kindergarten, my father taught us a handy phrase to use as a reply when we didn't know an answer: "Not knowing to any degree of accuracy, I dare not assert for fear of erring therein." With this personal coaching from Father, I felt I was ready for the stage.

In the first grade I was cast as the bumbling Cowslip in the Fall Flower Festival. While I had wanted the role of the Rose or the Red Geranium, I was rewarded when the audience applauded my dainty fall which ripped up my crepe paper petals and left me lying on the stage with my panties exposed.

My next major role was Mother Nature in the spring pageant. I wore a long blue gown trimmed in tinsel and carried a magic wand. As the fairy godmother of the world, I was to touch each little child who represented different elements of nature. As I tapped them with my scepter, each seedling was to burst forth in a sequence of spring. Unfortunately, this part never amounted to much. As I turned to transform my little brother, a lowly nasturtium, a trap door in the stage gave way and little James fell in. Somehow, after retrieving a frightened nasturtium, there didn't seem to be much point in going on, and we closed the show.

I next tried to be the "Queen of the May," but because of my weight, I was asked to sit on the base of the Maypole to hold it down while those slimmer forms danced lightly around me.

Even so, my father still had faith in my dramatic possibilities. He paid for weekly elocution lessons and encouraged my participation in every local talent show. By the time I was a senior in high school, I had won the Poetry Reading Contest and had the bit part of Cuckoo in our senior class play, *The Fighting Littles*. As I looked ahead to college, I was determined to become an actress.

In those days the answer to the nation's problems seemed to be in education: "If only people were educated, the country would surge ahead!" I agreed and threw myself wholeheartedly into my studies. Although I took college prep courses in Haverhill High School, I soon realized I couldn't get to college without money.

Working Girl

My first work experience was in Mitchell's Department Store selling chocolates, a heavenly job for a chubby fifteen-year-old.

The chocolates were in bins and I had to scoop them out by hand for each customer. Since the bins were not labeled, I had to memorize each filling by the different squiggles on top. To study them more closely I picked up each chocolate, and since I couldn't put the pieces back because I had touched them, I was "forced" to eat them! The first day I must have consumed a hundred chocolates—everything from lemon to caramel. I ate fewer the second day and by the end of two weeks the smell of chocolates made me ill.

I was a faithful worker and was soon promoted to Gloves. The lady in charge looked as if she had come straight off a cameo. She had snow white hair caught up in the back by jeweled combs. Little wisps of hair framed her face, and she always wore a black dress with a high collar right up to her chin. Tiny silk-covered buttons dotted the front of her dress and a white lace-edged hankie was always attached to her left wrist.

She was remote and serious and seemed to be constantly costumed as if she were playing the role of the old-maid aunt in a Victorian tragedy. While she hardly spoke to me except to give instructions, she became excited over selling gloves. She would work the leather gently over each of the customer's fingers and whisper, "Oh, this leather is so soft you could eat it." She prided herself on being able to spot a customer's size as the lady approached the counter, and she was always right. As much as I wanted to be a success at gloves, I couldn't develop a convincing whisper. I always pulled out the wrong size, and I had no innate love for leather. I was soon transferred to Books where there was nothing to eat or stroke.

I loved to read and the book department, hidden in a far corner of the basement, was a haven for me. The regular clerk who had been there for years had every shelf organized and alphabetized and there was little for me to do. I came in each noon from school in time for Mrs. Brown to go out to lunch, and while she was gone I would read. The few customers who did come found their own books. I just took their money and sent it off in the little metal boxes that shot up to the office on little tracks like elevated trains. Because I was a fast reader and Mrs. Brown took long lunch hours, I was able to finish many books.

One day while Mrs. Brown was out, I found a book hidden under some paper bags under the counter. When I pulled it out to put it back on its proper shelf, I saw the title, *Sex Techniques in Modern America*. We didn't have a shelf for books on sex, so I stuck it back under the bags.

I knew nothing about sex and had learned from my mother's look of shock at the mere mention of the word that it was a taboo topic. I knew, of course, it had something to do with babies and that it was negative. Mother often sighed over friends who were expecting by shaking her head and saying, "The poor thing is pregnant again." I began to wonder why people got pregnant if they didn't want babies. I wondered *why* and sometimes *how*.

The closest Mother had ever come to an explanation of sex was when she casually stated that the lady down the street seemed to get pregnant every time her husband hung his pants in the closet. This connection was confusing, but since I didn't want any babies at fourteen I really didn't care to know. I once asked my mother straight out where babies came from and she said uncomfortably, "When you're older, we'll talk about it." I never did get old enough and she never again brought up the subject.

Up to this time I had never really been interested, but as I thought about that hidden book I began to get curious.

What was there about sex that required a whole book?

The minute Mrs. Brown went out to lunch the next day I reached for the book. I went to the farthest corner of the basement behind the last row of bookshelves and sat on a high stool. I placed the book on a shelf so I would look as if I were working and began to read.

The first chapter was entitled "The Basics" and was both so shocking and fascinating, I was instantly transported to a world away from Mitchell's. When a customer said, "Pardon me," I gasped in fright, shoved the evidence behind some books and jumped off the stool. After I found what the customer wanted, I hurried back to my hideaway and began again.

As I swallowed up "The Basics," I suddenly lost respect for Mother and Father, realizing they must have engaged in such tasteless tactics at least three times. To illustrate the unpleasant suggestions, the book made absolutely disgusting diagrams that turned my stomach. But sick or not, I was compelled to go on. When Mrs. Brown returned, I put the book back under the paper bags and felt a little uncomfortable for the rest of the day.

The next day I could hardly wait to go to work. I had a new love for my job as I walked swiftly down Merrimack Street, into Mitchell's past Chocolates and Gloves, and down the stairs to Books. Mrs. Brown was delighted with my good humor and my suggestion that she take a long lunch hour.

As soon as she left I grabbed for the book and ran to my stool in the corner. I had been brought up to be scrupulously honest (my mother's instilled standards would have been applauded by the Puritan fathers). Therefore, this hidden, forbidden study was the most indecent thing I had ever done and it added a thrill of excitement to Mitchell's basement. I could hardly wait to get to my post each day, always in fear of being discovered which only heightened the excitement of reading a "dirty book."

While I didn't like the words or pictures I saw, and sometimes found myself nauseous and sweaty over a sordid thought, I couldn't put the book down. I would come to work feeling like the heroine in a spy story, wondering if I could keep my cover just one more day.

To make it easier to pick up quickly where I had left off, I put in a book mark and was both stunned and scared one day to discover the marker was moved to another page. Had I made a mistake? As soon as Mrs. Brown left for lunch the following noon, I opened the book and the marker had been changed again! Someone else was reading the book when I wasn't around. Who could it be?

There were only two people in the Book Department—frumpy, fiftyish Mrs. Brown and me. What would anyone her age need to know about sex? I felt a little uncomfortable as I read that day and I kept peeking around the bookcase to see if anyone was watching. No one seemed to be around, so I read on, and when I finished I put a new marker in my spot and left the other for my mystery partner.

Could it really be Mrs. Brown, or was there a night watchman or perhaps an early morning clerk I'd never seen? I never did find out, but the elusive mystic and I read secretly in tandem to the end.

From the time I was a young child, I never kept quiet about anything I learned. I once gave clear jitterbug instructions to neighborhood children from a diagram I tore out of a magazine. They all learned to dance even though I never could get my mind and feet together!

Because I liked to share whatever smattering of knowledge I picked up, I called my friends together. Five of us had a girls' club called the L.B.O.E.—Little Bit of Everything. As their leader, I summoned a secret session to preach the truths I had inhaled. Laden with ignorance and distorted thoughts, I began to teach the girls the facts of life. Today it is hard to believe how little we sheltered girls actually knew. But as I continued nightly to dispense sex education to my friends, we all grew up together.

My mother never did attempt to give me any biological explanations for life and I didn't need to ask. The exposés in this book more than filled my mind and at fifteen, untouched and unsought, I was looked up to by friends as a woman of the world.

A Lesson in Commitment

All through my junior year in high school I worked in Books and by summer I was ready for a new challenge. We high schoolers were feeling patriotic and were geared up to make supreme sacrifices for the highly publicized war effort, but we'd never found an available sacrifice to make. That is, not until my friend Ruthie Clark found one.

Her father worked in a factory and told her of some available summer jobs for girls at Hoyt and Worthings Tanning Factory and we applied. The man who interviewed us showed us a vast room full of women who were smoothly operating big machines and turning out bins of little things that looked like donuts. The man told us these "donuts" were chamois circles stuffed with kapok and were made to fit around the earphones that fighter pilots wore. He gave us a stirring message that made us feel we must seize the opportunity to work in this factory or be guilty of treason. Ruth accepted the job the minute she found it was piece work. Depending on how fast you worked, it was the ideal way to get rich quick. I wanted to sign up immediately, but my father had made me promise I would discuss it with him before taking the job.

I came home all excited over the prospects of making big money while helping to win the war. After I had explained the heroic aspects of the job and the ease with which the women operated the machines, my father told me he didn't want me working in a factory. He said I didn't have the strength or stamina for heavy work and I wouldn't enjoy the people who worked there. He felt I would soon get tired of the long walk from the bus, over the Merrimack River, to the factory, and I would want to quit.

I refuted his words by telling him I was strong and peppy and loved people. Furthermore, I enjoyed a good walk and I would not quit. Finally, my father made a deal with me. He said if I took the job against his better judgment, I would have to promise not to quit until the end of August. In all confidence and optimism I agreed.

"You must learn to think things over carefully before making a decision," he said. "You'll never amount to anything if you flit in and out of jobs. Once you make a commitment you must stay with it for the allotted time, whether you like it or not."

While I listened to what my father said, I didn't think his caution applied to me. Caught up in the pervasive patriotism of the day and lured by the prospects of gold, I went to work in the factory the following Monday morning.

The supervisor took Ruth and me to our huge machines which looked much larger up close than they had from a distance a few days before. Quickly Mr. Jay explained how to make chamois donuts.

"First, you take a piece of chamois out of the barrel and lay it in this circular mold with your left hand while reaching into the kapok bin with your right." He went on to explain that timed properly, my left hand should have the chamois placed down before my right hand got there with the kapok. It looked simple when he did it, but when I tried, my right hand got there first and I had the mold full of stuffing with no casing.

On the second try I got the chamois there first but I couldn't tuck it in with my left hand. I'd never used my left hand for anything before and it didn't work. I dumped the kapok in my right hand back into the bin and used two hands. Once I got the chamois placed correctly, I filled it with kapok and looked up eager for the next step. Ruth had already made three donuts.

Mr. Jay then showed me how to hold the edge of the chamois with my left hand so that it wouldn't slip out of the mold, pull down a big lever over my head to clamp the donut shut, and at the same time treadle fast with my right foot to sew the whole thing up. I never could quite do those steps all together!

By the end of the first day I completed a grand total of six chamois donuts. The average woman made 120 in an hour! Exhausted, I walked back to the bus stop. It took every remaining ounce of stamina I had to jump off the bus in front of the store, bounce in and tell Father what a great day I'd had in the mill.

The next morning I found Ruth had quit, and I was alone before my big machine with a pile of chamois on the left and a bin of kapok on the right. As I looked at my dim prospects of coordinated success, some of the regular girls walked by, and one asked, "Are you the kid who took all day to do six?" They all laughed at me and said, "You'll never get rich that way!"

I didn't like to be laughed at, so I jumped in and got to work. But when I reached up for the lever, pain shot up my arms and every part of my body hurt. My father was right. I didn't have the strength or the stamina for this kind of work. As I pulled the handle down one girl yelled, "Look, the kid is weak. She needs two hands." This brought hilarious laughter.

While the job was overwhelming in solitude, it was impossible with an audience. To make me feel worse, one overweight girl in a sleeveless print housedress stepped out in front and commanded, "Let's do it in rhythm!" She waved her flabby arms like a maestro and conducted their moves like orchestra while they all sang, "Laughing on the outside, crying on the inside, 'cause I'm so in love with you." I stood crying on the outside as they popped out donuts in unison on every beat. I wanted to quit.

Just then, Mr. Jay came in and saw me in tears. He yelled and the girls jumped back to their regular routine. In a kindly manner he took me aside and told me I just wasn't going to make it. I sobbed and said, "I can't quit. My father won't let me." He assumed that I had some ogre father who beat me each day before sending me to work, and he didn't know what to do.

"Let me try you on another job," he said with a sigh.

He led me to a counter covered with completed donuts and handed me a large pair of scissors. All I had to do was cut the chamois down close to the stitched seam, and it didn't have to be done in rhythm!

But this job didn't turn out too well either. My right hand became blistered and again Mr. Jay moved me. This time he made me an inspector. My third position in three days! I had to sit on a stool and inspect the donut seams to see if the cutters had cut too close. This titled job of "Inspector" lasted several days until one of the women from the machines spotted me in the inspection room and yelled to Mr. Jay, "How come the dummy got promoted?" He explained that I couldn't do anything else and had to be promoted. This didn't make sense to her, and she called in Sophie, the fat one in the housedress.

"Old Jay has promoted the dummy," she snarled. "We've been working our tails off for years for an inspector's job and this kid walks in here out of kindergarten and gets promoted. What do you think of that, Sophie?"

I could tell Sophie didn't think much of it. She pulled her massive self together and lumbered toward Mr. Jay like a bear. "Look here, old boy. We would hate to slow production and make your plant look unpatriotic, but it's this simple: Get the dummy off the stool and make me an inspector." I got off the stool, and she got on. I followed Mr. Jay into his little office and knew my factory days were over.

As Mr. Jay and I sat and stared at each other, a big, burly man with his T-shirt sleeves rolled up over his muscles came in and asked, "Hey, Jay, ya got anyone who knows how to glue?"

Mr. Jay, looking for a way to get me off his hands, said, "Do you think you could handle glue?" Any job seemed better than having to tell my father I'd failed, so I left with the T-shirt man. He had "Joe" tattooed on his arm, and I followed him into a big dimly lighted loft, piled high with boxes.

"We're backed up, and I need you to get these boxes labeled in a hurry," he said. Then he showed me each carton of "donuts" had a label sitting loosely on top. All I had to do was stick the label securely on each box so they would get to the right air bases and the waiting pilots. Again I felt patriotic as I thought of handsome Air Force officers in the war using these kapok-filled cushions I had shipped from Haverhill, Massachusetts.

While I was getting sentimental, Joe was setting up a huge vat of glue. He handed me a large paint brush and said, "All you do is stick the brush in the glue, wipe it over the back of the label, turn the label over, firm it down with your hand, and push the box away."

Joe handed me the brush and I noticed it was already sticky. As the day progressed, the brush glued itself firmly to my right hand. At lunch I couldn't separate me from the brush so I ate my sandwich with my left hand. By the end of summer I could comb my hair and put on lipstick with the brush glued to my right hand!

As I pasted my way through the heat of July and August, I had plenty of time to think over my mistake. Father was right and I was wrong. I had failed at machines, blistered at scissors, been pushed out of inspecting and spent the summer with a glue brush for a right hand. Father was also right about the people. They definitely weren't my type. I'm not sure I had a type at that point in life, but if I did, they were not it.

On my last day of work the women surprised me with a party on the loading dock where we ate lunch each day. They gave me a limp handful of flowers from Sophie's garden and a card with their signatures and a sentiment: "Congratulations, kid! We never thought you'd make it."

As I sat on the loading dock eating the ice cream, one

girl looked at me in the bright light. "You know," she said, "you have possibilities. You're not homely; you just haven't got yourself together yet."

I sat wide-eyed with my legs dangling over the edge of the dock as they surrounded me and began to show me how to shape up. I never considered them too stylish, but they sincerely wanted to help me. One had a make-up bag in her purse, and as she took it out, Sophie said, "You know, kid, your features aren't bad if you only knew what to do with yourself." As I sat there in the sun, the women made up my face, plucked my eyebrows and restyled my frizzy hair. Then as they stepped back and looked me over they said: "Not bad. Not bad."

Although I had to agree with my father that these women were not my type, I had become almost as attached to them as to my glue brush. That night I took my flowers home and enthusiastically told everyone what a great summer I had. I never spoke of the lessons I had learned, but I'm sure Father knew. He was just kind enough to never say, "I told you so."

"She Must Be Smart"

Although I had worked hard at Chocolates, Gloves, Books and Glue, I still didn't have enough money for college. But my assorted jobs had taught me one major lesson: I must go to college and become something better than a glue girl. With my future direction resolved, I set out to get a scholarship.

An athletic scholarship was out of the question. I couldn't dodge the dodge ball and was a failure at recess! And I was convinced I couldn't win anything for my beauty. The machine ladies had made that clear. As a child, when I stood next to my little brother James with his curly hair and big blue eyes, people would say, "Isn't he adorable!" There would then be a thirty-second pause while they looked me over and concluded, "She must be smart." If that's the best thing that can be said for you, you better get smart! So I tried.

In high school I threw myself into my studies and never went to the football games or school dances. This direction, however, was not so much a thirst for knowledge as it was the plain fact that no one ever asked me out. Today, my daughters look at my high school pictures and say, "Mother, I can see why nobody ever asked you out."

When I filled out my scholarship applications, I wrote movingly of my dramatic abilities, told of my varied occupations, sent copies of my High Honor Roll record, and listed completely my extracurricular activities: Poetry Club, Math Club, Yearbook, French Club and Drama Club. The combination must have been impressive as I received a tuition scholarship to Massachusetts State College. I was on my way to goal number one: get educated.

Reflections

Did you ever set goals for your life? How old were you when you began to focus on your future?

As I talk to young people today so few have any realistic goals. They assume they'll go through high school and probably continue on to college and then someday get a job. One boy I questioned said, "I don't care what I do as long as I have enough money for a red RX7 and my stereo equipment."

"Don't you need money for rent?" I asked.

"No, I'll just keep living at home."

His casual attitude toward life was so different from mine that I had to think it over. He didn't care to become anything as long as he had enough money to satisfy his desires.

When I was his age we were all hungry for a better life and we knew we had to work hard to get educated if we ever hoped for any measure of success. We had no desire to live with Mother forever and I surely wasn't about to spend my life in three rooms behind a store. My family had no car, no phone, no washing machine and no bath tub. Our total entertainment was one radio. No wonder I set goals and headed out of Haverhill. Little did I realize then that a social problem of the '90s would be adult children who don't want to leave home.

Have you been able to instill values and goals into your children?

What were some of your own goals at sixteen?

Which ones did you achieve?

Did your childhood deprivations cause you to make the tough times count?

As I look back on the lessons I learned from my odd jobs, I am grateful that my father made me promise to stick to my glue job, like it or not. Throughout my life his advice has helped me evaluate a position before accepting it and then to be reliable once I have taken the responsibility.

One summer in an un-airconditioned warehouse by a swamp was enough to teach me a new set of facts of life. I learned not to prejudge people because of their occupation or circumstances in life. The women I looked down upon as uneducated had hearts of gold and became my summer friends in a winter experience.

A few years ago Fred and I went back to Haverhill and retraced the walk I took from the bus, over the Merrimack River, down the dirt road to Hoyt and Worthings. Much to my surprise, the factory was still there and people were still working. The sign on the side of the brick wall was hardly legible and had not been painted since I worked there.

The workers were still eating their sandwiches on the loading dock right where I had eaten mine. I remembered how my feet dangled from the dock and how I ate with my right hand glued firmly to the brush. As Fred took pictures of me looking tearfully at the loading dock, a secretary came out of the office and asked if she could help us. I told her, "This factory changed my life. One summer here gave me the drive to work my way through college so I wouldn't have to glue labels forever."

I look back and praise my father for teaching me to be dependable and for helping me set goals for my future. I could still be in the factory with Sophie. It was a tough summer, but I learned to

Make the tough times count!

8

A Dedication to Education

I learned that in pouring at a social function, coffee outranks tea and the initials on the silver pot should always face the guest. With such important essentials under firm control, I was ready to meet the world.

In September, 1945, I arrived at the Trailways Bus stop in Amherst, Massachusetts, carrying everything I owned in two shopping bags with rope handles. I had stretched to put together five coordinated outfits and I had even bought two pairs of shoes. I had two itchy khaki blankets left over from my brother's brief stays at Boy Scout Camp, and a bag full of pencils, notebook paper, a Webster's Collegiate Dictionary and assorted high school term papers.

Carrying this inauspicious trivia, I took a local bus to the Massachusetts State College gymnasium where freshman registration was already in progress. After a two-hour wait, I received my schedule and a plethora of information on the glories of Old Bay State. As I looked these over and followed the line of coeds, I found myself in a gymnasium full of girls in their underwear. Before I had time to flee, a gym instructor blew a whistle and barked, "Strip down for your physicals."

As I clutched my printed forms to my bosom in a gesture of self-protection, the woman pointed straight at me and shouted, "And I do mean you." Never before had I undressed in front of anyone. Even with our open store policy, I always managed to wiggle out of my clothes under blankets. The instructor was staring at me. I knew there was no choice. Slowly I began unbuttoning my pink and white striped seersucker suit. My mother had always told me to wear good underwear in case I was in an accident, but I never anticipated this.

As I stood in my cotton panties and a limp unfilled bra in front of hundreds of girls, I forced a weak smile toward the gym lady who was watching me from the security of her warm Massachusetts State sweatshirt. It was then I noticed the line moving past a group of handsome young men in white coats and stethoscopes. When one winked at me I was horrified and tried to cover myself, but I had nothing but my arms, and they just wouldn't stretch far enough.

The man with the wink seemed to be mine. He approached with a thermometer and I heard his buddy say slyly, "You didn't get much of one this time." As I stood unclad in the cold gym waiting for my temperature to go up, the doctor took my pulse, looked me up and down and seemed disappointed.

When the basics were over, the men asked us all to lean over and touch our toes. I watched the others go down first and noticed the doctors focused on the voluptuous girls, who, in this unusual position, were close to falling out of their bras. They singled these girls out as having "bad backs" and asked them to go up and down a few times to see if they couldn't get themselves "loosened up." Obediently the girls exercised.

As I watched the men watching them, I concluded their interest was not in the girls' bad backs. One girl who was detained for further "corrective work" dared to ask where the doctors were from, and we learned they were med students from a distant school who had volunteered to screen the freshmen girls as a sacrificial goodwill project.

Humiliated by these mass physicals, I dressed quickly and left the gym with my shopping bags to find my way to Butterfield Hall. Along the walk I met another girl, Alison, who was also assigned to the same dorm.

When I first saw the path to Butterfield it appeared to go straight up to the sky. *No one short of Jack-and-the-Beanstalk could ever climb it,* I thought. Alison assured me it was possible to make it to the top, and we began a hike that I learned to take in stride at least twice a day for the next year. The boys on campus identified girls from Butterfield by the muscles in their legs. Since I didn't have any muscles to start with, the first few climbs were painful.

After Alison and I arrived exhausted at the front door of Butterfield, I got my room assignment from the housemother. Thankfully, it was on the first floor. I had asked for a private room since I had never had one and was relieved to find I was given a simple single room with a maple bed, desk, chair and dresser. For the first time in my life I had a place for my own things where no one else would touch them.

Alison directed me to the communal bathroom where both of us were fascinated by a series of strange elongated washbasins that went all the way down to the floor. We turned the handles and water ran from the top to the bottom like a waterfall. Neither one of us had ever seen such a strange contraption and we began to discuss its use. Alison said it was a foot bath. We both agreed that after such a miserable walk up the mountain each day it would be nice to rinse off our feet in cool water.

We decided there was no time like the present, took off our saddle shoes and bobby socks and began foot baths in separate units. As we stood there on one foot with the other in the waterfall, the proctor came in and began to shriek with laughter. I had already been embarrassed enough at the physicals and didn't appreciate anyone making fun of me. When she calmed down she explained that Butterfield had been designed as a boys' dorm before the men had gone off to war and the footbaths were really men's urinals. I wasn't too sure what a urinal was but pretended to grasp the idea quickly. With our new information, Alison and I spent the rest of the afternoon in the bathroom explaining to other confused girls that urinals were not foot baths.

Before we went to supper on our first Sunday evening, we were each asked to print our names on our doors. I taped together several pieces of notebook paper and fastened them on my door where I began to print FLORENCE in large black letters. Unfortunately, the dinner bell rang before I had completed my name and when I left to eat I had finished FLO and part of the R. Put together it read FLOP. By the time I came back from the meal, the girls on either side of me had decided my name was FLOP. From that moment on, Flop was my new nickname, hardly the right title for an aspiring actress.

Early Influences

To earn money to support myself in college, I applied for a job and became secretary to the dean of music, Doric Alviani. While I was as charmed by Doric as all the other girls in the college were, I could barely type and I knew no shorthand. I wasn't much of a secretary, but Doric was too kind and compassionate to fire me.

He asked what other things I could do. I volunteered to correct the student papers he had piled on his desk, and I also suggested I could help him direct the college musicals. Although he was doubtful I could do either, he gave me a try. I quickly read three music textbooks and with a little coaching from Doric, I was soon correcting all his quizzes and exams.

Besides working with Doric and unconsciously picking up his unique directional techniques, I studied Shakespeare and drama and attempted to fulfill my ambition of becoming an actress. I joined the Roister-Doister Drama Club and got the part of Ann Forrester in Dr. Frank Rand's version of *First Lady*. The following year a new speech teacher, Professor Arthur Niedeck, cast me in a small role as a type of temptress and then began the impossible task of making me into one.

I remember how he yelled from the back of the hall one night, "Get Flop a pair of falsies. Maybe that will help her out." The costume girl took me out to a back room and in front of several boys stuck two rubber pads in my bra. I slumped back onto the stage, and again the professor called, "Stand up straight and stick your chest out." I did the best I could, but it wasn't good enough. "Get the child another pair," he screamed.

Back I went and got filled out again. This time I walked in as sultry as I could, hoping he wouldn't continue to single out my deficiencies. As I took a deep breath and began my lines, I heard, "Ye gads, she needs another pair." Even with three sets of falsies, I didn't look like anything a man would leave his wife for, and my part was cut to a minimum.

On the closing night as I bowed with the rest at curtain call, I glanced down and noticed the falsies had slipped. I had three lumps: small, medium and large! I don't know how long I had looked like a deformed camel, but I guess if two were good, three were better.

After my failure as a provocative actress, Professor Niedeck suggested I forget acting and try directing. From that moment I changed my ambition and never again auditioned for a part.

As I was simultaneously trained by two outstanding artists, I learned two different styles of directing. Professor Niedeck was precise, natty and detail-conscious. He taught me how to plan every move of every actor before the first one stepped on stage to rehearse. He showed me how to block the action and make a thick prompt book which had every move, sound and light graphed out in different colors.

While Niedeck was meticulous, Doric was flamboyant, colorful, emotional and adorable. He never cared about what he told us yesterday if today's inspiration was better. We hung on his every word and worshipped him as a genius. While he never gave me detailed instructions in directing, he unconsciously taught me that without charisma you could never move the actors to greatness and triumph. I loved his feel for music and flair for the dramatic. As I absorbed the wisdom of these two different teachers, I tried to fuse Niedeck's organization and Doric's enthusiasm. I wanted to direct with command and style.

Another professor who influenced me greatly was a man with the unlikely name of Davey Crockett. He was short but made up for this deficiency with a booming, powerful voice. With perfect control he could raise and lower his tones and roll out his words in resonant cadenzas. He taught me how to breathe, how to project and how to think. He made me study Robert's Rules of Order until making a motion was second nature. He would engage me in a conversation until he found out my feelings on a certain subject and then assign me to take the opposite side in a debate. This training broadened my mind and helped me to be convincing on any topic. "Don't ever let your feelings get in the way of your material," he would say.

As the female delegate from Massachusetts State I wrote a political proposition to present to the 11th Annual Model Congress in 1947. After delivering my moving speech before the congress and judges, I was awarded the title of "Best Female College Speaker in New England." I felt it was only a matter of time before the U.S. Senate would discover me.

Spurred on by my success in congress, I decided to major in speech. Davey Crockett became my official advisor and planned the rest of my college courses. He helped me choose a balance of English, speech, drama, literature, psychology and education, and selected me as the one senior to do honors work in the field of speech. With his guidance and encouragement I kept studying, writing, speaking, directing and hoping to live up to his constant comment, "You'll be a great speaker some day, if you keep at it."

I wanted to keep at it. My father had given me a love for words, my elocution teachers had kept me memorizing poetry, Professor Niedeck had shown me the necessity for order in creativity, Davey Crockett had inspired me to modulate my voice and improve my delivery, and Doric had given my life meaning, color and flair.

Although speaking was my first love and I desired to be dramatic, I was not quite ready for high society. While I had left Haverhill, Haverhill had not left me. As I associated with students and faculty, I began to see I didn't have a feel for social graces. Living behind the store had not prepared me for the elegant life I desired.

Learning to Be a Lady

I reviewed my goals and decided I wanted to become a gracious lady. In between my studies and dramatics, I read books on etiquette and charm and began to file off a few of my rougher edges. As I filled in my gaps in the social graces, I began to feel better about myself. I signed up to take modeling lessons where I learned to do pivot turns, rise from chairs gracefully and frame myself in doorways like Loretta Young. (Although I didn't become a model, the experience gave me the confidence to narrate fashion shows many years later.) I had not planned to join a sorority, but I began to see that fraternal life provided an access to the refinements I needed to know.

My friend Alison had pledged Kappa Alpha Theta and

I followed her the second semester of my freshman year. Immediately the dignified housemother saw I had a teachable spirit and spent many hours sharing the specific differences between a woman and a lady. She showed me how to arrange the silver for a tea party and how to set a proper table, two needs that had never arisen while eating in the store.

The housemother also taught me where to seat the guest of honor at a formal dinner or club luncheon and how to introduce people according to protocol. I learned that in pouring at a social function, coffee outranks tea and the initials on the silver pot should always face the guest. With such important essentials under firm control, I was ready to meet the world.

As I helped set the tables for the sorority teas and began to insert ideas into the party plans, I discovered that I had a flair for entertaining. I became good friends with the sorority cook and learned the art of cooking from a pro. Often on weekends I would go to her home and she would show me special ways to make hors d'oeuvres, training me to become a gourmet cook.

Since I was eager to learn everything I could and wanted all the practice I could get, I was willing to assume the difficult job of house chairman in my senior year. I had been the sorority chaplain for two years where my chief function was to memorize and recite 1 Corinthians 13 at the weekly meetings, so I was excited when I was given the responsibility of directing all the physical functions of the house, including parties. Not wanting to do anything in a small way, I began to reorganize and revitalize every phase of sorority life.

One of my master creations was our fall rush party in October, 1948. Since the sororities tried to outdo each other in unusual themes, decorations and refreshments, I decided to turn the first floor of the sorority house into Coney Island. The dining room was filled with concession stands. We had ring toss games, dart boards and the most popular sport, throwing wet sponges at girls' heads stuck through a sheet. For refreshments we served sticky candied apples, popcorn balls that didn't quite hold together and bottles of Coca Cola.

The living room was the most exciting part of our project—we turned that into the beach. We got our boyfriends to borrow a coal truck and go several hours away to the Cape and fill the truck with white sand. We laid newspapers over the rug, and when the boys came back they put the chute through the front window and let two tons of sand pour in. Our guests were impressed with mounds of real sand in the sorority living room and shivered as they looked at us in our bathing suits sitting among the seashells with our pails and shovels.

The real winner was the party favor. At my suggestion, as each guest left we gave her a live fish in a beer can full of water. We had painted the cans black and put KAO on the front in luminous silver paint that shone in the dark. There was no way anyone could forget our Coney Island party as they fed their fish each day and saw KAO before their eyes even after their lights went out. The party was the talk of the campus and we filled our quota of new members.

Unfortunately, in my enthusiasm for the beach scene, I had not given any thought as to how we would remove the sand after the big night. We shoveled and shoveled and vacuumed and vacuumed, but when I returned for my fifth college reunion, the Thetas were still crunching across the carpet!

Reflections

How many of us grew up wanting to be in show business? We hoped someday to be discovered and sent off to Hollywood.

As I look back, I'm grateful for my professors who saw in me an ability to direct and consequently turned me in that direction. Even though I didn't become a leading lady, I can see how valuable my drama training has been in my Christian speaking, how my debating experience taught me to think logically and how my modeling lessons cured my feelings of being uncoordinated and clumsy.

Because I lapped up every word Doric and Professor Niedeck taught me, I was later able to direct musical comedies and teach speech on the high school and college level. I realize now that my time in college was more than an academic experience; it was a turning point in my life. I went in a young girl and came out a lady. My feeling of personal worth grew in four years from insecurity to confidence.

Have there been any turning points in your life? Have you made maximum use of your education? Do you regret your lack of education or training? It's never too late to learn. With adults taking courses as never before, there is no stigma to going back to school. If any deficiency in training has made you feel insecure, sign up for some courses and fill in your gaps with confidence.

It was not easy for me to work my way through college, but I'm grateful today that I'm able to

Make the tough times count!

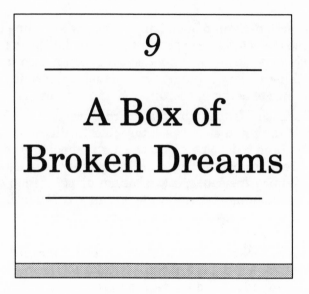

9

A Box of Broken Dreams

Had my dad not chosen that day to show me his box of broken dreams I would never have known about his talent.

During Christmas vacation of my senior year, my father took me into the den one afternoon and told me how proud he was of my achievements in speech and English. He reached in behind the piano and brought out a box of clippings he had kept hidden from the family. They were articles and letters he had written and sent to newspapers. There was even a response from Senator Henry Cabot Lodge to some advice Father had sent him. I asked him why he hadn't shown me these before. He responded that Mother had told him since he didn't have any education he shouldn't try to write. If he tried and failed, we'd all be humiliated.

At that moment I realized, in spite of all my father had taught me, I had never given him much credit for knowing anything. Like my mother, I had always felt that he didn't have the education necessary to be a success. In the past I had downgraded his ability and he had wisely waited until I was mature enough to share his hidden hobby.

Warmly, we discussed our mutual love of English and for the first time he shared that he had always wanted to be a politician. We laughed over how, when I was a child, he had made me sit and listen to political speeches on the radio.

As we discussed these and other subjects, Father brought the conversation back to his secret writing and he told me in confidence that he had sent an article to the editor of *Advance* magazine a few months before concerning the methods used in selecting delegates to our denominational conventions. He had looked each time the issue had come to see if his article had been published.

So far it had not been included and he said, "I guess I tried for something too big this time. Your mother is right. I don't have any talent."

The next day we three children decided to manage the store and let my father and mother take the first day off they had had together in twenty years. We felt we were old enough to handle everything and we joyfully sent them off to Boston. Besides, after working a seventeen-hour day, seven days a week, Father deserved a rest.

About supper time we looked out the window and saw Mother get off the bus alone. When she came in we asked where Father was. "Your father is dead," she said simply. She didn't cry. She just told us the story as we stood by in shock.

They had spent a beautiful day together and as they were walking through Park Street subway station, Father suddenly grabbed his heart and dropped to the cement. She said a nurse had been in the crowd of pushing people and knelt down to check him. She looked up at Mother and said, "He's dead," then slipped into a subway car and was gone. Mother told us how she just stood there in disbelief as busy commuters stepped over Father's form and went their way. A priest came by as a lone good Samaritan and said, "I'll call the police," and disappeared. For over an hour Mother kept watch over the body of her husband as indifferent people pushed and tripped around him.

She then told us how she had sat beside him in the ambulance, stayed with him in the emergency room where he was officially pronounced dead, and then had to take another lonesome ride to the city morgue where the man on duty had her go through Father's pockets and remove his belongings. After all this trauma, Mother took a bus from the morgue to North Station, the train to Haverhill, and then another bus home. She had faced the tragedy bravely and alone. As Mother told the tale, customers came in and listened, and soon we were all crying together.

We kept the store open for the next three days. Mother said Father had told her in the past, "Never close the store except for my funeral." Each time a person came in and asked, "Where's the old man?" we would reply, "He's dead."

The morning of the funeral, as I was going through the mail and reading the day's sympathy cards, I noticed the new issue of *Advance,* January 1949. As I glanced over it I discovered to my surprise that my father's article entitled "For More Democracy" was in print. It had come too late for him to see, and had he not chosen to share his secret ambition a few days before, I would never have looked in that issue of *Advance.*

We would have missed this fulfillment of Father's humble dream.

We did close the store for the funeral. I was the last to walk out with Mother. She leaned over the casket, kissed Father and said, "I love you, Chappie, I love you." Then with head up high, she walked quietly through the crowds of customers and friends who had gathered to say goodbye to an exceptional man.

Reflections

At the time of my father's death I had no idea of any good use I could make of this story. But now I know differently. I was grateful he had shared his heart with me and that I was the only one in the family who knew about his box of clippings.

Later when my mother closed the store, she left the old upright piano behind. Had my dad not chosen that day to show me his box of broken dreams I would never have known about his talent or the article in *Advance*. It was years before I told my mother about the clippings and showed her the article I had framed along with my father's picture. I also mounted the picture of Henry Cabot Lodge and the letter of thanks he had written.

Not only do I have these two framed memories on the wall over my desk for inspiration, but I have used this story as a key example in my book *Silver Boxes: The Gift of Encouragement.*

Have you ever suffered the loss of a loved one? How did you react? Have you been able to use something from this person's life to encourage others? Have you ever felt guilty over what you wished you'd done? I've been sorry that I didn't realize my father's talent sooner so that I could have given him encouraging words, but I am grateful he chose that day to show me his box. One more day would have been too late.

It was extremely difficult for my mother to be left with three children, no money and the store to run alone. I realize now how little I did to help her grieve and to be supportive of her emotional needs. But there were no books on grief in those days and we were told to be brave, put it behind you and get on with life.

My friend Marilyn Heavilin has given birth to five children. She lost two in infancy and one teen-age son was killed by a drunk driver. Because of the lack of under- standing people had about her grief and the thoughtless things well-meaning people said, she wrote the touching book *Roses in December*. God gives us memories so we might have roses in December. The response to this book was so enthusiastic that she followed it with *December's Song* and *When Your Dreams Die*. If you are in a grieving situation or know someone who is, read these tender, helpful books so you can

Make the tough times count!

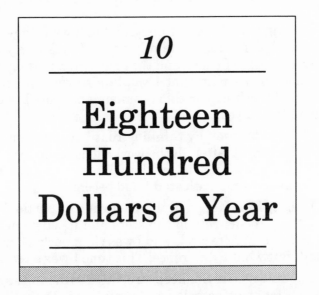

10

Eighteen Hundred Dollars a Year

I amused myself by thinking that I really should go back to Haverhill. After all the work I'd done on myself, it would be a shame not to let the folks at home see how intellectual and sophisticated I had become!

In June, 1949, I graduated from what had become the University of Massachusetts. I had full majors in English, speech and education plus honors in speech. With my B.A. and certificate as a teacher, I felt I had achieved my first goal in life: I was totally educated. Not only was I educated, but I also felt I had become a gracious lady. With these two milestones completed, I reviewed the plan for the rest of my life. I was now ready to pursue my remaining goals: money, clothes, popularity and marriage.

First I needed to get a job. I had received offers from interesting cities, but since my father's death my mother had not been well. She was lost without him and had become emotionally and physically exhausted with the overwhelming responsibilities of raising two young sons and running a business. Although I didn't want to return to Haverhill, I felt for the family's sake I must. I applied to Haverhill High School, and they gave me a job teaching English with the plan that I would also write a speech course and teach it. For this promising position I was to receive $1800 a year.

I amused myself by thinking that I really should go back to Haverhill. After all the work I'd done on myself, it would be a shame not to let the folks at home see how intellectual and sophisticated I had become!

I moved from Kappa Alpha Theta and its parties back to the three rooms behind the store and its customers. I had made a complete circle and I was right back where I'd started. But what a difference! This time I was a teacher.

I was steeped in Shakespeare, filled with multi-syllable words for every occasion and confident in the concepts of classroom teaching. My student teaching had been in high school speech, and the classes were above average, pre-trained, and with the regular teacher sitting in the room. I thoroughly enjoyed my time at Greenfield High School, and I expected my new job to be more of the same.

As I walked into the old red brick Haverhill High School Annex, Room 6, on my first day, I knew more than I thought I would ever need to know. I felt I was at the pinnacle of my intelligence and expectations. As the day wore on, however, I wore out. I discovered first-year teachers get the worst classes, and I was assigned five beauties. I had two classes of "Household Arts English" and soon learned that "Household Arts" was a fancy name for delinquent girls who were deficient in English. I also had two freshman classes and one group of sophomore boys. The five sections had two things in common—they were below average in intelligence and they were determined not to learn. Many of them couldn't read a word over two syllables and they thought a participle was a piece of fruit.

College had not prepared me for this. I had expected to use my large vocabulary and persuasive speech to sway students who would hang on my every word and thirst for more. Instead, I was fighting for survival, surrounded by rowdy kids who were doing time until they turned sixteen and could leave school. What good did it do me to understand calculus and love lyric poetry when these kids could neither add nor read?

As I looked at my household arts girls—dirty, disheveled, and disinterested—I realized they were light years away from understanding the innuendoes of *A Midsummer Night's Dream.* I knew they would laugh me out of the room if I tried to make sense out of little elves dropping love juice into Hermia's eyes as she lay sleeping in her chiffon gown in some shaded glade. Puck was right when he said, "What fools we mortals be." I abandoned Shakespeare and got down to the prosaic facts of life.

Shortly after one of the girls had been expelled for having "cooties," I introduced a hair washing party. I bought a large bottle of shampoo, lined up the girls, gave a speech on cleanliness and then washed each head. It was a humbling experience, but the girls thought it was the best thing they'd ever done in school, and I became their favorite teacher.

The first day I taught the sophomore boys, I walked to class wearing my leftover college clothes and my penny loafers. They all thought I was one of the pupils. One football-type called, "Sit next to me, honey," and several whistled. When they saw I was the teacher they began to laugh, and I was embarrassed. My education classes had been based on the premise that students were well-mannered and wanted to learn. What could be done with a wild group of louts who saw a young teacher as bait to be swallowed? I spent the first day letting them introduce themselves to me and the class. I learned many were veterans and as old as I was.

The text I had to teach was an edited version of *Julius Caesar,* and when I mentioned Shakespeare they groaned. But when I told them it was a man's story full of murders, they became interested. I played the whole thing like a Roman soap opera, with characters named Big Jule and The Brute. My boys actually became excited over the Ides of March and decided they wanted to act out the play. Some even fought over the leading roles. One teacher said, "I don't know how you did it, but those rowdy boys are truly interested in Shakespeare." I smiled.

Step One

I struggled through the year, pushed aside my courses on education and learned to live in the pits. I experienced first-hand the need for discipline and respect and developed a survival plan. Step one: Never let them know how scared you are or they'll jump in for the kill. I had a dramatic chance to practice Step One before I'd even written Step Two.

The school was having a contest to earn money for new band uniforms. Each homeroom had the responsibility to raise money in any way possible. My group decided to have an auction, and I was chosen to be the auctioneer.

In a moment of bravado I said, "Whatever you bring in, I'll auction off." "Anything?" they asked. "Yes," I said.

The day of the grand auction I walked in the front door of the High School Annex and saw my group huddled together whispering. They were normally loud so I knew trouble was brewing. I unlocked the door to our room and they followed in quietly. Those who had items to auction placed them on my desk. All eyes were staring as Angelo put down a corsage box and went quickly to his seat.

As he left, I heard something move in the box. Whatever was in there was alive! The class watched in unusual silence as I began the auction. (Step One: *Never let them know how scared you are . . .*) I sold every item on the desk before touching the box, and when I lifted it, the class in unison drew in its breath.

"This is our last item of the day," I said cheerfully. "Let's see what's inside."

Confidently I lifted off the cover. Staring up at me with bright eyes was a little white mouse. He trembled, and I realized he was as much afraid of me as I was of him.

As the class sat spellbound, I exclaimed, "Isn't he adorable!" Their mouths dropped in disbelief as I reached in and picked him up by the tail. He wiggled, and I felt sick to my stomach, but I held on and asked for the first bid. No one said a word.

"This dear little thing needs a nice home," I said. "What am I bid?" Slowly they began to speak, and soon all were anxious to own the mouse. We sold the pet for $3.50, and I kept him in my desk drawer for the rest of the day. Quickly my reputation as a brave auctioneer spread, and I was accepted into the Teachers' Hall of Fame.

As I overcame my opening jitters and settled in, I found it was possible to teach people who didn't want to learn. It was just much harder. I became creative, simplified my language and learned to laugh at myself. This combination, plus a loving hand of discipline for even the unlovable, brought me respect and popularity.

One day as I was correcting book reports, I found one that started, "Raucous, bold and daring was W. C. Fields." I knew the boy who wrote it had no idea what "raucous" meant, and I doubted he knew much more about W. C. Fields. I put his report aside and soon picked up another that opened with the same line, "Raucous, bold and daring was W. C. Fields." This girl was even less likely to have come up with such a sentence, and as I flipped through the pile of papers I found two more that started with the same line.

They could have copied the report from each other, but there wasn't one in the lot who could have written it.

I decided to check the *Reader's Digest* condensed book of the month in the school library, and there was the biography of W. C. Fields which began "Raucous, bold and daring . . . " Instead of calling in the four plagiarists, I decided to appeal to their honor to come to me and confess.

The next morning I said, "Some of you have cheated on your book reports, but I'm going to give you a chance to make it up to me. Whatever you have done that is dishonest, I will forgive you if you'll come in after school and confess. Since I know who you are, wouldn't it be better to come on your own than to be summoned? Surely you don't want to meet me on the street and have me think, *There is the boy who cheats.*"

The message fell on startled ears, and the class was forebodingly quiet for the remainder of the hour. When the next group filed in, I decided to try the talk again even though I had not found any obvious errors in their reports. Having given my plea once, I found the second time was better, longer and more moving with equally silencing results. I kept it up all day and could have sold it as a television pilot film by the time I had finished my fifth rendition.

When school closed that day, I waited for the four plagiarists to appear, and they did, along with thirty-eight other unapprehended cheats. I was so amazed at the results that I wasn't sure what to do. I quickly realized that if they were willing to turn themselves in, I had better listen and let each one think I had spotted his dishonest work. I called each repentant in separately, told him how proud I was of his willingness to confess and then listened to the most unbelievable tales of creative cheating I could have imagined. I forgave them all, had them write new reports in class and we all became good friends.

Pursuing Goal #3

By the end of my first year, I had collected my $1800 and was one of Haverhill High's most popular teachers. Additionally, I had fulfilled another of my original goals: to get clothes. My living expenses were almost nil as I lived rent-free in the three rooms behind the store with Mother and Ron. Somehow it never occurred to me that I should pay my mother room and board. I assumed that a woman of such humble means whose daughter had risen to such stature should be more than happy to support her. Therefore, with my first $1800 I set out to become well-dressed.

To achieve this goal, I headed each Saturday for "Filene's Basement" in Boston. This is an unusual store where people try on clothes in the aisles, and where every seven days all unsold items are marked down 25 percent. At the end of thirty days, if an item hasn't sold it is given to the Morgan Memorial. Week by week I closely watched a desired item lower in price until, just before it was to be given away, I snatched it up. This astute attention to shopping enabled me to purchase forty dresses, thirty suits, and twenty-five pairs of shoes in my first year and I proclaimed myself to be the best-dressed woman in Haverhill, Massachusetts.

In bringing us up, my mother had always had a conservative attitude on clothes. She believed that when you had only a few dresses, they should be so colorless and nondescript that people would not notice you were wearing the same thing all the time. Consequently, all my life I had been dressed so drably that, put against the wall in any given room, I would blend into the wallpaper and never be noticed.

When I was able to choose for myself, I bought the brightest and loudest clothes imaginable. They had stripes, checks or flowers, and were trimmed with ruffles, sequins or floating chiffon panels. I practiced walking like a model and entering rooms dramatically. Never again was I going to be unnoticed.

During my first two years of teaching, I achieved all but one of my goals. I was educated and refined, my salary was raised to $2200, and I was thrilled when I discovered one of my pupils had made a chart on how many days in a row Miss Chapman could go without wearing the same thing twice. For someone raised in a beige childhood, this was exciting beyond belief. By then I had attained some degree of social prominence, and I was the president of several organizations. I really should have been happy.

But what fear begins to creep into the heart of a single English teacher in the hills of Massachusetts?

Reflections

What was your first real job like?

How much did you earn that first year?

What adjustments did you have to make?

Isn't it amazing, when we look back, to realize how little we really knew? I had learned all the textbook answers to teaching but none of them worked with real people. I had taken modeling lessons and knew how to do pivot turns but none of my pupils cared. The only hope I had was to abandon the syllabus and get down to what my mother called "brass tacks." When I stopped trying to be somebody and began to meet the needs of these unpredictable and non-textbook cases, they responded and I received their respect. I had to learn to

Make the tough times count.

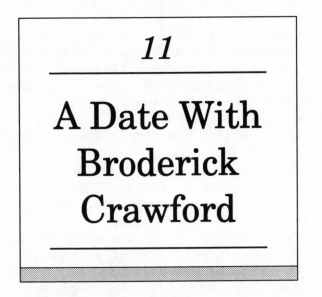

11

A Date With Broderick Crawford

Broderick actually put his arm around me during the performance. I knew he wasn't remotely interested in me, but I hoped my pupils watching in the balcony were impressed.

What fear does creep into the heart of a single English teacher in the hills of Massachusetts? What if I never get married! As I thought of my bleak future without a man, I began to panic.

I had never been popular with the boys. When I was fifteen my first romance with Chauncey DePew MacDonald III lasted one night. Chauncey's father was a friend of my Aunt Sadie and they had mutually arranged for Chauncey to take me bowling while he was home on leave from the Navy. I wanted to look my best and put on my one new outfit—a coral wool homemade dress with a Dutch hat to match, featuring big black velvet bows over each ear. To complete my bowling costume, I wore black patent leather shoes my mother had coated with vaseline so they wouldn't crack.

When Chauncey took his first look at his blind date, even I could sense his disappointment. Years later I realized how humiliated he must have been, showing up at the alleys in front of his friends with a fifteen-year-old girl in a fuzzy wool dress, flippy hat and slippery shoes. Worse than my looks was my lack of bowling skills. After one game where I actually scored eight points, Chauncey decided to take me home.

It was pouring rain as we drove through a dark back road in the woods. Suddenly he pulled the car off to one side, grabbed me, pushed me against the steering wheel and began to kiss me. I hadn't read the sex book yet and my mother's only words on the facts of life came back to me: "Good girls should never drink, smoke or get pregnant." I knew how not to drink and how not to smoke, but I had no idea how not to get pregnant. Maybe this was it.

I pulled away from Chauncey as fast as I could. "What is the matter with you, kid?" he said in disgust.

"Is this how you get pregnant?" I replied.

He never answered and within minutes he had me home. As I got out of the car, still bewildered, he muttered, "The boys on the ship will never believe this one."

A year later I had my second date with a boy named Amos Harrold. He was an artist and my mother thought he was very sweet. While I was grateful he never laid a hand on me, it wasn't until years later when he was discharged from the Navy for molesting his bunkmates that I understood the reason why.

After Amos, I set my heart on a handsome senior class president from a small town near Haverhill. Since I was from the big city, Bing Jordan noticed me when I appeared at his high school functions. We dated for many months and I tested his love by how many nights a week I could keep him sitting with me late enough to miss the last bus and then have to walk two miles home. I was proud that he cared enough to miss the bus almost every night. But when I left for my first year at college, I didn't want to be encumbered by a romance with a hometown boy who had no further education in mind. So I broke up with Bing and went off to Amherst to enter the big time.

I found my first love in a college calculus class. High school math had been easy, but college calculus was beyond my comprehension. I soon spotted a genius who knew all the answers, and I asked him for help.

Frank Rice was a pretty, frail boy who looked like he needed a mother. While he was not my idea of the college hero, he did know calculus, and we had a semester of mutual assistance. I mothered him and he did my math. At mid-term he joined the Navy and to make sure I was faithful, Frank left his best friend, Bill Howard, to take care of me. Bill was 6′4″, a track star, and we soon stopped talking about little Frank. Unfortunately, our romance never amounted to much because Bill had to run five miles every Saturday afternoon, and by the time we would get to the frat party and the low lights, Bill would fall asleep in a corner and someone else would have to take me back to the sorority.

When I returned to Haverhill after my first year in college, Bing looked better than I remembered. He had a good job and was willing to spend his money on me. We went steady that summer and all during my sophomore year and were engaged by the following August.

I was excited about the prospect of being a bride until Bing took me out to Georgetown, a suburb of Haverhill, and showed me the old farmhouse he was going to buy where we could spend the rest of our lives together in the wilderness. The thought of plodding through life in the remote reaches of Georgetown quickly brought me back to reality. I returned Bing's ring and went off to my junior year looking for new excitement.

I found intrigue first in my entomology class. The young lab instructor announced that we all had to collect a hundred different insects and mount them in a display box. The thought of bug catching appalled me, and I tearfully expressed the revulsion I felt at sticking a pin through a cockroach. My plight touched the instructor's heart and he volunteered to help me. Every afternoon we leaped together through the Amherst meadows with our nets in search of flying lepidoptera. My collection, full of rare species, was the first completed, and I never touched a single bug. And I got an A! However, once entomology was over, I lost interest in investigating insects and no longer found the instructor intriguing.

Soon my attention was drawn to Melvin Miller, the outstanding student in my speech class. Melvin was tall and handsome, but it was his keen mind and brilliant wit that impressed me. I was overwhelmed that he could take either side of a debate and be convincing enough to always win. Desperately I tried to equal him and was thrilled when the professor chose us as a team. We studied together each evening, held sequestered debates and searched for faulty syllogisms. We were two hearts that beat as one. I was ready to sign on for a lifetime symposium with him.

Because Mel wanted to be a lawyer but didn't have the money for further education, I soon became a one-woman crusade to get him a scholarship to graduate school. I gathered glowing letters from his professors and sent them with his applications. It was hard work but my efforts were rewarded when Mel received a tuition scholarship to Harvard Law School. However, he was still short of money and I pictured myself living in a Cambridge apartment, teaching school to help him become a lawyer. Whatever it would take, I was ready for the grand sacrifice.

At this moment in my young romantic life, Maria arrived on campus. She was an heiress to a Peruvian tin fortune and had gorgeous clothes that made the rest of us seem like rag dolls. The first time she met Mel, she looked up at him and said with her unusual accent, "You are sooo big." She followed him around the fraternity all evening, and two weeks later Mel told me Maria didn't want him to see me anymore. I cried, pleaded and reminded him of how much I had done for him. "You've been a good girl and a lot of fun to know," he said sadly, "but Maria is sooo rich."

When I came back for my senior year, Mel and Maria were engaged and I was heartbroken. I tried to figure out how to hurt him and when I found that Mel's fraternity president sat next to me in lyric poetry class, I set my mind on him. I reasoned that if I could show up at the Phi Sigma Kappa parties with the president, it would unnerve Mel.

Patrick Joseph O'Toole was a fragile fellow who seemed too shy to speak to girls, but I set out to change that. He had been absent from class for a week, and when he returned I introduced myself and volunteered to help make up his missing work. I was so helpful and kind that he repaid me by asking me to the first frat dance of the year. We went to every dance that year, and while Mel noticed I was there, he never seemed jealous.

We all graduated in June. I returned Pat's fraternity pin and Mel married the tin goddess. Thoroughly crushed at my failure to win the man I wanted, I decided to pursue my career without any serious romances.

Dating Life in Haverhill, Massachusetts

In the fall of 1951, when I felt I was close to "perfect," I began seriously to look for a husband. As a child I had been a Cinderella in need of change and I had first become aware of my possibilities that day on the loading dock when Sophie played fairy godmother. All through college I pursued self-improvement as if it might escape. My two years of teaching had given me the money and time to purchase the clothes, makeup and equipment necessary for the final touch, and on November 5, 1951, I knew I had arrived. I had a date with Broderick Crawford!

Broderick had won an Academy Award for *All the King's Men* and was on a promotion tour for a new film, *The Mob*. Since there were no resident movie stars in Haverhill to pair up with Broderick, the committee chose the only dramatic celebrity—me!

I was overwhelmed and went to Filene's to buy a new outfit. Chagrined at not having a Marilyn Monroe figure, I bought a red wool suit and black high-necked sweater, rather than a sequined gown with a plunging neckline, which might have been appropriate for a date with a star.

We met at the ticket booth in front of the Paramount Theater and Broderick didn't seem to get the message that I was his date. Perhaps because I didn't look like any date he'd ever had before! He didn't totally ignore me, but I wondered if he heard my name. To entertain him the committee told me to take Broderick for a spontaneous historical tour of old Haverhill.

I decided to start with the statue of Hannah Dustin scalping the Indians and then go on to John Greenleaf Whittier's birthplace. I had memorized much of Whittier's poetry and felt I could do a dramatic job of combining history with recitation. As I thought up a quick plan, I recalled, "Blessings on thee little man, Barefoot Boy with cheeks of tan."

While I was organizing my steps into history, Broderick turned to go into the theater. "Aren't you coming with me?" I asked, startled. "I'm going to take you to see Hannah Dustin scalping the Indians."

He looked at me and in his movie gangster voice said, "I don't need to see no Indians, honey. All I want is a stiff drink."

In an instant my tour of Haverhill's history evaporated. I followed him backstage where he had a large black tape recorder set up on a simple table. It was the same brand as the one I used in my speech classes and I commented on our similar choices.

"I bet yours doesn't have the same insides," he said as he opened the two doors where the tape reels were supposed to be to reveal a traveling bar.

My eyes betrayed my innocence as I looked at the

stemmed crystal, sterling silver jiggers and shakers and an assortment of bottles labeled Scotch and Whiskey all neatly arranged in what appeared to be a tape recorder. I watched stunned as Broderick poured drinks for the committee. I had been brought up to believe that abstention was the path to heaven and I was not about to throw away my salvation for a few drinks with a movie star.

By the time *The Mob* was ready to begin, Broderick was in a better mood and actually put his arm around me during the performance. I knew he wasn't remotely interested in me, but I hoped my pupils watching in the balcony were impressed.

After the show Broderick gave a few words from the stage, then posed with me for pictures for the *Haverhill Gazette*. While our brief encounter wasn't the greatest moment in history, it was the biggest event to hit Haverhill, and the *Gazette* filled a section of the paper that might have otherwise been blank. When the magic night was over, I still faced the dilemma of finding a husband.

In my own opinion at that time, I had perfected myself to such a high degree that there were few men left in Haverhill who were good enough for me. I had over-improved myself and realistically cut my choices to two men who I felt were my equals.

The first one was the local doctor. I dated him and learned he had four things in his favor. He had gone to Phillips Exeter Academy and graduated from Harvard Medical School. His father was president of the most prestigious bank in town, and he was an only child, sure to inherit the family fortune. These were impressive credentials for a husband at that point in my life, but there were two things that disturbed me. He had a strange and unusual attachment to his mother, and he was ugly.

I knew I was supposed to see beneath the surface to the inner beauty, but I didn't have that talent. I had always liked handsome men, so I asked myself, "Could you wake up every morning for the rest of your life and look at him and be happy?"

The answer to this caused me to turn toward the only other educated single man in town: the local priest. He was tall, dark, romantic and looked as if he were about to sing the lead in *Going My Way*. He was bright, witty and articulate, and whenever I saw him at one of the local cultural events, I would look at him and think, *What a waste.*

In those days eligible young girls didn't set their sights on the local priest, so instead I turned my attention toward the doctor. He was so unaggressive that during an entire year of dating, he never once kissed me good-night.

At the end of that year, the doctor decided to stay home with his mother, which is where he is today, and the priest ran away and married one of his parishioners. While the town was shocked, I was disappointed. I had put my efforts in the wrong direction. Who knows—if I had pursued the priest I might today be a Mother Superior!

Reflections

When you think back on some of the dates you had, do you laugh or cry? I shudder at how little I knew about the facts of life and how long it took me to learn. I remember how heartbroken I was when Mel turned me down after all I'd done for him and how humiliated I was trying to be sophisticated and worldly for Broderick.

I look back at my few boyfriends and wonder where I failed. Was I too insecure because of my background? Did I realize at the time I had no sense of style and no money for clothes?

What insecurities did you experience when you began to date? Were you one of those All-American beauties or a football hero? Or were you shy, afraid and easily intimidated? Those dating days were practice for future relationships and I hope we learned from our experiences how to make better choices.

12

Prince Charming

As Fred stared intently out to sea, he suddenly dropped a sentence I never could have predicted: "I'm sure you are a nice girl, but I know I could never marry you."

Discouraged in my search for a husband, I spent the summer of 1951 teaching drama in the woods of Maine. If eligible men were scarce in Haverhill, they were impossible to find in Maine where statistics show there are more cows than people. But one Friday evening, Janice, the sailing counselor, and I went on a pilgrimage to the social mecca of the area . . . the Howard Johnson's in Naples, Maine. This restaurant was so old that it didn't even have an orange roof! It was just a little gray shanty hanging over the edge of a stagnant pond full of floating fudgesicle wrappers, but it was the only place to go to look for men.

All the prestigious girls' camps in Maine made their counselors wear special uniforms when they went off the grounds so that if anyone got into trouble, the local sheriff would know to which camp she belonged. Although I felt

I had improved my looks, the uniform did nothing to help me. My camp counselor costume consisted of plain white sneakers, baggy blue slacks, a man's white shirt, black necktie and an itchy navy blue wool vest. Appliqued on the front of the vest was a large white felt pine tree with a big blue letter "T" that stood for Trebor, the name of the camp ("Robert" spelled backwards). Added to this was a heavy canvas crew hat that totally covered my short wispy hair. Janice had on an identical outfit; we looked like a pair of bookends.

After hitchhiking to Naples, Janice and I seductively draped ourselves over a rock in front of Howard Johnson's and began looking for action. As we surveyed the dreary boys passing by in equally unflattering camp uniforms, my glance stopped short. Through the mist, across the bridge over Brandy Pond came the handsomest looking young man I'd seen in the woods of Maine in many a summer. He was tall, blond, blue-eyed, with the build of a football player and the face of a movie star. *This is it,* said my heart. *This is the big moment you've been rehearsing for all these years.*

As I was trying to figure a way to meet this young man, the couple he was with ran over to Janice. They had been old college friends and while the three of them were reunioning, I rose gracefully from the rock, did a pivot turn and in the deepest tone that Davey Crockett had ever taught me said, "Hello."

He answered in a beautiful bass voice that made my studied tones seem weak. As he talked, I fell in love with his voice, and then his light blue eyes, and then his thick blond wavy hair, and then his tanned good-looking face, and then his broad shoulders and arms. Everything on him had been put together in the right places and in the right way.

He told me the couple with him was his brother Dick and his girlfriend Ruthie. As we all went into Howard Johnson's for ice cream, this dream man said his name was

Fred Littauer. Littauer, he explained, was the German word for someone from Lithuania. As the others talked about college, Fred told me he was in the Army and was from Larchmont, New York.

The next afternoon he called and asked me out. I was thrilled that he liked me. However, several months later he told me he hadn't asked me out because he had been impressed with me. Rather it was because he needed a date and I was the only single girl he knew in the woods of Maine.

While Fred waited to be discharged from the Army, he began to write letters which I answered within the hour. Since I wrote better than I looked, he enjoyed my correspondence, and at the end of the summer he accepted my invitation to come up to Haverhill for a weekend. I planned everything carefully and begged my two brothers not to say anything bad about me.

The first meal was an unbelievable experience. Just as Fred took his seat near the Coke machine, his plate began to move up and down. Quickly he jerked back and accidentally kicked over the quart of milk my mother always kept under the table. (During each meal she hid the milk so people in the store wouldn't see a bottle on the table and think we were unmannered.)

Fred helped Mother mop up the milk and I investigated and found my brother Ron had installed a "plate lifter" under the tablecloth. He could sit in his chair, squeeze a little bulb and the plate would jump up and down. When Fred wasn't looking, I swatted Ron and pinched him until he apologized. The apology was wasted because just as Fred started to cut his meat, the knife folded back on his knuckles and nicked him. We soon found that Ron had sent for a kit, "Trick Things for Your Table," and had saved them for Fred's arrival. As we tried to laugh and pass over these antics, Fred picked up his glass and as he drank, milk dripped steadily down his tie. Mother declared the dribble glass to be the last straw and sent Ron to bed.

To make up for my meager surroundings, I tried hard to impress Fred with my brains and personality. I even threw in how noble I had been to put my brother James through college after Father had died and left the family with a grand total of three hundred and twenty-eight dollars.

On Saturday we drove to my Aunt Sadie's cottage in Maine. In the afternoon we sat out on the rocks and watched the waves come in. As Fred stared intently out to sea, he suddenly dropped a sentence I never could have predicted: "I'm sure you are a nice girl, but I know I could never marry you."

I hadn't expected a proposal on the first visit, but was stunned as to why he would cross me off so quickly. I asked him how he had come to this devastating decision.

In a slow, thoughtful, business-like manner he said, "I've figured out how many miles it is from Larchmont to Haverhill, how many miles I get to the gallon, and how much gas costs." He then multiplied these amounts, threw in depreciation on the car and lunches, and like a computer came up with a total for one trip.

As I sat dumbfounded, he continued, "If I were going to court you properly," he always did everything properly, not a lot of fun, but properly, "I would have to come up twice a month." He then doubled the original amount and explained. "Frankly, when I look at these figures and then at yours, I don't feel it would be worth the investment."

Disturbed over what Fred had told me, I asked my brothers' advice. "Just forget stodgy old Fred," they said. "He doesn't have a sense of humor, isn't much fun anyway, and can't remember the punchline to jokes."

I followed their advice and forgot about my studied manners, marvelous vocabulary and pivot turns. Instead I went back to the natural way we lived before Fred came along. I decided if I had already lost him I would relax and ignore him until it was time for him to leave.

By Sunday evening Fred asked if he could stay one more day. "Ever since I told you I couldn't marry you, you have begun to shape up, and I'd like to stick around and see if you continue to improve." He stuck around two more days and then in the same business-like tone said, "I've altered my original estimate and I'm going to put you on a three-month probation period." Most girls would have sent him packing, but I had no one standing in the wings and felt a Fred in the hand was worth two in the bush.

My Visit to the Palace

We corresponded daily, and a few months later I was invited to his home for a weekend. I wanted to make sure I was dressed properly so I went to Filene's basement and bought a bright purple knit dress. I had to hunt to find matching suede shoes with grosgrain ribbon woven across the toe. As a finishing touch I bought a bunch of paper violets with long green stems to wear in my hair.

Fred had said little about his family, but I imagined his mother was elegant like that lady who gave me the paper dolls. She probably had lovely clothes and maybe even a fur. A fur—that's what I needed. Luckily Filene's was having a sale on furs and I selected what was called a grey kidskin cape for $99. It had broad shoulders like Joan Crawford wore and I was impressed with how I had put myself together. The purple dress and shoes, the violets behind one ear and the grey kidskin cape.

When the day for the big visit came, I dressed up in my new outfit, took the map Fred had given me in hand, and drove to Larchmont. As I got closer the homes got larger. I was overwhelmed and close to speechless when I arrived at a spacious English Tudor mansion and was met at the door by a German maid in uniform. As she escorted me inside, I noticed a sweeping circular staircase which led into a balcony surrounding the second floor. The huge foyer, central hall and stairs were carpeted in what appeared to be dark burgundy velvet. To the right was a long living room with an obviously expensive oriental rug, elegant furnishings and lamps, silk taffeta drapes and cornices, plus a massive stone fireplace. I had never been in such a home in my life.

There was no one else at home when I arrived and the maid, Anna, not knowing quite what to do with me, took me on a tour of the house. The spacious living room opened at one end into the library which led to a large screened porch. I had only seen home libraries in detective movies, and this one looked like the perfect setting in which to read the will of the murdered uncle to assorted eager relatives. One whole wall was lined with book shelves, and there was a long, comfortable coral couch with Chinese lamps at each end. The mahogany coffee table held impressive magazines and there was another Oriental rug on the floor. Then Anna, in her German accent, directed me to her favorite room, the kitchen, and explained how she rolled out pies and fancy cookies on the big marble table in the center. She gave me a little German tea cake with currant jelly on the top, and I knew she and I would be good friends.

Next to the kitchen on the right was Anna's room and bath and on the left was the breakfast room. I had never heard of a breakfast room before and couldn't imagine having a whole room set aside just for one hour a day. Beyond the breakfast room was an elegant formal dining room with a gleaming mahogany table and Chippendale chairs upholstered in blue-green brocade. I had never seen such chairs, but I could identify them from my college course on home furnishings. The long matching buffet had a shiny silver tea service in the center and sterling candelabra on each end. The wallpaper was a formal fleur-de-lis pattern and over the table was a dramatic crystal chandelier. My mind flashed back to the single hanging light bulb with the frosted glass shade that hung over our only table back in Haverhill. This place was like a fairy tale. I had always wanted to marry a Prince Charming and live happily ever after, and I could see that I was starting at the right place.

The upstairs balcony had many doors opening into the bedrooms, just like in the movies, and you could look from the balcony right down to the front door. Anna took me into the master suite, which was bigger than our entire three rooms at home. We Chapmans could have all lived quite comfortably in just this one room. There were two stately antique beds with blue silk spreads to match the drapes, two long dressers, an unusual dressing table, several chairs and a romantic moire French chaise lounge with soft colored cushions. The only thing missing from this room of my dreams was a fireplace.

As I imagined what life in this room could be, Anna suggested that I get settled and prepare for dinner. We passed several doors and I tried to peek in each one as she led me to the very last room. Anna showed me where I could hang my clothes and returned me to the study. I looked out the French windows to the sloping green lawns where the colored leaves were just beginning to drop from the big oak trees and realized I didn't belong in a mansion with a maid in uniform. Everything was just as I had dreamed, yet as I saw this grandiose home I realized I was still the same little girl from three rooms behind the store. And although I had been grooming myself for such a moment, I suddenly realized I didn't fit.

As a child, when I complained about our sparse surroundings, my mother would say, "Nothing's ever good enough for you. It's too bad you weren't born a queen." I knew her statement was sarcastic, but it always gave me a good feeling because I truly wanted to be a queen. I had been climbing for years to get a home like this.

As I reviewed my past, I realized I had lived a life of "If Onlys!" *If only* I could get educated, I could be happy. I had worked hard in school; I had a B. A. degree; I was an English and speech teacher; but education was not enough.

If only I could be a gracious lady. By the standards of Haverhill I felt secure, but standing in this mansion without even meeting the family, I was doubtful that I would ever measure up.

If only I could have money. Compared to my family and friends, I was rich. My $2200 a year was more than my father had ever earned. My salary gave me enough for clothes, a car and my brother Jim's college tuition. Yet, in an English Tudor mansion full of silver, antiques and oriental rugs, I felt poor.

If only I could be well-dressed. I had thought I was well-dressed, but perhaps I only had lots of clothes. My students loved my wardrobe and kept track of how many days I could go without wearing the same thing twice, but who knew how these clothes would look in New York.

If only I could be popular. Almost everyone in Haverhill knew me, but I was a total unknown outside of town, and I was way outside of town.

As I thought about how I achieved my goals, a wave of fear washed over me. Was it possible to achieve one's goals and still not be happy? I had spent twenty-three years in a determined quest for a dream. I had moved myself beyond my grandest vision, for here I was in New York, in a private room of the most elegant home I had ever seen, resting while a maid prepared dinner. I was excited and scared. What if I blew it? What if my years of preparation didn't quite fit the occasion? What if no one liked me?

As I mulled these thoughts I noticed a long grey DeSoto wind down the drive. The car stopped, and a young boy got out, hurried around the back of the car, and opened the door for his mother. It was my first view of Mrs. Littauer. Like a spy I watched unseen from behind the drapes. She stepped out of the car and walked quickly toward the house. She was wearing a full-length mink coat, and her blond hair had obviously just been styled. She was hardly the typical New England housewife. I was impressed with her fur coat, and I wondered what she would think of my $99 gray kidskin cape I had bought in Filene's basement.

At that point the front door opened, and I heard a most melodious "He-ello-oo—." I never knew "hello" could have so many syllables or sound so much like music. I wondered if I should go to meet her or wait to be summoned. Fortunately the decision was made for me as she called, "Where are you, dear?" Everything she said was like a line out of an opera, lyrical and beautiful.

How often I had dreamed of such a moment, and yet as Fred's mother looked at me, I knew I wasn't a beauty queen, but a kid from the country in a bright purple knit dress with matching shoes that suddenly seemed too loud. Do you know what happens to a gray kidskin cape when it stands next to a full length mink? It turns into what it is: dead goats!

If Mrs. Littauer was disappointed with her son's choice, she didn't show it. She greeted me with a big hug and said I looked "Lovely, dearie, lovely."

I met thirteen-year-old brother Billy as he carried in the groceries. We all ended up in the kitchen with Anna and tried in different ways to help. Mrs. Littauer quickly took command of any situation merely by her presence, and I felt quite insignificant. She looked far too good for a mother and had a figure in her cashmere sweater that my youth couldn't match. Everything about her was bright, charming and dynamic, and I decided she was the kind of woman I wanted to be.

As I tried to stay out of the way in the kitchen, two other brothers arrived. Dick, who managed one of the family millinery stores, was the one I had met with his girlfriend Ruthie at the Howard Johnson's in Naples, Maine. He seemed to have difficulty remembering who I was. Next came brother Steve, a tall, dark Air Force lieutenant with brown eyes. He was the same size as Fred but opposite in coloring. Finally Fred arrived from New York City after a hard day as assistant manager of Stouffer's Restaurant on Fifth Avenue.

When we sat down for dinner, I noticed all the sons

stood until their mother was seated and how Dick, as the eldest, held her chair. She sat graciously and regally at the end of the table while Anna in her black uniform and white ruffled apron served the food. In embarrassment, I thought of how Fred had eaten in the store, with my mother jumping up and down to wait on the customers and my brother Ron doing magic tricks during the meal. *Fred must like me a little,* I thought, *or he would never have brought me down here after seeing where I lived.*

The dinner conversation was all business. Dick reported the daily millinery sales and everyone commented on how it's always slow in October. Mrs. Littauer gave the figures for the other stores and comparisons were made. They next moved into an analysis of the stock market and were elated that most of their holdings were up. All I knew about the stock market was the little I had learned from a sophomore economics course.

Occasionally Fred's mother would turn and ask, "What grade is it you teach, dearie?" She seemed grateful that while I wasn't wealthy I at least had a job as a teacher. Occasionally I tried to drop a light thought into a heavy conversation, but my witty comments never seemed to find an open ear.

Throughout the weekend I discovered that what was smooth and sophisticated in Haverhill turned shoddy in New York. The only person with whom I could have any meaningful conversation was the maid.

The Big Question—Finally!

In spite of our differences in background, our courtship progressed properly as Fred had planned. I was so in awe of Fred's family, with their obvious wealth and finesse, that I subdued my behavior and hid my strong will and take-charge attitude. I struggled to learn all I could about the millinery business and stock market. I also observed how Fred's mother entertained, and I tried to become more like her.

While Fred and I never discussed marriage, we did

go back and forth twice a month and wrote almost daily. On October 11, 1952, I came down to New York City on the train and met Fred at Stouffer's on Fifth Avenue to attend a Broadway play. Instead of eating as we usually did where Fred worked, he took me to the Stouffer's by Central Park. Before we left for the theatre, he suggested we ride through the park in one of the horse-drawn carriages with the driver in the tall, silk hat carrying a whip.

Nothing could have been more romantic and I was eager to go. We sat huddled in the cab while the horse with his tinkling bells trotted through the park. Fred handed me a box from the florist. I was excited at the thought of flowers. The last corsage I had received was from Pat O'Toole at the senior prom. I opened the box and saw a large white orchid and another box. This one was green velvet, in the shape of a heart. With trembling hands almost too shaky to open it, I lifted it up and as I did, I gasped. There inside was the largest diamond I had ever seen with three small diamonds on each side.

"Will you be my wife?" asked Fred.

Mrs. Frederick Jerome Littauer, Jr., I thought, and then wondered, *How could I ever leave my brother Ron?* But only for an instant. "Yes, yes, yes!" I said through tear-filled eyes. I had never allowed myself to think of marriage as a real possibility, but now I began to make plans.

Reflections

Are you ever embarrassed when you think of how you looked years ago? Do you laugh at some of the things you wore and how little you really knew?

I had tried to be so smooth and sophisticated and yet I just missed. I had no idea of how Fred's mother must have felt when she viewed me in my violets and dead goats. It wasn't until I had teenagers of my own who brought home strange friends I was afraid they'd marry that I had any concept of the fear she must have experienced.

Can you remember the first time you met his mother—or her mother? What were you wearing? Did you say just the right things or were some of your words jumbled and senseless? On a scale of tough times, meeting the future mother-in-law is not the worst, but didn't you want to run and never come back? I was too far away from home to run and I was so impressed with the English Tudor mansion that I just stood there awe-struck and said to myself, "Florence, this is for you." I watched everything Fred's mother did and I became an eager pupil.

I wanted to be sure I would pass the test.

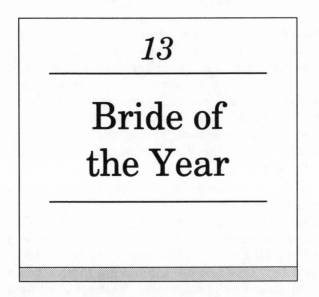

13

Bride of
the Year

*Had they seen me as the sophisticated lady I
tried to be, or did they know that under my wedding gown was a scared little girl from three
rooms behind her father's store?*

From the moment Fred slipped the diamond ring onto
my finger, I determined my wedding was going to be one
Haverhill would never forget. As a drama teacher in the
high school, I had a captive group of eager students ready
to make a production out of any slice of life. As I shared
my wedding plans, the students instantly volunteered to
help, and they organized the event as a giant-sized senior
class play.

We discussed a possible theme. Because I had always
wanted to be a queen, we decided to make it into a corona-
tion. The art class designed my tatted crown, the
woodshop boys made scepters for the bridesmaids out of
gold sprayed broomsticks, and the metal shop boys created
display racks for the wedding presents. We let it be known
that not only would the gifts be on display at the reception,

but each donor's name would be printed underneath their gift as well. There's no better way to increase the value of the wedding gifts! One would dare not bring a pot holder. Every girl who owned a strapless net dress was in my court. The home economics department planned the royal buffet, the auto shop borrowed a long white Cadillac from the owner of a shoe factory, and the high school band started practicing the Wedding March with my brother Ron at first trumpet.

At this moment in its history, *Life* magazine was doing a series called, "Life Goes to a Party." One of the more imaginative teens in our group wrote to *Life* and invited them to cover a teacher's wedding where the pupils were doing all the work. Amazingly, the idea appealed to *Life* and two weeks before the wedding I received a surprise call from *Life* photographer Yale Joel, telling me he had been assigned to cover my big event.

Poor little Haverhill went into instant redevelopment. At the thought of finding himself in print, the school principal became my best friend and ordered the janitors to polish the brass statue of The Thinker that brooded at the front door of Haverhill High. People I hardly knew asked to come to the wedding and absolute unknowns gave me showers. While my brothers and I were delirious over our own resident photographer, my mother hated every moment of this invasion of her privacy.

"I can't even go to the bathroom without a flashbulb going off!" she complained.

Mother had never shared my feeling for photographs and publicity and withdrew at the sight of a camera. As she withered, I blossomed. In my search for success, I never doubted that I would someday be on stage, but the presence of *Life* magazine was beyond even my confident calculations.

The *Haverhill Gazette* assigned a photographer and reporter to follow *Life's* photographer and reporter. When the *Haverhill Gazette* ran a front page picture of Yale Joel taking a picture of me, I was fascinated to find that my *Life* coverage was being covered! For two weeks *Life,* followed closely by the *Gazette,* recorded my every word and deed. By the time Yale Joel completed his assignment he had taken more than 200 pictures. The community was impressed and so was I.

As the wedding day approached, *Life* hired an electrician to rewire the interior of the church to accommodate their floodlights, the women's guild polished the pews and the janitor repainted the front door.

The day before the big event, Fred and his family arrived in Haverhill. In the frenzied excitement and preparation, I had almost forgotten about my husband-to-be. Suddenly Fred became the handsome leading man in a show where everyone knew their part but him. He had never even read the script! While Fred adjusted quietly to his role, I directed every move of the production with precision.

Choir Room Reflections

Finally the magic night arrived. I drove to the church in a gleaming white Cadillac while the police pushed a path for me through the crowds that filled the square between the big, gray church and our family store. My brothers and I had often played in this street, and now it was roped off for the event of the decade—my wedding.

I smiled, waved at my audience and tried to look like the queen I wanted to be. I held my crowned head high as I walked toward the waiting wedding party in my imported chantilly lace gown with a hoop skirt like those of the Southern heroines I had often read about. My sweeping white silk tissue faille court train was guided by two doting flowergirls who scattered rose petals as they walked. I carried a white silk pillow holding a circle of tatting to match the starched crown on my head. A large white orchid, to be used later as my corsage, accented the pillow which was hung with streamers of sweet peas and stephanotis.

The maid of honor was in turquoise silk and the bridesmaids wore candlelight yellow. They all carried the scepters made by the woodshop boys and decorated with gardenias, streamers and pearls by the home ec. girls.

As I stood that Saturday evening waiting for the Wedding March to begin, I felt I was the luckiest bride in the world. I had gone from living in three rooms behind my father's store to the promise of a large New York apartment; from being a plain unnoticed little girl to being practically worshipped by 2,000 high school students. What's more, I was moving from my humble background into a family which not only had money, but knew how to do everything with class. What more could a girl ask for? All the goals I had set for myself were being realized. I was marrying Prince Charming. I was to be in *Life*. And I hoped to live happily ever after.

I was jolted from my reverie by a phone call. It was Fred's Aunt Edie. She had lost her way and since she had driven all the way from New York, everything had to stop until she arrived.

I slipped into the music room to hide my disappointment and, as I looked around, I remembered how often I had sat on those little chairs while practicing with the junior choir. I had always wanted to be on the director's stool, and that night, all alone, I spread my long lace train over the high chair, then eased myself up on top. As I sat there, I wondered what *Life* would say about me.

Had they seen me as the sophisticated lady I tried to be, or did Yale Joel know that under my wedding gown was a scared little girl from three rooms behind her father's store? Would they feature shots of me in my elegant gown flanked by my flower girls, or would they infer I was a Cinderella whose shoes did not quite fit? I had spent my whole life training for this starring role, and I hoped *Life* would look at me from a positive point of view.

For years I had worked on my vocabulary. Inspired by my father, I had memorized every syllable in *Word*

Wealth and was able with ease and nonchalance to drop such gems as *magnanimous* and *mellifluous* into the right slots in sentences. I had learned the value of articulate alliteration and the impressive impact of biblical and Shakespearean quotations. Since my father had taught me Bible verses from the time I could talk, I needed only to brush up on my college Shakespeare to pepper my paragraphs.

I knew that "life's but a walking shadow" and that I might "suffer the slings and arrows of outrageous fortune" as I did "strut and fret my hour upon the stage."

In addition to my mental manipulations, I had worked to beautify my body. No fairy godmother waved her wand, but by diet, exercise and a Peter Pan padded bra, I had produced a commendable figure. With modeling lessons, I learned to walk well, do pivot turns and rise gracefully from my chair. With daily shampoos, I was able to fluff up my limp hair into a promising pageboy, and by proper application of mascara, I emphasized my eyes. I developed an instinct for showing up wherever the newspaper sent a photographer and learned by observation that if I wore a dark dress and stood sideways, I would always photograph slimmer than the rest. All of this self-improvement study had prepared me for this great moment when I would be "Queen for a Day."

As I sat on that high stool in the choir room, my gown flowing out around me, my crown on my head and my bouquet propped up on a music stand, I began to review the path that led me to *Life* and ask myself the question, "Can a simple school teacher from Haverhill find happiness in the big city?"

Aunt Edie finally arrived more than an hour late, having gone to the wrong church. Although the wedding party was a little wilted, we snapped to attention with the first commanding notes of the Wedding March. While the ceremony was short and unimpressive, it hardly mattered. Everyone was watching the photographer and smiling broadly hoping they would find themselves in *Life*.

After the ceremony the guests rushed into the fellow-ship hall for a drink of fruit punch prepared by the home economics department. The girls had also made tea sand-wiches, cookies and a wedding cake. As expected, the labeled gifts were a big hit. The ladies stood around dis-cussing who gave the most silver spoons and wondered why Mabel had sent an obviously second-hand plate.

The receiving line was endless. I had to kiss every pupil I ever had and hug every lady in the church. While the high school band played, Fred and I finally made the grand farewell. The police pushed back the crowds as the long white Cadillac holding Haverhill's "Our Miss Brooks" slowly passed the Riverside Variety Store.

I smiled and waved patronizingly as I had once seen Queen Elizabeth do from her gold carriage. The pupils screamed, cheered and threw baskets of confetti on us and themselves. With Fred's brother Steve at the wheel, we made as royal an exit as had ever been made from the Riverside Memorial Church.

The Honeymoon Was Over (Before It Had Begun)

As we drove into Boston I began to think about the trip ahead of us. The honeymoon had been planned to fulfill my Cinderella expectations. For weeks Fred and I had pored over travel folders. We selected a week in Bermuda as the best place for an ideal honeymoon. The biggest trip I had ever had was a tour of the Massachusetts State House when I was a Girl Scout and the idea of faraway Bermuda was overwhelming. After looking at pictures of petite cottages and azure seas I thought, *If only I could vacation there I could be happy*.

Getting to Bermuda from Haverhill, however, was another problem. After inquiries, Fred came up with an inspiring plan. We would spend our wedding night on a train! The thought of our first night together on a clanking train was hardly romantic. Fred comforted me by explain-ing that it wouldn't be an ordinary train with cracked leather seats. Rather, it would be a luxury locomotive with real rooms like a hotel. I liked the words *luxury* and *hotel* and romance once again filled my mind.

We arrived in Boston at midnight, drove to South Station and headed expectantly for our lavish suite. As we made our way toward the luxury locomotive, people pointed and giggled. I didn't know why at the time, but as I look back I can see it must have been the way we were dressed. My scarlet poodle-cloth going-away suit with a square double-breasted jacket and two rows of big pearl buttons, fit me as if I were wearing a red box tied with a huge white bow at the neck. To top it off, I wore a white straw hat edged in red velvet. The twenty-inch brim held a fluffy chiffon red rose and streamers down the back.

When we arrived at the gate to pick up our reserved passes, the clerk told us the train we had reserved had exploded and burned the day before. He assured us, however, the substitute train would be almost as good as the one we had anticipated. Disappointed, we entered the train, which may well have been the first Mr. Pullman ever produced, and were escorted to our suite.

When the porter opened the door, my dream of a romantic wedding night was immediately shattered. It was a cubicle less than half the size of our bedroom behind the store. I had expected to be traveling like a queen in a long, elegant car furnished like a European palace with a huge canopied bed. Instead we had an upper and lower berth, narrower than my cot at Camp Trebor. I began to cry.

The bathroom was so small we had to flatten against the wall to get the door shut. And the bedroom with its two bunks was so tiny that when Fred wanted to take a picture of me in my fluffy white negligee with pink satin rosebuds, he had to go into the hall and back against the far wall to get me in focus. Even then he missed the top of my head!

Fred calmed me down, and after agreeing that neither berth would accommodate both of us, he promptly went to sleep on the bottom bunk and I spent the night awake on the top bunk wondering how this could have ever happened to me. *If only* we could have been on the right train, I could have been happy.

Eventually morning came. Fred was alert; I was exhausted. I again put on my bright red suit and big hat and we went to the Hotel Commodore for a 6:30 A.M. breakfast. From the hotel we took a bus to the airport and flew to Bermuda hoping our disappointment was over.

Our honeymoon did improve when I saw the adorable pink cottage we were to stay in at Cambridge Beaches. But it was a little discouraging to find the bed was two couches on opposite sides of the room. Fred rearranged the furniture, put the couches together and our honeymoon began.

The first morning a waiter brought us a huge bowl of fresh strawberries and a lavish breakfast. We ate on our private patio that overlooked the ocean. It was a dream come true! But things were to change.

On our second afternoon Fred decided we should take a bicycle tour of the island. Unfortunately, Fred didn't know how totally uncoordinated I was. Within thirty seconds after renting a motorbike, I drove it straight into a stone wall and bent the front wheel. I had figured out how to start the motorbike but I had no idea how to stop it. Fred's enthusiasm for the trip was suddenly dimmed, but he courageously rented a second bicycle. I managed to drive, fearfully, for the rest of the afternoon.

Fred's idea of a beautiful honeymoon was to tour the ruins of old forts, and the next day we again took off on another bicycle tour. As I turned a corner on a sandy road, my bicycle skidded and fell over on top of me, twisting my right knee. I lay in a pained heap and as Fred turned and looked I could tell he was saddened with my plight, but obviously more annoyed with this delay in his plans.

Graciously, Fred told me he'd give me five minutes to rest and recover before going on. I thought he was cruel and inconsiderate but I had no choice—tears didn't impress him! Valiantly I pulled myself together, got back on the bicycle, and we inspected a few more forts. While Fred read every inscription on every doorway and perused every historical tidbit, I wept silently and wondered how this could have happened to me.

The following day my knee was swollen twice its normal size. When Fred saw I was unfit for the trails, he suggested I stay in bed. Since he didn't want to waste a day, he went off alone on another historical jaunt. I lay in bed all day in misery, wondering if all honeymoons were this dreadful.

On Friday we left for home aboard the Ocean Monarch, a huge ship that was like a floating hotel. I always loved romantic movies where the heroine sailed off on an ocean voyage while her friends wept and waved at the dock. I had read *Our Hearts Were Young and Gay* so many times I could feel the ocean swell whenever I picked up the book.

The ship did not disappoint me. It was greater than any movie I had seen or book I had read. Our stateroom was magnificent, and even though we were again dismayed to find double bunks, I was delighted with the flowers Fred ordered for our cabin.

Before the ship left Hamilton Harbor, Fred and I strolled hand in hand around the deck and relaxed on striped lounge chairs while dignified British waiters in red coats served us tea and crumpets. I was so excited with this storybook setting I hardly noticed my throbbing knee. However, the moment we cast off and Fred felt that first lurch, he raced for the rail. Within minutes he was deathly ill. He immediately retreated to our cabin and didn't emerge until we landed in New York Harbor.

To make matters worse, we ran into a hurricane with waves as high as the deck. As each wave smashed the wall of our stateroom, Fred groaned that he wished he were dead. Depressed to have my new husband wishing he were dead, and obviously having no fun, I left him alone and went off in search of something to brighten up a dull trip.

That afternoon as I limped around the deck, I met Tom, a handsome young Englishman whose wife was also sick. As our mates lay below in misery, we sipped tea and watched the huge waves from our deck chairs. All would have been perfect, but my knee became steadily worse and finally Tom took me to the ship's doctor. After the doctor examined it, he reprimanded me for my negligence in waiting so long to be treated. He told me I had torn the ligaments. After draining out a vial of fluid, he bound up the knee in an Ace bandage. Tom took tender care of me and we daringly concluded in jest that we hardy souls should have married each other. Although ladies on ships are supposed to have clandestine romances, I was not about to have one on my honeymoon.

Fred's mother met us at the dock in New York Harbor and was aghast to see what a week of marriage had done to us. Fred had lost ten pounds and looked green. I hobbled stiff-legged down the gang plank while he hung on to the ropes to keep from collapsing.

How to Be a Wife—Fred's Way

After we moved into our three-room apartment in Bronxville, New York, I was hit hard by the realization that after every wedding comes a marriage. Too few brides understand that the wedding is not necessarily the beginning of a great life, but the possible end of one. Our honeymoon had been a disappointment, but my hopes for the future were brighter. Unfortunately, when I returned from Bermuda, I became stupid overnight.

From being the urbane queen of Haverhill, Massachusetts, I quickly became Fred's own private Eliza Doolittle. What had looked so smooth and sophisticated in Haverhill suddenly turned shoddy in New York. While Fred had appeared to accept me just as I was before we were married, he found abundant faults in me as I took on the role of his wife. When our marriage was one week old he announced, "I'm going to put you on a training program. It will help you become a perfect wife. The first thing we have to do is get rid of your Boston accent."

"I don't have an accent," I snapped. "Everybody in Boston talks like me."

"Well, it may sound all right in Boston," said Fred, "but your accent will never be accepted in New York society."

I was crushed. I had thought my diction and intonation faultless. It distressed me that I had to learn to talk all over again. Every time I put an "r" where it shouldn't be (such as *idear*) or left one out (such as *paak* for park), Fred made me repeat the word three times correctly. For a person who talked as much and as fast as I did, this constant correction was unbearable. I soon stopped talking and communicated with Fred only in simple, one-syllable words that contained no r's!

The second lesson was teaching me how to walk. Since I had taken modeling and drama, I thought I knew how to walk quite nicely. When I defended myself, Fred pointed out that my feet turned out at the toes and his mother had always told him one should walk with one's toes straight ahead. Every night he made me practice by walking on the tiles on our foyer floor until I could go ten lengths without my toes lapping over the lines. What an exciting way to spend an evening!

My third lesson was how to answer the telephone. In Haverhill we just said "Hello," but Fred said this was uncouth. I had to pick up the phone and say, "Good evening, this is Florence Littauer. With whom did you wish to speak?" I thought this wordy and ridiculous, but Fred insisted and called several times a day to spot-check my responses.

My fourth and most difficult lesson was cooking. He analyzed every dish and then gave me an instant critique. Fred was in the restaurant business and knew far more about cooking than I did. He explained that one should never put two vegetables of the same color on the same plate. Also one should never put two vegetables of the same consistency together. In other words, I could never serve carrots and candied yams on the same plate, nor mashed potatoes and whipped turnips at the same time.

On one occasion Fred became upset because I gave him a sandwich on a paper plate. He told me he expected china service and then asked, "Where is the watercress?" In Haverhill we were lucky to get a sandwich on a napkin and whoever heard of watercress? If I had been asked to guess, I would have thought it was a little fish, like a sardine. Fortunately, I didn't have to ask. "Watercress," said Fred, "is a leafy garnish of a higher class than parsley; no sandwich should be served without it."

The other rule I found difficult to follow was that I must always preheat the dinner plates and pre-chill the salad plates. Fred made me recite to him, "Hot food on hot plates, cold food on cold plates."

On one of our first Saturday evenings after we were married, I served him hot dogs, baked beans and canned brown bread. I had eaten this tasty dish every Saturday night of my life. But when Fred saw it without even a sprig of parsley, he gave me a discouraged look and said, "What's this?"

"They're franks and beans," I said. "It's what everyone eats on Saturday night."

"Perhaps in Boston," he said, "but I never want to see canned baked beans again."

I cried and scraped the all-brown dinner down the garbage disposal—a part of my heritage ground up before my eyes!

The fifth lesson in my exciting bridal instruction course was on housekeeping. Fred's training in the restaurant had taught him to spot, with one sweep of his eye, every salt and pepper shaker that was out of place, every crooked picture frame and every waitress's bow that was not properly tied.

Likewise when he came home at night, he could, with one sweep of his eye, see everything I hadn't done properly. He would walk in the front door of our little apartment and immediately straighten the tilted pictures, rearrange the magazines on the coffee table so they were even from each edge and run his finger over the dressers to see if I had dusted. He would point out my sins of commission or omission, and with a condescending smile show me how to do everything better.

One night after watching me wash the dishes, Fred heaved a big sigh and told me I had made forty-two unnecessary moves. I had never heard of anyone counting the moves one made washing dishes, so I threw a big wet sponge at him. He was upset with my unladylike behavior and couldn't understand what had disturbed me.

"I'm sick of your constant instruction," I said.

He replied, "It's only natural for one who is more gifted to share his knowledge with one who is less fortunate."

So there it was—Fred's whole attitude toward marriage: a brilliant man trying to put up with a stupid woman. Surprisingly, in spite of Fred's critical attitude, I was grateful for a home of my own, and each morning I was able to bounce back from the previous day's instructions.

After Every Wedding Comes a Marriage

On May 18, 1953, our copy of *Life* arrived with a five-page spread entitled, "Pupils Help a Teacher Get Married." The copy was positive and complimentary, but there was one problem. Fred's name was never mentioned. I chuckled inwardly. The Littauers, who bought magazines for all the relatives, couldn't believe their family name had been omitted. In fact, the only clear picture of Fred was at the rehearsal, where I was instructing the pastor and Fred was looking down at his hand. *Life* said,

"Rehearsing wedding evening before ceremony, bride-groom looks confusedly at fingers."

As I looked over the pictures, I was delighted to see myself in print. I reread the article.

Pupils Help a Teacher Get Married: Admiring Teen-Agers Take Over Ceremony

When Florence Chapman, a high school teacher in Haverhill, Mass., announced her engagement last winter, her pupils promptly besieged her with offers to help out at her wedding. Miss Chapman, who teaches public speaking and dramatics, accepted their offers and began assigning their duties like homework. For the pupils, who designed the wedding costumes, decorated the reception hall, and helped prepare and serve the food at the reception itself, their teacher's wedding had everything that a class play would have, and romance too. Most of them had never been so close to an actual wedding before. But after it was all over and the bride and bridegroom had departed in a car driven by a pupil, one of the girls confessed, "It was lots of fun, but I'd rather get married more privately."

The wedding was the high point of my life, I thought after reading the article, *but it's slowly going down hill.*

I never stayed down for long and cheered myself on by beginning to make my little home a pleasant place to live, even if it wasn't too pleasant living there.

I had never had the opportunity to decorate anything beyond putting a blue Bates bedspread on my college cot. After papering the dinette in white paper with huge red roses, I decided to make the living room into a sort of opium den. I had never seen an opium den, of course, but I had picked up some ideas from Charlie Chan movies. I had a set of twenty silk padded Chinese paper dolls and used them as a focal point by gluing them to the living room wall at different heights.

After arranging the dolls in groupings, I then under-lined each section with strips of black plastic tape. Since we were without living room furniture, I took the odd pieces we had collected from relatives and painted them all in black glossy enamel. I made drapes out of bright red heavy cloth adorned with one-foot-high chartreuse Chinamen burning incense. I was thrilled with the consistent theme I had developed and knew the people in Haverhill would have been impressed. However, the relatives in New York were not. They somehow felt my opium den was not a fitting family image, and when Fred saw my Chinese dolls glued to the wall, he told me he thought the place looked like a first grade classroom. However, I didn't let these words discourage me. I was happy with my results and plunged into decorating the bedroom.

Gratefully, Fred said little about my draping the room in soft pink ruffles and I took his silence as a dubious compliment.

Next I decided to become a hostess. I invited some of Fred's family and friends over to play charades. I had spent days planning the party, and when the day came I made what I thought was an extremely clever dessert.

I bought little clay flower pots that were just the right size to hold my custard cups. I baked a half inch of cake batter in each cup, packed the cups with ice cream, and put them in the freezer. When it came time to serve the dessert, I whipped up a bowl of meringue which I spread in mounds on the cake and ice cream cups. I then slipped them into the oven and watched with delight as they puffed up and browned just perfectly. I then dropped each hot cup into a clay flower pot and stuck a real chrysanthemum into the meringue. For the final touch I placed a sugar cube soaked in brandy at the base of each flower and lit the cubes.

I carried the tray of flaming flower pots into the living room expecting Fred's acclaim. Instead he looked up and said, "What in the world have you done?" One of his sophisticated relatives gave a look that said, "What has the poor, gauche child come up with now?"

As I stood before them in my red Chinese gown, my adorable garden of desserts wilted before my eyes. By the time I served the last one, meringue was running down the pot and the chrysanthemum was on fire. Fred was embarrassed and I went to bed discouraged. As I drifted off to sleep, I thought what a hit my pots would have made back at the sorority.

Early Marital Advice

As the weeks passed I became more and more convinced that Fred and I were just two different people and there was little hope for a successful marriage. I began to ask the other girls in our apartment house how they were doing.

Most told me their marriages were no better than mine. I also learned from the other girls that my puritanical, Victorian morals and New England legalism had no place in the Fleetwood Arms Apartments.

My best friend was Gail. Her wealthy parents had left her in their big home while they had taken a six-month trip. When her parents returned, they discovered Gail's boyfriend, Joe, had been living with her, and their only daughter was two months pregnant. The parents insisted they marry immediately, which they did, and Gail's parents rented them the apartment next to ours.

Spoiled and lazy, Gail came each day to visit me. While I scrubbed and cleaned in a vain effort to please Fred, she sat and watched. Then just before Friendly Joe came home from work, Gail would wash off her makeup, flop down on my couch and pretend to be sick. When Joe came over to our apartment looking for her, she would moan about how ill she was and how it was his fault that she was pregnant in the first place. With a deep sense of guilt, Joe would help her back to their apartment and cook dinner.

I was wide-eyed with this game she played and knew I could never get away with such an act with Fred.

Then there was Thelma. She lived across the hall and was a little older and more worldly-wise than the rest of us. I had never met her traveling husband, but one day as I opened my hall door I saw a man unlocking Thelma's door and assumed it was her husband. I saw Thelma that evening and said, "I finally caught a glimpse of your Tom. He's really good looking." She seemed frightened and asked when I had seen him.

"I noticed him unlocking your door at lunch time," I said.

"Oh, that's not my husband," she said, "that's my friend Alex. He comes over every noon when Tom is out of town."

One night when Thelma knew Fred was working, she called and asked if I would like to come over to her apartment. "Alex has an adorable friend and he needs a date," she said. I told her primly I didn't do that sort of thing, and Thelma hung up in disgust.

Some time later Thelma told me I was naive and needed some broadening experiences. She, with Gail, suggested I have a baby. "A cute little thing around the house will take the pressure off your marriage." They also said a baby would keep my husband so happy he wouldn't have time to inspect my housework.

Fred had mentioned he wanted a namesake, but I wasn't in a hurry. Yet my marriage wasn't getting any better. Perhaps having a baby would remove the constant criticism of Fred's continuous training program. I marvel now that I was naive enough to believe a baby would make life easier. Anyone with an ounce of brains would have known that changing diapers at 2 A.M. would not revive a flagging marriage.

But before we began our program of potential parenthood, Fred was transferred to Cleveland to open a new restaurant in the Westgate Shopping Center. I was disappointed to have to tear apart my first home and pry the padded Chinese paper dolls off the wall, but I was excited about moving to a new state. Perhaps a fresh beginning and getting away from Fred's family was what our marriage needed.

We rented an attractive garden apartment in Cleveland and I began my decorating all over again. Within a few weeks I found I was pregnant, but by the time I had finished settling into my new home, Fred was promoted. Top management saw Fred as a master of detail and organization. The very qualities that bothered me impressed his superiors! They were grateful he could spot a sandwich without watercress, answer the telephone in a distinctive manner and walk with his feet straight ahead! So they sent him to Detroit to open the new Stouffer's at Northland.

Fred found us a beautiful apartment with a full basement; a first-floor living room, dinette and kitchen; and an upstairs with two bedrooms and a bath. It was almost a house.

Both of us excitedly became involved in our own projects. Fred worked extremely long hours and I decorated again and eagerly waited for our first child to be born. I was to learn later that our relationship was always best when our separate projects kept us apart—there was no time to bother each other!

Two weeks before I was due, I caught a terrible cold that turned into bronchial pneumonia. My condition became critical and the doctor decided to induce labor. However, he neglected to tell me or Fred what he was doing. Early the next morning I began to get sharp pains and I was taken unceremoniously off to the labor room and strapped to the sides of a large, white iron crib. There were at least thirty other women in similar cribs, all screaming in pain.

I had no idea having a baby was a public affair and I was mortified to be lying in agony in front of all these women. I asked the one nurse, who filed soberly through the room giving us all indiscriminate shots, if my husband knew I was in the labor room.

"I'm sure they've called him," she said brusquely.

They had not. While I was delivering Lauren Luise Littauer, Fred was home polishing his shoes. When he arrived that afternoon to see his wife who had pneumonia, he learned to his surprise that he had a daughter and a wife who was upset that he hadn't been present for the birth of his first child.

Due to my infection, the baby and I stayed in the hospital for over a week during which time Fred read three books on motherhood. By the time I got home, he already knew more about how to be a mother than I know to this day.

While I felt I was a semi-failure as a wife, cook and housekeeper, I thought genetically I would be a better mother than Fred. Instead of relieving the pressure in my marriage, Lauren only added to it. Fred now had a whole new training program for me. After two years of marriage, I was firmly convinced that in Fred's sight I was a total failure. It took my very best determination to keep my basic optimistic nature alive.

Reflections

Wouldn't you think that someone who had managed to work her way up from three rooms behind the store to an expensive New York apartment and five pages in *Life* ought to live happily ever after? I surely thought so until I got there.

As I look back with the advantage of hindsight I see that Fred and I got married for some of the wrong reasons. I equated happiness with money, a big house and good looks, all things I had so desperately wanted as I was growing up. I felt if I filled those voids I could be happy, and Fred seemed to answer my needs.

Little did I know that Fred had grown up feeling unloved by his busy parents and had been abused by a maid. Where there should have been love, he had nothing but extreme feelings of rejection. His mother had so domineered his life that Fred was eager to be in control of a female. I see now why he demanded I tell him I loved him whether I felt like it or not, why any light-hearted touch of humor came across as rejection, and why he was determined to break my will and be in control.

Since I felt like the poor girl from the country with no rights of my own, I accepted the situation and did whatever Fred instructed. He was never impolite or rude and he never hit me, but I just learned quickly that in turn for the nice home and money I had to play by his rules.

I once saw a sign in a store, "He who has the gold makes the rules." That's the way we lived. As I look back, I realize that I wanted money and a real home and Fred provided these. He needed love and acceptance and I tried to fill that huge, empty well inside him. But when Fred had business failures and didn't give me money, I stopped giving him the doting love he wanted. How we often marry to find someone who can fill our voids. And then when they fail to meet our every need, we assume we have married the wrong person.

When you think about it, can you see some deep emotional needs that you and your mate were craving to have filled when you married? Did you match up in your areas of emptiness? Have you matured emotionally and grown up together? Or has one of you made progress and the other refused to change? Isn't it amazing how we can look back and see our mistakes that were not recognizable at the time? Fred and I praise God today that He had a hold on us long before we had an awareness of our needs. Marriage isn't easy, but it is possible in retrospect to

Make the tough times count.

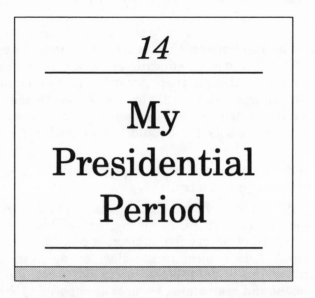

14

My Presidential Period

I had to admit that in those few moments, Ben had gotten closer to my heart and the problem of my marriage than anyone before him.

A year after Lauren was born, Fred left Stouffer's and took a job in New Haven, Connecticut, operating the food service of the Southern New England Telephone Company. He left Detroit ahead of Lauren and me to find us a place to live. One night he called, all excited. He had just rented a lovely home in Montowese and hoped I would like it even though both the living room and exterior were painted black. The thought of a black house depressed me but I had no choice since he had made a month's rent deposit. *We can always paint it,* I thought. Gratefully, when I arrived in Connecticut I found the house was not black, but forest green. Fred is color blind and to him it all looked black.

Life looked black to me as I settled into a lonely house in a town where I had no friends. I began to look for something more interesting than housework and child raising. Since I didn't seem to be good at either, I thought *if only* I had a challenging job I could be happy. I applied to the New Haven adult education program as an English teacher and although there wasn't an opening in the English department, they did have a desperate need for a teacher in a course called Elementary Psychology. The superintendent asked if I could handle such an assignment.

"I don't have credentials in psychology," I said, "but I'm willing to give it a try."

Within a week I read eight books on psychology and skimmed a dozen more. From my instant knowledge, I made up a list of twenty-five subjects of possible study and presented these choices to the class on opening night. Gratefully, the students chose topics like personality improvement and overcoming shyness as opposed to Freud's dream analysis and Sheinfeld's genetics. With my adult pupils' mandate clearly in hand, I went home and wrote a course. In order to teach two hours of class time twice a week, I studied six to eight hours each day. My group was thrilled that I cared enough to tailor the course to their needs.

As the year went on and other classes suffered from dropouts, my psychology class grew from thirty-five to more than fifty. I taught a second semester with most of the group returning and I was hired to teach psychology for a second year.

As I prepared for my second year, the North Haven board of education drafted me to teach a night course for women. The board didn't care what the subject matter was, as long as it appealed to women. I decided to make use of all the things Fred had spent years teaching me, plus a little psychology, and I designed a program called "Gracious Living." I was amazed at how much I had learned from Fred. Who would have thought I would ever enjoy teaching others the things I once hated to learn!

The following year I was hired as a full-time English

instructor at North Haven High School. Besides teaching English, I wrote two new courses in public speaking and creative writing. I also directed all the drama productions for the school and in 1958, my version of *The Boyfriend* won the top award at the New England Drama Festival. I was named best director of high school productions in New England. I attended a meeting of the Connecticut Speech and Drama Association and was elected president on my first visit before I'd even joined. On top again, my self-image brightened; I felt I no longer had to worry about what Fred thought of me. The town and even the state had accepted me!

Fred went into business for himself and when his food service company was doing well enough, we decided we should have another child. I was in my second year at North Haven High School when I became pregnant with what was supposed to be my husband's namesake, Frederick Jerome Littauer, III.

I kept on teaching and because I was careful with my weight and figure, no one knew I was expecting. I was also proud that pregnancy didn't slow me down. A-line dresses were in style and I modeled for a fashion show the day I delivered. After the show, my doctor examined me and in amazement said, "You are about to have this baby any minute. Get to the hospital immediately."

I was admitted to Yale-New Haven Hospital at 5 o'clock on October 29, 1958, and Marita Kathryn was born at 6 o'clock without my having one labor pain. The doctor was so amazed at my easy labor that he brought in a whole class of medical students who stood and stared at me throughout the entire delivery.

Doing Something Right

When Marita was six months old I began to escape the reality of my dull marriage by spending as much time out of the house as possible. Now that I no longer worked, I joined several different civic organizations and was elected president of the League of Women Voters in North

Haven, Connecticut. While I was giving my full attention to the League, Fred still talked of having a son. Reluctantly I agreed to try again.

In the fall of '59, I was both pregnant and president, and I decided I needed a maid. *If only* I had a maid, I could be happy. My husband's business was doing well and he felt there would be hope for the home if we had a real housekeeper. We hired Willie May Jones, a dignified black lady who took over my household completely. Finally I had a buffer between me and Fred. Whatever he complained about, I could say, "It's the maid's fault."

Years later I discovered from Lauren that each afternoon Willie May took my two little girls for a ride in her car and dropped into the back room of Joe's Cigar Store in the worst part of town to pick up money she had won playing the *numbers*. I didn't know what the *numbers* were. I just knew she called in some figures to someone each morning. She loved the combination of numbers on my license plate and "played it" frequently. In a year's time she picked up enough money from the man in the back room of the cigar store to buy a three-tenement house and quit working.

However, while Willie May was with us, I took advantage of the freedom and went out daily to save the world. Why should I stay home when Fred was spending every waking moment on his business? In three years he had gone from managing one cafeteria to being president of his own Mealtime Management with eighteen different accounts and a staff of over a hundred. I was happy and relieved that he had a whole staff to boss instead of just me.

He was so successful that one restaurant magazine called him "The Boy Wonder of the Food Service Industry." Fred responded by writing detailed manuals on every facet of his business. He was also asked to speak on the secrets of his success at the National Restaurant Convention in Chicago. But with all this exciting activity, he had little time for his family.

We decided we should expand our house now that financial security was assured and our third child was on the way. Fred began to design what he wanted and together we incorporated every conceivable convenience that any home could contain.

At this point I was called and asked if I could teach a freshman speech class at the University of Connecticut. The person hired had suddenly left town and the dean who knew me from the Speech and Drama Association had confidence that I could do it. I told him I was pregnant, but he said he didn't care if I turned green if I'd just help him out. I was thrilled to go back to teaching two days a week and once again I worked hard to prepare for each class. I kept my weight down, wore loose clothes, and stood behind the lectern so that the students were shocked when Fred arrived to give the final exam and told them I was in the hospital about to deliver.

On February 9, 1960, Frederick Jerome Littauer III was born in another painless delivery, watched this time by a group of student nurses who kept feeling my tummy and saying, "Are you sure it doesn't hurt?" It didn't, and I was thrilled to have produced our Freddie. My husband was even more excited. "Finally, you've done something right."

In March I was re-elected president of the League, and also appointed state budget director for the Connecticut League of Women Voters. In this position I traveled throughout the state to each local chapter, instructing them how to put together a budget— a topic on which Fred felt I was remarkably unqualified to speak.

Since I had always refused to make a budget for our household finances and had difficulty in balancing my checkbook, it was ironic that I would be running around telling others how to do what I could never do myself. Challenges such as the budget job had always fascinated me and I remember the summer I successfully taught archery at Camp Trebor when I was totally unable to get an arrow to the target myself. I did a quick study of the State League of Women Voters' Budget Book and learned enough to present the basic principles clearly.

That same year I was elected president of the Quinnipiac Valley Theatre. While in this position, in the ensuing years, I directed *Call Me Madam, Guys and Dolls, South Pacific,* and *Oklahoma.*

In March 1960 we began the construction of our new addition and in April, on our seventh wedding anniversary, Fred took me back to Bermuda for a one-week second honeymoon at Ariel Sands. I rode the bicycles cautiously and we flew both ways.

A Stranger's Insight

A week after we returned from Bermuda, I left for St. Louis as a delegate to the League of Women Voters' national convention. After Freddie's birth I returned to a size eight and treated myself to a whole new wardrobe. I packed the best of my wardrobe and headed for St. Louis with Ethel Libson, my League vice-president.

The first evening Ethel stayed in our room while I went across the street to the drugstore. As I walked alone through the lobby, I passed a noisy group of men who whistled at me. I was flattered and pleased they found me appealing. Fred had once said, "If there is one thing you don't have, it's sex appeal."

I crossed the street and began to realize I had devoted my life to becoming beautiful, but underneath I still felt like a plain, dull little girl from Haverhill. Fred never let me forget how he had saved me from being an old maid and how grateful I should be for his sacrifice.

As I struggled with my self-image I sensed someone following me. I walked quickly into the drugstore and sat down at the counter. When I ordered an orange juice, a voice next to me said, "I'll have one too and I'll pay for them both." I looked over to see a handsome, well-dressed man seated on the next stool.

Was this a pick-up? In my thirty-two years I had never been picked up. My premarriage romances had been ordinary, and my courtship with Fred so orderly and proper it eliminated any chance of suggestive excitement. While I viewed our marriage as routine and Fred's constant criticism a damper to any emotions, I had been a faithful wife. A strange shiver went through my body as I realized that good little me was sitting in a drugstore far from home with an unknown man who at that moment was paying for my orange juice. The plot was hardly the basis for a movie, but it held a first-time fascination for me.

As his gorgeous brown eyes looked me up and down, he leaned over and said, "I won you for the week."

"You won me!"

"Yes, I won you," he said. "We men are here for a shirtmaker's convention and were standing around the lobby looking for beautiful women. Frankly, the League of Women Voters aren't too appealing. We were discouraged with the flat-footed tweedy types and then you got off the elevator and we all said, 'That's more like it.' When you walked by in your slim silk dress and we whistled, you blushed and we knew we had a challenge. You were the best looking thing we'd seen, so we drew lots for you and I won. You are mine for the week and none of the others will try to take you away."

I was aghast at his explanation. The brightest thing I could think of was, "I'm married."

"So am I," he said. "But that doesn't mean a thing. You're away and I'm away and we wouldn't want to waste the week, would we?"

While I had never been a wasteful person, I thought it might be better to throw away this particular week than to use it the way he had in mind.

I explained what a fine moral person I was and how

faithful I had always been to my husband, but this only seemed to increase the challenge. He told me how it was possible to be true-blue at home and yet have fun at conventions. He explained he was a pillar of his community, a member of the school board on Long Island, and a model husband and father. "But what the little woman doesn't know won't hurt her," he said.

There was no way to get rid of this rather fascinating man, and I walked back to the hotel with him. He told me his name was Ben and he had come to sell Donmoor shirts. When we entered the lobby together, his friends applauded.

"Here's the winner," they said. "What a prize! If you change your mind, we'll take her."

I had never thought of myself as a prize and it was a nice feeling. We stood in the lobby and talked for awhile until I remembered Ethel and said, "I have to go to bed."

That statement brought roars from the group and they sent me off in the elevator—with Ben. "I can't invite you in because my friend Ethel is here," I said when we arrived at my door.

"You've got a roommate?" he asked, distressed.

"Yes," I said as I opened the door, stepped inside and gave him a wave goodnight.

Ethel and I laughed over my being the prize in a lottery and I knew that was the end of Ben. However, the next morning Ben was in the lobby waiting to take me to breakfast. I introduced him to Ethel and told him I had to eat with her. Ben wasn't too thrilled to meet Ethel, but asked her along.

After breakfast Ethel and I went to our League meetings, had lunch with the convention, and when I emerged at 4:00 P.M. there was Ben on a couch across from the door. When I looked surprised, he said, "I won you for a whole week, remember?"

I didn't quite know what to do with Ben. I had never

been won before. I didn't dare leave Ethel's side, so he took us both to dinner and to breakfast the following morning.

That afternoon Ethel went to a different meeting and I came out from the auditorium alone. Ben was ecstatic to find me without Ethel and asked me to come and look at his shirt display. I had been to many restaurant conventions and the displays were always out in a big ballroom with hundreds of people milling around. Certainly there was no harm in browsing through a few shirt racks.

We strolled toward the elevator, and he told me how much money he made a year in shirts. We got out on the second floor and walked toward what I assumed was going to be a ballroom. As I looked for the crowds, Ben unlocked a door labeled Donmoor Shirts, eased me into a room and shut the door behind him. There before me was a rack of shirts in his bedroom! As I gasped, Ben smiled, put his arm tightly around me and whispered, "I never thought I could pry you away from Ethel."

He eased me onto the edge of the bed and my back went rigid. "Relax," he said, "I'm not a rapist, just a nice average guy with a little free time on his hands. I wouldn't consider doing anything to you that you wouldn't enjoy."

The phrase was well put, but I was scared to death. How could I get out of the room unscathed and yet not appear like a dumb country kid? At the time it seemed important that I didn't appear unsophisticated by screaming. As these thoughts raced through my mind, Ben began to ask about my husband.

"Do you really love him?"

"I guess so," I said.

"You're not sure?"

I realized I was not. What was love, anyway? I was a dutiful wife but had to admit things were better when I didn't see too much of Fred. Maybe I didn't really love him. I never allowed myself to think of failing.

"Does your husband make you happy?"

"He provides for me very well. We are building a big addition to our home and he just bought me a beautiful black cherry Lincoln with leather interior."

"I didn't ask what you owned. I asked if your husband makes you happy. Do you get excited when you see him coming home?"

"Scared is more like it," I sighed. "I'm scared at what he's going to find wrong. But things are getting better now. I have a maid to do the housework and Fred is so busy that he doesn't come home until late at night."

"That doesn't sound like much of a marriage to me," said Ben. "You're each running around doing your own thing and not caring much about each other. You're so wrapped up in your big house, your maid and car, you don't even know you're miserable."

"I am not miserable. I have everything," I snapped defensively.

"Everything but love and contentment," he said. "You're as tight as a drum. I bet you keep yourself so busy climbing your social ladder you don't have time to think about how unhappy you are inside."

Ben had touched a raw nerve. My doctor had often told me I was an uptight person trying to appear happy. *Is it possible I do all these superhuman feats to prove to myself I'm happy?* I thought. I had never been too reflective and felt uncomfortable trying to analyze my motives. "I must be happy. I've achieved all my goals in life," I reassured myself out loud.

"Happiness is not achieving goals. It's being loved," said Ben softly. He whispered the word *loved* and gently pushed me down on the bed. Lying there confused, I looked up into his compassionate eyes and suddenly realized where I was. Virtuous me was alone in a hotel room with a strange man who was showing a warm interest in my marriage. Immediately it struck me that Ben didn't care a thing for my marriage. He had hit a sensitive spot and I had almost fallen for his line. I had to get away, but I didn't know how to retreat gracefully.

Here was a man who seemed to understand me. Oh, how I longed to be understood. Fred was so sure of himself, so businesslike, so proper, so serious, so busy, but Ben was a man who took it easy. He was fun to talk with. He cared about my inner feelings, and he was taking time out of a busy day to talk of love. The contrast overwhelmed me. I was in the wrong place but I was too content to leave.

"You don't know what you're missing," said Ben. "I want to help you find yourself." What a sweet thought. He wanted to help me.

The phone rang and brought me back to reality. While Ben took a shirt order, I got up and went to the door. Ben didn't try to stop me. "You'll be back," he said. "You need my help."

Maybe I needed his help, but I knew I wouldn't be back. Yet I had to admit that in those few moments, Ben had gotten closer to my heart and the problem of my marriage than anyone before him. None of my friends had ever seen beyond my exterior. Whenever Fred mentioned that our marriage wasn't as it should be, I always scoffed and told him I was content and the problem must be his. In my pursuit of happiness I had deceived myself and refused to believe my fairy-tale desires had not been totally fulfilled. But Ben had seen through me; he had hit a vulnerable spot.

I didn't go back. Ben followed me for the remainder of the week but never once did I leave Ethel's side.

On our last evening, Ben took Ethel and me to dinner. About 10:30 he called and invited me to his room after Ethel had gone to sleep. "Come on down," he said. "It's your last chance for happiness. Don't throw it away."

I thanked him for dinner, but I said firmly that I had no intention of ever seeing him again. Then he begged me to come so he could "save face" with his friends. I hated to ruin his reputation with his fellow shirtmakers, but I was more concerned with my own reputation.

"I may have won you for a week," he said, "but you didn't turn out to be much of a prize."

Fred met me at the plane and looked more handsome than I had remembered. He was impeccably dressed in a navy suit and striped tie, and his blond hair had touches of silver. Many women told me I was lucky to have such a handsome husband. And I was. *If only* he could love me just as I was, without all his instructions, I knew I could be happy.

I was glad Fred brought the girls. Lauren at five-and-a-half was a serious child who constantly wanted my attention. Marita was an eighteen-month-old bundle of bubbling energy who was always doing something she didn't want me to see. Both wore matching yellow organdy dresses with yellow bows in their hair.

I was proud.

That Elusive Happily Ever After

After my trip, I immediately got to work on the new part of the house. *If only* my house could be a showplace, I could be happy.

We finished the addition, complete with a twenty-by-twenty-foot bedroom, and to fulfill my childhood dreams, we topped it off with a huge fireplace and stereo speakers under our throne-type bed.

When the house was just the way I had envisioned, I began a round of lavish parties and exclusive social lunches. I opened my home for every imaginable pur-pose—board meetings, cast parties, the League of Women Voters tea—and crammed between all this activity, I de-cided to try to match my husband's skill at tennis.

I began by buying several adorable tennis dresses, a good racket and an hour of instruction. I learned where to plant my feet, how to move my body and how to swing the racket. *At last,* I thought, *here is a sport I can handle.* But in the second lesson, the teacher introduced the ball.

I could do professional pivots and swing in style, but could not quite connect the racket with the ball. Even when the instructor threw the ball right at the racket, I missed it. The instructor became discouraged faster than I did, and after six lessons said, "Mrs. Littauer, the best thing about your tennis is your attitude. It's great, but attitude alone won't win tennis games. I suggest you try another sport."

I never did try another sport; I just sat every weekend watching Fred win his matches. Once during a long tournament I was bored so I began reading a magazine. Fred left the court, stormed over to the fence and told me to put the magazine away and pay attention.

Week after week, year after year, I sat with Linda, his partner's wife, while we both pretended to love tennis. We clapped at the right times and hardly dared converse for fear of annoying the men. We stood by them when their pictures were taken and went to the dinners when they were honored. We were perfect country club wives, masking our true feelings. Fifteen years later I met Linda after her divorce and we confessed how miserable our tennis era had been.

Each weekend as I sat looking through chain link fences, I began to question the direction my life was taking. Ben had started me thinking when he told me I was unhappy and miserable. I denied that possibility, but as I sat bored, forbidden to read or talk, pretending to be interested in a little white ball, I wondered if I wasn't deceiving myself.

I knew I should be the happiest woman alive. I had achieved my goals. I had gone to college and become a teacher. I had closets full of clothes and enough money for cars, fur coats and exotic vacations. My house was a showplace. I had a maid, two well-dressed little girls and finally a son to please my husband. It was true that Fred's critical and negative nature bothered me, as did the knowledge that I would never measure up to his ideal of perfection, but I was not going to be defeated. For the first time in my life I had everything I wanted and I was determined to be happy forever.

Reflections

As I look back on this period of our marriage I realize it was a recess for both of us. Fred was wrapped up in his business and I was the professional president for every group in need of a leader. He was too busy and successful to feel rejected and I was so happy with the money and the lifestyle that I finally had confidence in my looks and social status.

I did not realize at that point that while Fred and I could communicate intellectually and socially, we had no relationship on an emotional level. We functioned totally in our minds. No wonder when Ben began to communicate on a feeling level, even for all the wrong reasons, I started to respond. Although we did nothing but talk, he did awaken me to the emotional vacuum in my marriage.

In counseling couples today I find many who are right where I was at that time. They are not fighting or unfaithful. They are intellectual, even spiritual, giants, but nothing's going on between them. I've had some tell me that they are so spiritual they don't need any real romance in their life. I shudder when someone shows a pride in sexual abstinence and I remember Ben's words, "You don't even know you're miserable."

Whenever we are functioning in a marriage relationship without heart, we are open to temptation. I've talked with Christian leaders who sincerely believed they were so like Paul that they needed no emotional communication—until that day when some weepy little lady threw herself upon him or some Ben touched a long-neglected chord. Suddenly feelings long suppressed came pounding on the pillow. At that point in my marriage I felt the best I had in years and yet I see now how vulnerable I was because I was functioning on a polite, intellectual level without realizing my emotions were sitting patiently below the surface waiting to be called forth at a moment's notice.

Where are you today in your marriage relationship? Are you a time-bomb waiting to go off? Would a good offer cause you to chuck it all and run away?

A well-known Christian radio personality in the midwest fell in love with his secretary. When he came to me in desperation he admitted he'd been too busy to pay attention to his wife who'd grown hard and cold by neglect. He knew if he continued with the secretary his whole denomination would turn against him and his ministry would be over. As we agreed intellectually and spiritually I asked, "If she walked in here right now and said, 'Come with me to Tahiti and start life all over again' what would you do?" He burst into sobs and said, "I'd go. I'd go."

A loveless marriage only lasts until someone lights a spark. If you're sitting in a placid relationship right now, these indifferent days are tough times. Do all you can humanly and prayerfully to communicate on a deeper level. Avoid temptation.

Make the tough times count.

15

Two Tragedies

I was faced with a tragedy that I could do nothing about. I had to learn that there were things in life money and willpower couldn't fix.

The fall of 1960 was a whirlwind of activity for Fred and me. Fred spent every working hour directing his business while I socialized, played bridge, rehearsed *Guys and Dolls* and saved the community. We got together on weekends at the Farms Country Club and concentrated on contentment and success. We were the image of what the world wanted for winners.

Although I didn't spend much time at home, I began to notice my beautiful son Freddie wasn't looking well. His china-blue eyes seemed glassy and he stopped smiling. He was seven months old but when he tried to sit up, he lost his balance. I would prop him up with pillows and try to tell myself that he looked just fine. Soon he began to scream in the night and when I would go in to him, his body would be stiff, his back arched and his fingers rigid. I would do everything I knew to comfort him and after a while he'd relax and go back to sleep.

After this had gone on for several weeks I took him to our pediatrician, Dr. Richard Granger, a personal friend. After a thorough examination, Dr. Granger called in a specialist and together they tapped Freddie, with no response. They rang little bells that he didn't seem to hear, and they flashed lights in his eyes that he didn't notice. With each test they became more concerned until finally they asked me to call my husband.

Fred was in the midst of a business conference and expressed annoyance that I had disturbed him. "The doctor wants you to come to his office and get your son's report," I said.

"I can't possibly leave work," answered Fred. "You get the report and bring it home."

By the time I got back to the doctor's office, I was in tears. It was hard for me to realize that Fred didn't care enough to be with me at such a difficult moment.

"Fred is not able to come," I said to Dr. Granger. "You'll have to tell me alone."

Tenderly, Dr. Granger put his arm around me and said softly, "Florence, I don't know how to tell you this, but your child appears to be hopelessly brain damaged. You might as well get your mind set to put him away, forget him and perhaps have another one."

Brain damaged? Put him away? Forget him? Have another one?

I stood there in shock, refusing to believe Dr. Granger's words. There's nothing in life that's hopeless, that somebody can't fix.

I pleaded, "Can't you fix him? Can't you do something? This child is my husband's namesake. We can't let anything happen to Freddie. Do whatever it takes. I'll get the money."

"Florence," said Dr. Granger, "this is one thing your money or your willpower can't do anything about. I'm afraid your Freddie is hopeless."

Dealing With the Hopeless

The word *hopeless* had never been in my vocabulary. I was determined to save my only son. But as I drove home late that afternoon with Freddie lying beside me in a baby seat, the word *hopeless* reverberated in my brain. I went to bed without eating and waited for Fred's return. He came in about 8 o'clock looking for me and dinner.

"You won't want dinner when you hear what the doctor said about Freddie. It's his brain; it doesn't work. He can't see, he can't hear, he's hopeless."

Confused and distraught, Fred said, "Somehow we'll get him fixed." He tried to comfort me, but every time Freddie screamed, I screamed. I was close to hysteria.

The next morning Fred called Dr. Granger for his advice. "We can't give up," he said. "We've got to save Freddie." Dr. Granger suggested a neurologist at Yale and we made an appointment for the following week. This time Fred left work and went with me.

The examining doctor gave Freddie every conceivable test. When he was ready to read us the results, Fred turned on his tape recorder. We wanted his exact words forever; but the words the doctor spoke were words we never did listen to again.

"He is blind. He is deaf. His brain does not work. He is hopeless. He's going to get worse and he probably won't live long."

I sat there holding my Freddie and Dr. Granger's words came back to me, "He's hopelessly brain damaged. You might as well put him away, forget him and have another one."

But how could I put this child away? How could I ever forget him? No, I could not run away from this problem, but I could have another baby.

The following week I asked Dr. Lach if he thought it would be safe for me to have another child. "After studying the reports on Freddie, I find no obvious cause for the baby's problems. It must have been some freak of nature that would probably never happen again."

We discussed every possible aspect of my situation and concluded the chances were one in a million that the brain damage would occur in another child. We assumed it was a one-of-a-kind situation and that it would be best for me to have another child as soon as possible.

Once I was pregnant, Dr. Lach enrolled me in a special program that Yale was conducting for expectant mothers who had already produced a brain-damaged child. I went through my interviews and tests and the results were all optimistic. The thought of a new baby gave me a touch of hope.

During the nine-month wait, I had time to re-evaluate my life. I began to realize I had always put my faith in me, in my own power to achieve things, and I had been quite successful. But now I was faced with a tragedy that I could do nothing about. I had to learn that there were things in life that money and willpower couldn't fix. When I had been discouraged in the past, I had cheered myself up by reviewing my accomplishments, but now my talents and achievements no longer made me happy.

As I paced the floor, clutching Freddie tightly to relieve the terror of his ten to twelve convulsions a day, it hardly mattered that I walked over plush carpeting. At night when he screamed and I jumped up, it made no difference that my bed was elevated on a platform and constructed like a throne. When I rocked him in the living room, I was no longer impressed with my custom-woven drapes that matched my Bjorn Winblad mural. What had been so important before was now trivial. When you're holding a dying child, the drapes and the wallpaper no longer matter. My only hope in those lonely empty nights was that my next child would be normal and I could put this nightmare behind me.

Christmas approached, but there was little to be

joyful about. I was pregnant, scared and I tried not to think about the chances of another problem child. As little Freddie's convulsions grew worse, a visiting nurse came in each day to give him shots to ease the severity of his spasms. For the sake of our girls we tried to have a normal Christmas season. Fred and I maintained that Little Brother would get better, for neither one of us could openly face the truth.

We had always taken pictures of the children and sent them, with a summary letter of our year, to friends and relatives. In December 1960, we tried to do the usual thing. We dressed the three children up in their Christmas finest, propped Freddie in a jump seat and hoped he would look normal.

At the best of times, taking pictures of three children is difficult, but this effort was almost impossible. Freddie kept falling over, bumping his head and crying. Each time he cried, Lauren, who sensed how sick he was, burst into tears. Marita would push him and say, "Sit up, Freddie. Sit up." A lump came in my throat as I watched this sad effort.

The whole idea was a mistake, but Fred was determined. He had all his camera equipment out and was going to take a picture, no matter if they were all crying. And soon they were. Freddie had a convulsion and screamed, Lauren got upset over his pain and sobbed, and Marita got mad because I wouldn't let her push Freddie. When all were crying, Fred captured the mood of our Christmas on film.

For some strange reason I decided to use the picture of three crying children for our annual newsletter with this caption, "The Littauers hope your New Year will be a howling success." I never hinted in the letter that we had a problem, and I closed the message with this paragraph:

> For all of you who have tried to take pictures of your children for a Christmas card, we dedicate ours as the ultimate in Christmas photos. After three sittings, 200

flash bulbs (of which half never worked), and a bottle of aspirin, we gave up on some lovely smiling photo which looks so casual and easy on other peoples' cards, and settled on the most typical pose of all. It shows how we felt after a fretful and frustrating day before the camera. We hope you'll think the whole thing is a scream as we did.

And so at the close of another year the happy, smiling Littauers wish you all a Merry Christmas and a most harmonious and prosperous New Year.

How could I have even written "the happy, smiling Littauers?" I had pursued happiness so passionately, I couldn't admit I had failed.

Sitting on new chairs at a new table in our newly expanded home, eating turkey served by a maid in uniform, we had the most miserable holiday in our lifetime. Fred and I picked at our food and gave each other presents that we hardly cared to open. While Marita was too young to understand our burdens, Lauren realized there was no Christmas spirit. As she opened Freddie's presents for him, she looked up and said, "Is Freddie ever going to get better?" I couldn't face her straight questions and felt tears welling up within me.

"I don't know," I choked.

"'I don't know' means no," she said as she hung her head sadly.

From that moment Lauren knew there was no hope, and while we never again verbalized it, we understood. When Freddie screamed in the night, I would run in to find Lauren already there, patting him while tears dropped on his rigid form. Few words passed between us, but we spent many silent hours uplifting each other by our presence. I began to realize what a deeply compassionate child I had in Lauren and in our time of mutual anguish we became close friends.

Fred found it just as hard to admit defeat. His defense was to work harder and not come home to view the convicting evidence. I continued my League and theater work and never told anyone but the closest of friends that I had a problem or was pregnant. I kept hoping for a secret solution.

My in-laws had long been members of a religious group that professed healing powers and, while I had resisted their strong suggestions to visit one of their practitioners, I finally gave in. Fred brightened at the thought that a miracle might take place and with his mother's help, found a learned gentleman who agreed to take our case. He had an elegant suite of offices on Park Avenue in New York City and each Tuesday afternoon of a long, hot summer, Fred and I would board the train from New Haven to take instruction in religious healing. From the beginning, the man made it clear the problem was mine, because unlike my husband, I was not a believer in their principles.

"When you can look at your son and say in faith that he is perfect, he will be perfect," said the man.

Each weekend I would go home and recite, "He is perfect. He is perfect," but with the first convulsion I would lose my faith. When I returned, the practitioner would gently chide me for my unbelief and repeat the prescription.

One week the gentleman came to our home and prayed over our child, but there was no change. When I was about eight months pregnant I refused to take any more trips to New York. Fred was disappointed in me and the program and I was weighted down with guilt. The fault had been clearly laid on me.

On August 14, 1961, Dr. Lach had me checked by the team of experts at Yale who had been observing and testing me throughout my pregnancy. They felt the time was right for me to deliver and began monitoring the heartbeat of my unborn child. They tested brain waves by inserting electrodes up to the baby's scalp, then wiring both me and the baby to a big machine. With a little help my labor started and the machines began to record. I watched, fascinated and frightened, as little marks went up and down on charts to indicate both heartbeat and brain waves.

"These lines are all normal," they said. "Your baby is going to be just fine."

I had another easy delivery, except this time the audience was smaller, just the team from this special program. My baby was born and we all rejoiced that I had a son. They removed the clamps that had been on his head during delivery and quickly tested his reactions.

"You will have no problem with this one," said the attending nurse. "He checks out perfectly normal."

When Fred was allowed in to see me, we wept for joy. We finally had our son. I named him after me: Laurence Chapman Littauer. I could hardly wait to get home and take care of my new baby.

When I arrived home, Freddie was gone. My husband had put him in a private children's hospital in northern Connecticut. I could never have made such a decision myself, and it wasn't an easy thing for Fred. He told me his whole life seemed to drain out of him when he placed his Frederick Jerome Littauer III into the arms of an unknown nurse in a home full of other hopelessly retarded babies.

Fred had redecorated the nursery and I brought little Larry home to a room stripped of any memories of our Freddie. We did all we could to forget the past and start over. I gave up my community positions, my charity presidencies—and put my hope in Larry.

Dark Times

On Valentine's Day, 1962, as I was preparing a party for Lauren and Marita, the phone rang. It was a nurse from the children's hospital calling to tell me my Freddie had died of pneumonia. Compassionately, she explained that a child without the ability to think doesn't know enough to cough, and so Freddie, with badly congested lungs, had choked to death in his crib. I was overcome with guilt. *If only I had kept him home, this wouldn't have happened,* I thought. I called Fred at work and he broke down and cried, "My Freddie is dead." He had clung to a hope that someday his namesake would be healed.

I shall never forget that private funeral held in a cold stark room of an old mortuary in Colebrook, Connecticut. I wore my black seal coat and still shivered as an unknown minister read a few uncomforting verses over the open casket that held the remains of our Frederick Jerome Littauer III. There were no flowers; there was no music. Just Fred and me, alone in our grief. We had told no one that our boy had died, and we stood in silence as we wept over our departed son. No longer was he beautiful, but bruised from banging his head on the crib rails during his frequent convulsions. No longer was he the hope of my husband, but the end of a bad dream.

A week after Freddie's funeral, when Larry was just six months old, I went in to pick him up from his nap. I called to him but he didn't respond. He had a blank look, his eyes were dull and I feared the worst. I grabbed him up, shook him and cried, "Smile, Larry, smile." But Larry didn't smile. Immediately I wrapped him up and rushed him to Dr. Granger's office. I literally shook with fear as I waited for Dr. Granger's answer. He gave Larry the same tests he had given my Freddie. "I don't know how to say this, Florence, but I'm afraid Larry has the same thing."

His words fell on me like a death knell. It was a repeat performance. I drove home on the same streets from the same doctor. Larry lay in the same car bed I had used for Freddie. I had to tell my two daughters the same story: They were going to lose another brother.

I woke up each morning hoping it was a bad dream, but it wasn't. Like his brother, Larry began to convulse, stiffen and scream, and he no longer smiled. These were lonesome times. Fred couldn't bear to come home, and I couldn't bear to go out.

One day a friend called to ask if I knew that Lauren

was arriving at school each morning in tears. When Lauren came home I asked her if this was true and she told me the children on the bus teased her every day. They would say things like, "Lauren's brother is no good. He won't ever walk; he's an idiot. He's a moron." As they said these things to her, she would begin to cry and they would laugh. By the time she got to school, she was a wreck.

When I asked her why she hadn't told me of this problem before, she said, "Mama, you have so much sadness on your mind. I didn't want to make it any worse."

I called some of the boys' mothers and instead of sympathy, I received defiant replies. They insisted their children would never say such things, and furthermore they didn't appreciate my accusations. I was shocked at their rebuffs and drove Lauren to and from school for the rest of the year.

Larry continued to get worse, and Dr. Granger made an appointment for him at Johns Hopkins Metabolic Research Unit in Baltimore, Maryland.

Dr. Robert Cook, director of the research unit, operated on Larry and I tried to prepare myself for the results. I asked Dr. Cook, "Is there any hope?"

Gripping the arms of the chair, I braced myself for his reply: "Come now, Mrs. Littauer, you know better than that." I did know better than to ask, but I was searching for some last unexpected ray of hope. There was none. To my horror, I learned my son had no real brain. Where there should have been gray matter and convolutions there was only a round ball, an inert mass.

I brought Larry home with a bandaged head and an empty mind; a child who no longer knew his mother. When our two daughters saw their second brother destroyed, swollen and vacant, they too were depressed. They cried when he cried and our home became a house of perpetual mourning. To save the emotional balance of our two girls and myself, we decided to put Larry in the same hospital where his brother had died just a few months before.

The doctors said he wouldn't live beyond the age of five or six. But they were wrong. He lived to be nineteen. When he died, he was the same size he had been when he was one year old. He had never grown, and for the eighteen years he existed in that private hospital, I never awoke one morning without the startling realization that I had a dying child. If only I could have a perfect baby boy, perhaps I could begin to rebuild my life. But my husband didn't care if he ever saw another baby. The desires had reversed. I was now the one who needed a new boy to replace my sons. After months of discussion, Fred finally consented to adoption.

After waiting a year, we drove to Danbury, Connecticut, where the licensed adoption agency brought out an adorable three-month-old baby boy with dark, curly hair and huge brooding brown eyes. As we looked at him, he seemed to analyze us. The three of us stared at each other while the case worker explained that he had been tested and appeared to be very advanced for his three months. We brought him home on my husband's birthday, February 19, 1964—a present for the whole family.

We had a joyful celebration and the party game was naming our new boy. He had been called Jeffrey at his foster home, so we all decided to put Frederick in front of that and have a new Freddie. A new child, we thought, would cheer us up.

But the memory of two failures haunted us. Unfortunately we wasted our suffering. Rather than bringing us closer together, the tragedies had wiped out whatever feelings Fred and I once had for each other. We were numb and began to look for new ways to amuse ourselves and escape the past. *If only* we could really forget, perhaps we could be happy.

Reflections

Statistics show that of couples who have experienced the birth of a retarded baby or the death of a child, 90 percent end up divorced. Since we had two abnormal sons and ultimately two deaths, it is truly a miracle that our marriage lasted at all. I look back now in disbelief that these tragedies happened and that we all survived.

I recall how hurt I was when Fred's mother did a genealogical check and announced that no one on their side had ever been brain damaged. Even my mother said, "Don't let anyone know about the boys. They'll think it's your fault." Additional guilt was heaped on me by the faith healer as well as friends who said, "If you were really a good mother you'd have kept the child at home."

I remember how hurt I was when friends stopped coming to see me. I thought they had abandoned me, but I realize now they just didn't know what to say. Lauren has written a most helpful book, *What You Can Say When You Don't Know What To Say,* helping people who want to be supportive to others in pain but just don't know how.

I wish I'd known what to do with the pain of grief, but Fred and I pushed our feelings underneath and tried to get on with life. There were no seminars in those days, no support groups for grieving parents, no books that showed how you could work through your pain and later make the tough times count.

We thought the children would get over it and forget, so we didn't talk about the loss of their brothers. It wasn't until years later that they told me of their hurts, and I was ashamed of myself when I read Lauren's chapter "The Forgotten Griever."

Have you been through difficult situations—a death, divorce, depression—and felt no one cared? People stayed away or took sides. No one seemed to know what to do with you. If you have, you can know how I felt in those heavy, hurtful hours.

Frequently, people ask me—or sometimes even tell me—what was wrong with my sons. Yale-New Haven Hospital and Johns Hopkins couldn't come up with any label except some kind of a degenerative brain disorder. After Lauren married and while Larry was still alive, we had some additional testing done at Loma Linda University Hospital in hopes of giving our daughter some genetic information. They fed the data into computers and found no other cases that matched Larry's pattern. On the amnio-centesis he came out as normal, showing that the flaw was not in the chromosomes but in the genes.

We wish we had answers to the questions, What was it? and Why did it happen twice? Why was each child beautiful and normal until six months old? Why did their brain power seem to shut off at one point and never go back on? Fred and I have had to learn that there are some things in life that defy explanations.

These were tough times—I'd hit the bottom after my years of trying to reach the top. As I look back now I could never say that I'd like to go through it all again, but I can say that those two tragedies showed me for the first time that there are things in life money and willpower can't do anything about.

As I look back on these double depressions, I realize that it was suffering through these dark years that gave me a compassion for others with problems. It is because I've been there that I can comfort those who give birth to abnormal babies or who lose a child in death. No one can say, "I know how you feel," if they've never been there. My book *Blow Away the Black Clouds* traces the steps I went through to get out of my depressions and gives hope to those in similar situations.

Never would I say losing my sons was a positive experience or I'm glad it happened, but I do have a heart for people with hurts that I did not have before.

By the grace of God, I have learned to make beauty out of ashes. I have learned to

Make the tough times count.

16

Good Time Charlie's

I dressed Lauren and Marita in matching dresses and I wore a bright red knit dress with a large brimmed white felt hat trimmed with a bunch of geraniums and streamers. I wanted to make sure they knew there was a new family in church. I'm sure they knew.

Forgetting wasn't easy. Everywhere I looked, there were reminders of my sons. When I rocked my new adopted Freddie, the motion brought back the hours I had spent in that same chair trying to soothe my dying sons. He was in their bed, he wore their clothes, he played with their toys. How could I ever forget them and move on?

Staying at home depressed me and I began to think about getting out. This time I no longer cared to be president of anything and found myself floundering for direction. There was no obvious avenue open for me.

Fred rarely came home. His food service business had expanded into four states, and he hid himself in his work. Defeat depressed him as much as it did me. We were programmed for success and we had failed. Our answer to defeat was to work harder and try to pretend these traumas had never happened.

One day, driving down North Haven's Washington Avenue, Fred noticed a "For Lease" sign on an old red building. It was a typical red New England barn with a second-story balcony around four sides. Fred felt it had great possibilities for a restaurant and arranged with the owner to see it.

"I think you're already too busy to begin looking for new fields to conquer," I said as we walked into the damp, empty barn.

"I think it will be perfect for a Roaring Twenties nightclub," said Fred, ignoring my comments.

I had learned that once Fred got an idea, there was no stopping him. I felt I might as well join him in this new business venture. As Fred became excited over this project, we found we had a common goal—something to work on together.

While Fred drew the designs, brought in carpenters to panel the walls, built a dance floor and stage, and made tables around the balcony, I visited antique shops and hung the treasures on the walls. Fred scouted out banjo players and singers, and I put together a group of young dancers who had been my drama students at North Haven High School. We created Twenties costumes with fringes and pearls and the girls began practicing the Charleston while workmen hammered around them. I found a bar that had been taken out of an old saloon, and Fred designed a modern kitchen for the limited food menu he had planned to supplement the beer and baskets of unshelled peanuts that would be on each table. The barn was soon transformed into a club and we decided to call it "Good Time Charlie's" with Fred as Charlie!

On opening night we invited every town dignitary and friend we could find and were pleased the following morning to find we had received coverage in the local newspaper. "It being a hot night last Friday, the *Chronicle* decided to go to a party at 'Good Time Charlie's, the new Roaring Twenties-type club opened up by Mr. and Mrs. Fred Littauer on Route 5 in North Haven. And what a night it was as these pictures show!"

The full-page spread displayed dynamic Holly Westin singing in her sequins, the band bursting with banjos, the Charlie girls flipping their fringes in the Charleston and the guests, including me, enjoying every minute of a raucous night.

Fred loved playing Charlie and became a different person when he donned his red striped shirt and black armband. He was able to forget the past and play in the present.

At first, I loved the glamour, clientele and activity at Charlie's. It became my new social center, a big home where I was the charming hostess. For awhile this movie-star era gave me an avenue of escape, but when I tried to make a suggestion to Fred, he told me to be quiet—it was his business, not mine. I had thought it was *our* club, but when I realized Fred didn't want my ideas, I began to lose interest in playing second banjo to Good Time Charlie. I grew tired of dressing up every night to be ignored by Fred and decided to abandon Fred to his Charlie girls. The most humiliating aspect of my departure was that Fred never seemed to notice I was gone. Again, I was alone.

About that time I noticed that a new professional theatre was about to open in New Haven and, true to form, I was soon involved in celebrity lunches and speaking at service clubs and churches. I became the paid director of volunteer services and I coordinated the activities of all who wanted to give time or money to the theatre. Life was again exciting and I blotted out my pain.

But underneath, I was lonesome and empty. I saw very little of my husband and I didn't like to go home much more than he did. The maid I had wasn't much of a cook, so eleven-year-old Lauren prepared dinner every night. A marriage counselor would have told us our life was headed in the wrong direction; however, we never asked one. We didn't even ask ourselves how we expected to hold a home together when Fred was out every night with his Charlie girls and I was running around in circles with a group of young actors. Instead of facing reality, we looked the other way and continued in our opposite directions.

Meeting Jesus Personally

About this time my sister-in-law, Ruthie, seeing the downward direction of our lives, invited me to attend a Christian Women's Club luncheon. A few months before, Ruthie had told us a preposterous story about how she and her husband Dick had watched Billy Graham on television. When he invited them to ask Jesus Christ to come into their lives, they got off the couch and knelt to pray in front of the television. They began to talk about Jesus as if they knew Him, and we branded them fanatics.

The last thing I wanted was for someone to tell me I needed religion. I had always been a good person, gone to church, taught Sunday school and given my time to charitable organizations. I was not interested in anything labeled "Christian Women's Club" which I expected would be full of somber, senile ladies in black dresses praying in a corner.

I kept refusing Ruthie's invitations, but she was persistent and I could see she wouldn't quit bugging me until I went once. The next time she asked me, she explained that the Christian Women's Club was to be held that month in the Old Mill Restaurant in Darien and that they were going to have a fashion show. I thought if these religious ladies liked clothes and ate in fine restaurants, they couldn't be too weird, so I decided to go.

On the specified day in August, 1965, I got dressed in a ruby red Ceil Chapman ensemble with spike heels to match, carried a new Lord and Taylor cut velvet handbag and wore a turban hat of satin and velvet with a large brooch on the front. I wanted to make sure those saintly ladies knew I was not one of them. And I'm sure they knew.

When I arrived at the Old Mill, I was impressed with the beauty of the surroundings and glad the luncheon wasn't in a stark social hall of some old church. At least the atmosphere was positive.

When Ruthie introduced me to the ladies on the club board, I was amazed that some of them were dressed as stylishly as I was. Much to my surprise, they seemed quite pleasant. I hadn't been prepared for bright, sharp women and didn't feel quite as confident and superior as I thought I would. The restaurant tables were elegantly decorated and in front of each plate was a place card: a flag on a toothpick stuck into a decorated marshmallow. I looked at mine and saw it had someone else's name. I whispered to Ruthie, "They have the wrong place card in front of me."

She returned, "It's not supposed to be your name. It's a prayer favor."

I had no idea what a prayer favor was and so I asked. "It has the name of a missionary on there," Ruthie explained. "You're supposed to take it home and put it by the kitchen sink and pray for her each time you see it."

"But I don't even know her," I said softly.

"That's all right. You can pray for people you don't know."

"I can?"

I looked around and saw ladies stuffing the little marshmallows into their handbags. I was not about to put a gummy marshmallow in my new handbag even with a missionary sticking out of it. But I didn't want to look unprayerful so I wrapped the little favor in a napkin and hoped it wouldn't melt all over the bottom of my bag.

As I waited somewhat apprehensively to see what was going to happen, an adorable girl began the meeting with the blessing. The fashion show was exceptional. I was impressed that the models were from the Christian Women's Club itself. I had never seen a more attractive group of ladies. By the time the speaker got up, I had completely changed my attitude. In fact, I felt a little in awe of the beautiful, joyful women surrounding me.

The speaker, Dr. Roy Gustafson from the Billy Graham team, was a tall, dignified, white-haired, intelligent and articulate gentleman. Not at all the weak, insipid religious type I had expected.

He caught my attention with a story of a woman who sounded so much like me I thought Ruthie must have given him advance information. He told a Cinderella story of an underprivileged girl who was determined to succeed in spite of her circumstances. After becoming socially prominent and well-dressed, she began to experience problems in her marriage. She was miserable inside, but never once had she let anyone know how she felt. I identified with the story—especially the part about never telling anyone her problems. I was proud that I had never told people about my problems and that some friends didn't even know I'd had the second son.

Then Dr. Gustafson got to the solution for the lady's life. She received Jesus Christ into her heart and asked Him to take away her sins and change her into what He wanted her to be. The lady hadn't sounded at all sinful. In fact, she seemed to be a nice, normal, well-intentioned person like me.

When Dr. Gustafson explained that all of us have sinned because we have fallen short of God's expectations, I became a little disturbed. I knew I wasn't perfect, but what did God expect of me? Then Dr. Gustafson explained that none of us are true Christians until we ask Christ to personally live in us. "Christian means 'Christ in me,'" he said.

Never in all my life had I heard any such statement. I thought I was a Christian because I wasn't Jewish, and my brother was an ordained minister. Then it was as if Dr. Gustafson read my mind. "It doesn't matter," he said, "if your relatives are religious. All that counts is the condition of your own heart. You don't get to heaven because your grandfather built a church."

He explained the need to individually open the door of our heart and let Jesus come in and live within us. The beautiful way he said, "Let Jesus come in," made me feel I should do it. He said we could ask Jesus Christ to come into our lives quietly within our own hearts and no one needed to know. *If I ever do such a thing,* I thought, *I surely won't let anyone know!*

"Romans 12:1,2," said Dr. Gustafson, "tells us what God wants us to do: 'Present your bodies a living sacrifice.' We are to give our whole selves to the Lord, not just our minds or our souls for an hour on Sunday."

Why not? What had I to lose? "Holy, acceptable unto God which is your reasonable service." Was I acceptable? I had always had perfect attendance at Sunday school. Would that do it? But then he said, "We don't become acceptable by our own works, but by God's grace—His willingness to take us as we are." As he spoke I was disappointed that my religious background didn't seem to count for much.

"Be not conformed to this world." We were not to make society our standard. It was a little late to tell me that, me the great social leader of the community. "But be ye transformed by the renewing of your mind." I sure could use a new mind. I worked hard to forget the memories of my boys. Was he telling me God could give me a new mind? "That you may prove what is that good, and acceptable and perfect, will of God." If God had a will for me, it surely had been far from perfect: two hopeless sons and a preoccupied husband.

"It doesn't matter what your past interests and gods have been," continued Dr. Gustafson. "If you willingly present your body to the Lord and ask Jesus Christ to come into your life, He will transform your mind and show you His plan for your future."

I knew he was speaking to me. I just hoped Ruthie

didn't know I was touched. *Lord Jesus,* I said in my mind as Dr. Gustafson began to pray, *I have tried to run my life the best way I knew how, and I've failed. I ask you to come into my life and take it over. I ask you to make me into what you want me to be. I present myself to You. In Jesus' name I pray. Amen.*

I had come into the meeting with my worldly veneer firmly in place, yet I left stripped to insignificance. Dr. Gustafson asked all those who had prayed with him to raise their hands while all eyes were closed and before I knew it, my hand was up. I was shocked. I wasn't the type to get emotional and start waving my hand. Yet, I was definitely there with my hand up and it felt right.

Pastor Frost

Nothing unusual happened in my life after that prayer. I began to think nothing would. What I didn't know was that Ruthie and Dick were praying for us. In fact, Ruthie and her next door neighbor met every morning to pray for our family. And Dick, after meeting Sherwood Frost, a young pastor from our town, asked him to visit us. Dick explained we weren't attending church and were in a spiritual vacuum.

So one Friday afternoon, as I was hurriedly heading out the door, I ran into a handsome man on my front step as he was about to ring the doorbell. "I'm Sherwood Frost, the pastor of the Evangelical Baptist Church," he said cheerily, "and thought you would like to come and visit next Sunday." I didn't like the sound of "evangelical" and blanched when he told me they met in an elementary school gymnasium. I was in a hurry and tried to discourage him from talking, but he didn't seem to sense my urgency.

"Do you believe in the Bible?" he asked.

"Some parts I do, and some parts I don't," I said.

"God didn't ask us to be judges of His Word," he said, "but to believe it all or forget it and stop playing at being a Christian."

I had never heard anyone say that before but I knew that was exactly what we had been doing. Fred had been brought up in one of the cults, and while I had never been interested in their doctrine, I had gone with him for ten long, dull years. After the sorrows of our sons, Fred substituted tennis for church on Sundays and for a time I went back to my childhood denomination. But that only lasted until one night at the bridge table when the minister had too much to drink, got angry at his wife and threw the rule book at her in a rage. Fred said to me later, "If that's supposed to be my spiritual leader, I don't need religion." We quit church completely and gave up on God.

However, Pastor Frost so impressed me that when Sunday came, I decided to go to church. I dressed Lauren and Marita in matching Polly Flinders dresses and I wore a bright red knit dress with a large brimmed white felt hat trimmed with a bunch of geraniums and streamers running down my back. I wanted to make sure they knew there was a new family in church and I'm sure they knew. We sat right in the front row so the pastor would see his visitation program had worked—and I'm sure he noticed.

When it was time for the sermon he asked us all to take out our Bibles. I'd never been to a church where they used Bibles or where the people had to do work. I thought that was the pastor's job. What does he have to do all week but study a few verses, make up a sermon and deliver it on Sunday? As I was thinking this, I noticed people were taking out Bibles from under their chairs and out of their handbags. I looked around, bewildered. The pastor pointed at me and said, "If you don't have a Bible this week, bring one next week."

I was humiliated that he had pointed me out as the only dummy in the group who didn't know enough to bring a Bible. *I don't have to come here and be insulted,* I thought. *I just won't come again.*

What I didn't realize is that when we commit our lives to Jesus He doesn't send us an imitation Moses with a big tablet commanding, "Thou shalt not have any fun anymore." Instead He begins to change our desires. When the next Sunday came I got up and got dressed for church. I wore a more subdued dress and no hat. My daughters had asked Fred if he'd come with us and much to my surprise he agreed.

As I started out the front door, I remembered the pastor's words, "If you don't have a Bible this week, bring one next week." I had no idea where I had a Bible. I knew I owned some because when we were children each time we won a contest we'd receive a Bible, but at that point I couldn't remember what I'd done with them. As I was searching my mind for a Bible, I glanced toward the coffee table and there was a Bible—the kind that you lay around the house to impress your friends with your spirituality.

It was a huge gold Bible, embossed on the top. The pages were edged in gold and it had a red velvet ribbon running through it. I looked over and said, "It sure is a Bible." I picked it up and went off to church with Fred and the girls.

I sat right up front again so the pastor would see that I indeed had brought a Bible. When he asked us to open the Word, I really opened the Word. It went over on the lap of the man next to me.

When Pastor Frost started the sermon he instructed us to underline a verse. *Underline,* I thought, *in this fancy Bible with the tissue paper pages and the gold edges?* The pastor noticed my surprise and stated, "If your Bible is too expensive to write in, get a cheaper one." This was the second Sunday in a row that the pastor had pointed me out as the dummy of the group—me who was used to being president of everything. After the service I asked the pastor quietly, "Where do you buy a cheap Bible?"

He replied, "I'll sell you one for 35 cents." That sounded cheap enough, so I bought a *Good News* Bible with the newsprint cover and that was the beginning of my Bible study. We never missed a Sunday after that and when Pastor Frost preached, he quoted directly from the Bible and told us clearly what God wanted us to do with our lives. I had never realized before, even though I'd been brought up in a church and could recite many Scripture verses, that the Bible was supposed to apply to me today.

Encouraged by the pastor, I started to read the New Testament in the *Good News* version. The first verse that spoke to me personally was Matthew 6:3 which says, "When you help a needy person, do it in such a way that even your closest friend will not know about it."

I had always helped the needy. From that moment at the charity Christmas party when I was seven, I knew it was better to be the one on stage giving out the gifts than the poor sad soul with his hands outstretched. But the verse said not to help needy people from a stage. It said to give in such a way that even my best friend won't know about it. *But what fun would it be to give if no one knew about it?* I thought. It never occurred to me to be quietly generous. I never purposely tried to show off, but as I thought about it, I made sure my philanthropies were presented at a peak viewing hour. Did the Bible mean my generosity was wrong? Was it possible to be good and not tell anyone? These were challenging questions and were the first theological truths I struggled with.

I was eager to learn and looked forward each Sunday to discovering something new. I underlined every meaningful passage in my Bible and became excited when I found thoughts that applied to me. Fred also bought a Bible and he began to neatly underline special verses as each Sunday he listened and applied the truths to himself.

After attending this little church for a year, Fred responded one Sunday when the pastor gave an invitation for those who wanted to become believing Christians. He raised his hand and committed his life to the Lord Jesus, just as I had done a year before.

The changes in me had been gradual, but it seemed that God transformed Fred overnight from a man who hardly ever came home to an avid Bible student. Night after night he sat at the table in our bedroom and studied. In amazement I watched his whole view of life improve. His superior attitude gave way to an admission that he wasn't perfect, and with all his material achievements, he realized he was a failure as a husband, as a father and even as a man.

One day he came home and said, "I'm closing Good Time Charlie's. I just don't feel right about that place anymore." Charlie's was making money and Fred had never shut down a winning enterprise, but that very night he locked the door on his former life.

A few months later the school tripled the rent on the gymnasium and the church held a prayer meeting at the pastor's home to seek God's solution to this financial problem. It was Fred's first prayer meeting. As they prayed, Fred thought about Charlie's. Why not make Good Time Charlie's into a church?

Within two weeks we turned our nightclub into a church. The band stand became the pulpit, the chairs were lined up on the dance floor, the empty bar made space for a classroom, and the kitchen was used for church suppers. Many people were curious to attend a church that had once been a nightclub and the attendance grew. To many it became "Saint Charlie's." Fred was the Patron Saint and I the Mother Superior!

What a time of fellowship we had at St. Charlie's. As excited new believers, we were in church every time the door opened. We became instant leaders and encouraged our friends to try a different, fun-kind of church, one that met in a night club. The piano that once played ragtime swung just as well on gospel songs, and did we ever sing! The pastor preached better, the hymns sounded better, and the people glowed with the joy of the Lord. We almost had as many people out Sunday evenings as we did in the mornings, and after the service we would have homemade cookies and cakes and sit at the tables around the balcony.

We were like one big, happy family.

While the ministry of St. Charlie's was the beginning of our spiritual growth, we soon learned that being a real Christian is not just going to church and being a nice person. It is a total commitment of a life to the Lord and a willingness to let Him direct your path. At first I wasn't sure how to let the Lord direct me. It was depressing for me to stay home, but I began to feel this was what I should do. One day Lauren said, "I hope I never have to grow up and get married and be miserable like you."

I was stunned. "What do you mean?" I asked.

"Well, you're always complaining," she said.

"I am not," I said. "I'm a cheerful person. Just ask my friends."

"I don't have to ask your friends," she said, "I live with you. You may not think you're complaining, but when you do the dishes, you always say how much you hate dishes, how Daddy's always late and how you were made for better things than this."

I couldn't believe I'd ever said such things, but I soon became aware that I muttered around the house with everything I did. While the pressures of our sons had relaxed, and I was in church as often as I could attend, I was still unhappy. I tried to be the life of the party outside of the home, but inside my children saw me as a bitter, angry, complaining woman. I didn't know quite what I was supposed to do with me.

Reflections

As I look back on my life in the '60s, I realize now that I was depressed. Because I didn't know how to handle depression I denied its existence and pushed down my anger.

I have learned that many of us don't know how to take a good look at our problems, label them for what they are and work to overcome them. Since I had always labored in my own strength and there was nothing I could do to restore my sons, I had given up and had tried to find challenging activities to occupy my mind so I wouldn't have to focus on my grief. I'm sure what I did was better than a nervous breakdown, but it was no long-range solution.

Some of you may have suffered a death in the family and have not been allowed to grieve. Friends and other family members have said, "Aren't you over it yet?" Or perhaps you have a spouse who hasn't grieved as you have and you don't think he cares. Many of us don't realize that different personalities grieve differently. Marilyn Heavilin's chapter "The Rose of Uniqueness" from her book *Roses in December* explains how to view a person's grief according to his or her natural temperament. Don't condemn your spouse if he or she reacts to death in a manner quite unlike your own.

I wish someone had told me that it was all right to cry. I regret that Fred and I never shared our grief together. Instead, we put it aside and pretended it never happened.

Today I meet so many people who have stuffed their defeats, depressions and abuses down inside them. They didn't know what else to do with them, so they swallowed them like a large pill. And that pill is still stuck in their throat causing headaches, nervous stomachs and undiagnosed pains. They don't want to be sick, but they just don't know how to get well.

Some of you may be like me—good moral people who don't deserve what's happened to you. Perhaps you've gone to church where everyone looks happy, even saintly, and you've thought you're the only one who hurts. Perhaps the pastor has only pasted platitudes over your problems and you've been afraid to mention them again. It isn't the pastor, the people, the pulpit or the pews that make a difference; it's the presence of the Lord, active and alive in your heart, that can change your life.

If you have any doubts about the power of the Lord in your life, ask Jesus to come in as I did that day at the Christian Women's Club. It's not the end of your problems, but it is the beginning of your solutions. And it will start you in the right direction so that someday you will be able to

Make the tough times count!

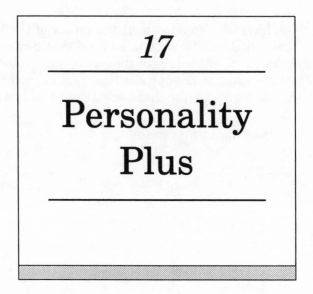

17

Personality Plus

There was a section in the book about the strengths of the Sanguine temperament. I could hardly wait to show Fred how much fun I really was.

Early in life I developed a talent for straightening out other people. Innately I believed I could spot faults in others and improve them if they would only listen to me. My mother called this my Cinderella complex—always ready to transform any damsel in distress.

I had grown up as the oldest child in a family of three and felt I was a born leader. When my father died, I simply took control of my family. My grieving mother, who was weak and exhausted, allowed my strong will to reign, and no one questioned my authority. It was the same when I taught school. My pupils doted on my every word. Not until my marriage had anyone ever suggested I needed help.

Meanwhile, Fred had been brought up believing he was God's perfect child and there was no such thing as sin. His mother encouraged this belief and told him he was

God's gift to women. Both of us entered marriage expecting the other to be grateful for receiving such a prize.

The result of this unreality was a constant battle of the wills. I thought everything should go my way, and Fred insisted it go his. I submitted on the surface, but underneath became more rebellious with each passing year. Dr. Lach once said to me, "In the beginning you fooled me. I thought you were as cool as you appeared, but I now know inside you're tied up in knots."

By the time God reached down and picked up the imperfect pieces of our marriage and began putting them back together, we were almost too antagonistic and apathetic to care. We each hoped the other would recognize his faults and improve. When we both asked the Lord Jesus to come into our lives and make us what He wanted us to be, we were at the bottom. We knew we were failures, and wanted to improve, but we were not sure how to begin.

As we groped for direction in our new Christian life, a friend gave us the book *Spirit-Controlled Temperament* by Tim LaHaye. I found myself on page thirteen: "Sparky Sanguine, the warm, buoyant, lively and 'enjoying' temperament. When he comes into a room of people, he has a tendency to lift the spirits of everyone present by his exuberant flow of conversation. He is a thrilling storyteller because his warm, emotional nature almost makes him relive the experience in the very telling of it."

Oh, how I loved to talk and oh, how I thought everyone but Fred enjoyed listening! Before marriage, I had been considered the life of the party. My brother Ron and I were frequently invited to social affairs just because we were hilarious. Often we rehearsed comedy lines on current topics of interest so that when someone brought up a subject, we would have a stock routine.

In adult life I did the same thing, often varying the story to fit the audience. Once Lauren, after hearing me regale my mother's church circle with one of my tales, said with a sigh, "That's the fifth time I've heard that story, and every time it has a different ending." Quickly I took her into the bedroom and told her she was never to make comments about my stories in public. My brother and I had always agreed we would support each others' tales, no matter how far they might travel from the truth.

Fred, who I thought had no sense of humor, called this lying. We called it "colorful speech."

As I read more of Sparky and his "disarming effect on many of his listeners," I was more convinced than ever I had married a dullard who couldn't appreciate my sense of humor. Fred just liked the straight facts. Before we were married he used to think I was amusing, but after twelve years of my fun and games, he groaned every time I repeated a story.

There was a section in the book about the strengths of the Sanguine temperament. I could hardly wait to show Fred how much fun I really was. But then I read the chapter on Sanguine weaknesses, and it sounded as if Fred had written them about me.

"His life is spent running from one target to another, and, unless disciplined, is not lastingly productive." Fred often pointed out that I seemed to run in circles, make a big production out of every little thing, and accomplish nothing at the end of the day. I felt I was a super achiever and had perfectly good reasons why my days looked incomplete. I never really listened to Fred, and I certainly never thought I was wrong.

Tim LaHaye went on to point out that the Sanguine temperament "can go overboard and become obnoxious by dominating, not just the major part of the conversation, but all of it." While Fred never called me obnoxious, he had for years told me I talked too much. "God hasn't appointed you official gap-filler in every flagging conversation," Fred said frequently. At dinner parties Fred often kicked me under the table when he thought I was too domineering. He also waved negatively from across the room if he heard my voice above the crowd. I barely tolerated his judgmental attitude and constant interruptions, and in twelve years it never once struck me I might possibly be obnoxious.

As I continued to read, I began to wonder if these verbal gifts I'd been so proud of may have a negative side. Did Fred have reason to be disturbed about me?

Fred also began to read the book and identified himself as a Melancholy. "Mr. Melancholy has strong perfectionist tendencies. His standard of excellence exceeds others." Fred began to realize that it was a positive trait to have high standards, but his wife couldn't live up to them, and his well-meaning instruction only made our marriage worse.

"He does not waste words like the Sanguine, but is usually very precise in stating exactly what he means." How true! Fred could say in ten words what took me a half hour! He opened his mouth only when he had something to say. I'd never thought of this as a strength, but the book said it was.

"Mr. Melancholy will be found to be very gloomy, depressed." Fred never seemed to be genuinely happy. No matter what I did, he would find something wrong with it. This attitude made me feel our marriage was hopeless. I gave up trying, and when I gave up, Fred became depressed. In retrospect, I see that living with me, a perpetual comedy act in search of an audience, was enough to send any serious man into a depression!

It was easy for an objective observer to see where each of us was wrong, but it took a miracle for us to begin to see ourselves as others saw us. We prayed for the ability to examine ourselves and began taking steps to break the judgmental patterns we had established in our lives. One day it dawned on me that just because Fred didn't see things as I did, he wasn't wrong; he was just different. As Fred and I looked further into the book, we found "Rocky Choleric. He is hot, quick, active, practical and strong-willed."

These adjectives belonged to both of us. After years of his criticizing me and my deflating him, our reactions were perched, ready to go, preprogrammed for hostility. Additionally, we both wanted to run the family our way. Fred wanted everything organized and charted out ahead. His idea of a great day was one in which he knew where he was going to be from 7:27 A.M. to midnight. He would get the children organized into a routine with tabulations of their activities on the wall.

I, on the other hand, preferred a day where if I didn't feel like doing anything, I didn't. When Fred went out of town, I would gather the children together and announce, "The ogre is gone. Now we can have some fun for a change." We'd sleep in late, ignore our duties, eat simple food and stay up late at night. I would keep reminding the children of what a great time they were having with fun-filled Mother and when Fred returned they would tell him, without my suggesting it, what a wonderful week they'd had while he was gone.

We were both strong leaders going in opposite directions, and the children didn't know which one to follow. "All we like sheep have gone astray," so far astray that as I look back, I'm amazed our family has been put back together. We were playing roulette with each other's emotions, and each thought it was the other's fault. It took a supernatural power to take our battles and bitterness and begin to change them to love.

We each started to pray, as the book suggested, that God would help us to accentuate our strengths and eliminate our weaknesses. When we did, God began a mighty miracle in our lives that resulted years later in my actually falling in love with my husband and giving him the genuine affection he'd been craving.

When I began to accept Fred unconditionally, he stopped caring whether the vegetables on the dinner plate were of a different color and texture and he ate whatever I gave him with pleasure.

Why had no one ever told us to look at ourselves first? Or perhaps someone had told us and we hadn't listened. Gratefully, God began to show both of us that we would never know true joy until we began to put our own interests aside and aim to please each other. We had so much to learn and so far to go.

Reflections

Surely God has a sense of humor. He reached down and took Fred out of Good Time Charlie's and me out of the Long Wharf Theatre and showed us the need for change in our lives. He turned our night club into a church and inspired us to study the Bible in a meaningful manner.

Can you believe that in one year's time Fred and I went from not knowing the Lord to owning a church?

Could I even know as I began to study *Spirit-Controlled Temperaments* that God would use this simple concept of self-analysis as the basis for a ministry I had neither asked for nor anticipated? I didn't know you could take examples from the tough times you'd had and use them to give other people hope.

Without knowing what we were doing, Fred and I became excited over our new understanding and I decided to invite in a few friends and make the four personalities into a parlor game. Little did I know that on the simplest and sketchiest information peoples' lives could be changed. As I shared how I found out I was a Sanguine who wanted to have fun and talk and that Fred was a Melancholy who didn't like frivolity and admired silence, couples began to nudge each other. "That's why you're like that! I thought you were out to get me."

We showed how we both were somewhat Choleric— wanting to be in charge and impatient when people didn't do it right. We used my mother as the Phlegmatic example, someone who caused no trouble and would do anything to keep peace and in her words, "not rock the boat."

The group had such a good time they asked if they could come back next week and learn more. As a Sanguine party-lover I was thrilled they wanted to run it all by again. Once Fred saw how much fun we were having, he decided to organize our class and take the fun out of it.

By the next Friday night Fred had made charts of the strengths and weaknesses and divided us up in groups. I took the Sanguines to the bedroom where we looked at our list and saw the first word was *talkative*. We were so excited to see other fun-loving storytelling people that we all began to talk at once, each one aiming to top the last story. When Fred walked in at the end of the hour we looked up stunned. Is our time up already? My, doesn't time fly when you're having fun!

Fred and his Melancholies had naturally finished their list exactly on time—not early or late but on time. He was depressed when he found out we had never gotten beyond talkative. He had made the mistake of putting the Phlegmatics in the family room with all the couches and when he went to check on them, they were all asleep. We had no Cholerics that night—they probably had important meetings to run. We learned by our second meeting that the four personalities concept was valid and when used as a simple measuring stick it could be the catalyst to a changed life.

Even I couldn't have dreamed at that time that I would later become friends with Tim and Beverly LaHaye and that I would go on to write *Personality Plus, Your Personality Tree, How to Get Along With Difficult People,* and *Personalities in Power*—all an outgrowth of that initial parlor game. I had no idea that the marriage problems Fred and I had would sound humorous to others and that our examples could encourage others and give them hope.

We were beginning to learn to

Make the tough times count!

18

Dying of Heart Attacks

I never did seem to have a name. I cried and thrashed and they watched the dials, assured that if I died the machine would tell them.

Before Fred and I got far in our new Christian life, we were stopped short. In April 1966, Dr. Lach decided to put me in the hospital for some exploratory work. After minor surgery, he explained that while there were a number of things wrong, none were serious, and he scheduled a major operation for May 11.

One afternoon as Fred was leaving to play tennis, I noticed he looked flushed and took his temperature. It was 100 degrees, but he refused to miss his match. The next day the doctor took tests which showed Fred had rheumatic fever.

During his month-long recuperation, Fred had time to read the Bible and one day found this verse in Solomon 1:6: "They made me the keeper of the vineyards; but mine own vineyard have I not kept." Fred meditated on this and began to realize he was the keeper of many vineyards. He watched over his food service business, was the president of Rotary, the country club tennis champ and finance chairman of our church. Yet this verse convicted him that he had failed to keep his own vineyard.

One Sunday after church, Fred shared how he had listed all his responsibilities and arranged them in order of importance. As he reviewed this list, God showed him he hadn't put me and the children first in his life.

"Business has always been most important, followed by tennis and civic activities," he said. I thought, *It's about time that came through to him!*

I had never been able to forget how neglected I had felt when the doctors told me about my first son's fatal condition and Fred had been too busy to come. As I began to dig up past negatives, Fred asked me to forgive him. I was stunned! In all our years together, Fred had never once told me he was sorry. I sat on the edge of the bed and cried in disbelief. His willingness to put me first came at a most crucial time as I was getting ready to leave for the hospital.

The surgery was to be a routine hysterectomy with some other repairs. However, when Dr. Lach began working on me, he came up with eleven other problems. Later he told me, "Nothing below your waist is where it was." What I expected to be a quick recovery was excruciatingly painful and endlessly slow.

Fred was still weak from his month-long bout with rheumatic fever, but he came to see me twice each day and cared for me in a new and tender way. We spent more quiet time together than we ever had before and reached a new depth in our relationship. He seemed genuinely interested in me and wanted me to come home so badly that he convinced Dr. Lach to let me leave before the catheter was removed. By the time I got home from the hospital, still connected to the little tube and plastic bag, Sophia, our new Greek maid, was in firm control of the house. "Just don't expect me to play nurse," she said. Fortunately my mother was there to care for me.

On Memorial Day good friends invited us for a family cookout and I begged Fred to let me go. Fred helped me to the car and the children were thrilled to be finally going somewhere. The cookout was the first fun I'd had in weeks. We ate hamburgers and out-of-season fresh corn and tomatoes from the agricultural experimental station where our friend worked. I lay on their chaise lounge basking in the joy of being among friends, out of the house and free of pain.

Hanging Between Life and Death

But when I got home that night, I began to experience new pain, this time in my chest. Nothing had been touched above my waist and I assumed I had indigestion from all I'd eaten at the party. At 2 A.M. I was jolted awake by a severe stab in my chest. As I sat up, a second pain gripped me. Fred awakened as I began to cry, and I became violently sick to my stomach. "I'm dying!" I screamed.

After Fred talked with Dr. Lach on the phone, I overheard him tell my mother, "The doctor thinks Florence may have a blood clot from the operation lodged in her heart. He hopes he can save her." My mother burst into tears as she remembered her sister who had died of an embolism after a similar operation.

When Lauren saw Grammie cry, she began to sob, "Don't leave us again, Mommy, don't leave us!"

I'll never forget the sight of Lauren and Mother standing in the driveway, clinging to each other in tears and Lauren crying, "Mommy come back! Don't die!" as the ambulance attendants lifted me onto a stretcher.

I didn't want to die, but I knew I was going to. I couldn't breathe. The attendant put an oxygen mask over my face and I began to relax. When I arrived at the hospital, Dr. Lach rushed me into X ray and then gave me a shot. As I passed out of my pain, I heard Dr. Lach tell Fred, "She may not live until morning."

When I next opened my eyes I saw a circle of white masks. Was I in heaven or a hospital? I had no idea. One of the masks had Dr. Lach's eyes. He had stood over me all night.

The X rays showed no blood clot, and the doctors decided I must have had a heart attack. I was moved from Emergency to the Cardiac floor where almost every patient had a beeping monitor above his door. In the weeks that followed, I heard many monitors stop and saw the rush of nurses followed by weeping relatives as the body was wheeled out for the last time. The fear of death invaded every room.

I was still uncomfortable from my operation and now fought to recover from my heart attack. In addition, a team of doctors came to see me every morning. I didn't mind their visit, but they stood around with their clipboards and looked me over as if I were a plastic model. They all seemed fascinated that a thirty-five-year-old woman, who hadn't moved a muscle in weeks, could have a heart attack.

"If we can keep her from having another attack, we will be able to save her," one doctor said with the detachment a dentist would have in trying to preserve a baby tooth.

"Let's keep her feet up and see if that helps," suggested one intern. They cranked up the end of the bed and I felt as if I were standing on my head. No one asked how I felt. They discussed my medication and agreed I should have my blood thinned. This was accomplished by inserting a needle in a vein by my right elbow and strapping my arm to a board.

After several days of standing on my head, half groggy, with my stiff arm, I again felt the pain and pushed the button for the nurse. Quickly she sent for the cardiogram machine and my team of experts. When they arrived, they never looked at me, but instead became fascinated with the machine as my pain increased.

"Watch the dials!" said one. "She's having another

one!" I never did seem to have a name. I cried and thrashed and they watched the dials, assured that if I died the machine would tell them.

The attack passed and the group left with the machine. The next morning when they came in, they seemed surprised to see me. "She's a hardy girl," they said. I kept wishing someone would say, "Mrs. Littauer, *you* are a hardy girl. Well done." But to this team I was only a case with a chart and a machine.

When Fred came in to visit that afternoon, a doctor told him I had had another heart attack and they were going to increase my anti-coagulant drug. "If she continues having these heart attacks, she will not live long," he said. "You should make plans for the care of your children in case they end up with no mother."

No mother, I thought. *No mother.* I had waited years to have a normal son and now that I had adopted Freddie, he was to have no mother?

I continued having one or two heart attacks a week. Each one would bring the nurse, the machine and the doctors, and each attack produced the same proclamations of imminent death and increases in my medications.

As the weeks passed, I became depressed. My tongue would no longer form words and my mind couldn't hold two thoughts together. I was too weak to eat and began to hate food so much I felt sick whenever I heard the shuffle of the tray girl's loose loafers. Day after day they set down food and picked it up untouched. No one ever noticed I hadn't eaten. I was so emaciated that my mother looked at me as if she were already at my funeral. After seeing me drugged and dying she begged Fred to do something. Fred pleaded with the doctors and they finally agreed, "If she can last a week without a heart attack, we'll let her go home to die."

At that point, going home to die seemed good. I prayed for a week free of attacks and the Lord answered my prayer. I passed a long, dull week and the doctors decided they would let me leave, but not without a few tests.

A Hospital Nightmare

I was tested for a number of things in my tilted bed, but one day I went for an unforgettable adventure. A tough nurse's aide was assigned to get me out of bed for the first time. I had been off some of the drugs for three days and I could talk slowly. The aide helped me sit up, then plunked me in a chair.

"Don't you dare move out of that chair," she said sternly. "You're very sick. The man next door disobeyed me and when he got up to walk by himself, he fell. He whacked his head right here on the edge of his bed, split his skull and bled all over the place."

Even if I could have moved, I wouldn't have dared disobey this frightening woman. Shortly after she left me sinking into the chair, an orderly arrived with a stretcher and told me to hop on. I explained I could no more hop on the stretcher than I could fly. He groaned, grabbed me under the arms and eased me onto the stretcher. As he pushed me down the hall, past the nurse's station, I noticed it was twelve noon. It was refreshing to see some other area than the square room I had lived in for almost five weeks. The orderly rang for the elevator and we landed in a basement.

"Where are we?" I asked.

"In the corridor that leads to underground tunnels which end up in other buildings," he said.

As we started down into an obvious tunnel, the boy spotted another orderly coming toward us with another unfortunate lady on his stretcher.

Immediately my boy yelled, "Chicken!" and charged forth, racing me in the direction of the other stretcher.

Just as we were about to crash, he swerved. "You're the chicken!" called the other boy as he whizzed by.

When I recovered, I asked him why he had tried to kill me. "We just like to play games," he said with a laugh.

"It gets dull wheeling old people around all day."

How ironic if I survive the heart attacks and die in a stretcher crash in a tunnel, I thought.

We arrived at the radio isotope building and my friend parked me in a hall and left. As I lay looking at the ceiling, I noticed that the fluorescent light fixture directly over me was hanging by only one wire. *Maybe I'll be killed by a lethal light fixture,* I thought.

I called to a passing doctor and pointed out the hanging tubes. "Oh, that's been like that since Christmas," he said. "Don't worry, it won't fall."

But lying alone in the hall, there wasn't much to do but worry. Soon a nurse came by and read the instructions the orderly had tucked under my feet. "You're to have a liver scan," she said. "I have to shoot this solution into your veins."

She found a vein on the top of my right hand, put in the needle and injected the liquid. Unfortunately she missed the vein and shot the solution into my hand. As I looked aghast, my hand immediately turned green. "Don't worry," she said, "it'll go away some day." It never did; the skin is still green around a large damaged vein on my right hand.

After the nurse succeeded on my other hand, she pushed me into a cool room and inserted me and the stretcher into a huge machine. It was July and very hot in the hospital and this one air-conditioned room seemed like heaven. I was exhausted from my stretcher ride, the chicken game, the fear of falling light fixtures and the blown-up vein. As soon as she pressed a few buttons and turned out the lights, I went off to sleep.

The next thing I remember was someone turning on a light. It was 4:30 P.M.!

As I tried to collect my senses, a night watchman walked around the room and jumped when he saw my head sticking out of the machine.

"What are you doing here?" he asked.

"I have no idea," I said. "Someone just pushed me into this room and left."

"You shouldn't be here," he exclaimed. "This building is closed."

"What do you want me to do?" I asked. "I'm strapped in this machine, too weak to move."

He ran out the door, made a frantic phone call, and I heard him say, "I just found some lady in the radio-isotope machine. No, I don't know who she is or how she got here. Just send someone to get her and quick. I don't want to be responsible for any of your people."

The watchman came back and looked at me. I looked at him. What was there to say to each other? In about five minutes a doctor arrived with an orderly. The doctor grabbed my wrist, read my name bracelet and told the orderly I belonged in 602 of the main building. Without so much as a hello, the doctor pulled a few switches that released me and the orderly wheeled me away.

As the orderly pushed me by the nurse's station, the head nurse called over, "Who have you got on that stretcher?"

"I don't know," said the boy, "just some lady from Room 602."

"That's the one that's missing!" she said happily. "She's back. She's back!"

I soon learned no one knew where I had been. When the nurse's aid returned and found me gone, she thought I had disobeyed her and wandered off. She reported my bad behavior to the head nurse. The cleaning woman was assigned to find me and she emptied the waste baskets in each room twice trying to locate me without letting anyone know a patient was missing.

At 4 P.M. the security office had tried unsuccessfully to reach my husband, so they called my mother to say they had lost me.

"How could you lose her?" Mother asked, almost collapsing.

"We really don't know," they said sheepishly. They had run out of searching ideas when I was calmly pushed out of the elevator at 5 P.M. in time for dinner.

Learning to Live Again

The next day the doctor team arrived with good news. "Your test results are all in," one said, "and you haven't been having heart attacks at all. Instead you have the worst gall bladder we've ever seen and now we're going to take it out." They all stood smiling proudly, impressed that after five weeks of treating me for the wrong problem, they could now remove my gall bladder.

Instead of being happy, I began to cry. I was ready to go home to die. I had prepared my mind for it, knowing that as a Christian I would go to heaven. Now life meant staying in the hospital and going through another major operation.

When they tested my blood it had been thinned so much it wouldn't coagulate. They quickly removed the needle for the anti-coagulant and changed it for another with a blood builder. Next the doctors told the nurse to take me off all tranquilizers and drugs and let me level off before the next operation.

I can now appreciate what a drug addict goes through in withdrawal. I became shaky, nervous, hot, cold, sick, wild—and I couldn't shut my eyes or sleep all night. I felt as if I were going insane. I asked for something to help me, but the nurse said, "Our instructions are that you are off all drugs."

After three days of withdrawal and blood building the doctors said I was ready.

The gall bladder operation was much more debilitating than it should have been. With the addition of new pain killers and medications, my ability to think was again shattered. The television faded in and out with my fantasies. I couldn't hold a book or focus on a phrase long enough to understand its meaning.

During the second evening after the operation, my private duty nurse made the mistake of not adjusting the flow of my intravenous fluid. While I was unconscious, the liquid poured into me at five times its normal rate. When Fred walked in to see me, he thought he was in the wrong room. My gaunt face was fat, my scrawny hands were stretched to their limit, and the nurse was asleep in the chair. Fred quickly awakened her and sent her home, deciding he could do better. For a week he slept on the hospital floor, jumping up each time I stirred or cried. He fed, bathed, and loved me in a way I had never known. I could hardly talk but my eyes said, "Thank you."

Before I left the hospital, the surgeon pulled out my drainage tubes and I felt as if all my intestines were being removed in one long rope. Fred took me home and I began a long, slow recovery.

I hadn't seen a mirror in weeks and was shocked at how I looked. My blond hair had grown out half brown and lay limp and shapeless on my head. My cheeks were sunken, my eyes never more than half open and I had lost more than twenty pounds. My hip bones stuck out and the skin on my legs hung in folds.

For someone who had spent her life working to be beautiful, the view in the mirror was the ultimate depressant. Fred kept reassuring me I would recover and look good again and often showed me how smooth and soft my feet had become with all this rest. I stared at my feet as the only improvement I could see and had Lauren paint my toenails. As I focused on my toes at the end of the bed, those ten small spots perked me up and I began to care about living again.

Reflections

If anyone in today's litigious society had the series of

blunders that were committed against me, they would sue the hospital for gross negligence and misdiagnosis. But we grew up feeling doctors were one step below angels and so we just accepted what had happened and tried to get me back on my feet.

One of the greatest problems was the withdrawal from the eleven drugs a day I had been on for five weeks. Tim Hansel, an author-friend who has an amazing sense of humor in spite of constant excruciating pain from a near fatal fall off a mountain, told me of the time when his pain pills had ceased to work and the doctors had taken him off all medication. "I never suffered so much in my life," he said. "I was climbing the walls in agony."

My heart went out to him, and my prayers also, as I remembered the pain of my attacks and the withdrawal anguish I went through. I can't think of any good that came out of my five weeks of blunders except that I now have a personal appreciation for pain and an understanding of addiction that I might not have learned in any less painful way. I now have a compassion for anyone addicted to anything. I no longer say, "Well, just don't do it anymore."

This new attitude is a result of daring to

Make the tough times count!

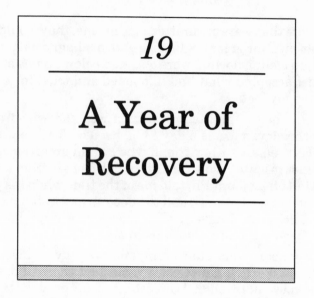

19

A Year of Recovery

I prayed I would be able to do dishes without reviewing Fred's wrongs, but a thirteen-year-old habit is difficult to break.

The unnecessary excess of drugs to prevent my supposed heart attacks had put my mind in neutral. When I read a page, I couldn't focus on what it said. Often I would start a sentence and forget what I was trying to say, and when my friends came for bridge, I could no longer remember what cards had been played.

I would go out of the house but my physical strength diminished rapidly. I would go to the supermarket and be too tired to finish my list. Months after I should have been well, I would find myself standing in the middle of a department store looking for a place to lie down. I had to tell myself to get moving and my mind would push my weary body home.

As I tried to coordinate my mind and body, I realized I hadn't read my Bible in months. In the hospital I had been too limp to hold a book and too confused to care.

Pastor Frost had visited me frequently and I knew my new friends at St. Charlie's were praying for my recovery. As soon as I felt I could concentrate, I started attending a Bible study at the church.

My "What Ifs?"

One day as I was worrying about whether I would ever again be able to speak in public, I read 2 Timothy 1:7: "For God hath not given us the spirit of fear; but of power, and of love, and of a sound mind."

I began to see I was still full of fear. I had spent the majority of my life in an "if only" anticipation—*if only* I could get my circumstances in order, I would be happy.

When I committed my life to Jesus Christ, He showed me that carpeting and cars were not the answer. He also showed me that I was part of my marriage problems and I began to move toward a life of faith in Christ instead of in me. But I had only taken a few baby steps in the Christian walk when I was stopped short and put on the sideline for months. Now I was emerging in fear. My "if only" had been replaced with "what ifs."

What if I could never really concentrate?

What if my memory never returned?

What if I couldn't speak again?

What if my haggard face didn't improve?

What if I couldn't regain my strength?

As these questions filled my mind, I reread the verse and saw that God had not given me the spirit of fear. I began to analyze my "what ifs." What was I truly afraid of? As I thought about this I was startled to realize my fears were all about me. *What if* I never could make me great again? My fears were not about war or famine or home or business. They were not about Fred or the children. They were about me. *What if* I couldn't rise again or meet my expectations of myself? As I concentrated on my fears about my own personal future, a disturbing thought flashed through my mind: "What difference does it make?"

What difference did it make whether I rose like the Phoenix from my mental ashes? Did Fred care if I got back on the stage? Were my children hoping I'd run off on the club circuit again? Had the League fallen apart without me? Had the theatre ceased production? Was there any great cry for my brilliance? The humbling answer was, "No!" Then what difference did it make whether I ever got going at top speed again?

I had to face it—I had never allowed myself to live a normal life. I had kept myself on an ambitious race for superiority. I had won, yet I ended up a failure. Now that I had been stopped and taken off my treadmill, I was afraid I would never again reach new heights. The fear didn't come from God, it came from me. I was afraid I couldn't accept me as I was. I wasn't directing anything. I didn't like me as a plain person. Stripped of titles and positions, I no longer felt I amounted to anything. I began to seriously reflect on the barrenness of my busy life. Before, I equated busyness and success with happiness. But I learned I could cry in a Lincoln Continental and shiver in a seal coat.

As I thought about myself I realized I had better accept myself just as I was. I didn't have a lot of energy, but I was no longer deathly ill, and for that I was grateful.

"For God hath not given us the spirit of fear, but of power." Whose power? His power. It surely was not going to be my power. My days of strength and leadership were apparently over and I was not willing to accept that all I needed was the Lord's power in my life.

"I can do all things through Christ which strengtheneth me" (Philippians 4:13). I had heard this verse in church but never claimed it for myself. Now I realized that once I was willing to give up my own plans, Christ would give me the strength to do what He wanted. But was I willing? I decided I didn't have much choice. It would no longer be my way, but His.

As I reflected more on 2 Timothy 1:7, I thought about

how I equated progress with love and realized I loved only those who pleased me. What an ugly thought! But I was not yet willing to face its full implication and went on to what had first attracted me to the verse: "a sound mind."

I needed a sound mind to get back into my old routine. As the thought hit me, I realized I had just decided, for the first time, not to push myself into new projects but to relax and wait for the Lord's strength and direction. It was going to be hard for me to let the Lord lead in my life.

Learning the Definition of Love

As I continued to read and study the Bible, I tried to apply the words of Scripture directly to me. One of the most difficult passages for me was the thirteenth chapter of 1 Corinthians. I had memorized this entire thirteenth chapter when I was chaplain of my college sorority but never thought about its meaning for me. I struggled with verse six: "Love does not keep a record of wrongs." I saw what it said and what it meant, but how did it apply to me? Before I had finished phrasing the question, the answer came: *You have a big record in your mind of all the things Fred has ever done wrong.*

What does that mean? I thought.

It means you don't love him.

Me not love Fred? I've lived with him for thirteen years. Of course, I love him.

I was trying to convince myself in the same strong, conclusive manner I had always used on others, but this time I couldn't. I had to open my mind to the possibility that I didn't love Fred. It was an unattractive thought for a model wife and I held court with myself.

Do you have a record of wrongs against the accused?

Only of things he's done really *wrong, Your Honor.*

Where do you keep your records?

Oh, only in my head, Sir.

How long have you kept this record?

Thirteen years.

How do you keep it fresh in your mind?

I rehearse it every day. You see, when I put my hands in dishwater, it triggers a switch in my head and I begin to review the list.

Very interesting. Then you do not love your husband?

Of course, I love my husband.

That's impossible, because our book says, "Love does not keep a record of wrongs." You have testified that you have a record of wrongs; therefore, you are guilty of not loving your husband.

Guilty as charged, Your Honor.

Once I admitted I was guilty, I had to make reparations, and I decided to start with the evidence: my record of wrongs. I prayed daily, sometimes hourly, that God would remove the list from my head. I prayed I would be able to do dishes without reviewing Fred's wrongs, but a thirteen-year-old habit is difficult to break.

As I continued to pray, the list began to disappear. But if Fred displeased me, it started all over again. Then a new thought came to me. When people give up smoking, they often chew gum to replace the habit. Perhaps I needed to fill the habit vacuum with something new; perhaps I should start a list of "rights."

I began by copying Philippians 4:8 and tacking it on a cabinet door where I could see it while doing dishes.

> Whatsoever things are TRUE,
> Whatsoever things are HONEST,
> Whatsoever things are JUST,
> Whatsoever things are PURE,
> Whatsoever things are of GOOD REPORT;
> if there be any VIRTUE and if there be any PRAISE,
> think on these things.

As I began to think on these things, I started to replace my negative list with some positives. Fred had always been true-blue to me. He was scrupulously honest, and certainly just and fair, and clean and lovely to look at. People in town spoke well of him; he was of good report. These were virtuous traits and I should have been willing to praise him, but because he rarely praised me, I was not about to go first. What a rebellious spirit! I won't be nice to you unless you're nice first. How childish!

Yet at the time I didn't consider myself childish. It took time, and as I studied the Scriptures, gradually I became more pliable and ceased searching for goals. I began to replace my record of wrongs with things worthy of praise, and as I became willing to be set on the sidelines forever, the Lord Jesus began to restore me. As I prayed, He worked. While I was weak, He was strong. As I studied His word, He rebuilt my mind. "God hath not given us the spirit of fear; but of power, and of love, and of a sound mind."

Reflections

In retrospect I see that God had to allow me to become weak so that He could become strong. Are there some points in your life where you have been ill or depressed and felt there was no hope? I can understand how you feel. I've been there. Have you found a verse that fit your situation so well you knew God wrote it just for you?

This time on the sidelines was a transition period for me where I finally learned to give up on myself and let the Lord take control. I'd been forced to accept my lack of power to change the fate of my babies, I'd been drugged into obedience in the hospital, but as I tried to re-enter the mainstream of life I was ready once more to take charge. A Choleric-out-of-control is depressed. As I look back I see that God would have kept me weak for years if I hadn't learned to give Him the control of my life so that He could show me how to

Make the tough times count!

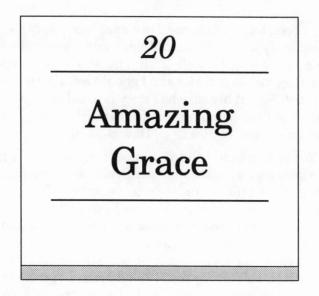

20

Amazing
Grace

*While we were too new in the Christian life at
that point to understand what they saw in us, we
realize now that they looked at us and thought,
"If only this couple would get turned on for the
Lord. What an impact they could have."*

Once I accepted the fact that I might never get better,
I began to get better. Once I ceased setting worldly goals,
I was given a reward. Once I gave control to God, He began
to bless my life.

In March of 1967, less than a year after my hospital
siege, a friend called to say she had a job commentating
fashion shows for a local store. They had booked two shows
on one day, and she wondered if I would be able to fill in
for her. I had always loved clothes and kept up with
current fashion. Even when I was too weak to read, I
flipped through *Vogue* and *Glamour*. I said yes and then
wondered if I would be able to handle the job.

I still had trouble with my memory, my words sometimes got mixed up, and I often got lost in the middle of a

sentence. Did I dare stand up and speak? I decided the Lord had opened this opportunity and would give me the strength to perform. I was excited about getting back on stage and began to prepare for the big day.

When it was time to choose the clothes for the show, I took Lauren along and we both learned from my friend how to "pull a show." While I had done some modeling and had commentated many club fashion shows, I never had to choose the clothes and accessories for each model. Together Lauren and I picked up the sense of selecting and coordinating the outfits and on the day of the show at the New Haven Country Club, we were ready. We had pulled the show, coordinated the accessories and reworked the lineup. I was to be on stage and thirteen-year-old Lauren was to direct the models and see that they got out on time and in the right order. To give the show an added touch, I had written a review of the season's fashion in verse.

The show went smoothly and the audience loved my poetry. Diane Brown, public relations director for R. H. Macy's in New Haven, observed the show and when it ended she told me how pleased she was with my work.

"Would you consider being the commentator for all the Macy's shows in Connecticut?" she asked. "I was impressed how smoothly the lineup moved."

"Oh, that's because Lauren was working backstage," I replied.

"We'll take her, too!" said Diane.

During the time Lauren and I worked for Macy's, Fred expanded his business to New York and decided to open an office there. When he checked rental prices, he found he could get an apartment for the same amount as a decent office. Fred met me one day when I was at Macy's in New York and took me to see an elegant new apartment building called The Churchill.

He had selected an apartment overlooking the East River with a clear view of the United Nations Building.

The view was breathtaking, and I was enthralled with the thought of a second home, a retreat in New York City. While Fred intended to use it for business, he told me to decorate it any way I wanted. "You've improved so much as a wife," he said, "I want to give you the best."

Nothing inspired me more than decorating a new home. This time it was extra special—Fred was also interested. Even though he said I could decorate it in any style, I wanted to please Fred for a change, and we shopped together.

As we divided our weekends between our two homes, we found our family time improving. Every other week we would leave on Friday for New York and spend the weekend in close fellowship in the apartment. We toured the city with the children and took horse-and-buggy rides in Central Park. Afternoons we wandered through the toys at F. A. O. Schwartz. For the first time in our married lives, Fred actually spent two days a week in our presence.

I was so deliriously happy with the attention he gave us, I couldn't do enough for him. I noticed that as I began to put his desires first, he started to enjoy my company. On Sunday mornings we would go to the Calvary Baptist Church where Dr. Stephen Olford would inspire us to improve our Christian lives. As we drove home on Sunday evenings, we would sing hymns and rejoice that we had each other.

Amazing Grace

While we spent much of the summer of '67 in our New York apartment, we settled into our Connecticut home in time for school. When we returned to church at Good Time Charlie's we were introduced to Grace Mintz, a bright, attractive girl in her early thirties. Grace had big green eyes, a radiant smile, and our family was immediately attracted to her.

We became acquainted with Grace and discovered that she had been a member of our church before we joined. She was divorced and was bringing up two little girls alone. We hadn't seen her before because she had been working as a secretary in the lay division of Campus Crusade for Christ in San Bernardino, California.

None of us in our little church had ever heard of Campus Crusade, but Grace began to change that. She made plans for a Crusade-sponsored Lay Institute for Evangelism in Connecticut and began promoting this among the pastors in our area. She wanted Fred and me to help her, but we were afraid of anything with such a heavy title as Lay Institute for Evangelism. Although we politely avoided promoting the Institute, Grace cheerfully kept us posted on her progress.

With no real help from anyone in the church or community, she single-handedly scheduled the Institute and visited almost every pastor in the New Haven area plus many in Bridgeport, Milford and Hartford. Few were willing to help. Undaunted, she arranged for a downtown New Haven church to lend her their social hall, and she persuaded Mike Hopping, a dentist from Atlanta, Georgia, and his wife Joyce to come and share their testimony. Throughout all of Grace's efforts to put on this Institute, Fred and I remained indifferent and had no intention of attending. We were a little reticent to get too religious.

As the October date approached we planned to spend that weekend in New York, but then Grace asked us if we would do her a big favor.

"Since you have the largest and the nicest home of anyone in church," she said, "I wonder if you would consider having Mike and Joyce Hopping stay with you while they're in New Haven."

She knew how to appeal to me! I was flattered to think my home was the best and quickly said I would be glad to take care of her guests. The Friday evening of the Lay Institute arrived, and Fred and I still had not planned to attend, even though the speakers would be spending the weekend in our home.

At dinner that evening, Fred said, "I really don't think

it's polite to have the speakers stay here and for us not to show enough interest to go and hear what they have to say."

We both concluded it would be embarrassing for Grace to bring the Hoppings to our home that evening if we hadn't gone to the program.

While Fred felt we ought to show interest out of moral obligation, I was afraid to attend. I didn't want to get involved with anything that had to do with "evangelism." Grace had said something about knocking on people's doors and sharing your faith, and I panicked at the thought that she might expect me to do the same. Fred said we should go, and I said only if he got a babysitter. The first girl he called said yes. My heart sank, but I had no choice.

Grace was delighted to see us that evening. "I just knew you would come," she said confidently. I wondered how she had this advance knowledge since we had just decided ourselves within the hour. Grace ushered us to the front row of a dingy basement room. I assumed she wanted to make sure we would pay attention, but I was very uncomfortable.

I pictured the Hoppings to be old, gloomy, pious people, but was pleasantly surprised to meet a young, attractive, dynamic couple. They shared the story of their married life and humorously pointed out their failures. Their experiences sounded just like ours. As they shared their Christian testimony and the changes the Lord had brought to their home, I began to see that Fred and I had a long way to go. We were impressed with their message and their inspiring example.

After the session, we took them home and sat up until 2 A.M. asking questions about how we could live out Christian principles in our daily lives. They gave us simple, factual steps to help us improve our marriage. They made it clear that once we invite Christ into our lives, He truly dwells in us and uses our bodies to do His will. We learned that, while a decision for Christ is a one-time commitment, we depend upon the power of the Holy Spirit to give us an abundant Christian life. We must appropriate the Holy Spirit's power daily and ask God in prayer to give us the strength and desire to do His will.

"Jesus came that we might have life, and that we might have it abundantly," they said.

I had been afraid that being a Christian would be dull, and I was relieved to see this personable couple had found an exciting relationship with Jesus Christ. Although God had already been working in our hearts, Mike and Joyce Hopping gave us a new understanding of how to live and enjoy a Spirit-filled life.

Fred and I had no intention of going to the Institute on Saturday. Fred had a full day of work at the office, and I had to prepare dinner for the Hoppings that night. The next morning, however, Fred got dressed and went to the meeting. He told me later that after listening to the Hoppings, God had spoken through them to him about his life.

After a gourmet dinner that had taken me all day to prepare, we again talked late into the night, questioning our guests and paying close attention to their answers. While we were too new in the Christian life at that point to understand what they saw in us, we realize now that they looked at us and thought, *If only this couple would get turned on for the Lord. What an impact they could have.*

Years later we often thought of others in the same way, but at that time we had no idea *we* were considered "baby Christians with growth potential."

The Hoppings encouraged us to take the week-long lay training offered by Campus Crusade in Arrowhead Springs above San Bernardino, California. There seemed to be no possibility of our getting to California for a week of Bible study, but the Hoppings emphasized that this experience would be extremely helpful in getting our Christian life underway.

On Sunday afternoon, the fifty people who attended the Institute were scheduled to go out into the community to witness. The idea of ringing doorbells and trying to convince perfect strangers they needed to invite Christ into their lives frightened and appalled me, and I stayed home. Fred, however, was braver than I and went off with a partner who had just committed his life to the Lord at the Institute the day before. They were to give the "Community Religious Survey," as they had been trained to do, to anyone who would listen. While I stayed home and prepared dinner, Fred knocked on doors.

At the third home Fred found a man raking leaves in the yard. When Fred asked if he had time to answer some questions on a survey, the man said, "I was just looking for an excuse to sit down." He was most hospitable and invited Fred and his partner inside.

Fred asked him all the questions on the survey, shared the "Four Spiritual Laws" gospel presentation, and at the conclusion asked, "Is there any reason why you would not want to pray and receive Christ into your life right now?"

"No, there isn't," said the man. "I would like to do this."

Fred was so shocked that he swallowed twice before leading the man in prayer. The man's name was Bernie Roop, and he began attending St. Charlie's. The last we heard, Bernie and his wife are still members of that church. Fred came home that afternoon excited that God had used him to reach a man who was ready and willing to commit his life to the Lord.

Sunday evening we stayed up late with the Hoppings again, and on Monday Fred took an unprecedented weekday off and took them sightseeing, then to their plane in New York. Every minute of our time together was filled with an insatiable desire for direction, and God used the Hoppings as Christian role models for us.

A Turning Point

The following month, Grace had a new plan and invited Hal Lindsey, who was then a traveling representative for Campus Crusade for Christ, to come to our little Charlie Church. Grace again asked us to keep the speaker in our home. That night we sat up again until two in the morning plying Hal with questions and, like the Hoppings, Hal insisted we go out to Arrowhead Springs to take the lay training.

Since Grace, the Hoppings and Hal Lindsey had all strongly suggested we go to California for Christian training, we began to consider the possibility. Grace provided us with information on activities at Arrowhead Springs, and in January of 1968 persuaded us to go. We took our pastor and his wife, Sherwood and Ruth Frost, and Grace asked some local businessmen to send three other Connecticut ministers to go with us.

We arrived in Los Angeles and took a little helicopter to San Bernardino. The shaky craft flew so low I could see the people on the ground, and I was frightened. A week later a helicopter crashed, and the service was discontinued.

The drive to Arrowhead Springs was beautiful. I was amazed at the tall palm trees, lush green lawns and bright smiling pansies in January! I was also impressed with the size and grandeur of the hotel. I was surprised to learn that Elizabeth Taylor had spent her first honeymoon on the sixth floor of the Arrowhead Springs hotel, then a resort for the Hollywood stars.

Our room was tastefully decorated, and later we all ate in the Candlelight Room, an ornate ballroom with a huge crystal chandelier in the center and candles doing double duty against the mirrored walls. I was overwhelmed. I had assumed that any religious retreat would be stark and barren, and we might expect to be called to prayer at four in the morning by a little monk with a tinkling bell.

I also expected a sparse diet and simple cots covered with khaki Army-surplus blankets to quicken our spirituality. I had presumed the staff would be seriously dedicated people who dressed in simple pilgrim style, carried large Bibles and seldom smiled. How wrong I was!

We spent the first evening in the Little Theatre, a former movie hall for the Hollywood set. Instead of watching risque movies, we sang hymns, listened to a fantastic pianist and enjoyed the rich fellowship of people in love with the Lord. After the singing and welcoming introductions, Dr. Bill Bright spoke to us.

I expected a big powerful man to leap on the stage and barrage us with a dynamic message. Instead, a short, unassuming man came quietly to the lectern and gave us a low-key talk on the founding of Campus Crusade for Christ. He told us how he began his ministry while operating a candy business and how it had grown from a handful of students at UCLA to an international organization with a staff of over 2,000.

"Campus Crusade is a worldwide movement," he said, "totally dedicated to one goal: to help fulfill the Great Commission of our Lord by taking the claims of Christ to the millions of students in every country of the world. Our special emphasis, though it is not our total thrust, is on the college and high school campuses, because we believe it is here that the main source of untapped manpower waits to be challenged and trained to help change the world."

He then said we were to be trained as laymen in order to go back to our own communities and become Christian leaders. We would receive biblical instruction plus helps in witnessing, teaching others and living the Christian life.

He concluded his quietly persuasive message by telling us to go to our rooms without saying a word to anyone and write down a list of all the sins in our lives. I knew this wouldn't take me long and I went quietly off to our room with Fred. No one said a word as we went through the lobby to the elevator. I had never been in an absolutely mute crowd before; it was a little creepy.

By the time we got to our room the silence was killing me, and as we shut the door, I opened my mouth to speak only to have Fred raise a finger and shush me. I could see he was genuinely moved and intended to follow through with the assignment.

He sat down at the desk and began to write. As I didn't want to appear too saintly, I also got out a piece of paper and sat on the edge of the bed. I expected to have difficulty writing bad things about me, but as I began to write, it was as if another hand took control and put down one fact after another.

An hour later Fred and I concluded our lists and were soberly ready for step two: prayerfully read over your list, confess that these are your sins and ask God to forgive you. We each did this quietly and then together went to the wastebasket where we slowly tore our lists in pieces and threw them away. This was to symbolize God's forgiveness, His cleansing and the promise that He would never again remember our sins.

By the time we completed this act, both of us were in tears. God had shown us sins in our lives we had never even thought of before. With almost no effort we had written pages of faults. It was hard for me to tear up a part of myself, even a bad part, but I did it. We threw our sins away and received God's forgiveness, and for the first time in our lives we were truly repentant of our newly admitted sins. We realized how we had hurt each other and apologized for our selfish lives.

That night was a turning point in our Christian experience. We had humbled ourselves before the Lord and one another, and God was ready to help us grow. I have learned since, the Lord is not pushy. He will not begin a work in a life until the person has been willing to look deeply into himself, pull out his sins and humbly confess them. When we are willing to be cleansed, He will forgive us of our faults and start to build a new life.

The next morning we could hardly wait to share our experience with others at the breakfast table. Later in class we memorized the "Four Spiritual Laws," an evangelistic pamphlet written by Dr. Bright to help the inexperienced share their faith with other people. It states simply: (1) God loves you and offers a wonderful plan for your life. (2) Man is sinful and separated from God, thus he cannot know and experience God's love and plan for his life. (3) Jesus Christ is God's only provision for man's sin. Through Him you can know and experience God's love and plan for your life. (4) We must individually receive Jesus Christ as Savior and Lord; then we can know and experience God's love and plan for our lives.

Once we learned how to use the Four Laws, we found out we were all going witnessing on Wednesday. When ringing doorbells was mentioned at our Lay Institute in Connecticut, I stayed home, but this time I was excited. I went off with a feeling of anticipation and a handful of "Community Religious Surveys" and the "Four Spiritual Laws" booklets.

When we arrived in West Covina, I thought I would have Fred to lean on, but our leader paired me with Ruth Frost, our pastor's wife. We were assigned a certain street and told to go to each house and ask if they would be willing to take a survey. If they were interested, we were to ask them the printed questions and share the Four Laws. When the reality of this process hit me, I wondered why I had come. Ruth was even more afraid than I, and we began to hope no one was home. But we looked down the long street and knew there was no chance that everyone would be on vacation.

Slowly we went to the first house. I rang the bell and a huge Great Dane jumped to the fence and looked down at us. I had never seen such a dog. He was as big as a horse! He barked ferociously, and Ruth and I clutched each other in genuine fear. Slowly we backed down the walk. There was no one home at the second house and the third had a teenager watching soap operas who had no time for us. The fourth home had a lady who was very pleasant, answered all the questions and said she would read the Four Laws later.

At the fifth home a sad lady came to the door and let us in. She was willing to take the survey and gave brief answers which indicated she had some religious background. We sat at her kitchen table and went over the Four Laws, explaining that God loved her and had a wonderful plan for her life. She didn't seem like the type to want any wonderful plan, but I proceeded anyway.

At the conclusion, I asked if there were any reason she would not like to pray to receive Christ right now and read the prayer at the end of the book with me. Instead of answering, she began to recite the prayer and finished the first line before I could join in. By the time we said "Amen," she was in tears and I was in shock. This event was the first time anyone had prayed with me to receive Christ.

"Does this mean that when I die, I will go to heaven for sure?" she asked.

I assured her she would. "The Bible tells us in John 3:16," I said, "that God so loved the world that He gave His only begotten Son, that whosoever believeth in Him should not perish, but have everlasting life."

"I asked my pastor this question," she said, "but he told me there was no way to know until I die. I've been worried about this and just last night prayed that God would send someone to tell me about heaven."

I was overwhelmed to realize that God had sent me, a totally inexperienced believer, to give this woman the assurance she was seeking. I know there were bells ringing in heaven and in my heart—a new believer entered the family of God.

As this dear lady didn't own a Bible, I spent the rest

of the afternoon introducing her to my New Testament and showing her how to study it. I've often wondered what I told her, I knew so little. Later I mailed her a *Good News* New Testament from Connecticut. A year later she wrote to tell me her house had burned down but she had saved her handbag and her Bible.

The next evening, as I was getting ready for bed, Fred showed me a little pocket New Testament.

"This Bible is really exciting," he said. He studied every minute he could find and began to pray for wisdom and knowledge. In six months Fred went from knowing almost nothing about the Bible to being able to find verses on any subject at a moment's notice. I couldn't believe how quickly he learned and how rapidly his whole personality changed. The more he studied, the more pleasant he became. One day a friend of ours said, "What's happened to Fred? He seems almost humble."

Revival in New Haven

By the time we returned from California, Grace had already planned another project. She had prayed for a second area-wide Lay Institute for Evangelism in New Haven and had gathered together a group of interested pastors. They asked Fred to be the chairman. Fred and I had seen the practical influence of such a conference and wanted to reach as many people as possible.

Fred and I also determined that if we were in charge of a Lay Institute, it was going to be the best. We were willing to spend as much time and energy as possible to insure a large audience. Since Fred had the weight of his business obligations and I was working for Macy's and keeping up two homes, we decided to look for someone to take care of the children. Through an ad in the Heidelberg newspaper, a German friend chose Gudrun Pitchel as our new mother's helper.

I pictured Gudrun to be a big, husky German girl straight off the farm, but when I met her, I was surprised to see she stood only four feet eleven inches, weighed ninety pounds, and was a size three. Gudrun spoke little English, and I knew no German, but from a note from our friend we learned she was twenty-four years old, was a professional dress designer and seamstress, and had taken the job to learn English. When I looked at her petite form next to mine, I thought I should be taking care of her. I wasn't sure how to communicate with her, but gratefully, Gudrun picked up English quickly. She was absolutely adorable, and we soon adopted her as one of the family.

She was a compulsive housekeeper, loved to make me clothes and adored the children. Fred and I were delighted with her service and gave ourselves wholeheartedly to the upcoming Lay Institute.

We arranged to have Arlis Priest, the director of public relations for Campus Crusade, as the main speaker. We rented the ballroom of the Hotel Taft in New Haven and encouraged Mike and Joyce Hopping to return. Grace asked Dave and Carolyn Petersen, a young couple from Syracuse, New York, to speak to the teen and college groups. Our biggest job was promotion—we were praying for 400 people.

Fred and I began speaking to any club, organization and church that would have us. The month before the Institute, I spoke thirty-seven times in thirty days. On the opening Sunday afternoon, the ballroom in the Hotel Taft was jammed with an overwhelming 700 participants. We didn't know how they all heard about it, but were excited to see what the Lord had done.

Instead of the number falling off during the week, it increased. By Tuesday we had outgrown the ballroom and moved to the First Congregational Church on the Green in New Haven. During that exciting week many people received Christ and hundreds learned for the first time how to appropriate the power of the Holy Spirit in their lives. It was the beginning of a revival in New Haven.

The following week Fred attended the President's Prayer Breakfast in Washington, D. C. and sat next to Dr.

Bill Bright. When Dr. Bright discovered Fred was in the food service business he asked Fred if he would be willing to come to Arrowhead Springs for a weekend and evaluate their food service. They arranged for Fred and me to come out on Memorial Day weekend.

Fred spent a day examining the food services and concluded that Campus Crusade was faced with an impossible situation. They had a new facility close to completion which was to feed and house 800 college students, but the new kitchen was totally inadequate for such a crowd. The new area, called The Village, was almost a mile away from the main hotel and was scheduled to handle 1400 people.

Fred gave his report to Dr. Bright and suggested that Campus Crusade get out of the food service operation and bring in an outside company. There were no available services in the San Bernardino area, and Fred agreed to bring some of his staff from the East to run the food service for the summer.

We flew home, Fred packed his clothes, and he left for what we expected to be a two-week period. But when he arrived back at Arrowhead Springs, he discovered the problem was greater than he had imagined. After working eighteen hours a day, seven days a week for two straight weeks, Fred called to tell me he didn't think he would get home that summer. He suggested I close our home, pack up the children and Gudrun, and spend the summer at the Arrowhead Springs hotel.

We moved into three rooms on the third floor, and while Fred worked in the hot kitchen, the children and I had a wonderful, relaxing summer. We ate in the Candlelight Room and swam in the same pool where Esther Williams had made many of her movies.

The Desires of Her Heart

Our good friend Grace Mintz also spent that summer at Arrowhead Springs, and through our mutual influence, five more people from New Haven came out for a Lay

Institute in August. By that time, Fred and I had taken staff training and were accepted as directors of the lay division for the state of Connecticut.

One afternoon Grace came to me and shared an unusual story. The previous year she had worked with Campus Crusade in Phoenix, Arizona. During that time she prayed constantly for God's guidance in her life. One night she was awakened from a sound sleep at 3 A.M. She said she felt the presence of the Lord and an inner voice saying, *Grace, go home to Connecticut and organize a Lay Institute there.* She debated with the Lord in prayer for the rest of the night.

"But Lord, how can you use me? I'm divorced. People won't accept me; I'm just a lone woman. Anyway Lord, I just want to meet and marry a nice Christian man to be a father to my girls."

As Grace gave her excuses, she suddenly seemed to hear the Lord say, *Grace, go home to Connecticut and work for me there for a year. After that, you'll be married.* A peace came over her and she never doubted she would one day be married to a Christian man.

Grace finished out her year in Phoenix and that summer went to Arrowhead Springs to attend the Institute of Biblical Studies before returning to Connecticut.

While at Arrowhead Springs, she heard Hal Lindsey speak on the topic, "Any Old Pot Will Do."

"If we're willing to be used," he said, "God can use us. It doesn't matter what our backgrounds, spiritual experiences, or our talents might be."

At that moment Grace realized it didn't matter what her qualifications for Christian service were, it mattered only that she be willing. She left the auditorium that night saying, "God is able to use any old pot or any old person who is willing to be emptied of self and filled with the Holy Spirit."

Grace became excited about what God was going to

do with her in Connecticut, and she soon met four young women from Connecticut who all agreed to pray fervently for their home state. They also prayed that Grace would be able to reach out to the Christian communities. Their specific prayer requests that summer were: (1) There would be two Lay Institutes in Connecticut during the next year; (2) Twelve people from Connecticut would come to California for training; (3) One couple would be raised up to join the Campus Crusade staff.

We never knew about Grace's covenant with the Lord and as she shared that God had answered all these prayer requests, I was stunned and delighted that Fred and I had been part of her covenant. It was amazing to me to realize that all the things that appeared to just "happen" that year in our lives had been part of a divine plan. Because Grace had been faithful and believed God for impossible things, our lives had been changed. Two Institutes had been held in New Haven, exactly twelve people had come to California, and we had joined Campus Crusade staff.

As Grace and I rejoiced over these answers to prayer, she hesitated a moment and said, "There is one other request that hasn't been fulfilled. I also prayed that God would give me a Christian husband and father for my two girls."

She told me she had claimed Psalms 37:4: "Delight thyself also in the Lord; and He shall give thee the desires of thine heart."

She hoped the Lord knew that the desires of her heart included not only revival in Connecticut, but a husband.

"Grace," I said as I put my arm around her shoulder, "maybe the Lord is still working on that. Let's keep praying for the desires of your heart."

The following week Grace left for Connecticut, thankful for the prayers but disappointed her personal desires seemed to have been forgotten.

None of us knew God was already working on Grace's

desires. During a Lay Institute at Arrowhead Springs in August, Grace had met Amy and Pat Booth, a couple from Dallas. They had taken a picture of Grace and shown it to their friend, Tommy McClain, an ordained minister and real estate investor. Tommy had recently lost his wife after an agonizing bout with cancer and was left with two sons to raise alone. When the Booths showed him Grace's picture and told him about her cheerful personality and sincere Christian commitment, he became interested and began to pray for the Lord's direction. About the first of September he felt led to call Grace from Dallas.

After talking on the phone several times that week, Tommy suggested he fly to New York, meet Grace and get acquainted.

"I can't meet an unknown man in a big city," she said.

"Haven't you been praying for a Christian husband?" asked Tommy.

There was nothing to do but admit it and with her faith challenged, she agreed to meet him.

On a Friday evening Tommy flew to New York, met Grace and put her up properly in a separate room. They spent Saturday in New York and Sunday going out to Connecticut where Tommy met Grace's two little girls. He also attended church with Grace at Good Time Charlie's and met the pastor and Grace's friends. Before he left Sunday evening, Tommy told Grace to pray about their future, and commit it to the Lord. A week later Tommy called to say it was clear in his mind that Grace should come to Dallas. After meeting Tommy's children, and the parents of Tommy's deceased wife Kathy, they knew the Lord wanted them together for life.

Thirteen days after they first met, Grace and Tommy were married. Grace had been faithful, had delighted herself in the Lord, had obeyed God, and the Lord gave her the desires of her heart.

In October, Grace and Tommy came back to Connecticut for a belated wedding reception. During the reception the pastor read a letter that Tommy's wife Kathy had written shortly before her death. She knew the Lord was taking her home to be with Him, and had written a thank you letter to the Lord for His sustaining power. She began by quoting Psalm 119:71: "It is good for me that I have been afflicted, that I might learn thy statutes."

It is hard for us to understand. But our understanding will have to be that God knows best. God has a plan. I cannot see it now, but whatever it is, it will be good—for me and perhaps for others. I know He has a blessing for us.

Lord, I so pray that if Your will is to take me that You will be ever so close and real to Tommy and the boys as well as our families. They will need strength. I know your grace is sufficient. Teach Brad and David the tenderness and complete healing power in death so they will never be bitter or question the reason. My wish would be that shortly You would lead Tommy to someone who would give him empathy and understanding. Someone he would love and she would return his love. I know Tommy well enough that he would never consider anyone who would not be a Christian mother to Brad and David and help them through their oncoming trials and frustrations.

And I pray they will completely open their hearts to her and accept her and show her the respect she deserves. Lord, help them to put me in the background and to love this new unity as if it was the first for them. May they not try to mold their new mother into my pattern but love her for what she is. No two people are alike and none of us is perfect. Goodness, the world doesn't need another Kathleen McClain anyway.

No work of fiction, no matter how great, would have equaled the gripping truth of that moment. God took a beautiful woman, rejected by her husband but devoted to the Lord, and moved her and her two daughters from Connecticut to Texas into the life of Tommy McClain. He took a lonesome widower with two sons to bring up, and gave him a new bride. Together as one they began a new life. Later they added a baby girl of their own. They built a lovely home, complete with a gymnasium, and opened it to the teenagers in their community. The McClain home became a center of Christian activity in Rockwall, Texas. Fred and I are grateful to God for bringing Grace into our lives and using her to bring us into Christian service.

Reflections

Once Fred and I had given the Lord control of our lives, He began the refining process and kept bringing Christian leaders onto our path. As Fred and I listened, they all seemed to say, "You two could really amount to something for the Lord if you ever got trained." We didn't even know what training was but we had learned enough to know that if God keeps sending you people saying the same thing, you had better listen.

Fred and I had first committed our lives to the Lord in desperation over the loss of our sons. We had given over control of our egos when we had felt weak and needed strength. We had attended seminars to learn about the Christian life. We had confessed our sins to the Lord. These steps, made in faith, prepared us for the one I never thought I'd do: door to door witnessing.

How great it is to look back and see that "the steps of a righteous man are ordered of the Lord." Our Christian growth is like our physical growth. We start out as babies drinking spiritual milk but step by step we grow up until one day we can walk and even witness. The Lord doesn't call us to any mission without giving us the strength to carry it out.

As I look back now and remember the fear we had of going to a Christian meeting and of witnessing to others, I can have compassion for those who come to our seminars and aren't sure if we will be too religious and serious or if they will be called on to recite some unknown verse. I also remember how different leaders encouraged us to study and get prepared for the call of God in ministry. Much of my life today is spent encouraging others to write, speak and become leaders.

Our amazing Grace lighted our path and we are grateful that she and Tommy, more than twenty years later, are still shining brightly for the Lord.

Have you experienced Christian growth in such a way that you can look back and see the steps as they were ordered by the Lord? Perhaps you've never looked at your life from that perspective. Why not review the past so that you can have faith today that the Lord will use you tomorrow? What is there about your life that you can use to encourage others? Don't waste it!

21

Bungalow One

As I prayed, God quieted my heart and showed me Philippians 4:11: "I have learned in whatsoever state I am, therewith to be content." I knew, for me, He meant the state of California.

When Grace left Arrowhead Springs for Connecticut, we expected to follow her back. We had been accepted as Connecticut lay directors for Campus Crusade, and I could hardly wait to put into practice all I had learned at staff training and move ahead with this new phase of our life.

But one day Dr. Bright called Fred to his office and explained that Colonel Irwin Stoll had resigned as director of conference services and hotel manager. Dr. Bright asked Fred to consider remaining in California to replace Col. Stoll. Surprised at this unexpected request, Fred knew that after three months in a hotel room I was anxious to return to my spacious home, my friends and my own Christian ministry.

When I first committed my life to the Lord at the Old Mill Restaurant, I asked the Lord to transform me into what He wanted me to be. In my own mind I was asking for help from some distant God, hoping He might be able to make me happy since the world had disappointed me. In reality, I switched my "if only" search from the secular disappointments to the Christian hope, but I didn't expect my prayer to alter my lifestyle.

As God began to work on me, my attitudes began to change. I sensed a gradual shifting from my focus on social events to Christian activities. As with everything in life, once I saw a new field I ran straight into it. I told God I was available and then tried to help Him out. I was constantly aiding His direction, which resulted in a seesaw Christian life.

I had already made my plans when Dr. Bright asked us to stay, so I immediately rejected the idea. I had spent years building a sound social reputation in Connecticut and felt I wielded considerable influence in the New Haven area. I just knew God wanted to use me to evangelize Connecticut. I knew also my connections would be helpful to the Lord and I told Him so. I had worked out God's plan for me and it didn't include a move to California. It never occurred to me He might have other plans.

I let Fred know my feelings clearly, but he wanted God's answer, not mine. Fred felt we should weigh each side of the question prayerfully and, in his organized way, he made a chart. On one side of the paper Fred wrote down all the reasons for staying in Connecticut, things like owning our home, having many friends, enjoying social acceptance and not having to move. On the other side of the paper he put the reasons for coming to California: things like leaving our security to trust the Lord, answering God's call to service, living in a Christian atmosphere and adjusting to a different lifestyle.

As Fred wrote these lists and prayed over them, it suddenly became clear to him that to stay in Connecticut was easy and to move to California would be a sacrifice. Fred felt we had lived a comfortable life too long and the

Lord was testing us to see if we were willing to give it all up, leave our family and friends, and go to California. After Fred made this pronouncement, the Lord encouraged him with Matthew 6:33: "Seek ye first the kingdom of God and His righteousness and all these things will be added unto you."

Fred believed if we followed God's sacrificial plan for our lives, we would be rewarded. I was not so sure. Why would God want to take things away from us? I didn't want to leave my home, my friends, my New York apartment, my job with Macy's or my secure life. I was willing to be a Christian leader but didn't want to give up anything to do it. Fred, however, wanted to find God's divine direction and felt sacrifice was a pivotal part of that plan. Fred knew he had received a clear call from the Lord, and I was waiting for him to come to his senses.

Listening When God Speaks

That Sunday we attended the Community Bible Church in San Bernardino, where Pastor John Emmans told the story of Nehemiah trying to encourage the Hebrews to go back to Jerusalem and build the wall. In applying this to our everyday lives, he said, "There may be some of you here this morning who are trying to decide what God wants you to do. The Lord wants you to be willing to go wherever He sends you. Are you willing to move when God says, 'Move'? Would you be willing this morning to agree with God if He were to ask you to move from one end of the country to the other, to leave your friends and family, to leave your reputation and your social life, to give it all up, and to follow God's sacrificial plan for your life?"

When I heard those unwelcome questions, I knew God was speaking to us. I knew I wasn't willing to give up my comfortable life. I also knew Fred was. Pastor Emmans ended his message by asking anyone to stand for prayer if they felt God was speaking to them about a new direction. At that point my husband rose and I slumped down. I knew his decision to move to California had been stamped with God's approval.

While I was upset over the thought of this drastic change, Fred was overjoyed and had a serene peace about him. Nothing I said disturbed him. When I told him he was wrong and I was right, he quietly asked, "Then how come I am calm and confident and you're doubtful and depressed?" I hated to admit he had a point. I was not about to give up my case.

At Fred's suggestion, I made an appointment to discuss my problem with Dr. Henry Brandt, a noted Christian psychologist who was spending his summer interviewing potential Campus Crusade for Christ staff. When I told Dr. Brandt about my indecision, he gave me a way to test whether the move to California was God's plan or Fred's.

It was a little after 4 P.M. when we began our conversation, and I knew Fred was in the hotel kitchen rushing to get supper ready for 1000 students, plus directing some fifty kitchen workers. Dr. Brandt suggested I go down to the kitchen at this hectic moment and ask my husband to sit down and talk with me. I told him I wasn't certain about such a move and didn't want to make a quick decision. I was sure Fred wouldn't have time to speak to me just before dinner, and what's more, he would get upset with me for disturbing him. I also told him Fred had already made up his mind and nothing I said would make him change.

As I gave Dr. Brandt my excuses as to why his suggestion wouldn't work, he said in a firm, but loving way, "You asked for my advice, and I have told you what to do. Now go and do it. If Fred won't see you to discuss the problem, then you will know he is behaving in the flesh. But if he leaves his work, sits down with you and agrees to postpone the decision, you will know the Holy Spirit is in control of the situation."

Dr. Brandt and I prayed and asked God to show me clearly what He wanted Fred and me to do. I left his office and went down to the huge kitchen full of people rushing to get dinner ready, stood on a platform above the kitchen and called to Fred. I expected him to say, "I'm much too busy to speak to you now. I'll talk to you later." Not only did I expect him to say this, I hoped he would.

But when I called, he came immediately and asked what I wanted. I told him I needed to talk to him about our big decision and wanted to do it now. To my amazement, he put down the towel in his hand, took me to a small, private dining room, smiled and sat down. I told him I was not yet ready to move to California, that I didn't have peace about it, and I wanted to postpone our decision for at least another week.

"I'm willing to wait," he said. "I don't want to move against your will. We both must be in agreement before we make the commitment."

When Fred said that, I began to cry. He couldn't understand why his agreeing with me was upsetting until I explained how Dr. Brandt had planned my mission. That gentle, Spirit-led conversation convinced me Fred was making a spiritual decision.

I spent the following week in prayer and Bible study, seeking God's confirmation on our future and waiting for His peace. As I prayed, God quieted my heart and showed me Philippians 4:11: "I have learned in whatsoever state I am, therewith to be content." I knew, for me, He meant the state of California.

Home Sweet Home

Once I had accepted that we were to move to California, I began to wonder where I would live and pictured buying a beautiful hillside home and maintaining the standard of living we were accustomed to in Connecticut. Imagine my shock when Fred told me Dr. Bright wanted us to live on campus at Arrowhead Springs.

"Where?" I asked. "In the hotel?"

"No," said Fred. "We can choose any bungalow we like

and I think you'll want Bungalow One."

I had no idea what Bungalow One had in store for me, but I'll never forget the afternoon Fred took me to look at what was to become my new home. The immediate surroundings were green and lush with little pools and waterfalls in front, but the bungalow was unbelievable.

The bungalows were built in the early '30s and had been used as individual motels by movie stars who came out from Hollywood for vacations. Bungalow One, next to the hotel, consisted of five rooms in a semi-circle set up like a train going around a curve. Each of the rooms had a motel door leading out to the central patio, and to go from one end of the house to the other, you had to go outdoors or go through every room as if you were on a train. There was a raised living room with a little porch in the center of the bungalow, and on each side were two bedrooms facing out on the patio. I couldn't imagine how I could make a home out of this antiquated motel with one living room and four bedrooms.

Not only was the layout peculiar, the condition of the bungalow was dreadful. The original carpeting was still on the floors with several places worn through to the cement. The ceiling was falling in chunks in every room. The bathtubs had been used to develop pictures, and the chemicals had eaten away the finish down to the black, rusty iron. The kitchen was a hot plate on a porch, and the place was infested with spiders. I took one look at this disaster and became homesick for my luxury in Connecticut. "Lord," I said, "when I told you I'd go anywhere, I surely didn't mean this."

But the Lord did mean this. I had to accept this house and try to make it a home. In spite of my feelings, I planned to renovate and decorate what appeared to be a hopeless impossibility.

While Fred worked in the kitchen, Gudrun and I spent our days sitting on the floor in Bungalow One with a pad, pencil and measuring tape which Gudrun called her "inch- es." Not only did we have to create ideas on how to reconstruct this abandoned building, but we also had to figure out where to put my twelve rooms of furniture. Every time I thought about my furniture, I got homesick and had to pray, "Lord, make me willing to move. You know I have no heart for this." I would then get back to my measuring and planning. The biggest problem was how to use the roomful of Spanish antiques we had bought in Madrid. The huge carved bookcase would overwhelm one of these motel rooms and yet it was my favorite piece. As I mentally placed my Connecticut furniture into this California cottage, most of it just wouldn't fit. What was I to do? I liked decorating challenges but this was too much!

Finally, I gave up worrying about what I had left in Connecticut and started to plan what I could do with what I had before me in California. Since Bungalow One had no kitchen, I had to create one from the porch. Gudrun and I decided to leave the beams on the porch roof in place and paint them in gold, orange and avocado, the hot decorator colors of that time. We ordered avocado appliances and Gudrun created Austrian shades in a flowered print. She sewed each little hoop on by hand and wove the fancy trim herself.

We planned to make the room behind the kitchen into a family room and converted the accompanying bathroom into a laundry room with an avocado washer and dryer. We designed the bedroom at the end of the house to be the master bedroom. The carpenters we hired totally gutted the antiquated bathroom and made a new bath and dress-ing room with gold and red flocked wallpaper, red sinks set in white marble counters, gold faucets and fixtures, and an unusual chandelier of Victorian ruby glass trimmed with crystals. It became the most dramatic room of the house. The high center room became our living room, and the two bedrooms on the other end of the house were for the children.

Lauren and I found some wild sheets on sale in

shocking pink and orange and painted the girls' room pink with orange trim to match the sheets. Gudrun made the sheets into bedspreads to be used on the bunkbeds we brought down from the hotel. When I got married, I had vowed my children would never sleep on bunkbeds, but I had to eat those words as we put Lauren, Marita and Gudrun into one room.

Once construction was underway and the children were registered in school, Fred and I flew back to Connecticut to pack our belongings. As I walked into my cold, quiet home where I had spent thirteen memorable years, I reflected on what the house had meant to me. When we had first bought this shingled New England ranch, I knew it would be my home for life. After a series of apartments and a small rented house, this spacious three-bedroom home seemed huge. We had moved in with an assortment of second-hand furniture and bit by bit had replaced the couches, tables and chairs until almost everything was new.

As our family grew, the house that had been bigger than anything I'd ever hoped to live in, seemed to close in on us and we had added six rooms and a large patio. The house had become almost a shrine to me and yet when I looked at it with no family in it, I realized it was no longer our home. I had lived in it, laughed in it, cried in it and now I was leaving it. I was here to pack up one life and ship it to California.

I had walked into this home with Lauren in my arms. I had added Marita and then Frederick Jerome Littauer, III. I looked at the rocker in the nursery and remembered the hours I had spent holding him, trying to soothe him. I saw the crib, empty at last, and I thought of the babies it had held: Lauren, in Detroit, then Marita, then Fred III, then Larry, and then our new Freddie. That one piece of furniture housed a fluctuating series of joys and tragedies. I would give it away. I never wanted to see it again.

For days Fred and I sorted, packed or discarded

everything we had gathered in thirteen years of living in one house. I reread the college term papers I had saved and wept over baby pictures of my boys. Fred worked on the principle that if you haven't used something in the last five years, you're not going to need it in the next five. As I cried, Fred filled up the trash cans.

My mother, who had moved from Haverhill to Connecticut to be near us, couldn't believe we were going to move away and leave her alone. Fred's family was sure we had been conned by a group of religious fanatics who were going to lock us up in a monastery and make the children live a drab, spartan existence. Our friends were in a state of shock that the Littauer home, an institution in North Haven, was closing its doors; and Fred's office staff couldn't believe he was going to leave the business in their hands and move across country.

Family, friends and business associates were at best confused and at worst afraid we'd lost our minds. To tell them God had instructed us to move would have confirmed their worst suppositions. Their pleading with us to change our plans made parting almost impossible, since I didn't want to leave North Haven in the first place.

Our church held a commissioning service on our last evening with them, dedicating us as the first full-time Christian workers to be sent out from St. Charlie's.

We stayed in our New York apartment that night and next morning went back to pack the car and take a final look at our home. It was stripped of everything that had made it home; its empty rooms signified the end of an era.

As I carried a box from the basement, I was stopped by some handprints on the stairway wall. I remembered the day Marita poured out a whole jar of bright blue poster paint onto the basement floor. She had put her little hand in the paint and printed it on the wall. The hand by the bottom step was dark and as the prints came up the stairs they became lighter and lighter 'til the top one became a shadow. I remembered how upset I'd been when she had shown me her blue hand and pointed proudly to her work. Yet, as I stood staring at those little fading handprints, I forgave her and I wondered how I could cut out that portion of the wall and take it with me to California.

By the time I had dried my eyes, Fred was ready to go. He had the trunk and back seat so full that the car was dragging on the driveway. Just as I was about to get into the car, I spotted a large dried flower and bird arrangement on top of the trash and remembered that a friend had given it to me when Larry was born. I couldn't leave it alone there in the garbage, so I plucked it from the trash and laid it on top of the boxes in the back seat. The branches stuck up high behind us and the flock of dead red birds followed us to California.

Four days later, after one of the sweetest times Fred and I ever spent together, we drove into Arrowhead Springs. For the first time we looked at it as home.

What the Lord Really Wants

Before I had finished arranging the furniture in Bungalow One, the Lord added more people to our family. A single girl named Dolores had joined staff and needed a place to live. We added another bed to the girl's room and she moved in. That gave us Lauren, Marita, Gudrun and Dolores in two doubledecker beds in one room. Freddie had the next bedroom to himself for a short while, until Fred's nine-year-old nephew Dwayne came out from Florida for a vacation. While he was visiting with us, his parents separated and asked if Dwayne could stay with us. We put a double-decker bed in Freddie's room and totaled six bodies stacked in layers in two rooms. My life had come full circle; I was now back to the same situation I had left fifteen years before when we all were piled tightly in one bedroom behind my father's store.

My mother had often wondered, "How can I ever bring up decent children in a place like this?" and had then gone on to bring up decent children. Now I was faced with the same question of bringing up decent children in a small space—eight of us in five rooms and a converted porch.

No longer did we have individual rights. It could no longer be my room, my towels, my toys; everything was everybody's. I began to realize how spoiled we were. We had become too possessive of our own things. Before, we each had our own record players and even a stereo that played through our mattress. Here we had one combination record player and radio and had to learn to like the same music. We were unable to get television so we spent our evenings playing games and talking as we'd never done before.

Fred decided we should pray together as a family each night, so we made a schedule. Gudrun and I would have dinner ready at 5:15. While the dinner sat in the oven, we would gather around the coffee table in the little family room. We made up prayer cards with headings on the top line such as Family Needs, Christian Workers and School Friends. We wrote dated prayer requests on each card and the children would take turns choosing a card and then praying for those specific requests. As the Lord answered our prayers, we dated the reply on the card. This scheduled prayer time each evening taught our children how to pray and showed them the reality of answered prayer. At 5:30 we would move to our crowded table on the porch and there never was an angry word.

As I accepted my new life in the old house, God began to fill my mind with Himself. I spent many hours in Bible study and took all the courses Campus Crusade had to offer. As I studied, listened and prayed, God began to train me for a new ministry.

Although I had not wanted to leave Connecticut, I could see after a year at Arrowhead Springs why the Lord had moved us. We could never have been trained so deeply and consistently if we had stayed in North Haven. We were too easily on the top without having started at the bottom. We had become Christian leaders before we knew what the Christian life was about. Fred and I had taught Bible studies in our home before we had studied the Bible.

In order for the Lord to teach us enough to teach others, He had to move us from our worldly surroundings and place us in a desert. I have since learned from Scripture that God frequently sends his children into a desert for training. This is just what He did with us.

While I was willing to give my time to serve the Lord, I never considered that true service demanded a humble spirit. If I thought about humility at all, I would have assumed humility to be a reward for those without talent. I had always been able to succeed at whatever project I embraced whether or not I knew anything about it. Yet I didn't brag about my accomplishments and had always put my efforts into positive, altruistic and now Christian activities. I always felt we should do the very best we could with whatever gifts we had been given. However, I learned, in Christian circles superiority was not necessarily applauded.

I felt I was a good speaker but I was seldom asked to speak. When I did speak and received an enthusiastic response, others who had been around longer were sometimes jealous. Once when I gave what I felt was a moving message, a staff member said, "You have too much charisma. There is so much of you that no one can see Jesus."

I always dressed well because I had a huge wardrobe. I felt I should be a good representative of Campus Crusade, yet one day a staff lady said to me, "You know what I'm afraid of about you, Florence? Someday you might have to wear the same dress twice." I drove a big gold Lincoln Continental and my neighbor would call out to me frequently, "Oh, there goes Mrs. Rich in her Lincoln."

I couldn't understand why, when I had given my life to come on staff, people looked at my strengths as problems. Was I supposed to be a silent soul in sackcloth and ashes riding on a donkey? I had left a twelve-room home for five rooms and a porch. I was willing to work in an organization full of young beauty queens even though I had always associated with older people so I could be the youthful spirit of the group. I had agreed to invest thousands of dollars in a bungalow I didn't own and pay rent to live in it besides. I had graciously played Martha to hosts of visitors who I knew would never be able to reciprocate. And most devastating of all, for the first time in my life, I had joined an organization where there was absolutely no hope that I would ever become president.

I had thought Campus Crusade would want to use my talents, but instead, all my achieved goals in life were wasting away. As I sat lonely and discouraged in Bungalow One asking the Lord why He had done this to me, I began to get an answer: *You needed to be humbled. You must learn I don't need your talents, your money, your cars, your clothes, your houses, your hospitality, your leadership. I can only use you when you have a broken spirit, when you are an empty vessel willing to be filled, when you have gotten yourself and your pride out of the way. I put you in a desert with people who don't appreciate you so you would finally give up.*

I finally gave up. If that's the way it's got to be, Lord, I'll quit. I felt alone, lost in a desert, but Jesus became my friend. I had always loved the hymn *In the Garden* and I used it as my baptism song. I had sung those words, "And He walks with me and He talks with me, and He tells me I am His own," but I never knew how it felt to have Jesus really walk and talk with me. As I isolated myself in my bedroom in Bungalow One, Jesus moved in. I asked Him, "For this I left everything behind?" and He answered, *You didn't leave anything you'll ever need. My grace is sufficient.*

While I thought I had given my life totally to the Lord, I began to realize I was proud of what I had given up. I had presented my body a living sacrifice and then wanted a badge for nobility. I was working for the Lord in my own strength and then looking for the glory. God resists the proud and gives grace to the humble. I wish I could say that humility fell upon my shoulders quickly like a queen's cloak. Instead it has come slowly, in pieces, like a patchwork quilt.

Once I willingly gave up my role as the Christian heroine, the Lord began to show me His new direction for my life. One day the superintendent of Sunday schools in Community Bible Church asked Fred and me to teach an adult Sunday school class. I felt totally unqualified to instruct anyone in the Bible. We told the superintendent this, but he continued to ask. Finally, Fred agreed we could put together a course on marriage since this was where God had already worked His greatest miracles in our lives.

We had never taken a course or read a book on marriage counseling, but as Fred often said, ignorance never kept me quiet! We proceeded to write a course and for our references used several Bibles, a large concordance and our lives. At the end of the thirteen weeks, after dividing the responsibility for teaching and writing between us, our attendance had risen from thirty-five to eighty-three.

News of the course spread and many people from outside the church began attending. We had touched a raw nerve. We improved it as the Lord gave new insights, wrote a weekly Bible study series to go along with the lectures, and by the time we had given the course four times we had an average attendance of 125. This course was the beginning of what became *After Every Wedding Comes a Marriage*.

A New Phase in Our Ministry

Just as the Lord led us to Arrowhead Springs, He led us away. Once I was willing to relax and let the Lord lead, I assumed He would use me at Campus Crusade for life. I pictured growing old in Bungalow One and becoming the sage of the hill, sitting in my rocking chair while young people came to me for wisdom and advice. But again, the Lord had other plans. Fred's Connecticut business needed attention, and because we had depleted our reserve money, we needed to get back to work. At that point we could have located anywhere in the world, but after searching for a place to live, the only place we had peace about was San Bernardino.

One day we found a secluded building lot cut out of a mountain which looked into the San Bernardino National Forest. We prayed and asked the Lord to direct us and give us a sign. A few days later a stock we owned went up sharply and we were able to sell it for a profit which gave us the exact amount we needed to buy the lot. When our offer was accepted, we took this as further confirmation that we should live in San Bernardino. Together, we designed a custom-made house to fit our pie-shaped lot.

With the lot paid for, we were able to get a mortgage for the exact amount of the building cost. Once the Lord had seen that I could live joyfully in a tiny home, He provided us with a big one. He had started my humbling process, and I knew He would help me handle a new home without it going to my head. I was eager to have some space again and Gudrun and I tackled the decorating of a new home with great excitement. What I thought up, she sewed up. She custom-made every curtain, drape, bedspread and pillow in the house.

Our new home was built of brick-colored Mexican slump block. The front entry was walled like a fortress with a redwood drawbridge that led over a recessed pool to a huge castle door complete with big iron hinges. The foyer, living room and dining room were all decorated like a Spanish castle with appropriate antiques. The carpeting was a four-inch white shag, the long Spanish couch was red velvet, and a rich tapestry hung on the rough plastered wall. A Spanish arched window led to a magnificent view of the city below and the olive groves in the canyon.

We designed the family room and kitchen to be large enough to hold groups for the Bible studies we planned to have. The walls were painted brick red to match the massive fireplace and hearth on the twenty-foot wall.

There was also a window-wall that looked out to a swimming pool and a direct view of Mt. McKinley.

Running the length of the long house was a hall with doors to each of the five bedrooms. Since we planned to place the family tree in the hall with pictures of our ancestors, we decided to decorate each room in the nationality of our varied backgrounds. We designed our bedroom and bath in ornate English for the Chapman part of the family. The walls were gold with flocked Victorian paper and I had my English father's picture framed on the wall. My collection of jasper Wedgwood gave touches of blue to this English retreat. Our study was Scotch with a plaid floor like my mother's MacDougall tartan and I hung up a clan map of Scotland, my grandfather's picture in his kilts, and my mother's first violin.

Freddie and Dwayne had the Littauer German room done like the courtyard of a Teutonic fort. I stood by the plasterers to make sure they made the walls look like stone. Gudrun designed an awning to go over the two beds which had been custom-made with drawers underneath. The carpet looked like plush red brick, and there were scenes of Germany on the wall.

Marita and Gudrun had a Swedish room after Fred's grandmother Klein and had two built-in beds fronted with Swedish arches filled with ruffled curtains. We did Lauren's room in Early American to commemorate our years in Connecticut. The wallpaper was little purple flowers, the carpet was purple shag, and Ethan Allen furniture lined the walls. Her double bed was canopied with white organdy, and swags of fluffy curtains were at the windows.

What had started out to be a comfortable house had become a show place which later was used for two different home tours. We dedicated our new residence to the Lord and His service on July 14, 1970.

By September 1 we were settled enough to begin thinking about starting a Bible study. I didn't consider myself to be a Bible scholar but was happy I knew more than I had two years before. At that time, Barbara Fain, a gifted Bible study teacher, began tutoring me in the Word. When she was out of town, she would have me substitute for her Bible study classes and this gave me experience.

One day she said to me, "The greatest thing about your teaching is that you are unencumbered by theological training and therefore, not deep enough to be confusing." I wasn't sure if this was a compliment, but at least I knew I wasn't going over people's heads.

When Barbara moved to Atlanta, Georgia, I was left to teach her Bible study class, and when we moved, I brought the class into my new home. On the first day sixty ladies arrived to start "The Survey of the New Testament" with an emphasis on practical applications. As the ladies tried to put into practice the truths of Scripture, their husbands noticed that their wives were becoming more loving and considerate and wanted to know what these Bible studies were about. The women soon asked for an evening class for couples.

This request prompted us to begin our Christian Home series. We printed invitations for the ladies to take home to their husbands and set aside thirteen Friday nights for study groups on marriage. We chose study leaders from among our friends and began to train them. Our plan was to have small discussion groups from 7:30 to 8:30 in different rooms throughout the house. Everyone would come into the family room at 8:30 for an hour's lecture, followed by refreshments. The response was good and we expected to have thirty to forty people who were willing to commit themselves to a thirteen-week marriage improvement course. But a week before our first scheduled class, something unbelievable happened to our new home.

Reflections

When I look back on our move to Bungalow One I can

hardly believe we did it. Only the Lord could have inspired us to leave a large, lavish home to camp out in Bungalow One. In retrospect I wish I'd learned humility faster so that the Lord could have spared me some of my humiliating experiences, but He continued to place me in deserts until I learned in whatsoever state I am therewith to be content. As I have shared my Bungalow One story, I've had women come rushing up to say, "I'm living in Bungalow One right now." I've been able to encourage them and show them Bungalow Two will be along any moment.

One great bonus of living in Bungalow One is that every house after that looks spacious and is a refreshing step up. I'm grateful now that I lived next door to Bill and Vonette Bright and that we've kept in touch over the years. I'm glad we met Glen and Marilyn Heavilin at that time and that they have remained friends.

At the Christian Booksellers Convention in Denver, July 1990, Fred and I spoke at the Here's Life Publishers breakfast along with the Brights, the Heavilins and Josh McDowell. I reminisced how we had all been at Arrowhead Springs in 1968-70 when Josh was but a child fresh out of college and how exciting it was to have the seven of us back together at one function after so many years apart.

The Lord does have His hand on all of us who are willing to take His direction—even if it means moving to the desert and living in Bungalow One.

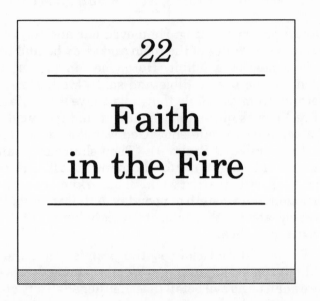

22

Faith
in the Fire

*We were told not to lift our heads and look out
the window no matter what. We didn't know if
we were going to crash into the water or on
land—we just knew we were going to crash.*

Friday the thirteenth began for us at 6:17 A.M. with
an earthquake. As we were jolted awake, Fred turned on
the radio and heard that besides the earthquake, a forest
fire had started in Big Bear, a mountain community
twenty miles away. As the day progressed, so did the fires,
fanned by 40 m.p.h. winds. By 5 P.M. when I put the meat
in the oven for a company dinner, I looked out to see the
entire sky behind Mt. McKinley a bright orange. The radio
reports ominously told how hot hurricane force winds were
wildly blasting the fire out of control, heading it toward
homes in the northeast section of San Bernardino where
we lived.

At 6:30 P.M. our little six-year-old Freddie, who had
been listening closely to the radio, called us and our dinner
guests into the living room and announced we were going

to have a prayer meeting. He moved our antique prayer bench into the center of the room and stood behind it like a little pastor in a pulpit. He opened in prayer, then handed me the family Bible and said, "Mother, read us something from the Bible that tells us we'll be safe from the fire." It was quite an assignment and I struggled to find a verse that would show God would save our home. Then I remembered Psalm 91: "Thou shalt not be afraid for the terror by night; nor for the arrow that flieth by day; nor for the pestilence that walketh in darkness; nor for the destruction that wasteth at noonday. A thousand shall fall at thy side, and ten thousand at thy right hand; but it shall not come nigh thee."

We prayed and claimed the promise that the fire would not come nigh unto us. We also claimed verse 10: "There shall be no evil befall thee, neither shall any plague come nigh thy dwelling."

We then saw God's condition. He states that if we put Him first in times of plenty, He will care for us in times of danger: "Because he hath set his love upon me, therefore will I deliver him: I will set him on high, because he hath known my name. He shall call upon me, and I will answer him."

We called upon Him and waited for His answer. As Freddie stood behind the bench, he pointed to each one of us in order and asked us to pray for our home. He concluded our meeting by thanking God ahead of time for the miracle He was going to perform. I knew then the Lord would save us—if only to reward the faith of this little child.

"The Lord Won't Let My House Burn"

When our last guests arrived at 7 P.M., we chatted over the clatter of fire trucks racing up our street. Before long we were startled by heavy footsteps on our front deck. Two big firemen knocked on the front door. "Prepare to evacuate," they said as I opened the door. "The fire has whipped up the back of Mt. McKinley and as soon as it comes over the top, you'll have to leave."

At exactly 8 o'clock, the first flames fanned over the summit and we left the dinner table to watch as the whole crest of the mountain was quickly outlined in fire. It was a majestic sight. The flames advanced in a straight path from as far as we could see, left and right, heading down the mountainside to the canyon below us. As I stood on the redwood deck watching the approaching fire, a fireman said, "Only a miracle could save this house."

The police made a roadblock at the bottom of the hill and only residents and relatives were allowed through. In order to get up the hill, our friends told the police they were our brothers and sisters. Later the officers said, "I never knew anyone to have so many brothers and sisters." Several friends came up with trucks ready to move us out and some came to take our children home with them. Freddie refused to leave. He wanted to stay and see the miracle he knew was about to happen. Lauren, unaware of our danger, was cheering at a high school football game many miles away, and Marita was already at a friend's home for the night. Dolores was cleaning up from the dinner and Gudrun was cheerfully serving coffee and leftovers to the firemen and friends.

At 9 P.M. Marita ran into the house and gathered up her two cages of pet mice to take back to her girlfriend's house.

"Don't you have any faith?" I called.

"I do," she said, "but the mice don't, so I'm taking them with me."

By this time the whole street was a mass of confusion. Policemen evacuated hysterical women and excited children; people with hastily rented moving vans loaded up priceless furnishings; one woman threw her sterling silver into the swimming pool. A reporter for the local newspaper, Harvey Feit, worked his way up the street through the turmoil to our house. When he interviewed us, he was amazed at the calm and joyful attitude in our home.

"How do you feel about your house being destroyed?" asked Harvey.

He was stunned at Fred's confident answer. "The Lord won't let my house burn. He gave it to us, and we use it for His work. If He wants it to stand, it will stand."

"Do you share your husband's faith that this house is not going to burn?" asked Harvey. "Yes," I said with an assurance I'd never known before. I could hardly wait to see how the Lord was going to do it.

During the long evening Fred made more coffee and Gudrun poured. There was an air of expectancy as we—family, friends and firemen—sipped, watched and prayed. We had received word from Campus Crusade that their prayer chain had been activated and hundreds were praying for our safety. Our church called to say that its members had been alerted and were also praying.

Throughout our home and on the roof, groups of friends gathered in prayer, and a few strangers who wandered in to watch remained to pray, several for the first time in their lives. A teenage boy, Paul Britton from across the street, asked Christ to come into his heart while standing on our roof holding a firehose. Because of his commitment that night, both his mother and father later became believing Christians and are now involved in Christian work.

About 10:30 the firemen insisted that all women and children leave before the fire reached our home. My friends ran quickly through the house and gathered possessions they thought I might want to save. One friend took all the gold-framed pictures off the family tree. I smiled as one girl went off into the night with my mother's cello under her arm. Freddie, Gudrun and Dolores left in one car and as Freddie kissed me goodbye, he whispered, "I'm sorry I can't stay to take care of you, Mother, but I'll be back as soon as it's over."

At 11 P.M. Lauren ran through the crowd, flung her arms around me and sobbed for joy to see me alive. She had been coming back to San Bernardino on the bus from the football game and suddenly realized the fire was burning "our mountain." By this time the fire had reached the bottom of the canyon nearest us and was starting up. We were all praying as the fire hit the olive trees. We hoped the green groves would slow the fire down, but the olive oil in the trees increased the fury of the fire and sent flames shooting fifty feet into the sky.

As the 60 m.p.h. winds moved the fire in a massive march toward our house, firemen turned on the hoses for the first time. I looked out of the kitchen window and saw an olive tree not twenty feet away burst into flames. A fireman told me I had to get out as the house would probably explode any minute. I kissed Fred goodbye and, with my Bible in hand, walked through the kitchen where a friend was pouring a cup of coffee. I'll never forget his question: "I hate to bother you at a time like this, but where do you keep your sugar?" I thought it hardly mattered whether his coffee had sugar or not, but I stopped long enough to hand him the sugar bowl.

As Lauren and I ran through the smoke to our car, the reporter called, "How does your faith look now?" We glanced back and saw the cliff behind the house flare up in a fence of fire and then, as the smoke enshrouded the silhouette, we could see the house no more. As we drove out of the yard, the firemen lifted the hoses over the car, making an archway to escape. We left, knowing Fred and his best friend Ralph Wagoner were still inside.

Still in the Miracle Business

Twenty minutes later, after a slow trip through the traffic to a friend's home, I called Fred and was relieved when he picked up the phone.

"Praise the Lord," he said, "the house is still here!" He then explained in jubilation how, as the hurricane-force winds whipped up the hill, the direction had suddenly changed, splitting the fire in two, sending half of it up the cliff behind the house and the rest down to the ravine below. For twenty minutes the smoke and flames had enveloped our home as Fred and his faithful friend Ralph watched through the windows and prayed for the Lord to save the house. Harvey Feit told Fred later that as he saw the flames shooting over the roof of the house, he was afraid it was gone. But then the smoke cleared and he said he looked in disbelief as the house came into view—whole and unharmed. God had covered our home with His protective hand.

One fireman later said, "I've never been a believing man before, but I was there and that was a miracle!" The next morning, November 14, 1970, the front page of the *San Bernardino Sun-Telegram* ran this headline: "The Lord Won't Let My House Burn—It Didn't." The story following the headline was the reporter's impression of his evening in our home.

SAN BERNARDINO—Fred Littauer stood looking out the patio door at the jagged line of flames advancing on his new house off the end of Manzanita Drive last night and said: "If the Lord wants this house to stand, it will stand."

At midnight, the Lord, with the help of some fifty firemen who stood fast in the face of forty-foot-high flames, saved Littauer's home. They also saved other homes in the exclusive residential area in the foothills of northeast San Bernardino.

Littauer, 41, who operates the food service for the Campus Crusade for Christ, was unwavering in his belief that his home would be saved despite its vulnerable position.

About three months old, the house on Aspen Drive was on a peninsula jutting toward the approaching wall of fire and the first in its path.

Littauer and his wife, who shared his faith, declined to move their furniture as some others did in less exposed locations.

"I'm not concerned," said Mrs. Littauer, "the furniture can be replaced."

She did take some "valuables" to the car. These included her Bible, notes and tapes she uses in teaching her Bible classes.

Their twelve-year-old daughter, Marita, one of their four children, dashed in, gathered up two cages of mice, and left.

City firemen, first on the scene, had time to prepare. They hooked up their hoses and waited.

At 11:40 P.M. the flames burst over the hill below the Littauer's home. Firemen turned on their hoses and began wetting down the brush on the surrounding slopes.

At the last minute, a crew of U.S. Forest Service firefighters arrived.

Sparks showered the area and thick, gagging smoke drove back the few remaining bystanders. But the firemen stayed, standing in the face of intense heat, and beat back the flames which circled in a giant U around the house and other exposed houses in the area.

At midnight it was over. Littauer looked through his patio door again at the ember-strewn slopes surrounding his home and said: "Good show, but we knew what was going to happen all the time."

The testimony of our faith was there for all to read. There was also a lighter side to the fire. One of our friends who had been there for dinner that night said later, "That was the most spectacular after-dinner entertainment I've ever seen."

Another asked, "How are you going to top that party?"

One friend said, "I think it's great to be on fire for the Lord, but I think you carried this to an extreme."

It was the Friday after the fire that we had scheduled the first session of our Christian Home Series. We planned for about forty guests with four trained couples to be group leaders. The cars began coming at 7 P.M. and by 7:30 when we were ready to start, ninety men and women had arrived. Many of the men who had not been interested before came to see the house God had spared. The publicity of the fire had doubled our anticipated attendance.

That week we hastily trained six new couples and asked our neighbors if we could borrow rooms in their homes for our groups. More came the following Friday, and we had ten discussion groups spread out in three houses.

The Miracles Never Cease

While the fire had been a catalyst for our Bible study, we had yet another miracle that year. Fred and I went to San Francisco for a long weekend before Christmas and enjoyed the usual tourist attractions. On our return we were in the air only ten minutes when the pilot announced that we had to return to San Francisco due to a faulty hydraulic system. "Don't worry," said the pilot, "there is an alternate plan and we're using it."

We came in low over the Bay and I saw the runway, but just as we were about to touch down, the pilot gunned the engines and took off almost straight up. He explained that there had been some planes on the runway, and he had decided it was better not to land. Later we found out the truth: When he had tried to slow down, he couldn't.

I looked at my watch. It was 10 A.M. Another ten minutes went by and the pilot told us he was going to try again, but that this time we should all get into the "brace position" as we were going to experience what he politely called an emergency landing.

We all had to study those cards in the seats that you never pay any attention to because you know you're not going to crash. Fred and I quickly memorized where the life rafts were, how to get the emergency door open and how to assume the brace position. We found this to be an ungainly posture created by putting your head on your knees, and locking your arms tightly under your legs to hold you firmly in one unit. The flight attendants looked slightly frantic as they hastily checked our positions and then doubled up themselves. We were told not to lift our heads and look out the window no matter what. We didn't know if we were going to crash into the water or on land—we just knew we were going to crash.

With our heads bowed, we prayed. Everybody prayed. There's nothing that makes a believer out of an agnostic faster than an impending plane crash. Finally, we hit the ground at full speed—swerved, shook, shuddered! The pilot instantly reversed all the engines and in one big heart attack, the plane rocked to a halt and the motors stopped dead. We held our breath waiting for an explosion, but nothing happened. As we raised our heads at 10:15 and looked out the window, we could see a circle of ambulances and fire trucks that had been prepared for the worst.

What we didn't know at the time was that our dear friend, Caroline Kinne, had played a part in our rescue. On the day of our flight, at exactly 10 A.M., Caroline, who was home recovering from an illness, was listening to the radio and when the announcer said it was 10 o'clock, our names came to her mind. She didn't know why, but she felt she should pray for our safety. She shut off the radio and for the next fifteen minutes prayed until she received a peace that we were safe. The next day she called us and asked if we had been in trouble. I quickly poured out our plane crash problems and told her it was a miracle that we were alive.

"Yes, it was a miracle," she said softly, and then she shared her part of God's plan for our lives.

Reflections

Have you ever been part of a miracle? We think back to Bible miracles like turning water into wine and healing lepers and know we've never personally been part of any such thing, yet God is still in the miracle business.

As I remember surviving several earthquakes, the raging flood that wiped out the only entrance bridge that connected Campus Crusade with the outside world, the wild forest fire that split graciously and went around our house instead of burning it, and the airplane crash that didn't quite crash, I realize that God has placed a big hand of protection over our lives. He has been our refuge and our fortress. He has saved us from deadly pestilence. He has covered us with his feathers. He has been our shield and rampart.

Because we love Him, He will rescue us and protect us.

What a set of promises from a God who knows us and cares.

Have there been miracles in your life that you've put out of your mind? Have you been spared when others have been harmed? Too often we feel we've survived by chance and not given God praise for His protection. He wants us to know His name and call upon Him—not just at moments of dire need, but daily. The Lord inhabits the praises of His people and He will respond when we call. He doesn't promise we will have no problems, but He will make beauty out of ashes. He will

Make the tough times count.

23

President of the Women's Club

Since there was a nucleus of women who feared I would capture the club, convert the members and carry them off to some religious retreat, I spent my year as first vice-president aiming for a low profile.

One fact that continues to amaze me in the Christian life is that God never wastes any talents or training we had before becoming believing Christians. Graciously, He doesn't write one script for all Christians to follow; rather, our roles are tailor-made to fit our unique personalities.

I had spent much of my life directing various secular women's organizations and the Lord let me use my experience in San Bernardino. When I had been at Arrowhead Springs for only a few months, Vonette Bright took me to the women's club of San Bernardino, a prestigious group of 350 civic-minded ladies. At her suggestion, I joined the club. Before I even paid my dues, I was given a minor board position with the impressive title of federation extension chairman. Since I have always felt Christian women in secular organizations should do a better-than-average job, I worked hard at my small assignment. At the end of the year I won a top district award.

In Federated Women's Clubs, anyone who wins an award attracts attention, and so the nomination committee decided I was a new hopeful. Vonette had been the membership chairman and third vice-president and I was nominated to replace her. I debated whether I should accept such a big position so quickly but felt confident that since I was asked, I should accept.

Shortly after the slate was announced I received two letters from ladies in the club. Both letters expressed shock that I, as a newcomer, had accepted the nomination for third vice-president. The letters accused me of trying to take over the club and one sentence read, "Even Jesus Christ had to die before He obtained the kingdom." The letters were bitter and vindictive and told me if I knew what was good for me, I would immediately withdraw my nomination.

In all my years of leadership, these were the first nasty letters I had ever received. I was aghast that anyone would write such words to me. The eight ladies who composed the two letters signed them with their first names and last initials. My natural curiosity was about to send me to the club yearbook to find out who these women were, but as I started toward the book, the Lord stopped me. It was as if He said, *I'm going to use you in this club, and you'll be more effective if you don't know who these ladies are.* I threw the letters away and asked God that if indeed He was directing me to continue with the club, He would cause me to completely forget the letters. I also prayed that if the letters were an indication I was to resign, I would be continuously upset. From the moment I threw the letters away, I never gave them another thought, and I left my name in nomination.

When election day came, I fully expected someone to nominate an opposing candidate from the floor. I waited anxiously as my name was read and the president asked if there were any additional nominations. After the traditional thirty-second pause, the president said, "Hearing no additional nominations, I declare the nomination for third vice-president be closed."

I knew the Lord had His hand on me. Within a week, the second vice-president became ill and resigned, and the first vice-president's husband was transferred and she had to leave town. Before I ever took office as third vice-president, I became the first vice-president!

Since there was a nucleus of women who feared I would capture the club, convert the members and carry them off to some religious retreat, I spent my year as first vice-president aiming for a low profile. I did nothing that was not asked of me, made no aggressive steps and tried to relieve my detractors of any serious worries. Since the by-laws stated that the first vice-president automatically is nominated for the next year's presidency, I was installed as president the following May. The signs of insurrection had disappeared.

Introducing the Club to Bible Study

One of the first areas the Lord laid upon my heart was to revitalize the ailing Religion Section. Each club is expected to have various section meetings that cover such topics as music, arts, crafts, drama, bridge, travel and religion, among many others. While most of our sections were functioning well, the Religion Section was close to failure.

I invited all ladies who would be interested in such a group to my home and asked what they felt we should do to strengthen the section. The only thing they agreed on was they did not want to do what they had done in the past. In a detached way, they had studied various types of religions—Buddhism, Hinduism, Judaism and Christianity. No one could think of what to do until my friend Lorna suggested we have a Bible study. They were unaccustomed to Bible studies, but accepted the idea. The next question was, Who would teach the Bible study? Lorna suggested me.

I was already conducting weekly Bible studies in my new home and didn't have time for an extra class, so I decided to shift my study group into the women's club. To make this move, I had to find a way for the club to allow non-members to attend the Bible study. Since any departure from the norm always requires a complete board approval, the section chairman had to ask permission to allow outsiders to come into the club. According to the by-laws, the only way we could do this was to turn our Bible studies into a special project and charge money from each lady who attended. We had never intended to charge admission to a Bible study, but it was the only way we could stay within the club rules. The last thing I wanted was a controversial Bible study. So we took care of the technicalities and laid plans for what was a new approach for the old Religion Section.

The first series I taught was on the Old Testament. I had never studied the Old Testament but I needed to eliminate any criticism that I was excluding Jewish club members. The first session drew thirty-five women, and by Christmas we had grown to sixty-five. The interest in Bible studies continued to increase and by the end of the year the section unanimously voted to have a Bible study project again.

As I conducted the business of the club as president, the Lord guided me to 1 Kings, where Rehoboam sought the counsel of the older men on how to be an effective leader. Samuel answered in 1 Kings 12:7: "If thou wilt be a servant unto this people this day and wilt serve them, and answer them, and speak good words to them, then they will be thy servants forever." I quietly adopted these words as my direction and prayed for a servant's attitude.

I kept my Christian teachings confined to the Thursday morning Bible studies, thus relieving the worried ladies of their concern about my capturing the club for the

Lord. When elections came up that year, there were no objections and I was chosen president for a second term.

The Bible studies increased in popularity and we made enough money from our admission charge to give a scholarship to Carmen Mayell, a deserving student at a Christian college. The following year we continued our study group and had our first club prayer breakfast. In 1973 we not only won the district award for religion, but were given a special honor at the state convention for "outstanding achievement in the area of spiritual values and ethics." The state chairman said we had won because of the Bible studies held in our club building. This was a major breakthrough and paved the way for other clubs to have Bible studies with the approval of the California Federation of Women's Clubs.

I taught these studies for ten years until my traveling schedule made a weekly commitment impossible. Our prayer breakfasts provided an evangelistic outreach and, because of their success, the district started a prayer breakfast, then the state and ultimately the national convention for Federated Women's Clubs of America instituted a prayer breakfast. All this because our local group was willing to step out and bring the Lord into a secular organization in an inoffensive way that changed lives.

One woman summed it up when she returned after a year away and said, "I don't know what's happened in this club, but everyone seems nicer."

Reflections

The Lord has given me a ministry of encouragement and I have often been able to help women have an impact in their community by assuming leadership in secular organizations. The Lord Jesus went out among the worldly people and He loved them where they were. He didn't make every dinner party into an evangelistic rally but He let His light shine so that people could see the difference.

Unfortunately, the world perceives Christians today as standing against everything society wants or enjoys. Non-Christians become quickly defensive when they sense someone is out to convert them. But they do appreciate hard workers who do what they say they'll do and who have an above-average sense of responsibility. If you wish to have an influence for good in your community, here are some suggestions.

1. *Don't choose a group that is obviously anti-God.* In selecting an organization to work in, find one that has some basic moral principles. When I read the by-laws of the Federated Women's Clubs I found a section that said we were to invest in the spiritual values of our members. I quoted this by-law in proposing Bible studies in the clubhouse. It's amazing what's in the by-laws of any organization and you can be safe in assuming that the average member has never read them.

2. *Be willing to do insignificant jobs well.* Don't try to be president before doing some small chores and doing them better than anyone else has ever done them before.

3. *Become program chairman.* This office gives the best opportunity for influencing what speakers come into the group. You can't have an altar call at each meeting, but you can bring in speakers with a moral message and keep out some of the perverted possibilities waiting to pollute the minds of the public.

4. *Remember that there are leadership vacuums everywhere.* Few people want the responsibility that comes with being chairman or president. I was in one church where the pastor had encouraged his people to go to political caucuses and volunteer for leadership positions. When they reported in the next Sunday, many had become local party chairmen on the first meeting and almost all who had done as the pastor instructed had come away with some party office. I was impressed with how easy it is to become a leader when you are willing to volunteer and work conscientiously.

I know several women who have become PTA presidents and have been able to influence school programs and sometimes even curriculum from a position of leadership.

5. *Don't be discouraged by fellow Christians who reprimand you for "leaving the faith" for worldly pursuits.* If you feel called to serve in a secular organization, respond in the knowledge that the Lord will bless your efforts. In Philippians 2:14,15 it says: "Do all things without murmurings or disputings that you may be blameless and harmless, the sons of God without rebuke, in the middle of a crooked and perverse nation among whom you shine as lights in the world."

We are surely in a crooked and perverse nation, so go out and shine!

For those of you interested in understanding the biblical rationale for Christian activism in local politics, I would suggest you read *The Blue Book for Grassroots Politics* by Charles Phillips (Oliver Nelson). This is a complete and practical handbook for anyone interested in how to have an impact on our country's moral and spiritual values and laws.

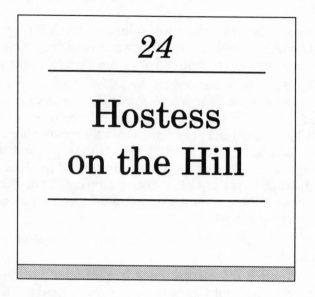

24

Hostess
on the Hill

Though the move was a difficult step of faith to take, God blessed the sacrifice through expanding our ministry in ways we never would have imagined.

My children now look back on our days in the spacious house in the foothills of the San Bernardino mountains as "Mother's Hostess on the Hill Era." And in retrospect, it was.

At the time of the fire I had promised the Lord that if He would spare our home I'd dedicate it to Christian hospitality and entertaining the saints. We had constant open house. People came for dinner and stayed for weeks, sometimes years. We had a monthly covered dish supper and never knew how many would arrive. We would set up tables and chairs in our family room, turning it into a candlelit restaurant. On the second Saturday of every month about fifty people brought a casserole, salad or dessert, plus any friends, and we all met for dinner, fellowship and a program.

For eight years we maintained a well-kept hospitable home and loved every aspect of what God had given us to do. I was playing Martha, serving all who entered, plus I taught the women's club Bible study, a teen study, a couples' Friday night study and a Wednesday lunch Bible study at Norton Air Force Base. But as our speaking ministry increased, we began to wonder if this hospitality phase of our life should come to an end.

When I had moved into this home I had especially designed a study with built-in desks for Fred and me and bookshelves containing every kind of reference material imaginable. I knew when I designed the study that I wanted to write a book, but in eight busy years I hadn't composed so much as a chapter. I had created scores of original Bible messages but I had never written a book. People kept asking me, "Do you have any of this in writing?" Every time I answered no, I felt ashamed. I had all the equipment but no product; somewhat like a woman with a beautiful kitchen who can't cook.

Fred occasionally mentioned that the house was too much for me, but each time I'd dive into my chores with new energy just to show him I could handle it. At that point I was teaching a Bible study on Hebrews and when I got to chapter twelve on laying aside the weights that keep us from running the race, I prayed and asked the Lord to show me if there was anything holding me down. Immediately the house came to my mind. I rejected that thought, but it kept returning: *Your house is a heavy weight; it's slowing you down.*

I pointed out to the Lord how I had used this home to glorify Him, and how many people had heard His Word here for the first time in their lives. The message kept coming back: *Sell your house.*

Not wanting to believe these words, I put a few conditions on the sale of our home. It would have to sell quickly so we could be re-established by September for our son Fred to go to junior high school, and we would have to get close to the asking price. If it didn't sell, I would assume I should cut back on my speaking and continue to entertain and teach. Not wanting to make this an easy job for the Lord, I listed the house with the agency our daughter Lauren worked for under the conditions that they wouldn't advertise, put it in multiple listing or place a sign out front. For this house to sell, it would take a miracle.

A few days later I answered the door bell to find a lady from the real estate office. She wanted to look the house over. She was obviously a Choleric personality, as she walked briskly through the house without even opening any closet doors. When she had completed her brief tour she said, "I'll take it."

"Just like that?" I asked.

"I came through here once on a home tour you had and I vowed if this house ever came on the market, I'd buy it."

And she did. Quickly and at the right price.

Surely I had no excuse. I had asked the Lord to show me if anything was keeping me from doing His will. He had given me bad news and I had made it as difficult as possible. When the house sold in spite of me, I had to agree with the Lord and begin packing. It is never easy to leave a home that has become part of you and the thought of taking apart this dream house and packing it up was especially hard. Once again I was leaving my castle where I had planned to live happily ever after.

I walked from room to room and cried. I looked at each decorative detail that Gudrun and I had so carefully constructed. How could I leave behind the striped awnings over Freddie's beds or the Swedish arches built in front of Marita's beds with the Austrian shades that could be let down to hide her away? That house was a part of me and I loved every inch of it.

How well I remember the day when the new owner and her decorator came. He was an imperious man who barely gave me a token hello. Each room he entered appalled him. "Oh, my dear, this will never do. How could they have painted the family room brick red? We'll have to tear out these cheap little arches and pull down these tacky canopies over the beds. This is a much bigger job than I ever anticipated."

I couldn't believe he thought everything I loved was tasteless and should be removed as soon as possible. By the time he left I wondered if interior design schools had a course called Disdain 101 to teach the students how to scoff at the decorating attempts of others.

We had to relocate quickly and Lauren found us a Spanish style condominium in Redlands. In one fell swoop we got rid of our encumbrances, the weights that slowed me down, and we moved from a six-bedroom house to a 1300-square-foot condo. It was like living in a motel and almost like returning to Bungalow One.

Since I no longer had room for a study at home, I sent Marita out to find me an office where I could write. A college sophomore at that time and noted for her ability to charm others, Marita located a four-room office in an old building in the center of Redlands. The price was $200 a month, but by the time she concluded the agreement, the owner rented it to us for $80. Marita, assorted boyfriends and my son Fred painted and wallpapered the main room and we moved in furniture left over from our former home.

I never would have found the time to write if I had stayed in my castle on the hill, but within one year's time in my office I had written my first two books and increased my speaking engagements. Though the move was a difficult step of faith to take, God blessed the sacrifice through expanding our ministry in ways we never would have imagined.

Reflections

As I look back on that traumatic move, I realize how

easy it is to go up in life and how difficult it is to come down. Yet I know even more surely today that the move was right. I had prayed for guidance, using God's Word as a foundation, and He gave me clear direction. I have learned that when I pray and get an answer I don't like, it is usually the Lord speaking. I don't have to pray for direction to find a shopping mall. I can find them on my own in nearly every city.

Often people ask, "How do you know God's will for your life?"

Before you can hear God's instruction you have to be studying His Word. Be open to certain verses or passages as they draw your attention. Second, you have to be seeking His direction in prayer and then listening for His answer. When you do spend time daily in study and prayer, you will receive the Lord's counsel. Conversely, if you never have time for study and only shoot up prayers on the run, you may not ever hear His counsel or know His will.

Not every answer is what we want to hear, but as we fellowship closely with the Lord we become so in tune that we turn automatically in His direction.

Leaving my dream home was not an easy or exciting thing to do, but in retrospect it was the right thing to do. As the Lord has blessed us we have been able to

Make the tough times count!

25

Saying It
With Class

*We all have a story to tell, but many of us don't
realize that our difficulties and dilemmas, once
we've had a degree of healing, can be used to
encourage others.*

In the fall of 1980 the Lord used a verse to call me to
a new ministry. I had already been challenged by an article
predicting that the '80s was to be the decade of the active
woman and that women were going to be looking for all
kinds of training. I knew that Christian women were going
to be part of the active decade and I wondered who would
be training them and what they would be learning. At this
point I was studying in the Amplified Bible and found 2
Timothy 2:2:

And the instructions which you have heard from me
along with many witnesses, transmit and entrust as a
deposit to reliable and faithful men who will be competent
and qualified to teach others also.

As I studied, I realized how perfectly this verse fit my

241

story and how it challenged me to move in a new direction. I looked at my life as an everlasting training program. I had been receiving instructions forever. I remembered my father teaching me verses and poems, my mother trying to make me into a violinist like her, and my Aunt Sadie giving me piano lessons. Although I didn't have much innate musical talent, I did learn to read music and have enough of an appreciation for the melody, rhythm and style that I was later able to direct musical comedies.

I thought of my teachers and Sunday school instructors who had filled me with information and Bible stories. My high school years of serious study in order to get a scholarship to college. The extra-curricular activities in drama, poetry reading, debates, yearbook, French club and public speaking. My three college majors of English, speech and education, six years of high school teaching, one course of instructing Gracious Living, two terms of teaching psychology to adults and one year of teaching public speaking on the college level.

Added to that were my endless years of being president of everything and my understanding of Roberts Rules of Order. Plus the intense Bible study I had done and the many Christian speakers I had heard. That added up to *instructions* I had heard from God, parents, teachers, speakers, plus all my life experiences and *many other witnesses.*

What did the verse say I was to do with my own special package of learning? *Transmit*—send across. I was to teach it to others. *Entrust* as in a deposit. I was to help others become Christian leaders and speakers and writers, considering my instructions as a *deposit* in the lives of others with the possible hope that someday I might see some interest on my deposit.

Who was I to teach? *Faithful* and *reliable* people who I knew loved the Lord Jesus and could be counted on to use and not waste the information.

What would happen to these people? If I taught them

all I knew, they would become *competent* and *qualified* to *train others also*. What a way to multiply my life and make the tough times count.

Once I accepted the call, I invited forty women to come to California to be trained. Thirty-five accepted and I began to write the first CLASS, Christian Leaders and Speakers Seminars. I had assumed everyone who attended my seminars would be above average in every way and relatively trouble-free. I was going to take people with no problems and send them out to take care of those who had them. But what I learned in that last week of January 1981 was that all of us have been through traumatic times. We all have a story to tell, but many of us don't realize that our difficulties and dilemmas, once we've had a degree of healing, can be used to encourage others.

In our select group of thirty-five Christian women leaders, we had seven incest or child abuse victims, several divorces and an assortment of other major problems including drug and alcohol abuse. How exciting it was to see each woman realize she didn't need to be ashamed of her past but she could use her victimization and victories as inspiration for others in similar circumstances. She could make her tough times count!

As our CLASS ministry grew, we began using a survey called "Troubles in River City" (we got the name from the song of that title in *The Music Man*). We listed every problem we could think of and had the participants check off all of those that had happened to them or to immediate family members. In the last ten years we have added new traumas that we hadn't thought of in 1980 and we have watched the progression of problems increase. Along the way we learned that our purpose in teaching CLASS was not just to train others to speak but to help them find healing in their own lives first.

Carol came to CLASS as an experienced Bible study teacher who wanted to brush up on her technique. During the section on the four personalities she began to think,

Who am I really? She knew all the things she did, but she did not know who she was. She took her Personality Profile and was somewhat even in every personality type. I explained to her, "Either this means you are so Phlegmatic you have difficulty deciding on the words and their meaning, or you are so perfectly balanced you are about to ascend, or you've spent your life trying so hard to please everyone—be all things to all people—that you have no idea who you really are."

"It's the last one," she said quickly.

As we talked, I found she had grown up in an alcoholic home where she had learned to cover up bad situations and deny that there were any problems. In doing this she had covered up her true personality. As a Christian she was devout, legalistic and almost too sweet to be real. She had created "good little spiritual Carol."

She went home eager to find out who she really was and be done with any hypocrisy. As she read through *Your Personality Tree* she was convicted by the chapter on masking. She had been hiding behind a false face of wishful thinking. As she began to write her prayers daily and ask the Lord to show her truth—that the truth might set her free—she uncovered some sexual abuse by her alcoholic father. She set on a course of recovery from her revelation of reality and she now teaches on overcoming childhood traumas and leads support groups to help others who have had similar problems.

Carol came to pick up some new ideas for teaching her Bible studies, learned she needed some help in her own life and progressed into a ministry of far greater depth and heart than she had ever thought possible.

We have seen thousands of Carols and hundreds of men come through our CLASS in the past ten years who have been open to God's leading first in their own lives and then in meeting the needs of others.

Reflections

As I look back over the ten years of CLASS, I rejoice in what the Lord has done with so many of our alums. From my modest thought of training thirty-five women in 1981, CLASS has grown each year and has graduated over 7000. From the simple start in the basement of a bank in Redlands, California, CLASS has expanded to the Hilton International Hotel in Brisbane, Australia, and to Auckland, New Zealand, where Dame Catherine Tizard, mayor of Auckland and Governor General of New Zealand, attended. She had only meant to give an opening greeting but was so fascinated she stayed to the end. When I asked her to give a closing comment, she said, "I came to scoff and stayed to worship."

In ten years we have trained movie stars and mothers, teenagers and senior citizens, Bible teachers and businessmen, pastors and politicians to communicate more effectively whether speaking to one or one thousand. Our original thrust was to show people with something to say how to put their message into a form simple enough to reach the minds and hearts of the listeners and clear enough to be used of God to change people's lives.

We still follow this principle, but we have added the necessity of "becoming real" before ministering to others. As we saw the number of Christian leaders who were avoiding or denying their own problems, we moved slowly but surely into helping each CLASS member review their past, take off any mask they had put on for any reason and become the real person God intended them to be. In doing this, solid ministries have been created that depend on a genuine relationship with the Lord for their foundation. Whenever there has been a vague feeling of personal confusion or blockage between the individual and God, we have worked to clear away the clouds.

In order to bring Christian leaders in touch with reality and into a solid relationship with the Lord, we use the concept of the four personalities as a measuring stick.

When people come out confused or with opposite personalities, we lead them into a prayerful study of our book,
Freeing Your Mind From Memories That Bind and a
disciplined daily writing of their prayers, asking the Lord
to take off their masks and make them real. Some are
hesitant, but the majority eagerly respond and report later
that they feel truly free for the first time in their adult
lives.

The Lord has done a stripping job in my life and in
Fred's over these ten years; He has brought us to a humbling point of relying on Him and not ourselves. We have
put away any pretenses we might have had and He has
given us a gentleness and gracious spirit that can only
exist when the peace that passes all understanding is in
control.

Fred and I work with many gifted people at CLASS.
Our director of training is Patsy Clairmont of Brighton,
Michigan, who has been with us from the original CLASS.
When Patsy first came, she had no idea what God was
going to do with her life. She had been giving book reviews
at women's retreats and was known as "God's Little
Bookie." Petite, precious and powerfully packaged, Patsy
has gone from agrophobia and insecurity to becoming one
of the outstanding female communicators in America
today. Her unique sense of humor, transparent personality and depth of scriptural knowledge combine to make her
a human dynamo.

God has transformed Patsy from a frightened country
girl to a gifted presenter of His Word. He has healed her
from many pains of her past and is using her to help others.
When Patsy spoke on Focus on the Family, her message,
"God Uses Cracked Pots—and I Am the Visual Aid," received so many requests that it placed on the list of all-time
favorites. Since then, Dr. Dobson has offered her a contract
for a book of the same name. If no other life but Patsy's
has been transformed, CLASS would be considered successful.

Our director of management and manuscripts, Marilyn Heavilin, first came to CLASS a year and a half after her teenage son Nathan had been killed by a drunk driver. Marilyn was still grieving the loss of Nathan and only came to CLASS because I wanted her to tape a message on how to grieve and work through your pain. As she began to speak on this subject, I encouraged her to write her story. As we worked together on the foundation of *Roses in December*, we found we had many similarities in our lives. Her Matthew was born six months before my Freddie (February 9, 1960); her Mellyn within a few days of Larry (August 14, 1961). And within the next two years two of her babies died. Marilyn had multiple surgeries at almost the same time I was in the hospital. While Fred was put to bed with rheumatic fever, her husband Glen was suffering with debilitating migraine headaches.

As couples we were in deep depression and in need of supernatural healing. That's when the Lord picked us up from Connecticut and the Heavilins from Indiana and put us both down in the desert of San Bernardino at Campus Crusade for Christ headquarters. When we found each other with our almost identical lives of trauma and tragedy, we knew God had brought us together for a reason. We share a bond of love and mutual support that can only be formed by those who can say to each other, "I know what it was like. I've been there."

The Lord brought us together and allowed me to encourage Marilyn to write, speak and train others to make the tough times count.

In 1981 our daughter Marita was the child of our CLASS, but as she matured, she created new aspects and avenues of Christian leadership. She is the founder and co-chairman with Marilyn of the Southern California Women's Retreat, and now serves as our director of Christian Leaders, Authors and Speakers Services. Marita is a speaker herself, and she trains speakers through CLASS. She books speaking engagements in churches and conferences all over the country for those who have been through CLASS and she has formed a media publicity service available to major publishers to get their authors on radio and TV talk shows to promote their books. With Marilyn, Marita receives manuscripts, evaluates them and places them in the hands of publishers who might not otherwise read them.

Our daughter Lauren helped me put on the first CLASS and she has served with us frequently throughout the last ten years. She has her own ministry as a grief consultant to those women who are hurting from the loss of a child, from a miscarriage or from the birth of a retarded or handicapped baby.

Lauren's first priority is to her three sons and her husband Randy, but the Lord has used her informally to give words of encouragement to those in need. Her book, *What You Can Say When You Don't Know What to Say,* has been used by individuals, pastors and counselors to show well-meaning people what to say to those in need.

Lauren's son Randy is our first grandson and when he was little I took him to hear me speak. One day he said to me, "When I grow up, I'm going to be a speaker." I was thrilled and encouraged him. When he was about five he mentioned to me, "Someday I'm going to be a fireman." I pretended to be disappointed and replied, "I thought you were going to be a speaker." Quickly he recouped, "I'm going to speak on fires!"

Our second grandson Jonathan is a Sanguine and he loves to talk. When he was five I taught him about the personalities and then gave him the video tapes of *Your Personality Tree.* By the time he was six, he was a junior expert on the subject. I took him with me on a local speaking engagement and on the way I asked him, "Do you know why I'm bringing you along today?"

Immediately he answered, "You're going to talk about me and you want the people to see the real thing."

I introduced him as the surprise guest speaker and

handed him the microphone. He talked brightly for fifteen minutes on a child's view of the personalities, ending with: "It is not my job to make Randy Sanguine like me; nor is it his job to make me Melancholy like him. We have to learn to accept each other as we are."

The ladies were amazed at his maturity and knowledge and they clapped loudly. When the applause died down, little Jonathan, still holding the mike, said, "I do have time to stay and sign autographs."

We seem to have here a chip off the old grandmother.

Little Bryan is still too young to put on the platform, but he is very verbal and will surely add his words of wisdom in a family of communicators.

The Lord has blessed CLASS and those who have so faithfully served over the last ten years. He has given us the people and abilities to take those who come with a story to tell and show them how to communicate the truth as speakers and authors.

As I have been faithful in giving "the instructions" I have received from the Lord and many others to "faithful and reliable people," I've been blessed and they have become "competent and qualified to train others also."

I learned the hard way—without a mentor—and I've determined to share all I know with those who want to learn that they might be saved some time, some errors and some effort. In the words of the French writer Etienne De Grellet (1773-1855):

I shall pass through this world but once. If, therefore, there be any kindness I can show, or any good thing I can do, let me do it now; let me not defer or neglect it, for I shall not pass this way again.

I want to help you

Make the tough times count!

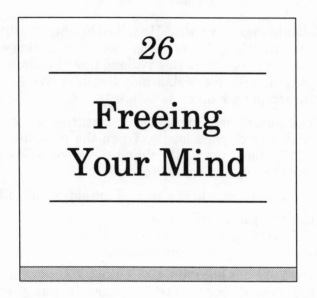

26

Freeing Your Mind

We were all so naive at the beginning, confident that there were no people with childhood sexual or emotional abuse in our church or even in our circle of personal friends.

In 1988, spurred on by the needs of people in Christian leadership to become aware of the reality of abuse in "good church families," the needs of the leaders themselves to work through the pain in their own lives and the needs of the hurting, neglected and dysfunctional families whose symptoms were being ignored, Fred and I determined to write something we could put in the hands of the hurting to help them heal. I envisioned a pamphlet with a few steps to wholeness, but as we set out to give answers to the problems we had been encountering in the churches and in CLASS, the "pamphlet" grew into a 300-page book that sold more copies in its first three months than my others had sold in their first year.

The response to *Freeing Your Mind From Memories That Bind* was so overwhelming that we were deluged with calls and letters pouring out pitiful problems and begging for help. One letter had the word HELP! printed all around the piece of paper like a border.

In his melancholy way, Fred wanted to collect data to analyze the extent of childhood sexual abuse and its effects on the adult life. He created a "Survey of Emotional Responses" to gather statistics on how many people showed symptoms of having been sexually abused in childhood but weren't consciously aware of any specific incidents. In surveying more than 2000 people in various Christian conferences, we found that 25 percent of the women had not been abused, 25 percent had been abused and were aware of it, and 50 percent had been abused (displayed the same symptoms as the abused victims) and yet didn't realize it. They had blanked out their traumatic past.

In men we found 40 percent were not harmed, 10 percent were and knew it and 50 percent were and didn't know it. The information on these surveys and other responses to *Freeing Your Mind* plus an amplification of the steps to restoration are now in Fred's book *The Promise of Healing.*

Reflections

As we look back over this ten-year period, we are amazed at what has happened to us and to the people who have come to CLASS. We were all so naive at the beginning, confident that there were no people with childhood sexual or emotional abuse in our church or even in our circle of personal friends. And yet as time has passed and cases have piled up on top of each other, we have had to face some hard truths. We desire to help the Christian community come to some degree of awareness on this issue. No longer can we say to hurting people: "Just pray about it and it will go away"; "Forgive him and you'll be happy"; "You're just not walking in victory . . . or in the Spirit . . . or as a Christian should."

Fred and I never set out to seek a ministry with desperate people. I only wanted to train leaders to go out and train other leaders. But I decided we all need to find the source of our problems and gain some degree of healing before we can minister to others.

Perhaps you have had some abuse in your childhood: emotionally, physically, mentally or sexually. Perhaps you've denied it, covered it over or thought that's what happened to everyone.

Perhaps you have suffered migraine headaches, stomach problems, undiagnosed ailments or chronic depression and just thought you had to live with it.

Perhaps you've worked hard and somehow not quite made it, failed just before you reached success, self-destructed when you should have achieved the goal.

Any of these unexplained failures or emotional and physical symptoms could stem from some problems so far back that you have never connected your childhood traumas with your adult dilemmas. Begin today to prayerfully ask the Lord if there's some connection you've missed, some childhood abuse you've blocked out. Get a copy of *Freeing Your Mind From Memories That Bind* and carefully go over the sections of "identification," "explanation" and "restoration." As you pull the loose ends of your life together, the Lord will use you to help others.

As Fred and I have been faithful to God's call, He has equipped us to handle the hurting without counting the cost in time or dollars. As we have taught others to speak and write from their own heart issues, we have been blessed to see many published books written by potential authors we encouraged. As we have been open and transparent about our own lives, we have been able to show thousands of others—many just like you—how to

Make the tough times count!

27

Confronting in Love

Because Fred had always been a loving husband, polite, gracious and generous, I had denied or ignored any recognition of deep-seated problems in his life.

All of us like stories that have happy endings. Women love to see Cinderella marry Prince Charming, ride off into the sunset, buy a big castle with a moat and raise adorable little children and fluffy little dogs. Men dream of business and financial success and some hope to be athletic heroes.

Fred and I were typical. We really thought we could get married and live happily ever after, but right from the start we found we were nothing alike and didn't see eye to eye on anything. We didn't think our church backgrounds would make much difference, but we couldn't agree on a mutual denomination. We found out our personalities didn't match; I wanted fun and he wanted things perfect. We thought we'd have adorable children who'd grow up to be brilliant and successful, but we lost our two longed-for sons. I thought Fred would make lots of money and we'd live in lavish houses. Sometimes he did and sometimes we did. But sometimes we didn't. Our whole life story could be charted out in the ups and downs of houses.

When we committed our lives to the Lord Jesus we thought, *This is the answer. Now we'll be happy.* The adoption of Freddie certainly should have cheered us up. But I had operations, depression, disappointments. We moved to the desert of California to go into full-time Christian service. Surely God would bless such dedication, but after losing money on our Connecticut home and putting money into Bungalow One, we were forced to leave it all and move on.

We built a big house and entertained the saints. I pictured living in that home forever, that home the Lord protected from the fire, but with financial problems and a call from the Lord we sold the dream and moved to a tiny condominium. We started CLASS. We moved to a normal house. I wrote seventeen books, and I spoke all over the country. Did we finally get to Happy Ever After time? Were the tough times over? I thought so.

Caring Enough to Confront

Throughout our married life I had little to do with Fred's businesses. I had married him expecting financial security and yet through all our years we had never really reached it. We'd had many good years, but then something would happen and Fred's plans often failed. He always had logical excuses and I had no choice but to believe him. He was always optimistic and couldn't see why a loss of money bothered me. "It's only money," he'd say. He never understood that because I had grown up poor in a store I had a desperate desire to be financially secure. I didn't need to be rich; I just needed to know the bills were paid.

As my speaking and writing ministry grew, I had even less to do with Fred's business. He always led me to believe things were going well until I came home from one weekend retreat to find we'd had some major financial losses and some legal entanglements. There was no dishonesty or malicious intent, but the situation was upsetting and humiliating.

Marita and I discussed what we should do about Fred's apparent inability to succeed for any length of time. We were also concerned about the anger he seemed to have pent up inside him. I had never really thought of him as angry before because he never yelled or hit me. Yet as Marita and I talked over the situation, I realized that the reason he didn't display his anger was because I had learned to avoid triggering it. As long as I was supportive and submissive, he didn't get mad. If I questioned his decisions or directions, he'd give me what I called "The Look," a flash from his eyes that said, "I dare you." I never dared.

Because Fred had always been a loving husband, polite, gracious and generous, I had denied or ignored any recognition of deep-seated problems in his life. But this financial and legal turmoil brought up feelings I didn't know I had.

I tried to tell Fred that I felt he had some hurts in his past he hadn't dealt with, but he flatly denied it. When I suggested I felt he had an odd relationship with his mother, he angrily defended her and said sternly to me, "Don't you ever say a bad thing about my mother."

I continued trying different approaches to make him realize the source of what I felt was a long-range problem, not just the financial crisis of the moment. He could not see that his repeated business difficulties were anything more than occasional bad luck.

When I felt I was getting nowhere, Marita and I decided we needed a time of confrontation. With our friend and counselor Lana Bateman as the outside, objective party, we asked to speak with Fred about a serious matter. When we told him we saw a lot of anger inside him, he denied it and got angry. As we enumerated examples, he began to listen and suddenly his reaction softened and he agreed to see a male counselor we had already consulted.

In the interim we were functioning as usual.

One day as we were waiting to appear on the PTL Club with Gary McSpadden, we turned on the television monitor to see Becky Tirabassi. Becky has a testimony of teen-age alcoholism. She pledged to the Lord that if He would save her, she'd spend at least one hour a day in written prayer. As Fred watched her story, the Lord convicted him that he should write his prayers and he began the next day.

During the three months before he went for his two weeks of intensive therapy, Fred wrote out his prayers each day. By the time he got to the counseling he was ready for God to do a great work.

In counseling, Fred learned that he was a victim of rejection by both his mother and father. They were always working and never came to any of his sporting events or performances. Instead of encouraging young Fred, his mother had, in fact, told him he'd never succeed at anything. Little did we understand at the time that Fred's inability to stay on top for long was a fulfillment of that prophecy of doom.

He also learned that his mother had a lot of anger in her that spilled out on Fred as a child. He was always made to say he was sorry even when the situation was not his fault. He'd stuffed his anger inside him because he couldn't vent it on her. As we look back now, he had unconsciously done the same with me. Whatever the problem, I had to apologize. After a while I had learned to do it without feeling, as a cheap price for peace.

When Fred told the therapist that after his father's death his mother had moved him into her bedroom and made him her new husband in every way but sexually, the counselor explained this was an emotional form of sexual abuse.

Fred did not come home healed; instead, he was confused, introspective and remote. He had done what we'd asked him to do and he felt worse. He continued his written prayer, began to read everything he could on rejection and abuse, and spent hours in Bible study seeking God's answers for his life. Gradually we saw changes: "The Look" was gone and there was a new peace in his demeanor. As Marita and I saw the difference, we encouraged him. The Lord began to bring people to him who had hidden their pains of the past and couldn't figure out why they were angry. As Fred helped others, he developed steps that God used to heal him and those he counseled.

So much happened so quickly. As Fred became vulnerable and willing to share and as the Lord used him to help others, he felt strongly led to write *Freeing Your Mind From Memories That Bind*. He had never written before and really had never planned to, but as he says now, that was because he had nothing to say. Now he does.

The Lord has given him a special gift for uncovering the root of people's problems and filling in the gaps in their memories. We have learned that until someone finds out the *cause* of their problems (the source of the pain), the symptoms don't go away. The Lord only heals what we bring to Him.

As Fred has been the instrument in encouraging others to write their prayers daily, he has continued this discipline himself and I can attest to it. Through his "seeking first the kingdom of God" each day he has also uncovered that fact that he was a victim of sexual abuse sometime before the age of two-and-a-half. He tells about this in his book *The Promise of Healing*.

The Lord showed Fred that he should get out of business ventures and trust that we could support ourselves in speaking, writing and ministering to others. With the Lord's blessing this has become possible. Now as we travel full-time together, being home only a few days a month, we have learned to love each other in a new dimension and feel as if we are on a perpetual honeymoon. We've faced our problems squarely. We've sought the Lord's wisdom and He has helped us to make the tough times count.

Reflections

What has all this meant to our marriage? It means that as Fred has dealt with his own hidden hurts and has come to a closer relationship with the Lord, he has become a real person.

Fred never intended to be a phony. None of us do, but the repressed anger and rejections in Fred's past had caused him to live an artificial life. He didn't realize this nor did I, but in retrospect I see how difficult it was to love a person who wasn't genuine. There was always that missing piece to the puzzle. We had learned to function well together. We even admired each other's talents, but we didn't know what love really was. Since we got along so much better than everyone else we knew, we thought we had a good marriage but we were missing the key ingredient. We could communicate intellectually, socially and spiritually, but not emotionally.

Does any of this sound like you? Do you have a marriage or relationship that seems to be missing something? Maybe it's time to prayerfully confront your mate and think about the possibility that there may be some childhood problems that are still influencing your behavior today. If you wish to look together at possible damaging emotions from the past, use the questions in *Freeing Your Mind From Memories That Bind*. We've had people ask each other these background questions and discover things about each other they never knew before.

Marilyn and Glen Heavilin, both on our CLASS staff, used the *Freeing Your Mind* questions as a conversational tool on a long trip. As Glen drove, he asked Marilyn questions about her childhood. "Tell me about the house you lived in as a young child." "How do you feel about that house?" "Did you ever have babysitters?"

As Marilyn answered yes to that question, a scene formed in her mind that was so vivid she was able to describe the carpet on the floor, the color of the couch, the clothes she had on and the clothes the babysitter—a teenage boy—was wearing. This event happened more than forty-eight years ago, but Marilyn was able to recall a very uncomfortable situation with this young boy which she now realizes created fears that she has been dealing with since that time. She also remembered the bathrobe she was wearing and that her parents left her because she was ill.

Shortly after recalling this memory, Marilyn was able to verify with her mother the reality of what she remembered. Because she had whooping cough, Marilyn had been left with this boy for a short while so her parents could attend a wedding.

Marilyn says, "Although I have been with others when they retrieved memories from their childhood, I must admit I wondered sometimes if these events really happened. It seemed almost too easy. But God allowed me to see through my own experience that if we are really seeking the truth in order to be more usable vessels, He is willing to reveal the truth to us with very little fanfare or effort on our part. All we need is a willing spirit. When the time is right, the truth will be revealed to us. I needed to be released from these fears that followed me from childhood, and when I was willing to confront the issue in prayer, God allowed me to be released from my past."

Marilyn is typical of many who have some hidden hurts in their lives that they have not even known about and, therefore, have not dealt with or brought to the Lord for healing. You may need to examine your own life or encourage your spouse to seek counsel. If there is resistance or if you have a situation where there needs to be some personal confrontation, I'd suggest a few guidelines.

1. *Determine if there is a need to confront.* Is the behavior of the individual in question threatening the emotional health of at least one other family member? Is there any physical abuse going on? Is there an addiction—drugs, alcohol, gambling, pornography—that shows no signs of stopping? Are there continued business failures

or other patterns that are damaging to the family? Is there a fear of blow-ups, temper tantrums, fits of rage?

If any of these types of problems exist now and are getting worse and not better, there is a need for confrontation. I have talked with women who have been beaten and abused by their husbands who felt it was their cross to bear. They felt if they were really submissive enough and Christian enough, he would stop tomorrow. In my experience, women who tolerate abuse in a marriage over a long period of time do so because they were abused as children. They have learned to "take it." Be sure to check your own emotional stability before attempting to confront someone else.

2. *Seek the Lord's direction.* Do not hastily jump into a confrontation or you may end up defeated. Daily write to the Lord in prayer, asking His guidance in the situation. Make sure you are spiritually ready and divinely inspired.

3. *Read at least one book on confrontation* to better prepare you for what may happen.

4. *Find an independent, outside person* who is willing to stand with you as a mediator, not an attacker. Explain the situation as objectively as possible and have this individual ready to do the confronting if necessary.

5. *Enlist family support.* It's almost impossible to implement family change if the group is not with you. If they all feel you are off balance, you will need some family counseling first to decide where the problems are rooted and what the others feel should be done.

6. *Develop a plan for possible solutions.* Before we expressed to Fred that we felt he would benefit from counseling, we had talked with a therapist about the situation and knew when he had a block of time available. Don't go into any confrontation until you have looked into possible solutions and have the phone numbers of professional help in hand.

7. *Be willing to hang tough.* No confrontation is easy

and the person may turn on you and try to browbeat or reason you into changing your mind. He or she has probably already done that many times in spontaneous confrontations you've had in the past. You must be prepared and determined that life cannot go on like it is any longer.

8. *Be prepared for the worst.* We don't want to approach this meeting with a negative attitude, but we must be alert to the possibility that the person we confront will pack up and leave.

9. *Set an appropriate time.* No time is perfect for a confrontation, but make sure you choose a time when the individual will be under the least amount of stress and when he or she is not under a time pressure to leave.

10. *Approach with love.* Don't make the confrontation an attack. It is shocking enough for the person to find himself in a position where everyone seems to have suddenly turned against him. Continue to say, "We love you. We want the best for you, but we need some changes made." Be willing to modify your own behavior and compromise in minor areas as long as the confronted person is willing to take major steps.

These suggestions are from what I learned personally. They are not a complete manual on confrontation, but they will at least give you some guidelines if confrontation is necessary.

Our time of facing reality was not easy, but it was necessary and the changes have been remarkable. God has blessed our ministry and given us a new depth and understanding. He has

Made the tough times count!

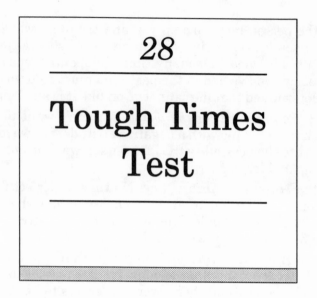

28

Tough Times Test

Check off the answer which is closest to your feelings.

	Column A	Column B	Column C
1. When you think of that ideal childhood in a garden of verses, a meadow of daisies or a fountain of blessings, do you feel you were surrounded by flowers?	⎯⎯ Never	⎯⎯ Sometimes	⎯⎯ Always
2. As you look back, were your childhood days dull, drab and without beauty?	⎯⎯ Always	⎯⎯ Often	⎯⎯ Never
3. Did you wish for a better home or car? Did you wish you could live on the other side of the tracks?	⎯⎯ Definitely	⎯⎯ Sometimes	⎯⎯ Never

4. Do you remember

Christmases as disappoint-
ing or quarrelsome?

Many	A few	None

5. When you look back, was
substance abuse a part
of your childhood?

Constantly	Often	Never

6. When you think of the
clothes you wore as a child,
what is your first reaction?

Hated them	Okay	Loved them

7. Was there any shame or
ridicule attached to your clothes,
shoes or hair as a child?

Always	Sometimes	Never

8. Was there anything stuck
on you (nickname, reputation,
family problems) that you
couldn't seem to shake off?
What was it? _____
Did this bother you?

All through childhood	Sometimes	For a brief time

9. Did you set specific goals
for yourself?

Never	Once	Definitely

10. Did either parent teach
you positive principles that
have helped you in life?

Not really	Off and on	Often

11. Where did you learn
the facts of life?

Friends	Books	Parents

12. Did you ever feel that
getting out of your hometown
was your only hope for success?

Yes	Didn't matter	No

13. Would you feel better about
yourself if you had more

education?

	Definitely	Perhaps	No

14. Were there any deaths in the family when you were young?

	More than one	One	None

15. From teen years to now, how many deaths of family members or close friends have you experienced?

	Several	One	None

16. Do you feel you were allowed to grieve? Were you encouraged to share your feelings about these deaths?

	Not at all	Once	Yes

17. Were you encouraged to study and get an education?

	Not at all	One parent	Constantly

18. Did financial or emotional problems exist in your family?

	Constantly	Occasionally	Never

19. Was there divorce in your family (parents, sisters, brothers, yourself)?

	More than one	One	None

20. Did you have a parent who leaned on you for support and/or drained you emotionally?

	Both	One	Neither

21. Were you ever in a position where you were embarrassed about your body (doctor's office, physicals, group showers)?

	Several times	Once	Never

22. Did getting married raise

your feeling of worth and
give you more confidence?

_____	_____	_____
Not at all	At first	Yes

23. Was your honeymoon
a positive experience?

_____	_____	_____
No	Average	Great

24. Do you feel your mate set
out to make you over?

_____	_____	_____
Definitely	A little	No

25. Do you both communicate on
an emotional, heart-felt level?

_____	_____	_____
Seldom	Off and on	Yes

26. Have you been tempted
to be unfaithful?

_____	_____	_____
Often	Once	Never

27. Have you ever longed for
someone who really would
understand you?

_____	_____	_____
Often	Sometimes	I have one

28. Have you (or your mate)
had any problem pregnancies
or miscarriages?

_____	_____	_____
More than one	One	None

29. Have you (or your mate)
given birth to a baby with
birth defects or retardation?

_____	_____	_____
More than one	One	None

30. Do you feel you've worked
through the grief of these
traumatic births?

_____	_____	_____
Very little	Somewhat	Completely

31. Have you had
major surgery?

_____	_____	_____
More than once	Once	Never

32. Have you experienced
any misdiagnosis or neglect?

_____	_____	_____
Each time	Once	Never

33. Have you ever had feelings
of rejection or loneliness?

For years	In the past	Never

34. Were you sexually abused
or touched inappropriately
as a child?

Many times	Once	Never

35. Have you given complete
control of your life to
the Lord?

No	Sometimes	Yes

36. Have you been so hungry
for the Lord that you've stayed
up half the night to talk with
Him?

Never	Occasionally	Often

37. Have you thought the Lord
couldn't use you because you
were divorced, untrained or
for any other reason?

Definitely	Occasionally	No

38. Have you ever had to move
from a home you loved to one
less desirable?

Many times	Once	Never

39. Have you and your mate
ever disagreed on what the
Lord was calling you to do?

Frequently	Occasionally	Never

40. Have you experienced a
major catastrophe, such as
fire, flood or earthquake?

More than once	Once	Never

41. How would you classify
your leadership roles?

Troubled	Accepted	Praised

42. How would you classify
your witnessing attempts?

Offensive	Not tried	Successful

43. Do you use your house
for Christian hospitality?

Never	Sometimes	Often

44. Have you used your
tough times to help others?

Never	Sometimes	Often

45. How would you
classify your memory?

Lots of gaps	Wanders	Clear

46. How would you describe
your brothers and sisters?

Emotionally unstable	A little mixed up	Emotionally stable

47. Do you ever feel insecure
about who you really are?

Often	Sometimes	Never

48. Have you thought of
your life as difficult?

Yes	Occasionally	Never

49. Have you failed when you
could have succeeded?

Often	Once	Never

50. Have you realized in the
past that God would make
the tough times count?

No	A little	Yes

Now add up each column and give yourself 3 points
for each answer in Column A, 2 points for Column B and
1 point for Column C.

	Number	Points	Total
Column A	_____	x 3	= _____
Column B	_____	x 2	= _____
Column C	_____	x 1	= _____

Grand Total _____

Now that you have taken the Tough Times Test, what are you going to do with the results to make them count?

If you scored 50 or below, your life has been relatively trouble free. You are emotionally balanced and have little difficulty in human relationships. You may not understand someone whose life has been one calamity after another, but you have the ability to develop compassion and concern for those in perpetual problems if you so desire. Help others find the steps to hope and healing. God can use you in a mighty way as you make yourself available to minister to those in need.

If your score is between 51 and 90, you have had your share of problems, but you've not been defeated by them. You have made the best of bad situations and you have learned from your own mistakes. If you wish to go beyond the average and make the tough times count, read the steps to making the tough times count (below) and follow those that apply to you.

If your score is above 90, you can surely say you have experienced tough times. But that doesn't mean you are a failure or a hopeless human being. My score was 102, and most people would feel I have lived a positive and productive life. Your score only means that you are now at a point where God can begin to work in you in a new and powerful way.

The apostle Paul prayed fervently to have God remove his "thorn in his flesh." In writing to the Corinthians, he summed up his situation by saying his problems kept him from glorying in himself and from exalting himself above measure: "So for the sake of Christ, I am well pleased and take pleasure in infirmities, insults, hardships, persecutions, perplexities and distresses; for when I am weak (in human strength), then am I [truly] strong—able, powerful in divine strength" (2 Corinthians 12:10, Amplified).

There are few people in the world who have not suffered, but often as Christians we are made to feel that if we were really spiritual we'd be healthy, wealthy and wise. Author Oswald Chambers writes that when we finally get to the end of ourselves God will begin to use us in a new way:

> As long as you think there is something in you, He cannot choose you because you have ends of your own to serve; but if you have let Him bring you to the end of your self-sufficiency then He can choose you to go with Him. . . . The comradeship of God is made up out of men who know their poverty. He can do nothing with the man who thinks he is of use to God.[1]

Fred and I can attest to that.

Steps to Making the Tough Times Count

1. Know your poverty.

Because you have read this book and taken the Tough Times Test, you now know that you and I are poverty cases. I grew up poor in the Depression and thought that once I got some money and position I'd never be poor again. But over and over I've been brought to a point of poverty of the spirit, a place where I wanted to give up, a time when I thought my efforts were of no avail. Jesus says in His beatitudes, "Blessed are the poor in spirit; for theirs is the kingdom of Heaven" (Matthew 5:3, KJV). When we get to the point of poverty, the Lord can move in a mighty way.

2. Set aside a time of seeking.

Don't sit in poverty and wait for the Lord to drop spiritual riches in your lap, but set aside some time to evaluate your life. You've gone through this book and know what has happened in my life. I had to analyze myself and seek wisdom from the Lord and help from respected friends. I spent a full day in counsel and prayer with Lana Bateman going back over my life and dealing with each area of hurt or bitterness. Fred gave up two weeks to receive guidance from a counselor and uncover the roots of his rejections. Together we spend hours each week in Bible study and prayer and help others to uncover the source of their problems so they may move on to the solutions.

3. *Understand your personality.*

When we first started working with the four basic personalities in 1967, we did it as a parlor game. But I was amazed to see people's lives changed as they suddenly understood the source of their relationship problems. Using the Personality Profile as a tool has helped so many thousands of people to understand their strengths and weaknesses: The Sanguine who wants to have fun but is undisciplined; the Choleric who takes control but is often bossy; the Melancholy who aims for perfection but gets depressed when things go wrong; and the Phlegmatic who is peaceful, well-liked and inoffensive but would rather rest than work.

As we used the Personalities as the core of our messages, we began to find people who "didn't come out right." They had conflicting scores on their Personality Profile. By working with them we found that somewhere along the line they had been forced to put on a mask for survival. Many had been abused or lived in dysfunctional homes; almost all had deep feelings of rejection. The study of the personalities went far beyond what we had originally tried as a simple game.

If you have not worked with the personalities or have looked at them superficially, I would suggest you start with *Personality Plus* and *Your Personality Tree* and make this study a family project. *Your Personality Tree* is set up with discussion questions and plans for a family tree scrapbook.

4. *Read anything pertaining to your problem area.*

Today there are good Christian books on just about every possible area of need. As you read, highlight anything that speaks to you specifically and then go back and reread it. Buy magazines that have articles which relate to your problems.

5. *Pray specifically.*

In James 1:5 we read that if any lack wisdom, we can ask God for it. Proverbs tells us that wisdom is more precious than gold. And yet few people pray specifically for wisdom in their own area of need. In his counseling situations, Fred has found that when an abuse victim asks God to show him where the abuse first started, a scene usually comes before him as he prays. Many have gone to counseling for years and prayed in general, but they have never asked for the wisdom to find the specific source of their pain. The Holy Spirit brings recall of what we need to know in order to be healed. Whatever your need may be, we strongly recommend a daily discipline of written prayer, pouring out your concerns to the Lord.

6. *Free your mind.*

If you feel that because of your repeated problems you need some extra help, you may be right. Turn to the Survey of Emotions and Experience on page 279 and check off any that now apply or ever have applied to you. If you check more than 10, you probably need to get *Freeing Your Mind From Memories That Bind* and work through the entire book carefully.

We have received tremendous response from people who had never understood why they had continual tough times until they read *Freeing Your Mind* and prayed specifically for wisdom. Suddenly their past problems have come into focus and they could see their pattern of victimization and/or rejection.

7. *Look for the lesson.*

Whatever your problems may be and whatever circumstances you've lived through, look for the lesson. What have you learned about yourself? Has there been a consistency about the problems you've faced? What moral is there to your story? Have you acted upon what you've learned? Do you need to confront some issue or some person? Have you just hoped it would all go away someday?

Our heartaches are only of some value if we've looked them over and learned from them. James says, "Is your life full of difficulties and temptations? Then be happy, for when the way is rough, your patience has a chance to grow. So let it grow, and don't try to squirm out of your problems. For when your patience is finally in full bloom, then you will be ready for anything, strong in character, full and complete" (James 1:2-4, TLB).

Don't just wish the problems away; look for the lesson, learn it and apply it.

8. *Help others in similar situations.*

One of the best ways to lessen our own pain and make the tough times count is to help others who are in a similar situation. You don't have to be a registered psychologist to say, "I know how you hurt. I've been there."

You might be thinking, "How will I find people to help?" You don't have to look; just let God know you're ready. If He agrees with you, He will send those who can use your special touch. I find them in ladies' rooms, at airports and in supermarket lines. They see the compassion and concern in your eyes and they pour out their life story. When you are ready, God will do the selecting.

The greatest thrill I have is to see those who come to CLASS doubting that God could ever use them, suddenly see the light and begin to make the tough times count.

I lived through poverty and charity dresses. I learned the hard way that after every wedding comes a marriage. I suffered with double deaths and depression. I lived through floods, fires, earthquakes and a plane crash. I went through surgeries and searchings.

But with the guidance of the Lord Jesus, I've been able to know and accept my poverty, set aside time for introspection, seeking and study, understand my personality strengths and weaknesses, read extensively on many subjects of interest, pray specifically for Fred's willingness to seek counsel, watch him free his mind from memories that bind, find the lessons in adverse circumstances and help others in similar situations.

I can't say that I'd like to ever experience those tough times again, but I do know I'm a stronger person today because I've worked through them and the Lord has made beauty out of ashes.

One day when my son Fred was ten years old, he said, "Mother, I'm sorry for the problems you've had with your two boys, but I was just thinking. If it hadn't been for them, I wouldn't be your son. I would have been born anyway, and someone else would have adopted me, but it wouldn't have been you, and I might not even be a Christian today."

While I would never want to repeat the trials or troubles in my life, Fred's words reminded me that "All things work together for good to them that love God, to them who are called according to His purpose" (Romans 8:28, KJV).

The verse doesn't say everything that happens *is* good but that someday, down the line, God will redeem the tragedies and use the lessons for good. But not to everyone; only to those who love God and are called according to His purpose. I am so grateful today that our family loves the Lord and He has called us to help others

Make the tough times count!

Epilogue

All Cinderella stories end with the transformed heroine and her Prince Charming riding off toward their castle to live happily ever after. While I programmed myself for this fairy-tale existence, knowing that *if only* I could achieve my goals I would be happy, the traumas of my life brought me from romance to reality.

While the Declaration of Independence guarantees the pursuit of happiness, neither government action nor personal determination assures we will find it. If anyone ever tried to pull life all together, I did. If anyone ever had the strength and drive for success, I did. Yet, I learned that as long as we seek perfect circumstances, we'll *never* be happy.

I started out as a poor little girl in need of a transformation. I looked for a nonexistent fairy godmother and when I couldn't find her, remade myself. I married a Prince Charming and decorated a whole series of castles, yet when my walls were attacked, I crumbled. I had to admit defeat and reach out to Jesus, who provided the transforming power I had looked for all my life.

While my circumstances have never reached perfection, the Lord has given me the ability to rise above my problems. He has taught me through one verse, 1 Corinthians 10:13, that I am not the first person to have problems, nor the last, but He will help me bear my burdens: "There hath no temptation taken you but such as is common to man: but God is faithful, who will not suffer you to be tempted above that ye are able; but will with the temptation also make a way of escape, that ye may be able to bear it."

While I do not enjoy tragedies, God gives me the ability to bear them, to have joy in adversity and, most of all, to make the tough times count.

As I have searched for the keys to happiness I've found no human guarantee, but I have found who holds my future. The Lord Jesus himself says, "I will give you the keys of the Kingdom of Heaven." (Matt. 16:19 NKJV)

I'll meet you there!

Family Photos

Florence Marcia Chapman, c. 1929

Three Rooms Behind a Store, c. 1937

Clockwise from left: Walter Chapman, Florence, Jim, Ron

The Littauer Family Home, c. 1952

"I was overwhelmed and close to speechless when I arrived at a spacious English Tudor mansion."

Marita Littauer, Fred, Florence, Katie Chapman
April 11, 1953

"What more could a girl ask for? I was marrying Prince
Charming. I was to be in *Life*. And I hoped to live happily
ever after."

Life's Party

ON LAST DAY in school Miss Chapman presents new teacher, Edwin Johnson, to one of her classes.

Pupils Help A Teacher Get Married

ADMIRING TEEN-AGERS TAKE OVER CEREMONY

When Florence Chapman, a high school teacher in Haverhill, Mass., announced her engagement last winter, her pupils promptly besieged her with offers to help out at her wedding. Miss Chapman, who teaches public speaking and dramatics, accepted their offers and began assigning their duties like homework. For the pupils, who designed the wedding costumes, decorated the reception hall and helped prepare and serve the food at the reception itself, their teacher's wedding had everything that a class play would have and romance too. Most of them had never been so close to an actual wedding before. But after it was all over and the bride and bridegroom had departed—in a car driven by a pupil —one of the girls confessed, "It was lots of fun but I'd rather get married more privately."

CLASS PRESENT is complete china place setting in her pattern. "Look at her shaking!" said someone.

SURPRISE SHOWER in school auditorium ends with real shower of confetti released by boys above.

A Page from LIFE Magazine
May 18, 1953

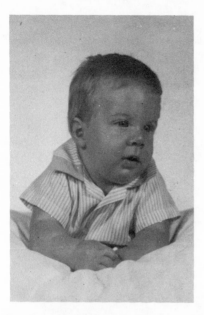

Frederick Jerome Littauer, III
6 months old

Laurence Chapman Littauer
6 months old

Our New Family, 1964
Freddie, Marita, Lauren

A GREAT TIME AT "GOOD TIME CHARLIE'S"

It being a hot night last Friday, the Chronicle decided to go to a party at "Good Time Charlie's", the new, Roaring Twenties-type night club opened up by Mr. and Mrs. Fred Littauer on Route 5 in North Haven.

And what a night it was, as these pictures show.

A handpicked combo plays hot jazz.

Charles Messier laughs it up with Mrs. Clinton B. Scoble.

t but happy! L-r are William s. Edward Davis, Mrs. Don vard Davis, Louis Guyott,

Don Campion Mrs. Guyott and Mrs. Gamble.

In center photo, just for fun Mrs. Schiavone dons her Parisian sequin dress of the 20' era for the evening at Good Time Charlie's. She's pictured with Mr. Schiavone.

At lower right, Mrs. Frederick Littauer chats with Michael Schiavone, Charles Scholhamer and Joseph Schiavone.

A Page from the CHRONICLE
July 15, 1965

Fred and Florence Littauer